TALES FROM THE ARABIC

Of the Breslau and Calcutta (1814-18) editions of
The Book of the Thousand Nights and One Night
not occurring in the other printed texts of the
work, Now first done into English

By John Payne

First published in 1884

Published by Left of Brain Books

Copyright © 2023 Left of Brain Books

ISBN 978-1-396-32460-4

First Edition

PUBLISHER'S PREFACE

About the Book

"Arabic in terms of the number of speakers, is the largest living member of the Semitic language family. Classified as Central Semitic, it is closely related to Hebrew and Aramaic, and has its roots in a Proto-Semitic common ancestor. In ISO 639-3, modern Arabic is classified as a macrolanguage with 27 sub-languages. These varieties are spoken throughout the Arab world, and Standard Arabic is widely studied and used throughout the Islamic world.

Modern Standard Arabic derives from Classical Arabic, the only surviving member of the Old North Arabian dialect group, attested epigraphically since the 6th century. It has been a literary language and the liturgical language of Islam since the 7th century."

(Quote from wikipedia.org)

About the Author

"John Payne (1842 - 1916) was an English poet and translator, from Devon. Initially he pursued a legal career, and associated with Dante Gabriel Rossetti. Later he became involved with limited edition publishing, and the Villon Society.

He is now best known for his translation of Boccaccio's Decameron and The Arabian Nights."

(Quote from wikipedia.org)

CONTENTS

VOLUME THE FIRST

ASLEEP AND AWAKE[1]

THERE was once [at Baghdad], in the Khalifate of Haroun er Reshid, a man, a merchant, who had a son by name Aboulhusn el Khelia.[2] The merchant died and left his son great store of wealth, which he divided into two parts, one of which he laid up and spent of the other half; and he fell to companying with Persians[3] and with the sons of the merchants and gave himself up to good eating and good drinking, till all that he had with him of wealth[4] was wasted and gone; whereupon he betook himself to his friends and comrades and boon-companions and expounded to them his case, discovering to them the failure of that which was in his hand of wealth; but not one of them took heed of him neither inclined unto him.

So he returned to his mother (and indeed his spirit was broken), and related to her that which had happened to him and what had betided him from his friends, how they, had neither shared with him nor requited him with speech. "O Aboulhusn," answered she, "on this wise are the sons[5] of this time: if thou have aught, they make much of thee,[6] and if thou have nought, they put thee away [from them]." And she went on to condole with him, what while he bewailed himself and his tears flowed and he repeated the following verses:

> An if my substance fail, no one there is will succour me,
> But if my wealth abound, of all I'm held in amity.
> How many a friend, for money's sake, hath companied with me!
> How many an one, with loss of wealth, hath turned mine enemy!

Then he sprang up [and going] to the place wherein was the other half of his good, [took it] and lived with it well; and he swore that he would never again consort with those whom he knew, but would company only with the stranger nor entertain him but one night and that, whenas it morrowed, he would never know him more. So he fell to sitting every night on the bridge[7] and looking on every one who passed by him; and if he saw him to be a stranger, he made friends with him and carried him to his house, where he caroused with him till the morning. Then he dismissed him and would never more salute him nor ever again drew near unto him neither invited him.

On this wise he continued to do for the space of a whole year, till, one day, as he sat on the bridge, according to his custom, expecting who should come to him, so he might take him and pass the night with him, behold, [up came] the Khalif and Mesrour, the swordsman of his vengeance, disguised [in merchants' habits] as of their wont. So he looked at them and rising up, for that he knew them not, said to them, "What say ye? Will you go with me to my dwelling-place, so ye may eat what is ready and dr nk what is at hand, to wit, bread baked in the platter[8] and meat cooked and wine clarified?" The Khalif refused this, but he conjured him and said to him, "God on thee, O my lord, go with me, for thou art my guest t nis night, and disappoint not my expectation concerning thee!" And he ceased not to press him till he consented to him; whereat Aboulhusn rejoiced and going on before him, gave not over talking with him till they came to his [house and he carried the Khalif into the] saloon. Er Reshid entered and made his servant abide at the door; and as soon as he was seated, Aboulhusn brought him somewhat to eat; so he ate, and Aboulhusn ate with him, so eating might be pleasant to him. Then he removed the tray and they washed their hands and the Khalif sat down again; whereupon Aboulhusn set on the drinking vessels and seating himself by his side, fel to filling and giving him to drink and entertaining him with discourse.

His hospitality pleased the Khalif and the goodliness of his fashion, and he said to him, "O youth, who art thou? Make me acquainted wi h thyself, so I may requite thee thy kindness." But Aboulhusn smiled and said, "O my lord, far be it that what is past should recur and that I be in company with thee at other than this time!" "Why so?" asked the Khalif. 'And why wilt thou not acquaint me with thy case?" And Aboulhusn said, "Know, O my lord, that my story is extraordinary and that there is a cause for this affair." Quoth the Khalif, "And what is the cause?" And he answered, "The cause hath a tail." The Khalif laughed at his words and Aboulhusn said, "I will explain to thee this [saying] by the story of the lackpenny and the cook. Know, O my lord, that

STORY OF THE LACKPENNY AND THE COOK.

One of the good-for-noughts found himself one day without aught and the world was straitened upon him and his patience failed; so he lay down to sleep and gave not over sleeping till the sun burnt him and the foam came out upon his mouth, whereupon he arose, and he was penniless and had not so much as one dirhem. Presently, he came to the shop of a cook, who had set up therein his pans[9] [over the fire] and wiped his scales and washed his saucers and swept his shop and sprinkled it; and indeed his oils[10] were clear[11] and his spices fragrant and he himself stood behind his cooking-pots [waiting for custom]. So the lackpenny went up to him and saluting him, said to him, 'Weigh me half a dirhem's worth of meat and a quarter of a dirhem's worth of kouskoussou[12] and the like of bread.' So the cook weighed out to him [that which he sought] and the lackpenny entered the shop, whereupon the cook set the food before him and he ate till he had gobbled up the whole and licked the saucers and abode perplexed, knowing not how he should do with the cook concerning the price of that which he had eaten and turning his eyes about upon everything in the shop.

Presently, he caught sight of an earthen pan turned over upon its mouth; so he raised it from the ground and found under it a horse's tail, freshly cut off, and the blood oozing from it; whereby he knew that the cook adulterated his meat with horses' flesh. When he discovered this default, he rejoiced therein and washing his hands, bowed his head and went out; and when the cook saw that he went and gave him nought, he cried out, saying, 'Stay, O sneak, O slink-thief!' So the lackpenny stopped and said to him, 'Dost thou cry out upon me and becall [me] with these words, O cuckold?' Whereat the cook was angry and coming down from the shop, said, 'What meanest thou by thy speech, O thou that devourest meat and kouskoussou and bread and seasoning and goest forth with "Peace[13] [be on thee!]," as it were the thing had not been, and payest down nought for it?' Quoth the lackpenny, 'Thou liest, O son of a cuckold!' Wherewith the cook cried out and laying hold of the lackpenny's collar, said, 'O Muslims, this fellow is my first customer[14] this day and he hath eaten my food and given me nought.'

So the folk gathered together to them and blamed the lackpenny and said to him, 'Give him the price of that which thou hast eaten.' Quoth he, 'I gave him a dirhem before I entered the shop;' and the cook said, 'Be everything I sell this day forbidden[15] to me, if he gave me so much as the name of a piece of money! By Allah, he gave me nought, but ate my food and went out and [would have] made off, without aught [said I]' 'Nay,' answered the lackpenny, 'I gave thee a dirhem,' and he reviled the cook, who returned his abuse; whereupon he dealt him a cuff and they gripped and grappled and throttled each other. When the folk saw them on this wise, they came up to them and said to them, 'What is this strife between you, and no cause for it?' 'Ay, by Allah,' replied the lackpenny, 'but there is a cause for it, and the cause hath a tail!' Whereupon, 'Yea, by Allah,' cried the cook, 'now thou mindest me of thyself and thy dirhem! Yes, he gave me a dirhem and [but] a quarter of the price is spent. Come back and take the rest of the price of thy dirhem.' For that he understood what was to do, at the mention of the tail; and I, O my brother," added Aboulhusn, "my story hath a cause, which I will tell thee."

The Khalif laughed at his speech and said, "By Allah, this is none other than a pleasant tale! Tell me thy story and the cause." "With all my heart," answered Aboulhusn. "Know, O my lord, that my name is Aboulhusn el Khelia and that my father died and left me wealth galore, of which I made two parts. One I laid up and with the other I betook myself to [the enjoyment of the pleasures of] friendship [and conviviality] and consorting with comrades and boon-companions and with the sons of the merchants, nor did I leave one but I caroused with him and he with me, and I spent all my money on companionship and good cheer, till there remained with me nought [of the first half of my good]; whereupon I betook myself to the comrades and cup-companions upon whom I had wasted my wealth, so haply they might provide for my case; but, when I resorted to them and went round about to them all, I found no avail in one of them, nor broke any so much as a crust of bread in my face. So I wept for myself and repairing to my mother, complained to her of my case. Quoth she, 'On this wise are friends; if thou have aught, they make much of thee and devour thee, but, if thou have nought, they cast thee off and chase thee away.' Then I brought out the other half of my money and bound myself by an oath that I would never more entertain any, except one night, after which I would never again salute him nor take note of him; hence my saying to thee, 'Far be it that what is past should recur!' For that I will never again foregather with thee, after this night."

When the Khalif heard this, he laughed heartily and said, "By Allah, O my brother, thou art indeed excused in this matter, now that I know the cause and that the cause hath a tail. Nevertheless if it please God, I will not sever myself from thee." "O my guest," replied Aboulhusn, "did I not say to thee, 'Far be it that what is past should recur! For that I will never again foregather with any'?" Then the Khalif rose and Aboulhusn set before him a dish of roast goose and a cake of manchet-bread and sitting down, fell to cutting off morsels and feeding the Khalif therewith. They gave not over eating thus till they were content, when Aboulhusn brought bowl and ewer and potash[16] and they washed their hands.

Then he lighted him three candles and three lamps and spreading the drinking-cloth, brought clarified wine, limpid, old and fragrant, the scent whereof was as that of virgin musk. He filled the first cup and saying, "O my boon-companion, by thy leave, be ceremony laid aside between us! I am thy slave; may I not be afflicted with thy loss!" drank it off and filled a second cup, which he handed to the Khalif, with a reverence. His fashion pleased the Khalif and the goodliness of his speech and he said in himself, "By Allah, I will assuredly requite him for this!" Then Aboulhusn filled the cup again and handed it to the Khalif, reciting the following verses:

Had we thy coming known, we would for sacrifice Have poured thee out heart's blood or blackness of the eyes;
Ay, and we would have spread our bosoms in thy way, That so thy feet might fare on eyelids, carpet-wise.

When the Khalif heard his verses, he took the cup from his hand and kissed it and drank it off and returned it to Aboulhusn, who made him an obeisance and filled and drank. Then he filled again and kissing the cup thrice, recited the following verses:

Thy presence honoureth us and we Confess thy magnanimity;
If thou forsake us, there is none Can stand to us instead of thee.

Then he gave the cup to the Khalif, saying, "Drink [and may] health and soundness [attend it]! It doth away disease and bringeth healing and setteth the runnels of health abroach."

They gave not over drinking and carousing till the middle of the night, when the Khalif said to his host, "O my brother, hast thou in thy heart a wish thou wouldst have accomplished or a regret thou wouldst fain do away?" "By Allah," answered he, "there is no regret in my heart save that I am not gifted with dominion and the power of commandment and prohibition, so I might do what is in my mind!" Quoth the Khalif, "For God's sake, O my brother, tell me what is in thy mind!" And Aboulhusn said, "I would to God I might avenge myself on my neighbours, for that in my neighbourhood is a mosque and therein four sheikhs, who take it ill, whenas there cometh a guest to me, and vex me with talk and molest me in words and threaten me that they will complain of me to the Commander of the Faithful, and indeed they oppress me sore, and I crave of God the Most High one day's dominion, that I may beat each of them with four hundred lashes, as well as the Imam of the mosque, and parade them about the city of Baghdad and let call before them, 'This is the reward and the least of the reward of whoso exceedeth [in talk] and spiteth the folk and troubleth on them their joys.' This is what I wish and no more."

Quoth the Khalif, "God grant thee that thou seekest! Let us drink one last cup and rise before the dawn draw near, and to-morrow night I will be with thee again." "Far be it!" said Aboulhusn. Then the Khalif filled a cup and putting therein a piece of Cretan henbane, gave it to his host and said to him, "My life on thee, O my brother, drink this cup from my hand!" "Ay, by thy life," answered Aboulhusn, "I will drink it from thy hand." So he took it and drank it off; but hardly had he done so, when his head forewent his feet and he fell to the ground like a slain man; whereupon the Khalif went out and said to his servant Mesrour, "Go in to yonder young man, the master of the house, and take him up and bring him to me at the palace; and when thou goest out, shut the door."

So saying, he went away, whilst Mesrour entered and taking up Aboulhusn, shut the door after him, and followed his master, till he reached the palace, what while the night drew to an end and the cocks cried out, and set him down before the Commander of the Faithful, who laughed at him. Then he sent for Jaafer the Barmecide and when he came before him, he said to him, "Note this young man and when thou seest him to-morrow seated in my place of estate and on the throne of my Khalifate and clad in my habit, stand thou in attendance upon him and enjoin the Amirs and grandees and the people of my household and the officers of my realm to do the like and obey him in that which he shall command them; and thou, if he bespeak thee of anything, do it and hearken unto him and gainsay him not in aught in this coming day." Jaafer answered with, "Hearkening and obedience,"[17] and withdrew, whilst the Khalif went in to the women of the palace, who came to him, and he said to them, "Whenas yonder sleeper awaketh to-morrow from his sleep, kiss ye the earth before him and make obeisance to him and come round about him and clothe him in the [royal] habit and do him the service of the Khalifate and deny not aught of his estate, but say to him, 'Thou art the Khalif.'" Then he taught them what they should say to him and how they should do with him and withdrawing to a privy place, let down a curtain before himself and slept.

Meanwhile, Aboulhusn gave not over snoring in his sleep, till the day broke and the rising of the sun drew near, when a waiting-woman came up to him and said to him, "O our lord [it is the hour of] the morning- prayer." When he heard the girl's words, he laughed and opening his eyes, turned them about the place and found himself in an apartment the walls whereof were painted with gold and ultramarine and its ceiling starred with red gold. Around it were sleeping-chambers, with curtains of gold-embroidered silk let down over their doors, and all about vessels of gold and porcelain and crystal and furniture and carpets spread and lamps burning before the prayer-niche and slave-girls and eunuchs and white slaves and black slaves and boys and pages and attendants. When he saw this, he was confounded in his wit and said, "By Allah, either I am dreaming, or this is Paradise and the Abode of Peace!"[18] And he shut his eyes and went to sleep again. Quoth the waiting-woman, "O my lord, this is not of thy wont, O Commander of the Faithful!"

Then the rest of the women of the palace came all to him and lifted him into a sitting posture, when he found himself upon a couch, stuffed all with floss-silk and raised a cubit's height from the ground.[19] So they seated him upon it and propped him up with a pillow, and he looked at the apartment and its greatness and saw those eunuchs and slave-girls in attendance upon him and at his head, whereat he laughed at himself and said, "By Allah, it is not as I were on wake, and [yet] I am not asleep!" Then he arose and sat up, whilst the damsels laughed at him and hid [their laughter] from him; and he was confounded in his wit and bit upon his finger. The bite hurt him and he cried "Oh!" and was vexed; and the Khalif watched him, whence he saw him not, and laughed.

Presently Aboulhusn turned to a damsel and called to her; whereupon she came to him and he said to her, "By the protection of God, O damsel, am I Commander of the Faithful?" "Yes, indeed," answered she; "by the protection of God thou in this time art Commander of the Faithful." Quoth he, "By Allah, thou liest, O thousandfold strumpet!" Then he turned to the chief eunuch and called to him, whereupon he came to him and kissing the earth before him, said, "Yes, O Commander of the Faithful." "Who is Commander of the Faithful?" asked Aboulhusn. "Thou," replied the eunuch and Aboulhusn said, "Thou liest, thousandfold catamite that thou art!"

Then he turned to another eunuch and said to him, "O my chief,[20] by the protection of God, am I Commander of the Faithful?" "Ay, by Allah, O my lord!" answered he. "Thou in this time art Commander of the Faithful and Vicar of the Lord of the Worlds." Aboulhusn laughed at himself and misdoubted of his reason and was perplexed at what he saw and said, "In one night I am become Khalif! Yesterday I was Aboulhusn the Wag, and to-day I am Commander of the Faithful." Then the chief eunuch came up to him and said, "O Commander of the Faithful, (the name of God encompass thee!) thou art indeed Commander of the Faithful and Vicar of the Lord of the Worlds!" And the slave-girls and eunuchs came round about him, till he arose and abode wondering at his case.

Presently, one of the slave-girls brought him a pair of sandals wrought with raw silk and green silk and embroidered with red gold, and he took them and put them in his sleeve, whereat the slave cried out and said, "Allah! Allah! O my lord, these are sandals for the treading of thy feet, so thou mayst enter the draught-house." Aboulhusn was confounded and shaking the sandals from his sleeve, put them on his feet, whilst the Khalif [well-nigh] died of laughter at him. The slave forewent him to the house of easance, where he entered and doing his occasion, came out into the chamber, whereupon the slave- girls brought him a basin of gold and an ewer of silver and poured water on his hands and he made the ablution.

Then they spread him a prayer-carpet and he prayed. Now he knew not how to pray and gave not over bowing and prostrating himself, [till he had prayed the prayers] of twenty inclinations,[21] pondering in himself the while and saying, "By Allah, I am none other than the Commander of the Faithful in very sooth! This is assuredly no dream, for all these things happen not in a dream." And he was convinced and determined in himself that he was Commander of the Faithful; so he pronounced the Salutation[22] and made an end[23] of his prayers; whereupon the slaves and slave-girls came round about him with parcels of silk and stuffs[24] and clad him in the habit of the Khalifate and gave him the royal dagger in his hand. Then the chief eunuch went out before him and the little white slaves behind him, and they ceased not [going] till they raised the curtain and brought him into the hall of judgment and the throne-room of the Khalifate. There he saw the curtains and the forty doors and El Ijli and Er Recashi[25] and Ibdan and Jedim and Abou Ishac [26] the boon-companions and beheld swords drawn and lions [27] encompassing [the throne] and gilded glaives and death-dealing bows and Persians and Arabs and Turks and Medes and folk and peoples and Amirs and viziers and captains and grandees and officers of state and men of war, and indeed there appeared the puissance of the house of Abbas [28] and the majesty of the family of the Prophet.

So he sat down upon the throne of the Khalifate and laid the dagger in his lap, whereupon all [present] came up to kiss the earth before him and called down on him length of life and continuance [of glory and prosperity]. Then came forward Jaafer the Barmecide and kissing the earth, said, "May the wide world of God be the treading of thy feet and may Paradise be thy dwelling-place and the fire the habitation of thine enemies! May no neighbour transgress against thee nor the lights of fire die out for thee, [29]O Khalif of [all] cities and ruler of [all] countries!"

Therewithal Aboulhusn cried out at him and said, "O dog of the sons of Bermek, go down forthright, thou and the master of the police of the city, to such a place in such a street and deliver a hundred dinars to the mother of Aboulhusn the Wag and bear her my salutation. [Then, go to such a mosque] and take the four sheikhs and the Imam and beat each of them with four hundred lashes and mount them on beasts, face to tail, and go round with them about all the city and banish them to a place other than the city; and bid the crier make proclamation before them, saying, 'This is the reward and the least of the reward of whoso multiplieth words and molesteth his neighbours and stinteth them of their delights and their eating and drinking!'" Jaafer received the order [with submission] and answered with ["Hearkening and] obedience;" after which he went down from before Aboulhusn to the city and did that whereunto he had bidden him.

Meanwhile, Aboulhusn abode in the Khalifate, taking and giving, ordering and forbidding and giving effect to his word, till the end of the day, when he gave [those who were present] leave and permission [to withdraw], and the Amirs and officers of state departed to their occasions. Then the eunuchs came to him and calling down on him length of life and continuance [of glory and prosperity], walked in attendance upon him and raised the curtain, and he entered the pavilion of the harem, where he found candles lighted and lamps burning and singing-women smiting [on instruments of music]. When he saw this, he was confounded in his wit and said in himself, "By Allah, I am in truth Commander of the Faithful!" As soon as he appeared, the slave-girls rose to him and carrying him up on to the estrade,[30] brought him a great table, spread with the richest meats. So he ate thereof with all his might, till he had gotten his fill, when he called one of the slave-girls and said to her, "What is thy name?' "My name is Miskeh," replied she, and he said to another, "What is thy name?" Quoth she, "My name is Terkeh." Then said he to a third, "What is thy name?" "My name is Tuhfeh," answered she; and he went on to question the damsels of their names, one after another, [till he had made the round of them all], when he rose from that place and removed to the wine-chamber.

He found it every way complete and saw therein ten great trays, full of all fruits and cakes and all manner sweetmeats. So he sat down and ate thereof after the measure of his sufficiency, and finding there three troops of singing-girls, was amazed and made the girls eat. Then he sat and the singers also seated themselves, whilst the black slaves and the white slaves and the eunuchs and pages and boys stood, and the slave-girls, some of them, sat and some stood. The damsels sang and warbled all manner melodies and the place answered them for the sweetness of the songs, whilst the pipes cried out and the lutes made accord with them, till it seemed to Aboulhusn that he was in Paradise and his heart was cheered and his breast dilated. So he sported and joyance waxed on him and he bestowed dresses of honour on the damsels and gave and bestowed, challenging this one and kissing that and toying with a th rd, plying one with wine and another with meat, till the night fell down.

All this while the Khalif was diverting himself with watching him and laughing, and at nightfall he bade one of the slave-girls drop a piece of henbane in the cup and give it to Aboulhusn to drink. So she did as he bade her and gave Aboulhusn the cup, whereof no sooner had he drunken than his head forewent his feet [and he fell down, senseless]. Therewith the Khalif came forth from behind the curtain, laughing, and calling to the servant who had brought Aboulhusn to the palace, said to him, "Carry this fellow to his own place." So Mesrour took him up [and carrying him to his own house], set him down in the saloon. Then he went forth from him and shutting the saloon-door upon him, returned to the Khalif, who slept till the morrow.

As for Aboulhusn, he gave not over sleeping till God the Most High brought on the morning, when he awoke, crying out and saying, "Ho, Tuffaheh! Ho, Rahet el Culoub! Ho, Miskeh! Ho, Tuhfeh!" And he gave not over calling upon the slave-girls till his mother heard him calling upon strange damsels and rising, came to him and said, "The name of God encompass thee! Arise,

O my son, O Aboulhusn! Thou dreamest." So he opened his eyes and finding an old woman at his head, raised his eyes and said to her, "Who art thou?" Quoth she, "I am thy mother;" and he answered, "Thou liest! I am the Commander of the Faithful, the Vicar of God." Whereupon his mother cried out and said to him, "God preserve thy reason! Be silent, O my son, and cause not the loss of our lives and the spoiling of thy wealth, [as will assuredly betide,] if any hear this talk and carry it to the Khalif."

So he rose from his sleep and finding himself in his own saloon and his mother by him, misdoubted of his wit and said to her, "By Allah, O my mother, I saw myself in a dream in a palace, with slave-girls and servants about me and in attendance upon me, and I sat upon the throne of the Khalifate and ruled. By Allah, O my mother, this is what I saw, and verily it was not a dream!" Then he bethought himself awhile and said, "Assuredly, I am Aboulhusn el Khelia, and this that I saw was only a dream, and [it was in a dream that] I was made Khalif and commanded and forbade." Then he bethought himself again and said, "Nay, but it was no dream and I am no other than the Khalif, and indeed I gave gifts and bestowed dresses of honour." Quoth his mother to him, "O my son, thou sportest with thy reason: thou wilt go to the hospital and become a gazing-stock. Indeed, that which thou hast seen is only from the Devil and it was a delusion of dreams, for whiles Satan sporteth with men's wits in all manner ways."

Then said she to him, "O my son, was there any one with thee yester-night?" And he bethought himself and said, "Yes; one lay the night with me and I acquainted him with my case and told him my story. Doubtless, he was from the Devil, and I, O my mother, even as thou sayst truly, am Aboulhusn el Khelia." "O my son," rejoined she, "rejoice in tidings of all good, for yesterday's record is that there came the Vivier Jaafer the Barmecide [and his company] and beat the sheikhs of the mosque and the Imam, each four hundred lashes; after which they paraded them about the city, making proclamation before them and saying, 'This is the reward and the least of the reward of whoso lacketh of goodwill to his neighbours and troubleth on them their lives!' and banished them from Baghdad. Moreover, the Khalif sent me a hundred dinars and sent to salute me." Whereupon Aboulhusn cried out and said to her, "O old woman of ill-omen, wilt thou contradict me and tell me that I am not the Commander of the Faithful? It was I who commanded Jaafer the Barmecide to beat the sheikhs and parade them about the city and make proclamation before them and who sent thee the hundred dinars and sent to salute thee, and I, O beldam of ill-luck, am in very deed the Commander of the Faithful, and thou art a liar, who would make me out a dotard."

So saying, he fell upon her and beat her with a staff of almond-wood, till she cried out, "[Help], O Muslims!" and he redoubled the beating upon her, till the folk heard her cries and coming to her, [found] Aboulhusn beating her and saying to her, "O old woman of ill-omen, am I not the Commander of the Faithful? Thou hast enchanted me!" When the folk heard his words, they said, "This man raveth," and doubted not of his madness. So they came in upon him and seizing him, pinioned him and carried him to the hospital. Quoth the superintendant, "What aileth this youth?" And they said, "This is a madman." "By Allah," cried Aboulhusn, "they lie against me! I am no madman, but the Commander of the Faithful.' And the superintendant answered him, saying, "None lieth but thou, O unluckiest of madmen!"

Then he stripped him of his clothes and clapping on his neck a heavy chain, bound him to a high lattice and fell to drubbing him two bouts a day and two anights; and on this wise he abode the space of ten days. Then his mother came to him and said, "O my son, O Aboulhusn, return to thy reason, for this is the Devil's doing." Quoth he, "Thou sayst sooth, O my mother, and bear thou witness of me that I repent [and forswear] that talk and turn from my madness. So do thou deliver me, for I am nigh upon death." So his mother went out to the superintendant and procured his release and he returned to his own house.

Now this was at the beginning of the month, and when it was the end thereof, Aboulhusn longed to drink wine and returning to his former usance, furnished his saloon and made ready food and let bring wine; then, going forth to the bridge, he sat there, expecting one whom he should carouse withal, as of his wont. As he sat thus, behold, up came the Khalif [and Mesrour] to him; but Aboulhusn saluted them not and said to them, "No welcome and no greeting to the perverters![31] Ye are no other than devils." However, the Khalif accosted him and said to him, "O my brother, did I not say to thee that I would return to thee?" Quoth Aboulhusn, "I have no need of thee; and as the byword says in verse:

'Twere fitter and better my loves that I leave, For, if the eye see not, the heart will not grieve.

And indeed, O my brother, the night thou camest to me and we caroused together, I and thou, it was as if the Devil came to me and troubled me that night." "And who is he, the Devil?" asked the Khalif. "He is none other than thou," answered Aboulhusn; whereat the Khalif smiled and sitting down by him, coaxed him and spoke him fair, saying, "O my brother, when I went out from thee, I forgot [to shut] the door [and left it] open, and belike Satan came in to thee." Quoth Aboulhusn, "Ask me not of that which hath betided me. What possessed thee to leave the door open, so that the Devil came in to me and there befell me with him this and that?" And he related to him all that had befallen him, from first to last, aud there is no advantage in the repetition of it; what while the Khalif laughed and hid his laughter.

Then said he to Aboulhusn, "Praised be God who hath done away from thee that which irked thee and that I see thee in weal!" And Aboulhusn said, "Never again will I take thee to boon-companion or sitting-mate; for the byword saith, 'Whoso stumbleth on a stone and returneth thereto, blame and reproach be upon him.' And thou, O my brother, nevermore will I entertain thee nor use companionship with thee, for that I have not found thy commerce propitious to me."[32] But the Khalif blandished him and conjured him, redoubling words upon him with "Verily, I am thy guest; reject not the guest," till Aboulhusn took him and [carrying him home], brought him into the saloon and set food before him and friendly entreated him in speech. Then he told him all that had befallen him, whilst the Khalif was like to die of hidden laughter; after which Aboulhusn removed the tray of food and bringing the wine-tray, filled a cup and emptied it out three times, then gave it to the Khalif, saying, "O boon-companion mine, I am thy slave and let not that which I am about to say irk thee, and be thou not vexed, neither do thou vex me." And he recited these verses:

No good's in life (to the counsel list of one who's purpose-whole,) An if thou be not drunken still and gladden not thy soul.
Ay, ne'er will I leave to drink of wine, what while the night on me Darkens, till drowsiness bow down my head upon my bowl.
In wine, as the glittering sunbeams bright, my heart's contentment is, That banishes hence, with various joys, all kinds of care and dole.

When the Khalif heard these his verses, he was moved to exceeding delight and taking the cup, drank it off, and they ceased not to drink and carouse till the wine rose to their heads. Then said Aboulhusn to the Khalif, "O boon-companion mine, of a truth I am perplexed concerning my affair, for meseemed I was Commander of the Faithful and ruled and gave gifts and largesse, and in very deed, O my brother, it was not a dream." "These were the delusions of sleep," answered the Khalif and crumbling a piece of henbane into the cup, said to him, "By my life, do thou drink this cup." And Aboulhusn said, "Surely I will drink it from thy hand." Then he took the cup from the Khalifs hand and drank it off, and no sooner had it settled in his belly than his head forewent his feet [and he fell down senseless].

Now his parts and fashions pleased the Khalif and the excellence of his composition and his frankness, and he said in himself, "I will assuredly make him my cup- companion and sitting-mate." So he rose forthright and saying to Mesrour, "Take him up," [returned to the palace]. Accordingly, Mesrour took up Aboulhusn and carrying him to the palace of the Khalifate, set him down before Er Reshid, who bade the slaves and slave- girls encompass him about, whilst he himself hid in a place where Aboulhusn could not see him.

Then he commanded one of the slave-girls to take the lute and strike it at Aboulhusn's head, whilst the rest smote upon their instruments. [So they played and sang,] till Aboulhusn awoke at the last of the night and heard the noise of lutes and tabrets and the sound of the pipes and the singing of the slave-girls, whereupon he opened his eyes and finding himself in the palace, with the slave-girls and eunuchs about him, exclaimed, 'There is no power and no virtue but in God the Most High, the Supreme! Verily, I am fearful of the hospital and of that which I suffered therein aforetime, and I doubt not but the Devil is come to me again, as before. O my God, put thou Satan to shame!" Then he shut his eyes and laid his head in his sleeve and fell to laughing softly and raising his head [bytimes], but [still] found the apartment lighted and the girls singing.

Presently, one of the eunuchs sat down at his head and said to him, "Sit up, O Commander of the Faithful, and look on thy palace and thy slave-girls." Quoth Aboulhusn, "By the protection of God, am I in truth Commander of the Faithful and dost thou not lie? Yesterday, I went not forth neither ruled, but drank and slept, and this eunuch cometh to rouse me up." Then he sat up and bethought himself of that which had betided him with his mother and how he had beaten her and entered the hospital, and he saw the marks of the beating, wherewithal the superintendant of the hospital had beaten him, and was perplexed concerning his affair and pondered in himself, saying, "By Allah, I know not how my case is nor what is this that betideth me!"

Then he turned to a damsel of the damsels and said to her, "Who am I?" Quoth she, "Thou art the Commander of the Faithful;" and he said, "Thou liest, O calamity![33] If I be indeed the Commander of the Faithful, bite my finger." So she came to him and bit it with her might, and he said to her, "It sufficeth." Then he said to the chief eunuch, "Who am I?" And he answered, "Thou art the Commander of the Faithful." So he left him and turning to a little white slave, said to him, "Bite my ear;" and he bent down to him and put his ear to his mouth. Now the slave was young and lacked understanding; so he closed his teeth upon Aboulhusn's ear with his might, till he came near to sever it; and he knew not Arabic, so, as often as Aboulhusn said to him, "It sufficeth," he concluded that he said, "Bite harder," and redoubled his bite and clenched his teeth upon the ear, whilst the damsels were diverted from him with hearkening to the singing-girls, and Aboulhusn cried out for succour from the boy and the Khalif [well-nigh] lost his senses for laughter.

Then he dealt the boy a cuff and he let go his ear, whereupon Aboulhusn put off his clothes and abode naked, with his yard and his arse exposed, and danced among the slave-girls. They bound his hands and he wantoned among them, what while they [well-nigh] died of laughing at him and the Khalif swooned away for excess of laughter. Then he came to himself and going forth to Aboulhusn, said to him, "Out on thee, O Aboulhusn! Thou slayest me with laughter." So he turned to him and knowing him, said to him, "By Allah, it is thou slayest me and slayest my mother and slewest the sheikhs and the Imam of the Mosque!"

Then the Khalif took him into his especial favour and married him and bestowed largesse on him and lodged him with himself in the palace and made him of the chief of his boon-companions, and indeed he was preferred with him above them and the Khalif advanced him over them all. Now they were ten in number, to wit, El Ijli and Er Recashi and Ibdan and Hassan el Feresdec and El Lauz and Es Seker and Omar et Tertis and Abou Nuwas[34] and Abou Ishac en Nedim and Aboulhusn el Khelia, and by each of them hangeth a story that is told in other than this book. And indeed Aboulhusn became high in honour with the Khalif and favoured above all, so that he sat with him and the Lady Zubeideh bint el Casim and married the latter's treasuress, whose name was Nuzhet el Fuad.

Aboulhusn abode with his wife in eating and drinking and all delight of life, till all that was with them was spent, when he said to her, "Harkye, O Nuzhet el Fuad!" "At thy service," answered she, and he said, "I have it in mind to play a trick on the Khalif and thou shalt do the like with the Lady Zubeideh, and we will take of them, in a twinkling, two hundred dinars and two pieces of silk." "As thou wilt," answered she; "but what thinkest thou to do?" And he said,"We will feign ourselves dead and this is the trick. I will die before thee and lay myself out, and do thou spread over me a kerchief of silk and loose [the muslin of] my turban over me and tie my toes and lay on my heart a knife, and a little salt.[35] Then let down thy hair and betake thyself to thy mistress Zubeideh, tearing thy dress and buffeting thy face and crying out. She will say to thee, 'What aileth thee?' and do thou answer her, saying, 'May thy head outlive Aboulhusn el Khelia! For ne is dead." She will mourn for me and weep and bid her treasuress give thee a hundred dinars and a piece of silk and will say to thee, 'Go lay him out and carry him forth [to burial].' So do thou take of her the hundred dinars and the piece of silk and come back, and when thou returnest to me, I will rise up and thou shalt lie down in my place, and I will go to the Khalif and say to him, 'May thy head outlive Nuzhet el Fuad!' and tear my dress and pluck at my beard. He will mourn for thee and say to his treasurer, 'Give Aboulhusn a hundred dinars and a piece of silk.' Then he will say to me, 'Go; lay her out and carry her forth;' and I will come back to thee."

Therewith Nuzhet el Fuad rejoiced and said, "Indeed, this is an excellent device." [Then Aboulhusn stretched himself out] forthright and she shut his eyes and tied his feet and covered him with the kerchief and did what [else] her lord had bidden her; after which she rent her dress and uncovering her head, let down her hair and went in to the Lady Zubeideh, crying out and weeping, When the princess saw her in this case, she said to her, "What plight is this [in which I see thee]? What is thy story and what maketh thee weep?" And Nuzhet el Fuad answered, weeping and crying out the while, "O my lady, may thy head live and mayst thou survive Aboulhusn el Khelia! For he is dead." The Lady Zubeideh mourned for him and said, "Alas for Aboulhusn el Khelia!" And she wept for him awhile. Then she bade her treasuress give Nuzhet el Fuad a hundred dinars and a piece of silk and said to her, "O Nuzhet el Fuad, go, lay him out and carry him forth."

So she took the hundred dinars and the piece of silk and returned to her dwelling, rejoicing, and went in to Aboulhusn and told him what had befallen, whereupon he arose and rejoiced and girt his middle and danced and took the hundred dinars and the piece of silk and laid them up. Then he laid out Nuzhet el Fuad and did with her even as she had done with him; after which he rent his clothes and plucked out his beard and disordered his turban [and went forth] and gave not over running till he came in to the Khalif, who was sitting in the hall of audience, and he in this plight, beating upon his breast. Quoth the Khalif to him, "What aileth thee, O Aboulhusn!" And he wept and said, "Would thy boon-companion had never been and would his hour had never come!" "Tell me [thy case,]" said the Khalif; and Aboulhusn said, "O my lord, may thy head outlive Nuzhet el Fuad!" Quoth the Khalif, "There is no god but God!" And he smote hand upon hand. Then he comforted Aboulhusn and said to him, "Grieve not, for we will give thee a concubine other than she." And he bade the treasurer give him a hundred dinars and a piece of silk. So the treasurer gave him what the Khalif bade him, and the latter said to him,"Go, lay her out and carry her forth and make her a handsome funeral." So Aboulhusn took that which he had given him and returning to his house, rejoicing, went in to Nuzhet el Fuad and said to her, "Arise, for the wish is accomplished unto us." So she arose and he laid before her the hundred dinars and the piece of silk, whereat she rejoiced, and they added the gold to the gold and the silk to the silk and sat talking and laughing at one another.

Meanwhile, when Aboulhusn went out from the presence of the Khalif and went to lay out Nuzhet el Fuad, the prince mourned for her and dismissing the divan, arose and betook himself, leaning upon Mesrour, the swordsman of his vengeance, [to the pavilion of the harem, where he went in] to the Lady Zubeideh, that he might condole with her for her slave-girl. He found the princess sitting weeping and awaiting his coming, so she might condole with him for [his boon-companion] Aboulhusn el Khelia. So he said to her, "May thy head outlive thy slave-girl Nuzhet el Fuad!" And she answered, saying, "O my lord, God preserve my slave-girl! Mayst thou live and long survive thy boon-companion Aboulhusn el Khelia! For he is dead."

The Khalif smiled and said to his eunuch, "O Mesrour, verily women are little of wit. I conjure thee, by Allah, say, was not Aboulhusn with me but now?" ["Yes, O Commander of the Faithful," answered Mesrour] Quoth the Lady Zubeideh, laughing from a heart full of wrath, "Wilt thou not leave thy jesting? Is it not enough that Aboulhusn is dead, but thou must kill my slave-girl also and bereave us of the two and style me little of wit?"

"Indeed," answered the Khalif, "it is Nuzhet el Fuad who is dead." And Zubeideh said, "Indeed he hath not been with thee, nor hast thou seen him, and none was with me but now but Nuzhet el Fuad, and she sorrowful, weeping, with her clothes torn. I exhorted her to patience and gave her a hundred dinars and a piece of silk; and indeed I was awaiting thy coming, so I might condole with thee for thy boon- companion Aboulhusn el Khelia, and was about to send for thee." The Khalif laughed and said, "None is dead but Nuzhet el Fuad;" and she, "No, no, my lord; none is dead but Aboulhusn."

With this the Khalif waxed wroth, and the Hashimi vein[36] started out from between his eyes and he cried out to Mesrour and said to him, "Go forth and see which of them is dead." So Mesrour went out, running, and the Khalif said to Zubeideh, "Wilt thou lay me a wager?" "Yes," answered she; "I will wager, and I say that Aboulhusn is dead." "And I," rejoined the Khalif, "wager and say that none is dead save Nuzhet el Fuad; and the stake shall be the Garden of Pleasance against thy palace and the Pavilion of Pictures." So they [agreed upon this and] abode awaiting Mesrour, till such time as he should return with news.

As for Mesrour, he gave not over running till he came to the by-street, [wherein was the house] of Aboulhusn el Khelia. Now the latter was sitting reclining at the lattice, and chancing to look round, saw Mesrour running along the street and said to Nuzhet el Fuad, "Meseemeth the Khalif, when I went forth from him, dismissed the Divan and went in to the Lady Zubeideh, to condole with her [for thee;] whereupon she arose and condoled with him [for me,] saying, 'God greaten thy recompence for [the loss of] Aboulhusn el Khelia!' And he said to her, 'None is dead save Nuzhet el Fuad, may thy head outlive her!' Quoth she, 'It is not she who is dead, but Aboulhusn el Khelia, thy boon-companion.' And he to her, 'None is dead but Nuzhet el Fuad.' And they gainsaid one another, till the Khalif waxed wroth and they laid a wager, and he hath sent Mesrour the swordbearer to see who is dead. Wherefore it were best that thou lie down, so he may see thee and go and acquaint the Khalif and confirm my saying." So Nuzhet el Fuad stretched herself out and Aboulhusn covered her with her veil and sat at her head, weeping.

Presently, in came Mesrour the eunuch to him and saluted him and seeing Nuzhet el Fuad stretched out, uncovered her face and said, "There is no god but God! Our sister Nuzhet el Fuad is dead. How sudden was the [stroke of] destiny! May God have mercy on thee and acquit thee of responsibility!" Then he returned and related what had passed before the Khalif and the Lady Zubeideh, and he laughing. "O accursed one,' said the Khalif, "is this a time for laughter? Tell us which is dead of them." "By Allah, O my lord," answered Mesrour, "Aboulhusn is well and none is dead but Nuzhet el Fuad." Quoth the Khalif to Zubeideh, "Thou hast lost thy pavilion in thy play," and he laughed at her and said to Mesrour, "O Mesrour, tell her what thou sawest." "Verily, O my lady," said the eunuch, "I ran without ceasing till I came in to Aboulhusn in his house and found Nuzhet el Fuad lying dead and Aboulhusn sitting at her head, weeping. I saluted him and condoled with him and sat down by his side and uncovered the face of Nuzhet el Fuad and saw her dead and her face swollen. So I said to him, 'Carry her out forthright [to burial], so we may pray over her.' He answered, 'It is well;' and I left him to lay her out and came hither, that I might tell you the news."

The Khalif laughed and said, "Tell it again and again to thy lady lack-wit." When the Lady Zubeideh heard Mesrour's words [and those of the Khalif,] she was wroth and said, "None lacketh wit but he who believeth a black slave." And she reviled Mesrour, whilst the Khalif laughed. Mesrour was vexed at this and said to the Khalif, "He spoke sooth who said, 'Women lack wit and religion.'" Then said the Lady Zubeideh to the Khalif, "O Commander of the Faithful, thou sportest and jestest with me, and this slave hoodwinketh me, to please thee; but I will send and see which is dead of them." And he answered, saying, "Send one who shall see which is dead of them." So the Lady Zubeideh cried out to an old woman, a stewardess, and said to her, "Go to the house of Nuzhet el Fuad in haste and see who is dead and loiter not." And she railed at her.

The old woman went out, running, whilst the Khalif and Mesrour laughed, and gave not over running till she came into the street. Aboulhusn saw her and knowing her, said to his wife, "O Nuzhet el Fuad, meseemeth the Lady Zubeideh hath sent to us to see who is dead and hath not given credence to Mesrour's report of thy death; so she hath despatched the old woman, her stewardess, to discover the truth; wherefore it behoveth me to be dead in my turn, for the sake of thy credit with the Lady Zubeideh." Accordingly, he lay down and stretched himself out, and she covered him and bound his eyes and feet and sat at his head, weeping.

Presently, the old woman came in to her and saw her sitting at Aboulhusn's head, weeping and lamenting; and when she saw the old woman, she cried out and said to her, "See what hath betided me! Indeed, Aboulhusn is dead and hath left me alone and forlorn!" Then she cried out and tore her clothes and said to the old woman, "O my mother, how good he was!" Quoth the other, "Indeed thou art excused, for thou wast used to him and he to thee." Then she considered what Mesrour had reported to the Khalif and the Lady Zubeideh and said to her, "Indeed, Mesrour goeth about to sow discord between the Khalif and the Lady Zubeideh." "And what is the [cause of] discord, O my mother?" asked Nuzhet el Fuad. "O my daughter," answered the old woman, "Mesrour came to the Khalif and the Lady Zubeideh and gave them news of thee that thou wast dead and that Aboulhusn was well. "And Nuzhet el Fuad said to her, "O my aunt, I was with my lady but now and she gave me a hundred dinars and a piece of silk; and now see my condition and that which hath befallen me! Indeed, I am bewildered, and how shall I do, and I alone, forlorn? Would God I had died and he had lived!"

Then she wept and the old woman with her and the latter went up to Aboulhusn and uncovering his face, saw his eyes bound and swollen for the binding. So she covered him again and said, "Indeed, O Nuzhet el Fuad, thou art afflicted in Aboulhusn!" Then she condoled with her and going out from her, ran without ceasing till she came in to the Lady Zubeideh and related to her the story; and the princess said to her, laughing, "Tell it over again to the Khalif, who maketh me out scant of wit and lacking of religion, and to this ill-omened slave, who presumeth to contradict me." Quoth Mesrour, "This old woman lieth; for I saw Aboulhusn well and Nuzhet el Fuad it was who lay dead." "It is thou that liest," rejoined the stewardess, "and wouldst fain sow discord between the Khalif and the Lady Zubeideh." And he said, "None lieth but thou, O old woman of ill-omen, and thy lady believeth thee, and she doteth." Whereupon the Lady Zubeideh cried out at him, and indeed she was enraged at him and at his speech and wept.

Then said the Khalif to her, "I lie and my eunuch lieth, and thou liest and thy waiting-woman lieth; so methinks we were best go, all four of us together, that we may see which of us telleth the truth." Quoth Mesrour, "Come, let us go, that I may put this ill-omened old woman to shame[37] and deal her a sound drubbing for her lying." And she answered him, saying, "O dotard, is thy wit like unto my wit? Indeed, thy wit is as the hen's wit." Mesrour was incensed at her words and would have laid violent hands on her, but the Lady Zubeideh warded him off from her and said to him, "Her sooth-fastness will presently be distinguished from thy sooth-fastness and her leasing from thy leasing."

Then they all four arose, laying wagers with one another, and went forth, walking, from the palace-gate [and fared on] till they came in at the gate of the street in which Aboulhusn el Khelia dwelt. He saw them and said to his wife Nuzhet el Fuad, "Verily, all that is sticky is not a pancake and not every time cometh the jar off safe.[38] ' Meseemeth the old woman hath gone and told her lady and acquainted her with our case and she hath disputed with Mesrour the eunuch and they have laid wagers with one another about our death and are come to us, all four, the Khalif and the eunuch and the Lady Zubeideh and the old woman." When Nuzhet el Fuad heard this, she started up from her lying posture and said, "How shall we do?" And he said, "We will both feign ourselves dead and stretch ourselves out and hold our breath." So she hearkened unto him and they both lay down on the siesta[-carpet] and bound their feet and shut their eyes and covered themselves with the veil and held their breath.

Presently, up came the Khalif and the Lady Zubeideh and Mesrour and the old woman and entering, found Aboulhusn and his wife both stretched out [apparently] dead; which when the Lady Zubeideh saw, she wept and said, "They ceased not to bring [ill] news of my slave- girl, till she died; methinketh Aboulhusn's death was grievous to her and that she died after him."[39]. Quoth the Khalif, "Thou shalt not forestall me with talk and prate. She certainly died before Aboulhusn, for he came to me with his clothes torn and his beard plucked out, beating his breast with two bricks, and I gave him a hundred dinars and a piece of silk and said to him, 'Go, carry her forth [and bury her] and I will give thee a concubine other than she and handsomer, and she shall be in stead of her.' But it would appear that her death was no light matter to him and he died after her;[40] so it is I who have beaten thee and gotten thy stake."

The Lady Zubeideh answered him many words and the talk waxed amain between them. At last the Khalif sat down at the heads of the pair and said, "By the tomb of the Apostle of God (may He bless and preserve him!) and the sepulchres of my fathers and forefathers, whoso will tell me which of them died before the other, I will willingly give him a thousand dinars!" When Aboulhusn heard the Khalifs words, he sprang up in haste and said, "I died first, O Commander of the Faithful! Hand over the thousand dinars and quit thine oath and the conjuration by which thou sworest." Then Nuzhet el Fuad rose also and stood up before the Khalif and the Lady Zubeideh, who both rejoiced in this and in their safety, and the princess chid her slave-girl. Then the Khalif and the Lady Zubeideh gave them joy at their well-being and knew that this [pretended] death was a device to get the money; and the princess said to Nuzhet el Fuad, "Thou shouldst have sought of me that which thou desiredst, without this fashion, and not have consumed my heart for thee." And she said, "Indeed, I was ashamed, O my lady."

As for the Khalif, he swooned away for laughing and said, "O Aboulhusn, thou wilt never cease to be a wag and do rarities and oddities!" Quoth he, "O Commander of the Faithful, I played off this trick, for that the money was exhausted, which thou gavest me, and I was ashamed to ask of thee again. When I was single, I could never keep money; but since thou marriedst me to this damsel here, if I possessed thy wealth, I should make an end of it. So, when all that was in my hand was spent, I wrought this trick, so I might get of thee the hundred dinars and the piece of silk; and all this is an alms from our lord. But now make haste to give me the thousand dinars and quit thee of thine oath."

The Khalif and the Lady Zubeideh laughed and returned to the palace; and he gave Aboulhusn the thousand dinars, saying, "Take them as a thank-offering for thy preservation from death," whilst the princess did the like with Nuzhet el Fuad. Moreover, the Khalif increased Aboulhusn in his stipends and allowances, and he [and his wife] ceased not [to live] in joy and contentment, till there came to them the Destroyer of Delights and Sunderer of Companies, he who layeth waste the palaces and peopleth the tombs.

THE KHALIF OMAR BEN ABDULAZIZ AND THE POETS
41

IT is said that, when the Khalifate devolved on Omar ben Abdulaziz[42] (of whom God accept), the poets [of the time] resorted to him, as they had been used to resort to the Khalifs before him, and abode at his door days and days, but he gave them not leave to enter, till there came to Omar Adi ben Artah,[43] who stood high in esteem with him. Jerir[44] accosted him and begged him to crave admission for them [to the Khalif]. "It is well," answered Adi and going in to Omar, said to him, "The poets are at thy door and have been there days and days; yet hast thou not given them leave to enter, albeit their sayings are abiding[45] and their arrows go straight to the mark." Quoth Omar, "What have I to do with the poets?" And Adi answered, saying, "O Commander of the Faithful, the Prophet (whom God bless and preserve) was praised [by a poet] and gave [him largesse,] and therein[46] is an exemplar to every Muslim." Quoth Omar, "And who praised him?" "Abbas ben Mirdas[47] praised him," replied Adi, "and he clad him with a suit and said, 'O Bilal,[48] cut off from me his tongue!'" "Dost thou remember what he said?" asked the Khalif; and Adi said, "Yes." "Then repeat it," rejoined Omar. So Adi recited the following verses:

I saw thee, O thou best of all the human race, display A book that came to teach the Truth to those in error's way.
Thou madest known to us therein the road of righteousness, When we had wandered from the Truth, what while in gloom it lay.
A dark affair thou littest up with Islam and with proof Quenchedst the flaming red-coals of error and dismay.
Mohammed, then, I do confess, God's chosen prophet is, And every man requited is for that which he doth say.
The road of right thou hast made straight, that erst was crooked grown; Yea, for its path of old had fall'n to ruin and decay.
Exalted mayst thou be above th' empyrean heaven of joy And may God's glory greater grow and more exalted aye!

"And indeed," continued Adi, "this ode on the Prophet (may God bless and keep him!) is well known and to comment it would be tedious." Quoth

Omar, "Who is at the door?" "Among them is Omar ibn [Abi] Rebya the Cureishite,"[49] answered Adi, and the Khalif said, "May God show him no favour neither quicken him! Was it not he who said ... ?" And he recited the following verses:

Would God upon that bitterest day, when my death calls for me,
What's 'twixt thine excrement and blood[50] I still may smell of thee!
Yea, so but Selma in the dust my bedfellow may prove, Fair fall it thee! In heaven or hell I reck not if it be.

"Except," continued the Khalif, "he were the enemy of God, he had wished for her in this world, so he might after [repent and] return to righteous dealing. By Allah, he shall not come in to me! Who is at the door other than he?" Quoth Adi, "Jemil ben Mamer el Udhri[51] is at the door;" and Omar said, "It is he who says in one of his odes" ... [And he recited the following:]

Would we may live together and when we come to die, God grant the death-sleep bring me within her tomb to lie!
For if "Her grave above her is levelled" it be said, Of life and its continuance no jot indeed reck I.

"Away with him from me! Who is at the door?" "Kutheiyir Azzeh,"[52] replied Adi, and Omar said, "It is he who says in one of his odes ... " [And he repeated the following verses:]

Some with religion themselves concern and make t their business all;
Sitting,[53] they weep for the pains of hell and still for mercy bawl!
If they could hearken to Azzeh's speech, as I, I hearken to it, They straight would humble themselves to her and prone before her fall.

"Leave the mention of him. Who is at the door?" Quoth Adi, "El Akhwes el Ansari."[54] "God the Most High put him away and estrange him from His mercy!" cried Omar. "Is it not he who said, berhyming on a man of Medina his slave-girl, so she might outlive her master ... ?" [And he repeated the following line:]

God [judge] betwixt me and her lord! Away With her he flees me and I follow aye.

"He shall not come in to me. Who is at the door, other than he?" "Heman ben Ghalib el Ferezdec,"[55] answered Adi; and Omar said, "It is he who saith, glorying in adultery ..." [And he repeated the following verses:]

The two girls let me down from fourscore fathoms' height, As swoops a hawk, with wings all open in full flight;
And when my feet trod earth, "Art slain, that we should fear," Quoth they, "or live, that we may hope again thy sight?"

"He shall not come in to me. Who is at the door, other than he?" "El Akhtel et Teghlibi,"[56] answered Adi; and Omar said, "He is the unbeliever who says in his verse ..." [And he repeated the following:]

Ramazan in my life ne'er I fasted, nor e'er Have I eaten of flesh, save in public[57] it were.
No exhorter am I to abstain from the fair, Nor to love Mecca's vale for my profit I care;
Nor, like others a little ere morning appear who bawl, "Come to safety!"[58] I stand up to prayer.
Nay, at daybreak I drink of the wind-freshened wine And prostrate me[59] instead in the dawn-whitened air.

"By Allah, he treadeth no carpet of mine! Who is at the door other than he?" "Jerir ibn el Khetefa," answered Adi; and Omar said, "It is he who saith ... " [And he recited as follows:]

But for the spying of the eyes [ill-omened,] we had seen Wild cattle's eyes and antelopes' tresses of sable sheen.
The huntress of th' eyes[60] by night came to me. "Turn in peace," [Quoth I to her;] "This is no time for visiting, I ween."

"If it must be and no help, admit Jerir." So Adi went forth and admitted Jerir, who entered, saying:

He, who Mohammed sent, as prophet to mankind, Hath to a just high-priest[61] the Khalifate assigned.
His justice and his truth all creatures do embrace; The erring he corrects and those of wandering mind.
I hope for present[62] good [and bounty at thy hand,] For souls of men are still to present[63] good inclined.

Quoth Omar, "O Jerir, keep the fear of God before thine eyes and say nought but the truth." And Jerir recited the following verses:

How many, in Yemameh,[64] dishevelled widows plain! How many a weakling orphan unsuccoured doth remain,
For whom is thy departure even as a father's loss! To fly or creep, like nestlings, alone, they strive in vain.
Now that the clouds have broken their promise to our hope, We trust the Khalif's bounty will stand to us for rain.[65]

When the Khalif heard this, he said, "By Allah, O Jerir, Omar possesseth but a hundred dirhems."[66] [And he cried out to his servant, saying,] "Ho, boy! give them to him." Moreover, he gave him the ornaments cf his sword; and Jerir went forth to the [other] poets, who said to him, "What is behind thee?"[67] And he answered, "A man who giveth to the poor and denieth the poets, and I am well-pleased with him."[68]

EL HEJJAJ AND THE THREE YOUNG MEN [69]

THEY tell that El Hejjaj[70] once commanded the Master of Police [of Bassora] to go round about [the city] by night, and whomsoever he found [abroad] after nightfall, that he should strike off his head. So he went round one night of the nights and came upon three youths staggering from side to side, and on them signs of [intoxication with] wine. So the officers laid hold of them and the captain of the watch said to them, "Who are ye that ye transgress the commandment of the [lieutenant of the] Commander of the Faithful and come abroad at this hour?" Quoth one of the youths, "I am the son of him to whom [all] necks[71] abase themselves, alike the nose-pierced[72] of them and the [bone-]breaker;[73] they come to him in their own despite, abject and submissive, and he taketh of their wealth[74] and of their blood."

The master of police held his hand from him, saying, "Belike he is of the kinsmen of the Commander of the Faithful," and said to the second, "Who art thou?" Quoth he, "I am the son of him whose rank[75] time abaseth not, and if it descend[76] one day, it will assuredly return [to its former height]; thou seest the folk [crowd] in troops to the light of his fire, some standing around it and some sitting." So the master of the police refrained from slaying him and said to the third, "Who art thou?" Quoth he, "I am the son of him who plungeth through the ranks[77] with his might and correcteth[78] them with the sword,[79] so that they stand straight;[80] his feet are not loosed from the stirrup,[81] whenas the horsemen on the day of battle are weary." So the master of police held his hand from him also, saying, "Belike, he is the son of a champion of the Arabs."

Then he kept them under guard, and when the morning morrowed, he referred their case to El Hejjaj, who caused bring them before him and enquiring into their affair, found that the first was the son of a barber-surgeon, the second of a [hot] bean-seller and the third of a weaver. So he marvelled at their readiness of speech[82] and said to his session-mates, "Teach your sons deportment;[83] for, by Allah, but for their ready wit, I had smitten off their heads!"

HAROUN ER RESHID AND THE WOMAN OF THE BARMECIDES [84]

THEY tell that Haroun er Reshid was sitting one day to do away grievances, when there came up to him a woman and said to him, "O Commander of the Faithful, may God accomplish thine affair and cause thee rejoice in that which He hath given thee and increase thee in elevation! Indeed, thou hast done justice[85] and wrought equitably."[86] Quoth the Khalif to those who were present with him, "Know ye what this woman meaneth by her saying?" And they answered, "Of a surety, she meaneth not otherwise than well, O Commander of the Faithful." "Nay," rejoined Haroun; "she purposeth only in this an imprecation against me. As for her saying, 'God accomplish thine affair!' she hath taken it from the saying of the poet, 'When an affair is accomplished, its abatement[87] beginneth. Beware of cessation, whenas it is said, "It is accomplished."' As for her saying 'God cause thee rejoice in that which He hath given thee,' she took it from the saying of God the Most High, 'Till, whenas they rejoiced in that which they were given, we took them suddenly and lo, they were confounded!'[88] As for her saying, 'God increase thee in elevation!' she took it from the saying of the poet, 'No bird flieth and riseth up on high, but, like as he flieth, he falleth.' And as for her saying, 'Indeed, thou hast done justice and wrought equitably,' it is from the saying of the Most High, '[If ye deviate[89] or lag behind or turn aside, verily, God of that which ye do is aware;'[90] and] 'As for the transgressors,'[91] they are fuel for hell[-fire]."[92]

Then he turned to the woman and said to her, "Is it not thus?" "Yes, O Commander of the Faithful," answered she; and he said, "What prompted thee to this?" Quoth she, "Thou slewest my father and my mother and my kinsfolk and tookest their goods." "Whom meanest thou?" asked the Khalif, and she replied, "I am of the house of Bermek."[93] Then said he to her, "As for the dead, they are of those who are past away, and it booteth not to speak of them; but, as for that which I took of wealth, it shall be restored to thee, yea, and more than it." And he was bountiful to her to the utmost of munificence.

THE TEN VIZIERS; OR THE HISTORY OF KING AZADBEKHT AND HIS SON [94]

THERE was once, of old days, a king of the kings, whose name was Azadbekht; his [capital] city was called Kuneim Mudoud and his kingdom extended to the confines of Seistan and from the frontiers of Hindustan to the sea He had ten viziers, who ordered his state and his dominion, and he was possessed of judgment and exceeding wisdom. One day he went forth with certain of his guards to the chase and fell in with an eunuch on horseback, holding in his hand the halter of a mule, which he led along. On the mule's back was a litter of gold-inwoven brocade, garded about with an embroidered band set with gold and jewels, and over against the litter was a company of horsemen. When King Azadbekht saw this, he separated himself from his companions and making for the mule and the horsemen, questioned the latter, saying, "To whom belongeth this litter and what is therein?". The eunuch answered, (for he knew not that he was King Azadbekht,) saying, "This litter belongeth to Isfehend, vizier to King Azadbekht, and therein is his daughter, whom he purposeth to marry to Zad Shah the King."

As the eunuch was speaking with the king, behold, the damsel raised a corner of the curtain that shut in the litter, so she might look upon the speaker, and saw the king. When Azadbekht beheld her and noted her fashion and her loveliness (and indeed never set story-teller[95] eyes on her like,) his soul inclined to her and she took hold upon his heart and he was ravished by her sight. So he said to the eunuch, "Turn the mule's head and return, for I am King Azadbekht and I will marry her myself, for that Isfehend her father is my vizier and he will accept of this affair and it will not be grievous to him." "O king," answered the eunuch, "may God prolong thy continuance, have patience till I acquaint my lord her father, and thou shalt take her in the way of approof, for it befitteth thee not neither is it seemly unto thee that thou take her on this wise, seeing that it will be an affront to her father if thou take her without his knowledge." Quoth Azadbekht, "I have not patience [to wait] till thou go to her father and return, and no dishonour will betide him, if I marry her." "O my lord," rejoined the eunuch, "nought that is done in haste is long of durance nor doth the heart rejoice therein; and indeed it behoveth thee not to take her on this foul wise. Whatsoever betideth thee, destroy not thyself with [undue] haste, for I know that her father's breast will be straitened by this affair and this that thou dost will not profit thee." But the king said, "Verily, Isfehend is [my boughten] servant and a slave of my slaves, and I reck not of her father, if he be vexed or pleased." So saying, he drew the reins of the mule and carrying the damsel, whose name was Behrjaur, to his house, married her.

Meanwhile, the eunuch betook himself, he and the horsemen, to her father and said to him, "O my lord, the king is beholden to thee for many years' service and thou hast not failed him a day of the days; and now, behold, he hath taken thy daughter against thy wish and without thy permission." And he related to him what had passed and how the king had taken her by force. When Isfehend heard the eunuch's story, he was exceeding wroth and assembling many troops, said to them, "Whenas the king was occupied with his women [and concerned not himself with the affairs of his kingdom], we took no reck of him; but now he putteth out his hand to our harem; wherefore methinketh we should do well to look us out a place, wherein we may have sanctuary."

Then he wrote a letter to King Azadbekht, saying to him, "I am a servant of thy servants and a slave of thy slaves and my daughter s a handmaid at thy service, and may God the Most High prolong thy days and appoint thy times [to be] in delight and contentment! Indeed, I still went girded of the waist in thy service and in caring for the preservation of thy dominion and warding off thine enemies from thee; but now I abound yet more than before in zeal and watchfulness, for that I have taken this to charge upon myself, since my daughter is become thy wife." And he despatched a messenger to the king with the letter and a present.

When the messenger came to King Azadbekht and he read the letter and the present was laid before him, he rejoiced with an exceeding joy and occupied himself with eating and drinking, hour after hour. But the chief Vizier of his Viziers came to him and said, "O king, know that Isfehend the Vizier is thine enemy, for that his soul liketh not that which thou hast done with him, and the message that he hath sent thee [is a trick; so] rejoice thou not therein, neither be thou deluded by the sweetness of his words and the softness of his speech." The king hearkened [not] to his Vizier's speech, but made light of the matter and presently, [dismissing it from his thought], busied himself with that which he was about of eating and drinking and merrymaking and delight

Meanwhile, Isfehend the Vizier wrote a letter and despatched it to all the Amirs, acquainting them with that which had betided him with King Azadbekht and how he had taken his daughter by force and adding, "And indeed he will do with you more than he hath done with me." When the letter reached the chiefs [of the people and troops], they all assembled together to Isfehend and said to him, "What is to do with him?"[96] So he discovered to them the affair of his daughter and they all agreed, of one accord, that they should endeavour for the slaughter of the king and taking horse with their troops, set out, intending for him. Azadbekht knew not [of their design] till the noise [of the invasion] beset his capital city, when he said to his wife Behrjaur, "How shall we do?" And she answered, saying, "Thou knowest best and I am at thy commandment." So he let bring two swift horses and bestrode one himself, whilst his wife mounted the other. Then they took what they might of gold and went forth, fleeing, in the night, to the desert of Kerman; what while Isfehend entered the city and made himself king.

Now King Azadbekht's wife was big with child and the pains of labour took her in the mountain; so they alighted at the mountain-foot, by a spring of water, and she gave birth to a boy as he were the moon. Behrjaur his mother pulled off a gown of gold-inwoven brocade and wrapped the child therein, and they passed the night [in that place], what while she gave him suck till the morning. Then said the king to her, "We are hampered by this child and cannot abide here nor can we carry him with us; so methinks we were better leave him here and go, for Allah is able to send him one who shall take him and rear him." So they wept over him exceeding sore and left him beside the spring, wrapped in the gown of brocade: then they laid at his head a thousand dinars in a bag and mounting their horses, departed, fleeing.

Now, by the ordinance of God the Most High, a company of thieves fell in upon a caravan hard by that mountain and made prize of that which was with them of merchandise. Then they betook themselves to the mountain, so they might share their booty, and looking at the foot thereof, espied the gown of brocade. So they descended, to see what it was, and finding the child wrapped therein and the gold laid at his head, marvelled and said, "Extolled be the perfection of God! By what wickedness cometh this child here?" Then they divided the money between them and the captain of the thieves took the boy and made him his son and fed him with sweet milk and dates, till he came to his house, when he appointed him a nurse, who should rear him.

Meanwhile, King Azadbekht and his wife stayed not in their flight till they came to [the court of] the King of Fars,[97] whose name was Kutrou.[98] When they presented themselves to him, he entreated them with honour and entertained them handsomely, and Azadbekht told him his story, first and last. So he gave him a great army and wealth galore and he abode with him some days, till he was rested, when he made ready with his host and setting out for his own dominions, waged war upon Isfehend and falling in upon the capital, defeated the rebel vizier and slew him. Then he entered the city and sat down on the throne of his kingship; and whenas he was rested and the kingdom was grown peaceful for him, he despatched messengers to the mountain aforesaid in quest of the child; but they returned and informed the king that they had not found him.

As time went on, the boy, the son of the king, grew up and fell to stopping the way[99] with the thieves, and they used to carry him with them, whenas they went a-thieving. They sallied forth one day upon a caravan in the land of Seistan, and there were in that caravan strong and valiant men and with them merchandise galore. Now they had heard that in that land were thieves; so they gathered themselves together and made ready their arms and sent out spies, who returned and gave them news of the thieves. Accordingly, they prepared for battle, and when the robbers drew near the caravan, they fell in upon them and they fought a sore battle. At last the folk of the caravan overmastered the thieves, by dint of numbers, and slew some of them, whilst the others fled. Moreover they took the boy, the son of King Azadbekht, and seeing him as he were the moon, possessed of beauty and grace, brightfaced and comely of fashion, questioned him, saying, "Who is thy father, and how camest thou with these thieves?" And he answered, saying, "I am the son of the captain of the thieves." So they took him and carried him to the capital of his father King Azadbekht

When they reached the city, the king heard of their coming and commanded that they should attend him with what befitted [of their merchandise]. So they presented themselves before him, [and the boy with them,] whom when the king saw, he said to them, "To whom belongeth this boy?" And they answered, "O king, we were going in such a road, when there came out upon us a sort of robbers; so we made war upon them and overcame them and took this boy prisoner. Then we questioned him, saying, 'Who is thy father?' and he answered, 'I am the captain's son of the thieves.'" Quoth the king, "I would fain have this boy." And the captain of the caravan said, "God maketh thee gift of him, O king of the age, and we all are thy slaves." Then the king dismissed [the people of] the caravan and let carry the youth into his palace and he became as one of the servants, what while his father the king knew not that he was his son. As time went on, the king observed in him good breeding and understanding and knowledge[100] galore and he pleased him; so he committed his treasuries to his charge and straitened the viziers' hand therefrom, commanding that nought should be taken forth therefrom except by leave of the youth. On this wise he abode a number of years and the king saw in him nought but fidelity and studiousness in well-doing.

Now the treasuries aforetime had been in the viziers' hand, so they might do with them what they would, and when they came under the youth's hand, that of the viziers was straitened from them, and the youth became dearer to the king than a son and he could not brook to be separated from him. When the viziers saw this, they were jealous of him and envied him and cast about for a device against him whereby they might oust him from the king's favour, but found no opportunity. At last, when came the destined hour,[101] it chanced that the youth one day drank wine and became drunken and wandered from his wits; so he fell to going round about within the palace of the king and fate led him to the lodging of the women, in which there was a little sleeping-chamber, where the king lay with his wife. Thither came the youth and entering the chamber, found there a couch spread, to wit, a sleeping place, and a candle burning. So he cast himself on the couch, marvelling at the paintings that were in the chamber, and slept and slumbered heavily till eventide, when there came a slave-girl, bringing with her all the dessert, eatables and drinkables, that she was wont to make ready for the king and his wife, and seeing the youth lying on his back, (and none knowing of his case and he in his drunkenness unknowing where he was,) thought that he was the king asleep on his bed; so she set the censing-vessel and laid the essences by the couch, then shut the door and went away.

Presently, the king arose from the wine-chamber and taking his wife by the hand, repaired with her to the chamber in which he slept. He opened the door and entering, saw the youth lying on the bed, whereupon he turned to his wife and said to her, "What doth this youth here? This fellow cometh not hither but on thine account." Quoth she, "I have no knowledge of him." With this, the youth awoke and seeing the king, sprang up and prostrated himself before him, and Azadbekht said to him, "O vile of origin,[102] O lack-loyalty, what hath prompted thee to outrage my dwelling?" And he bade imprison him in one place and the woman in another.

The First Day.

OF THE USELESSNESS OF ENDEAVOUR AGAINST PERSISTENT ILL FORTUNE.

When the morning morrowed and the king sat on the throne of his kingship, he summoned the chief of his viziers and said to him, "What deemest thou of this that yonder robber-youth hath done? Behold, he hath entered my house and lain down on my bed and I fear lest there be an intrigue between him and the woman. How deemest thou of the affair?" "God prolong the king's continuance!" replied the vizier. "What sawest thou in this youth [to make thee trust in him]? Is he not vile of origin, the son of thieves? Needs must a thief revert to his vile origin, and whoso reareth the young of the serpent shall get of them nought but biting. As for the woman, she is not at fault; for, since [the] time [of her marriage with thee] till now, there hath appeared from her nought but good breeding and modesty; and now, if the king give me leave, I will go to her and question her, so I may discover to thee the affair."

The king gave him leave for this and the vizier betook himself to the queen and said to her, "I am come to thee, on account of a grave reproach, and I would have thee be truthful with me in speech and tell me how came the youth into the sleeping-chamber." Quoth she, "I have no knowledge whatsoever [of it]" and swore to him a solemn oath thereof, whereby he knew that she had no knowledge of the matter and that she was not at fault and said to her, "I will teach thee a device, where- with thou mayst acquit thyself and thy face be whitened before the king." "What is it?" asked she; and he answered, saying, "When the king calleth for thee and questioneth thee of this, say thou to him, 'Yonder youth saw me in the privy-chamber and sent me a message, saying, "I will give thee a hundred jewels, to whose price money may not avail, so thou wilt suffer me to foregather with thee." I laughed at him who bespoke me with these words and rebuffed him; but he sent again to me, saying, "An thou fall not in with my wishes, I will come one of the nights, drunken, and enter and lie down in the sleeping-chamber, and the king will see me and kill me; so wilt thou be put to shame and thy face will be blackened with him and thine honour abased."' Be this thy saying to the king, and I will presently go to him and repeat this to him." Quoth the queen, "And I also will say thus."

So the vizier returned to the king and said to him, "Verily, this youth hath merited grievous punishment, after abundance of bounty [bestowed on him], and it may not be that a bitter kernel should ever become sweet; but, as for the woman, I am certified that there is no fault in her." Then he repeated to the king the story which he had taught the queen, which when Azadbekht heard, he rent his clothes and bade fetch the youth. So they brought him and stationed him before the king, who let bring the head-sman, and the folk all fixed their eyes upon the youth, so they might see what the king should do with him.

Then said Azadbekht to him (and indeed his words were [prompted] by anger and those of the youth by presence of mind and good breeding), "I bought thee with my money and looked for fidelity from thee, wherefore I chose thee over all my grandees and servants and made thee keeper of my treasuries. Why, then, hast thou outraged my honour and entered my house and played the traitor with me and tookest no thought unto that which I have done thee of benefits?" "O king," answered the youth, "I did this not of my choice and freewill and I had no [evil] intent in being there; but, of the littleness of my luck, I was driven thither, for that fate was contrary and fair fortune lacking. Indeed, I had striven with all endeavour that nought of foul should proceed from me and kept watch over myself, lest default appear in me; but none may avail to make head against ill fortune, nor doth endeavour profit in case of lack of luck, as appeareth by the example of the merchant who was stricken with ill luck and his endeavour profited him not and he succumbed to the badness of his fortune." "What is the story of the merchant," asked the king, "and how was his luck changed upon him by the sorriness of his fortune?" "May God prolong the king's continuance!" answered the youth.

Story of the Unlucky Merchant.

"There was once a man, a merchant, who was fortunate in trade, and at one time his [every] dirhem profited [him] fifty. Presently, his luck turned against him and he knew it not; so he said in himself, 'I have wealth galore, yet do I weary myself and go round about from country to country; I were better abide in my own country and rest myself in my house from this travail and affliction and sell and buy at home.' Then he made two parts of his money, with one whereof he bought wheat in summer, saying, 'When the winter cometh, I will sell it at a great profit.' But, when the winter came, wheat became at half the price for which he had bought it, whereat he was sore concerned and left it till the next year. However, next year, the price fell yet lower and one of his friends said to him, 'Thou hast no luck in this wheat; so do thou sell it at whatsoever price.' Quoth the merchant, 'This long while have I profited and it is allowable that I lose this time. God is all- knowing! If it abide [with me] half a score years, I will not sell it save at a profit.'

Then, in his anger, he walled up the door of the granary with clay, and by the ordinance of God the Most High, there came a great rain and descended from the roofs of the house wherein was the wheat [so that the latter rotted]; and needs must the merchant give the porters five hundred dirhems from his purse, so they should carry it forth and cast it without the city, for that the smell of it was noisome. So his friend said to him, 'How often did I tell thee thou hadst no luck in wheat? But thou wouldst not give ear to my speech, and now it behoveth thee to go to the astrologer and question him of thy star.' Accordingly the merchant betook himself to the astrologer and questioned him of his star, and the astrologer said to him, 'Thy star is unpropitious. Put not thy hand to any business, for thou wilt not prosper therein.' However, he paid no heed to the astrologer's words and said in himself, 'If I do my occasion,[103] I am not afraid of aught.' Then he took the other part of his money, after he had spent therefrom three years, and built [therewith] a ship, which he loaded with all that seemed good to him and all that was with him and embarked on the sea, so he might travel.

The ship tarried with him some days, till he should be certified what he would do,[104] and he said, 'I will enquire of the merchants what this merchandise profiteth and in what country it lacketh and how much is the gain thereon.' [So he questioned them and] they directed him to a far country, where his dirhem should profit a hundredfold. Accordingly, he set sail and steered for the land in question; but, as he went, there blew on him a tempestuous wind and the ship foundered. The merchant saved himself on a plank and the wind cast him up, naked as he was, on the seashore, hard by a town there. So he praised God and gave Him thanks for his preservation; then, seeing a great village hard by, he betook himself thither and saw, seated therein, a very old man, whom he acquainted with his case and that which had betided him. The old man grieved sore for him, when he heard his story, and set food before him. So he ate and the old man said to him, 'Abide here with me, so I may make thee my steward and factor over a farm I have here, and thou shall have of me five dirhems [105] a day.' 'God make fair thy reward,' answered the merchant, 'and requite thee with benefits!'

So he abode in this employ, till he had sowed and reaped and threshed and winnowed, and all was sheer in his hand and the owner appointed neither inspector nor overseer, but relied altogether upon him. Then he bethought himself and said, 'I misdoubt me the owner of this grain will not give me my due; so I were better take of it, after the measure of my hire; and if he give me my due, I will restore him that which I have taken.' So he took of the grain, after the measure of that which fell to him, and hid it in a privy place. Then he carried the rest to the old man and meted it out to him, and he said to him, 'Come, take [of the grain, after the measure of] thy hire, for which I agreed with thee, and sell it and buy with the price clothes and what not else; and though thou abide with me half a score years, yet shall thou still have this wage and I will acquit it to thee thus.' Quoth the merchant in himself, 'Indeed, I have done a foul thing in that I look it without his leave.'

Then he went to fetch that which he had hidden of the grain, but found it not and returned, perplexed and sorrowful, to the old man, who said to him, 'What aileth thee to be sorrowful?' And he answered, 'Methought thou wouldst not pay me my due; so I took of the grain, after the measure of my hire; and now thou hast paid me my due and I went to bring back to thee that which I had hidden from thee, but found it gone, for those who had happened upon it had stolen it.' The old man was wroth, when he heard this, and said to the merchant, 'There is no device [can cope] with ill luck! I had given thee this, but, of the sorriness of thy luck and thy fortune, thou hast done this deed, O oppressor of thine own self! Thou deemedst I would not acquit thee thy wage; but, by Allah, nevermore will I give thee aught.' And he drove him away from him.

So the merchant went forth, afflicted, sorrowful, weeping, [and wandered on along the sea-shore], till he came to a sort of divers diving in the sea for pearls. They saw him weeping and mourning and said to him, 'What is thy case and what maketh thee weep?' So he acquainted them with his history, from first to last, whereby they knew him and said to him, 'Art thou [such an one] son of such an one?' 'Yes,' answered he; whereupon they condoled with him and wept sore for him and said to him, 'Abide here till we dive for thy luck this next time and whatsoever betideth us shall be between us and thee.' Accordingly, they dived and brought up ten oysters, in each two great pearls; whereat they marvelled and said to him, 'By Allah, thy luck hath returned and thy good star is in the ascendant!' Then they gave him ten pearls and said to him, 'Sell two of them and make them thy capital [whereon to trade]; and hide the rest against the time of thy straitness.' So he took them, joyful and contented, and addressed himself to sew eight of them in his gown, keeping the two others in his mouth; but a thief saw him and went and advertised his mates of him; whereupon they gathered together upon him and took his gown and departed from him. When they were gone away, he arose, saying, 'These two pearls [in my mouth] will suffice me,' and made for the [nearest] city, where he brought out the pearls [and repairing to the jewel- market, gave them to the broker], that he might sell them.

Now, as destiny would have it, a certain jeweller of the town had been robbed of ten pearls, like unto those which were with the merchant; so, when he saw the two pearls in the broker's hand, he said to him, 'To whom do these pearls belong?' and the broker answered, 'To yonder man.' [The jeweller looked at the merchant and] seeing him in sorry case and clad in tattered clothes, misdoubted of him and said to him (purposing to surprise him into confession), 'Where are the other eight pearls?' The merchant thought he asked him of those which were in the gown and answered, 'The thieves stole them from me.' When the jeweller heard his reply, he doubted not but that it was he who had taken his good; so he laid hold of him and haling him before the chief of the police, said to him, 'This is the man who stole my pearls: I have found two of them upon him and he confesseth to the other eight.'

Now the magistrate knew of the theft of the pearls; so he bade clap the merchant in prison. Accordingly they imprisoned him and flogged him, and he abode in the prison a whole year, till, by the ordinance of God the Most High, the Master of Police arrested one of the divers aforesaid and imprisoned him in the prison where the merchant lay. He saw the latter and knowing him, questioned him of his case; whereupon he told them his story and that which had befallen him, and the diver marvelled at the sorriness of his luck. So, when he came forth of the prison, he acquainted the Sultan with the merchant's case and told him that it was he who had given him the pearls. The Sultan bade bring him forth of the prison and questioned him of his story, whereupon he told him all that had befallen him and the Sultan pitied him and assigned him a lodging in his own palace, together with an allowance for his living.

Now the lodging in question adjoined the king's house, and whilst the merchant was rejoicing in this and saying, 'Verily, my luck hath returned and I shall live in this king's shadow the rest of my life,' he espied an opening walled up with stones and clay. So he pulled out the stones and clearing away the earth from the opening, found that it was a window giving upon the lodging of the king's women. When he saw this, he was affrighted and rising in haste, fetched clay and stopped it up again. But one of the eunuchs saw him and misdoubting of him, repaired to the Sultan and told him of this. So he came and seeing the stones pulled out, was wroth with the merchant and said to him, 'Is this my recompense from thee, that thou seekest to violate my harem?' And he bade pluck out his eyes. So they did as he commanded and the merchant took his eyes in his hand and said, 'How long [wilt thou afflict me], O star of ill-omen? First my wealth and now my life!' And he bewailed himself, saying, 'Endeavour profiteth me nought against evil fortune. The Compassionate aided me not and endeavour was useless.'

On like wise, O king," continued the youth, "whilst fortune was favourable to me, all that I did came to good; but now that it is grown contrary to me, everything turneth against me."

When the youth had made an end of his story, the king's anger subsided a little and he said, "Restore him to the prison, for the day draweth to an end, and tomorrow we will took into his affair."

OF LOOKING TO THE ISSUES OF AFFAIRS.

When it was the second day, the second of the king's viziers, whose name was Beheroun, came in to him and said, "God advance the king! This that yonder youth hath done is a grave matter and a foul deed and a heinous against the household of the king." So Azadbekht bade fetch the youth, because of the saying of the vizier; and when he came into his presence, he said to him, "Out on thee, O youth! Needs must I slay thee by the worst of deaths, for indeed thou hast committed a grave crime, and I will make thee a warning to the folk." "O king," answered the youth, "hasten not, for the looking to the issues of affairs is a pillar of the realm and [a cause of] continuance and sure stablishment for the kingship. Whoso looketh not to the issues of affairs, there befalleth him that which befell the merchant, and whoso looketh to the issues of affairs, there betideth him of joyance that which betided the merchant's son." "And what is the story of the merchant and his son?" asked the king. "O king," answered the youth,

Story of the Merchant and His Sons.

"There was once a man, a merchant, who had a wife and abundant wealth. He set out one day on a journey with merchandise, leaving his wife big with child, and said to her, 'If it be the will of God the Most High, I will return before the birth of the child.' Then he took leave of her and setting out, journeyed from country to country till he came to the court of one of the kings and foregathered with him. Now this king was in need of one who should order his affairs and those of his kingdom and seeing the merchant well-bred and intelligent, he charged him abide with him and entreated him with honour and munificence. After awhile, he sought of the king leave to go to his own house, but the latter would not consent to this; whereupon he said to him, 'O king, suffer me go and see my children and come again.' So he gave him leave for this and took surety of him for his return. Moreover, he gave him a purse, wherein were a thousand gold dinars, and the merchant embarked in a ship and set sail, intending for his own country.

Meanwhile, news came to his wife that her husband had taken service with King Such-an-one; so she arose and taking her two sons, (for she had given birth to twin boys in his absence,) set out for those parts. As fate would have it, they happened upon an island and her husband came thither that very night in the ship. [When the woman heard of the coming of the ship], she said to her children, 'This ship cometh from the country where your father is; so go ye to the sea-shore, that ye may enquire of him.' So they repaired to the sea-shore and [going up into the ship], fell to playing about it and occupied themselves with their play till the evening.

Now the merchant their father lay asleep in the ship, and the crying of the boys troubled him; so he rose to call out to them [and silence them] and let the purse [with the thousand dinars therein] fall among the bales of merchandise. He sought for it and finding it not, buffeted his head and seized upon the boys, saying, 'None took the purse but you. Ye were playing about the bales, so ye might steal somewhat, and there was none here but you.' Then he took a staff and laying hold of the children, fell to beating them and flogging them, whilst they wept, and the sailors came round about them and said, 'The boys of this island are all thieves and robbers.' Then, of the greatness of the merchant's wrath, he swore that, if they brought not out the purse, he would drown them in the sea; so when [by reason of their denial] his oath became binding upon him, he took the two boys and lashing them [each] to a bundle of reeds, cast them into the sea.

Presently, the mother of the two boys, finding that they tarried from her, went searching for them, till she came to the ship and fell to saying, 'Who hath seen two boys of mine? Their fashion is thus and thus and their age thus and thus.' When they heard her words, they said, 'This is the description of the two boys who were drowned in the sea but now.' Their mother heard and fell to calling on them and saying, 'Alas, my anguish for your loss, O my sons! Where was the eye of your father this day, that it might have seen you?' Then one of the crew questioned her, saying, 'Whose wife art thou?' And she answered, 'I am the wife of such an one the merchant. I was on my way to him, and there hath befallen me this calamity.' When the merchant heard her speech, he knew her and rising to his feet, rent his clothes and buffeted his head and said to his wife, 'By Allah, I have destroyed my children with mine own hand! This is the end of whoso looketh not to the issues of affairs.' Then he fell a-wailing and weeping over them, he and his wife, and he said, 'By Allah, I shall have no ease of my life, till I light upon news of them!' And he betook himself to going round about the sea, in quest of them, but found them not.

Meanwhile, the wind carried the two children [out to sea and thence driving them] towards the land, cast them up on the sea-shore. As for one of them, a company of the guards of the king of those parts found him and carried him to their master, who marvelled at him with an exceeding wonderment and adopted him to his son, giving out to the folk that he was his [very] son, whom he had hidden,[106] of his love for him. So the folk rejoiced in him with an exceeding joy, for the king's sake, and the latter appointed him his heir-apparent and the inheritor of his kingdom. On this wise, a number of years passed, till the king died and they crowned the youth king in his room. So he sat down on the throne of his kingship and his estate flourished and his affairs prospered.

Meanwhile, his father and mother had gone round about all the islands of the sea in quest of him and his brother, hoping that the sea might have cast them up, but found no trace of them; so they despaired of finding them and took up their abode in one of the islands. One day, the merchant, being in the market, saw a broker, and in his hand a boy he was calling for sale, and said in himself, 'I will buy yonder boy, so I may console myself with him for my sons.' So he bought him and carried him to his house; and when his wife saw him, she cried out and said, 'By Allah, this is my son!' So his father and mother rejoiced in him with an exceeding joy and questioned him of his brother; but he answered, 'The sea parted us and I knew not what became of him.' Therewith his father and mother consoled themselves with him and on this wise a number of years passed.

Now the merchant and his wife had taken up their abode in a city in the land whereof their [other] son was king, and when the boy [whom they had found] grew up, his father assigned unto him merchandise, so he might travel therewith. So he set out and entered the city wherein his brother was king. News reached the latter that there was a merchant come thither with merchandise befitting kings. So he sent for him and the young merchant obeyed the summons and going in to him, sat down before him. Neither of them knew the other; but blood stirred between them and the king said to the young merchant, 'I desire of thee that thou abide with me and I will exalt thy station and give thee all that thou desirest and cravest.' So he abode with him awhile, quitting him not; and when he saw that he would not suffer him to depart from him, he sent to his father and mother and bade them remove thither to him. So they addressed them to remove to that island, and their son increased still in honour with the king, albeit he knew not that he was his brother.

It chanced one night that the king sallied forth without the city and drank and the wine got the mastery of him and he became drunken. So, of the youth's fearfulness for him, he said, 'I will keep watch myself over the king this night, seeing that he deserveth this from me, for that which he hath wrought with me of kindnesses.' So he arose forthright and drawing his sword, stationed himself at the door of the king's pavilion. Now one of the royal servants saw him standing there, with the drawn sword in his hand, and he was of those who envied him his favour with the king; so he said to him, 'Why dost thou on this wise at this season and in the like of this place?' Quoth the youth, 'I am keeping watch over the king myself, in requital of his bounties to me.'

The servant said no more to him, but, when it was morning, he acquainted a number of the king's servants with this and they said, 'This is an opportunity for us. Come let us assemble together and acquaint the king with this, so the young merchant may lose favour with him and he rid us of him and we be at rest from him.' So they assembled together and going in to the king, said to him, 'We have a warning we would give thee.' Quoth he, 'And what is your warning?' And they said, 'Yonder youth, the merchant, whom thou hast taken into favour and whose rank thou hast exalted above the chiefs of the people of thy household, we saw yesterday draw his sword and offer to fall upon thee, so he might slay thee.' When the king heard this, his colour changed and he said to them, 'Have ye proof of this?' Quoth they, 'What proof wouldst thou have? If thou desire this, feign thyself drunken again this night and lie down, as if asleep, and watch him, and thou wilt see with thine eyes all that we have named to thee.'

Then they went to the youth and said to him, 'Know that the king thanketh thee for thy dealing yesternight and exceedeth in [praise of] thy good deed;' and they prompted him to do the like again. So, when the next night came, the king abode on wake; watching the youth; and as for the latter, he went to the door of the pavilion and drawing his sword, stood in the doorway. When the king saw him do thus, he was sore disquieted and bade seize him and said to him, 'Is this my requital from thee? I showed thee favour more than any else and thou wouldst do with me this vile deed.' Then arose two of the king's servants and said to him, 'O our lord, if thou command it, we will strike off his head.' But the king said, 'Haste in slaying is a vile thing, for it[107] is a grave matter; the quick we can slay, but the slain we cannot quicken, and needs must we look to the issue of affairs. The slaying of this [youth] will not escape us.'[108] Therewith he bade imprison him, whilst he himself returned [to the city] and despatching his occasions, went forth to the chase.

Then he returned to the city and forgot the youth; so the servants went in to him and said to him, 'O king, if thou keep silence concerning yonder youth, who would have slain thee, all thy servants will presume upon thee, and indeed the folk talk of this matter.' With this the king waxed wroth and saying, 'Fetch him hither,' commanded the headsman to strike off his head. So they [brought the youth and] bound his eyes; and the headsman stood at his head and said to the king, 'By thy leave, O my lord, I will strike off his head.' But the king said, 'Stay, till I look into his affair. Needs must I put him to death and the slaying of him will not escape [me].' So he restored him to the prison and there he abode till it should be the king's will to put him to death.

Presently, his father and his mother heard of the matter; whereupon the former arose and going up to the place, wrote a letter and [presented it to the king, who] read it, and behold, therein was written, saying, 'Have pity on me, so may God have pity on thee, and hasten not in the slaughter [of my son]; for indeed I acted hastily in a certain affair and drowned his brother in the sea, and to this day I drink the cup of his anguish. If thou must needs kill him, kill me in his stead.' Therewith the old merchant prostrated himself before the king and wept; and the latter said to him, 'Tell me thy story.' 'O my lord,' answered the merchant, 'this youth had a brother and I [in my haste] cast them both into the sea.' And he related to him his story from first to last, whereupon the king cried out with an exceeding great cry and casting himself down from the throne, embraced his father and brother and said to the former, 'By Allah, thou art my very father and this is my brother and thy wife is our mother.' And they abode weeping, all three.

Then the king acquainted the people [of his court] with the matter and said to them,' O folk, how deem ye of my looking to the issues of affairs?' And they all marvelled at his wisdom and foresight. Then he turned to his father and said to him, 'Hadst thou looked to the issue of thine affair and dealt deliberately in that which thou didst, there had not betided thee this repentance and grief all this time.' Then he let bring his mother and they rejoiced in each other and lived all their days in joy and gladness. What then," continued the young treasurer, "is more grievous than the lack of looking to the issues of affairs? Wherefore hasten thou not in the slaying of me, lest repentance betide thee and sore concern."

When the king heard this, he said, "Restore him to the prison till the morrow, so we may look into his affair; for that deliberation in affairs is advisable and the slaughter of this [youth] shall not escape [us]."

The Third Day.

OF THE ADVANTAGES OF PATIENCE.

When it was the third day, the third vizier came in to the king and said to him, "O king, delay not the affair of this youth, for that his deed hath caused us fall into the mouths of the folk, and it behoveth that thou slay him presently, so the talk may be estopped from us and it be not said, 'The king saw on his bed a man with his wife and spared him.'"* The king was chagrined by this speech and bade bring the youth. So they brought him in shackles, and indeed the king's anger was roused against him by the speech of the vizier and he was troubled; so he said to him, "O base of origin, thou hast dishonoured us and marred our repute, and needs must I do away thy life from the world." Quoth the youth, "O king, make use of patience in all thine affairs, so wilt thou attain thy desire, for that God the Most High hath appointed the issue of patience [to be] in abounding good, and indeed by patience Abou Sabir ascended from the pit and sat down upon the throne." "Who was Abou Sabir," asked the king, "and what is his story?" And the youth answered, saying, "O king,

STORY OF ABOU SABIR.

There was once a man, a headman [of a village], by name Abou Sabir, and he had much cattle and a fair wife, who had borne him two sons. They abode in a certain village and there used to come thither a lion and devour Abou Sabir's cattle, so that the most part thereof was wasted and his wife said to him one day, 'This lion hath wasted the most part of our cattle. Arise, mount thy horse and take thy men and do thine endeavour to kill him, so we may be at rest from him.' But Abou Sabir said, 'Have patience, O woman, for the issue of patience is praised. This lion it is that transgresseth against us, and the transgressor, needs must Allah destroy him. Indeed, it is our patience that shall slay him, and he that doth evil, needs must it revert upon him.' A little after, the king went forth one day to hunt and falling in with the lion, he and his troops, gave chase to him and ceased not [to follow] after him till they slew him. This came to Abou Sabir's knowledge and he said to his wife, 'Said I not to thee, O woman, that whoso doth evil, it shall revert upon him? Belike, if I had sought to slay the lion myself, I had not availed against him, and this is the issue of patience.'

It befell, after this, that a man was slain in Abou Sabir's village; wherefore the Sultan caused plunder the village, and they plundered the headman's goods with the rest So his wife said to him, 'All the Sultan's officers know thee; so do thou prefer thy plaint to the king, that he may cause thy beasts to be restored to thee.' But he said to her, 'O woman, said I not to thee that he who doth evil shall suffer it? Indeed, the king hath done evil, and he shall suffer [the consequences of] his deed, for whoso taketh the goods of the folk, needs must his goods be taken.' A man of his neighbours heard his speech, and he was an envier of his; so he went to the Sultan and acquainted him therewith, whereupon he sent and plundered all [the rest of] his goods and drove him forth from the village, and his wife [and children] with him. So they went wandering in the desert and his wife said to him, 'All that hath befallen us cometh of thy slothfulness in affairs and thy default.' But he said to her, 'Have patience, for the issue of patience is good.'

Then they went on a little, and thieves met them and despoiling them of that which remained with them, stripped them of their raiment and took the children from them; whereupon the woman wept and said to her husband, 'O man, put away from thee this folly and arise, let us follow the thieves, so haply they may have compassion on us and restore the children to us.' 'O woman,' answered he, 'have patience, for he who doth evil shall be requited with evil and his wickedness shall revert upon him. Were I to follow them, most like one of them would take his sword and smite off my head and slay me; but have patience, for the issue of patience is praised.' Then they fared on till they drew near a village in the land of Kirman, and by it a river of water. So he said to his wife, 'Abide thou here, whilst I enter the village and look us out a place wherein we may take up our lodging.' And he left her by the water and entered the village.

Presently, up came a horseman in quest of water, so he might water his horse. He saw the woman and she was pleasing in his sight; so he said to her, 'Arise, mount with me and I will take thee to wife and entreat thee kindly.' Quoth she, 'Spare me, so may God spare thee! Indeed, I have a husband.' But he drew his sword and said to her, 'An thou obey me not, I will smite thee and kill thee.' When she saw his malice, she wrote on the ground in the sand with her finger, saying, 'O Abou Sabir, thou hast not ceased to be patient, till thy wealth is gone from thee and thy children and [now] thy wife, who was more precious in thy sight than everything and than all thy wealth, and indeed thou abidest in thy sorrow all thy life long, so thou mayst see what thy patience will profit thee.' Then the horseman took her, and setting her behind him, went his way.

As for Abou Sabir, when he returned, he saw not his wife and read what was written on the ground, wherefore he wept and sat [awhile] sorrowing. Then said he to himself, 'O Abou Sabir, it behoveth thee to be patient, for belike there shall betide [thee] an affair yet sorer than this and more grievous;' and he went forth wandering at a venture, like to the love-distraught, the madman, till he came to a sort of labourers working upon the palace of the king, by way of forced labour. When [the overseers] saw him, they laid hold of him and said to him, 'Work thou with these folk at the palace of the king; else will we imprison thee for life.' So he fell to working with them as a labourer and every day they gave him a cake of bread. He wrought with them a month's space, till it chanced that one of the labourers mounted a ladder and falling, broke his leg; whereupon he cried out and wept. Quoth Abou Sabir to him, 'Have patience and weep not; for thou shall find ease in thy patience.' But the man said to him, 'How long shall I have patience?' And he answered, saying, 'Patience bringeth a man forth of the bottom of the pit and seateth him on the throne of the kingdom.'

Now the king was seated at the lattice, hearkening to their talk, and Abou Sabir's words angered him; so he bade bring him before him and they brought him forthright. Now there was in the king's palace an underground dungeon and therein a vast deep pit, into which the king caused cast Abou Sabir, saying to him, 'O lackwit, now shall we see how thou wilt come forth of the pit to the throne of the kingdom.' Then he used to come and stand at the mouth of the pit and say, 'O lackwit, O Abou Sabir, I see thee not come forth of the pit and sit down on the king's throne!' And he assigned him each day two cakes of bread, whilst Abou Sabir held his peace and spoke not, but bore with patience that which betided him.

Now the king had a brother, whom he had imprisoned in that pit of old time, and he had died [there]; but the folk of the realm thought that he was alive, and when his [supposed] imprisonment grew long, the king's officers used to talk of this and of the tyranny of the king, and the report spread abroad that the king was a tyrant, wherefore they fell upon him one day and slew him. Then they sought the well and brought out Abou Sabir therefrom, deeming him the king's brother, for that he was the nearest of folk to him [in favour] and the likest, and he had been long in the prison. So they doubted not but that he was the prince in question and said to him, 'Reign thou in thy brother's room, for we have slain him and thou art king in his stead.' But Abou Sabir was silent and spoke not a word; and he knew that this was the issue of his patience. Then he arose and sitting down on the king's throne, donned the royal raiment and discovered justice and equity and the affairs [of the realm] prospered [in his hand]; wherefore the folk obeyed him and the people inclined to him and many were his troops.

Now the king, who had plundered Abou Sabir['s goods] and driven him forth of his village, had an enemy; and the latter took horse against him and overcame him and captured his [capital] city; wherefore he addressed himself to flight and came to Abou Sabir's city, craving protection of him and seeking that he should succour him. He knew not that the king of the city was the headman whom he had despoiled; so he presented himself before him and made complaint to him; but Abou Sabir knew him and said to him, 'This is somewhat of the issue of patience. God the Most High hath given me power over thee.' Then he bade his guards plunder the [unjust] king and his attendants; so they plundered them and stripping them of their clothes, put them forth of his country. When Abou Sabir's troops saw this, they marvelled and said, 'What is this deed that the king doth? There cometh a king to him, craving protection, and he despoileth him! This is not of the fashion of kings.' But they dared not [be]speak [him] of this.

After this, news came to the king of robbers in his land; so he set out in quest of them and ceased not to follow after them, till he seized on them all, and behold, they were the [very] thieves who had despoiled him [and his wife] by the way and taken his children. So he bade bring them before him, and when they came into his presence, he questioned them, saying, 'Where are the two boys ye took on such a day?' Quoth they, 'They are with us and we will present them to our lord the king for slaves to serve him and give him wealth galore that we have gotten together and divest ourselves of all that we possess and repent from sin and fight in thy service.' Abou Sabir, however, paid no heed to their speech, but took all their good and bade put them all to death. Moreover, he took the two boys and rejoiced in them with an exceeding joy, whereat the troops murmured among themselves, saying, 'Verily, this is a greater tyrant than his brother! There come to him a sort of robbers and seek to repent and proffer two boys [by way of peace-offering], and he taketh the two boys and all their good and slayeth them!'

After this came the horseman, who had taken Abou Sabir's wife, and complained of her to the king that she would not give him possession of herself, avouching that she was his wife. The king bade bring her before him, that he might hear her speech and pronounce judgment upon her. So the horseman came with her before him, and when the king saw her, he knew her and taking her from her ravisher, bade put the latter to death. Then he became aware of the troops, that they murmured against him and spoke of him as a tyrant; so he turned to his officers and viziers and said to them, 'As for me, by God the Great, I am not the king's brother! Nay, I am but one whom the king imprisoned upon a word he heard from me and used every day to taunt me therewith. Ye think that I am the king's brother; but I am Abou Sabir and God hath given me the kingship in virtue of my patience. As for the king who sought protection of me and I despoiled him, it was he who first wronged me, for that he despoiled me aforetime and drove me forth of my native land and banished me, without due [cause]; wherefore I requited him with that which he had done to me, in the way of lawful vengeance. As for the thieves who proffered repentance, there was no repentance for them with me, for that they began upon me with foul [dealing] and waylaid me by the road and despoiled me and took my good and my sons. Now these two boys, that I took of them and whom ye deemed slaves, are my very sons; so I avenged myself on the thieves of that which they did with me aforetime and requited them with equity. As for the horseman whom I slew, the woman I took from him was my wife and he took her by force, but God the Most High hath restored her [to me]; so this was my right, and my deed that I have done was just, albeit ye, [judging] by the outward of the matter, deemed that I had done this by way of tyranny.' When the folk heard this, they marvelled and fell prostrate before him; and they redoubled in esteem for him and exceeding affection and excused themselves to him, marvelling at that which God had done with him and how He had given him the kingship by reason of his longsuffering and his patience and how he had raised himself by his patience from the bottom of the pit to the throne of the kingdom, what while God cast down the [late] king from the throne into the pit.[109] Then Abou Sabir foregathered with his wife and said to her, 'How deemest thou of the fruit of patience and its sweetness and the fruit of haste and its bitterness? Verily, all that a man doth of good and evil, he shall assuredly abide.' On like wise, O king," continued the young treasurer, "it behoveth thee to practise patience, whenas it is possible to thee, for that patience is of the fashion of the noble, and it is the chiefest of their reliance, especially for kings."

When the king heard this from the youth, his anger subsided; so he bade restore him to the prison, and the folk dispersed that day.

The Fourth Day.

OF THE ILL EFFECTS OF PRECIPITATION.

When it was the fourth day, the fourth vizier, whose name was Zoushad, made his appearance and prostrating himself to the king, said to him, "O king, suffer not the talk of yonder youth to delude thee, for that he is not a truth-teller. So long as he abideth on life, the folk will not give over talking nor will thy heart cease to be occupied with him." "By Allah," cried the king, "thou sayst sooth and I will cause fetch him this day and slay him before me." Then he commanded to bring the youth; so they brought him in shackles and he said to him, "Out on thee! Thinkest thou to appease my heart with thy prate, whereby the days are spent in talk? I mean to slay thee this day and be quit of thee." "O king," answered the youth, "it is in thy power to slay me whensoever thou wilt, but haste is of the fashion of the base and patience of that of the noble. If thou put me to death, thou wilt repent, and if thou desire to bring me back to life, thou wilt not be able thereunto. Indeed, whoso acteth hastily in an affair, there befalleth him what befell Bihzad, son of the king." Quoth the king, "And what is his story?" "O king," replied the young treasurer,

STORY OF PRINCE BIHZAD.

"There was once, of old time, a king and he had a son [ramed Bihzad], there was not in his day a goodlier than he and he loved to consort with the folk and to sit with the merchants and converse with them. One day, as he sat in an assembly, amongst a number of folk, he heard them talking of his own goodliness and grace and saying, 'There is not in his time a goodlier than he.' But one of the company said, 'Indeed, the daughter of King Such-an-one is handsomer than he.' When Bihzad heard this saying, his reason fled and his heart fluttered and he called the last speaker and said to him, 'Repeat to me that which thou saidst and tell me the truth concerning her whom thou avouchest to be handsomer than I and whose daughter she is.' Quoth the man, 'She is the daughter of King Such-an-one;' whereupon Bihzad's heart clave to her and his colour changed.

The news reached his father, who said to him, 'O my son, this damsel to whom thy heart cleaveth is at thy commandment and we have power over her; so wait till I demand her [in marriage] for thee.' But the prince said, 'I will not wait.' So his father hastened in the matter and sent to demand her of her father, who required of him a hundred thousand dinars to his daughter's dowry. Quoth Bihzad's father, 'So be it,' and paid down what was in his treasuries, and there remained to his charge but a little of the dower. So he said to his son, 'Have patience, O my son, till we gather together the rest of the money and send to fetch her to thee, for that she is become thine.' Therewith the prince waxed exceeding wroth and said, 'I will not have patience;' so he took his sword and his spear and mounting his horse, went forth and fell to stopping the way, [so haply that he might win what lacked of the dowry].

It chanced one day that he fell in upon a company of folk and they overcame him by dint of numbers and taking him prisoner, pinioned him and carried him to the lord of that country. The latter saw his fashion and grace and misdoubting of him, said, 'This is no robber's favour. Tell me truly, O youth, who thou art.' Bihzad thought shame to acquaint him with his condition and chose rather death for himself; so he answered, 'I am nought but a thief and a bandit.' Quoth the king, 'It behoveth us not to act hastily in the matter of this youth, but that we look into his affair, for that haste still engendereth repentance.' So he imprisoned him in his palace and assigned him one who should serve him.

Meanwhile, the news spread abroad that Bihzad, son of the king, was lost, whereupon his father sent letters in quest of him [to all the kings and amongst others to him with whom he was imprisoned]. When the letter reached the latter, he praised God the Most High for that he had not anydele hastened in Bihzad's affair and letting bring him before himself, said to him, 'Art thou minded to destroy thyself?' Quoth Bihzad, '[I did this] for fear of reproach;' and the king said, 'An thou fear reproach, thou shouldst not practise haste [in that thou dost]; knowest thou not that the fruit of haste is repentance? If we had hasted, we also, like unto thee, we had repented.'

Then he conferred on him a dress of honour and engaged to him for the completion of the dowry and sent to his father, giving him the glad news and comforting his heart with [the tidings of] his son's safety; after which he said to Bihzad, Arise, O my son, and go to thy father.' 'O king,' rejoined the prince, 'complete thy kindness to me by [hastening] my going-in to my wife; for, if I go back to my father, till he send a messenger and he return, promising me, the time will be long.' The king laughed and marvelled at him and said to him, 'I fear for thee from this haste, lest thou come to shame and attain not thy desire.' Then he gave him wealth galore and wrote him letters, commending him to the father of the princess, and despatched him to them. When he drew near their country, the king came forth to meet him with the people of his realm and assigned him a handsome lodging and bade hasten the going-in of his daughter to him, in compliance with the other king's letter. Moreover, he advised the prince's father [of his son's coming] and they busied themselves with the affair of the damsel.

When it was the day of the going-in,[110] Bihzad, of his haste and lack of patience, betook himself to the wall, which was between himself and the princess's lodging and in which there was a hole pierced, and looked, so he might see his bride, of his haste. But the bride's mother saw him and this was grievous to her; so she took from one of the servants two red-hot iron spits and thrust them into the hole through which the prince was looking. The spits ran into his eyes and put them out and he fell down aswoon and joyance was changed and became mourning and sore concern. See, then, O king," continued the youth, "the issue of the prince's haste and lack of deliberation, for indeed his haste bequeathed him long repentance and his joy was changed to mourning; and on like wise was it with the woman who hastened to put out his eyes and deliberated not. All this was the doing of haste; wherefore it behoveth the king not to be hasty in putting me to death, for that I am under the grasp of his hand, and what time soever thou desirest my slaughter, it shall not escape [thee]."

When the king heard this, his anger subsided and he said, "Carry him back to prison till to-morrow, to we may look into his affair."

The Fifth Day

OF THE ISSUES OF GOOD AND EVIL ACTIONS.

When it was the fifth day, the fifth Vizier, whose name was Jehrbaur, came in to the king and prostrating himself before him, said, "O king, it behoveth thee, if thou see or hear that one look on thy house,[111] that thou put out his eyes. How then should it be with him whom thou sawest midmost thy house and on thy very bed, and he suspected with thy harem, and not of thy lineage nor of thy kindred? Wherefore do thou away this reproach by putting him to death. Indeed, we do but urge thee unto this for the assurance of thine empire and of our zeal for thy loyal counselling and of our love to thee. How can it be lawful that this youth should live for a single hour?"

Therewith the king was filled with wrath and said, "Bring him forthright," So they brought the youth before him, shackled, and the king said to him, "Out on thee! Thou hast sinned a great sin and the time of thy life hath been long;[112] but needs must we put thee to death, for that there is for us no ease in thy life after this," "O king," answered he, "know that I, by Allah, am guiltless, and by reason of this I hope for life, for that he who is guiltless of offence goeth not in fear of punishment neither maketh great his mourning and his concern; but whoso hath sinned, needs must his sin be expiated upon him, though his life be prolonged, and it shall overtake him, even as it overtook Dadbin the king and his vizier." "How was that?" asked Azadbekht, and the youth said,

STORY OF KING DADBIN AND HIS VIZIERS.

"There was once a king in the land of Teberistan, by name Dadbin, and he had two viziers, called one Zourkhan and the other Kardan. The Vizier Zourkhan had a daughter, there was not in her time a handsomer than she nor yet a chaster nor a more pious, for she was a faster, a prayer and a worshipper of God the Most High, and her name was Arwa. Now Dadbin heard tell of her charms; so his heart clave to her and he called the vizier [her father] and said to him, 'I desire of thee that thou marry me to thy daughter.' Quoth Zourkhan, 'Allow me to consult her, and if she consent, I will marry thee with her.' And the king said, 'Hasten unto this.'

So the vizier went in to his daughter and said to her, 'O my daughter, the king seeketh thee of me and desireth to marry thee.' 'O my father,' answered she 'I desire not a husband and if thou wilt marry me, marry me not but with one who shall be below me in rank and I nobler than he, so he may not turn to other than myself nor lift his eyes upon me, and marry me not to one who is nobler than I, lest I be with him as a slave-girl and a serving-woman.' So the vizier returned to the king and acquainted him with that which his daughter had said, whereat he redoubled in desire and love-liking for her and said to her father, 'An thou marry me not to her of good grace, I will take her by force in thy despite.' The vizier again betook himself to his daughter and repeated to her the king's words, but she replied, 'I desire not a husband.' So he returned to the king and told him what she said, and he was wroth and threatened the vizier, whereupon the latter took his daughter and fled with her.

When this came to the king's knowledge, he despatched troops in pursuit of Zourkhan, to stop the road upon him, whilst he himself went out and overtaking the vizier, smote him on the head with his mace and slew him. Then he took his daughter by force and returning to his dwelling-place, went in to her and married her. Arwa resigned herself with patience to that which betided her and committed her affair to God the Most High; and indeed she was used to serve Him day and night with a goodly service in the house of King Dabdin her husband.

It befell one day that the king had occasion to make a journey; so he called his Vizier Kardan and said to him, 'I have a trust to commit to thy care, and it is yonder damsel, my wife, the daughter of the Vizier [Zourkhan], and I desire that thou keep her and guard her thyself, for that there is not in the world aught dearer to me than she.' Quoth Kardan in himself, 'Of a truth, the king honoureth me with an exceeding honour [in entrusting me] with this damsel.' And he answered 'With all my heart.'

When the king had departed on his journey, the vizier said in himself, 'Needs must I look upon this damsel whom the king loveth with all this love.' So he hid himself in a place, that he might look upon her, and saw her overpassing description; wherefore he was confounded at her and his wit was dazed and love got the mastery of him, so that he said to her, saying, 'Have pity on me, for indeed I perish for the love of thee.' She sent back to him, saying, 'O vizier, thou art in the place of trust and confidence, so do not thou betray thy trust, but make thine inward like unto thine outward[113] and occupy thyself with thy wife and that which is lawful to thee. As for this, it is lust and [women are all of] one taste.[114] And if thou wilt not be forbidden from this talk, I will make thee a byword and a reproach among the folk.' When the vizier heard her answer, he knew that she was chaste of soul and body; wherefore he repented with the utmost of repentance and feared for himself from the king and said, 'Needs must I contrive a device wherewithal I may destroy her; else shall I be disgraced with the king.'

When the king returned from his journey, he questioned his vizier of the affairs of his kingdom and the latter answered, 'All is well, O king, save a vile matter, which I have discovered here and wherewith I am ashamed to confront the king; but, if I hold my peace thereof, I fear lest other than I discover it and I [be deemed to] have played traitor to the king in the matter of my [duty of] loyal warning and my trust.' Quoth Dabdin, 'Speak, for thou art none other than a truth-teller, a trusty one, a loyal counsellor in that which thou sayest, undistrusted in aught.' And the vizier said, 'O king, this woman to whose love thy heart cleaveth and of whose piety thou talkest and her fasting and praying, I will make plain to thee that this is craft and guile.' At this, the king was troubled and said, 'What is to do?' 'Know,' answered the vizier, 'that some days after thy departure, one came to me and said to me, "Come, O vizier, and look." So I went to the door of the [queen's] sleeping-chamber and beheld her sitting with Aboulkhair, her father's servant, whom she favoureth, and she did with him what she did, and this is the manner of that which I saw and heard.'

When Dabdin heard this, he burnt with rage and said to one of his eunuchs,[115] 'Go and slay her in her chamber.' But the eunuch said to him, 'O king, may God prolong thy continuance! Indeed, the killing of her may not be at this time; but do thou bid one of thine eunuchs take her up on a camel and carry her to one of the trackless deserts and cast her down there; so, if she be at fault, God shall cause her to perish, and if she be innocent, He will deliver her, and the king shall be free from sin against her, for that this damsel is dear to thee and thou slewest her father by reason of thy love for her.' Quoth the king, 'By Allah, thou sayst sooth!' Then he bade one of his eunuchs carry her on a camel to one of the far-off deserts and there leave her and go away, and he forbade [him] to prolong her torment. So he took her up and betaking himself with her to the desert, left her there without victual or water and returned, whereupon she made for one of the [sand-]hills and ranging stones before her [in the form of a prayer-niche], stood praying.

Now it chanced that a camel-driver, belonging to Kisra the king, lost certain camels and the king threatened him, if he found them not, that he would slay him. So he set out and plunged into the deserts till he came to the place where the damsel was and seeing her standing praying, waited till she had made an end of her prayer, when he went up to her and saluted her, saying, 'Who art thou?' Quoth she, 'I am a handmaid of God.' 'What dost thou in this desolate place?' asked he, and she said, 'I serve God the Most High.' When he saw her beauty and grace, he said to her, 'Harkye! Do thou take me to husband and I will be tenderly solicitous over thee and use thee with exceeding compassion and I will further thee in obedience to God the Most High.' But she answered, saying, 'I have no need of marriage and I desire to abide here [alone] with my Lord and His service; but, if thou wouldst deal compassionately with me and further me in the obedience of

God the Most High, carry me to a place where there is water and thou wilt have done me a kindness.'

So he carried her to a place wherein was running water and setting her down on the ground, left her and went away, marvelling at her. After he left her, he found his camels, by her blessing, and when he returned, King Kisra asked him, 'Hast thou found the camels?' ['Yes,' answered he] and acquainted him with the affair of the damsel and set out to him her beauty and grace; whereupon the king's heart clave to her and he mounted with a few men and betook himself to that place, where he found the damsel and was amazed at her, for that he saw her overpassing the description wherewith the camel-driver had described her to him. So he accosted her and said to her, 'I am King Kisra, greatest of the kings. Wilt thou not have me to husband?' Quoth she, 'What wilt thou do with me, O king, and I a woman abandoned in the desert?' And he answered, saying, 'Needs must this be, and if thou wilt not consent to me, I will take up my sojourn here and devote myself to God's service and thine and worship Him with thee.'

Then he bade set up for her a tent and another for himself, facing hers, so he might worship God with her, and fell to sending her food; and she said in herself, 'This is a king and it is not lawful for me that I suffer him forsake his subjects and his kingdom for my sake. So she said to the serving-woman, who used to bring her the food, 'Speak to the king, so he may return to his women, for he hath no need of me and I desire to abide in this place, so I may worship God the Most High therein.' The slave-girl returned to the king and told him this, whereupon he sent back to her, saying, 'I have no need of the kingship and I also desire to abide here and worship God with thee in this desert.' When she found this earnestness in him, she consented to his wishes and said, 'O king, I will consent unto thee in that which thou desirest and will be to thee a wife, but on condition that thou bring me Dadbin the king and his Vizier Kardan and his chamberlain[116] and that they be present in thine assembly, so I may speak a word with them in thy presence, to the intent that thou mayest redouble in affection for me.' Quoth Kisra, 'And what is thine occasion unto this?' So she related to him her story from first to last, how she was the wife of Dadbin the king and how the latter's vizier had miscalled her honour.

When King Kisra heard this, he redoubled in loveliking for her and affection and said to her, 'Do what thou wilt.' So he let bring a litter and carrying her therein to his dwelling-place, married her and entreated her with the utmost honour. Then he sent a great army to King Dadbin and fetching him and his vizier and the chamberlain, caused bring them before him, unknowing what he purposed with them. Moreover, he caused set up for Arwa a pavilion in the courtyard of his palace and she entered therein and let down the curtain before herself. When the servants had set their seats and they had seated themselves, Arwa raised a corner of the curtain and said, 'O Kardan, rise to thy feet, for it befitteth not that thou sit in the like of this assembly, before this mighty King Kisra.' When the vizier heard these words, his heart quaked and his joints were loosened and of his fear, he rose to his feet. Then said she to him, 'By the virtue of Him who hath made thee stand in this place of standing [up to judgment], and thou abject and humiliated, I conjure thee speak the truth and say what prompted thee to lie against me and cause me go forth from my house and from the hand of my husband and made thee practise thus against a man,[117] a true believer, and slay him. This is no place wherein leasing availeth nor may prevarication be therein.'

When the vizier was ware that she was Arwa and heard her speech, he knew that it behoved him not to lie and that nought would avail him but truth-speaking; so he bowed [his head] to the ground and wept and said, 'Whoso doth evil, needs must he abide it, though his day be prolonged. By Allah, I am he who hath sinned and transgressed, and nought prompted me unto this but fear and overmastering desire and the affliction written upon my forehead;[118] and indeed this woman is pure and chaste and free from all fault.' When King Dadbin heard this, he buffeted his face and said to his vizier, 'God slay thee! It is thou that hast parted me and my wife and wronged me!' But Kisra the king said to him, 'God shall surely slay thee, for that thou hastenedst and lookedst not into thine affair and knewest not the guilty from the guiltless. Hadst thou wrought deliberately, the false had been made manifest to thee from the true; so where was thy judgment and thy sight?"

Then said he to Arwa, "What wilt thou that I do with them?" And she answered, saying, "Accomplish on them the ordinance of God the Most High;[119] the slayer shall be slain and the transgressor transgressed against, even as he transgressed against us; yea, and the well-doer, good shall be done unto him, even as he did unto us." So she gave [her officers] commandment concerning Dadbin and they smote him on the head with a mace and slew him, and she said, "This is for the slaughter of my father." Then she bade set the vizier on a beast [and carry him] to the desert whither he had caused carry her [and leave him there without victual or water]; and she said to him, "An thou be guilty, thou shalt abide [the punishment of] thy guilt and perish of hunger and thirst in the desert; but, if there be no guilt in thee, thou shalt be delivered, even as I was delivered."

As for the eunuch, the chamberlain, who had counselled King Dadbin [not to slay her, but] to [cause] carry her to the desert [and there abandon her], she bestowed on him a sumptuous dress of honour and said to him, "The like of thee it behoveth kings to hold in favour and set in high place, for that thou spokest loyally and well, and a man is still requited according to his deed." And Kisra the king invested him with the governance of one of the provinces of his empire. Know, therefore, O king," continued the youth, "that whoso doth good is requited therewith and he who is guiltless of sin and reproach feareth not the issue of his affair. And I, O king, am free from guilt, wherefore I trust in God that He will show forth the truth and vouchsafe me the victory over enemies and enviers."

When the king heard this, his wrath subsided and he said, "Carry him back to the prison till the morrow, so we may look into his affair.'

The Sixth Day

OF TRUST IN GOD.

When it was the sixth day, the viziers' wrath redoubled, for that they had not compassed their desire of the youth and they feared for themselves from the king; so three of them went in to him and prostrating themselves before him, said to him, "O king, indeed we are loyal counsellors to thy dignity and tenderly solicitous for thee. Verily, thou persistest long in sparing this youth alive and we know not what is thine advantage therein. Every day findeth him yet on life and the talk redoubleth suspicions on thee; so do thou put him to death, that the talk may be made an end of." When the king heard this speech, he said, "By Allah, indeed, ye say sooth and speak rightly!" Then he let bring the young treasurer and said to him, "How long shall I look into thine affair and find no helper for thee and see them all athirst for thy blood?"

"O king," answered the youth, "I hope for succour only from God, not from created beings: if He aid me, none can avail to harm me, and if He be with me and on my side, because of the truth, who is it I shall fear, because of falsehood? Indeed, I have made my intent with God a pure and sincere intent and have severed my expectation from the help of the creature; and whoso seeketh help [of God] findeth of his desire that which Bekhtzeman found." Quoth the king, "Who was Bekhtzeman and what is his story?" "O king," replied the youth,

STORY OF KING BEKHTZEMAN.

"There was once a king of the kings, whose name was Bekhtzeman, and he was a great eater and drinker and carouser. Now enemies of his made their appearance in certain parts of his realm and threatened him; and one of his friends said to him, 'O king, the enemy maketh for thee: be on thy guard against him.' Quoth Bekhtzeman, 'I reck not of him, for that I have arms and wealth and men and am not afraid of aught.' Then said his friends to him, 'Seek aid of God, O king, for He will help thee more than thy wealth and thine arms and thy men.' But he paid no heed to the speech of his loyal counsellors, and presently the enemy came upon him and waged war upon him and got the victory over him and his trust in other than God the Most High profited him nought. So he fled from before him and seeking one of the kings, said to him, 'I come to thee and lay hold upon thy skirts and take refuge with thee, so thou mayst help me against mine enemy.'

The king gave him money and men and troops galore and Bekhtzeman said in himself, 'Now am I fortified with this army and needs must I conquer my enemy therewith and overcome him;' but he said not, 'With the aid of God the Most High.' So his enemy met him and overcame him again and he was defeated and put to the rout and fled at a venture. His troops were dispersed from him and his money lost and the enemy followed after him. So he sought the sea and passing over to the other side, saw a great city and therein a mighty citadel. He asked the name of the city and to whom it belonged and they said to him, 'It belongeth to Khedidan the king.' So he fared on till he came to the king's palace aud concealing his condition, passed himself off for a horseman[120] and sought service with King Khedidan, who attached him to his household and entreated him with honour; but his heart still clave to his country and his home.

Presently, it chanced that an enemy attacked King Khedidan; so he sent out his troops to him and made Bekhtzeman head of the army. Then they went forth to the field and Khedidan also came forth and ranged his troops and took the spear and sallied out in person and fought a sore battle and overcame his enemy, who fled, he and his troops, ignominiously. When the king and his army returned in triumph, Bekhtzeman said to him, 'Harkye, O king! Meseemeth this is a strange thing of thee that thou art compassed about with this vast army, yet dost thou apply thyself in person to battle and adventurest thyself.' Quoth the king, 'Dost thou call thyself a cavalier and a man of learning and deemest that victory is in abundance of troops?' 'Ay,' answered Bekhtzeman; 'that is indeed my belief.' Anc Khedidan said, 'By Allah, then, thou errest in this thy belief! Woe and again woe to him whose trust is in other than God! Indeed, this army is appointed only for adornment and majesty, and victory is from God alone. I too, O Bekhtzeman, believed aforetime that victory was in the multitude of men, and an enemy came out against me with eight hundred men, whilst I had eight hundred thousand. I trusted in the number of my troops, whilst mine enemy trusted in God; so he defeated me and routed me and I was put to a shameful flight and hid myself in one of the mountains, where I met with a recluse, [who had] withdrawn [himself from the world]. So I joined myself to him and complained to him of my case and acquainted him with all that had befallen me. Quoth he, "Knowest thou why this befell thee and thou wast defeated?" "I know not," answered I, and he said, "Because thou puttest thy trust in the multitude of thy troops and reliedst not upon God the Most High. Hadst thou put thy trust in God and believed in Him that it is He [alone] who advantageth and endamageth thee, thine enemy had not availed to cope with thee. Return unto God." So I returned to myself and repented at the hands of the solitary, who said to me, "Turn back with what remaineth to thee of troops and confront thine enemies, for, if their intents be changed from God, thou wilt overcome them, wert thou alone." When I heard these words, I put my trust in God the Most High, and gathering together those who remained with me, fell upon mine enemies at unawares in the night. They deemed us many and fled on the shamefullest wise, whereupon I entered my city and repossessed myself of my place by the might of God the Most High, and now I fight not out [trusting] in His aid.'

When Bekhtzeman heard this, he awoke from his heedlessness and said, 'Extolled be the perfection of God the Great! O king, this is my case and my story, nothing added and nought diminished, for I am King Bekhtzeman and all this happened to me; wherefore I will seek the gate of God['s mercy] and repent unto Him.' So he went forth to one of the mountains and there worshipped God awhile, till one night, as he slept, one appeared to him in a dream and said to him, 'O Bekhtzeman, God accepteth thy repentance and openeth on thee [the gate of succour] and will further thee against thine enemy.' When he was certified of this in the dream, he arose and turned back, intending for his own city; and when he drew near thereunto, he saw a company of the king's retainers, who said to him, 'Whence art thou? We see that thou art a stranger and fear for thee from this king, for that every stranger who enters this city, he destroys him, of his fear of King Bekhtzeman.' Quoth Bekhtzeman, 'None shall hurt him nor advantage him save God the Most High.' And they answered, saying, 'Indeed, he hath a vast army and his heart is fortified in the multitude of his troops.'

When King Bekhtzeman heard this, his heart was comforted and he said in himself, 'I put my trust in God. If He will, I shall overcome mine enemy by the might of God the Most High.' So he said to the folk, ' Know ye not who I am?' and they answered, ' No, by Allah.' Quoth he, 'I am King Bekhtzeman.' When they heard this and knew that it was indeed he, they dismounted from their horses and kissed his stirrup, to do him honour, and said to him, 'O king, why hast thou thus adventured thyself?' Quoth he, 'Indeed, my life is a light matter to me and I put my trust in God the Most High, looking to Him for protection.' And they answered him, saying, 'May this suffice thee! We will do with thee that which is in our power and whereof thou art worthy: comfort thy heart, for we will succour thee with our goods and our lives, and we are his chief officers and the most in favour with him of all folk. So we will take thee with us and cause the folk follow after thee, for that the inclination of the people, all of them, is to thee.' Quoth he, 'Do that unto which God the Most High enableth you.'

So they carried him into the city and hid him with them. Moreover, they agreed with a company of the king's chief officers, who had aforetime been those of Bekhtzeman, and acquainted them with this; whereat they rejoiced with an exceeding joy. Then they assembled together to Bekhtzeman and made a covenant and handfast [of fealty] with him and fell upon the enemy at unawares and slew him and seated King Bekhtzeman again on the throne of his kingship. And his affairs prospered and God amended his estate and restored His bounty to him, and he ruled his subjects justly and abode in the obedience of the Most High. On this wise, O king," continued the young treasurer, "he with whom God is and whose intent is pure, meeteth nought but good. As for me, I have no helper other than God, and I am content to submit myself to His ordinance, for that He knoweth the purity of my intent."

With this the king's wrath subsided and he said, "Restore him to the prison till the morrow, so we may look into his affair."

The Seventh Day.

OF CLEMENCY.

When it was the seventh day, the seventh vizier, whose name was Bihkemal, came in to the king and prostrating himself to him, said, "O king, what doth thy long-suffering with this youth advantage thee? Indeed the folk talk of thee and of him. Why, then, dost thou postpone the putting him to death?" The vizier's words aroused the king's anger and he bade bring the youth. So they brought him before him, shackled, and Azadbekht said to him, "Out on thee! By Allah, after this day there abideth no deliverance for thee from my hand, for that thou hast outraged mine honour, and there can be no forgiveness for thee."

"O king," answered the youth, "there is no great forgiveness save in case of a great crime, for according as the offence is great, in so much is forgiveness magnified and it is no dishonour to the like of thee if he spare the like of me. Verily, Allah knoweth that there is no fault in me, and indeed He commandeth unto clemency, and no clemency is greater than that which spareth from slaughter, for that thy forgiveness of him whom thou purposest to put to death is as the quickening of a dead man; and whoso doth evil shall find it before him, even as it was with King Bihkerd." "And what is the story of King Bihkerd?" asked the king. "O king," answered the youth,

STORY OF KING BIHKERD.

"There was once a king named Bihkerd aed he had wealth galore and many troops; but his deeds were evil and he would punish for a slight offence and never forgave. He went forth one day to hunt and one of his servants shot an arrow, which lit on the king's ear and cut it off. Quoth Bihkerd, 'Who shot that arrow?' So the guards brought him in haste the offender, whose name was Yetrou, and he of his fear fell down on the ground in a swoon. Then said the king, 'Put him to death;' but Yetrou said, 'O King, this that hath befallen was not of my choice nor of my knowledge; so do thou pardon me, in the hour of thy power over me, for that clemency is of the goodliest of things and belike it shall be [in this worlc] a provision and a good work [for which thou shall be requited] one of these days, and a treasure [laid up to thine account] with God in the world to come. Pardon me, therefore, and fend off evil from me, so shall God fend off from thee evil the like thereof.' When the king heard this, it pleased him and he pardoned the servant, albeit he had never before pardoned any.

Now this servant was of the sons of the kings and had fled from his father, on account of an offence he had committed. Then he went and took service with King Bihkerd and there happened to him what happened. After awhile, it chanced that a man recognized him and went and told his father, who sent him a letter, comforting his heart and mind and [beseeching him] to return to him. So he returned to his father, who came forth to meet him and rejoiced in him, and the prince's affairs were set right with him.

It befell, one day of the days, that King Bihkerd embarked in a ship and put out to sea, so he might fish; but the wind blew on them and the ship foundered. The king won ashore on a plank, unknown of any, and came forth, naked, on one of the coasts; and it chanced that he landed in the country whereof the father of the youth aforesaid, [his sometime servant], was king. So he came in the night to the gate of the latter's city and [finding it shut], took up his lodging [for the night] in a burying-place there.

When the morning morrowed and the folk came forth of the city, they found a murdered man cast down in a corner of the burial-ground and seeing Bihkerd there, doubted not but it was he who had slain him; so they laid hands on him and carried him up to the king and said to him, 'This fellow hath slain a man.' The king bade imprison him; [so they clapped him in prison] and he fell a-saying in himself, what while he was in the prison, 'All that hath befallen me is of the abundance of my sins and my tyranny, for, indeed, I have slain much people unrighteously and this is the requital of my deeds and that which I have wrought aforetime of oppression.' As he was thus pondering in himself, there came a bird and lighted down on the coign of the prison, whereupon, of his much eagerness in the chase, he took a stone and cast it at the bird.

Now the king's son was playing in the exercise-ground with the ball and the mall, and the stone lit on his ear and cut it off, whereupon the prince fell down in a swoon. So they enquired who had thrown the stone and [finding that it was Bihkerd,] took him and carried him before the prince, who bade put him to death. Accordingly, they cast the turban from his head and were about to bind his eyes, when the prince looked at him and seeing him cropped of an ear, said to him, 'Except thou wert a lewd fellow, thine ear had not been cut off.' 'Not so, by Allah!' answered Bihkerd. 'Nay, but the story [of the loss] of my ear is thus and thus, and I pardoned him who smote me with an arrow and cut off my ear.' When the prince heard this, he looked in his face and knowing him, cried out and said, 'Art thou not Bihkerd the king?' 'Yes,' answered he, and the prince said to him 'What bringeth thee here?' So he told him all that had betided him and the folk marvelled and extolled the perfection of God the Most High.

Then the prince rose to him and embraced him and kissed him and entreated him with honour. Moreover, he seated him in a chair and bestowed on him a dress of honour; and he turned to his father and said to him, 'This is the king who pardoned me and this is his ear that I cut off with an arrow; and indeed he deserveth pardon from me, for that he pardoned me.' Then said he to Bihkerd, 'Verily, the issue of clemency hath been a provision for thee [in thine hour of need].' And they entreated him with the utmost kindness and sent him back to his own country in all honour and worship Know, then, O King," continued the youth, "that there is no goodlier thing than clemency and that all thou dost thereof, thou shalt find before thee, a treasure laid up for thee."

When the king heard this, his wrath subsided and he said, "Carry him back to the prison till the morrow, so we may look into his affair."

The Eighth Day.

OF ENVY AND MALICE.

When it was the eighth day, the viziers all assembled and took counsel together and said, "How shall we do with this youth, who baffleth us with his much talk? Indeed, we fear lest he be saved and we fall [into perdition]. Wherefore, let us all go in to the king and unite our efforts to overcome him, ere he appear without guilt and come forth and get the better of us." So they all went in to the king and prostrating themselves before him, said to him, "O king, have a care lest this youth beguile thee with his sorcery and bewitch thee with his craft. If thou heardest what we hear, thou wouldst not suffer him live, no, not one day. So pay thou no heed to his speech, for we are thy viziers, [who endeavour for] thy continuance, and if thou hearken not to our word, to whose word wilt thou hearken? See, we are ten viziers who testify against this youth that he is guilty and entered not the king's sleeping-chamber but with evil intent, so he might put the king to shame and outrage his honour; and if the king slay him not, let him banish him his realm, so the tongue of the folk may desist from him."

When the king heard his viziers' words, he was exceeding wroth and bade bring the youth, and when he came in to the king, the viziers all cried out with one voice, saying, "O scant o' grace, thinkest thou to save thyself from slaughter by craft and guile, that thou beguilest the king with thy talk and hopest pardon for the like of this great crime which thou hast committed?" Then the king bade fetch the headsman, so he might smite off his head; whereupon each of the viziers fell a-saying, "I will slay him;" and they sprang upon him. Quote the youth, "O king, consider and ponder these men's eagerness. Is this of envy or no? They would fain make severance between thee and me, so there may fall to them what they shall plunder, as aforetime." And the king said to him, "Consider their testimony against thee." "O king," answered the young man, "how shall they testify of that which they saw not? This is but envy and rancour; and thou, if thou slay me, thou wilt regret me, and I fear lest there betide thee of repentance that which betided Ilan Shah, by reason of the malice of his viziers." "And what is his story?" asked Azadbekht. "O king," replied the youth,

STORY OF ILAN SHAH AND ABOU TEMAM.

"There was once a merchant named Abou Temam, and he was a man of understanding and good breeding, quick-witted and truthful in all his affairs, and he had wealth galore. Now there was in his land an unjust king and a jealous, and Abou Temam feared for his wealth from this king and said, 'I will remove hence to another place where I shall not be in fear.' So he made for the city of Ilan Shah and built himself a palace therein and transporting his wealth thither, took up his abode there. Presently, the news of him reached King Ilan Shah; so he sent to bid him to his presence and said to him, 'We know of thy coming to us and thine entry under our allegiance, and indeed we have heard of thine excellence and wit and generosity; so welcome to thee and fair welcome! The land is thy land and at thy commandment, and whatsoever occasion thou hast unto us, it is [already] accomplished unto thee; and it behoveth that thou be near our person and of our assembly.' Abou Temam prostrated himself to the king and said to him, 'O king, I will serve thee with my wealth and my life, but do thou excuse me from nearness unto thee, for that, [if I took service about thy person], I should not be safe from enemies and enviers.' Then he addressed himself to serve the king with presents and largesses, and the king saw him to be intelligent, well-bred and of good counsel; so he committed to him the ordinance of his affairs and in his hand was the power to bind and loose.

Now Ilan Shah had three viziers, in whose hands the affairs [of the kingdom] were [aforetime] and they had been used to leave not the king night nor day; but they became shut out from him by reason of Abou Temam and the king was occupied with him to their exclusion. So they took counsel together upon the matter and said, 'What counsel ye we should do, seeing that the king is occupied from us with yonder man, and indeed he honoureth him more than us? But now come, let us cast about for a device, whereby we may remove him from the king.' So each of them spoke forth that which was in his mind, and one of them said, 'The king of the Turks hath a daughter, whose like there is not in the world, and whatsoever messenger goeth to demand her in marriage, her father slayeth him. Now our king hath no knowledge of this; so, come, let us foregather with him and bring up the talk of her. When his heart is taken with her, we will counsel him to despatch Abou Temam to seek her hand in marriage; whereupon her father will slay him and we shall be quit of him, for we have had enough of his affair."

Accordingly, they all went in to the king one day (and Abou Temam was present among them,) and mentioned the affair of the damsel, the king's daughter of the Turks, and enlarged upon her charms, till the king's heart was taken with her and he said to them, 'We will send one to demand her in marriage for us; but who shall be our messenger?' Quoth the viziers, 'There is none for this business but Abou Temam, by reason of his wit and good breeding;' and the king said, 'Indeed, even as ye say, none is fitting for this affair but he.' Then he turned to Abou Temam and said to him, 'Wilt thou not go with my message and seek me [in marriage] the king's daughter of the Turks?' and he answered, 'Hearkening and obedience, O king.'

So they made ready his affair and the king conferred on him a dress of honour, and he took with him a present and a letter under the king's hand and setting out, fared on till he came to the [capital] city of Turkestan. When the king of the Turks knew of his coming, he despatched his officers to receive him and entreated him with honour and lodged him as befitted his rank. Then he entertained him three days, after which he summoned him to his presence and Abou Temam went in to him and prostrating himself before him, as beseemeth unto kings, laid the present before him and gave him the letter.

The king read the letter and said to Abou Temam, "We will do what behoveth in the matter; but, O Abou Temam, needs must thou see my daughter and she thee, and needs must thou hear her speech and she thine.' So saying, he sent him to the lodging of the princess, who had had notice of this; so that they had adorned her sitting-chamber with the costliest that might be of utensils of gold and silver and the like, and she seated herself on a throne of gold, clad in the most sumptuous of royal robes and ornaments. When Abou Temam entered, he bethought himself and said, 'The wise say, he who restraineth his sight shall suffer no evil and he who guardeth his tongue shall hear nought of foul, and he who keepeth watch over his hand, it shall be prolonged and not curtailed.'[121] So he entered and seating himself on the ground, [cast down his eyes and] covered his hands and feet with his dress.[122] Quoth the king's daughter to him, 'Lift thy head, O Abou Temam, and look on me and speak with me.' But he spoke not neither raised his head, and she continued, 'They sent thee but that thou mightest look on me and speak with me, and behold, thou speakest not at all. Take of these pearls that be around thee and of these jewels and gold and silver. But he put not forth his hand unto aught, and when she saw that he paid no heed to anything, she was angry and said, 'They have sent me a messenger, blind, dumb and deaf.'

Then she sent to acquaint her father with this; whereupon the king called Abou Temam to him and said to him, 'Thou camest not but to see my daughter. Why, then, hast thou not looked upon her?' Quoth Abou Temam, 'I saw everything.' And the king said, 'Why didst thou not take somewhat of that which thou sawest of jewels and the like? For they were set for thee.' But he answered, 'It behoveth me not to put out my hand to aught that is not mine.' When the king heard his speech, he gave him a sumptuous dress of honour and loved him exceedingly and said to him, 'Come, look at this pit.' So Abou Temam went up [to the mouth of the pit] and looked, and behold, it was full of heads of men; and the king said to him, 'These are the heads of ambassadors, whom I slew, for that I saw them without loyalty to their masters, and I was used, whenas I saw an ambassador without breeding, [123]to say, "He who sent him is less of breeding than he, for that the messenger is the tongue of him who sendeth him and his breeding is of his master's breeding; and whoso is on this wise, it befitteth not that he be akin to me."[124] So, because of this, I used to put the messengers to death; but, as for thee, thou hast overcome us and won my daughter, of the excellence of thy breeding; so be of good heart, for she is thy master's.' Then he sent him back to king Ilan Shah with presents and rarities and a letter, saying, 'This that I have done is in honour of thee and of thine ambassador.'

When Abou Temam returned with [news of] the accomplishment of his errand and brought the presents and the letter, King Ilan Shah rejoiced in this and redoubled in showing him honour and made much of him. Some days thereafterward, the king of Turkestan sent his daughter and she went in to King Ilan Shah, who rejoiced in her with an exceeding joy and Abou Temam's worth was exalted in his sight. When the viziers saw this, they redoubled in envy and despite and said, 'An we contrive us not a device to rid us of this man, we shall perish of rage.' So they bethought them [and agreed upon] a device they should practise.

Then they betook themselves to two boys affected to the [special] service of the king, who slept not but on their knee,[125] and they lay at his head, for that they were his pages of the chamber, and gave them each a thousand dinars of gold, saying, 'We desire of you that ye do somewhat for us and take this gold as a provision against your occasion.' Quoth the boys, 'What is it ye would have us do?' And the viziers answered, 'This Abou Temam hath marred our affairs for us, and if his case abide on this wise, he will estrange us all from the king's favour; and what we desire of you is that, when ye are alone with the king and he leaneth back, as he were asleep, one of you say to his fellow, "Verily, the king hath taken Abou Temam into his especial favour and hath advanced him to high rank with him, yet is he a transgressor against the king's honour and an accursed one." Then let the other of you ask, "And what is his transgression?" And the first make answer, "He outrageth the king's honour and saith, 'The King of Turkestan was used, whenas one went to him to seek his daughter in marriage, to slay him; but me he spared, for that she took a liking to me, and by reason of this he sent her hither, because she loved me.'" Then let his fellow say, "Knowest thou this for truth?" And the other reply, "By Allah, this is well known unto all the folk, but, of their fear of the king, they dare not bespeak him thereof; and as often as the king is absent a-hunting or on a journey, Abou Temam comes to her and is private with her."' And the boys answered, 'We will say this.'

Accordingly, one night, when they were alone with the king and he leant back, as he were asleep, they said these words and the king heard it all and was like to die of rage and said in himself, 'These are young boys, not come to years of discretion, and have no intrigue with any; and except they had heard these words from some one, they had not spoken with each other thereof.' When it was morning, wrath overmastered him, so that he stayed not neither deliberated, but summoned Abou Temam and taking him apart, said to him, 'Whoso guardeth not his lord's honour,[126] what behoveth unto him?' Quoth Abou Temam, 'It behoveth that his lord guard not his honour.' 'And whoso entereth the king's house and playeth the traitor with him,' continued the king, 'what behoveth unto him?' And Abou Temam answered, 'He shall not be left on life.' Whereupon the king spat in his face and said to him, 'Both these things hast thou done.' Then he drew his dagger on him in haste and smiting him in the belly, slit it and he died forthright; whereupon the king dragged him to a well that was in his palace and cast him therein.

After he had slain him, he fell into repentance and mourning and chagrin waxed upon him, and none, who questioned him, would he acquaint with the cause thereof, nor, of his love for his wife, did he tell her of this, and whenas she asked him of [the cause of] his grief, he answered her not. When the viziers knew of Abou Temam's death, they rejoiced with an exceeding joy and knew that the king's grief arose from regret for him. As for Ilan Shah, he used, after this, to betake himself by night to the sleeping-chamber of the two boys and spy upon them, so he might hear what they said concerning his wife. As he stood one night privily at the door of their chamber, he saw them spread out the gold before them and play with it and heard one of them say, 'Out on us! What doth this gold profit us? For that we cannot buy aught therewith neither spend it upon ourselves. Nay, but we have sinned against Abou Temam and done him to death unjustly.' And the other answered, 'Had we known that the king would presently kill him, we had not done what we did.'

When the king heard this, he could not contain himself, but rushed in upon them and said to them, 'Out on you! What did ye? Tell me.' And they said, 'Pardon, O king.' Quoth he, 'An ye would have pardon from God and me, it behoveth you to tell me the truth, for nothing shall save you from me but truth-speaking.' So they prostrated themselves before him and said, 'By Allah, O king, the viziers gave us this gold and taught us to lie against Abou Teman, so thou mightest put him to death, and what we said was their words.' When the king heard this, he plucked at his beard, till he was like to tear it up by the roots and bit upon his fingers, till he well-nigh sundered them in twain, for repentance and sorrow that he had wrought hastily and had not delayed with Abou Temam, so he might look into his affair.

Then he sent for the viziers and said to them, 'O wicked viziers, ye thought that God was heedless of your deed, but your wickedness shall revert upon you. Know ye not that whoso diggeth a pit for his brother shall fall into it? Take from me the punishment of this world and to-morrow ye shall get the punishment of the world to come and requital from God.' Then he bade put them to death; so [the headsman] smote off their heads before the king, and he went in to his wife and acquainted her with that wherein he had transgressed against Abou Temam; whereupon she grieved for him with an exceeding grief and the king and the people of his household left not weeping and repenting all their lives. Moreover, they brought Abou Temam forth of the well and the king built him a dome[127] in his palace and buried him therein.

See, then, O august king," continued the youth, "what envy doth and injustice and how God caused the viziers' malice revert upon their own necks; and I trust in God that He will succour me against all who envy me my favour with the king and show forth the truth unto him. Indeed, I fear not for my life from death; only I fear lest the king repent of my slaughter, for that I am guiltless of offence, and if I knew that I were guilty of aught, my tongue would be mute."

When the king heard this, he bowed [his head] in perplexity and confusion and said, "Carry him back to the prison till the morrow, so we may look into his affair."

The Ninth Day

OF DESTINY OR THAT WHICH IS WRITTEN ON THE FOREHEAD.

When it was the ninth day, the viziers [foregathered and] said, one to another, "Verily, this youth baffleth us, for as often as the king is minded to put him to death, he beguileth him and ensorcelleth him with a story; so what deem ye we should do, that we may slay him and be at rest from him?" Then they took counsel together and were of accord that they should go to the king's wife [and prompt her to urge the king to slaughter the youth. So they betook themselves to her] and said to her, "Thou art heedless of this affair wherein thou art and this heedlessness will not profit thee; whilst the king is occupied with eating and drinking and diversion and forgetteth that the folk beat upon tabrets and sing of thee and say, 'The king's wife loveth the youth;' and what while he abideth on life, the talk will increase and not diminish." Quoth she, "By Allah, it was ye set me on against him, and what shall I do [now]?" And they answered, "Do thou go in to the king and weep and say to him, 'Verily, the women come to me and tell me that I am become a byword in the city, and what is thine advantage in the sparing of this youth? If thou wilt not slay him, slay me, so this talk may be estopped from us.'"

So she arose and tearing her clothes, went in to the king, in the presence of the viziers, and cast herself upon him, saying, "O king, falleth my shame not upon thee and fearest thou not reproach? Indeed, this is not of the behoof of kings that their jealousy over their women should be thus [laggard]. Thou art heedless and all the folk of the realm prate of thee, men and women. So either slay him, that the talk may be cut off, or slay me, if thy soul will not consent to his slaughter." Thereupon the king's wrath waxed hot and he said to her, "I have no pleasure in his continuance [on life] and needs must I slay him this day. So return to thy house and comfort thy heart."

Then he bade fetch the youth; so they brought him before him and the viziers said, "O base of origin, out on thee! Thy term is at hand and the earth hungereth for thy body, so it may devour it." But he answered them, saying, "Death is not in your word nor in your envy; nay, it is an ordinance written upon the forehead; wherefore, if aught be written upon my forehead, needs must it come to pass, and neither endeavour nor thought-taking nor precaution will deliver me therefrom; [but it will surely happen] even as happened to King Ibrahim and his son." Quoth the king, "Who was King Ibrahim and who was his son?" And the youth said, "O king,

STORY OF KING IBRAHIM AND HIS SON.

There was once a king of the kings, by name Ibrahim, to whom the kings abased themselves and did obedience; but he had no son and was straitened of breast because of this, fearing lest the kingship go forth of his hand. He ceased not vehemently to desire a son and to buy slave-girls and lie with them, till one of them conceived, whereat he rejoiced with an exceeding joy and gave gifts and largesse galore. When the girl's months were accomplished and the season of her delivery drew near, the king summoned the astrologers and they watched for the hour of her child-bearing and raised astrolabes [towards the sun] and took strait note of the time. The damsel gave birth to a male child, whereat the king rejoiced with an exceeding joy, and the people heartened each other with the glad news of this.

Then the astrologers made their calculations and looked into his nativity and his ascendant, whereupon their colour changed and they were confounded. Quoth the king to them, 'Acquaint me with his horoscope and ye shall have assurance and fear ye not of aught' 'O king,' answered they, 'this child's nativity denotes that, in the seventh year of his age, there is to be feared for him from a lion, which will attack him; and if he be saved from the lion, there will betide an affair yet sorer and more grievous.' 'What is that?' asked the king; and they said, 'We will not speak, except the king command us thereto and give us assurance from [that which we] fear.' Quoth the king, 'God assure you!' And they said, 'If he be saved from the lion, the king's destruction will be at his hand.' When the king heard this, his colour changed and his breast was straitened; but he said in himself, 'I will be watchful and do my endeavour and suffer not the lion to eat him. It cannot be that he will kill me, and indeed the astrologers lied.'

Then he caused rear him among the nurses and matrons; but withal he ceased not to ponder the saying of the astrologers and indeed his life was troubled. So he betook himself to the top of a high mountain and dug there a deep pit and made in it many dwelling-places and closets and filled it with all that was needful of victual and raiment and what not else and made in it conduits of water from the mountain and lodged the boy therein, with a nurse who should rear him. Moreover, at the first of each month he used to go to the mountain and stand at the mouth of the pit and let down a rope he had with him and draw up the boy to him and strain him to his bosom and kiss him and play with him awhile, after which he would let him down again into the pit to his place and return; and he used to count the days till the seven years should pass by.

When came the time [of the accomplishment] of the foreordered fate and the fortune graven on the forehead and there abode for the boy but ten days till the seven years should be complete, there came to the mountain hunters hunting wild beasts and seeing a lion, gave chase to him. He fled from them and seeking refuge in the mountain, fell into the pit in its midst. The nurse saw him forthright and fled from him into one of the closets; whereupon the lion made for the boy and seizing upon him, tore his shoulder, after which he sought the closet wherein was the nurse and falling upon her, devoured her, whilst the boy abode cast down in a swoon. Meanwhile, when the hunters saw that the lion had fallen into the pit, they came to the mouth thereof and heard the shrieking of the boy and the woman; and after awhile the cries ceased, whereby they knew that the lion had made an end of them.

Presently, as they stood by the mouth of the pit, the lion came scrambling up the sides and would have issued forth; but, as often as he showed his head, they pelted him with stones, till they beat him down and he fell; whereupon one of the hunters descended into the pit and despatched him and saw the boy wounded; after which he went to the cabinet, where he found the woman dead, and indeed the lion had eaten his fill of her. Then he noted that which was therein of clothes and what not else, and advising his fellows thereof, fell to passing the stuff up to them. Moreover, he took up the boy and bringing him forth of the pit, carried him to their dwelling-place, where they dressed his wounds and he grew up with them, but acquainted them not with his affair; and indeed, when they questioned him, he knew not what he should say, for that he was little, when they let him down into the pit. The hunters marvelled at his speech and loved him with an exceeding love and one of them took him to son and abode rearing him with him [and instructing him] in hunting and riding on horseback, till he attained the age of twelve and became a champion, going forth with the folk to the chase and to the stopping of the way.

It chanced one day that they sallied forth to stop the way and fell in upon a caravan in the night; but the people of the caravan were on their guard; so they joined battle with the robbers and overcame them and slew them and the boy fell wounded and abode cast down in that place till the morrow, when he opened his eyes and finding his comrades slain, lifted himself up and rose to walk in the way. Presently, there met him a man, a treasure-seeker, and said to him, 'Whither goest thou, O youth?' So he told him what had betided him and the other said, 'Be of good heart, for that [the season of] thy fair fortune is come and God bringeth thee joy and solace. I am one who am in quest of a hidden treasure, wherein is vast wealth. So come with me, that thou mayst help me, and I will give thee wealth, wherewith thou shalt provide thyself thy life long.' Then he carried the youth to his dwelling and dressed his wound, and he abode with him some days, till he was rested; when he took him and two beasts and all that he needed, and they fared on till they came to a precipitous mountain.

Here the treasure-seeker brought out a book and reading therein, dug in the crest of the mountain five cubits deep, whereupon there appeared to him a stone. He pulled it up and behold, it was a trap-door covering the mouth of a pit. So he waited till the [foul] air was come forth from the midst of the pit, when he bound a rope about the boy's middle and let him down to the bottom, and with him a lighted flambeau. The boy looked and beheld, at the upper end of the pit, wealth galore; so the treasure-seeker let down a rope and a basket and the boy fell to filling and the man to drawing up, till the latter had gotten his sufficiency, when he loaded his beasts and did his occasion, whilst the boy looked for him to let down to him the rope and draw him up; but he rolled a great stone to the mouth of the pit and went away.

When the boy saw what the treasure-seeker had done with him he committed his affair to God (extolled be His perfection and exalted be He!) and abode perplexed concerning his case and said, 'How bitter is this death!' For that indeed the world was darkened on him and the pit was blinded to him. So he fell a-weeping and saying, 'I was delivered from the lion and the thieves and now is my death [appointed to be] in this pit, where I shall die lingeringly.' And he abode confounded and looked for nothing but death. As he pondered [his affair], behold, he heard a sound of water running with a mighty noise; so he arose and walked in the pit, following after the sound, till he came to a corner and heard the mighty running of water. So he laid his ear to the sound of the current and hearing it a great strength, said in himself, 'This is the running of a mighty water and needs must I die in this place, be it to-day or to-morrow: so I will cast myself into the water and not die a lingering death in this pit.'

Then he braced up his courage and gathering his skirts about him, threw himself into the water, and it bore him along with an exceeding might and carrying him under the earth, stayed not till it brought him out into a deep valley, wherethrough ran a great river, that welled up from under the earth. When he found himself on the surface of the earth, he abode perplexed and dazed all that day; after which he came to himself and rising, fared on along the valley, till he came to an inhabited land and a great village in the dominions of the king his father. So he entered the village and foregathered with its inhabitants, who questioned him of his case; whereupon he related to them his history and they marvelled at him, how God had delivered him from all this. Then he took up his abode with them and they loved him exceedingly.

To return to the king his father. When he went to the pit, as of his wont, and called the nurse, she returned him no answer, whereat his breast was straitened and he let down a man who [found the nurse dead and the boy gone and] acquainted the king therewith; which when he heard, he buffeted his head and wept passing sore and descended into the midst of the pit, so he might see how the case stood. There he found the nurse slain and the lion dead, but saw not the boy; so he [returned and] acquainted the astrologers with the verification of their words, and they said, 'O king, the lion hath eaten him; destiny hath been accomplished upon him and thou art delivered from his hand; for, had he been saved from the lion, by Allah, we had feared for thee from him, for that the king's destruction should have been at his hand.' So the king left [sorrowing for] this and the days passed by and the affair was forgotten.

Meanwhile, the boy [grew up and] abode with the people of the village, and when God willed the accomplishment of His ordinance, the which endeavour availeth not to avert, he went forth with a company of the villagers, to stop the way. The folk complained of them to the king, who sallied out with a company of his men and surrounded the highwaymen and the boy with them, whereupon the latter drew forth an arrow and launched it at them, and it smote the king in his vitals and wounded him. So they carried him to his house, after they had laid hands upon the youth and his companions and brought them before the king, saying, 'What biddest thou that we do with them?' Quoth he, 'I am presently in concern for myself; so bring me the astrologers.' Accordingly, they brought them before him and He said to them, 'Ye told me that my death should be by slaying at the hand of my son: how, then, befalleth it that I have gotten my death-wound on this wise of yonder thieves?' The astrologers marvelled and said to him, 'O king, it is not impossible to the lore of the stars, together with the fore-ordinance of God, that he who hath smitten thee should be thy son.'

When Ibrahim heard this, he let fetch the thieves and said to them, 'Tell me truly, which of you shot the arrow that wounded me.' Quoth they, 'It was this youth that is with us.' Whereupon the king fell to looking upon him and said to him, 'O youth, acquaint me with thy case and tell me who was thy father and thou shalt have assurance from God.' 'O my lord,' answered the youth, 'I know no father; as for me, my father lodged me in a pit [when I was little], with a nurse to rear me, and one day, there fell in upon us a lion, which tore my shoulder, then left me and occupied himself with the nurse and rent her in pieces; and God vouchsafed me one who brought me forth of the pit.' Then he related to him all that had befallen him, first and last; which when Ibrahim heard, he cried out and said, 'By Allah, this is my very son!' And he said to him, 'Uncover thy shoulder.' So he uncovered it and behold, it was scarred.

Then the king assembled his nobles and commons and the astrologers and said to them, 'Know that what God hath graven upon the forehead, be it fair fortune or calamity, none may avail to efface, and all that is decreed unto a man he must needs abide. Indeed, this my caretaking and my endeavour profited me nought, for that which God decreed unto my son, he hath abidden and that which He decreed unto me hath betided me. Nevertheless, I praise God and thank Him for that this was at my son's hand and not at the hand of another, and praised be He for that the kingship is come to my son!' And he strained the youth to his breast and embraced him and kissed him, saying, 'O my son, this matter was on such a wise, and of my care and watchfulness over thee from destiny, I lodged thee in that pit; but caretaking availed not.' Then he took the crown of the kingship and set it on his son's head and caused the folk and the people swear fealty to him and commended the subjects to his care and enjoined him to justice and equity. And he took leave of him that night and died and his son reigned in his stead.

On like wise, O king," continued the young treasurer, "is it with thee. If God have written aught on my forehead, needs must it befall me and my speech to the king shall not profit me, no, nor my adducing to him of [illustrative] instances, against the fore-ordinance of God. So with these viziers, for all their eagerness and endeavour for my destruction, this shall not profit them; for, if God [be minded to] save me, He will give me the victory over them."

When the king heard these words, he abode in perplexity and said, "Restore him to the prison till the morrow, so we may look into his affair, for the day draweth to an end and I mean to put him to death on exemplary wise, and [to-morrow] we will do with him that which he meriteth."

The Tenth Day.

OF THE APPOINTED TERM,[128] WHICH, IF IT BE ADVANCED, MAY NOT BE DEFERRED AND IF IT BE DEFERRED, MAY NOT BE ADVANCED.

When it was the tenth day, (now this day was called El Mihrjan[129] and it was the day of the coming in of the folk, gentle and simple, to the king, so they might give him joy and salute him and go forth), the counsel of the viziers fell of accord that they should speak with a company of the notables of the city [and urge them to demand of the king that he should presently put the youth to death]. So they said to them, "When ye go in to-day to the king and salute him, do ye say to him, 'O king, (to God be the praise!) thou art praiseworthy of policy and governance, just to all thy subjects; but this youth, to whom thou hast been bountiful, yet hath he reverted to his base origin and wrought this foul deed, what is thy purpose in his continuance [on life]? Indeed, thou hast prisoned him in thy house, and every day thou hearest his speech and thou knowest not what the folk say.'" And they answered with "Hearkening and obedience."

So, when they entered with the folk and had prostrated themselves before the king and given him joy and he had raised their rank, [they sat down]. Now it was the custom of the folk to salute and go forth, so, when they sat down, the king knew that they had a word that they would fain say. So he turned to them and said, "Ask your need." And the viziers also were present. Accordingly, they bespoke him with all that these latter had taught them and the viziers also spoke with them; and Azadbekht said to them, "O folk, I know that this your speech, there is no doubt of it, proceedeth from love and loyal counsel to me, and ye know that, were I minded to slay half these folk, I could avail to put them to death and this would not be difficult to me; so how shall I not slay this youth and he in my power and under the grip of my hand? Indeed, his crime is manifest and he hath incurred pain of death and I have only deferred his slaughter by reason of the greatness of the offence; for, if I do this with him and my proof against him be strengthened, my heart is healed and the heart of the folk; and if I slay him not to-day, his slaughter shall not escape me to-morrow."

Then he bade fetch the youth and when he was present before him, he prostrated himself to him and prayed for him; whereupon quoth the king to him, "Out on thee! How long shall the folk upbraid me on thine account and blame me for delaying thy slaughter? Even the people of my city blame me because of thee, so that I am grown a talking-stock among them, and indeed they come in to me and upbraid me [and urge me] to put thee to death. How long shall I delay this? Indeed, this very day I mean to shed thy blood and rid the folk of thy prate."

"O king," answered the youth, "if there have betided thee talk because of me, by Allah, by Allah the Great, those who have brought on thee this talk from the folk are these wicked viziers, who devise with the folk and tell them foul things and evil concerning the king's house; but I trust in God that He will cause their malice to revert upon their heads. As for the king's menace of me with slaughter, I am in the grasp of his hand; so let not the king occupy his mind with my slaughter, for that I am like unto the sparrow in the hand of the fowler; if he will, he slaughtereth him, and if he will, he looseth him. As for the delaying of my slaughter, it [proceedeth] not [from] the king, but from Him in whose hand is my life; for, by Allah, O king, if God willed my slaughter, thou couldst not avail to postpone it, no, not for a single hour. Indeed, man availeth not to fend off evil from himself, even as it was with the son of King Suleiman Shah, whose anxiety and carefulness for the accomplishment of his desire of the new-born child [availed him nothing], for his last hour was deferred how many a time! and God saved him until he had accomplished his [foreordained] period and had fulfilled [the destined term of] his life."

"Out on thee!" exclaimed the king. "How great is thy craft and thy talk! Tell me, what was their story." And the youth said, "O king,

STORY OF KING SULEIMAN SHAH AND HIS SONS.

There was once a king named Suleiman Shah, who was goodly of polity and judgment, and he had a brother who died and left a daughter. So Suleiman Shah reared her on the goodliest wise and the girl grew up, endowed with reason and perfection, nor was there in her time a fairer than she. Now the king had two sons, one of whom he had appointed in himself that he would marry her withal, and the other purposed in himself that he would take her. The elder son's name was Belehwan and that of the younger Melik Shah, and the girl was called Shah Khatoun.

One day, King Suleiman Shah went in to his brother's daughter and kissing her head, said to her, 'Thou art my daughter and dearer to me than a child, for the love of thy father deceased; wherefore I am minded to marry thee to one of my sons and appoint him my heir apparent, so he may be king after me. Look, then, which thou wilt have of my sons, for that thou hast been reared with them and knowest them.' The damsel arose and kissing his hand, said to him, 'O my lord, I am thine handmaid and thou art the ruler over me; so whatsoever pleaseth thee, do, for that thy wish is higher and more honourable and nobler [than mine] and if thou wouldst have me serve thee, [as a handmaid], the rest of my life, it were liefer to me than any [husband].'

The king approved her speech and bestowed on her a dress of honour and gave her magnificent gifts; after which, for that his choice had fallen upon his younger son, Melik Shah, he married her with him and made him his heir apparent and caused the folk swear fealty to him. When this came to the knowledge of his brother Belehwan and he was ware that his younger brother had been preferred over him, his breast was straitened and the affair was grievous to him and envy entered into him and rancour; but he concealed this in his heart, whilst fire raged therein because of the damsel and the kingship.

Meanwhile Shah Khatoun went in to the king's son and conceived by him and bore a son, as he were the resplendent moon. When Belehwan saw this that had betided his brother, jealousy and envy overcame him; so he went in one night to his father's house and coming to his brother's lodging, saw the nurse sleeping at the chamber-door, with the cradle before her and therein his brother's child asleep. Belehwan stood by him and fell to looking upon his face, the radiance whereof was as that of the moon, and Satan insinuated himself into his heart, so that he bethought himself and said, 'Why is not this child mine? Indeed, I am worthier of him than my brother, [yea], and of the damsel and the kingship.' Then envy got the better of him and anger spurred him, so that he took out a knife and setting it to the child's gullet, cut his throat and would have severed his windpipe.

So he left him for dead and entering his brother's chamber, saw him asleep, with the damsel by his side, and thought to slay her, but said in himself, 'I will leave the damsel for myself.' Then he went up to his brother and cutting his throat, severed his head from his body, after which he left him and went away. Therewithal the world was straitened upon him and his life was a light matter to him and he sought his father Suleiman Shah's lodging, that he might slay him, but could not win to him. So he went forth from the palace and hid himself in the city till the morrow, when he repaired to one of his father's strengths and fortified himself therein.

Meanwhile, the nurse awoke, that she might give the child suck, and seeing the bed running with blood, cried out; whereupon the sleepers and the king awoke and making for the place, found the child with his throat cut and the cradle running over with blood and his father slain and dead in his sleeping chamber. So they examined the child and found life in him and his windpipe whole and sewed up the place of the wound. Then the king sought his son Belehwan, but found him not and saw that he had fled; whereby he knew that it was he who had done this deed. and this was grievous to the king and to the people of his realm and to the lady Shah Katoun. So the king laid out his son Melik Shah and buried him and made him a mighty funeral and they mourned passing sore; after which he addressed himself to the rearing of the infant

As for Belehwan, when he fled and fortified himself, his power waxed amain and there remained for him but to make war upon his father, who had cast his affection upon the child and used to rear him on his knees and supplicate God the Most High that he might live, so he might commit the commandment to him. When he came to five years of age, the king mounted him on horseback and the people of the city rejoiced in him and invoked on him length of life, so he might take his father's leavings[130] and [heal] the heart of his grandfather.

Meanwhile, Belehwan the froward addressed himself to pay court to Caesar, King of the Greeks,[131] and seek help of him in making war upon his father, and he inclined unto him and gave him a numerous army. His father the king heard of this and sent to Caesar, saying, 'O king of illustrious might, succour not an evil-doer. This is my son and he hath done thus and thus and cut his brother's throat and that of his brother's son in the cradle.' But he told not the King of the Greeks that the child [had recovered and] was alive. When Caesar heard [the truth] of the matter, it was grievous to him and he sent back to Suleiman Shah, saying, 'If it be thy will, O king, I will cut off his head and send it to thee.' But he made answer, saying, 'I reck not of him: the reward of his deed and his crimes shall surely overtake him, if not to-day, then to-morrow.' And from that day he continued to correspond with Caesar and to exchange letters and presents with him.

Now the king of the Greeks heard tell of the damsel[132] and of the beauty and grace wherewith she was gifted, wherefore his heart clave to her and he sent to seek her in marriage of Suleiman Shah, who could not refuse him. So he arose and going in to Shah Khatoun, said to her, 'O my daughter, the king of the Greeks hath sent to me to seek thee in marriage. What sayst thou?' She wept and answered, saying, 'O king, how canst thou find it in thy heart to bespeak me thus? Abideth there husband for me, after the son of my uncle?' 'O my daughter,' rejoined the king, 'it is indeed as thou sayest; but let us look to the issues of affairs. Needs must I take account of death, for that I am an old man and fear not but for thee and for thy little son; and indeed I have written to the king of the Greeks and others of the kings and said, "His uncle slew him," and said not that he [hath recovered and] is living, but concealed his affair. Now hath the king of the Greeks sent to demand thee in marriage, and this is no thing to be refused and fain would we have our back strengthened with him."[133] And she was silent and spoke not.

So King Suleiman Shah made answer unto Caesar with 'Hearkening and obedience.' Then he arose and despatched her to him, and Cassar went in to her and found her overpassing the description wherewithal they had described her to him; wherefore he loved her with an exceeding love and preferred her over all his women and his love for Suleiman Shah was magnified; but Shah Khatoun's heart still clave to her son and she could say nought. As for Suleiman Shah's rebellious son, Belehwan, when he saw that Shah Khatoun had married the king of the Greeks, this was grievous to him and he despaired of her. Meanwhile, his father Suleiman Shah kept strait watch over the child and cherished him and named him Melik Shah, after the name of his father. When he reached the age of ten, he made the folk swear fealty to him and appointed him his heir apparent, and after some days, [the hour of] the old king's admission [to the mercy of God] drew near and he died.

Now a party of the troops had banded themselves together for Belehwan; so they sent to him and bringing him privily, went in to the little Melik Shah and seized him and seated his uncle Belehwan on the throne of the kingship. Then they proclaimed him king and did homage to him all, saying, 'Verily, we desire thee and deliver to thee the throne of the kingship; but we wish of thee that thou slay not thy brother's son, for that on our consciences are the oaths we swore to his father and grandfather and the covenants we made with them.' So Belehwan granted them this and imprisoned the boy in an underground dungeon and straitened him. Presently, the heavy news reached his mother and this was grievous to her; but she could not speak and committed her affair to God the Most High, daring not name this to King Caesar her husband, lest she should make her uncle King Suleiman Shah a liar.

So Belehwan the froward abode king in his father's room and his affairs prospered, what while the young Melik Shah lay in the underground dungeon four full-told years, till his charms faded and his favour changed. When God (extolled be His perfection and exalted be He!) willed to relieve him and bring him forth of the prison, Belehwan sat one day with his chief officers and the grandees of his state and discoursed with them of the story of King Suleiman Shah and what was in his heart. Now there were present certain viziers, men of worth, and they said to him, 'O king, verily God hath been bountiful unto thee and hath brought thee to thy wish, so that thou art become king in thy father's stead and hast gotten thee that which thou soughtest. But, as for this boy, there is no guilt in him, for that, from the day of his coming into the world, he hath seen neither ease nor joyance, and indeed his favour is faded and his charms changed [with long prison]. What is his offence that he should merit this punishment? Indeed, it is others than he who were to blame, and God hath given thee the victory over them, and there is no fault in this poor wight.' Quoth Belehwan, 'Indeed, it is as ye say; but I am fearful of his craft and am not assured from his mischief; belike the most part of the folk will incline unto him.' 'O king,' answered they, 'what is this boy and what power hath he? If thou fear him, send him to one of the frontiers.' And Belehwan said, 'Ye say sooth: we will send him to be captain over such an one of the marches.'

Now over against the place in question was a host of enemies, hard of heart, and in this he purposed the youth's slaughter. So he bade bring him forth of the underground dungeon and caused him draw near to him and saw his case. Then he bestowed on him a dress of honour and the folk rejoiced in this. Moreover, he tied him an ensign[134] and giving him a numerous army, despatched him to the region aforesaid, whither all who went were still slain or made prisoners. So Melik Shah betook himself thither with his army and when it was one of the days, behold, the enemy fell in upon them in the night; whereupon some of his men fled and the rest the enemy took; and they took Melik Shah also and cast him into an underground dungeon, with a company of his men. There he abode a whole year in evil plight, whilst his fellows mourned over his beauty and grace.

Now it was the enemy's wont, at every year's end, to bring forth their prisoners and cast them down from the top of the citadel to the bottom. So they brought them forth, at the end of the year, and cast them down, and Melik Shah with them. However, he fell upon the [other] men and the earth touched him not, for his term was [God-]guarded. Now those that were cast down there were slain and their bodies ceased not to lie there till the wild beasts ate them and the winds dispersed them. Melik Shah abode cast down in his place, aswoon, all that day and night, and when he recovered and found himself whole, he thanked God the Most High for his safety [and rising, fared on at a venture]. He gave not over walking, unknowing whither he went and feeding upon the leaves of the trees; and by day he hid himself whereas he might and fared on all his night at hazard; and thus he did some days, till he came to an inhabited land and seeing folk there, accosted them and acquainted them with his case, giving them to know that he had been imprisoned in the fortress and that they had cast him down, but God the Most High had delivered him and brought him off alive.

The folk took compassion on him and gave him to eat and drink and he abode with them awhile. Then he questioned them of the way that led to the kingdom of his uncle Belehwan, but told them not that he was his uncle. So they taught him the way and he ceased not to go barefoot, till he drew near his uncle's capital, and he naked and hungry, and indeed his body was wasted and his colour changed. He sat down at the gate of the city, and presently up came a company of King Belehwan's chief officers, who were out a-hunting and wished to water their horses. So they lighted down to rest and the youth accosted them, saying, 'I will ask you of somewhat, wherewith do ye acquaint me.' Quoth they, 'Ask what thou wilt.' And he said, 'Is King Belehwan well?' They laughed at him and answered, 'What a fool art thou, O youth! Thou art a stranger and a beggar, and what concern hast thou with the king's health?' Quoth he, 'Indeed, he is my uncle;' whereat they marvelled and said, 'It was one question[135] and now it is become two.' Then said they to him, 'O youth, it is as thou wert mad. Whence pretendest thou to kinship with the king? Indeed, we know not that he hath aught of kinsfolk, except a brother's son, who was prisoned with him, and he despatched him to wage war upon the infidels, so that they slew him.' 'I am he,' answered Melik Shah, 'and they slew me not, but there betided me this and that.'

They knew him forthright and rising to him, kissed his hands and rejoiced in him and said to him, 'O our lord, in good sooth, thou art a king and the son of a king, and we desire thee nought but good and beseech [God to grant] thee continuance. Consider how God hath rescued thee from this thy wicked uncle, who sent thee to a place whence none came ever off alive, purposing not in this but thy destruction; and indeed thou fellest into [peril of] death and God delivered thee therefrom. So how wilt thou return and cast thyself again into thine enemy's hand? By Allah, save thyself and return not to him again. Belike thou shall abide upon the face of the earth till it please God the Most High [to vouchsafe thee relief]; but, if thou fall again into his hand, he will not suffer thee live a single hour.'

The prince thanked them and said to them, 'God requite you with all good, for indeed ye give me loyal counsel; but whither would ye have me go?' Quoth they, 'Get thee to the land of the Greeks, the abiding-place of thy mother.' And he said, 'My grandfather Suleiman Shah, when the King of the Greeks wrote to him, demanding my mother in marriage, concealed my affair and hid my secret; [and she hath done the like,] and I cannot make her a liar.' 'Thou sayst sooth,' rejoined they; 'but we desire thine advantage, and even if thou tookest service with the folk, it were a means of thy continuance [on life].' Then each of them brought out to him money and gave to him and clad him and fed him and fared on with him a parasang's distance till they brought him far from the city, and giving him to know that he was safe, departed from him, whilst he fared on till he came forth of the dominions of his uncle and entered those [of the king] of the Greeks. Then he entered a village and taking up his abode therein, betook himself to serving one there in ploughing and sowing and the like.

As for his mother, Shah Khatoun, great was her longing for her son and she [still] thought of him and news of him was cut off from her, wherefore her life was troubled and she forswore sleep and could not make mention of him before King Caesar her husband. Now she had an eunuch who had come with her from the court of her uncle King Suleiman Shah, and he was intelligent, quickwitted, a man of good counsel. So she took him apart one day and said to him, 'Thou hast been my servant from my childhood to this day; canst thou not therefore avail to get me news of my son, for that I cannot speak of his matter?' 'O my lady,' answered he, 'this is an affair that thou hast concealed from the first, and were thy son here, it would not be possible for thee to harbour him, lest thine honour fall into suspicion with the king; for they would never credit thee, since the news hath been spread abroad that thy son was slain by his uncle.' Quoth she, 'The case is even as thou sayst and thou speakest truly; but, provided I know that my son is alive, let him be in these parts pasturing sheep and let me not see him nor he me.' And he said to her, 'How shall we contrive in this affair?' 'Here are my treasures and my wealth,' answered she. 'Take all thou wilt and bring me my son or else news of him.'

Then they agreed upon a device between them, to wit, that they should feign an occasion in their own country, under pretext that she had there wealth buried from the time of her husband Melik Shah and that none knew of it but this eunuch who was with her, wherefore it behoved that he should go and fetch it. So she acquainted the king her husband with this and sought of him leave for the eunuch to go: and the king granted him permission for the journey and charged him cast about for a device, lest any get wind of him. Accordingly, the eunuch disguised himself as a merchant and repairing to Belehwan's city, began to enquire concerning the youth's case; whereupon they told him that he had been prisoned in an underground dungeon and that his uncle had released him and dispatched him to such a place, where they had slain him. When the eunuch heard this, it was grievous to him and his breast was straitened and he knew not what he should do.

It chanced one day that one of the horsemen, who had fallen in with the young Melik Shah by the water and clad him and given him spending-money, saw the eunuch in the city, disguised as a merchant, and recognizing him, questioned him of his case and of [the reason of] his coming. Quoth he, 'I come to sell merchandise.' And the horseman said, 'I will tell thee somewhat, if thou canst keep it secret.' 'It is well,' answered the eunuch; 'what is it?' And the other said, 'We met the king's son Melik Shah, I and certain of the Arabs who were with me, and saw him by such a water and gave him spending-money and sent him towards the land of the Greeks, near his mother, for that we feared for him, lest his uncle Belehwan should kill him.' Then he told him all that had passed between them, whereupon the eunuch's countenance changed and he said to the cavalier, 'Assurance!' 'Thou shalt have assurance,' answered the other, 'though thou come in quest of him.' And the eunuch rejoined, saying, 'Truly, that is my errand, for there abideth no repose for his mother, lying down or rising up, and she hath sent me to seek news of him.' Quoth the cavalier, 'Go in safety, for he is in a [certain] part of the land of the Greeks, even as I said to thee.'

The eunuch thanked him and blessed him and mounting, returned upon his way, following the trace, whilst the cavalier rode with him to a certain road, when he said to him, 'This is where we left him.' Then he took leave of him and returned to his own city, whilst the eunuch fared on along the road, enquiring of the youth in every village he entered by the description which the cavalier had given him, and he ceased not to do thus till he came to the village where the young Melik Shah was. So he entered and lighting down therein, made enquiry after the prince, but none gave him news of him; whereat he abode perplexed concerning his affair and addressed himself to depart. Accordingly he mounted his horse [and set out homeward]; but, as he passed through the village, he saw a cow bound with a rope and a youth asleep by her side, with the end of the halter in his hand; so he looked at him and passed on and took no heed of him in his heart; but presently he stopped and said in himself; 'If he of whom I am in quest be come to the like [of the condition] of yonder sleeping youth, by whom I passed but now, how shall I know him? Alas, the length of my travail and weariness! How shall I go about in quest of a wight whom I know not and whom, if I saw him face to face, I should not know?'

Then he turned back, pondering upon that sleeping youth, and coming to him, as he slept, lighted down from his horse and sat down by him. He fixed his eyes upon his face and considered him awhile and said in himself, 'For aught I know, this youth may be Melik Shah.' And he fell a-hemming and saying, 'Harkye, O youth!' Whereupon the sleeper awoke and sat up; and the eunuch said to him, 'Who is thy father in this village and where is thy dwelling?' The youth sighed and answered, 'I am a stranger;' and the eunuch said, 'From what land art thou and who is thy father?' Quoth the other, 'I am from such a land,' and the eunuch ceased not to question him and he to answer him, till he was certified of him and knew him. So he rose and embraced him and kissed him and wept over his case. Moreover, he told him that he was going about in quest of him and informed him that he was come privily from the king his mother's husband and that his mother would be content [to know] that he was alive and well, though she saw him not.

Then he re-entered the village and buying the prince a horse, mounted him thereon and they ceased not going, till they came to the frontier of their own country, where there fell robbers upon them by the way and took all that was with them and pinioned them; after which they cast them into a pit hard by the road and went away and left them to die there, and indeed they had cast many folk into that pit and they had died.

The eunuch fell a-weeping in the pit and the youth said to him, 'What is this weeping and what shall it profit here?' Quoth the eunuch, 'I weep not for fear of death, but of pity for thee and the sorriness of thy case and because of thy mother's heart and for that which thou hast suffered of horrors and that thy death should be this abject death, after the endurance of all manner stresses.' But the youth said, 'That which hath betided me was forewrit to me and that which is written none hath power to efface; and if my term be advanced, none may avail to defer it.'[136] Then they passed that night and the following day and the next night and the next day [in the pit], till they were weak with hunger and came near upon death and could but groan feebly.

Now it befell, by the ordinance of God the Most High and His providence, that Caesar, king of the Greeks, the husband of Melik Shah's mother Shah Khatoun, [went forth to the chase that day]. He started a head of game, he and his company, and chased it, till they came up with it by that pit, whereupon one of them lighted down from his horse, to slaughter it, hard by the mouth of the pit. He heard a sound of low moaning from the bottom of the pit} so he arose and mounting his horse, waited till the troops were assembled. Then he acquainted the king with this and he bade one of his servants [descend into the pit]. So the man descended and brought out the youth [and the eunuch], aswoon.

They cut their bonds and poured wine into their gullets, till they came to themselves, when the king looked at the eunuch and recognizing him, said, 'Harkye, such an one!' 'Yes, O my lord the king,' replied the man and prostrated himself to him; whereat the king marvelled with an exceeding wonder and said to him, 'How earnest thou to this place and what hath befallen thee?" Quoth the eunuch, 'I went and took out the treasure and brought it hither; but the [evil] eye was behind me and I unknowing. So the thieves took us alone here and seized the money and cast us into this pit, so we might die of hunger, even as they had done with other than we; but God the Most High sent thee, in pity to us.'

The king marvelled, he and his company, and praised God the Most High for that he had come thither; after which he turned to the eunuch and said to him, 'What is this youth thou hast with thee?' 'O king,' answered he, 'this is the son of a nurse who belonged to us and we left him little. I saw him to-day and his mother said to me, 'Take him with thee.' So I brought him with me, that he might be a servant to the king, for that he is an adroit and quickwitted youth.' Then the king fared on, he and his company, and the eunuch and the youth with them, what while he questioned the former of Belehwan and his dealing with his subjects, and he answered, saying, 'As thy head liveth, O king, the folk with him are in sore straits and not one of them desireth to look on him, gentle or simple.'

[When the king returned to his palace,] he went in to his wife Shah Khatoun and said to her, 'I give thee the glad news of thine eunuch's return.' And he told her what had betided and of the youth whom he had brought with him. When she heard this, her wits fled and she would have cried out, but her reason restrained her, and the king said to her, 'What is this? Art thou overcome with grief for [the loss of] the treasure or [for that which hath befallen] the eunuch?' 'Nay, as thy head liveth, O king!' answered she. 'But women are fainthearted.' Then came the servant and going in to her, told her all that had befallen him and acquainted her with her son's case also and with that which he had suffered of stresses and how his uncle had exposed him to slaughter and he had been taken prisoner and they had cast him into the pit and hurled him from the top of the citadel and how God had delivered him from these perils, all of them; and he went on to tell her [all that had betided him], whilst she wept.

Then said she to him, 'When the king saw him and questioned thee of him, what saidst thou to him?' And he answered, 'I said to him, "This is the son of a nurse who belonged to us. We left him little and he grew up; so I brought him, that he might be servant to the king,"' Quoth she, 'Thou didst well.' And she charged him to be instant in the service of the prince. As for the king, he redoubled in kindness to the eunuch and appointed the youth a liberal allowance and he abode going in to the king's house and coming out therefrom and standing in his service, and every day he grew in favour with him; whilst, as for Shah Khatoun, she used to stand a-watch for him at the windows and balconies and gaze upon him, and she on coals of fire on his account, yet could she not speak.

On this wise she abode a great while and indeed yearning for him came nigh to slay her; so she stood and watched for him one day at the door of her chamber and straining him to her bosom, kissed him on the cheek and breast. At this moment, out came the master of the king's household and seeing her embracing the youth, abode amazed. Then he asked to whom that chamber belonged and was answered, 'To Shah Khatoun, wife of the king,' whereupon he turned back, trembling as [one smitten by] a thunderbolt. The king saw him quaking and said to him, 'Out on thee! what is the matter?' 'O king,' answered he, 'what matter is graver than that which I see?' 'What seest thou?' asked the king and the officer said, 'I see that yonder youth, who came with the eunuch, he brought not with him but on account of Shah Khatoun; for that I passed but now by her chamber door, and she was standing, watching; [and when the youth came up,] she rose to him and clipped him and kissed him on his cheek.'

When the king heard this, he bowed [his head] in amazement and perplexity and sinking into a seat, clutched at his beard and shook it, till he came nigh to pluck it out. Then he arose forthright and laid hands on the youth and clapped him in prison. Moreover, he took the eunuch also and cast them both into an underground dungeon in his house, after which he went in to Shah Khatoun and said to her, 'Thou hast done well, by Allah, O daughter of nobles, O thou whom kings sought in marriage, for the excellence of thy repute and the goodliness of the reports of thee! How fair is thy semblance! May God curse her whose inward is the contrary of her outward, after the likeness of thy base favour, whose outward is comely and its inward foul, fair face and foul deeds! Verily, I mean to make of thee and of yonder good-for-nought an example among the folk, for that thou sentest not thine eunuch but of intent on his account, so that he took him and brought him into my house and thou hast trampled my head with him; and this is none other than exceeding hardihood; but thou shall see what I will do with you.'

So saying, he spat in her face and went out from her; whilst Shah Khatoun made him no answer, knowing that, if she spoke at that time, he would not credit her speech. Then she humbled herself in supplication to God the Most High and said, 'O God the Great, Thou knowest the hidden things and the outward parts and the inward' If an advanced term[137] be [appointed] to me, let it not be deferred, and if a deferred one, let it not be advanced!' On this wise she passed some days, whilst the king fell into perplexity and forswore meat and drink and sleep and abode knowing not what he should do and saying [in himself], 'If I kill the eunuch and the youth, my soul will not be solaced, for they are not to blame, seeing that she sent to fetch him, and my heart will not suffer me to slay them all three. But I will not be hasty in putting them to death, for that I fear repentance.' Then he left them, so he might look into the affair.

Now he had a nurse, a foster-mother, on whose knees he had been reared, and she was a woman of understanding and misdoubted of him, but dared not accost him [with questions]. So she went in to Shah Khatoun and finding her in yet sorrier plight than he, asked her what was to do; but she refused to answer. However, the nurse gave not over coaxing and questioning her, till she exacted of her an oath of secrecy. So the old woman swore to her that she would keep secret all that she should say to her, whereupon the queen related to her her history from first to last and told her that the youth was her son. With this the old woman prostrated herself before her and said to her, 'This is an easy matter.' But the queen answered, saying, 'By Allah, O my mother, I choose my destruction and that of my son rather than defend myself by avouching a thing whereof they will not credit me; for they will say, "She avoucheth this, but that she may fend off reproach from herself" And nought will avail me but patience.' The old woman was moved by her speech and her intelligence and said to her, 'Indeed, O my daughter, it is as thou sayst, and I hope in God that He will show forth the truth. Have patience and I will presently go in to the king and hear what he saith and contrive somewhat in this matter, if it be the will of God the Most High.'

Then she arose and going in to the king, found him with his head between his knees, and he lamenting. So she sat down by him awhile and bespoke him with soft words and said to him, 'Indeed, O my son, thou consumest mine entrails, for that these [many] days thou hast not mounted to horse, and thou lamentest and I know not what aileth thee.' 'O my mother,' answered he, '[this my chagrin] is due to yonder accursed woman, of whom I still deemed well and who hath done thus and thus.' Then he related to her the whole story from first to last, and she said to him, 'This thy concern is on account of a worthless woman.' Quoth he, 'I was but considering by what death I should slay them, so the folk may [be admonished by their fate and] repent.' And she said, 'O my son, beware of haste, for it engendereth repentance and the slaying of them will not escape [thee]. When thou art assured of this affair, do what thou wilt.' 'O my mother,' rejoined he;

'there needeth no assurance concerning him for whom she despatched her eunuch and he fetched him.'

But she said, 'There is a thing wherewith we will make her confess, and all that is in her heart shall be discovered to thee.' 'What is that?' asked the king, and she answered, 'I will bring thee a hoopoe's heart,[138] which, when she sleepeth, do thou lay upon her heart and question her of all thou wilt, and she will discover this unto thee and show forth the truth to thee." The king rejoiced in this and said to his nurse, 'Hasten and let none know of thee.' So she arose and going in to the queen, said to her, 'I have done thine occasion and it is on this wise. This night the king will come in to thee and do thou feign thyself asleep; and if he ask thee of aught, do thou answer him, as if in thy sleep.' The queen thanked her and the old woman went away and fetching the hoopoe's heart, gave it to the king.

Hardly was the night come, when he went in to his wife and found her lying back, [apparently] asleep; so he sat down by her side and laying the hoopoe's heart on her breast, waited awhile, so he might be certified that she slept. Then said he to her, 'Shah Khatoun, Shah Khatoun, is this my recompense from thee?' Quoth she, 'What offence have I committed?' And he, 'What offence can be greater than this? Thou sentest after yonder youth and broughtest him hither, on account of the desire of thy heart, so thou mightest do with him that for which thou lustedst.' 'I know not desire,' answered she. 'Verily, among thy servants are those who are comelier and handsomer than he; yet have I never desired one of them.' 'Why, then,' asked he, 'didst thou lay hold of him and kiss him!' And she said, 'This is my son and a piece of my heart; and of my longing and love for him, I could not contain myself, but sprang upon him and kissed him.' When the king heard this, he was perplexed and amazed and said to her, 'Hast thou a proof that this youth is thy son? Indeed, I have a letter from thine uncle King Suleiman Shah, [wherein he giveth me to know] that his unck Belehwan cut his throat.' 'Yes,' answered she, 'he did indeed cut his throat, but severed not the windpipe; so my uncle sewed up the wound and reared him, [and he lived,] for that his hour was not come.'

When the king heard this, he said, 'This proof sufficeth me,' and rising forthright in the night, let bring the youth and the eunuch. Then he examined the former's throat with a candle and saw [the scar where] it [had been] cut from ear to ear, and indeed the place had healed up and it was like unto a stretched-out thread. Therewithal the king fell down prostrate to God, [in thanksgiving to Him] for that He had delivered the prince from all these perils and from the stresses that he had undergone, and rejoiced with an exceeding joy for that he had wrought deliberately and had not made haste to slay him, in which case sore repentance had betided him. As for the youth," continued the young treasurer, "he was not saved but because his term was deferred, and on like wise, O king, is it with me; I too have a deferred term, which I shall attain, and a period which I shall accomplish, and I trust in God the Most High that He will give me the victory over these wicked viziers."

When the youth had made an end of his speech, the king said, "Carry him back to the prison;" and when they had done this, he turned to the viziers and said to them, "Yonder youth looseth his tongue upon you, but I know your affectionate solicitude for the welfare of my empire and your loyal counsel to me; so be of good heart, for all that ye counsel me I will do." When they heard tnese words, they rejoiced and each of them said his say Then said the king, "I have not deferred his slaughter but to the intent that the talk might be prolonged and that words might abound, and I desire [now] that ye sit up for him a gibbet without the town and make proclamation among the folk that they assemble and take him and carry him in procession to the gibbet, with the crier crying before him and saying, 'This is the recompense of him whom the king delighted to favour and who hath betrayed him!'" The viziers rejoiced, when they heard this, and slept not that night, of their joy; and they made proclamation in the city and set up the gibbet.

The Eleventh Day.

OF THE SPEEDY RELIEF OF GOD.

When it was the eleventh day, the viziers betook them early in the morning to the king's gate and said to him, "O king, the folk are assembled from the king's gate to the gibbet, so they may see [the execution of] the king's commandment on the youth." So the king bade fetch the prisoner and they brought him; whereupon the viziers turned to him and said to him, "O vile of origin, doth any hope of life remain with thee and lookest thou still for deliverance after this day?" "O wicked viziers," answered he, "shall a man of understanding renounce hope in God the Most High? Indeed, howsoever a man be oppressed, there cometh to him deliverance from the midst of stress and life from the midst of death, [as is shown by the case of] the prisoner and how God delivered him." "What is his story?" asked the king; and the youth answered, saying, "O king, they tell that

STORY OF THE PRISONER AND HOW GOD GAVE HIM RELIEF.

There was once a king of the kings, who had a high palace, overlooking a prison of his, and he used to hear in the night one saying, 'O Ever-present Deliverer, O Thou whose relief is nigh, relieve Thou me!' One day the king waxed wroth and said, "Yonder fool looketh for relief from [the consequences of] his crime. 'Then said he to his officers, 'Who is in yonder prison?' And they answered, 'Folk upon whom blood hath been found.'[139] So the king bade bring the man in question before him and said to him, 'O fool, little of wit, how shall thou be delivered from this prison, seeing that thine offence is great?' Then he committed him to a company of his guards and said to them, 'Take this fellow and crucify him without the city.'

Now it was the night-season. So the soldiers carried him without the city, thinking to crucify him, when, behold, there came out upon them thieves and fell in on them with swords and [other] weapons. Thereupon the guards left him whom they purposed to put to death [and took to flight], whilst the man who was going to slaughter fled forth at a venture and plunging into the desert, knew not whither he went before he found himself in a thicket and there came out upon him a lion of frightful aspect, which snatched him up and set him under him. Then he went up to a tree and tearing it up by the roots, covered the man therewith and made off into the thicket, in quest of the lioness.

As for the man, he committed his affair to God the Most High, relying upon Him for deliverance, and said in himself, 'What is this affair?' Then he did away the leaves from himself and rising, saw great plenty of men's bones there, of those whom the lion had devoured. He looked again and saw a heap of gold lying alongside a girdle;[140] whereat he marvelled and gathering up the gold in his skirts, went forth of the thicket and fled in affright at hazard, turning neither to the right nor to the left, in his fear of the lion; till he came to a village and cast himself down, as he were dead. He lay there till the day appeared and he was rested from his fatigue, when he arose and burying the gold, entered the village. Thus God gave him relief and he came by the gold."

Then said the king, "How long wilt thou beguile us with thy prate, O youth? But now the hour of thy slaughter is come." And he bade crucify him upon the gibbet. [So they carried him to the place of execution] and were about to hoist him up [upon the cross,] when, behold, the captain of the thieves, who had found him and reared him,[141] came up at that moment and asked what was that assembly and [the cause of] the crowds gathered there. They told him that a servant of the king had committed a great crime and that he was about to put him to death. So the captain of the thieves pressed forward and looking upon the prisoner, knew him, whereupon he went up to him and embraced him and clipped him and fell to kissing him upon his mouth. Then said he, "This is a boy whom I found under such a mountain, wrapped in a gown of brocade, and I reared him and he fell to stopping the way with us. One day, we set upon a caravan, but they put us to flight and wounded some of us and took the boy and went their way. From that day to this I have gone round about the lands in quest of him, but have not lighted on news of him [till now;] and this is he."

When the king heard this, he was certified that the youth was his very son; so he cried out at the top of his voice and casting himself upon him, embraced him and wept and said, "Had I put thee to death, as was my intent, I should have died of regret for thee." Then he cut his bonds and taking his crown from his head, set it on that of his son, whereupon the people raised cries of joy, whilst the trumpets sounded and the drums beat and there befell a great rejoicing. They decorated the city and it was a glorious day; the very birds stayed their flight in the air, for the greatness of the clamour and the noise of the crying. The army and the folk carried the prince [to the palace] in magnificent procession, and the news came to his mother Behrjaur, who came forth and threw herself upon him. Moreover, the king bade open the prison and bring forth all who were therein, and they held high festival seven days and seven nights and rejoiced with a mighty rejoicing; whilst terror and silence and confusion and affright fell upon the viziers and they gave themselves up for lost.

After this the king sat, with his son by his side and the viziers sitting before him, and summoned his chief officers and the folk of the city. Then the prince turned to the viziers and said to them, "See, O wicked viziers, that which God hath done and the speedy [coming of] relief." But they answered not a word and the king said, "It sufficeth me that there is nothing alive but rejoiceth with me this day, even to the birds in the sky, but ye, your breasts are straitened. Indeed, this is the greatest of ill-will in you to me, and had I hearkened to you, my regret had been prolonged and I had died miserably of grief." "O my father," quoth the prince, "but for the fairness of thy thought and thy judgment and thy longanimity and deliberation in affairs, there had not bedded thee this great joyance. Hadst thou slain me in haste, repentance would have been sore on thee and long grief, and on this wise doth he who ensueth haste repent."

Then the king sent for the captain of the thieves and bestowed on him a dress of honour,[142] commanding that all who loved the king should put off [their raiment and cast it] upon him.[143] So there fell dresses of honour [and other presents] on him, till he was wearied with their much plenty, and Azadbekht invested him with the mastership of the police of his city. Then he bade set up other nine gibbets beside the first and said to his son, "Thou art guiltless, and yet these wicked viziers endeavoured for thy slaughter." "O my father," answered the prince, "I had no fault [in their eyes] but that I was a loyal counsellor to thee and still kept watch over thy good and withheld their hands from thy treasuries; wherefore they were jealous and envied me and plotted against me and sought to slay me," Quoth the king, "The time [of retribution] is at hand, O my son; but what deemest thou we should do with them in requital of that which they did with thee? For that they have endeavoured for thy slaughter and exposed thee to public ignominy and soiled my honour among the kings."

Then he turned to the viziers and said to them, "Out on ye! What liars ye are! What excuse is left you?" "O king," answered they, "there abideth no excuse for us and our sin hath fallen upon us and broken us in pieces. Indeed we purposed evil to this youth and it hath reverted upon us, and we plotted mischief against him and it hath overtaken us; yea, we digged a pit for him and have fallen ourselves therein." So the king bade hoist up the viziers upon the gibbets and crucify them there, for that God is just and ordaineth that which is right. Then Azadbekht and his wife and son abode in joyance and contentment, till there came to them the Destroyer of Delights and they died all; and extolled be the perfection of the [Ever-]Living One, who dieth not, to whom be glory and whose mercy be upon us for ever and ever! Amen.

JAAFER BEN YEHYA AND ABDULMEILIK BEN SALIH THE ABBASIDE [144]

IT is told of Jaafer ben Yehya the Barmecide that he sat down one day to drink and being minded to be private (with his friends), sent for his boon-companions, in whom he delighted, and charged the chamberlain[145] that he should suffer none of the creatures of God the Most High to enter, save a man of his boon-companions, by name Abdulmelik ben Salih,[146] who was behindhand with them. Then they donned coloured clothes,[147] for that it was their wont, whenas they sat in the wine-chamber, to don raiment of red and yellow and green silk, and sat down to drink, and the cups went round and the lutes pulsed.

Now there was a man of the kinsfolk of the Khalif [Haroun er Reshid], by name Abdulmelik ben Salih ben Ali ben Abdallah ben el Abbas,[148] who was great of gravity and piety and decorousness, and Er Reshid was used instantly to require of him that he should keep him company in his carousals and drink with him and had proffered him, to this end, riches galore, but he still refused. It chanced that this Abdulmelik es Salih came to the door of Jaafer ben Yehya, that he might bespeak him of certain occasions of his, and the chamberlain, doubting not but he was the Abdulmelik ben Salih aforesaid, whom Jaafer had charged him admit and that he should suffer none but him to enter, allowed him to go in to his master.

When Jaafer saw him, his reason was like to depart for shame and he knew that the chamberlain had been deceived by the likeness of the name; and Abdulmelik also perceived how the case stood and confusion was manifest to him in Jaafer's face. So he put on a cheerful favour and said, "No harm be upon you![149] Bring us of these dyed clothes." So they brought him a dyed gown[150] and he put it on and sat discoursing cheerily with Jaafer and jesting with him. Then said he, "Give us to drink of your wine." So they poured him out a pint and he said, "Be ye indulgent with us, for we have no wont of this." Then he chatted and jested with them till Jaafer's breast dilated and his constraint ceased from him and his shamefastness, and he rejoiced in this with an exceeding joy and said to Abdulmelik, "What is thine errand?" Quoth the other, "I come (may God amend thee!) on three occasions, whereof I would have thee bespeak the Khalif; to wit, firstly, I have on me a debt to the amount of a thousand thousand dirhems,[151] which I would have discharged; secondly, I desire for my son the office of governor of a province, whereby his rank may be raised; and thirdly, I would fain have thee marry him to a daughter of the Khalif, for that she is his cousin and he is a match for her." And Jaafer said, "God accomplished! unto thee these three occasions. As for the money, it shall presently be carried to thy house; as for the government, I make thy son viceroy of Egypt; and as for the marriage, I give him to wife such an one, the daughter of our Lord the Commander of the Faithful, at a dowry of such and such a sum. So depart in the assurance of God the Most High."

So Abdulmelik went away to his house, whither he found that the money had foregone him, and on the morrow Jaafer presented himself before the Khalif and acquainted him with what had passed and that he had appointed Abdulmelik's son governor of Egypt and had promised him his daughter in marriage. Er Reshid approved of this and confirmed the appointment and the marriage. [Then he sent for the young man] and he went not forth of the palace of the Khalif till he wrote him the patent [of investiture with the government] of Egypt; and he let bring the Cadis and the witnesses and drew up the contract of marriage.

ER RESHID AND THE BARMECIDES [152]

IT is said that the most extraordinary of that which happened to Er Reshid was as follows: His brother El Hadi,[153] when he succeeded to the Khalifate, enquired of a seal-ring of great price, that had belonged to his father El Mehdi,[154] and it came to his knowledge that Er Reshid had taken it. So he required it of the latter, who refused to give it up, and El Hadi insisted upon him, but he still denied the seal-ring of the Khalifate. Now this was on the bridge [over the Tigris], and he threw the ring into the river. When El Hadi died and Er Reshid succeeded to the Khalifate, he came in person to that bridge, with a seal-ring of lead, which he threw into the river at the same place, and bade the divers seek it. So they did [his bidding] and brought up the first ring, and this was reckoned [an omen] of Er Reshid's good fortune and [a presage of] the continuance of his reign.[155]

When Er Reshid came to the throne, he invested Jaafer ben Yehya ben Khalid el Bermeki[156] with the vizierate. Now Jaafer was eminently distinguished for generosity and munificence, and the stories of him to this effect are renowned and are written in the books. None of the viziers attained to the rank and favour which he enjoyed with Er Reshid, who was wont to call him brother[157] and used to carry him with him into his house. The period of his vizierate was nineteen years,[158] and Yehya one day said to his son Jaafer, "O my son, what time thy reed trembleth, water it with kindness."[159] Opinions differ concerning the reason of Jaafer's slaughter, but the better is as follows. Er Reshid could not brook to be parted from Jaafer nor from his [own] sister Abbaseh, daughter of El Mehdi, a single hour, and she was the loveliest woman of her time; so he said to Jaafer, "I will marry thee to her, that it may be lawful to thee to look upon her, but thou shalt not touch her." [Accordingly, they were married] and they used both to be present in Er Reshid's sitting chamber. Now the Khalif would rise bytimes [and go forth] from the chamber, and they being both young and filled with wine, Jaafer would rise to her and swive her. She conceived by him and bore a handsome boy and fearing Er Reshid, despatched the newborn child by one of her confidants to Mecca the Holy, may God the Most High advance it in honour and increase it in venerance and nobility and magnification! The affair abode concealed till there befell despite between Abbaseh and one of her slave-girls, whereupon the latter discovered the affair of the child to Er Reshid and acquainted him with its abiding-place. So, when the Khalif made the pilgrimage, he despatched one who brought him the boy and found the affair true, wherefore he caused befall the Barmecides that which befell.[160]

IBN ES SEMMAK AND ER RESHID [161]

IT is related that Ibn es Semmak[162] went in one day to Er Reshid and the Khalif, being athirst, called for drink. So his cup was brought him, and when he took it, Ibn es Semmak said to him, "Softly, O Commander of the Faithful! If thou wert denied this draught, with what wouldst thou buy it?" "With the half of my kingdom," answered the Khalif; and Ibn es Semmak said, "Drink and God prosper it to thee!" Then, when he had drunken, he said to him, "If thou wert denied the going forth of the draught from thy body, with what wouldst thou buy its issue?" "With the whole of my kingdom," answered Er Reshid: and Ibn es Semmak said, "O Commander of the Faithful, verily, a kingdom that weigheth not in the balance against a draught [of water] or a voiding of urine is not worth the striving for." And Haroun wept.

EL MAMOUN AND ZUBEIDEH [163]

IT is said that El Mamoun[164] came one day upon Zubeideh, mother of El Amin,[165] and saw her moving her lips and muttering somewhat he understood not; so he said to her, "O mother mine, dost thou imprecate [curses] upon me, for that I slew thy son and despoiled him of his kingdom?" "Not so, by Allah, O Commander of the Faithful!" answered she, and he said, "What then saidst thou?" Quoth she, "Let the Commander of the Faithful excuse me." But he was instant with her, saying, "Needs must thou tell it." And she replied, "I said, 'God confound importunity!'" "How so?" asked the Khalif, and she said, "I played one day at chess with the Commander of the Faithful [Haroun er Reshid] and he imposed on me the condition of commandment and acceptance.[166] He beat me and bade me put off my clothes and go round about the palace, naked; so I did this, and I incensed against him. Then we fell again to playing and I beat him; so I bade him go to the kitchen and swive the foulest and sorriest wench of the wenches thereof. [I went to the kitchen] and found not a slave-girl fouler and filthier than thy mother;[167] so I bade him swive her. He did as I bade him and she became with child by him of thee, and thus was I [by my unlucky insistance] the cause of the slaying of my son and the despoiling him of his kingdom." When El Mamoun heard this, he turned away, saying, "God curse the importunate!" to wit, himself, who had importuned her till she acquainted him with that matter.

EN NUMAN AND THE ARAB OF THE BENOU TAI [168]

IT is said that En Numan[169] had two boon-companions, one of whom was called Ibn Saad and the other Amrou ben el Melik, and he became one night drunken and bade bury them alive; so they buried them. When he arose on the morrow, he enquired for them and was acquainted with their case, whereupon he built over them a monument and appointed to himself a day of ill-luck and a day of good-luck. If any met him on his day of ill-omen, he slew him and with his blood he washed the monument aforesaid, the which is a place well known in Cufa; and if any met him on his day of grace, he enriched him.

Now there accosted him once, on his day of ill-omen, an Arab of the Benou Tai,[170] and En Numan would have put him to death; but the Arab said, "God quicken the king! I have two little girls and have made none guardian over them; so, if the king see fit to grant me leave to go to them, I will give him the covenant of God[171] that I will return to him, whenas I have appointed them a guardian." En Numan had compassion on him and said to him, "If a man will be surety for thee of those who are with us, [I will let thee go], and if thou return not, I will put him to death." Now there was with En Numan his vizier Sherik ben Amrou; so the Tai[172] looked at him and said,

Sherik ben Amrou, what device avails the hand of death to stay? O brother of the brotherless, brother of all th' afflicted, say.
Brother of En Numan, with thee lies an old man s anguish to allay, A graybeard slain, may God make fair his deeds upon the Reckoning-Day!
Quoth Sherik, "On me be his warranty, may God assain the king!" So the Tai departed, after a term had been assigned him for his coming.

When the appointed day arrived, En Numan sent for Sherik and said to him, "Verily the first part of this day is past." And Sherik answered, "The king hath no recourse against me till it be eventide." When it evened, there appeared one afar off and En Numan fell to looking upon him and on Sherik, and the latter said to him, "Thou hast no right over me till yonder fellow come, for belike he is my man." As he spoke, up came the Tai in haste and En Numan said "By Allah, never saw I [any] more generous than you two! I know not whether of you is the more generous, this one who became warrant for thee in [danger of] death or thou who returnest unto slaughter." Then said he to Sherik, "What prompted thee to become warrant for him, knowing that it was death?" And he said, "[I did this] lest it be said, 'Generosity hath departed from viziers.'" Then said En Numan to the Tai, "And thou, what prompted thee to return, knowing that therein was death and thine own destruction?" Quoth the Arab, "[I did this] lest it be said, 'Fidelity hath departed from the folk.'" And En Numan said, "By Allah, I will be the third of you,[173] lest it be said, 'Clemency hath departed from kings.'" So he pardoned him and bade abolish the day of ill-omen; whereupon the Arab recited the following verses:

Full many a man incited me to infidelity, But I refused, for all the talk wherewith they set on me.
I am a man in whom good faith's a natural attribute; The deeds of every upright man should with his speech agree.

Quoth En Numan, "What prompted thee to keep faith, the case being as thou sayest?" "O king," answered the Arab, "it was my religion." And En Numan said, "What is thy religion?" "The Christian," replied the other. Quoth the king, "Expound it unto me." [So the Tai expounded it to him] and En Numan became a Christian.[174]

FIROUZ AND HIS WIFE [175]

A certain king sat one day on the roof of his palace, diverting himself with looking about him, and presently, chancing to look aside, he espied, on [the roof of] a house over against his palace, a woman, never saw his eyes her like. So he turned to those who were present and said to them, "To whom belongeth yonder house?" "To thy servant Firouz," answered they, "and that is his wife." So he went down, (and indeed love had made him drunken and he was passionately enamoured of her), and calling Firouz, said to him, "Take this letter and go with it to such a city and bring me the answer." Firouz took the letter and going to his house, laid it under his head and passed that night. When the morning morrowed, he took leave of his wife and set out for the city in question, unknowing what the king purposed against him.

As for the king, he arose in haste and disguising himself, repaired to the house of Firouz and knocked at the door. Quoth Firouz's wife, "Who is at the door?" And he answered, saying, "I am the king, thy husband's master." So she opened the door and he entered and sat down, saying, "We are come to visit thee." Quoth she, "I seek refuge [with God] from this visitation, for indeed I deem not well thereof." And the king said, "O desire of hearts, I am thy husband's master and methinks thou knowest me not." "Nay," answered she, "I know thee, O my lord and master, and I know thy purpose and that which thou seekest and that thou art my husband's lord. I understand what thou wishest, and indeed the poet hath forestalled thee in his saying of the following verses, in reference to thy case:

Your water I'll leave without drinking, for there Too many already have drunken whilere.
When the flies light on food, from the platter my hand I raise, though my spirit should long for the fare;
And whenas the dogs at a fountain have lapped, The lions to drink of the water forbear."

Then said she, "O king, comest thou to a [watering-]place whereat thy dog hath drunken and wilt thou drink thereof?" The king was abashed at her and at her words and went out from her, but forgot his sandal in the house.

As for Firouz, when he went forth from his house, he sought the letter, but found it not; so he returned home. Now his return fell in with the king's going forth and he found the latter's sandal in his house, whereat his wit was dazed and he knew that the king had not sent him away but for a purpose of his own. However, he held his peace and spoke not a word, but, taking the letter, went on his errand and accomplished it and returned to the king, who gave him a hundred dinars. So Firouz betook himself to the market and bought what beseemeth women of goodly gifts and returning to his wife, saluted her and gave her all that he had brought and said to her, "Arise [go] to thy father's house." "Wherefore?" asked she, and he said, "Verily, the king hath been bountiful to me and I would have thee show forth this, so thy father may rejoice in that which he seeth upon thee." "With all my heart," answered she and arising forthright, betook herself to the house of her father, who rejoiced in her coming and in that which he saw upon her; and she abode with him a month's space, and her husband made no mention of her.

Then came her brother to him and said, "O Firouz, an thou wilt not acquaint me with the reason of thine anger against thy wife, come and plead with us before the king." Quoth he, "If ye will have me plead with you, I will do so." So they went to the king and found the cadi sitting with him; whereupon quoth the damsel's brother, "God assist our lord the cadi! I let this man on hire a high-walled garden, with a well in good case and trees laden with fruit; but he beat down its walls and ruined its well and ate its fruits, and now he desireth to return it to me." The cadi turned to Firouz and said to him, "What sayst thou, O youth?" And he answered, "Indeed, I delivered him the garden in the goodliest of case." So the cadi said to the brother, "Hath he delivered thee the garden, as he saith?" And the other replied, "No; but I desire to question him of the reason of his returning it." Quoth the cadi, "What sayst thou, O youth?" And Firouz answered, "I returned it in my own despite, for that I entered it one day and saw the track of the lion; wherefore I feared lest, if I entered it again, the lion should devour me. So that which I did, I did of reverence to him and for fear of him."

Now the king was leaning back upon the cushion, when he heard the man's words, he knew the purport thereof; so he sat up and said, "Return to thy garden in all assurance and ease of heart; for, by Allah, never saw I the like of thy garden nor stouter of ward than its walls over its trees!" So Firouz returned to his wife, and the cadi knew not the truth of the affair, no, nor any of those who were in that assembly, save the king and the husband and the damsel's brother.[176]

KING SHAH BEKHT AND HIS VIZIER ER REHWAN [177]

THERE was once, of old days and in bygone ages and times, a king of the kings of the time, by name Shah Bekht, who had troops and servants and guards galore and a vizier called Er Rehwan, who was wise, understanding, a man of good counsel and a cheerful acceptor of the commandments of God the Most High, to whom belong might and majesty. The king committed to him the affairs of his kingdom and his subjects and said according to his word, and on this wise he abode a long space of time.

Now this vizier had many enemies, who envied him his high place and still sought to do him hurt, but found no way thereunto, and God, in His fore-knowledge and His fore-ordinance from time immemorial, decreed that the king dreamt that the Vizier Er Rehwan gave him a fruit from off a tree and he ate it and died. So he awoke, affrighted and troubled, and when the vizier had presented himself before him [and withdrawn] and the king was alone with those in whom he trusted, he related to them his dream and they counselled him to send for the astrologers and interpreters [of dreams] and commended to him a sage, for whose skill and wisdom they vouched. So the king sent for him and entreated him with honour and made him draw near to himself. Now there had been private with the sage in question a company of the vizier's enemies, who besought him to slander the vizier to the king and counsel him to put him to death, in consideration of that which they promised him of wealth galore; and he agreed with them of this and told the king that the vizier would slay him in the course of the [ensuing] month and bade him hasten to put him to death, else would he surely slay him.

Presently, the vizier entered and the king signed to him to cause avoid the place. So he signed to those who were present to withdraw, and they departed; whereupon quoth the king to him, "How deemest thou, O excellent vizier, O loyal counsellor in all manner of governance, of a vision I have seen in my sleep?" "What is it, O king?" asked the vizier, and Shah Bekht related to him his dream, adding, "And indeed the sage interpreted it to me and said to me, 'An thou put not the vizier to death within a month, he will slay thee.' Now I am exceeding both to put the like of thee to death, yet do I fear to leave thee on life. What then dost thou counsel me that I should do in this matter?" The vizier bowed his head awhile, then raised it and said, "God prosper the king! Verily, it skills not to continue him on life of whom the king is afraid, and my counsel is that thou make haste to put me to death."

When the king heard his speech, he turned to him and said, "It is grievous to me, O vizier of good counsel." And he told him that the [other] sages testified [to the correctness of their fellow's interpretation of the dream]; whereupon Er Rehwan sighed and knew that the king went in fear of him; but he showed him fortitude and said to him, "God assain the king! My counsel is that the king accomplish his commandment and execute his ordinance, for that needs must death be and it is liefer to me that I die, oppressed, than that I die, an oppressor. But, if the king see fit to defer the putting of me to death till the morrow and will pass this night with me and take leave of me, when the morrow cometh, the king shall do what he will."

Then he wept till he wet his gray hairs and the king was moved to compassion for him and granted him that which he sought and vouchsafed him that night's respite.

The First Night of the Month

When it was eventide, the king caused avoid his sitting chamber and summoned the vizier, who presented himself and making his obeisance to the king, kissed the earth before him and bespoke him as follows:

STORY OF THE MAN OF KHORASSAN, HIS SON AND HIS GOVERNOR.

"There was once a man of Khorassan and he had a son, whose improvement he ardently desired; but the young man sought to be alone and to remove himself from his father's eye, so he might give himself up to pleasance and delight. So he sought of his father [leave to make] the pilgrimage to the Holy House of God and to visit the tomb of the Prophet (whom God bless and keep!). Now between them and Mecca was a journey of five hundred parasangs; but his father could not gainsay him, for that the law of God made this[178] incumbent on him and because of that which he hoped for him of improvement [therefrom]. So he joined unto him a governor, in whom he trusted, and gave him much money and took leave of him. The son set out on the holy pilgrimage[179] with the governor and abode on that wise, spending freely and using not thrift.

Now there was in his neighbourhood a poor man, who had a slave-girl of surpassing beauty and loveliness, and the youth became enamoured of her and suffered grief and concern for the love of her and her loveliness, so that he was like to perish for passion; and she also loved him with a love yet greater than his love for her. So she called an old woman who used to visit her and acquainted her with her case, saying, 'An I foregather not with him, I shall die.' The old woman promised her that she would do her endeavour to bring her to her desire; so she veiled herself and repairing to the young man, saluted him and acquainted him with the girl's case, saying, 'Her master is a covetous man; so do thou invite him [to thy lodging] and tempt him with money, and he will sell thee the damsel.'

Accordingly, he made a banquet, and stationing himself in the man's way, invited him and carried him to his house, where they sat down and ate and drank and abode in discourse. Presently, the young man said to the other, 'I hear that thou hast with thee a slave-girl, whom thou desirest to sell.' And he answered, saying, 'By Allah, O my lord, I have no mind to sell her!' Quoth the youth, 'I hear that she cost thee a thousand dinars, and I will give thee six hundred, to boot.' And the other said, 'I sell her to thee [at that price].' So they fetched notaries, who drew up the contract of sale, and the young man counted out to the girl's master half the purchase money, saying, 'Let her be with thee till I complete to thee the rest of the price and take my slave-girl.' The other consented to this and took of him a bond for the rest of the money, and the girl abode with her master, on deposit.

As for the youth, he gave his governor a thousand dirhems and despatched him to his father, to fetch money from him, so he might pay the rest of the girl's price, saying to him, 'Be not [long] absent.' But the governor said in himself, 'How shall I go to his father and say to him, "Thy son hath wasted thy money and wantoned it away"?[180] With what eye shall I look on him, and indeed, I am he in whom he confided and to whom he hath entrusted his son? Indeed, this were ill seen. Nay, I will fare on to the pilgrimage[181] [with the caravan of pilgrims], in despite of this fool of a youth; and when he is weary [of waiting], he will demand back the money [he hath already paid] and return to his father, and I shall be quit of travail and reproach.' So he went on with the caravan to the pilgrimage[182] and took up his abode there.

Meanwhile, the youth abode expecting his governor's return, but he returned not; wherefore concern and chagrin waxed upon him, because of his mistress, and his longing for her redoubled and he was like to slay himself. She became aware of this and sent him a messenger, bidding him to her. So he went to her and she questioned him of the case; whereupon he told her what was to do of the matter of his governor, and she said to him, 'With me is longing the like of that which is with thee, and I misdoubt me thy messenger hath perished or thy father hath slain him; but I will give thee all my trinkets and my clothes, and do thou sell them and pay the rest of my price, and we will go, I and thou, to thy father.'

So she gave him all that she possessed and he sold 't and paid the rest of her price; after which there remained to him a hundred dirhems. These he spent and lay that night with the damsel in all delight of life, and his soul was like to fly for joy; but when he arose in the morning, he sat weeping and the damsel said to him, 'What aileth thee to weep?' And he said, 'I know not if my father be dead, and he hath none other heir but myself; and how shall I win to him, seeing I have not a dirhem?' Quoth she, 'I have a bracelet; do thou sell it and buy small pearls with the price. Then bray them and fashion them into great pearls, and thereon thou shalt gain much money, wherewith we may make our way to thy country.' So he took the bracelet and repairing to a goldsmith, said to him, 'Break up this bracelet and sell it.' But he said, 'The king seeketh a good[183] bracelet; I will go to him and bring thee the price thereof.' So he carried the bracelet to the Sultan and it pleased him greatly, by reason of the goodliness of its workmanship. Then he called an old woman, who was in his palace, and said to her, 'Needs must I have the mistress of this bracelet, though but for a single night, or I shall die.' And the old woman answered, 'I will bring her to thee.'

So she donned a devotee's habit and betaking herself to the goldsmith, said to him, 'To whom belongeth the bracelet that is in the king's hand?' Quoth he, 'It belongeth to a man, a stranger, who hath bought him a slave-girl from this city and lodgeth with her in such a place.' So the old woman repaired to the young man's house and knocked at the door. The damsel opened to her and seeing her clad in devotee's apparel,[184] saluted her and said to her, ' Belike thou hast an occasion with us?' 'Yes,' answered the old woman; 'I desire privacy and ablution.'[185] Quoth the girl, 'Enter.' So she entered and did her occasion and made the ablution and prayed. Then she brought out a rosary and began to tell her beads thereon, and the damsel said to her, 'Whence comest thou, O pilgrim?'[186] Quoth she '[I come] from [visiting] the Idol[187] of the Absent in such a church.[188] There standeth up no woman [to prayer] before him, who hath an absent friend and discovereth to him her need, but he acquainteth her with her case and giveth her tidings of her absent one.' 'O pilgrim,' said the damsel, 'we have an absent one, and my lord's heart cleaveth to him and I desire to go to the idol and question him of him.' Quoth the old woman, '[Wait] till to-morrow and ask leave of thy husband, and I will come to thee and go with thee in weal.'

Then she went away, and when the girl's master came, she sought his leave to go with the old woman and he granted her leave. So the beldam took her and carried her to the king's door. The damsel entered with her, unknowing whither she went, and beheld a goodly house and chambers adorned [with gold and colours] that were no idol's chambers. Then came the king and seeing her beauty and grace, went up to her, to kiss her; whereupon she fell down in a fit and strove with her hands and feet. When he saw this, he was solicitous for her and held aloof from her and left her; but the thing was grievous to her and she refused meat and drink, and as often as the king drew near her, she fled from him in affright, wherefore he swore by Allah that he would not approach her, save with her consent, and fell to guerdoning her with trinkets and raiment, but she only redoubled in aversion to him.

Meanwhile, the youth her master abode expecting her; but she returned not and his heart forbode him of the draught [of separation]; so he went forth at hazard, distraught and knowing not what he should do, and fell to strewing dust upon his head and crying out, 'The old woman hath taken her and gone away!' The boys followed him with stones and pelted him, saying, 'A madman! A madman!' Presently, the king's chamberlain, who was a man of age and worth, met him, and when he saw his youth, he forbade the boys and drove there away from him, after which he accosted him and questioned him of his case. So he told him how it was with him and the chamberlain said to him, 'Fear not: all shall yet be well with thee. I will deliver thy slave-girl for thee: so calm thy trouble.' And he went on to speak him fair and comfort him, till he put faith in his speech.

Then he carried him to his house and stripping him of his clothes, clad him in rags; after which he called an old woman, who was his stewardess, and said to her. 'Take this youth and clap on his neck this iron chain and go round about with him in all the thoroughfares of the city; and when thou hast made an end of this, go up with him to the palace of the king.' And he said to the youth, 'In whatsoever place thou seest the damsel, speak not a syllable, but acquaint me with her place and thou shall owe her deliverance to none but me.' The youth thanked him and went with the old woman on such wise as the chamberlain bade him. She fared on with him till they entered the city [and made the round thereof]; after which she went up to the palace of the king and fell to saying, 'O people of affluence, look on a youth whom the devils take twice in the day and pray for preservation from [a like] affliction!' And she ceased not to go round about with him till she came to the eastern wing[189] of the palace, whereupon the slave-girls came out to look upon him and when they saw him they were amazed at his beauty and grace and wept for him.

Then they told the damsel, who came forth and looked upon him and knew him not. But he knew her; so he bowed his head and wept. She was moved to compassion for him and gave him somewhat and returned to her place, whilst the youth returned with the stewardess to the chamberlain and told him that she was in the king's house, whereat he was chagrined and said, 'By Allah, I will assuredly contrive a device for her and deliver her!' Whereupon the youth kissed his hands and feet. Then he turned to the old woman and bade her change her apparel and her favour. Now this old woman was goodly of speech and nimble of wit; so he gave her costly and delicious perfumes and said to her, 'Get thee to the king's slave girls and sell them these [perfumes] and make thy way to the damsel and question her if she desire her master or not.' So the old woman went out and making her way to the palace, went in to the damsel and drew near her and recited the following verses:

God keep the days of love-delight! How dearly sweet they were! How joyous and how solaceful was life in them whilere!
Would he were not who sundered us upon the parting day! How many a body hath he slain, how many a bone laid bare?
Sans fault of mine, my blood and tears he shed and beggared me Of him I love, yet for himself gained nought thereby whate'er.

When the damsel heard these verses, she wept till her clothes were drenched and drew near the old woman, who said to her, 'Knowest thou such an one?' And wept and said, 'He is my lord. Whence knowest thou him?' 'O my lady,' answered the old woman, 'sawst thou not the madman who came hither yesterday with the old woman? He was thy lord. But this is no time for talk. When it is night, get thee to the top of the palace [and wait] on the roof till thy lord come to thee and contrive for thy deliverance.' Then she gave her what she would of perfumes and returning to the chamberlain, acquainted him with that which had passed, and he told the youth.

When it was eventide, the chamberlain let bring two horses and great store of water and victual and a saddle-camel and a man to show them the way. These he hid without the town, whilst he and the young man took with them a long rope, made fast to a staple, and repaired to the palace. When they came thither, they looked and beheld the damsel standing on the roof. So they threw her the rope and the staple; whereupon she [made the latter fast to the parapet and] wrapping her sleeves about her hands, slid down [the rope] and landed with them. They carried her without the town, where they mounted, she and her lord, and fared on, whilst the guide forewent them, directing them in the way, and they gave not over going night and day till they entered his father's house. The young man saluted his father, who rejoiced in him, and he related to him all that had befallen him, whereupon he rejoiced in his safety.

As for the governor, he wasted all that was with him and returned to the city, where he saw the youth and excused himself to him. Then he questioned him of what had befallen him and he told him, whereat he marvelled and returned to companionship with him; but the youth ceased to have regard for him and gave him not stipends, as of his [former] wont, neither discovered to him aught of his secrets. When the governor saw that there was no profit for him with the young Khorassani, he returned to the king, the ravisher of the damsel, and told him what the chamberlain had done and counselled him to slay the latter and incited him to recover the damsel, [promising] to give his friend to drink of poison and return. So the king sent for the chamberlain and upbraided him; whereupon he fell upon him and slew him and the king's servants fell upon the chamberlain and slew him.

Meanwhile, the governor returned to the youth, who questioned him of his absence, and he told him that he had been in the city of the king who had taken the damsel. When the youth heard this, he misdoubted of the governor and never again trusted him in aught, but was still on his guard against him. Then the governor made great store of sweetmeats and put in them deadly poison and presented them to the youth. When the latter saw the sweetmeats, he said in himself, 'This is an extraordinary thing of the governor! Needs must there be mischief in this sweetmeat, and I will make proof of it upon himself.' So he made ready victual anc set on the sweetmeat amongst it and bade the governor to his house and set food before him. He ate and amongst the rest, they brought nim the poisoned sweetmeat; so he ate thereof and died forthright; whereby the youth knew that this was a plot against himself and said, 'He who seeketh his fortune of his own [unaided] might[190] attaineth it not.' Nor (cont nued the vizier) is this, O king of the age, more extraordinary than the story of the druggist and his wife and the singer."

When King Shah Bekht heard his vizier's story, he gave him leave to withdraw to his own house and he abode there the rest of the night and the next day till the evening.

The Second Night of the Month

When the evening evened, the king sat in his privy sitting-chamber and his mind was occupied with the story of the singer and the druggist. So he called the vizier and bade him tell the story. "It is well," answered he, "They tell, O my lord, that

STORY OF THE SINGER AND THE DRUGGIST.

There was once in the city of Hemadan[191] a young man of comely aspect and excellently skilled in singing to the lute, and he was well seen of the people of the city. He went forth one day of his city, with intent to travel, and gave not over journeying till his travel brought him to a goodly city. Now he had with him a lute and what pertained thereto,[192] so he entered and went round about the city till he fell in with a druggist, who, when he espied him, called to him. So he went up to him and he bade him sit down. Accordingly, he sat down by him and the druggist questioned him of his case. The singer told him what was in his mind and the other took him up into his shop and brought him food and fed him. Then said he to him, 'Arise and take up thy lute and beg about the streets, and whenas thou smellest the odour of wine, break in upon the drinkers and say to them, "I am a singer." They will laugh and say, "Come, [sing] to us." And when thou singest, the folk will know thee and bespeak one another of thee; so shall thou become known in the city and thine affairs will prosper.'

So he went round about, as the druggist bade him, till the sun grew hot, but found none drinking. Then he entered a by-street, that he might rest himself, and seeing there a handsome and lofty house, stood in its shade and fell to observing the goodliness of its ordinance. As he was thus engaged, behold, a window opened and there appeared thereat a face, as it were the moon. Quoth she,[193] 'What aileth thee to stand there? Dost thou want aught?' And he answered, 'I am a stranger,' and acquainted her with his case; whereupon quoth she, 'What sayst thou to meat and drink and the enjoyment of a fair-face[d one] and getting thee what thou mayst spend?' 'O my lady,' answered he, 'this is my desire and that in quest whereof I am going about.'

So she opened the door to him and brought him in. Then she seated him at the upper end of the room and set food before him. So he ate and drank and lay with her and swived her. Then she sat down in his lap and they toyed and laughed and kissed till the day was half spent, when her husband came home and she could find nothing for it but to hide the singer in a rug, in which she rolled him up. The husband entered and seeing the place disordered[194] and smelling the odour of wine, questioned her of this. Quoth she, 'I had with me a friend of mine and I conjured her [to drink with me]; so we drank a jar [of wine], she and I, and she went away but now, before thy coming in.' Her husband, (who was none other than the singer's friend the druggist, that had invited him and fed him), deemed her words true and went away to his shop, whereupon the singer came forth and he and the lady returned to their sport and abode on this wise till eventide, when she gave him money and said to him, 'Come hither to-morrow in the forenoon.' 'It is well,' answered he and departed; and at nightfall he went to the bath.

On the morrow, he betook himself to the shop of his friend the druggist, who welcomed him and questioned him of his case and how he had fared that day. Quoth the singer, 'May God requite thee with good, O my brother! For that thou hast directed me unto easance!' And he related to him his adventure with the woman, till he came to the mention of her husband, when he said, 'And at midday came the cuckold her husband and knocked at the door. So she wrapped me in the mat, and when he had gone about his business, I came forth and we returned to what we were about.' This was grievous to the druggist and he repented of having taught him [how he should do] and misdoubted of his wife. So he said to the singer, 'And what said she to thee at thy going away?' And the other answered, 'She bade me come back to her on the morrow. So, behold, I am going to her and I came not hither but that I might acquaint thee with this, lest thy heart be occupied with me.' Then he took leave of him and went his way. As soon as the druggist was assured that he had reached the house, he cast the net over his shop[195] and made for his house, misdoubting of his wife, and knocked at the door.

Now the singer had entered and the druggist's wife said to him, 'Arise, enter this chest.' So he entered it and she shut the lid on him and opened to her husband, who came in, in a state of bewilderment, and searched the house, but found none and overlooked the chest. So he said in himself, 'The house [of which the singer spoke] is one which resembleth my house and the woman is one who resembles my wife,' and returned to his shop; whereupon the singer came forth of the chest and falling upon the druggist's wife, did his occasion and paid her her due and weighed down the scale for her.[196] Then they ate and drank and kissed and clipped, and on this wise they abode till the evening, when she gave him money, for that she found his weaving good,[197] and made him promise to come to her on the morrow.

So he left her and slept his night and on the morrow he repaired to the shop of his friend the druggist and saluted him. The other welcomed him and questioned him of his case; whereupon he told him how he had fared, till he came to the mention of the woman's husband, when he said, 'Then came the cuckold her husband and she clapped me into the chest and shut the lid on me, whilst her addlepated pimp of a husband went round about the house, top and bottom; and when he had gone his way, we returned to what we were about.' With this, the druggist was certified that the house was his house and the wife his wife, and he said, 'And what wilt thou do to-day?' Quoth the singer, 'I shall return to her and weave for her and full her yarn,[198] and I came but to thank thee for thy dealing with me.'

Then he went away, whilst the fire was loosed in the heart of the druggist and he shut his shop and betaking himself to his house, knocked at the door. Quoth the singer, 'Let me get into the chest, for he saw me not yesterday.' 'Nay,' answered she, 'wrap thyself up in the rug.' So he wrapped himself up in the rug and stood in a corner of the room, whilst the druggist entered and went straight to the chest, but found it empty. Then he went round about the house and searched it from top to bottom, but found nothing and no one and abode between belief and disbelief, and said in himself, 'Belike, I suspect my wife of that which is not in her.' So he was certified of her innocence and returned to his shop, whereupon out came the singer and they abode on their former case, as of wont, till eventide, when she gave him one of her husband's shirts and he took it and going away, passed the night in his lodging.

On the morrow, he repaired to the druggist, who saluted him and came to meet him and rejoiced in him and smiled in his face, deeming his wife innocent. Then he questioned him of his yesterday's case and he told him how he had fared, saying, 'O my brother, when the cuckold knocked at the door, I would have entered the chest; but his wife forbade me and rolled me up in the rug. The man entered and thought of nothing but the chest; so he broke it open and abode as he were a madman, going up and coming down. Then he went his way and I came out and we abode on our wonted case till eventide, when she gave me this shirt of her husband's; and behold, I am going to her.'

When the druggist heard the singer's words, he was certified of the case and knew that the calamity, all of it, was in his own house and that the wife was his wife; and he saw the shirt, whereupon he redoubled in certainty and said to the singer, 'Art thou now going to her?' 'Yes, O my brother,' answered he and taking leave of him, went away; whereupon the druggist started up, as he were a madman, and ungarnished his shop.[199] Whilst he was thus engaged, the singer won to the house, and presently up came the druggist and knocked at the door. The singer would have wrapped himself up in the rug, but she forbade him and said to him, 'Get thee down to the bottom of the house and enter the oven[200] and shut the lid upon thyself.' So he did as she bade him and she went down to her husband and opened the door to him, whereupon he entered and went round about the house, but found no one and overlooked the oven. So he stood meditating and swore that he would not go forth of the house till the morrow.

As for the singer, when his [stay in the oven] grew long upon him, he came forth therefrom, thinking that her husband had gone away. Then he went up to the roof and looking down, beheld his friend the druggist; whereat he was sore concerned and said in himself, 'Alas, the disgrace of it! This is my friend the druggist, who dealt kindly with me and wrought me fair and I have requited him with foul' And he feared to return to the druggist; so he went down and opened the first door and would have gone out; but, when he came to the outer door, he found it locked and saw not the key. So he stole up again to the roof and cast himself down into the [next] house. The people of the house heard him and hastened to him, deeming him a thief. Now the house in question belonged to a Persian; so they laid hands on him and the master of the house began to beat him, saying to him, 'Thou art a thief.' 'Nay,' answered he, 'I am no thief, but a singing-man, a stranger. I heard your voices and came to sing to you.'

When the folk heard his words, they talked of letting him go; but the Persian said, 'O folk, let not his speech beguile you. This fellow is none other than a thief who knoweth how to sing, and when he happeneth on the like of us, he is a singer.' 'O our lord,' answered they, 'this man is a stranger, and needs must we release him.' Quoth he, 'By Allah, my heart revolteth from this fellow! Let me make an end of h'm with beating.' But they said, 'Thou mayst nowise do that' So they delivered the singer from the Persian, the master of the house, and seated him amongst them, whereupon he fell to singing to them and they rejoiced in him.

Now the Persian had a mameluke,[201] as he were the full moon, and he arose [and went out], and the singer followed him and wept before him, professing love to him and kissing his hands and feet. The mameluke took compassion on him and said to him, 'When the night cometh and my master entereth [the harem] and the folk go away, I will grant thee thy desire; and I lie in such a place.' Then the singer returned and sat with the boon-companions, and the Persian rose and went out, he and the mameluke beside him. [Then they returned and sat down.][202] Now the singer knew the place that the mameluke occupied at the first of the night; but it befell that he rose from his place and the candle went out. The Persian, who was drunken, fell over on his face, and the singer, supposing him to be the mameluke, said, 'By Allah, it is good!' and threw himself upon him and clipped him, whereupon the Persian started up, crying out, and laying hands on the singer, pinioned him and beat him grievously, after which he bound him to a tree that was in the house.[203]

Now there was in the house a fair singing-girl and when she saw the singer pinioned and bound to the tree, she waited till the Persian lay down on his couch, when she arose and going to the singer, fell to condoling with him over what had betided him and ogling him and handling his yard and rubbing it, till it rose on end. Then said she to him, 'Do thou swive me and I will loose thy bonds, lest he return and beat thee again; for he purposeth thee evil.' Quoth he, 'Loose me and I will do.' But she said, 'I fear that, [if I loose thee], thou wilt not do. But I will do, and thou standing; and when I have done, I will loose thee.' So saying, she pulled up her clothes and sitting down on the singer's yard, fell to going and coming.

Now there was in the house a ram, with which the Persian used to butt, and when he saw what the woman did, he thought she would butt with him; so he broke his halter and running at her, butted her and broke her head. She fell on her back and cried out; whereupon the Persian started up from sleep in haste and seeing the singing-girl [cast down on her back] and the singer with his yard on end, said to the latter, 'O accursed one, doth not what thou hast already done suffice thee?' Then he beat him soundly and opening the door, put him out in the middle of the night.

He lay the rest of the night in one of the ruins, and when he arose in the morning, he said, 'None is to blame. I sought my own good, and he is no fool who seeketh good for himself; and the druggist's wife also sought good for herself; but destiny overcometh precaution and there remaineth no abiding for me in this town.' So he went forth from the city. Nor (added the vizier) is this story, extraordinary though it be, more extraordinary than that of the king and his son and that which bedded them of wonders and rarities."

When the king heard this story, he deemed it pleasant and said, "This story is near unto that which I know and meseemeth I should do well to have patience and hasten not to slay my vizier, so I may get of him the story of the king and his son." Then he gave the vizier leave to go away to his own house; so he thanked him and abode in his house all that day.

The Third Night of the Month

When it was the time of the evening meal, the king repaired to the sitting-chamber and summoning the vizier, sought of him the story he had promised him; and the vizier said, "They avouch, O king, that

STORY OF THE KING WHO KNEW THE QUINTESSENCE[204] OF THINGS.

There came to a king of the kings, in his old age, a son, who grew up comely, quick-witted and intelligent, and when he came to years of discretion and became a young man, his father said to him, 'Take this kingdom and govern it in my stead, for I desire to flee [from the world] to God the Most High and don the gown of wool and give myself up to devotion.' Quoth the prince, 'And I also desire to take refuge with God the Most High.' And the king said, 'Arise, let us flee forth and make for the mountains and worship in them, for shamefastness before God the Most High.'

So they gat them raiment of wool and clothing themselves therewith, went forth and wandered in the deserts and wastes; but when some days had passed over them, they became weak for hunger and repented them of that which they had done, whenas repentance profted them not, and the prince complained to his father of weariness and hunger. 'Dear my son,' answered the king, 'I did with thee that which behoved me,[205] but thou wouldst not hearken to me, and now there is no means of returning to thy former estate, for that another hath taken the kingdom and become its defender; but I will counsel thee of somewhat, wherein do thou pleasure me.' Quoth the prince, 'What is it?' And his father said, 'Take me and go with me to the market and sell me and take my price and do with it what thou wilt, and I shall become the property of one who will provide for my support,' 'Who will buy thee of me,' asked the prince, 'seeing thou art a very old man? Nay, do thou rather sell me, for the demand for me will be greater.' But the king said, 'An thou wert king, thou wouldst require me of service.'

So the youth obeyed his father's commandment and taking him, carried him to the slave-dealer and said to the latter, 'Sell me this old man.' Quoth the dealer, 'Who will buy this fellow, and he a man of fourscore?' Then said he to the king, 'In what crafts dost thou excel?' Quoth he, 'I know the quintessence of jewels and I know the quintessence of horses and that of men; brief, I know the quintessence of all things.' So the dealer took him and went about, offering him for sale to the folk; but none would buy. Presently, up came the overseer of the [Sultan's] kitchen and said, 'What is this man?' And the dealer answered, 'This is a slave for sale.' The cook marvelled at this and bought the king for ten thousand dirhems, after questioning him of what he could do. Then he paid down the money and carried him to his house, but dared not employ him in aught of service; so he appointed him an allowance, such as should suffice for his livelihood, and repented him of having bought him, saying, 'What shall I do with the like of this fellow?'

Presently, the king [of the city] was minded to go forth to his garden,[206] a-pleasuring, and bade the cook forego him thither and appoint in his stead one who should dress meat for the king, so that, when he returned, he might find it ready. So the cook fell a-considering of whom he should appoint and was bewildered concerning his affair. As he was on this wise, the old man came to him and seeing him perplexed how he should do, said to him, 'Tell me what is in thy mind; belike, I may avail to relieve thee.' So he acquainted him with the king's wishes and he said, 'Have no care for this, but leave me one of the serving-men and go thou in peace and surety, for I will suffice thee of this.' So the cook departed with the king, after he had brought the old man what he needed and left him a man of the guards.

When he was gone, the old man bade the trooper wash the kitchen-vessels and made ready passing goodly food. When the king returned, he set the meat before him, and he tasted food whose like he had never known; whereat he marvelled and asked who had dressed it. So they acquainted him with the old man's case and he summoned him to his presence and awarded him a handsome recompense.[207] Moreover, he commanded that they should cook together, he and the cook, and the old man obeyed his commandment.

Awhile after this, there came two merchants to the king with two pearls of price and each of them avouched that his pearl was worth a thousand dinars, but there was none who availed to value them. Then said the cook, 'God prosper the king! Verily, the old man whom I bought avouched that he knew the quintessence of jewels and that he was skilled in cookery. We have made proof of him in cookery and have found him the skilfullest of men; and now, if we send after him and prove him on jewels, [the truth or falsehood of] his pretension will be made manifest to us.'

So the king bade fetch the old man and he came and stood before the Sultan, who showed him the two pearls. Quoth he, 'As for this one, it is worth a thousand dinars.' And the king said, 'So saith its owner.' 'But for this other,' continued the old man, 'it is worth but five hundred.' The folk laughed and marvelled at his saying, and the merchant, [the owner of the second pearl], said to him, 'How can this, which is greater of bulk and purer of water and more perfect of rondure, be less of worth than that?' And the old man answered, 'I have said what is with me.'[208] Then said the king to him, 'Indeed, the outward appearance thereof is like unto that of the other pearl; why then is it worth but the half of its price?' 'Yes,' answered the old man, '[its outward resembleth the other]; but its inward is corrupt.' 'Hath a pearl then an outward and an inward?' asked the merchant, and the old man said, 'Yes. In its inward is a boring worm; but the other pearl is sound and secure against breakage.' Quoth the merchant, 'Give us a token of this and prove to us the truth of thy saying.' And the old man answered, 'We will break the pearl. If I prove a, liar, here is my head, and if I speak truth, thou wilt have lost thy pearl.' And the merchant said, 'I agree to that.' So they broke the pearl and it was even as the old man had said, to wit, in its midst was a boring worm.

The king marvelled at what he saw and questioned him of [how he came by] the knowledge of this. 'O king,' answered the old man, 'this [kind of] jewel is engendered in the belly of a creature called the oyster and its origin is a drop of rain and it is firm to the touch [and groweth not warm, when held in the hand]; so, when [I took the second pearl and felt that] it was warm to the touch, I knew that it harboured some living thing, for that live things thrive not but in heat.'[209] So the king said to the cook, 'Increase his allowance.' And he appointed to him [fresh] allowances.

Awhile after this, two merchants presented themselves to the king with two horses, and one said, 'I ask a thousand dinars for my horse,' and the other, 'I seek five thousand for mine.' Quoth the cook, 'We have experienced the old man's just judgment; what deemeth the king of fetching him?' So the king bade fetch him, and when he saw the two horses, he said, 'This one is worth a thousand and the other two thousand dinars.' Quoth the folk, 'This [horse that thou judgeth the lesser worth] is an evident thoroughbred and he is younger and swifter and more compact of limb than the other, ay, and finer of head and clearer of skin and colour. What token, then, hast thou of the truth of thy saying?' And the old man said, 'This ye say is all true, but his sire is old and this other is the son of a young horse. Now, when the son of an old horse standeth still [to rest,] his breath returneth not to him and his rider falleth into the hand of him who followeth after him; but the son of a young horse, if thou put him to speed and make him run, [then check him] and alight from off him, thou wilt find him untired, by reason of his robustness.'

Quoth the merchant, 'Indeed, it is as the old man avoucheth and he is an excellent judge.' And the king said, 'Increase his allowance.' But the old man stood still and did not go away. So the king said to him, 'Why dost thou not go about thy business?' And he answered, 'My business is with the king.' 'Name what thou wouldst have,' said the king, and the other replied, 'I would have thee question me of the quintessences of men, even as thou hast questioned me of the quintessences of horses.' Quoth the king, 'We have no occasion to question thee of [this].' But the old man replied, 'I have occasion to acquaint thee.' 'Say what thou pleasest,' rejoined the king, and the old man said, 'Verily, the king is the son of a baker.' Quoth the king 'How knowest thou that?' And the other replied, 'Know, O king, that I have examined into degrees and dignities[210] and have learnt this.'

Thereupon the king went in to his mother and questioned her of his father, and she told him that me king her husband was weak;[211] 'wherefore,' quoth she, 'I feared for the kingdom, lest it pass away, after his death; so I took to my bed a young man, a baker, and conceived by him [and bore a son]; and the kingship came into the hand of my son, to wit, thyself.' So the king returned to the old man and said to him, 'I am indeed the son of a baker; so do thou expound to me the means whereby thou knewest me for this.' Quoth the other, 'I knew that, hadst thou been a king's son, thou wouldst have given largesse of things of price, such as rubies [and the like]; and wert thou the son of a Cadi, thou hadst given largesse of a dirhem or two dirhems, and wert thou the son of a merchant, thou hadst given wealth galore. But I saw that thou guerdonest me not but with cakes of bread [and other victual], wherefore I knew that thou wast the son of a baker.' Quoth the king, 'Thou hast hit the mark.' And he gave him wealth galore and advanced him to high estate."

This story pleased King Shah Bekht and he marvelled thereat; but the vizier said to him, "This story is not more extraordinary than that of the rich man who married his fair daughter to the poor old man." The king's mind was occupied with the [promised] story and he bade the vizier withdraw to his lodging. So he [returned to his house and] abode there the rest of the night and the whole of the following day.

The Fourth Night of the Month.

When the evening evened, the king withdrew to his privy sitting-chamber and bade fetch the vizier. When he presented himself before him, he said to him, "Tell me the story of the wealthy man who married his daughter to the poor old man." "It is well," answered the vizier. "Know, O puissant king, that

STORY OF THE RICH MAN WHO GAVE HIS FAIR DAUGHTER IN MARRIAGE TO THE POOR OLD MAN.

A certain wealthy merchant had a fair daughter, who was as the full moon, and when she attained the age of fifteen, her father betook himself to an old man and spreading him a carpet in his sitting-chamber, gave him to eat and caroused with him. Then said he to him, 'I desire to marry thee to my daughter.' The other excused himself, because of his poverty, and said to him, 'I am not worthy of her nor am I a match for thee.' The merchant was instant with him, but he repeated his answer to him, saying, 'I will not consent to this till thou acquaint me with the reason of thy desire for me. If I find it reasonable, I will fall in with thy wish; and if not, I will not do this ever.'

'Know, then,' said the merchant, 'that I am a man from the land of China and was in my youth well-favoured and well-to-do. Now I made no account of womankind, one and all, but followed after boys, and one night I saw, in a dream, as it were a balance set up, and it was said by it, "This is the portion of such an one." Presently, I heard my own name; so I looked and beheld a woman of the utmost loathliness; whereupon I awoke in affright and said, "I will never marry, lest haply this loathly woman fall to my lot." Then I set out for this city with merchandise and the voyage was pleasant to me and the sojourn here, so that I took up my abode here awhile and got me friends and factors, till I had sold all my merchandise and taken its price and there was left me nothing to occupy me till the folk[212] should depart and depart with them.

One day, I changed my clothes and putting money in my sleeve, sallied forth to explore the holes and corners of this city, and as I was going about, I saw a handsome house. Its goodliness pleased me; so I stood looking on it, and behold, a lovely woman [at the lattice]. When she saw me, she made haste and descended, whilst I abode confounded. Then I betook myself to a tailor there and questioned him of the house and to whom it belonged. Quoth he, "It belongeth to such an one the notary, may God curse him!" "Is he her father?" asked I; [and he replied, "Yes."] So I repaired in haste to a man, with whom I had been used to deposit my goods for sale, and told him that I desired to gain access to such an one the notary. Accordingly he assembled his friends and we betook ourselves to the notary's house. When we came in to him, we saluted him and sat with him, and I said to him, "I come to thee as a suitor, desiring the hand of thy daughter in marriage." Quoth he, "I have no daughter befitting this man." And I rejoined, "God aid thee! My desire is for thee and not for her."[213] But he still refused and his friends said to him, "This is an honourable man and thine equal in estate, and it is not lawful to thee that thou hinder the girl of her fortune." Quoth he to them, "Verily, my daughter whom ye seek is passing foul-favoured and in her are all blameworthy qualities." And I said, "I accept her, though she be as thou sayest." Then said the folk, "Extolled be the perfection of God! A truce to talk! [The thing is settled;] so say the word, how much wilt thou have [to her dowry]?" Quoth he, "I must have four thousand dinars." And I said, "Hearkening and obedience."

So the affair was concluded and we drew up the contract of marriage and I made the bride-feast; but on the wedding-night I beheld a thing[214] than which never made God the Most High aught more loathly. Methought her people had contrived this by way of sport; so I laughed and looked for my mistress, whom I had seen [at the lattice], to make her appearance; but saw her not. When the affair was prolonged and I found none but her, I was like to go mad for vexation and fell to beseeching my Lord and humbling myself in supplication to Him that He would deliver me from her. When I arose in the morning, there came the chamber-woman and said to me, "Hast thou occasion for the bath?" "No," answered I; and she said, "Art thou for breakfast?" But I replied, "No;" and on this wise I abode three days, tasting neither meat nor drink.

When the damsel[215] saw me in this plight, she said to me, "O man, tell me thy story, for, by Allah, an I may avail to thy deliverance, I will assuredly further thee thereto." I gave ear to her speech and put faith in her loyalty and told her the story of the damsel whom I had seen [at the lattice] and how I had fallen in love with her; whereupon quoth she, "If the girl belong to me, that which I possess is thine, and if she belong to my father, I will demand her of him and deliver her to thee." Then she fell to calling slave-girl after slave-girl and showing them to me, till I saw the damsel whom I loved and said, "This is she." Quoth my wife, "Let not thy heart be troubled, for this is my slave-girl. My father gave her to me and I give her to thee. So comfort thyself and be of good heart and cheerful eye."

Then, when it was night, she brought her to me, after she had adorned her and perfumed her, and said to her, "Gainsay not this thy lord in aught that he shall seek of thee." When she came to bed with me, I said in myself, "Verily, this damsel[216] is more generous than I!" Then I sent away the slave-girl and drew not nigh unto her, but arose forthright and betaking myself to my wife, lay with her and did away her maidenhead. She straightway conceived by me and accomplishing the time of her pregnancy, gave birth to this dear little daughter; in whom I rejoiced, for that she was lovely to the utterest, and she hath inherited her mother's wit and her father's comeliness.

Indeed, many of the notables of the people have sought her of me in marriage, but I would not marry her to any, for that, one night, I saw, in a dream, the balance aforesaid set up and men and women being weighed, one against the other, therein, and meseemed I saw thee [and her] and it was said to me, "This is such a man,[217] the allotted portion of such a woman."[218] Wherefore I knew that God the Most High had allotted unto her none other than thyself, and I choose rather to marry thee to her in my lifetime than that thou shouldst marry her after my death.'

When the poor man heard the merchant's story, he became desirous of marrying his daughter. So he took her to wife and was vouchsafed of her exceeding love. Nor," added the vizier, "is this story more extraordinary than that of the rich man and his wasteful heir."

When the king heard his vizier's story, he was assured that he would not slay him and said, "I will have patience with him, so I may get of him the story of the rich man and his wasteful heir." And he bade him depart to his own house.

The Fifth Night of the Month

When the evening evened, the king sat in his privy closet and summoning the vizier, required of him the promised story. So Er Rehwan said, "Know, O king, that

STORY OF THE RICH MAN AND HIS WASTEFUL SON.

There was once a sage of the sages, who had three sons and sons' sons, and when they waxed many and their posterity multiplied, there befell dissension between them. So he assembled them and said to them, 'Be ye one hand[219] against other than you and despise[220] not [one another,] lest the folk despise you, and know that the like of you is as the rope which the man cut, when it was single; then he doubled [it] and availed not to cut it; on this wise is division and union. And beware lest ye seek help of others against yourselves[221] or ye will fall into perdition, for by whosesoever means ye attain your desire,[222] his word[223] will have precedence of[224] your word. Now I have wealth which I will bury in a certain place, so it may be a store for you, against the time of your need.'

Then they left him and dispersed and one of the sons fell to spying upon his father, so that he saw him hide the treasure without the city. When he had made an end of burying it, he returned to his house; and when the morning morrowed, his son repaired to the place where he had seen his father bury the treasure and dug and took it and went his way. When the [hour of the] old man's admission [to the mercy of God] drew nigh, he called his sons to him and acquainted them with the place where he had hidden his riches. As soon as he was dead, they went and dug up the treasure and found wealth galore, for that the money, which the first son had taken by stealth, was on the surface and he knew not that under it was other money. So they took it and divided it and the first son took his share with the rest and laid it to that which he had taken aforetime, behind [the backs of] his father and his brethren. Then he took to wife the daughter of his father's brother and was vouchsafed by her a male child, who was the goodliest of the folk of his time.

When the boy grew up, his father feared for him from poverty and change of case, so he said to him, 'Dear my son, know that in my youth I wronged my brothers in the matter of our father's good, and I see thee in weal; but, if thou [come to] need, ask not of one of them nor of any other, for I have laid up for thee in yonder chamber a treasure; but do not thou open it until thou come to lack thy day's food.' Then he died, and his wealth, which was a great matter, fell to his son. The young man had not patience to wait till he had made an end of that which was with him, but rose and opened the chamber, and behold, it was [empty and its walls were] whitened, and in its midst was a rope hanging down and half a score bricks, one upon another, and a scroll, wherein was written, 'Needs must death betide; so hang thyself and beg not of any, but kick away the bricks, so there may be no escape[225] for thee, and thou shall be at rest from the exultation of enemies and enviers and the bitterness of poverty.'

When the youth saw this, he marvelled at that which his father had done and said, 'This is a sorry treasure.' Then he went forth and fell to eating and drinking with the folk, till nothing was left him and he abode two days without tasting food, at the end of which time he took a handkerchief and selling it for two dirhems, bought bread and milk with the price and left it on the shelf [and went out. Whilst he was gone,] a dog came and took the bread and spoiled the milk, and when the man returned and saw this, he buffeted his face and went forth, distraught, at a venture. Presently, he met a friend of his, to whom he discovered his case, and the other said to him, 'Art thou not ashamed to talk thus? How hast thou wasted all this wealth and now comest telling lies and saying, "The dog hath mounted on the shelf," and talking nonsense?' And he reviled him.

So the youth returned to his house, and indeed the world was grown black in his eyes and he said, 'My father said sooth.' Then he opened the chamber door and piling up the bricks under his feet, put the rope about his neck and kicked away the bricks and swung himself off; whereupon the rope gave way with him [and he fell] to the ground and the ceiling clove in sunder and there poured down on him wealth galore, So he knew that his father meant to discipline[226] him by means of this and invoked God's mercy on him. Then he got him again that which he had sold of lands and houses and what not else and became once more in good case. Moreover, his friends returned to him and he entertained them some days.

Then said he to them one day, 'There was with us bread and the locusts ate it; so we put in its place a stone, a cubit long and the like broad, and the locusts came and gnawed away the stone, because of the smell of the bread.' Quoth one of his friends (and it was he who had given him the lie concerning the dog and the bread and milk), 'Marvel not at this, for mice do more than that.' And he said, 'Go to your houses. In the days of my poverty, I was a liar [when I told you] of the dog's climbing upon the shelf and eating the bread and spoiling the milk; and to-day, for that I am rich again, I say sooth [when I tell you] that locusts devoured a stone a cubit long and a cubit broad.' They were confounded at his speech and departed from him; and the youth's good flourished and his case was amended.[227] Nor," added the vizier,"is this stranger or more extraordinary than the story of the king's son who fell in love with the picture."

Quoth the king, "Belike, if I hear this story, I shall gain wisdom from it; so I will not hasten in the slaying of this vizier, nor will I put him to death before the thirty days have expired." Then he gave him leave to withdraw, and he went away to his own house.

The Sixth Night of the Month

When the day departed and the evening came, the king sat in his privy chamber and summoned the vizier, who presented himself to him and he questioned him of the story. So the vizier said, "Know, O august king, that

THE KING'S SON WHO FELL IN LOVE WITH THE PICTURE.

There was once, in a province of Persia, a king of the kings, who was mighty of estate, endowed with majesty and venerance and having troops and guards at his command; but he was childless. Towards the end of his life, his Lord vouchsafed him a male child, and the boy grew up and was comely and learned all manner of knowledge. He made him a private place, to wit, a lofty palace, builded with coloured marbles and [adorned with] jewels and paintings. When the prince entered the palace, he saw in its ceiling the picture [of a woman], than whom he had never beheld a fairer of aspect, and she was compassed about with slave-girls; whereupon he fell down in a swoon and became distraught for love of her. Then he sat under the picture, till, one day, his father came in to him and finding him wasted of body and changed of colour, by reason of his [continual] looking on that picture, thought that he was ill and sent for the sages and physicians, that they might medicine him. Moreover, he said to one of his boon- companions, 'If thou canst learn what aileth my son, thou shalt have of me largesse.' So the courtier went in to the prince and spoke him fair and cajoled him, till he confessed to him that his malady was caused by the picture. Then he returned to the king and told him what ailed his son, whereupon he transported the prince to another palace and made his former lodging the guest-house; and whosoever of the Arabs was entertained therein, he questioned of the picture, but none could give him tidings thereof.

One day, there came a traveller and seeing the picture, said, 'There is no god but God! My brother wrought this picture.' So the king sent for him and questioned him of the affair of the picture and where was he who had wrought it. 'O my lord,' answered the traveller, 'we are two brothers and one of us went to the land of Hind and fell in love with the king's daughter of the country, and it is she who is the original of the portrait. In every city he entereth, he painteth her portrait, and I follow him, and long is my journey.' When the king's son heard this, he said,'Needs must I travel to this damsel.' So he took all manner rarities and store of riches and journeyed days and nights till he entered the land of Hind, nor did he win thereto save after sore travail. Then he enquired of the King of Hind and he also heard of him.

When the prince came before him, he sought of him his daughter in marriage, and the king said, 'Indeed, thou art her equal, but none dare name a man to her, because of her aversion to men.' So the prince pitched his tents under the windows of the princess's palace, till one day he got hold of one of her favourite slave-girls and gave her wealth galore. Quoth she to him, 'Hast thou a wish?' 'Yes,' answered he and acquainted her with his case; and she said, 'Indeed thou puttest thyself in peril.' Then he abode, flattering himself with false hopes, till all that he had with him was gone and the servants fled from him; whereupon quoth he to one in whom he trusted, 'I am minded to go to my country and fetch what may suffice me and return hither.' And the other answered, 'It is for thee to decide.' So they set out to return, but the way was long to them and all that the prince had with him was spent and his company died and there abode but one with him, on whom he loaded what remained of the victual and they left the rest and fared on. Then there came out a lion and ate the servant, and the prince abode alone. He went on, till his beast stood still, whereupon he left her and fared on afoot till his feet swelled.

Presently he came to the land of the Turks,[228] and he naked and hungry and having with him nought but somewhat of jewels, bound about his fore-arm. So he went to the bazaar of the goldsmiths and calling one of the brokers, gave him the jewels. The broker looked and seeing two great rubies, said to him, 'Follow me.' So he followed him, till he brought him to a goldsmith, to whom he gave the jewels, saying, 'Buy these.' Quoth he, 'Whence hadst thou these?' And the broker replied, 'This youth is the owner of them.' Then said the goldsmith to the prince, 'Whence hadst thou these rubies?' And he told him all that had befallen him and that he was a king's son. The goldsmith marvelled at his story and bought of him the rubies for a thousand dinars.

Then said the prince to him, 'Make ready to go with me to my country.' So he made ready and went with the prince till he drew near the frontiers of his father's kingdom, where the people received him with the utmost honour and sent to acquaint his father with his son's coming. The king came out to meet him and they entreated the goldsmith with honour. The prince abode awhile with his father, then set out, [he and the goldsmith] to return to the country of the fair one, the daughter of the King of Hind; but there met him robbers by the way and he fought the sorest of battles and was slain. The goldsmith buried him and marked his grave[229] and returned, sorrowing and distraught to his own country, without telling any of the prince's death.

To return to the king's daughter of whom the prince went in quest and on whose account he was slain. She had been used to look out from the top of her palace and gaze on the youth and on his beauty and grace; so she said to her slave-girl one day, 'Harkye! What is come of the troops that were encamped beside my palace?' Quoth the maid, 'They were the troops of the youth, the king's son of the Persians, who came to demand thee in marriage, and wearied himself on thine account, but thou hadst no compassion on him.' 'Out on thee!' cried the princess. 'Why didst thou not tell me?' And the damsel answered, 'I feared thy wrath.' Then she sought an audience of the king her father and said to him, 'By Allah, I will go in quest of him, even as he came in quest of me; else should I not do him justice.'

So she made ready and setting out, traversed the deserts and spent treasures till she came to Sejestan, where she called a goldsmith to make her somewhat of trinkets. [Now the goldsmith in question was none other than the prince's friend]; so, when he saw her, he knew her (for that the prince had talked with him of her and had depictured her to him) and questioned her of her case. She acquainted him with her errand, whereupon he buffeted his face and rent his clothes and strewed dust on his head and fell a-weeping. Quoth she, 'Why dost thou thus?' And he acquainted her with the prince's case and how he was his comrade and told her that he was dead; whereat she grieved for him and faring on to his father and mother, [acquainted them with the case].

So the prince's father and his uncle and his mother and the grandees of the realm repaired to his tomb and the princess made lamentation over him, crying aloud. She abode by the tomb a whole month; then she let fetch painters and caused them limn her portraiture and that of the king's son. Moreover, she set down in writing their story and that which had befallen them of perils and afflictions and set it [together with the pictures], at the head of the tomb; and after a little, they departed from the place. Nor," added the vizier, "is this more extraordinary, O king of the age, than the story of the fuller and his wife and the trooper and what passed between them."

With this the king bade the vizier go away to his lodging, and when he arose in the morning, he abode his day in his house.

The Seventh Night of the Month.

At eventide the king sat [in his privy sitting-chamber] and sending for the vizier, said to him, "Tell me the story of the fuller and his wife." "With all my heart," answered the vizier. So he came forward and said, "Know, O king of the age, that

STORY OF THE FULLER AND HIS WIFE.

There was once in a certain city a woman fair of favour, who had to lover a trooper. Her husband was a fuller, and when he went out to his business, the trooper used to come to her and abide with her till the time of the fuller's return, when he would go away. On this wise they abode awhile, till one day the trooper said to his mistress, 'I mean to take me a house near unto thine and dig an underground passage from my house to thy house, and do thou say to thy husband, "My sister hath been absent with her husband and now they have returned from their travels; and I have made her take up her sojourn in my neighbourhood, so I may foregather with her at all times. So go thou to her husband the trooper and offer him thy wares [for sale], and thou wilt see my sister with him and wilt see that she is I and I am she, without doubt. So, Allah, Allah, go to my sister's husband and give ear to that which he shall say to thee."'

Accordingly, the trooper bought him a house near at hand and made therein an underground passage communicating with his mistress's house. When he had accomplished his affair, the wife bespoke her husband as her lover had lessoned her and he went out to go to the trooper's house, but turned back by the way, whereupon quoth she to him, 'By Allah, go forthright, for that my sister asketh of thee.' So the dolt of a fuller went out and made for the trooper's house, whilst his wife forewent him thither by the secret passage, and going up, sat down beside her lover. Presently, the fuller entered and saluted the trooper and his [supposed] wife and was confounded at the coincidence of the case.[230] Then doubt betided him and he returned in haste to his dwelling; but she forewent him by the underground passage to her chamber and donning her wonted clothes, sat [waiting] for him and said to him, 'Did I not bid thee go to my sister and salute her husband and make friends with them?' Quoth he, 'I did this, but I misdoubted of my affair, when I saw his wife.' And she said, 'Did I not tell thee that she resembleth me and I her, and there is nought to distinguish between us but our clothes? Go back to her.'

So, of the heaviness of his wit, he believed her and turning back, went in to the trooper; but she had foregone him, and when he saw her beside her lover, he fell to looking on her and pondering. Then he saluted her and she returned him the salutation; and when she spoke, he was bewildered. So the trooper said to him, 'What ails thee to be thus?' And he answered, 'This woman is my wife and the voice is her voice.' Then he rose in haste and returning to his own house, saw his wife, who had foregone him by the secret passage. So he went back to the trooper's house and saw her sitting as before; whereupon he was abashed before her and sitting down in the trooper's sitting-chamber, ate and drank with him and became drunken and abode without sense all that day till nightfall, when the trooper arose and shaving off some of the fuller's hair (which was long and flowing) after the fashion of the Turks, clipped the rest short and clapped a tarboush on his head.

Then he thrust his feet into boots and girt him with a sword and a girdle and bound about his middle a quiver and a bow and arrows. Moreover, he put money in his pocket and thrust into his sleeve letters-patent addressed to the governor of Ispahan, bidding him assign to Rustem Khemartekeni a monthly allowance of a hundred dirhems and ten pounds of bread and five pounds of meat and enrol him among the Turks under his commandment. Then he took him up and carrying him forth, left him in one of the mosques.

The fuller gave not over sleeping till sunrise, when he awoke and finding himself in this plight, misdoubted of his affair and imagined that he was a Turk and abode putting one foot forward and drawing the other back. Then said he in himself, 'I will go to my dwelling, and if my wife know me, then am I Ahmed the fuller; but, if she know me not, I am a Turk.' So he betook himself to his house; but when the artful baggage his wife saw him, she cried out in his face, saying, 'Whither away, O trooper? Wilt thou break into the house of Ahmed the fuller, and he a man of repute, having a brother-in-law a Turk, a man of high standing with the Sultan? An thou depart not, I will acquaint my husband and he will requite thee thy deed.'

When he heard her words, the dregs of the drunkenness wrought in him and he imagined that he was indeed a Turk. So he went out from her and putting his hand to his sleeve, found therein a scroll and gave it to one who read it to him. When he heard that which was written in the scroll, his mind was confirmed in the false supposition; but he said in himself, 'Maybe my wife seeketh to put a cheat on me; so I will go to my fellows the fullers; and if they know me not, then am I for sure Khemartekeni the Turk.' So he betook himself to the fullers and when they espied h m afar off, they thought that he was one of the Turks, who used to wash their clothes with them without payment and give them nothing.

Now they had complained of them aforetime to the Sultan, and he said, 'If any of the Turks come to you, pelt them with stones.' So, when they saw the fuller, they fell upon him with sticks and stones and pelted him; whereupon quoth he [in himself], 'Verily, I am a Turk and knew it not.' Then he took of the money in his pocket and bought him victua [for the journey] and hired a hackney and set out for Ispahan, leaving his wife to the trooper. Nor," added the vizier, "is this more extraordinary than the story of the merchant and the old woman and the king."

The vizier's story pleased King Shah Bekht and his heart clave to the story of the merchant and the old woman; so he bade Er Rehwan withdraw to his lodging, and he went away to his house and abode there the next day.

The Eight Night of the Month

When the evening evened, the king sat in his privy chamber and bade fetch the vizier, who presented himself before him, and the king required of him the promised story. So the vizier answered, "With all my heart. Know, O king, that

STORY OF THE OLD WOMAN, THE MERCHANT AND THE KING

There was once in a city of Khorassan a family of affluence and distinction, and the townsfolk used to envy them for that which God had vouchsafed them. As time went on, their fortune ceased from them and they passed away, till there remained of them but one old woman. When she grew feeble and decrepit, the townsfolk succoured her not with aught, but put her forth of the city, saying, 'This old woman shall not harbour with us, for that we do her kindness and she requiteth us with evil.' So she took shelter in a ruined place and strangers used to bestow alms upon her, and on this wise she abode a while of time.

Now the uncle's son of the king of the city had aforetime disputed [the kingship] with him, and the people misliked the king; but God the Most High decreed that he should get the better of his cousin. However, jealousy of him abode in his heart and he acquainted the vizier, who hid it not and sent [him] money. Moreover, he fell to summoning [all strangers who came to the town], man after man, and questioning them of their faith and their worldly estate, and whoso answered him not [to his liking], he took his good.[231] Now a certain wealthy man of the Muslims was on a journey and it befell that he arrived at that city by night, unknowing what was to do, and coming to the ruin aforesaid, gave the old woman money and said to her, 'No harm upon thee.' Whereupon she lifted up her voice and prayed [for him], He set down his merchandise by her [and abode with her] the rest of the night and the next day.

Now thieves had followed him, so they might rob him of his good, but availed not unto aught; wherefore he went up to the old woman and kissed her head and exceeded in munificence to her. Then she [warned him of that which awaited strangers entering the town and] said to him, 'I like not this for thee and I fear mischief for thee from these questions that the vizier hath appointed for the confrontation of the ignorant.' And she expounded to him the case according to its fashion. Then said she to him, 'But have no concern: only carry me with thee to thy lodging, and if he question thee of aught, whilst I am with thee, I will expound the answers to thee.' Se he carried her with him to the city and established her in his lodging and entreated her kindly.

Presently, the vizier heard of the merchant's coming; so he sent to him and let bring him to his house and talked with him awhile of his travels and of that which he had abidden therein, and the merchant answered him thereof. Then said the vizier, 'I will put certain questions to thee, which if thou answer me, it will be well [for thee].' And the merchant rose and made him no answer. Quoth the vizier, 'What is the weight of the elephant?' The merchant was perplexed and returned him no answer and gave himself up for lost. Then said he, 'Grant me three days' time.' So the vizier granted him the delay he sought and he returned to his lodging and related what had passed to the old woman, who said, 'When the morrow cometh, go to the vizier and say to him, "Make a ship and launch it on the sea and put in it an elephant, and when it sinketh in the water, [under the beast's weight], mark the place to which the water riseth. Then take out the elephant and cast in stones in its place, till the ship sink to the mark aforesaid; whereupon do thou take out the stones and weigh them and thou wilt know the weight of the elephant"'

So, when he arose in the morning, he repaired to the vizier and repeated to him that which the old woman had taught him; whereat the vizier marvelled and said to him, 'What sayst thou of a man, who seeth in his house four holes, and in each a viper offering to come out and kill him, and in his house are four staves and each hole may not be stopped but with the ends of two staves? How shall he stop all the holes and deliver himself from the vipers?' When the merchant heard this, there betided him [of concern] what made him forget the first and he said to the vizier, 'Grant me time, so I may consider the answer.' 'Go out,' replied the vizier, 'and bring me the answer, or I will seize thy good.'

The merchant went out and returned to the old woman, who, seeing him changed of colour, said to him, 'What did he ask thee, [may God confound] his hoariness?' So he acquainted her with the case and she said to him, 'Fear not; I will bring thee forth of this [strait].' Quoth he, 'God requite thee with good!' And she said, 'To-morrow go to him with a stout heart and say, "The answer to that whereof thou askest me is that thou put the heads of two staves into one of the holes; then take the other two staves and lay them across the middle of the first two and stop with their heads the second hole and with their butts the fourth hole. Then take the butts of the first two staves and stop with them the third hole."'[232]

So he repaired to the vizier and repeated to him the answer; and he marvelled at its justness and said to him, 'Go; by Allah, I will ask thee no more questions, for thou with thy skill marrest my foundation.'[233] Then he entreated him friendly and the merchant acquainted him with the affair of the old woman; whereupon quoth the vizier, 'Needs must the man of understanding company with those of understanding.' Thus did this weak woman restore to that man his life and good on the easiest wise. Nor," added the vizier, "is this more extraordinary than the story of the credulous husband."

When the king heard this story, he said, "How like is this to our own case!" Then he bade the vizier retire to his lodging; so he withdrew to his house and on the morrow he abode at home [till the king should summon him to his presence.]

The Ninth Night of the Month.

When the night came, the king sat in his privy chamber and sending after the vizier, sought of him the promised story; and he said, "Know, O august king, that

STORY OF THE CREDULOUS HUSBAND

There was once of old time a foolish, ignorant man, who had wealth galore, and his wife was a fair woman, who loved a handsome youth. The latter used to watch for her husband's absence and come to her, and on this wise he abode a long while. One day, as the woman was private with her lover, he said to her, 'O my lady and my beloved, if thou desire me and love me, give me possession of thyself and accomplish my need in thy husband's presence; else will I never again come to thee nor draw near thee, what while I abide on life.' Now she loved him with an exceeding love and could not brook his separation an hour nor could endure to vex him; so, when she heard his words, she said to him, ['So be it,] in God's name, O my beloved and solace of mine eyes, may he not live who would vex thee!' Quoth he, 'To-day?' And she said, 'Yes, by thy life,' and appointed him of this.

When her husband came home, she said to him, 'I desire to go a-pleasuring.' And he said, ' With all my heart.' So he went, till he came to a goodly place, abounding in vines and water, whither he carried her and pitched her a tent beside a great tree; and she betook herself to a place beside the tent and made her there an underground hiding-place, [in which she hid her lover]. Then said she to her husband, 'I desire to mount this tree.' And he said, 'Do so.' So she climbed up and when she came to the top of the tree, she cried out and buffeted her face, saying, 'Lewd fellow that thou art, are these thy usages? Thou sworest [fidelity to me] and liedst.' And she repeated her speech twice and thrice.

Then she came down from the tree and rent her clothes and said, 'O villain, if these be thy dealings with me before my eyes, how dost thou when thou art absent from me?' Quoth he, 'What aileth thee?' and she said, 'I saw thee swive the woman before my very eyes.' 'Not so, by Allah!' cried he. 'But hold thy peace till I go up and see.' So he climbed the tree and no sooner did he begin to do so than up came the lover [from his hiding-place] and taking the woman by the legs, [fell to swiving her]. When the husband came to the top of the tree, he looked and beheld a man swiving his wife. So he said, 'O strumpet, what doings are these?' And he made haste to come down from the tree to the ground; [but meanwhile the lover had returned to his hiding- place] and his wife said to him, What sawest thou?' 'I saw a man swive thee,' answered he; and she said, 'Thou liest; thou sawest nought and sayst this but of conjecture.'

On this wise they did three times, and every time [he climbed the tree] the lover came up out of the underground place and bestrode her, whilst her husband looked on and she still said, 'O liar, seest thou aught?' 'Yes,' would he answer and came down in haste, but saw no one and she said to him, 'By my life, look and say nought but the truth!' Then said he to her, 'Arise, let us depart this place,[234] for it is full of Jinn and Marids.' [So they returned to their house] and passed the night [there] and the man arose in the morning, assured that this was all but imagination and illusion. And so the lover accomplished his desire.[235] Nor, O king of the age," added the vizier, "is this more extraordinary than the story of the king and the tither."

When the king heard this from the vizier, he bade him go away [and he withdrew to his house].

The Tenth Night of the Month.

When it was eventide, the king summoned the vizier and sought of him the story of the King and the Tither, and he said, "Know, O king, that

STORY OF THE UNJUST KING AND THE TITHER.

There was once a king of the kings of the earth, who dwelt in a populous[236] city, abounding in good; but he oppressed its people and used them foully, so that he ruined[237] the city; and he was named none other than tyrant and misdoer. Now he was wont, whenas he heard of a masterful man[238] in another land, to send after him and tempt him with money to take service with him; and there was a certain tither, who exceeded all his brethren in oppression of the people and foulness of dealing. So the king sent after him and when he stood before him, he found him a mighty man[239] and said to him, 'Thou hast been praised to me, but meseemeth thou overpassest the description. Set out to me somewhat of thy sayings and doings, so I may be dispensed therewith from [enquiring into] all thy circumstance.' 'With all my heart,' answered the other. 'Know, O king, that I oppress the folk and people[240] the land, whilst other than I wasteth[241] it and peopleth it not.'

Now the king was leaning back; so he sat up and said, 'Tell me of this.' 'It is well,' answered the tither. 'I go to the man whom I purpose to tithe and circumvent him and feign to be occupied with certain business, so that I seclude myself therewith from the folk; and meanwhile the man is squeezed after the foulest fashion, till nothing is left him. Then I appear and they come in to me and questions befall concerning him and I say, "Indeed, I was ordered worse than this, for some one (may God curse him!) hath slandered him to the king." Then I take half of his good and return him the rest publicly before the folk and send him away to his house, in all honour and worship, and he causeth the money returned to be carried before him, whilst he and all who are with him call down blessings on me. So is it published in the city that I have returned him his money and he himself saith the like, so he may have a claim on me for the favour due to whoso praiseth me. Then I feign to forget him till some time[242] hath passed over him, when I send for him and recall to him somewhat of that which hath befallen aforetime and demand [of him] somewhat privily. So he doth this and hasteneth to his dwelling and sendeth what I bid him, with a glad heart. Then I send to another man, between whom and the other is enmity, and lay hands upon him and feign to the first man that it is he who hath traduced him to the king and taken the half of his good; and the people praise me.'[243]

The king marvelled at this and at his dealing and contrivance and invested him with [the control of] all his affairs and of his kingdom and the land abode [under his governance] and he said to him, 'Take and people.'[244] One day, the tither went out and saw an old man, a woodcutter, and with him wood; so he said to him, 'Pay a dirhem tithe for thy load.' Quoth the old man, 'Behold, thou killest me and killest my family.' 'What [meanest thou]?'

said the tither. 'Who killeth the folk?' And the other answered, 'If thou suffer me enter the city, I shall sell the wood there for three dirhems, whereof I will give thee one and buy with the other two what will support my family; but, if thou press me for the tithe without the city, the load will sell but for one dirhem and thou wilt take it and I shall abide without food, I and my family. Indeed, thou and I in this circumstance are like unto David and Solomon, on whom be peace!' ['How so?' asked the tither, and the woodcutter said], 'Know that

STORY OF DAVID AND SOLOMON.

Certain husbandmen once made complaint to David (on whom be peace!) against certain owners of sheep, whose flocks had fallen upon their crops by night and devoured them, and he bade value the crops [and that the shepherds should make good the amount]. But Solomon (on whom be peace!) rose and said, "Nay, but let the sheep be delivered to the husbandmen, so they may take their milk and wool, till they have repaid themselves the value of their crops; then let the sheep return to their owners." So David withdrew his own ordinance and caused execute that of Solomon; yet was David no oppressor; but Solomon's judgment was more pertinent and he showed himself therein better versed in jurisprudence.'[245]

When the tither heard the old man's speech, he relented towards him and said to him, 'O old man, I make thee a present of that which is due from thee, and do thou cleave to me and leave me not, so haply I may get of thee profit that shall do away from me my errors and guide me into the way of righteousness.' So the old man followed him, and there met him another with a load of wood. Quoth the tither to him, 'Pay what is due from thee.' And he answered, 'Have patience with me till to-morrow, for I owe the hire of a house, and I will sell another load of wood and pay thee two days' tithe.' But he refused him this and the old man said to him, 'If thou constrain him unto this, thou wilt enforce him quit thy country, for that he is a stranger here and hath no domicile; and if he remove on account of one dirhem, thou wilt lose [of him] three hundred and threescore dirhems a year. Thus wilt thou lose the much in keeping the little.' Quoth the tither, 'I give him a dirhem every month to the hire of his lodging.'

Then he went on and presently there met him a third woodcutter and he said to him, 'Pay what is due from thee.' And he answered, 'I will pay thee a dirhem when I enter the city; or take of me four danics[246] [now].' Quoth the tither, 'I will not do it,' but the old man said to him, 'Take of him the four danics presently, for it is easy to take and hard to restore.' 'By Allah,' quoth the tither, 'it is good!' and he arose and went on, crying out, at the top of his voice and saying, 'I have no power to-day [to do evil].' Then he put off his clothes and went forth wandering at a venture, repenting unto his Lord. Nor," added the vizier, "is this story more extraordinary than that of the thief who believed the woman and sought refuge with God against falling in with her like, by reason of her cunning contrivance for herself."

When the king heard this, he said in himself, "Since the tither repented, in consequence of the admonitions [of the woodcutter], it behoves that I spare this vizier, so I may hear the story of the thief and the woman." And he bade Er Rehwan withdraw to his lodging.

The Eleventh Night of the Month.

When the evening came and the king sat in his privy chamber, he summoned the vizier and required of him the story of the thief and the woman. Quoth the vizier, "Know, O king, that

STORY OF THE THIEF AND THE WOMAN.

A certain thief was a [cunning] workman and used not to steal aught, till he had spent all that was with him; moreover, he stole not from his neighbours, neither companied with any of the thieves, lest some one should come to know him and his case get wind. On this wise he abode a great while, in flourishing case, and his secret was concealed, till God the Most High decreed that he broke in upon a poor man, deeming that he was rich. When he entered the house, he found nought, whereat he was wroth, and necessity prompted him to wake the man, who was asleep with his wife. So he aroused him and said to him, 'Show me thy treasure.'

Now he had no treasure; but the thief believed him not and insisted upon him with threats and blows. When he saw that he got no profit of him, he said to him, 'Swear by the oath of divorce from thy wife[247] [that thou hast nothing].' So he swore and his wife said to him, 'Out on thee! Wilt thou divorce me? Is not the treasure buried in yonder chamber?' Then she turned to the thief and conjured him to multiply blows upon her husband, till he should deliver to him the treasure, concerning which he had sworn falsely. So he drubbed him grievously, till he carried him to a certain chamber, wherein she signed to him that the treasure was and that he should take it up.

So the thief entered, he and the husband; and when they were both in the chamber, she locked on them the door, which was a stout one, and said to the thief, 'Out on thee, O fool! Thou hast fallen [into the trap] and now I have but to cry out and the officers of the police will come and take thee and thou wilt lose thy life, O Satan!' Quoth he, 'Let me go forth;' and she said, 'Thou art a man and I am a woman; and in thy hand is a knife and I am afraid of thee.' Quoth he, 'Take the knife from me.' So she took the knife from him and said to her husband, 'Art thou a woman and he a man? Mar his nape with beating, even as he did with thee; and if he put out his hand to thee, I will cry out and the police will come and take him and cut him in sunder.' So the husband said to him, 'O thousand-horned,[248] O dog, O traitor, I owe thee a deposit,[249] for which thou dunnest me.' And he fell to beating him grievously with a stick of live-oak, whilst he called out to the woman for help and besought her of deliverance; but she said, 'Abide in thy place till the morning, and thou shalt see wonders.' And her husband beat him within the chamber, till he [well- nigh] made an end of him and he swooned away.

Then he left beating him and when the thief came to himself, the woman said to her husband, 'O man, this house is on hire and we owe its owners much money, and we have nought; so how wilt thou do?' And she went on to bespeak him thus. Quoth the thief, 'And what is the amount of the rent?' 'It will be fourscore dirhems,' answered the husband; and the thief said, 'I will pay this for thee and do thou let me go my way.' Then said the wife, 'O man, how much do we owe the baker and the greengrocer?' Quoth the thief, 'What is the sum of this?' And the husband said, 'Sixscore dirhems.' 'That makes two hundred dirhems,' rejoined the other; 'let me go my way and I will pay them.' But the wife said, 'O my dear one, and the girl groweth up and needs must we marry her and equip her and [do] what else is needful' So the thief said to the husband, 'How much dost thou want?' And he answered, 'A hundred dirhems, in the way of moderation.'[250] Quoth the thief, 'That makes three hundred dirhems.' And the woman said, 'O my dear one, when the girl is married, thou wilt need money for winter expenses, charcoal and firewood and other necessaries.' 'What wouldst thou have?' asked the thief; and she said, 'A hundred dirhems.' 'Be it four hundred dirhems,' rejoined he; and she said, 'O my dear one and solace of mine eyes, needs must my husband have capital in hand, wherewith he may buy merchandise and open him a shop.' 'How much will that be?' asked he, and she said, 'A hundred dirhems.' Quoth the thief, '[That makes five hundred dirhems; I will pay it;] but may I be divorced from my wife if all my possessions amount to more than this, and that the savings of twenty years! Let me go my way, so I may deliver them to thee.' 'O fool,' answered she, 'how shall I let thee go thy way? Give me a right token.' [So he gave her a token for his wife] and she cried out to her young daughter and said to her, 'Keep this door.'

Then she charged her husband keep watch over the thief, till she should return, and repairing to his wife, acquainted her with his case and told her that her husband the thief had been taken and had compounded for his release, at the price of seven hundred dirhems, and named to her the token. So she gave her the money and she took it and returned to her house. By this time, the dawn had broken; so she let the thief go his way, and when he went out, she said to him, 'O my dear one, when shall I see thee come and take the treasure?' 'O indebted one,' answered he, 'when thou needest other seven hundred dirhems, wherewithal to amend thy case and that of thy children and to discharge thy debts.' And he went out, hardly believing in his deliverance from her. Nor," added the vizier, "is this more extraordinary than the story of the three men and our Lord Jesus."

And the king bade him depart to his own house.

The Twelfth Night of the Month.

When it was eventide, the king summoned the vizier and bade him tell the [promised] story, "Hearkening and obedience," answered he. "Know, O king, that

STORY OF THE THREE MEN AND OUR LORD JESUS.

Three men once went out in quest of riches and came upon a block of gold, weighing a hundred pounds. When they saw it, they took it up on their shoulders and fared on with it, till they drew near a certain city, when one of them said, 'Let us sit in the mosque, whilst one of us goes and buys us what we may eat." So they sat down in the mosque and one of them arose and entered the city. When he came therein, his soul prompted him to play his fellows false and get the gold for himself alone. So he bought food and poisoned it; but, when he returned to his comrades, they fell upon him and slew him, so they might enjoy the gold without him. Then they ate of the [poisoned] food and died, and the gold abode cast down over against them.

Presently, Jesus, son of Mary (on whom be peace!) passed by and seeing this, besought God the Most High for tidings of their case; so He told him what had betided them, whereat great was his wonderment and he related to his disciples what he had seen. Quoth one of them, 'O Spirit of God,[251] nought resembleth this but my own story.' 'How so?' asked Jesus, and the other said,

THE DISCIPLE'S STORY.

'I was aforetime in such a city and hid a thousand dirhems in a monastery there. After awhile, I went thither and taking the money, bound it about my middle. [Then I set out to return] and when I came to the desert, the carrying of the money was burdensome to me. Presently, I espied a horseman pricking after me; so I [waited till he came up and] said to him, "O horseman, carry this money [for me] and earn reward and recompense [from God]." "Nay," answered he; "I will not do it, for I should weary myself and weary my horse." Then he went on, but, before he had gone far, he said in himself, "If I take up the money and spur my horse and forego him, how shall he overtake me?" And I also said in myself, "Verily, I erred [in asking him to carry the money]; for, had he taken it and made off, I could have done nought." Then he turned back to me and said to me, "Hand over the money, that I may carry it for thee." But I answered him, saying, "That which hath occurred to thy mind hath occurred to mine also; so go in peace."'

Quoth Jesus (on whom be peace!), 'Had these dealt prudently, they had taken thought for themselves; but they neglected the issues of events; for that whoso acteth prudently is safe and conquereth,[252] and whoso neglecteth precaution perisheth and repenteth.' Nor," added the vizier," is this more extraordinary nor goodlier than the story of the king, whose kingdom was restored to him and his wealth, after he had become poor, possessing not a single dirhem."

When the king heard this, he said in himself "How like is this to my own story in the matter of the vizier and his slaughter! Had I not used precaution, I had put him to death." And he bade Er Rehwan depart to his own house.

The Thirteenth Night of the Month.

When the evening evened, the king sent for the vizier to his privy sitting chamber and bade him [tell] the [promised] story. So he said, "Hearkening and obedience. They avouch, O king, that

STORY OF THE DETHRONED KING WHOSE KINGDOM AND GOOD WERE RESTORED TO HIM.

There was once, in a city of Hind, a just and beneficent king, and he had a vizier, a man of understanding, just in his judgment, praiseworthy in his policy, in whose hand was the governance of all the affairs of the realm; for he was firmly stablished in the king's favour and high in esteem with the folk of his time, and the king set great store by him and committed himself to him in all his affairs, by reason of his contrivance for his subjects, and he had helpers[253] who were content with him.

Now the king had a brother, who envied him and would fain have been in his place; and when he was weary of looking for his death and the term of his life seemed distant unto him, he took counsel with certain of his partisans and they said, 'The vizier is the king's counsellor and but for him, there would be left the king no kingdom.' So the king's brother cast about for the ruin of the vizier, but could find no means of accomplishing his design; and when the affair grew long upon him, he said to his wife, 'What deemest thou will advantage us in this?' Quoth she, 'What is it?' And he replied, 'I mean in the matter of yonder vizier, who inciteth my brother to devoutness with all his might and biddeth him thereto, and indeed the king is infatuated with his counsel and committeth to him the governance of all things and matters.' Quoth she, 'Thou sayst truly; but how shall we do with him?' And he answered, 'I have a device, so thou wilt help me in that which I shall say to thee.' Quoth she, 'Thou shall have my help in whatsoever thou desirest.' And he said, 'I mean to dig him a pit in the vestibule and dissemble it artfully.'

So he did this, and when it was night, he covered the pit with a light covering, so that, whenas the vizier stepped upon it, it would give way with him. Then he sent to him and summoned him to the presence in the king's name, and the messenger bade him enter by the privy door. So he entered in thereat, alone, and when he stepped upon the covering of the pit, it gave way with him and he fell to the bottom; whereupon the king's brother fell to pelting him with stones. When the vizier saw what had betided him, he gave himself up for lost; so he stirred not and lay still. The prince, seeing him make no motion, [deemed him dead]; so he took him forth and wrapping him up in his clothes, cast him into the billows of the sea in the middle of the night. When the vizier felt the water, he awoke from the swoon and swam awhile, till a ship passed by him, whereupon he cried out to the sailors and they took him up.

When the morning morrowed, the people went seeking for him, but found him not; and when the king knew this, he was perplexed concerning his affair and abode unknowing what he should do. Then he sought for a vizier to fill his room, and the king's brother said, 'I have a vizier, a sufficient man.' 'Bring him to me,' said the king. So he brought him a man, whom he set at the head of affairs; but he seized upon the kingdom and clapped the king in irons and made his brother king in his stead. The new king gave himself up to all manner of wickedness, whereat the folk murmured and his vizier said to him, 'I fear lest the Indians take the old king and restore him to the kingship and we both perish; wherefore, if we take him and cast him into the sea, we shall be at rest from him; and we will publish among the folk that he is dead.' And they agreed upon this. So they took him up and carrying him out to sea, cast him in.

When he felt the water, he struck out, and gave not over swimming till he landed upon an island, where he abode five days, finding nothing which he might eat or drink; but, on the sixth day, when he despaired of himself, he caught sight of a passing ship; so he made signals to the crew and they came and took him up and fared on with him to an inhabited country, where they set him ashore, naked as he was. There he saw a man tilling; so he sought guidance of him and the husbandman said, 'Art thou a stranger?' 'Yes,' answered the king and sat with him and they talked. The husbandman found him quickwitted and intelligent and said to him, 'If thou sawest a comrade of mine, thou wouldst see him the like of what I see thee, for his case is even as thy case, and he is presently my friend.'

Quoth the king, 'Verily, thou makest me long to see him. Canst thou not bring us together?' 'With all my heart,' answered the husbandman, and the king sat with him till he had made an end of his tillage, when he carried him to his dwelling-place and brought him in company with the other stranger, aud behold, it was his vizier. When they saw each other, they wept and embraced, and the husbandman wept for their weeping; but the king concealed their affair and said to him, 'This is a man from my country and he is as my brother.' So they abode with the husbandman and helped him for a wage, wherewith they supported themselves a long while. Meanwhile, they sought news of their country and learned that which its people suffered of straitness and oppression.

One day, there came a ship and in it a merchant from their own country, who knew them and rejoiced in them with an exceeding joy and clad them in goodly apparel. Moreover, he acquainted them with the manner of the treachery that had been practised upon them and counselled them to return to their own land, they and he with whom they had made friends,[254] assuring them that God the Most High would restore them to their former estate. So the king returned and the folk joined themselves to him and he fell upon his brother and his vizier and took them and clapped them in prison.

Then he sat down again upon the throne of his kingship, whilst the vizier stood before him, and they returned to their former estate, but they had nought of the [goods of the world]. So the king said to his vizier, 'How shall we avail to abide in this city, and we in this state of poverty?' And he answered, 'Be at thine ease and have no concern.' Then he singled out one of the soldiers[255] and said to him, 'Send us thy service[256] for the year.' Now there were in the city fifty thousand subjects[257] and in the hamlets and villages a like number; and the vizier sent to each of these, saying, 'Let each of you get an egg and lay it under a hen.' So they did this and it was neither burden nor grievance to them.

When twenty days had passed by, each [egg] was hatched, and the vizier bade them pair the chickens, male and female, and rear them well. So they did this and it was found a charge unto no one. Then they waited for them awhile and after this the vizier enquired of the chickens and was told that they were become fowls. Moreover, they brought him all their eggs and he bade set them; and after twenty days there were hatched from each [pair] of them thirty or five-and-twenty or fifteen [chickens] at the least. The vizier let note against each man the number of chickens that pertained to him, and after two months, he took the old hens and the cockerels, and there came to him from each man nigh half a score, and he left the [young] hens with them. On like wise he sent to the country folk and let the cocks abide with them. So he got him young ones [galore] and appropriated to himself the sale of the fowls, and on this wise he got him, in the course of a year, that which the regal estate required of the king and his affairs were set right for him by the vizier's contrivance. And he peopled[258] the country and dealt justly by his subjects and returned to them all that he took from them and lived a happy and prosperous life. Thus good judgment and prudence are better than wealth, for that understanding profiteth at all times and seasons. Nor," added the vizier, "is this more extraordinary than the story of the man whose caution slew him."

When the king heard his vizier's words, he marvelled with the utmost wonderment and bade him retire to his lodging. [So Er Rehwan withdrew to his house and abode there till eventide of the next day, when he again presented himself before the king.]

The Fourteenth Night of the Month.

When the vizier returned to the king, the latter sought of him the story of the man whose caution slew him and be said, "Know, O august king, that

STORY OF THE MAN WHOSE CAUTION WAS THE CAUSE OF HIS DEATH.

There was once a man who was exceeding cautious over himself, and he set out one day on a journey to a land abounding in wild beasts. The caravan wherein he was came by night to the gate of a city; but the warders refused to open to them; so they passed the night without the city, and there were lions there. The man aforesaid, of the excess of his caution, could not fix upon a place wherein he should pass the night, for fear of the wild beasts and reptiles; so he went about seeking an empty place wherein he might lie.

Now there was a ruined building hard by and he climbed up on to a high wall and gave not over clambering hither and thither, of the excess of his carefulness, till his feet betrayed him and he slipped [and fell] to the bottom and died, whilst his companions arose in the morning in health [and weal]. Now, if he had overmastered his corrupt[259] judgment and submitted himself to fate and fortune fore-ordained, it had been safer and better [for him]; but he made light of the folk and belittled their wit and was not content to take example by them; for his soul whispered him that he was a man of understanding and he imagined that, if he abode with them, he would perish; so his folly cast him into perdition. Nor," added the vizier, "is this more extraordinary than the story of the man who was lavish of his house and his victual to one whom he knew not"

When the king heard this, he said, "I will not isolate myself from the folk and slay my vizier." And he bade him depart to his dwelling.

The Fifteenth Night of the Month.

When the evening evened, the king let fetch the vizier and required of him the [promised] story. So he said, "Know, O king, that

STORY OF THE MAN WHO WAS LAVISH OF HIS HOUSE AND HIS VICTUAL TO ONE WHOM HE KNEW NOT.

There was once an Arab of [high] rank and [goodly] presence, a man of exalted generosity and magnanimity, and he had brethren, with whom he consorted and caroused, and they were wont to assemble by turns in each other's houses. When it came to his turn, he made ready in his house all manner goodly and pleasant meats and dainty drinks and exceeding lovely flowers and excellent fruits, and made provision of all kinds of instruments of music and store of rare apothegms and marvellous stories and goodly instances and histories and witty anedotes and verses and what not else, for there was none among those with whom he was used to company but enjoyed this on every goodly wise, and in the entertainment he had provided was all whereof each had need. Then he sallied forth and went round about the city, in quest of his friends, so he might assemble them; but found none of them in his house.

Now in that town was a man of good breeding and large generosity, a merchant of condition, young of years and bright of face, who had come to that town from his own country with great store of merchandise and wealth galore. He took up his abode therein and the place was pleasant to him and he was lavish in expenditure, so that he came to the end of all his good and there remained with him nothing save that which was upon him of raiment. So he left the lodging wherein he had abidden in the days of his affluence, after he had wasted[260] that which was therein of furniture, and fell to harbouring in the houses of the townsfolk from night to night.

One day, as he went wandering about the streets, he espied a woman of the utmost beauty and grace, and what he saw of her charms amazed him and there betided him what made him forget his present plight. She accosted him and jested with him and he besought her of foregathering and companionship. She consented to this and said to him, 'Let us go to thy lodging.' With this he repented and was perplexed concerning his affair and grieved for that which must escape him of her company by reason of the straitness of his hand,[261] for that he had no jot of spending money. But he was ashamed to say, 'No,' after he had made suit to her; so he went on before her, bethinking him how he should rid himself of her and casting about for an excuse which he might put off on her, and gave not over going from street to street, till he entered one that had no issue and saw, at the farther end, a door, whereon was a padlock.

So he said to her, 'Do thou excuse me, for my servant hath locked the door, and who shall open to us?' Quoth she, 'O my lord, the padlock is worth [but] half a score dirhems.' So saying, she tucked up [her sleeves] from fore-arms as they were crystal and taking a stone, smote upon the padlock and broke it. Then she opened the door and said to him, 'Enter, O my lord.' So he entered, committing his affair to God, (to whom belong might and majesty,) and she entered after him and locked the door from within. They found themselves in a pleasant house, comprising all[262] weal and gladness; and the young man went on, till he came to the sitting-chamber, and behold, it was furnished with the finest of furniture [and arrayed on the goodliest wise for the reception of guests,] as hath before been set out, [for that it was the house of the man aforesaid].

He [seated himself on the divan and] leant upon a cushion, whilst she put out her hand to her veil and did it off. Then she put off her heavy outer clothes and discovered her charms, whereupon he embraced her and kissed her and swived her; after which they washed and returned to their place and he said to her, 'Know that I have little knowledge [of what goes on] in my house, for that I trust to my servant; so arise thou and see what the boy hath made ready in the kitchen.' Accordingly, she arose and going down into the kitchen, saw cooking pots over the fire, wherein were all manner of dainty meats, and manchet-bread and fresh almond-and-honey cakes. So she set bread on a dish and ladled out [what she would] from the pots and brought it to him.

They ate and drank and sported and made merry awhile of the day; and as they were thus engaged, up came the master of the house, with his friends, whom he had brought with him, that they might carouse together, as of wont. He saw the door opened and knocked lightly, saying to his friends, 'Have patience with me, for some of my family are come to visit me; wherefore excuse belongeth [first] to God the Most High, and then to you.'[263] So they took leave of him and went their ways, whilst he gave another light knock at the door. When the young man heard this, he changed colour and the woman said to him, 'Methinks thy servant hath returned.' 'Yes,' answered he; and she arose and opening the door to the master of the house, said to him, 'Where hast thou been? Indeed, thy master is wroth with thee.' 'O my lady,' answered he, 'I have but been about his occasions.'

Then he girt his middle with a handkerchief and entering, saluted the young merchant, who said to him, 'Where hast thou been?' Quoth he, 'I have done thine errands;' and the youth said, 'Go and eat and come hither and drink.' So he went away, as he bade him, and ate. Then he washed and returning to the saloon, sat down on the carpet and fell to talking with them; whereupon the young merchant's heart was comforted and his breast dilated and he addressed himself to joyance. They abode in the most delightsome life and the most abounding pleasance till a third part of the night was past, when the master of the house arose and spreading them a bed, invited them to lie down. So they lay down and the youth abode on wake, pondering their affair, till daybreak, when the woman awoke and said to her companion, 'I wish to go.' So he bade her farewell and she departed; whereupon the master of the house followed her with a purse of money and gave it to her, saying, 'Blame not my master,' and made his excuse to her for the young merchant.

Then he returned to the youth and said to him, 'Arise and come to the bath.' And he fell to shampooing his hands and feet, whilst the youth called down blessings on him and said, 'O my lord, who art thou? Methinks there is not in the world the like of thee, no, nor a pleasanter than thy composition.' Then each of them acquainted the other with his case and condition and they went to the bath; after which the master of the house conjured the young merchant to return with him and summoned his friends. So they ate and drank and he related to them the story, wherefore they praised the master of the house and glorified him; and their friendship was complete, what while the young merchant abode in the town, till God vouchsafed him a commodity of travel, whereupon they took leave of him and he departed; and this is the end of his story. Nor," added the vizier, "O king of the age, is this more marvellous than the story of the rich man who lost his wealth and his wit."

When the king heard the vizier's story, it pleased him and he bade him go to his house.

The Sixteenth Night of the Month.

When the evening evened, the king sat in his sitting- chamber and sending for his vizier, bade him relate the story of the wealthy man who lost his wealth and his wit. So he said, "Know, O king, that

STORY OF THE IDIOT AND THE SHARPER.

There was once a man of fortune, who lost his wealth, and chagrin and melancholy got the mastery of him, so that he became an idiot and lost his wit. There abode with him of his wealth about a score of dinars and he used to beg alms of the folk, and that which they gave him he would gather together and lay to the dinars that were left him. Now there was in that town a vagabond, who made his living by sharping, and he knew that the idiot had somewhat of money; so he fell to spying upon him and gave not over watching him till he saw him put in an earthen pot that which he had with him of money and enter a deserted ruin, where he sat down, [as if] to make water, and dug a hole, in which he laid the pot and covering it up, strewed earth upon the place. Then he went away and the sharper came and taking what was in the pot, covered it up again, as it was.

Presently, the idiot returned, with somewhat to add to his hoard, but found it not; so he bethought him who had followed him and remembered that he had found the sharper aforesaid assiduous in sitting with him and questioning him. So he went in quest of him, assured that he had taken the pot, and gave not over looking for him till he espied him sitting; whereupon he ran to him and the sharper saw him. [Then the idiot stood within earshot] and muttered to himself and said, 'In the pot are threescore dinars and I have with me other score in such a place and to-day I will unite the whole in the pot.' When the sharper heard him say this to himself, muttering and mumbling after his fashion, he repented him of having taken the dinars and said, 'He will presently return to the pot and find it empty;

wherefore that[264] for which I am on the look-out will escape me; and meseemeth I were best restore the dinars [to their place], so he may see them and leave all that is with him in the pot, and I can take the whole.'

Now he feared [to return to the pot then and there], lest the idiot should follow him to the place and find nothing and so his plan be marred. So he said to him, 'O Ajlan,[265] I would have thee come to my lodging and eat bread with me." So the idiot went with him to his lodging and he seated him there and going to the market, sold somewhat of his clothes and pawned somewhat from his house and bought dainty food. Then he betook himself to the ruin and replacing the money in the pot, buried it again; after which he returned to his lodging and gave the idiot to eat and drink, and they went out together. The sharper went away and hid himself, lest the idiot should see him, whilst the latter repaired to his hiding- place and took the pot

Presently, the sharper came to the ruin, rejoicing in that which he deemed he should get, and dug in the place, but found nothing and knew that the idiot had tricked him. So he buffeted his face, for chagrin, and fell to following the other whithersoever he went, so he might get what was with him, but availed not unto this, for that the idiot knew what was in his mind and was certified that he spied upon him, [with intent to rob him]; so he kept watch over himself. Now, if the sharper had considered [the conse-quences of] haste and that which is begotten of loss therefrom, he had not done thus. Nor," continued the vizier, "is this story, O king of the age, rarer or more extraordinary or more diverting than the story of Khelbes and his wife and the learned man and that which befell between them."

When the king heard this story, he renounced his purpose of putting the vizier to death and his soul prompted him to continue him on life. So he bade him go away to his house.

The Seventeenth Night of the Month.

When the evening evened, the king summoned the vizier, and when he presented himself, he required of him the [promised] story. So he said, "Hearkening and obedience. Know, O august king, that

STORY OF KHELBES AND HIS WIFE AND THE LEARNED MAN.

There was once a man hight Khelbes, who was a lewd fellow, a calamity, notorious for this fashion, and he had a fair wife, renowned for beauty and loveliness. A man of his townsfolk fell in love with her and she also loved him. Now Khelbes was a crafty fellow and full of tricks, and there was in his neighbourhood a learned man, to whom the folk used to resort every day and he told them stories and admonished them [with moral instances]; and Khelbes was wont to be present in his assembly, for the sake of making a show before the folk.

Now this learned man had a wife renowned for beauty and loveliness and quickness of wit and understanding and the lover cast about for a device whereby he might win to Khelbes's wife; so he came to him and told him, as a secret, what he had seen of the learned man's wife and confided to him that he was enamoured of her and besought him of help in this. Khelbes told him that she was distinguished to the utterest for chastity and continence and that she exposed herself not to suspicion; but the other said, 'I cannot renounce her, [firstly,] because the woman inclineth to me and coveteth my wealth, and secondly, because of the greatness of my love for her; and nothing is wanting but thy help.' Quoth Khelbes, 'I will do thy will;' and the other said, 'Thou shalt have of me two dirhems a day, on condition that thou sit with the learned man and that, when he riseth from the assembly, thou speak a word notifying the breaking up of the session.' So they agreed upon this and Khelbes entered and sat in the assembly, whilst the lover was assured in his heart that the secret was safe with him, wherefore he rejoiced and was content to pay the two dirhems.

Then Khelbes used to attend the learned man's assembly, whilst the other would go in to his wife and abide with her, on such wise as he thought good, till the learned man arose from his session; and when Khelbes saw that he purposed rising, he would speak a word for the over to hear, whereupon he went forth from Khelbes's wife, and the latter knew not that calamity was in his own house. At last the learned man, seeing Khelbes do on this wise every day, began to misdoubt of him, more by token of that which he knew of his character, and suspicion grew upon him; so, one day, he advanced the time of his rising before the wonted hour and hastening up to Khelbes, laid hold of him and said to him, 'By Allah, an thou speak a single syllable, I will do thee a mischief!' Then he went in to his wife, with Khelbes in his grasp, and behold, she was sitting, as of her wont, nor was there about her aught of suspicious or unseemly.

The learned man bethought him awhile of this, then made for Khelbes's house, which adjoined his own, still holding the latter; and when they entered, they found the young man lying on the bed with Khelbes's wife; whereupon quoth he to him, 'O accursed one, the calamity is with thee and in thine own house!' So Khelbes put away his wife and went forth, fleeing, and returned not to his own land. This, then," continued the vizier, "is the consequence of lewdness, for whoso purposeth in himself craft and perfidy, they get possession of him, and had Khelbes conceived of himself that[266] which he conceived of the folk of dishonour and calamity, there had betided him nothing of this. Nor is this story, rare and extraordinary though it be, more extraordinary or rarer than that of the pious woman whose husband's brother accused her of lewdness."

When the king heard this, wonderment gat hold of him and his admiration for the vizier redoubled; so he bade him go to his house and return to him [on the morrow], according to his wont. Accordingly, the vizier withdrew to his lodging, where he passed the night and the ensuing day.

VOLUME THE SECOND

KING SHAH BEKHT AND HIS VIZIER ER REHWAN
(CONTINUED)

The Eighteenth Night of the Month.

WHEN the evening evened, the king summoned the vizier and required of him the [promised] story; so he said, "It is well. Know, O king, that

STORY OF THE PIOUS WOMAN ACCUSED OF LEWDNESS.

There was once a man of Nishapour,[267] who had a wife of the utmost loveliness and piety, and he was minded to set out on the pilgrimage. So he commended his wife to the care of his brother and besought him to aid her in her affairs and further her to her desires till he should return, so they both abode alive and well. Then he took ship and departed and his absence was prolonged. Meanwhile, the brother went in to his brother's wife, at all times and seasons, and questioned her of her circumstances and went about her occasions; and when his visits to her were prolonged and he heard her speech and looked upon her face, the love of her gat hold upon his heart and he became distraught with passion for her and his soul prompted him [to evil]. So he besought her to lie with him, but she refused and chid him for his foul deed, and he found him no way unto presumption;[268] wherefore he importuned her with soft speech and gentleness.

Now she was righteous in all her dealings and swerved not from one word;[269] so, when he saw that she consented not unto him, he misdoubted that she would tell his brother, when he returned from his journey, and said to her, 'An thou consent not to this whereof I require thee, I will cause thee fall into suspicion and thou wilt perish.' Quoth she, 'Be God (extolled be His perfection and exalted be He!) [judge] betwixt me and thee, and know that, shouldst thou tear me limb from limb, I would not consent to that whereto thou biddest me.' His folly[270] persuaded him that she would tell her husband; so, of his exceeding despite, he betook himself to a company of people in the mosque and told them that he had witnessed a man commit adultery with his brother's wife. They believed his saying and took act of his accusation and assembled to stone her. Then they dug her a pit without the city and seating her therein, stoned her, till they deemed her dead, when they left her.

Presently a villager passed by [the pit and finding] her [alive,] carried her to his house and tended her, [till she recovered]. Now, he had a son, and when the young man saw her, he loved her and besought her of herself; but she refused and consented not to him, whereupon he redoubled in love and longing and despite prompted him to suborn a youth of the people of his village and agree with him that he should come by night and take somewhat from his father's house and that, when he was discovered, he should say that she was of accord with him in this and avouch that she was his mistress and had been stoned on his account in the city. So he did this and coming by night to the villager's house, stole therefrom goods and clothes; whereupon the old man awoke and seizing the thief, bound him fast and beat him, to make him confess. So he confessed against the woman that she had prompted him to this and that he was her lover from the city. The news was bruited abroad and the people of the city assembled to put her to death; but the old man, with whom she was, forbade them and said, 'I brought this woman hither, coveting the recompense [of God,] and I know not [the truth of] that which is said of her and will not suffer any to hurt her.' Then he gave her a thousand dirhems, by way of alms, and put her forth of the village. As for the thief, he was imprisoned for some days; after which the folk interceded for him with the old man, saying, 'This is a youth and indeed he erred;' and he released him.

Meanwhile, the woman went out at hazard and donning devotee's apparel, fared on without ceasing, till she came to a city and found the king's deputies dunning the towns-folk for the tribute, out of season. Presently, she saw a man, whom they were pressing for the tribute; so she enquired of his case and being acquainted therewith, paid down the thousand dirhems for him and delivered him from beating; whereupon he thanked her and those who were present. When he was set free, he accosted her and besought her to go with him to his dwelling. So she accompanied him thither and supped with him and passed the night. When the night darkened on him, his soul prompted him to evil, for that which he saw of her beauty and loveliness, and he lusted after her and required her [of love]; but she repelled him and bade him fear God the Most High and reminded him of that which she had done with him of kindness and how she had delivered him from beating and humiliation.

However, he would not be denied, and when he saw her [constant] refusal of herself to him, he feared lest she should tell the folk of him. So, when he arose in the morning, he took a scroll and wrote in it what he would of forgery and falsehood and going up to the Sultan's palace, said, '[I have] an advisement [for the king].' So he bade admit him and he delivered him the writ that he had forged, saying, 'I found this letter with the woman, the devotee, the ascetic, and indeed she is a spy, a secret informer against the king to his enemy; and I deem the king's due more incumbent on me than any other and his advisement the first [duty], for that he uniteth in himself all the people, and but for the king's presence, the subjects would perish; wherefore I have brought [thee] warning.' The king put faith in his words and sent with him those who should lay hands upon the woman and put her to death; but they found her not.

As for the woman, whenas the man went out from her, she resolved to depart; so she went forth, saying in herself, 'There is no journeying for me in woman's attire.' Then she donned men's apparel, such as is worn of the pious, and set out and wandered over the earth; nor did she leave going till she entered a certain city. Now the king of that city had an only daughter in whom he gloried and whom he loved, and she saw the devotee and deeming her a pilgrim youth, said to her father, 'I would fain have this youth take up his abode with me, so I may learn of him wisdom and renunciation and religion.' Her father rejoiced in this and commanded the [supposed] pilgrim to take up his sojourn with his daughter in his palace. Now they were in one place and the king's daughter was strenuous to the utterest in continence and chastity and nobility of mind and magnanimity and devotion to the worship of God; but the ignorant slandered her[271] and the folk of the realm said, 'The king's daughter loveth the pilgrim youth and he loveth her.'

Now the king was a very old man and destiny decreed the ending of his term of life; so he died and when he was buried, the folk assembled and many were the sayings of the people and of the king's kinsfolk and officers, and they took counsel together to slay the princess and the young pilgrim, saying, 'This fellow dishonoureth us with yonder strumpet and none accepteth dishonour but the base.' So they fell upon them and slew the princess, without questioning her of aught; whereupon the pious woman (whom they deemed a boy) said to them, 'Out on ye, O misbelievers I Ye have slain the pious lady.' Quoth they, 'Lewd fellow that thou art, dost thou bespeak us thus? Thou lovedst her and she loved thee, and we will slay thee without mercy.' 'God forbid!' answered she, 'Indeed, the affair is the contrary of this.' 'What proof hast thou of that?' asked they, and she said, 'Bring me women.' So they brought her women, and when they looked on her, they found her a woman.

When the townsfolk saw this, they repented of that which they had done and the affair was grievous to them; so they sought pardon [of God] and said to her, ' By the virtue of Him whom thou servest, do thou seek pardon for us [of God!]' Quoth she, 'As for me, I may no longer abide with you and I am about to depart from you.' Then they humbled themselves in supplication to her and wept and said to her, 'We conjure thee, by the virtue of God the Most High, that thou take upon thyself the governance of the kingdom and of the subjects.' But she refused; whereupon they came up to her and wept and gave not over supplicating her, till she consented and abode in the kingship. Her first commandment was that they should bury the princess and build over her a dome[272] and she abode in that palace, worshipping God the Most High and ruling the people with justice, and God (extolled be His perfection and exalted be He!) vouchsafed her, by reason of the excellence of her piety and her patience and continence, the acceptance of her prayers, so that she sought not aught of Him to whom belong might and majesty, but He granted her prayer; and her report was noised abroad in all countries.

So the folk resorted to her from all parts and she used to pray God (to whom belong might and majesty) for the oppressed and God granted him relief, and against his oppressor, and He broke him in sunder. Moreover, she prayed for the sick and they were made whole; and on this wise she abode a great space of time. As for her husband, when he returned from the pilgrimage, his brother and the neighbours acquainted him with his wife's affair, whereat he was sore concerned and misdoubted of their story, for that which he knew of her chastity and prayerfulness; and he wept for her loss.

Meanwhile, she prayed to God the Most High that He would establish her innocence in the eyes of her husband and the folk. So He sent down upon her husband's brother a sore disease and none knew a remedy for him; wherefore he said to his brother, ' In such a city is a pious woman, a recluse, and her prayers are answered; so do thou carry me to her, that she may pray for me and God (to whom belong might and majesty) may make me whole of this sickness.' Accordingly, he took him up and fared on with him, till they came to the village where dwelt the old man, who had rescued the woman from the pit and carried her to his dwelling and tended her there, [till she recovered].

Here they halted and took up their lodging with the old man, who questioned the husband of his case and that of his brother and the reason of their journey, and he said, 'I purpose to go with my brother, this sick man, to the holy woman, her whose prayers are answered, so she may pray for him and God may make him whole by the blessing of her prayers.' Quoth the villager, 'By Allah, my son is in a parlous plight for sickness and we have heard that the holy woman prayeth for the sick and they are made whole. Indeed, the folk counsel me to carry him to her, and behold, I will go in company with you. And they said, 'It is well.' So they passed the night in that intent and on the morrow they set out for the dwelling of the holy woman, this one carrying his son and that his brother.

Now the man who had stolen the clothes and forged a lie against the pious woman, pretending that he was her lover, sickened of a sore sickness, and his people took him up and set out with him to visit the holy woman, and Destiny brought them all together by the way. So they fared on, till they came to the city wherein the man dwelt for whom she had paid a thousand dirhems, to deliver him from torment, and found him about to travel to her, by reason of a sickness that had betided him. So they all fared on together, unknowing that the holy woman was she whom they had so foully wronged, and ceased not going till they came to her city and foregathered at the gates of her palace, to wit, that wherein was the tomb of the king's daughter.

Now the folk used to go in to her and salute her and crave her prayers; and it was her wont to pray for none till he had confessed to her his sins, when she would seek pardon for him and pray for him that he might be healed, and he was straightway made whole of sickness, by permission of God the Most High. [So, when the four sick men were brought in to her,] she knew them forthright, though they knew her not, and said to them, ' Let each of you confess his sins, so I may crave pardon for him and pray for him.' And the brother said, 'As for me, I required my brother's wife of herself and she refused; whereupon despite and folly[273] prompted me and I lied against her and accused her to the townsfolk of adultery; so they stoned her and slew her unjustly and unrighteously; and this is the issue of unright and falsehood and of the slaying of the [innocent] soul, whose slaughter God hath forbidden.'

Then said the young man, the villager's son, 'And I, O holy woman, my father brought us a woman who had been stoned, and my people tended her till she recovered. Now she was surpassing of beauty; so I required her of herself; but she refused and clave fast to God (to whom belong might and majesty), wherefore folly[274] prompted me, so that I agreed with one of the youths that he should steal clothes and coin from my father's house. Then I laid hands on him [and carried him] to my father and made him confess. So he avouched that the woman was his mistress from the city and had been stoned on his account and that she was of accord with him concerning the theft and had opened the doors to him, and this was a lie against her, for that she had not yielded to me in that which I sought of her. So there befell me what ye see of punishment." And the young man, the thief, said, 'I am he with whom thou agreedst concerning the theft and to whom thou openedst the door, and I am he who avouched against her falsely and calumniously and God (extolled be His perfection and exalted be He!) knoweth that I never did evil with her, no, nor knew her in any wise before then.'

Then said he whom she had delivered from torture and for whom she had paid a thousand dirhems and who had required her of herself in his house, for that her beauty pleased him, and [when she refused to yield to him] had forged a letter against her and treacherously denounced her to the Sultan and requited her bounty with ingratitude, 'I am he who wronged her and lied against her, and this is the issue of the oppressor's affair.'

When she heard their words, in the presence of the folk, she said, 'Praise be to God, the King who availeth unto all things, and blessing upon His prophets and apostles!' Then quoth she [to the assembly], ' Bear witness, O ye who are present, to these men's speech, and know that I am that woman whom they confess that they wronged.' And she turned to her husband's brother and said to him, 'I am thy brother's wife and God (extolled be His perfection and exalted be He !) delivered me from that whereinto thou castedst me of false accusation and suspect and from the frowardness whereof thou hast spoken, and [now] hath He shown forth my innocence, of His bounty and generosity. Go, for thou art absolved of the wrong thou didst me.' Then she prayed for him and he was made whole of his sickness.

Then said she to the villager's son, 'Know that I am the woman whom thy father delivered from harm and stress and whom there betided from thee of false accusation and frowardness that which thou hast named.' And she craved pardon for him and he was made whole of his sickness. [Then said she to the thief, 'I am she against whom thou liedst, avouching that I was thy mistress, who had been stoned on thine account, and that I was of accord with thee concerning the robbing of the villager's house and had opened the doors to thee.' And she prayed for him and he was made whole of his sickness.] Then said she to [the townsman], him of the tribute, 'I am she who gave thee the [thousand] dirhems and thou didst with me what thou didst.' And she craved pardon for him and prayed for him and he was made whole; whereupon the folk marvelled at her oppressors, who had been afflicted alike, so God (extolled be His perfection and exalted be He!) might show forth her innocence before witnesses.

Then she turned to the old man who had delivered her from the pit and prayed for him and gave him presents galore and among them a myriad of money;[275] and they all departed from her, except her husband. When she was alone with him, she made him draw near unto her and rejoiced in his coming and gave him the choice of abiding with her. Moreover, she assembled the people of the city and set out to them his virtue and worth and counselled them to invest him with the charge of their governance and besought them to make him king over them. They fell in with her of this and he became king and took up his abode amongst them, whilst she gave herself up to her religious exercises and abode with her husband on such wise as she was with him aforetime.[276] Nor," added the vizier, "is this story, O king of the time, more extraordinary or more delightful than that of the journeyman and the girl whose belly he slit and fled."

When King Shah Bekht heard this, he said, "Most like all they say of the vizier is leasing and his innocence will appear, even as that of the pious woman appeared." Then he comforted the vizier's heart and bade him go to his house.

The Nineteenth Night of the Month.

When the evening evened, the king bade fetch the vizier and required of him the story of the journeyman and the girl. So he said, "Hearkening and obedience. Know, O august king, that

STORY OF THE JOURNEYMAN AND THE GIRL.

There was once, of old time, in one of the tribes of the Arabs, a woman great with child by her husband, and they had a hired servant, a man of excellent understanding. When the woman came to [the time of her] delivery, she gave birth to a maid-child in the night and they sought fire of the neighbours. So the journeyman went in quest of fire.

Now there was in the camp a wise woman,[277] and she questioned him of the new-born child, if it was male or female. Quoth he, 'It is a girl;' and she said, 'She shall do whoredom with a hundred men and a journeyman shall marry her and a spider shall slay her.' When the journeyman heard this, he returned upon his steps and going in to the woman, took the child from her by wile and slit its paunch. Then he fled forth into the desert at a venture and abode in strangerhood what [while] God willed.

He gained him wealth and returning to his native land, after twenty years' absence, alighted in the neighbourhood of an old woman, whom he bespoke fair and entreated with liberality, requiring of her a wench whom he might lie withal. Quoth she, 'I know none but a certain fair woman, who is renowned for this fashion.'[278] Then she described her charms to him and made him lust after her, and he said, 'Hasten to her forthright and lavish unto her that which she asketh, [in exchange for her favours].' So the old woman betook herself to the damsel and discovered to her the man's wishes and bade her to him; but she answered, saying, 'It is true that I was on this [fashion of] whoredom [aforetime]; but now I have repented to God the Most High and hanker no more after this; nay, I desire lawful marriage; so, if he be content with that which is lawful, I am at his service.'

The old woman returned to the man and told him what the damsel said; and he lusted after her, by reason of her beauty and her repentance; so he took her to wife, and when he went in to her, he loved her and she also loved him. On this wise they abode a great while, till one day he questioned her of the cause of a mark[279] he espied on her body, and she said, 'I know nought thereof save that my mother told me a marvellous thing concerning it.' 'What was that?' asked he, and she answered, 'She avouched that she gave birth to me one night of the nights of the winter and despatched a hired man, who was with us, in quest of fire for her. He was absent a little while and presently returning, took me and slit my belly and fled. When my mother saw this, affliction overcame her and compassion possessed her; so she sewed up my belly and tended me till, by the ordinance of God (to whom belong might and majesty), the wound healed up."

When her husband heard this, he said to her, 'What is thy name and what are the names of thy father and mother?' She told him their names and her own, whereby he knew that it was she whose belly he had slit and said to her, 'And where are thy father and mother?' 'They are both dead,' answered she, and he said, 'I am that journeyman who slit thy belly.' Quoth she, 'Why didst thou that?' And he replied, 'Because of a saying I heard from the wise woman.' 'What was it?' asked his wife, and he said, 'She avouched that thou wouldst play the harlot with a hundied men and that I should after take thee to wife.' Quoth she, 'Ay, I have whored it with a hundred men, no more and no less, and behold, thou hast married me.' 'Moreover,' continued her husband, 'the wise woman foresaid, also, that thou shouldst die, at the last of thy life, of the bite of a spider. Indeed, her saying hath been verified of the harlotry and the marriage, and I fear lest her word come true no less in the matter of thy death.'

Then they betook themselves to a place without the city, where he builded him a mansion of solid stone and white plaster and stopped its inner [walls] and stuccoed them; yea, he left not therein cranny nor crevice and set in it two serving-women to sweep and wipe, for fear of spiders. Here he abode with his wife a great while, till one day he espied a spider on the ceiling and beat it down. When his wife saw it, she said, 'This is that which the wise woman avouched would kill me; so, by thy life [I conjure thee], suffer me to slay it with mine own hand.' Her husband forbade her from this, but she conjured him to let her kill the spider; then, of her fear and her eagerness, she took a piece of wood and smote it. The wood broke in sunder, of the force of the blow, and a splinter from it entered her hand and wrought upon it, so that it swelled. Then her arm swelled also and the swelling spread to her side and thence grew till it reached her heart and she died. Nor," added the vizier, "is this more extraordinary or more wonderful than the story of the weaver who became a physician by his wife's commandment."

When the king heard this, his admiration redoubled and he said, "Of a truth, destiny is forewritten to all creatures, and I will not accept[280] aught that is said against my vizier the loyal counsellor." And he bade him go to his house.

The Twentieth Night of the Month.

When the evening evened, the king let call his vizier and he presented himself before him, whereupon he required of him the hearing of the [promised] story. So he said, "Hearkening and obedience. Know, O king. that

STORY OF THE WEAVER WHO BECAME A PHYSICIAN BY HIS WIFE'S COMMANDMENT.

There was once, in the land of Fars,[281] a man who took to wife a woman higher than himself in rank and nobler of lineage, but she had no guardian to preserve her from want. It misliked her to marry one who was beneath her; nevertheless, she married him, because of need, and took of him a bond in writing to the effect that he would still be under her commandment and forbiddance and would nowise gainsay her in word or deed. Now the man was a weaver and he bound himself in writing to pay his wife ten thousand dirhems, [in case he should make default in the condition aforesaid].

On this wise they abode a long while till one day the wife went out in quest of water, whereof she had need, and espied a physician who had spread a carpet in the Thereon he had set out great store of drugs and implements of medicine and he was speaking and muttering [charms], whilst the folk flocked to him and compassed him about on every side. The weaver's wife marvelled at the largeness of the physician's fortune[282] and said in herself, 'Were my husband thus, he would have an easy life of it and that wherein we are of straitness and misery would be enlarged unto him.'

Then she returned home, troubled and careful; and when her husband saw her on this wise, he questioned her of her case and she said to him, 'Verily, my breast is straitened by reason of thee and of the simpleness of thine intent. Straitness liketh me not and thou in thy [present] craft gaiuest nought; so either do thou seek out a craft other than this or pay me my due[283] and let me go my way.' Her husband chid her for this and admonished her;[284] but she would not be turned from her intert and said to him, 'Go forth and watch yonder physician how he doth and leam from him what he saith.' Quoth he, 'Let not thy heart be troubled: I will go every day to the physician's assembly.'

So he fell to resorting daily to the physician and committing to memory his sayings and that which he spoke of jargon, till he had gotten a great matter by heart, and all this he studied throughly and digested it. Then he returned to his wife and said to her, 'I have committed the physician's sayings to memory and have learned his fashion of muttering and prescribing and applying remedies[285] and have gotten by heart the names of the remedies and of all the diseases, and there abideth nought [unaccomplished] of thy commandment. What wilt thou have me do now?' Quoth she, 'Leave weaving and open thyself a physician's shop.' But he answered, 'The people of my city know me and this affair will not profit me, save in a land of strangerhood; so come, let us go out from this city and get us to a strange land and [there] live.' And she said, 'Do as thou wilt.'

So he arose and taking his weaving gear, sold it and bought with the price drugs and simples and wrought himself a carpet, with which they set out and journeyed to a certain village, where they took up their abode. Then the man donned a physician's habit and fell to going round about the hamlets and villages and country parts; and he began to earn his living and make gain. Their affairs prospered and their case was bettered; wherefore they praised God for their present ease and the village became to them a home.

[On this wise he abode a pretty while] and the days ceased not and the nights to transport him from country to country, till he came to the land of the Greeks and lighted down in a city of the cities thereof, wherein was Galen the Sage; but the weaver knew him not, nor was he ware who he was. So he went forth, according to his wont, in quest of a place where the folk might assemble together, and hired Galen's courtyard.[286] There he spread his carpet and setting out thereon his drugs and instruments of medicine, praised himself and his skill and vaunted himself of understanding such as none but he might claim.

Galen heard that which he avouched of his understanding and it was certified unto him and established in his mind that the man was a skilled physician of the physicians of the Persians and [he said in himself], 'Except he had confidence in his knowledge and were minded to confront me and contend with me, he had not sought the door of my house neither spoken that which he hath spoken.' And concern gat hold upon Galen and doubt. Then he looked out upon[287] the weaver and addressed himself to see what he should do, whilst the folk began to flock to him and set out to him their ailments, and he would answer them thereof [and prescribe for them], hitting the mark one while and missing it another, so that there appeared unto Galen of his fashion nothing whereby his mind might be assured that he had formed a just opinion of his skill.

Presently, up came a woman with a phial of urine, and when the [mock] physician saw the phial afar off, he said to her, 'This is the urine of a man, a stranger.' 'Yes,' answered she; and he continued, 'Is he not a Jew and is not his ailment indigestion?' 'Yes,' replied the woman, and the folk marvelled at this; wherefore the man was magnified in Galen's eyes, for that he heard speech such as was not of the usage of physicians, seeing that they know not urine but by shaking it and looking into it anear neither know they a man's water from a woman's water, nor a stranger's [from a country-man's], nor a Jew's from a Sherifs.[288] Then said the woman, 'What is the remedy?' Quoth the weaver, 'Pay down the fee.' So she paid him a dirhem and he gave her medicines contrary to that ailment and such as would aggravate the patient's malady.

When Galen saw what appeared to him of the [mock] physician's incapacity, he turned to his disciples and pupils and bade them fetch the other, with all his gear and drugs. So they brought him into his presence on the speediest wise, and when Galen saw him before him, he said to him, 'Knowest thou me?' ' No,' answered the other, 'nor did I ever set eyes on thee before this day.' Quoth the sage, 'Dost thou know Galen?' And the weaver said, 'No.' Then said Galen, 'What prompted thee to that which thou dost?' So he related to him his story and gave him to know of the dowry and the obligation by which he was bound with regard to his wife, whereat Galen marvelled and certified himself of the matter of the dower.

Then he bade lodge him near himself and was bountiful to him and took him apart and said to him, 'Expound to me the story of the phial and whence then knewest that the water therein was that of a man, and he a stranger and a Jew, and that his ailment was indigestion?' ' It is well,' answered the weaver. ' Thou must know that we people of Persia are skilled in physiognomy[289] and I saw the woman to be rosy-cheeked, blue-eyed and tall. Now these attributes belong to women who are enamoured of a man and are distraught for love of him;[290] moreover, I saw her consumed [with anxiety]; wherefore I knew that the patient was her husband. As for his strangerhood, I observed that the woman's attire differed from that of the people of the city, wherefore I knew that she was a stranger; and in the mouth of the phial I espied a yellow rag,[291] whereby I knew that the patient was a Jew and she a Jewess. Moreover, she came to me on the first day [of the week];[292] and it is the Jews' custom to take pottages[293] and meats that have been dressed overnight[294] and eat them on the Sabbath day,[295] hot and cold, and they exceed in eating; wherefore indigestion betideth them. On this wise I was directed and guessed that which thou hast heard.'

When Galen heard this, he ordered the weaver the amount of his wife's dowry and bade him pay it to her and divorce her. Moreover, he forbade him from returning to the practice of physic and warned him never again to take to wife a woman of better condition than himself; and he gave him his spending-money and bade him return to his [former] craft. Nor," added the vizier, "is this more extraordinary or rarer than the story of the two sharpers who cozened each his fellow."

When King Shah Bekht heard this, he said in himself, "How like is this story to my present case with this vizier, who hath not his like!" Then he bade him depart to his own house and come again at eventide.

The Twenty-First Night of the Month.

When came the night, the vizier presented himself before the king, who bade him relate the [promised] story. So he said, "Hearkening and obedience. Know, Out

STORY OF THE TWO SHARPERS WHO CHEATED EACH HIS FELLOW.

There was once, in the city of Baghdad, a man, [by name El Merouzi,][296] who was a sharper and plagued[297] the folk with his knavish tricks, and he was renowned in all quarters [for roguery]. [He went out one day], carrying a load of sheep's dung, and took an oath that he would not return to his lodging till he had sold it at the price of raisins. Now there was in another city a second sharper, [by name Er Razi,][298] one of its people, who [went out the same day], bearing a load of goat's dung, which he had sworn that he would not sell but at the price of dried figs.

So each of them fared on with that which was with him and gave not over going till they met in one of the inns[299] and each complained to the other of that which he had abidden of travel [in quest of custom] and of the lack of demand for his wares. Now each of them had it in mind to cheat his fellow; so El Merouzi said to Er Razi, 'Wilt thou sell me that?' 'Yes,' answered he, and the other continued, 'And wilt thou buy that which is with me?' Er Razi assented; so they agreed upon this and each of them sold his fellow that which was with him [in exchange for the other's ware]; after which they bade each other farewell and parted. As soon as they were out of each other's sight, they examined their loads, to see what was therein, and one of them found that he had a load of sheep's dung and the other that he had a load of goat's dung; whereupon each of them turned back in quest of his fellow. They met in the inn aforesaid and laughed at each other and cancelling their bargain, agreed to enter into partnership and that all that they had of money and other good should be in common between them, share and share alike.

Then said Er Razi to El Merouzi, 'Come with me to my city, for that it is nearer [than thine].' So he went with him, and when he came to his lodging, he said to his wife and household and neighbours, 'This is my brother, who hath been absent in the land of Khorassan and is come back.' And he abode with him in all honour and worship three days' space. On the fourth day, Er Razi said to him, 'Know, O my brother, that I purpose to do somewhat' 'What is it?' asked El Merouzi. Quoth the other, 'I mean to feign myself dead and do thou go to the market and hire two porters and a bier. [Then come back and take me up and go round about the streets and markets with me and collect alms on my account.]300

Accordingly El Merouzi repaired to the market and fetching that which he sought, returned to Er Razi's house, where he found the latter cast down in the vestibule, with his beard tied and his eyes shut; and indeed, his colour was paled and his belly blown out and his limbs relaxed. So he deemed him in truth dead and shook him; but he spoke not; and he took a knife and pricked him in the legs, but he stirred not. Then said Er Razi, 'What is this, O fool?' And El Merouzi answered, 'Methought thou wast dead in very sooth.' Quoth Er Razi, 'Get thee to seriousness and leave jesting.' So he took him up and went with him to the market and collected [alms] for him that day till eventide, when he carried him back to his lodging and waited till the morrow.

Next morning, he again took up the bier and went round with it as before, in quest of alms. Presently, the master of police, who was of those who had given alms on account of the supposed dead man on the previous day, met him; so he was angered and fell on the porters and beat them and took the [supposed] dead body, saying, 'I will bury him and earn the reward [of God].'[301] So his men took him up and carrying him to the prefecture, fetched grave-diggers, who dug him a grave. Then they bought him a shroud and perfumes[302] and fetched an old man of the quarter, to wash him. So he recited over him [the appointed prayers and portions of the Koran] and laying him on the bench, washed him and shrouded him. After he had shrouded him, he voided;[303] so he renewed the washing and went away to make his ablutions,[304] whilst all the folk departed, likewise, to make the [obligatory] ablution, previously to the funeral.

When the dead man found himself alone, he sprang up, as he were a Satan, and donning the washer's clothes,[305] took the bowls and water-can and wrapped them up in the napkins. Then be took his shroud under his arm and went out. The doorkeepers thought that he was the washer and said to him, 'Hast thou made an end of the washing, so we may tell the Amir?' 'Yes,' answered the sharper and made off to his lodging, where he found El Merouzi soliciting his wife and saying to her, 'Nay, by thy life, thou wilt never again look upon his face; for that by this time he is buried. I myself escaped not from them but after travail and trouble, and if he speak, they will put him to death.' Quoth she, 'And what wilt thou have of me?' 'Accomplish my desire of thee,' answered he, 'and heal my disorder, for I am better than thy husband.' And he fell a-toying with her.

When Er Razi heard this, he said, 'Yonder wittol lusteth after my wife; but I will do him a mischief.' Then he rushed in upon them, and when El Merouzi saw him, he marvelled at him and said to him, 'How didst thou make thine escape?' So he told him the trick he had played and they abode talking of that which they had collected from the folk [by way of alms], and indeed they had gotten great store of money. Then said El Merouzi, 'Verily, mine absence hath been prolonged and fain would I return to my own country.' Quoth Er Rasi,' As thou wilt;' and the other said, 'Let us divide the money we have gotten and do thou go with me to my country, so I may show thee my tricks and my fashions.' 'Come to-morrow,' replied Er Razi, 'and we will divide the money.'

So El Merouzi went away and the other turned to his wife and said to her, 'We have gotten us great plenty of money, and yonder dog would fain take the half of it; but this shall never be, for that my mind hath been changed against him, since I heard him solicit thee; wherefore I purpose to play him a trick and enjoy all the money; and do not thou cross me.' 'It is well,' answered she, and he said to her, '[To-morrow] at day-peep I will feign myself dead and do thou cry out and tear thy hair, whereupon the folk will flock to me. Then lay me out and bury me, and when the folk are gone away [from the burial-place], do thou dig down to me and take me; and have no fear for me, for I can abide two days in the tomb [without hurt].' And she answered, 'Do what thou wilt.'

So, when it was the foredawn hour, she tied his beard and spreading a veil over him, cried out, whereupon the people of the quarter flocked to her, men and women. Presently, up came El Merouzi, for the division of the money, and hearing the crying [of the mourners], said, 'What is to do?" Quoth they, 'Thy brother is dead;' and he said in himself, 'The accursed fellow putteth a cheat on me, so he may get all the money for himself, but I will do with him what shall soon bring him to life again.' Then he rent the bosom of his gown and uncovered his head, weeping and saying, 'Alas, my brother! Alas, my chief! Alas, my lord!' And he went in to the men, who rose and condoled with him. Then he accosted Er Razi's wife and said to her, 'How came his death about?' 'I know not,' answered she, 'except that, when I arose in the morning, I found him dead.' Moreover, he questioned her of the money and good that was with her, but she said, 'I have no knowledge of this and no tidings.'

So he sat down at the sharper's head, and said to him, 'Know, O Razi, that I will not leave thee till after ten days and their nights, wherein I will wake and sleep by thy grave. So arise and be not a fool.' But he answered him not and El Merouzi [drew his knife and] fell to sticking it into the other's hands and feet, thinking to make him move; but [he stirred not and] he presently grew weary of this and concluded that the sharper was dead in good earnest. [However, he still misdoubted of the case] and said in himself, 'This fellow is dissembling, so he may enjoy all the money.' Therewith he addressed himself to prepare him [for burial] and bought him perfumes and what [not else] was needed. Then they brought him to the washing-place and El Merouzi came to him and heating water till it boiled and bubbled and a third of it was wasted,[306] fell to pouring it on his skin, so that it turned red and blue and blistered; but he abode still on one case [and stirred not].

So they wrapped him in the shroud and set him on the bier. Then they took up his bier and bearing him to the burial-place, laid him in the grave[307] and threw the earth over him; after which the folk dispersed, but El Merouzi and the widow abode by the tomb, weeping, and gave not over sitting till sundown, when the woman said to him, 'Come, let us go to the house, for this weeping will not profit us, nor will it restore the dead.' 'By Allah,' answered the sharper, 'I will not budge hence till I have slept and waked by this tomb ten days, with their nights!' When she heard this his speech, she feared lest he should keep his word and his oath, and so her husband perish; but she said in herself, 'This fellow dissembleth: if I go away and return to my house, he will abide by him a little while and go away.' And El Merouzi said to her, 'Arise, thou, and go away.'

So she arose and returned to her house, whilst El Merouzi abode in his place till the night was half spent, when he said to himself, 'How long [is this to last]? Yet how can I let this knavish dog die and lose the money? Methinks I were better open the tomb on him and bring him forth and take my due of him by dint of grievous beating and torment.' Accordingly, he dug him up and pulled him forth of the tomb; after which he betook himself to an orchard hard by the burial-ground and cut thence staves and palm sticks. Then he tied the dead man's legs and came down on him with the staff and beat him grievously; but he stirred not. When the time grew long on him, his shoulders became weary and he feared lest some one of the watch should pass on his round and surprise him. So he took up Er Razi and carrying him forth of the cemetery, stayed not till he came to the Magians' burying-place and casting him down in a sepulchre[308] there, rained heavy blows upon him till his shoulders failed him, but the other stirred not Then he sat down by his side and rested; after which he rose and renewed the beating upon him, [but to no better effect; and thus he did] till the end of the night

Now, as destiny would have it, a band of thieves, whose use it was, whenas they had stolen aught, to resort to that place and divide [their booty], came thither [that night], as of their wont; and they were ten in number and had with them wealth galore, which they were carrying. When they drew near the sepulchre, they heard a noise of blows within it and the captain said, 'This is a Magian whom the angels[309] are tormenting.' So they entered [the burial-ground] and when they came over against El Merouzi, he feared lest they should be the officers of the watch come upon him, wherefore he [arose and] fled and stood among the tombs.[310] The thieves came up to the place and finding Er Razi bound by the feet and by him near seventy sticks, marvelled at this with an exceeding wonderment and said, 'God confound thee! This was sure an infidel, a man of many crimes; for, behold, the earth hath rejected him from her womb, and by my life, he is yet fresh! This is his first night [in the tomb] and the angels were tormenting him but now; so whosoever of you hath a sin upon his conscience, let him beat him, as a propitiatory offering to God the Most High.' And the thieves said, 'We all have sins upon our consciences.'

So each of them went up to the [supposed] dead man and dealt him nigh upon a hundred blows, exclaiming the while, one, 'This is for[311] my father!' and another, 'This is for my grandfather!' whilst a third said, 'This is for my brother!' and a fourth, 'This is for my mother!' And they gave not over taking turns at him and beating him, till they were weary, what while El Merouzi stood laughing and saying in himself, 'It is not I alone who have entered into sin against him. There is no power and no virtue save in God the Most High, the Supreme!'

Then the thieves addressed themselves to sharing their booty and presently fell out concerning a sword that was among the spoil, who should take it. Quoth the captain, 'Methinks we were better prove it; so, if it be good, we shall know its worth, and if it be ill, we shall know that.' And they said, 'Try it on this dead man, for he is fresh.' So the captain took the sword and drawing it, poised it and brandished it; but, when Er Razi saw this, he made sure of death and said in himself, 'I have borne the washing and the boiling water and the pricking with the knife and the grave and its straitness and all this [beating], trusting in God that I might be delivered from death, and [hitherto] I have been delivered; but, as for the sword, I may not brook that, for but one stroke of it, and I am a dead man.'

So saying, he sprang to his feet and catching up the thigh-bone of one of the dead, cried out at the top of his voice, saying, 'O ye dead, take them!' And he smote one of them, whilst his comrade [El Merouzi] smote another and they cried out at them and buffeted them on the napes of their necks; whereupon the thieves left that which was with them of plunder and fled; and indeed their wits forsook them [for terror] and they stayed not in their flight till they came forth of the Magians' burial-ground and left it a parasang's length behind them, when they halted, trembling and affrighted for the soreness of that which had betided them of fear and amazement at the dead.

As for Er Razi and El Merouzi, they made peace with each other and sat down to share the booty. Quoth El Merouzi, 'I will not give thee a dirhem of this money, till thou pay me my due of the money that is in thy house.' And Er Razi said 'I will not do it, nor will I subtract this from aught of my due.' So they fell out upon this and disputed with one another and each went saying to his fellow, 'I will not give thee a dirhem!' And words ran high between them and contention was prolonged.

Meanwhile, when the thieves halted, one of them said to the others, 'Let us return and see;' and the captain said, 'This thing is impossible of the dead: never heard we that they came to life on this wise. So let us return and take our good, for that the dead have no occasion for good.' And they were divided in opinion as to returning: but [presently they came to a decision and] said, 'Indeed, our arms are gone and we cannot avail against them and will not draw near the place where they are: only let one of us [go thither and] look at it, and if he hear no sound of them, let him advertise us what we shall do.' So they agreed that they should send a man of them and assigned him [for this service] two parts [of the booty].

Accordingly, he returned to the burial-ground and gave not over going till he stood at the door of the sepulchre, when he heard El Merouzi say to his fellow, 'I will not give thee a single dirhem of the money!' The other said the like and they were occupied with contention and mutual revilement and talk. So the thief returned in haste to his fellows, who said, 'What is behind thee?' Quoth he, 'Get you gone and flee for your lives and save yourselves, O fools; for that much people of the dead are come to life and between them are words and contention.' So the thieves fled, whilst the two sharpers retained to Er Razi's house and made peace with one another and laid the thieves' purchase to the money they had gotten aforetime and lived a while of time. Nor, O king of the age," added the vizier, "is this rarer or more marvellous than the story of the four sharpers with the money-changer and the ass."

When the king heard this story, he smiled and it pleased him and he bade the vizier go away to his own house.

The Twenty-Second Night of the Month.

When the evening evened, the king summoned the vizier and required of him the hearing of the [promised] story. So he said, "Hearkening and obedience. Know, O king, that

STORY OF THE SHARPERS WITH THE MONEY-CHANGER AND THE ASS.

Four sharpers once plotted against a money-changer, a man of abounding wealth, and agreed upon a device for the taking of somewhat of his money. So one of them took an ass and laying on it a bag, wherein was money, lighted down at the money-changer's shop and sought of him change for the money. The money- changer brought out to him the change and bartered it with him, whilst the sharper was easy with him in the matter of the exchange, so he might give him confidence in himself. [As they were thus engaged,] up came the [other three] sharpers and surrounded the ass; and one of them said, '[It is] he,' and another said, 'Wait till I look at him.' Then he fell to looking on the ass and stroking him from his mane to his crupper; whilst the third went up to him and handled him and felt him from head to tail, saying, ' Yes, [it is] in him.' Quoth another, ['Nay,] it is not in him.' And they gave not over doing the like of this.

Then they accosted the owner of the ass and chaffered with him and he said, 'I will not sell him but for ten thousand dirhems.' They offered him a thousand dirhems; but he refused and swore that he would not sell the ass but for that which he had said. They ceased not to add to their bidding, till the price reached five thousand dirhems, whilst their fellow still said, 'I will not sell him but for ten thousand dirhems.' The money-changer counselled him to sell, but he would not do this and said to him, 'Harkye, gaffer! Thou hast no knowledge of this ass's case. Concern thyself with silver and gold and what pertaineth thereto of change and exchange; for indeed the virtue of this ass passeth thy comprehension. To every craft its craftsman and to every means of livelihood its folk.'

When the affair was prolonged upon the three sharpers, they went away and sat down a little apart; then they came up to the money-changer privily and said to him, 'If thou canst buy him for us, do so, and we will give thee a score of dirhems.' Quoth he, 'Go away and sit down afar from him.' So they did his bidding and the money-changer went up to the owner of the ass and gave not over tempting him with money and cajoling him and saying, 'Leave yonder fellows and sell me the ass, and I will reckon him a gift from thee,' till he consented to sell him the ass for five thousand and five hundred dirhems. Accordingly the money-changer counted down to him five thousand and five hundred dirhems of his own money, and the owner of the ass took the price and delivered the ass to him, saying, 'Whatsoever betideth, though he abide a deposit about thy neck,[312] sell him not to yonder rogues for less than ten thousand dirhems, for that they would fain buy him because of a hidden treasure whereof they know, and nought can guide them thereto but this ass. So close thy hand on him and gainsay me not, or thou wilt repent.'

So saying, he left him and went away, whereupon up came the three other sharpers, the comrades of him of the ass, and said to the money-changer, 'God requite thee for us with good, for that thou hast bought him! How can we requite thee!' Quoth he, 'I will not sell him but for ten thousand dirhems.' When they heard this, they returned to the ass and fell again to examining him and handling him. Then said they to the money-changer, 'We were mistaken in him. This is not the ass we sought and he is not worth more than half a score paras to us.' Then they left him and offered to go away, whereat the money-changer was sore chagrined and cried out at their speech, saying, 'O folk, ye besought me to buy him for you and now I have bought him, ye say, "We were deceived [in him], and he is not worth more than ten paras to us."' Quoth they, 'We supposed that in him was that which we desired; but, behold, in him is the contrary of that which we want; and indeed he hath a default, for that he is short of back.' And they scoffed at him and went away from him and dispersed.

The money-changer thought they did but finesse with him, that they might get the ass at their own price; but, when they went away from him and he had long in vain awaited their return, he cried out, saying, 'Woe!' and 'Ruin!' and 'Alack, my sorry chance!' and shrieked aloud and tore his clothes. So the people of the market assembled to him and questioned him of his case; whereupon he acquainted them with his plight and told them what the sharpers had said and how they had beguiled him and how it was they who had cajoled him into buying an ass worth half a hundred dirhems[313] for five thousand and five hundred.[314] His friends blamed him and a company of the folk laughed at him and marvelled at his folly and his credulity in accepting the sharpers' talk, without suspicion, and meddling with that which he understood not and thrusting himself into that whereof he was not assured.

On this wise, O King Shah Bekht," continued the vizier, "is the issue of eagerness for [the goods of] the world and covetise of that which our knowledge embraceth not; indeed, [whoso doth thus] shall perish and repent Nor, O king of the age, (added he) is this story more extraordinary than that of the sharper and the merchants."

When the king heard this story, he said in himself, "Verily, had I given ear to the sayings of my courtiers and inclined to the idle prate [of those who counselled me] in the matter of [the slaying of] my vizier, I had repented to the utterest of repentance, but praised be God, who hath disposed me to mansuetude and long-suffering and hath endowed me with patience!" Then he turned to the vizier and bade him return to his dwelling and [dismissed] those who were present, as of wont.

The Twenty-Third Night of the Month.

When the evening evened, the king sent after the vizier and when he presented himself before him, he required of him the hearing of the [promised] story. So he said, "Hearkening and obedience. Know, O illustrious lord, that

STORY OF THE SHARPER AND THE MERCHANTS.

There was once aforetime a certain sharper, who [was so eloquent that he] would turn the ear inside out, and he was a man of understanding and quick wit and skill and perfection. It was his wont to enter a town and [give himself out as a merchant and] make a show of trafficking and insinuate himself into the intimacy of people of worth and consort with the merchants, for he was [apparently] distinguished for virtue and piety. Then he would put a cheat on them and take [of them] what he might spend and go away to another city; and he ceased not to do thus a great while.

It befell one day that he entered a certain city and sold somewhat that was with him of merchandise and got him friends of the merchants of the place and fell to sitting with them and entertaining them and inviting them to his lodging and his assembly, whilst they also invited him to their houses. On this wise he abode a long while, till he was minded to leave the city; and this was bruited abroad among his friends, who were concerned for parting from him. Then he betook himself to him of them, who was the richest of them in substance and the most apparent of them in generosity, and sat with him and borrowed his goods; and when he was about to take leave, he desired him to give him the deposit that he had left with him. 'And what is the deposit?' asked the merchant. Quoth the sharper, 'It is such a purse, with the thousand dinars therein.' And the merchant said, 'When didst thou give it me?' 'Extolled be the perfection of God!' replied the sharper. 'Was it not on such a day, by such a token, and thus and thus?' 'I know not of this,' rejoined the merchant, and words were bandied about between them, whilst the folk [who were present also] disputed together concerning their affair and their speech, till their voices rose high and the neighbours had knowledge of that which passed between them.

Then said the sharper, 'O folk, this is my friend and I deposited with him a deposit, but he denieth it; so in whom shall the folk put trust after this?' And they said, 'This [315] is a man of worth and we have found in him nought but trustiness and loyality and good breeding, and he is endowed with understanding and generosity. Indeed, he avoucheth no falsehood, for that we have consorted with him and mixed with him and he with us and we know the sincerity of his religion.' Then quoth one of them to the merchant, 'Harkye, such an one! Bethink thee and consult thy memory. It may not be but that thou hast forgotten.' But he said, 'O folk, I know nothing of that which he saith, for indeed he deposited nought with me.' And the affair was prolonged between them. Then said the sharper to the merchant, 'I am about to make a journey and have, praised be God the Most High, wealth galore, and this money shall not escape me; but do thou swear to me.' And the folk said, 'Indeed, this man doth justice upon himself.'[316] Whereupon the merchant fell into that which he misliked[317] and came near upon [suffering] loss and ill repute.

Now he had a friend, who pretended to quickwittedness and understanding; so he came up to him privily and said to him, 'Let me do, so I may put the change on this trickster, for I know him to be a liar and thou art near upon having to pay the money; but I will turn suspicion from thee and say to him, "The deposit is with me and thou erredst in imagining that it was with other than myself," and so divert him from thee.' 'Do so,' replied the merchant, 'and rid the folk of their [false] debts.'

So the friend turned to the sharper and said to him, 'O my lord, O such an one, thou goest under a delusion. The purse is with me, for it was with me that thou depositedst it, and this elder is innocent of it.' But the sharper answered him with impatience and impetuosity, saying, 'Extolled be the perfection of God! As for the purse that is with thee, O noble and trusty man, I know that it is in the warrant of God anc my heart is at ease concerning it, for that it is with thee as it were with me; but I began by demanding that which I deposited with this man, of my knowledge that he coveteth the folk's good.' At this the friend was ccnfounded and put to silence and returned not an answer; [and the] only [result of his interference was that] each of them [318] paid a thousand dinars.

So the sharper took the two thousand dinars and made off; and when he was gone, the merchant said to his friend, the [self-styled] man of wit and intelligence, 'Harkye, such an one! Thou and I are like unto the hawk and the locust.' 'What was their case?' asked the other; and the merchant said,

STORY OF THE HAWK AND THE LOCUST.

'There was once, of old time, a hawk who made himself a nest hard by that of a locust, and the latter gloried in his neighbourhooc and betaking herself to him, saluted him and said, "O my lord and chief of the birds, indeed the nearness unto thee delighteth me and thou honourest me with thy neighbourhood and my soul is fortified with thee." The hawk thanked her for this and there ensued friendship between them. One day, the locust said to the hawk, "O chief of the birds, how cometh it that I see thee alone, solitary, having with thee no friend of thy kind of the birds, to whom thou mayst incline in time of easance and of whom thou mayst seek succour in time of stress? Indeed, it is said, 'Man goeth about seeking the ease of his body and the preservation of his strength, and in this there is nought more necessary to him than a friend who shall be the completion of his gladness and the mainstay of his life and on whom shall be his dependence in his stress and in his ease.' Now I, albeit I ardently desire thy weal in that which beseemeth thy condition, yet am I weak [and unable] unto that which the soul craveth; but, if thou wilt give me leave, I will seek out for thee one of the birds who shall be conformable unto thee in thy body and thy strength." And the hawk said, "I commit this to thee and rely upon thee therein."

Therewithal, O my brother, the locust fell to going round about among the company of the birds, but saw nought resembling the hawk in bulk and body save the kite and deemed well of her. So she brought the hawk and the kite together and counselled the former to make friends with the latter. Now it chanced that the hawk fell sick and the kite abode with him a long while [and tended him] till he recovered and became whole and strong; wherefore he thanked her [and she departed from him]. But after awhile the hawk's sickness returned to him and he needed the kite's succour. So the locust went out from him and was absent from him a day, after which she returned to him with a[nother] locust, [319]saying, "I have brought thee this one." When the hawk saw her, he said, "God requite thee with good! Indeed, thou hast done well in the quest and hast been subtle in the choice."

All this, O my brother,' continued the merchant, 'befell because the locust had no knowledge of the secret essence that lieth hid in apparent bodies. As for thee, O my brother, (may God requite thee with good!) thou wast subtle in device and usedst precaution; but precaution sufficeth not against fate, and fortune fore-ordained baffleth contrivance. How excellent is the saying of the poet! And he recited the following verses:

It chances whiles that the blind man escapes a pit, Whilst he who is clear of sight falls into it.
The ignorant man may speak with impunity A word that is death to the wise and the ripe of wit.
The true believer is pinched for his daily bread, Whilst infidel rogues enjoy all benefit.
Where is a man's resource and what can he do? It is the Almighty's will; we most submit.

Nor," added the vizier, "is this, O king of the age, more extraordinary or stranger than the story of the king and his chamberlain's wife; nay, the latter is rarer than this and more delightsome."

When the king heard this story, he was fortified in his resolve to spare the vizier and to leave haste in an affair whereof he was not assured; so he comforted him and bade him withdraw to his lodging.

The Twenty-Fourth Night of the Month.

When it was night, the king summoned the vizier and sought of him the hearing of the [promised] story. "Hearkening and obedience," replied Er Rehwan, "Know, O august king, that

STORY OF THE KING AND HIS CHAMBERLAIN'S WIFE.

There was once, of old days and in bygone ages and times, a king of the kings of the Persians, who was passionately addicted to the love of women. His courtiers bespoke him of the wife of a chamberlain of his chamberlains, for that she was endowed with beauty and loveliness and perfection, and this prompted him to go in to her. When she saw him, she knew him and said to him, 'What prompteth the king unto this that he doth?' And he answered, saying, 'Verily, I yearn after thee with an exceeding yearning and needs must I enjoy thy favours.' And he gave her of wealth that after the like whereof women hanker; but she said, 'I cannot do that whereof the king speaketh, for fear of my husband.' And she refused herself to him with the most rigorous of refusals and would not do his desire. So the king went out, full of wrath, and forgot his girdle in the place.

Presently, her husband entered and saw the girdle and knew it. Now he was ware of the king's love for women; so he said to his wife, ' What is this that I see with thee?' Quoth she, 'I will tell thee the truth,' and recounted to him the story; but he believed her not and doubt entered into his heart. As for the king, he passed that night in chagrin and concern, and when it morrowed, he summoned the chamberlain and investing him with the governance of one of his provinces, bade him betake himself thither, purposing, after he should have departed and come to his destination, to foregather with his wife. The chamberlain perceived [his intent] and knew his design; so he answered, saying, 'Hearkening and obedience. I will go and set my affairs in order and give such charges as may be necessary for the welfare of my estate; then will I go about the king's occasion.' And the king said, 'Do this and hasten.'

So the chamberlain went about that which he needed and assembling his wife's kinsfolk, said to them, 'I am resolved to put away my wife.' They took this ill of him and complained of him and summoning him before the king, sat pleading with him. Now the king had no knowledge of that which had passed; so he said to the chamberlain, 'Why wilt thou put her away and how can thy soul consent unto this and why takest thou unto thyself a goodly piece of land and after forsakest it? 'May God amend the king!' answered the husband. 'By Allah, O king, I saw therein the track of the lion and fear to enter the land, lest the lion devour me; and indeed the like of my affair with her is that which befell between the old woman and the draper's wife.' 'What is their story?' asked the king; and the chamberlain said, 'Know, O king, that

STORY OF THE OLD WOMAN AND THE DRAPER'S WIFE.

There was once a man of the drapers, who had a fair wife, and she was curtained [320] and chaste. A certain young man saw her coming forth of the bath and loved her and his heart was occupied with her. So he cast about [to get access to her] with all manner of devices, but availed not to win to her; and when he was weary of endeavour and his patience was exhausted for weariness and his fortitude failed him and he was at an end of his resources against her, he complained of this to an old woman of ill-omen, [321]who promised him to bring about union between him and her. He thanked her for this and promised her all manner of good; and she said to him, "Get thee to her husband and buy of him a turban-cloth of fine linen, and let it be of the goodliest of stuffs."

So he repaired to the draper and buying of him a turban-cloth of lawn, returned with it to the old woman, who took it and burned it in two places. Then she donned devotees' apparel and taking the turban-cloth with her, went to the draper's house and knocked at the door. When the draper's wife saw her, she opened to her and received her kindly and made much of her and welcomed her. So the old woman went in to her and conversed with her awhile. Then said she to her, "[I desire to make] the ablution [preparatory] to prayer." So the wife brought her water and she made the ablution and standing up to pray, prayed and did her occasion. When she had made an end of her prayers, she left the turban-cloth in the place of prayer and went away.

Presently, in came the draper, at the hour of evening prayer, and sitting down in the place where the old woman had prayed, looked about him and espied the turban. He knew it [for that which he had that day sold to the young man] and misdoubted of the case, wherefore anger appeared in his face and he was wroth with his wife and reviled her and abode his day and his night, without speaking to her, what while she knew not the cause of his anger. Then she looked and seeing the turban-cloth before him and noting the traces of burning thereon, understood that his anger was on account of this and concluded that he was wroth because it was burnt.

When the morning morrowed, the draper went out, still angered against his wife, and the old woman returned to her and found her changed of colour, pale of face, dejected and heart-broken. [So she questioned her of the cause of her dejection and she told her how her husband was angered against her (as she supposed) on account of the burns in the turban-cloth.] "O my daughter," rejoined the old woman, "be not concerned; for I have a son, a fine-drawer, and he, by thy life, shall fine-draw [the holes] and restore the turban-cloth as it was. "The wife rejoiced in her saying and said to her, "And when shall this be?" "To-morrow, if it please God the Most High," answered the old woman, "I will bring him to thee, at the time of thy husband's going forth from thee, and he shall mend it and depart forthright." Then she comforted her heart and going forth from her, returned to the young man and told him what had passed.

Now, when the draper saw the turban-cloth, he resolved to put away his wife and waited but till he should get together that which was obligatory on him of the dowry and what not else,[322] for fear of her people. When the old woman arose in the morning, she took the young man and carried him to the draper's house. The wife opened the door to her and the ill-omened old woman entered with him and said to the lady, "Go, fetch that which thou wouldst have fine-drawn and give it to my son." So saying, she locked the door on her, whereupon the young man forced her and did his occasion of her and went forth. Then said the old woman to her, "Know that this is my son and that he loved thee with an exceeding love and was like to lose his life for longing after thee. So I practised on thee with this device and came to thee with this turban-cloth, which is not thy husband's, but my son's. Now have I accomplished my desire; so do thou trust in me and I will put a trick on thy husband for the setting thee right with him, and thou wilt be obedient to me and to him and to my son."[323] And the wife answered, saying, "It is well. Do so."

So the old woman returned to the lover and said to him, "I have skilfully contrived the affair for thee with her; [and now it behoveth us to amend that we have marred]. So go now and sit with the draper and bespeak him of the turban-cloth, [saying, 'The turban-cloth I bought of thee I chanced to burn in two places; so I gave it to a certain old woman, to get mended, and she took it and went away, and I know not her dwelling-place '] When thou seest me pass by, rise and lay hold of me [and demand of me the turban-cloth], to the intent that I may amend her case with her husband and that thou mayst be even with her." So he repaired to the draper's shop and sat down by him and said to him, "Thou knowest the turban-cloth I bought of thee?" "Yes," answered the draper, and the other said, "Knowest thou what is come of it?" "No," replied the husband, and the youth said, "After I bought it of thee, I fumigated myself[324] and it befell that the turban-cloth was burnt in two places. So I gave it to a woman, whose son, they said, was a fine-drawer, and she took it and went away with it; and I know not her abiding-place." When the draper heard this, he misdoubted him [of having wrongly suspected his wife] and marvelled at the story of the turban-cloth, and his mind was set at ease concerning her.

Presently, up came the old woman, whereupon the young man sprang to his feet and laying hold of her, demanded of her the turban-cloth. Quoth she, "Know that I entered one of the houses and made the ablution and prayed in the place of prayer; and I forgot the turban-cloth there and went out. Now I know not the house in which I prayed, nor have I been directed[325] thereto, and I go round about every day till the night, so haply I may light on it, for I know not its owner." When the draper heard this, he said to the old woman, "Verily, Allah restoreth unto thee vhat which thou hast lost. Rejoice, for the turban-cloth is with me and in my house." And he arose forthright and gave her the turban-cloth, as it was. She gave it to the young man, and the draper made his peace with his wife and gave her raiment and jewellery, [by way of peace-offering], till she was content and her heart was appeased. [326]

When the king heard his chamberlain's story, he was confounded and abashed and said to him, 'Abide on thy wonted service and till thy land, for that the lion entered it, but marred it not, and he will never more return thither.'[327] Then he bestowed on him a dress of honour and made him a sumptuous present; and the man returned to his wife and people, rejoicing and glad, for that his heart was set at rest concerning his wife. Nor," added the vizier, "O king of the age, is this rarer or more extraordinary than the story of the fair and lovely woman, endowed with amorous grace, with the foul-favoured man."

When the king heard the vizier's speech, he deemed it goodly and it pleased him; so he bade him go away to his house, and there he abode his day long.

The Twenty-fifth Night of the Month.

When the evening evened, the king summoned his vizier and bade him tell the [promised] story. So he said, "It is well. Know, O king, that

STORY OF THE FOUL-FAVOURED MAN AND HIS FAIR WIFE.

There was once a man of the Arabs who had a number of sons, and amongst them a boy, never was seen a fairer than he of favour nor a more accomplished in loveliness, no, nor a more perfect of wit. When he came to man's estate, his father married him to the daughter of one of his uncles, and she excelled not in beauty, neither was she praiseworthy of attributes; wherefore she pleased not the youth, but he bore with her, for kinship's sake.

One day, he went forth in quest of certain stray camels of his and fared on all his day and night till eventide, when he [came to an Arab encampment and] was fain to seek hospitality of one of the inhabitants. So he alighted at one of the tents of the camp and there came forth to him a man of short stature and loathly aspect, who saluted him and lodging him in a corner of the tent, sat entertaining him with talk, the goodliest that might be. When his food was dressed, the Arab's wife brought it to the guest, and he looked at the mistress of the tent and saw a favour than which no goodlier might be. Indeed, her beauty and grace and symmetry amazed him and he abode confounded, looking now at her and now at her husband. When his looking grew long, the man said to him, 'Harkye, O son of the worthy! Occupy thyself with thine own concerns, for by me and this woman hangeth a rare story, that is yet goodlier than that which thou seest of her beauty; and when we have made an end of our food, I will tell it thee.'

So, when they had made an end of eating and drinking, the young man asked his host for the story, and he said, 'Know that in my youth I was even as thou seest me in the matter of loathliness and foul favour; and I had brethren of the comeliest of the folk; wherefore my father preferred them over me and used to show them kindness, to my exclusion, and employ me, in their room [in menial service], like as one employeth slaves. One day, a she-camel of his went astray and he said to me, "Go thou forth in quest of her and return not but with her." Quoth I, "Send other than I of thy sons." But he would not consent to this and reviled me and insisted upon me, till the matter came to such a pass with him that he took a whip and fell to beating me. So I arose and taking a riding-camel, mounted her and sallied forth at a venture, purposing to go out into the deserts and return to him no more. I fared on all my night [and the next day] and coming at eventide to [the encampment of] this my wife's people, alighted down with her father, who was a very old man, and became his guest.

When the night was half spent, I arose [and went forth the tent] to do an occasion of mine, and none knew of my case save this woman. The dogs misdoubted of me and followed me and gave not over besetting me, till I fell on my back into a deep pit, wherein was water, and one of the dogs fell in with me. The woman, who was then a girl in the first bloom of youth, full of strength and spirit, was moved to pity on me, for that wherein I was fallen, and coming to me with a rope, said to me, "Lay hold of this rope." So I laid hold of the rope and clung to it and she pulled me up; but, when I was halfway up, I pulled her [down] and she fell with me into the pit; and there we abode three days, she and I and the dog.

When her people arose in the morning and saw her not, they sought her in the camp, but, finding her not and missing me also, doubted not but she had fled with me. Now she had four brothers, as they were falcons, and they mounted and dispersed in quest of us. When the day dawned [on the fourth morning], the dog began to bark and the other dogs answered him and coming to the mouth of the pit, stood howling to him. My wife's father, hearing the howling of the dogs, came up and standing at the brink of the pit, [looked in and] beheld a marvel. Now he was a man of valour and understanding, an elder versed[328] in affairs so he fetched a rope and bringing us both forth, questioned us of our case. I told him all that had betided and he abode pondering the affair.

Presently, her brothers returned, whereupon the old man acquainted them with the whole case and said to them, "O my sons, know that your sister purposed not aught but good, and if ye slay this man, ye will earn abiding reproach and ye will wrong him, ay, and wrong yourselves and your sister, to boot; for indeed there appeareth no cause [of offence] such as calleth for slaughter, and it may not be denied that this incident is a thing the like whereof may well betide and that he may well have been baffled by the like of this chance." Then he turned to me and questioned me of my lineage; so I set forth to him my genealogy and he said, "A man of equal rank, honourable [and] understanding." And he offered me [his daughter in] marriage. I consented to him of this and marrying her, took up my abode with him and God the Most High hath opened on me the gates of weal and fortune, so that I am become the most abounding in substance of the folk of the tribe; and He hath stablished me in that which He hath given me of His bounties.'

The young man marvelled at his story and lay the night with him; and when he arose in the morning, he found his strays. So he took them and returning [to his family.], acquainted them with what he had seen and that which had betided him. Nor," added the vizier, "is this more marvellous or rarer than the story of the king who lost kingdom and wealth and wife and children and God restored them unto him and requited him with a kingdom more magnificent than that which he had lost and goodlier and rarer and greater of wealth and elevation."

The vizier's story pleased the king and he bade depart to his dwelling.

The Twenty-Sixth Night of the Month.

When came the night, the king summoned his vizier and bade him tell the story of the king who lost kingdom and wife and wealth. "Hearkening and obedience," replied Er Rehwan. "Know, O king, that

STORY OF THE KING WHO LOST KINGDOM AND WIFE AND WEALTH AND GOD RESTORED THEM TO HIM.

There was once a king of the kings of Hind, who was goodly of polity, praiseworthy in administration, just to his subjects, beneficent to men of learning and piety and asceticism and devoutness and worship and shunning traitors and froward folk and those of lewc life. On this wise of polity he abode in his kingship what God the Most High willed of days and hours and years, and he married the daughter of his father's brother, a beautiful and lovesome woman, endowed with brightness and perfection, who had been reared in the king's house in splendour and delight. She bore him two sons, the comeliest that might be of boys. Then came fore-ordained fate, which there is no warding off, and God the Most High raised up against the king another king, who came forth upon his realm, and all the folk of the city, who had a mind unto evil and lewdness, joined themselves unto him. So he fortified himself against the king and made himself master of his kingdom, putting his troops to the rout and slaying his guards.

The king took his wife, the mother of his sons, and what he might [of good] and saved himself and fled in the darkness of the night, unknowing whither he should go. When travel grew sore upon them, there met them robbers by the way, who took all that was with them, [even to their clothes], so that there was left unto each of them but a shirt and trousers; yea, they left them without victual or camels or [other] riding-cattle, and they ceased not to fare on afoot, till they came to a coppice, to wit, a garden of trees, on the shore of the sea. Now the road which they would have followed was crossed by an arm of the sea, but it was scant of water. So, when they came to that place, the king took up one of his children and fording the water with him, set him down on the other bank and returned for his other son. Him also he set by his brother and returning for their mother, took her up and passing the water with her, came to the place [where he had left his children], but found them not. Then he looked at the midst of the island and saw there an old man and an old woman, engaged in making themselves a hut of reeds. So he put down his wife over against them and set off in quest of his children, but none gave him news of them and he went round about right and left, but found not the place where they were.

Now the children had entered the coppice, to make water, and there was there a forest of trees, wherein, if a horseman entered, he might wander by the week, [before finding his way out], for none knew the first thereof from the last. So the boys entered therein and knew not how they should return and went astray in that wood, to an end that was willed of God the Most High, whilst their father sought them, but found them not. So he returned to their mother and they abode weeping for their children. As for these latter, when they entered the wood, it swallowed them up and they went wandering in it many days, knowing not where they had entered, till they came forth, at another side, upon the open country.

Meanwhile, the king and queen abode in the island, over against the old man and woman, and ate of the fruits that were in the island and drank of its waters, till, one day, as they sat, there came a ship and moored to the side of the island, to fill up with water, whereupon they[329] looked at each other and spoke. The master of the ship was a Magian and all that was therein, both men and goods, belonged to him, for that he was a merchant and went round about the world. Now covetise deluded the old man, the owner of the island, and he went up [into the ship] and gave the Magian news of the king's wife, setting out to him her charms, till he made him yearn unto her and his soul prompted him to use treachery and practise upon her and take her from her hnsband. So he sent to her, saying, 'With us in the ship is a woman with child, and we fear lest she be delivered this night. Hast thou skill in the delivering of women?' And she answered, 'Yes.' Now it was the last of the day; so he sent to her to come up into the ship and deliver the woman, for that the pangs of labour were come upon her; and he promised her clothes and spending-money. Accordingly, she embarked in all assurance, with a heart at ease for herself, and transported her gear to the ship; but no sooner was she come thither than the anchors were weighed and the canvas spread and the ship set sail.

When the king saw this, he cried out and his wife wept in the ship and offered to cast herself into the sea; but the Magian bade the sailors lay hands on her. So they seized her and it was but a little while ere the night darkened and the ship disappeared from the king's eyes; whereupon he swooned away for excess of weeping and lamentation and passed his night bewailing his wife and children.

When the morning morrowed, he recited the following verses:

> How long, O Fate, wilt thou oppress and baffle me?
> Tell me, was ever yet a mortal spared of thee?
> Behold, my loved ones all are ta'en from me away.
> They left me and content forthright forsook my heart,
> Upon that day my loves my presence did depart;
> My pleasant life for loss of friends is troubled aye.
> By Allah, I knew not their worth nor yet how dear
> A good it is to have one's loved ones ever near,
> Until they left my heart on fire without allay.
> Ne'er shall I them forget, nay, nor the day they went
> And left me all forlorn, to pine for languishment,
> My severance to bewail in torment and dismay.
> I make a vow to God, if ever day or night
> The herald of good news my hearing shall delight,
> Announcing the return o' th' absent ones,
> I'll lay Upon their threshold's dust my cheeks and to my soul,
> "Take comfort, for the loved are come again,"
> I'll say. If for my loved ones' loss I rent my heart for do e,
> Before I rent my clothes, reproach me not, I pray.

He abode weeping for the loss of his wife and children till the morning, when he went forth wandering at a venture, knowing not what he should do, and gave not over faring along the sea-shore days and nights, unknowing whither he went and taking no food therein other than the herbs of the earth and seeing neither man nor beast nor other living thing, till his travel brought him to the top of a mountain. He took up his sojourn in the mountain and abode there [awhile] alone, eating of its fruits and drinking of its waters. Then he came down thence and fared on along the high road three days, at the end of which time he came upon tilled fields and villages and gave not over going till he sighted a great city on the shore of the sea and came to the gate thereof at the last of the day. The gatekeepers suffered him not to enter; so he abode his night anhungred, and when he arose in the morning, be sat down hard by the gate.

Now the king of the city was dead and had left no son, and the townsfolk fell out concerning who should be king over them: and their sayings differed and their counsels, so that turmoil was like to betide between them by reason of this. At last, after long dissension, they came to an accord and agreed to leave the choice to the late king's elephant and that he unto whom he consented should be king and that they would not contest the commandment with him. So they made oath of this and on the morrow, they brought out the elephant and came forth to the utterward of the city; nor was there man or woman left in the place but was present at that time. Then they adorned the elephant and setting up the throne on his back, gave him the crown in his trunk; and he went round about examining the faces of the folk, but stopped not with any of them till he came to the banished king, the forlorn, the exile, him who had lost his children and his wife, when he prostrated himself to him and placing the crown on his head, took him up and set him on his back.

Thereupon the folk all prostrated themselves and gave one another joy of this and the drums of good tidings beat before him, and he entered the city [and went on] till he came to the House of Justice and the audience-hall of the palace and sat down on the throne of the kingdom, with the crown on his head; whereupon the folk came in to him to give him joy and offer up prayers for him. Then he addressed himself, after his wont in the kingship, to ordering the affairs of the folk and ranging the troops according to their ranks and looking into their affairs and those of all the people. Moreover, he released those who were in the prisons and abolished the customs dues and gave dresses of honour and bestowed gifts and largesse and conferred favours on the amirs and viziers and dignitaries, and the chamberlains and deputies presented themselves before him and did him homage. So the people of the city rejoiced in him and said, 'Indeed this is none other than a king of the greatest of the kings.'

Moreover, he assembled the sages and the theologians and the sons of the kings and devised with them and asked them questions and problems and examined with them into many things of all fashions that might direct him to well-doing in the kingly office; and he questioned them also of subtleties and religious obligations and of the laws of the kingdom and the fashions of administration and of that which it behoveth the king to do of looking into the affairs of the people and repelling the enemy [from the realm] and fending off his malice with war; wherefore the people's contentment redoubled and their joy in that which God the Most High had vouchsafed them of his elevation to the kingship over them. So he upheld the ordinance of the realm and the affairs thereof abode established upon the accepted customs.

Now the late king had left a wife and a daughter, and the people would fain have married the latter to the new king, to the intent that the kingship might not pass out of the old royal family. So they proposed to him that he should take her to wife, and he promised them this, but put them off from him,[330] of his respect for the covenant he had made with his former wife, to wit, that he would take none other to wife than herself. Then he betook himself to fasting by day and standing up by night [to pray], giving alms galore and beseeching God (extolled be His perfection and exalted be He!) to reunite him with his children and his wife, the daughter of his father's brother.

When a year had elapsed, there came to the city a ship, wherein were merchants and goods galore. Now it was of their usance, from time immemorial, that, when there came a ship to the city, the king sent unto it such of his servants as he trusted in, who took charge of the goods, so they might be [first of all] shown to the king, who bought such of them as befitted him and gave the merchants leave to sell the rest. So he sent, as of wont, one who should go up to the ship and seal up the goods and set over them who should keep watch over them.

To return to the queen his wife. When the Magian fled with her, he proffered himself to her and lavished unto her wealth galore, but she rejected his suit and was like to slay herself for chagrin at that which had befallen and for grief for her separation from her husband. Moreover, she refused meat and drink and offered to cast herself into the sea; but the Magian shackled her and straitened her and clad her in a gown of wool and said to her, 'I will continue thee in misery and abjection till thou obey me and consent to my wishes.' So she took patience and looked for God to deliver her from the hand of that accursed one; and she ceased not to travel with him from place to place till he came with her to the city wherein her husband was king and his goods were put under seal.

Now the woman was in a chest and two youths of the pages of the late king, who were now in the new king's service, were those who had been charged with the guardianship of the vessel and the goods. When the evening evened on them, the two youths fell a-talking and recounted that which had befallen them in their days of childhood and the manner of the going forth of their father and mother from their country and royal estate, whenas the wicked overcame their land, and [called to mind] how they had gone astray in the forest and how fate had made severance between them and their parents; brief, they recounted their story, from beginning to end. When the woman heard their talk, she knew that they were her very sons and cried out to them from the chest, saying, 'I am your mother such an one, and the token between you and me is thus and thus.' The young men knew the token and falling upon the chest, broke the lock and brought out their mother, who strained them to her breast, and they fell upon her and swooned away, all three.

When they came to themselves, they wept awhile and the folk assembled about them, marvelling at that which they saw, and questioned them of their case. So the young men vied with each other who should be the first to discover the story to the folk; and when the Magian saw this, he came up, crying out, 'Alas!' and 'Woe worth the day!' and said to them, 'Why have ye broken open my chest? I had in it jewels and ye have stolen them, and this damsel is my slave-girl and she hath agreed with you upon a device to take the good.' Then he rent his clothes and called aloud for succour, saying, 'I appeal to God and to the just king, so he may quit me of these wrong-doing youths!' Quoth they, 'This is our mother and thou stolest her.' Then words waxed many between them and the folk plunged into talk and prate and discussion concerning their affair and that of the [pretended] slave-girl, and the strife waxed amain between them, so that [at last] they carried them up to the king.

When the two young men presented themselves before him and set forth their case to him and to the folk and the king heard their speech, he knew them and his heart was like to fly for joyance in them: the tears poured from his eyes at their sight and that of his wife, and he thanked God the

Most High and praised Him for that He had reunited [him with] them. Then he dismissed the folk who were present about him and bade commit the Magian and the woman and the two youths to his armoury[331] [for the night], commanding that they should keep guard over them till God caused the morning morrow, so he might assemble the cadis and the judges and assessors and judge between them, according to the Holy Law, in the presence of the four cadis. So they did his bidding and the king passed the night praying and praising God the Most High for that which He had vouchsafed him of kingship and puissance and victory over[332] him who had wronged him and thanking Him who had reunited him with his family.

When the morning morrowed, he assembled the cadis and judges and assessors and sending for the Magian and the two youths and their mother, questioned them of their case, whereupon the two young men began and said, 'We are the sons of the king Such-an-one and enemies and wicked men got the mastery of out realm; so our father fled forth with us and wandered at a venture, for fear of the enemies.' [And they recounted to him all that had betided them, from beginning to end.] Quoth he, 'Ye tell a marvellous story; but what hath [Fate] done with your father?' 'We know not how fortune dealt with him after our loss,' answered they; and he was silent.

Then he turned to the woman and said to her, 'And thou, what sayst thou?' So she expounded to him her case and recounted to him all that had betided her and her husband, first and last, up to the time when they took up their abode with the old man and woman who dwelt on the sea-shore. Then she set out that which the Magian had practised on her of knavery and how he had carried her off in the ship and all that had betided her of humiliation and torment, what while the cadis and judges and deputies hearkened to her speech. When the king heard the last of his wife's story, he said, 'Verily, there hath betided thee a grievous matter; but hast thou knowledge of what thy husband did and what came of his affair?' 'Nay, by Allah,' answered she; 'I have no knowledge of him, save that I leave him no hour unremembered in fervent prayer, and never, whilst I live, will he cease to be to me the father of my children and my father's brother's son and my flesh and my blood.' Then she wept and the king bowed his head, whilst his eyes brimmed over with tears at her story.

Then he raised his head to the Magian and said to him, 'Say thy say, thou also.' So the Magian said, 'This is my slave-girl, whom I bought with my money from such a land and for so many dinars, and I made her my favourite[333] and loved her with an exceeding love and gave her charge over my good; but she betrayed me in my substance and plotted with one of my servants to slay me, tempting him by promising him that she would be his wife. When I knew this of her and was certified that she purposed treason against me, I awoke [from my heedlessness] and did with her that which I did, of fear for myself from her craft and perfidy; for indeed she is a beguiler with her tongue and she hath taught these two youths this pretence, by way of trickery and of her perfidy and malice: so be thou not deluded by her and by her talk.'

'Thou liest, O accursed one,' cried the king and bade lay hands on him and clap him in irons. Then he turned to the two youths, his sons, and strained them to his breast, weeping sore and saying, 'O all ye who are present of cadis and assessors and officers of state, know that these twain are my sons and that this is my wife and the daughter of my father's brother; for that I was king aforetime in such a region.' And he recounted to them his history from beginning to end, nor is there aught of profit in repetition; whereupon the folk cried out with weeping and lamentation for the stress of that which they heard of marvellous chances and that rare story. As for the king's wife, he caused carry her into his palace and lavished upon her and upon her sons all that behoved and beseemed them of bounties, whilst the folk flocked to offer up prayers for him and give him joy of [his reunion with] his wife and children.

When they had made an end of pious wishes and congratulations, they besought the king to hasten the punishment of the Magian and heal their hearts of him with torment and humiliation. So he appointed them for a day on which they should assemble to witness his punishment and that which should betide him of torment, and shut himself up with his wife and sons and abode thus private with them three days, during which time they were sequestered from the folk. On the fourth day the king entered the bath, and coming forth, sat down on the throne of his kingship, with the crown on his head, whereupon the folk came in to him, according to their wont and after the measure of their several ranks and degrees, and the amirs and viziers entered, ay, and the chamberlains and deputies and captains and men of war and the falconers and armbearers. Then he seated his two sons, one on his right and the other on his left hand, whilst all the folk stood before him and lifted up their voices in thanksgiving to God the

Most High and glorification of Him and were strenuous in prayer for the king and in setting forth his virtues and excellences.

He returned them the most gracious of answers and bade carry the Magian forth of the town and set him on a high scaffold that had been builded for him there; and he said to the folk, 'Behold, I will torture him with all kinds of fashions of torment.' Then he fell to telling them that which he had wrought of knavery with the daughter of his father's brother and what he had caused betide her of severance between her and her husband and how he had required her of herself, but she had sought refuge against him with God (to whom belong might and majesty) and chose rather humiliation than yield to his wishes, notwithstanding stress of torment; neither recked she aught of that which he lavished to her of wealth and raiment and jewels.

When the king had made an end of his story, he bade the bystanders spit in the Magian's face and curse him; and they did this. Then he bade cut out his tongue and on the morrow he bade cut off his ears and nose and pluck out his eyes. On the third day he bade cut off his hands and on the fourth his feet; and they ceased not to lop him limb from limb, and each member they cast into the fire, after its cutting-off, before his face, till his soul departed, after he had endured torments of all kinds and fashions. The king bade crucify his trunk on the city-wall three days' space; after which he let burn it and reduce its ashes to powder and scatter them abroad in the air.

Then the king summoned the cadi and the witnesses and bade them many the old king's daughter and sister to his own sons; so they married them, after the king had made a bride-feast three days and displayed their brides to them from eventide to peep of day. Then the two princes went in to their brides and did away their maidenhead and loved them and were vouchsafed children by them.

As for the king their father, he abode with his wife, their mother, what while God (to whom belong might and majesty) willed, and they rejoiced in reunion with each other. The kingship endured unto them and glory and victory, and the king continued to rule with justice and equity, so that the people loved him and still invoked on him and on his sons length of days and durance; and they lived the most delightsome of lives till there came to them the Destroyer of Delights and Sunderer of Companies, He who layeth waste the palaces and peopleth the tombs; and this is all that hath come down to us of the story of the king and his wife and children. Nor," added the vizier, "if this story be a solace and a diversion, is it pleasanter or more diverting than that of the young man of Khorassan and his mother and sister."

When King Shah Bekht heard this story, it pleased him and he bade the vizier go away to his own house.

The Twenty-Seventh Night of the Month

When the evening came, the king bade fetch the vizier; so he presented himself before him and the king bade him tell the [promised] story. So he said, "Hearkening and obedience. Know, O king (but God alone knoweth His secret purpose and is versed in all that is past and was foredone among bygone peoples), that

STORY OF SELIM AND SELMA.

There was once, in the parts of Khorassan, a man of the affluent of the country, who was a merchant of the chiefest of the merchants and was blessed with two children, a son and a daughter. He was assiduous in rearing them and making fair their education, and they grew up and throve after the goodliest fashion. He used to teach the boy, who taught his sister all that he learnt, so that the girl became perfect in the knowledge of the Traditions of the Prophet and in polite letters, by means of her brother. Now the boy's name was Selim and that of the girl Selma. When they grew up and waxed, their father built them a mansion beside his own and lodged them apart therein and appointed them slave-girls and servants to tend them and assigned unto each of them pensions and allowances and all that they needed of high and low, meat and bread and wine and raiment and vessels and what not else. So Selim and Selma abode in that mansion, as they were one soul in two bodies, and they used to sleep on one couch; and rooted in each one's heart was love and affection and familiar friendship [for the other of them].

One night, when the night was half spent, as Selim and Selma sat talking and devising with each other, they heard a noise below the house; so they looked out from a lattice that gave upon the gate of their father's mansion and saw a man of goodly presence, whose clothes were hidden by a wide cloak, which covered him. He came up to the gate and laying hold of the door-ring, gave a light knock; whereupon the door opened and out came their sister, with a lighted flambeau, and after her their mother, who saluted the stranger and embraced him, saying, 'O beloved of my heart and light of mine eyes and fruit of mine entrails, enter.' So he entered and shut the door, whilst Selim and Selma abode amazed.

Then Selim turned to Selma and said to her, 'O sister mine, how deemest thou of this calamity and what counsellest thou thereanent?' 'O my brother,' answered she, 'indeed I know not what I shall say concerning the like of this; but he is not disappointed who seeketh direction [of God], nor doth he repent who taketh counsel. One getteth not the better of the traces of burning by[334] haste, and know that this is an affliction that hath descended on us; and we have need of management to do it away, yea, and contrivance to wash withal our shame from our faces.' And they gave not over watching the gate till break of day, when the young man opened the door and their mother took leave of him; after which he went his way and she entered, she and her handmaid.

Then said Selim to his sister, 'Know that I am resolved to slay yonder man, if he return this next night, and I will say to the folk, "He was a thief," and none shall know that which hath befallen. Moreover, I will address myself to the slaughter of whosoever knoweth that which is between yonder fellow and my mother.' But Selma said, ' I fear lest, if thou slay him in our dwelling-place and he savour not of robberhood,[335] suspicion will revert upon ourselves, and we cannot be assured but that he belongeth unto folk whose mischief is to be feared and their hostility dreaded,[336] and thus wilt thou have fled from privy shame to open shame and abiding public dishonour.' 'How then deemest thou we should do?' asked Selim and she said, 'Is there nothing for it but to slay him? Let us not hasten unto slaughter, for that the slaughter of a soul without just cause is a grave [matter].'

(When Shehriyar heard this, he said in himself, 'By Allah, I have indeed been reckless in the slaying of women and girls, and praised be God who hath occupied me with this damsel from the slaughter of souls, for that the slaughter of souls is a grave [matter!] By Allah, if Shah Bekht spare the vizier, I will assuredly spare Shehrzad!' Then he gave ear to the story and heard her say to her sister:)

Quoth Selma to Selim, 'Hasten not to slay him, but ponder the matter and consider the issue to which it may lead; for whoso considereth not the issues [of his actions], fortune is no friend to him.' Then they arose on the morrow and occupied themselves with devising how they should turn away their mother from that man, and she forebode mischief from them, by reason of that which she saw in their eyes of alteration, for that she was keen of wit and crafty. So she took precaution for herself against her children and Selma said to Selim, 'Thou seest that whereinto we have fallen through this woman, and indeed she hath gotten wind of our purpose and knoweth that we have discovered her secret. So, doubtless, she will plot against us the like of that which we plot for her; for indeed up to now she had concealed her affair, and now she will forge lies against us; wherefore, methinks, there is a thing [fore-]written to us, whereof God (extolled be His perfection and exalted be He!) knew in His foreknowledge and wherein He executeth His ordinances.' 'What is that?' asked he, and she said, 'It is that we arise, I and thou, and go forth this night from this land and seek us a land wherein we may live and witness nought of the doings of yonder traitress; for whoso is absent from the eye is absent from the heart, and quoth one of the poets in the following verse:

Twere better and meeter thy presence to leave, For, if the eye see not, the heart doth not grieve.'

Quoth Selim to her, 'It is for thee to decide and excellent is that which thou counsellest; so let us do this, in the name of God the Most High, trusting in Him for grace and guidance.' So they arose and took the richest of their clothes and the lightest of that which was in their treasuries of jewels and things of price and gathered together a great matter. Then they equipped them ten mules and hired them servants of other than the people of the country; and Selim bade his sister Selma don man's apparel. Now she was the likest of all creatures to him, so that, [when she was clad in man's attire,] the folk knew no difference between them, extolled be the perfection of Him who hath no like, there is no God but He! Then he bade her mount a horse, whilst he himself bestrode another, and they set out, under cover of the night. None of their family nor of the people of their house knew of them; so they fared on into the wide world of God and gave not over going night and day two months' space, at the end of which time they came to a city on the sea-shore of the land of Mekran, by name Es Sherr, and it is the first city in Sind.

They lighted down without the place and when they arose in the morning, they saw a populous and goodly city, fair of seeming and great, abounding in trees and streams and fruits and wide of suburbs. So the young man said to his sister Selma, 'Abide thou here in thy place, till I enter the city and examine it and make assay of its people and seek out a place which we may buy and whither we may remove. If it befit us, we will take up our abode therein, else will we take counsel of departing elsewhither.' Quoth she, 'Do this, trusting in the bounty of God (to whom belong might and majesty) and in His blessing.'

So he took a belt, wherein were a thousand dinars, and binding it about his middle, entered the city and gave not over going round about its streets and markets and gazing upon its houses and sitting with those of its folk whose aspect bespoke them men of worth, till the day was half spent, when he resolved to return to his sister and said in himself, 'Needs must I buy what we may eat of ready-[dressed] food] I and my sister.' Accordingly, he accosted a man who sold roast meat and who was clean [of person], though odious in his [means of getting a] living, and said to him, 'Take the price of this dish [of meat] and add thereto of fowls and chickens and what not else is in your market of meats and sweetmeats and bread and arrange it in dishes.' So the cook set apart for him what he desired and calling a porter, laid it in his basket, and Selim paid the cook the price of his wares, after the fullest fashion.

As he was about to go away, the cook said to him, 'O youth, doubtless thou art a stranger?' And he answered, 'Yes.' Quoth the cook, 'It is reported in one of the Traditions [of the Prophet that he said,] "Loyal admonition is [a part] of religion;" and the understanding say, "Admonition is of the characteristics of the true believers." And indeed that which I have seen of thy fashions pleaseth me and I would fain give thee a warning.' 'Speak out thy warning,' rejoined Selim, 'and may God strengthen thine affair!' Then said the cook, 'Know, O my son, that in this our country, whenas a stranger entereth therein and eateth of flesh-meat and drinketh not old wine thereon, this is harmful unto him and engendereth in him dangerous disorders. Wherefore, if thou have provided thee somewhat thereof,[337] [it is well;] but, if not, look thou procure it, ere thou take the meat and carry it away.' 'May God requite thee with good!' rejoined Selim. 'Canst thou direct me where it is sold?' And the cook said, 'With me is all that thou seekest thereof.' 'Is there a way for me to see it?' asked the young man; and the cook sprang up and said, 'Pass on.' So he entered and the cook showed him somewhat of wine; but he said, 'I desire better than this.' Whereupon he opened a door and entering, said to Selim, 'Enter and follow me.'

Selim followed him till he brought him to an underground chamber and showed him somewhat of wine that was to his mind. So he occupied him with looking upon it and taking him at unawares, sprang upon him from behind and cast him to the earth and sat upon his breast. Then he drew a knife and set it to his jugular; whereupon there betided Selim [that wherewithal] God made him forget all that He had decreed [unto him],[338] and he said to the cook, 'Why dost thou this thing, O man? Be mindful of God the Most High and fear Him. Seest thou not that I am a stranger? And indeed [I have left] behind me a defenceless woman. Why wilt thou slay me?' Quoth the cook, 'Needs must I slay thee, so I may take thy good.' And Selim said, 'Take my good, but slay me not, neither enter into sin against me; and do with me kindness, for that the taking of my money is lighter[339] than the taking of my life.'

'This is idle talk,' answered the cook. 'Thou canst not deliver thyself with this, O youth, for that in thy deliverance is my destruction.' Quoth Selim, 'I swear to thee and give thee the covenant of God (to whom belong might and majesty) and His bond, that He took of His prophets, that I will not discover thy secret ever.' But the cook answered, saying, 'Away! Away! This may no wise be.' However, Selim ceased not to conjure him and make supplication to him and weep, while the cook persisted in his intent to slaughter him. Then he wept and recited the following verses:

Haste not to that thou dost desire, for haste is still unblest; Be merciful to men, as thou on mercy reckonest;
For no hand is there but the hand of God is over it And no oppressor but shall be with worse than he opprest.

Quoth the cook, 'Nothing will serve but I must slay thee, O fellow; for, if I spare thee, I shall myself be slain.' But Selim said, 'O my brother, I will counsel thee somewhat[340] other than this.' 'What is it?' asked the cook. 'Say and be brief, ere I cut thy throat' And Selim said, '[Do thou suffer me to live and] keep me, that I may be a servant unto thee, and I will work at a craft, of the crafts of the skilled workmen, wherefrom there shall return to thee every day two dinars.' Quoth the cook, 'What is the craft?' and Selim said, 'The cutting [and polishing] of jewels.'

When the cook heard this, he said in himself, 'It will do me no hurt if I imprison him and shackle him and bring him what he may work at. If he tell truth, I will let him live, and if he prove a liar, I will slay him.' So he took a pair of stout shackles and clapping them on Selim's legs, imprisoned him within his house and set over him one who should guard him. Then he questioned him of what tools he needed to work withal. Selim set forth to him that which he required, and the cook went out from him and presently returning, brought him all he needed. So Selim sat and wrought at his craft; and he used every day to earn two dinars; and this was his wont and usance with the cook, whilst the latter fed him not but half his fill.

To return to his sister Selma. She awaited him till the last of the day, but he came not; and she awaited him a second day and a third and a fourth, yet there came no news of him, wherefore she wept and beat with her hands on her breast and bethought her of her affair and her strangerhood and her brother's absence; and she recited the following verses:

Peace on thee! Would our gaze might light on thee once more! So should our hearts be eased and eyes no longer sore.
Thou only art the whole of our desire; indeed Thy love is hid within our hearts' most secret core.

She abode awaiting him thus till the end of the month, but discovered no tidings of him neither happened upon aught of his trace; wherefore she was troubled with an exceeding perturbation and despatching her servants hither and thither in quest of him, abode in the sorest that might be of grief and concern. When it was the beginning of the new month, she arose in the morning and bidding cry him throughout the city, sat to receive visits of condolence, nor was there any in the city but betook himself to her, to condole with her; and they were all concerned for her, nothing doubting but she was a man.

When three nights had passed over her with their days of the second month, she despaired of him and her tears dried not up. Then she resolved to take up her abode in the city and making choice of a dwelling, removed thither. The folk resorted to her from all parts, to sit with her and hearken to her speech and witness her good breeding; nor was it but a little while ere the king of the city died and the folk fell out concerning whom they should invest with the kingship after him, so that strife was like to betide between them. However, the men of judgment and understanding and the folk of experience counselled them to make the youth king who had lost his brother, for that they doubted not but Selma was a man. They all consented unto this and betaking themselves to Selma, proffered her the kingship. She refused, but they were instant with her, till she consented, saying in herself, 'My sole desire in [accepting] the kingship is [to find] my brother.' Then they seated her on the throne of the kingdom and set the crown on her head, whereupon she addressed herself to the business of administration and to the ordinance of the affairs of the people; and they rejoiced in her with the utmost joy.

Meanwhile, Selim abode with the cook a whole year's space, earning him two dinars every day; and when his affair was prolonged, the cook inclined unto him and took compassion on him, on condition that, if he let him go, he should not discover his fashion to the Sultan, for that it was his wont every little while to entrap a man and carry him to his house and slay him and take his money and cook his flesh and give it to the folk to eat. So he said to him, 'O youth, wilt thou that I release thee from this thy plight, on condition that thou be reasonable and discover not aught of thine affair ever?' And Selim answered, 'I will swear to thee by whatsoever oath thou choosest that I will keep thy secret and will not speak one syllable against thy due, what while I abide on life.' Quoth the cook, 'I purpose to send thee forth with my brother and cause thee travel with him on the sea, on condition that thou be unto him a boughten slave; and when he cometh to the land of Hind, he shall sell thee and thus wilt thou be delivered from prison and slaughter.' And Selim said, 'It is well: be it as thou sayst, may God the Most High requite thee with good!'

Therewithal the cook equipped his brother and freighting him a ship, embarked therein merchandise. Then he committed Selim unto him and they set out and departed with the ship. God decreed them safety, so that they arrived [in due course] at the first city [of the land of Hind], the which is known as El Mensoureh, and cast anchor there. Now the king of that city had died, leaving a daughter and a widow, who was the quickest-witted of women and gave out that the girl was a boy, so that the kingship might be stablished unto them. The troops and the amirs doubted not but that the case was as she avouched and that the princess was a male child; so they obeyed her and the queen mother took order for the matter and used to dress the girl in man's apparel and seat her on the throne of the kingship, so that the folk might see her. Accordingly, the grandees of the kingdom and the chief officers of the realm used to go in to her and salute her and do her service and go away, nothing doubting but she was a boy.

On this wise they abode months and years and the queen-mother ceased not to do thus till the cook's brother came to the town in his ship, and with him Selim. So he landed with the youth and showed him to the queen, [that she might buy him]. When she saw him, she augured well of him; so she bought him from the cook's brother and was kind to him and entreated him with honour. Then she fell to proving him in his parts and making assay of him in his affairs and found in him all that is in kings' sons of understanding and breeding and goodly manners and qualities.

So she sent for him in private and said to him, 'I purpose to do thee a service, so thou canst but keep a secret.' He promised her all that she desired and she discovered to him her secret in the matter of her daughter, saying, 'I will marry thee to her and commit to thee the governance of her affair and make thee king and ruler over this city.' He thanked her and promised to uphold all that she should order him, and she said to him, 'Go forth to such an one of the neighbouring provinces privily.' So he went forth and on the morrow she made ready bales and gear and presents and bestowed on him a great matter, all of which they loaded on the backs of camels.

Then she gave out among the folk that the king's father's brother's son was come and bade the grandees and troops go forth to meet him. Moreover, she decorated the city in his honour and the drums of good tidings beat for him, whilst all the king's household [went out to meet him and] dismounting before him, [escorted him to the city and] lodged him with the queen-mother in her palace. Then she bade the chiefs of the state attend his assembly; so they presented themselves before him and saw of his breeding and accomplishments that which amazed them and made them forget the breeding of those who had foregone him of the kings.

When they were grown familiar with him, the queen-mother fell to sending [privily] for the amirs, one by one, and swearing them to secrecy; and when she was assured of their trustworthiness, she discovered to them that the king had left but a daughter and that she had done this but that she might continue the kingship in his family and that the governance should not go forth from them; after which she told them that she was minded to marry her daughter with the new-comer, her father's brother's son, and that he should be the holder of the kingship. They approved of her proposal and when she had discovered the secret to the last of them [and assured herself of their support], she published the news abroad and sent for the cadis and assessors, who drew up the contract of marriage between Selim and the princess, and they lavished gifts upon the troops and overwhelmed them with bounties. Then was the bride carried in procession to the young man and the kingship was stablished unto him and the governance of the realm.

On this wise they abode a whole year, at the end of which time Selim said to the queen-mother, 'Know that my life is not pleasing to me nor can I abide with you in contentment till I get me tidings of my sister and learn in what issue her affair hath resulted and how she hath fared after me. Wherefore I will go and be absent from you a year's space; then will I return to you, so it please God the Most High and I accomplish of this that which I hope.' Quoth she, 'I will not trust to thy word, but will go with thee and help thee to that which thou desirest of this and further thee myself therein.' So she took a ship and loaded it with all manner things of price, goods and treasures and what not else. Moreover, she appointed one of the viziers, a man in whom she trusted and in his fashion and ordinance, to rule the realm in their absence, saying to him, 'Abide [in the kingship] a full-told year and ordain all that whereof thou hast need.

Then the old queen and her daughter and son-in-law embarked in the ship and setting sail, fared on till they came to the land of Mekran. Their arrival there befell at the last of the day; so they passed the night in the ship, and when the day was near to break, the young king went down from the ship, that he might go to the bath, and made for the market. As he drew near the bath, the cook met him by the way and knew him; so he laid hands on him and binding his arms fast behind him, carried him to his house, where he clapped the old shackles on his feet and straightway cast him back into his whilom place of duresse.

When Selim found himself in that sorry plight and considered that wherewith he was afflicted of tribulation and the contrariness of his fortune, in that he had been a king and was now returned to shackles and prison and hunger, he wept and groaned and lamented and recited the following verses:

My fortitude fails, my endeavour is vain; My bosom is straitened. To Thee, I complain,
O my God! Who is stronger than Thou in resource? The Subtle, Thou knowest my plight and my pain.

To return to his wife and her mother. When the former arose in the morning and her husband returned not to her with break of day, she forebode all manner of calamity and straightway despatched her servants and all who were with her in quest of him; but they happened not on any trace of him neither fell in with aught of his news. So she bethought herself concerning her affair and complained and wept and groaned and sighed and blamed perfidious fortune, bewailing that sorry chance and reciting these verses:

God keep the days of love-delight! How passing sweet they were! How joyous and how solaceful was life in them whilere!
Would he were not, who sundered us upon the parting-day! How many a body hath he slain, how many a bone laid bare!
Sans fault of mine, my blood and tears he shed and beggared me Of him I love, yet for himself gained nought thereby whate'er.

When she had made an end of her verses, she considered her affair and said in herself, 'By Allah, all these things have betided by the ordinance of God the Most High and His providence and this was written and charactered upon the forehead.' Then she landed and fared on till she came to a spacious place, where she enquired of the folk and hired a house. Thither she straightway transported all that was in the ship of goods and sending for brokers, sold all that was with her. Then she took part of the price and fell to enquiring of the folk, so haply she might scent out tidings [of her lost husband]. Moreover, she addressed herself to lavishing alms and tending the sick, clothing the naked and pouring water upon the dry ground of the forlorn. On this wise she abode a whole year, and every little while she sold of her goods and gave alms to the sick and the needy; wherefore her report was bruited abroad in the city and the folk were lavish in her praise.

All this while, Selim lay in shackles and strait prison, and melancholy possessed him by reason of that whereinto he had fallen of that tribulation. Then, when troubles waxed on him and affliction was prolonged, he fell sick of a sore sickness. When the cook saw his plight (and indeed he was like to perish for much suffering), he loosed him from the shackles and bringing him forth of the prison, committed him to an old woman, who had a nose the bigness of a jug, and bade her tend him and medicine him and serve him and entreat him kindly, so haply he might be made whole of that his sickness. So the old woman took him and carrying him to her lodging, fell to tending him and giving him to eat and drink; and when he was quit of that torment, he recovered from his malady.

Now the old woman had heard from the folk of the lady who gave alms to the sick, and indeed [the news of] her bounties reached both poor and rich; so she arose and bringing out Selim to the door of her house, laid him on a mat and wrapped him in a mantle and sat over against him. Presently, it befell that the charitable lady passed by them, which when the old woman saw, she rose to her and offered up prayers for her, saying, 'O my daughter, O thou to whom pertain goodness and beneficence and charity and almsdoing, know that this young man is a stranger, and indeed want and vermin and hunger and nakedness and cold slay him.' When the lady heard this, she gave her alms of that which was with her; and indeed her heart inclined unto Selim, [but she knew him not for her husband].

The old woman received the alms from her and carrying it to Selim, took part thereof herself and with the rest bought him an old shirt, in which she clad him, after she had stripped him of that he had on. Then she threw away the gown she had taken from off him and arising forthright, washed his body of that which was thereon of filth and scented him with somewhat of perfume. Moreover, she bought him chickens and made him broth; so he ate and his life returned to him and he abode with her on the most solaceful of life till the morrow.

Next morning, the old woman said to him, 'When the lady cometh to thee, do thou arise and kiss her hand and say to her, "I am a strange man and indeed cold and hunger slay me;" so haply she may give thee somewhat that thou mayst expend upon thy case.' And he answered, 'Hearkening and obedience.' Then she took him by the hand and carrying him without her house, seated him at the door. As he sat, behold, the lady came up to him, whereupon the old woman rose to her and Selim kissed her hand and offered up prayers for her. Then he looked on her and when he saw her, he knew her for his wife; so he cried out and wept and groaned and lamented; whereupon she came up to him and cast herself upon him; for indeed she knew him with all knowledge, even as he knew her. So she laid hold of him and embraced him and called to her serving-men and attendants and those who were about her; and they took him up and carried him forth of that place.

.

When the old woman saw this, she cried out to the cook from within the house, and he said to her, 'Go before me.' So she forewent him and he ran after her till he [overtook the party and] catching hold of Selim, said [to the latter's wife,] 'What aileth thee to take my servant?' Whereupon she cried out at him, saying, 'Know that this is my husband, whom I had lost.' And Selim also cried out, saying, 'Mercy! Mercy! I appeal to God and to the Sultan against this Satan!' Therewith the folk gathered together to them forthright and loud rose the clamours and the cries between them; but the most part of them said, 'Refer their affair to the Sultan.' So they referred the case to the Sultan, who was none other than Selim's sister Selma.

[Then they went up to the palace and] the interpreter went in to Selma and said to her, 'O king of the age, here is an Indian woman, who cometh from the land of Hind, and she hath laid hands on a young man, a servant, avouching that he is her husband, who hath been missing these two years, and she came not hither but on his account, and indeed these many days she hath done almsdeeds [in the city]. And here is a man, a cook, who avoucheth that the young man is his slave.' When the queen heard these words, her entrails quivered and she groaned from an aching heart and called to mind her brother and that which had betided him. Then she bade those who were about her bring them before her, and when she saw them, she knew her brother and was like to cry aloud; but her reason restrained her; yet could she not contain herself, but she must needs rise up and sit down. However, she enforced herself unto patience and said to them, 'Let each of you acquaint me with his case.'

So Selim came forward and kissing the earth before the [supposed] king, praised him and related to him his story from beginning to end, till the time of their coming to that city, he and his sister, telling him how he had entered the place and fallen into the hands of the cook and that which had betided him [with him] and what he had suffered from him of beating and bonds and shackles and pinioning. Moreover, he told him how the cook had made him his brother's slave and how the latter had sold him in Hind and he had married the princess and become king and how life was not pleasant to him till he should foregather with his sister and how the cook had fallen in with him a second time and acquainted her with that which had betided him of sickness and disease for the space of a full-told year.

When he had made an end of his speech, his wife came forward forthright and told her story, from first to last, how her mother bought him from the cook's partner and the people of the kingdom came under his rule; nor did she leave telling till she came, in her story, to that city [and acquainted the queen with the manner of her falling in with her lost husband]. When she had made an end of her story, the cook exclaimed, 'Alack, what impudent liars there be! By Allah, O king, this woman lieth against me, for this youth is my rearling[341] and he was born of one of my slave-girls. He fled from me and I found him again.

When the queen heard the last of the talk, she said to the cook, 'The judgment between you shall not be but in accordance with justice.' Then she dismissed all those who were present and turning to her brother, said to him, 'Indeed thy soothfastness is established with me and the truth of thy speech, and praised be God who hath brought about union between thee and thy wife! So now begone with her to thy country and leave [seeking] thy sister Selma and depart in peace.' But Selim answered, saying, 'By Allah, by the virtue of the All-knowing King, I will not turn back from seeking my sister till I die or find her, if it please God the Most High!' Then he called his sister to mind and broke out with the following verses from a heart endolored, afflicted, disappointed, saying:

O thou that blamest me for my heart and railest at my ill, Hadst them but tasted my spirit's grief, thou wouldst excuse me still.
By Allah, O thou that chid'st my heart concerning my sister's love, Leave chiding and rather bemoan my case and help me to my will.
For indeed I am mated with longing love in public and privily, Nor ever my heart, alas I will cease from mourning, will I or nill.
A fire in mine entrails burns, than which the fire of the hells denounced For sinners' torment less scathing is: it seeketh me to slay.

When his sister Selma heard what he said, she could no longer contain herself, but cast herself upon him and discovered to him her case. When he knew her, he threw himself upon her [and lay without life] awhile; after which he came to himself and said, 'Praised be God, the Bountiful, the Beneficent!' Then they complained to each other of that which they had suffered for the anguish of separation, whilst Selim's wife abode wondered at this and Selma's patience and constancy pleased her. So she saluted her and thanked her for her fashion, saying, 'By Allah, O my lady, all that we are in of gladness is of thy blessing alone; so praised be God who hath vouchsafed us thy sight!' Then they abode all three in joy and happiness and delight three days, sequestered from the folk; and it was bruited abroad in the city that the king had found his brother, who was lost years agone.

On the fourth day, all the troops and the people of the realm assembled together to the [supposed] king and standing at his gate, craved leave to enter. Selma bade admit them; so they entered and paid her the service of the kingship and gave her joy of her brother's safe return. She bade them do suit and service to Selim, and they consented and paid him homage; after which they kept silence awhile, so they might hear what the king should command. Then said Selma, 'Harkye, all ye soldiers and subjects, ye know that ye enforced me to [accept] the kingship and besought me thereof and I consented unto your wishes concerning my investment [with the royal dignity]; and I did this [against my will]; for know that I am a woman and that I disguised myself and donned man's apparel, so haply my case might be hidden, whenas I lost my brother. But now, behold, God hath reunited me with my brother, and it is no longer lawful to me that I be king and bear rule over the people, and I a woman; for that there is no governance for women, whenas men are present. Wherefore, if it like you, do ye set my brother on the throne of the kingdom, for this is he; and I will busy myself with the worship of God the Most High and thanksgiving [to Him] for my reunion with my brother. Or, if it like you, take your kingship and invest therewith whom ye will.'

Thereupon the folk all cried out, saying, 'We accept him to king over us!' And they did him suit and service and gave him joy of the kingship. So the preachers preached in his name[342] and the poets praised him; and he lavished gifts upon the troops and the officers of his household and overwhelmed them with favours and bounties and was prodigal to the people of justice and equitable dealings and goodly usance and polity. When he had accomplished this much of his desire, he caused bring forth the cook and his household to the divan, but spared the old woman who had tended him, for that she had been the cause of his deliverance. Then they assembled them all without the town and he tormented the cook and those who were with him with all manner of torments, after which he put him to death on the sorriest wise and burning him with fire, scattered his ashes abroad in the air.

Selim abode in the governance, invested with the sultanate, and ruled the people a whole year, after which he returned to El Mensoureh and sojourned there another year. And he [and his wife] ceased not to go from city to city and abide in this a year and that a year, till he was vouchsafed children and they grew up, whereupon he appointed him of his sons, who was found fitting, to be his deputy in [one] kingdom [and abode himself in the other]; and he lived, he and his wife and children, what while God the Most High willed. Nor," added the vizier, "O king of the age, is this story rarer or more extraordinary than that of the king of Hind and his wronged and envied vizier."

When the king heard this, his mind was occupied [with the story he had heard and that which the vizier promised him], and he bade the latter depart to his own house.

The Twenty-Eighth and Last Night of the Month

When the evening evened, the king summoned the vizier and bade him tell the story of the King of Hind and his vizier. So he said, "Hearkening and obedience. Know, O king of august lineage, that

STORY OF THE KING OF HIND AND HIS VIZIER.

There was once in the land of Hind a king of illustrious station, endowed with understanding and good sense, and his name was Shah Bekht. He had a vizier, a man of worth and intelligence, prudent in counsel, conformable to him in his governance and just in his judgment; wherefore his enviers were many and many were the hypocrites, who sought in him faults and set snares for him, so that they insinuated into King Shah Bekht's eye hatred and rancour against him and sowed despite against him in his heart; and plot followed after plot, till [at last] the king was brought to arrest him and lay him in prison and confiscate his good and avoid his estate.[343]

When they knew that there was left him no estate that the king might covet, they feared lest he be brought to release him, by the incidence of the vizier's [good] counsel upon the king's heart, and he return to his former case, so should their plots be marred and their ranks degraded, for that they knew that the king would have need of that which he had known from that man nor would forget that wherewith he was familiar in him. Now it befell that a certain man of corrupt purpose[344] found a way to the perversion of the truth and a means of glozing over falsehood and adorning it with a semblance of fair-seeming and there proceeded from him that wherewith the hearts of the folk were occupied, and their minds were corrupted by his lying tales; for that he made use of Indian subtleties and forged them into a proof for the denial of the Maker, the Creator, extolled be His might and exalted be He! Indeed, God is exalted and magnified above the speech of the deniers. He avouched that it is the planets[345] that order the affairs of all creatures and he set down twelve mansions to twelve signs [of the Zodiac] and made each sign thirty degrees, after the number of the days of the month, so that in twelve mansions there are three hundred and threescore [degrees], after the number of the days of the year; and he wrought a scheme, wherein he lied and was an infidel and denied [God]. Then he got possession of the king's mind and the enviers and haters aided him against the vizier and insinuated themselves into his favour and corrupted his counsel against the vizier, so that he suffered of him that which he suffered and he banished him and put him away.

So the wicked man attained that which he sought of the vizier and the case was prolonged till the affairs of the kingdom became disordered, by dint of ill governance, and the most part of the king's empery fell away from him and he came nigh unto ruin. Therewithal he was certified of the loyalty of his [late] skilful vizier and the excellence of his governance and the justness of his judgment. So he sent after him and brought him and the wicked man before him and summoning the grandees of his realm and the chiefs of his state to his presence, gave them leave to talk and dispute and forbade the wicked man from that his lewd opinion.[346] Then arose that wise and skilful vizier and praised God the Most High and lauded Him and glorified Him and hallowed Him and attested His unity and disputed with the wicked man and overcame him and put him to silence; nor did he cease from him till he enforced him to make confession of repentance [and turning away] from that which he had believed.

Therewith King Shah Bekht rejoiced with an exceeding great joy and said, 'Praise be to God who hath delivered me from yonder man and hath preserved me from the loss of the kingship and the cessation of prosperity from me!' So the affair of the vizier returned to order and well-being and the king restored him to his place and advanced him in rank. Moreover, he assembled the folk who had missaid of him and destroyed them all, to the last man. And how like," continued the vizier, "is this story unto that of myself and King Shah Bekht, with regard to that whereinto I am fallen of the changing of the king's heart and his giving credence to others against me; but now is the righteousness of my dealing established in thine eyes, for that God the Most High hath inspired me with wisdom and endowed thee with longanimity and patience [to hearken] from me unto that which He allotted unto those who had foregone us, till He hath shown forth my innocence and made manifest unto thee the truth. For now the days are past, wherein it was avouched to the king that I should endeavour for the destruction of my soul,[347] [to wit,] the month; and behold, the probation time is over and gone, and past is the season of evil and ceased, by the king's good fortune." Then he bowed his head and was silent.[348]

When King Shah Bekht heard his vizier's speech, he was confounded before him and abashed and marvelled at the gravity of his understanding and his patience. So he sprang up to him and embraced him and the vizier kissed his feet. Then the king called for a sumptuous dress of honour and cast it over Er Rehwan and entreated him with the utmost honour and showed him special favour and restored him to his rank and vizierate. Moreover he imprisoned those who had sought his destruction with leasing and committed unto himself to pass judgment upon the interpreter who had expounded to him the dream. So the vizier abode in the governance of the realm till there came to them the Destroyer of Delights; and this (added Shehrzad) is all, O king of the age, that hath come down to us of King Shah Bekht and his vizier.

SHEHRZAD AND SHEHRIYAR.

As for King Shehriyar, he marvelled at Shehrzad with the utmost wonder and drew her near to his heart, of his much love for her; and she was magnified in his eyes and he said in himself, "By Allah, the like of this woman is not deserving of slaughter, for indeed the time affordeth not her like. By Allah, I have been heedless of mine affair, and had not God overcome me with His mercy and put this woman at my service, so she might adduce to me manifest instances and truthful cases and goodly admonitions and edifying traits, such as should restore me to the [right] road, [I had come to perdition!]. Wherefore to God be the praise for this and I beseech Him to make my end with her like unto that of the vizier and Shah Bekht." Then sleep overcame the king and glory be unto Him who sleepeth not!

When it was the Nine hundred and thirtieth Night, Shehrzad said, "O king, there is present in my thought a story which treateth of women's craft and wherein is a warning to whoso will be warned and an admonishment to whoso will be admonished and whoso hath discernment; but I fear lest the hearing of this lessen me with the king and lower my rank in his esteem; yet I hope that this will not be, for that it is a rare story. Women are indeed corruptresses; their craft and their cunning may not be set out nor their wiles known. Men enjoy their company and are not careful to uphold them [in the right way], neither do they watch over them with all vigilance, but enjoy their company and take that which is agreeable and pay no heed to that which is other than this. Indeed, they are like unto the crooked rib, which if thou go about to straighten, thou distortest it, and which if thou persist in seeking to redress, thou breakest it; wherefore it behoveth the man of understanding to be silent concerning them."

"O sister mine," answered Dinarzad, "bring forth that which is with thee and that which is present to thy mind of the story concerning the craft of women and their wiles, and have no fear lest this endamage thee with the king; for that women are like unto jewels, which are of all kinds and colours. When a [true] jewel falleth into the hand of him who is knowing therein, he keepeth it for himself and leaveth that which is other than it. Moreover, he preferreth some of them over others, and in this he is like unto the potter, who filleth his oven with all the vessels [he hath moulded] and kindleth fire thereunder. When the baking is at an end and he goeth about to take forth that which is in the oven, he findeth no help for it but that he must break some thereof, whilst other some are what the folk need and whereof they make use, and yet other some there be that return to their whilom case. Wherefore fear thou not to adduce that which thou knowest of the craft of women, for that in this is profit for all folk."

Then said Shehrzad, "They avouch, O king, (but God [alone] knowest the secret things,) that

EL MELIK EZ ZAHIR RUKNEDDIN BIBERS EL BUNDUCDARI AND THE SIXTEEN OFFICERS OF POLICE

THERE was once in the land [of Egypt and] the city of Cairo, [under the dynasty] of the Turks,[349] a king of the valiant kings and the exceeding mighty Sultans, by name El Melik ez Zahir Rukneddin Bibers el Bunducdari.[350] He was used to storm the Islamite strongholds and the fortresses of the Coast[351] and the Nazarene citadels, and the governor of his [capital] city was just to the folk, all of them. Now El Melik ez Zahir was passionately fond of stories of the common folk and of that which men purposed and loved to see this with his eyes and hear their sayings with his ears, and it befell that he heard one night from one of his story-tellers[352] that among women are those who are doughtier than men of valour and greater of excellence and that among them are those who will do battle with the sword and others who cozen the quickest-witted of magistrates and baffle them and bring down on them all manner of calamity; whereupon quoth the Sultan, 'I would fain hear this of their craft from one of those who have had to do theiewith, so I may hearken unto him and cause him tell.' And one of the story-tellers said, 'O king, send for the chief of the police of the town.'

Now Ilmeddin Senjer was at that time Master of Police and he was a man of experience, well versed in affairs: so the king sent for him and when he came before him, he discovered to him that which was in his mind. Quoth Ilmeddin Senjer, 'I will do my endeavour for that which our lord the Sultan seeketh.' Then he arose and returning to his house, summoned the captains of the watch and the lieutenants of police and said to them, 'Know that I purpose to marry my son and make him a bride-feast, and it is my wish that ye assemble, all of you, in one place. I also will be present, I and my company, and do ye relate that which ye have heard of extraordinary occurrences and that which hath betided you of experiences.' And the captains and sergeants and agents of police made answer to him, saying, 'It is well: in the name of God! We will cause thee see all this with thine eyes and hear it with thine ears.' Then the master of police arose and going up to El Melik ez Zahir, informed him that the assembly would take place on such a day at his house; and the Sultan said, 'It is well,' and gave him somewhat of money for his expenses.

When the appointed day arrived, the chief of the police set apart for his officers a saloon, that had windows ranged in order and giving upon the garden, and El Melik ez Zahir came to him, and he seated himself, he and the Sultan, in the alcove. Then the tables were spread unto them for eating and they ate; and when the cup went round amongst them and their hearts were gladdened with meat and drink, they related that which was with them and discovered their secrets from concealment. The first to relate was a man, a captain of the watch, by name Muineddin, whose heart was engrossed with the love of women; and he said, 'Harkye, all ye people of [various] degree, I will acquaint you with an extraordinary affair which befell me aforetime. Know that

THE FIRST OFFICER'S STORY.

When I entered the service of this Amir,[353] I had a great repute and every lewd fellow feared me of all mankind, and whenas I rode through the city, all the folk would point at me with their fingers and eyes. It befell one day, as I sat in the house of the prefecture, with my back against a wall, considering in myself, there fell somewhat in my lap, and behold, it was a purse sealed and tied. So I took it in my hand and beheld, it had in it a hundred dirhems,[354] but I found not who threw it and I said, "Extolled be the perfection of God, the King of the Kingdoms!"[355] Another day, [as I sat on like wise,] somewhat fell on me and startled me, and behold, it was a purse like the first. So I took it and concealing its affair, made as if I slept, albeit sleep was not with me.

One day, as I was thus feigning sleep, I felt a hand in my lap, and in it a magnificent purse. So I seized the hand and behold, it was that of a fair woman. Quoth I to her, "O my lady, who art thou?" And she said, "Rise [and come away] from here, that I may make myself known to thee." So I arose and following her, fared on, without tarrying, till she stopped at the door of a lofty house, whereupon quoth I to her,"O my lady, who art thou? Indeed, thou hast done me kindness, and what is the reason of this?" "By Allah," answered she, "O Captain Mum, I am a woman on whom desire and longing are sore for the love of the daughter of the Cadi Amin el Hukm. Now there was between us what was and the love of her fell upon my heart and I agreed with her upon meeting, according to possibility and convenience. But her father Amin el Hukm took her and went away, and my heart cleaveth to her and love-longing and distraction are sore upon me on her account."

I marvelled at her words and said to her, "What wouldst thou have me do?" And she answered, "O Captain Muin, I would have thee give me a helping hand." Quoth I, "What have I to do with the daughter of the Cadi Amin el Hukm?" And she said, "Know that I would not have thee intrude upon the Cadi's daughter, but I would fain contrive for the attainment of my wishes.' This is my intent and my desire, and my design will not be accomplished but by thine aid." Then said she, "I mean this night to go with a stout heart and hire me trinkets of price; then will I go and sit in the street wherein is the house of Amin el Hukm; and when it is the season of the round and the folk are asleep, do thou pass, thou and those who are with thee of the police, and thou wilt see me sitting and on me fine raiment and ornaments and wilt smell on me the odour of perfumes; whereupon do thou question me of my case and I will say, 'I come from the Citadel and am of the daughters of the deputies[356] and I came down [into the town,] to do an occasion; but the night overtook me at unawares and the Zuweyleh gate was shut against me and all the gates and I knew not whither I should go this night Presently I saw this street and noting the goodliness of its ordinance and its cleanness, took shelter therein against break of day.' When I say this to thee with all assurance[357] the chief of the watch will have no suspicion of me, but will say, 'Needs must we leave her with one who will take care of her till morning.' And do thou rejoin, 'It were most fitting that she pass the night with Amin el Hukm and lie with his family and children till the morning.' Then do thou straightway knock at the Cadi's door, and thus shall I have gained admission into his house, without inconvenience, and gotten my desire; and peace be on thee!" And I said to her, "By Allah, this is an easy matter."

So, when the night darkened, we sallied forth to make our round, attended by men with sharp swords, and went round about the streets and compassed the city, till we came to the by-street where was the woman, and it was the middle of the night Here we smelt rich scents and heard the clink of earrings; so I said to my comrades, "Methinks I spy an apparition," And the captain of the watch said, "See what it is." So I came forward and entering the lane, came presently out again and said, "I have found a fair woman and she tells me that she is from the Citadel and that the night surprised her and she espied this street and seeing its cleanness and the goodliness of its ordinance, knew that it appertained to a man of rank and that needs must there be in it a guardian to keep watch over it, wherefore she took shelter therein." Quoth the captain of the watch to me, "Take her and carry her to thy house." But I answered, "I seek refuge with Allah![358] My house is no place of deposit[359] and on this woman are trinkets and apparel [of price]. By Allah, we will not deposit her save with Amin el Hukrn, in whose street she hath been since the first of the darkness; wherefore do thou leave her with him till the break of day." And he said, "As thou wilt." Accordingly, I knocked at the Cadi's door and out came a black slave of his slaves, to whom said I, "O my lord, take this woman and let her be with you till break of day, for that the lieutenant of the Amir Ilmeddin hath found her standing at the door of your house, with trinkets and apparel [of price] on her, and we feared lest her responsibility be upon you;[360] wherefore it is most fit that she pass the night with you." So the slave opened and took her in with him.

When the morning morrowed, the first who presented himself before the Amir was the Cadi Amin el Hukm, leaning on two of his black slaves; and he was crying out and calling [on God] for aid and saying, "O crafty and perfidious Amir, thou depositedst with me a woman [yesternight] and broughtest her into my house and my dwelling-place, and she arose [in the night] and took from me the good of the little orphans,[361] six great bags, [containing each a thousand dinars,[362] and made off;] but as for me, I will say no more to thee except in the Sultan's presence."[363] When the Master of the Police heard these words, he was troubled and rose and sat down; then he took the Cadi and seating him by his side, soothed him and exhorted him to patience, till he had made an end of talk, when he turned to the officers and questioned them. They fixed the affair on me and said, "We know nothing of this affair but from Captain Muinedd n." So the Cadi turned to me and said, "Thou wast of accord with this woman, for she said she came from the Citadel."

As for me, I stood, with my head bowed to the earth, forgetting both Institutes and Canons,[364] and abode sunk in thought, saying, "How came I to be the dupe of yonder worthless baggage?" Then said the Amir to me, "What aileth thee that thou answerest not?" And I answerec, saying, "O my lord, it is a custom among the folk that he who hath a payment to make at a certain date is allowed three days' grace; [so do thou have patience with me so long,] and if, [by the end of that time,] the culprit be not found, I will be answerable for that which is lost." When the folk heard my speech, they all deemed it reasonable and the Master of Police turned to the Cadi and swore to him that he would do his utmost endeavour to recover the stolen money and that it should be restored to him. So he went away, whilst I mounted forthright and fell to going round about the world without purpose, and indeed I was become under the dominion of a woman without worth or honour; and I went round about on this wise all that my day and night, but happened not upon tidings of her; and thus I did on the morrow.

On the third day I said to myself, "Thou art mad or witless!" For I was going about in quest of a woman who knew me and I knew her not, seeing that indeed she was veiled, [whenas I saw her]. Then I went round about the third day till the hour of afternoon prayer, and sore was my concern and my chagrin, for I knew that there abode to me of my life but [till] the morrow, when the chief of the police would seek me. When it was the time of sundown, I passed through one of the streets, and beheld a woman at a window. Her door was ajar and she was clapping her hands and casting furtive glances at me, as who should say, "Come up by the door." So I went up, without suspicion, and when I entered, she rose and clasped me to her breast 1 marvelled at her affair and she said to me, "I am she whom thou depositedst with Amin el Hukm." Quoth I to her, "O my sister, I have been going round and round in quest of thee, for indeed thou hast done a deed that will be chronicled in history and hast cast me into slaughter[365] on thine account." "Sayst thou this to me," asked she, "and thou captain of men?" And I answered, "How should I not be troubled, seeing that I am in concern [for an affair] that I turn over and over [in my mind], more by token that I abide my day long going about [searching for thee] and in the night I watch its stars [for wakefulness]?" Quoth she, "Nought shall betide but good, and thou shalt get the better of him."

So saying, she rose [and going] to a chest, took out therefrom six bags full of gold and said to me, "This is what I took from Amin el Hukm's house. So, if thou wilt, restore it; else the whole is lawfully thine; and if thou desire other than this, [thou shalt have it;] for I have wealth in plenty and I had no design in this but to marry thee." Then she arose and opening [other] chests, brought out therefrom wealth galore and I said to her, "O my sister, I have no desire for all this, nor do I covet aught but to be quit of that wherein I am." Quoth she, "I came not forth of the [Cadi's] house without [making provision for] thine acquittance."

Then said she to me, "To-morrow morning, when 'Amin el Hukm cometh, have patience with him till he have made an end of his speech, and when he is silent, return him no answer; and if the prefect say to thee, 'What ailest thee that thou answereth him not?' do thou reply, 'O lord, know that the two words are not alike, but there is no [helper] for him who is undermost[366], save God the Most High.'[367] The Cadi will say, 'What is the meaning of thy saying," The two words are not alike"?' And do thou make answer, saying, 'I deposited with thee a damsel from the palace of the Sultan, and most like some losel of thy household hath transgressed against her or she hath been privily murdered. Indeed, there were on her jewels and raiment worth a thousand dinars, and hadst thou put those who are with thee of slaves and slave-girls to the question, thou hadst assuredly lit on some traces [of the crime].' When he heareth this from thee, his agitation will redouble and he will be confounded and will swear that needs must thou go with him to his house; but do thou say, 'That will I not do, for that I am the party aggrieved, more by token that I am under suspicion with thee.' If he redouble in calling [on God for aid] and conjure thee by the oath of divorce, saying, 'Needs must thou come,' do thou say, 'By Allah, I will not go, except the prefect come also.'

When thou comest to the house, begin by searching the roofs; then search the closets and cabinets; and if thou find nought, humble thyself unto the Cadi and make a show of abjection and feign thyself defeated, and after stand at the door and look as if thou soughtest a place wherein to make water, for that there is a dark corner there. Then come forward, with a heart stouter than granite, and lay hold upon a jar of the jars and raise it from its place. Thou wilt find under it the skirt of a veil; bring it out publicly and call the prefect in a loud voice, before those who are present. Then open it and thou wilt find it full of blood, exceeding of redness,[368] and in it [thou wilt find also] a woman's shoes and a pair of trousers and somewhat of linen." When I heard this from her, I rose to go out and she said to me, "Take these hundred dinars, so they may advantage thee; and this is my guest-gift to thee." So I took them and bidding her farewell, returned to my lodging.

Next morning, up came the Cadi, with his face like the ox-eye,[369] and said, "In the name of God, where is my debtor and where is my money?" Then he wept and cried out and said to the prefect, "Where is that ill-omened fellow, who aboundeth in thievery and villainy?" Therewith the prefect turned to me and said, "Why dost thou not answer the Cadi?" And I replied, "O Amir, the two heads[370] are not equal, and I, I have no helper but God; but, if the right be on my side, it will appear." At this the Cadi cried out and said, "Out on thee, O ill-omened fellow! How wilt thou make out that the right is on thy side?" "O our lord the Cadi," answered I, "I deposited with thee a trust, to wit, a woman whom we found at thy door, and on her raiment and trinkets of price. Now she is gone, even as yesterday is gone; and after this thou turnest upon us and makest claim upon me for six thousand dinars. By Allah, this is none other than gross unright, and assuredly some losel of thy household hath transgressed against her!"

With this the Cadi's wrath redoubled and he swore by the most solemn of oaths that I should go with him and search his house. "By Allah," replied I, "I will not go, except the prefect be with us; for, if he be present, he and the officers, thou wilt not dare to presume upon me." And the Cadi rose and swore an oath, saying, "By Him who created mankind, we will not go but with the Amir!" So we repaired to the Cadi's house, accompanied by the prefect, and going up, searched high and low, but found nothing; whereupon fear gat hold upon me and the prefect turned to me and said, "Out on thee, O ill-omened fellow! Thou puttest us to shame before the men." And I wept and went round about right and left, with the tears running down my face, till we were about to go forth and drew near the door of the house. I looked at the place [behind the door] and said, "What is yonder dark place that I see?" And I said to the sergeants, "Lift up this jar with me." They did as I bade them and I saw somewhat appearing under the jar and said, "Rummage and see what is under it." So they searched and found a woman's veil and trousers full of blood, which when I beheld, I fell down in a swoon.

When the prefect saw this, he said, "By Allah, the captain is excused!" Then my comrades came round about me and sprinkled water on my face, [till I came to myself,] when I arose and accosting the Cadi, who was covered with confusion, said to him, "Thou seest that suspicion is fallen on thee, and indeed this affair is no light matter, for that this woman's family will assuredly not sit down under her loss." Therewith the Cadi's heart quaked and he knew that the suspicion had reverted upon him, wherefore his colour paled and his limbs smote together; and he paid of his own money, after the measure of that which he had lost, so we would hush up the matter for him.[371] Then we departed from him in peace, whilst I said in myself, "Indeed, the woman deceived me not."

After that I tarried till three days had elapsed, when 1 went to the bath and changing my clothes, betook myself to her house, but found the door locked and covered with dust. So I questioned the neighbours of her and they said, "This house hath been empty these many days; but three days agone there came a woman with an ass, and yesternight, at eventide, she took her gear and went away." So I turned back, confounded in my wit, and every day [after this, for many a day,] I inquired of the inhabitants [of the street] concerning her, but could light on no tidings of her. And indeed I marvelled at the eloquence of her tongue and [the readiness of] her speech; and this is the most extraordinary of that which hath betided me.'

When El Melik ez Zahir heard Muineddin's story, he marvelled thereat Then rose another officer and said, 'O lord, bear what befell me in bygone days.

THE SECOND OFFICER'S STORY.

I was once an officer in the household of the Amir Jemaleddin El Atwesh El Mujhidi, who was invested with the governance of the Eastern and Western districts,[372] and I was dear to his heart and he concealed from me nought of that which he purposed to do; and withal he was master of his reason.[373] It chanced one day that it was reported to him that the daughter of such an one had wealth galore and raiment and jewe s and she loved a Jew, whom every day she invited to be private with her, and they passed the day eating and drinking in company and he lay the night with her. The prefect feigned to give no credence to this story, but one night he summoned the watchmen of the quarter and questioned them of this. Quoth one of them, "O my lord, I saw a Jew enter the street in question one night; but know not for certain to whom he went in." And the prefect said, "Keep thine eye on him henceforth and note what p ace he entereth." So the watchman went out and kept his eye on the Jew.

One day, as the prefect sat [in his house], the watchman came in to him and said, "O my lord, the Jew goeth to the house of such an one." Whereupon El Atwesh arose and went forth alone, taking with him none but myself. As he went along, he said to me, "Indeed, this [woman] is a fat piece of meat."[374] And we gave not over going till we came to the door of the house and stood there till a slave-girl came out, as if to buy them somewhat. We waited till she opened the door, whereupon, without further parley, we forced our way into the house and rushed in upon the girl, whom we found seated with the Jew in a saloon with four estrades, and cooking-pots and candles therein. When her eyes fell on the prefect, she knew him and rising to her feet, said, "Welcome and fair welcome! Great honour hath betided me by my lord's visit and indeed thou honourest my dwelling."

Then she carried him up [to the estrade] and seating him on the couch, brought him meat and wine and gave him to drink; after which she put off all that was upon her of raiment and jewels and tying them up in a handkerchief, said to him, "O my lord, this is thy portion, all of it." Moreover she turned to the Jew and said to him, "Arise, thou also, and do even as I." So he arose in haste and went out, scarce crediting his deliverance. When the girl was assured of his escape, she put out her hand to her clothes [and jewels] and taking them, said to the prefect, "Is the requital of kindness other than kindness? Thou hast deigned [to visit me and eat of my victual]; so now arise and depart from us without ill-[doing]; or I will give one cry and all who are in the street will come forth." So the Amir went out from her, without having gotten a single dirhem; and on this wise she delivered the Jew by the excellence of her contrivance.'

The folk marvelled at this story and as for the prefect and El Melik ez Zahir, they said, 'Wrought ever any the like of this device?' And they marvelled with the utterest of wonderment Then arose a third officer and said, 'Hear what betided me, for it is yet stranger and more extraordinary.

THE THIRD OFFICER'S STORY

I was one day abroad on an occasion with certain of my comrades, and as we went along, we fell in with a company of women, as they were moons, and among them one, the tallest and handsomest of them. When I saw her and she saw me, she tarried behind her companions and waited for me, till I came up to her and bespoke her. Quoth she, "O my lord, (God favour thee!) I saw thee prolong thy looking on me and imagined that thou knewest me. If it be thus, vouchsafe me more knowledge of thee." "By Allah," answered I, "I know thee not, save that God the Most High hath cast the love of thee into my heart and the goodliness of thine attributes hath confounded me and that wherewith God hath gifted thee of those eyes that shoot with arrows; for thou hast captivated me." And she rejoined, "By Allah, I feel the like of that which thou feelest; so that meseemeth I have known thee from childhood."

Then said I, "A man cannot well accomplish all whereof he hath need in the market-places." "Hast thou a house?" asked she. "No, by Allah," answered I; "nor is this town my dwelling-place." "By Allah," rejoined she, "nor have I a place; but I will contrive for thee." Then she went on before me and I followed her till she came to a lodging-house and said to the housekeeper, "Hast thou an empty chamber?" "Yes," answered she; and my mistress said, "Give us the key." So we took the key and going up to see the room, entered it; after which she went out to the housekeeper and [giving her a dirhem], said to her, "Take the key-money,[375] for the room pleaseth us, and here is another dirhem for thy trouble. Go, fetch us a pitcher of water, so we may [refresh ourselves] and rest till the time of the noonday siesta pass and the heat decline, when the man will go and fetch the [household] stuff." Therewith the housekeeper rejoiced and brought us a mat and two pitchers of water on a tray and a leather rug.

We abode thus till the setting-in of the time of mid-afternoon, when she said, "Needs must I wash before I go." Quoth I, "Get water wherewithal we may wash," and pulled out from my pocket about a score of dirhems, thinking to give them to her; but she said, "I seek refuge with God!" and brought out of her pocket a handful of silver, saying, "But for destiny and that God hath caused the love of thee fall into my heart, there had not happened that which hath happened." Quoth I, "Take this in requital of that which thou hast spent;" and she said, "O my lord, by and by, whenas companionship is prolonged between us, thou wilt see if the like of me looketh unto money and gain or no." Then she took a pitcher of water and going into the lavatory, washed[376] and presently coming forth, prayed and craved pardon of God the Most High for that which she had done.

Now I had questioned her of her name and she answered, "My name is Rihaneh," and described to me her dwelling-place. When I saw her make the ablution, I said in myself, "This woman doth on this wise, and shall I not do the like of her?" Then said I to her, "Belike thou wilt seek us another pitcher of water?" So she went out to the housekeeper and said to her, "Take this para and fetch us water therewith, so we may wash the flags withal." Accordingly, the housekeeper brought two pitchers of water and I took one of them and giving her my clothes, entered the lavatory and washed.

When I had made an end of washing, I cried out, saying, "Harkye, my lady Rihaneh!" But none answered me. So I went out and found her not; and indeed she had taken my clothes and that which was therein of money, to wit, four hundred dirhems. Moreover, she had taken my turban and my handkerchief and I found not wherewithal to cover my nakedness; wherefore I suffered somewhat than which death is less grievous and abode looking about the place, so haply I might espy wherewithal to hide my shame. Then I sat a little and presently going up to the door, smote upon it; whereupon up came the housekeeper and I said to her, "O my sister, what hath God done with the woman who was here?" Quoth she, "She came down but now and said, 'I am going to cover the boys with the clothes and I have left him sleeping. If he awake, tell him not to stir till the clothes come to him.'" Then said I, "O my sister, secrets are [safe] with the worthy and the freeborn. By Allah, this woman is not my wife, nor ever in my life have I seen her before this day!" And I recounted to her the whole affair and begged her to cover me, informing her that I was discovered of the privities.

She laughed and cried out to the women of the house, saying, "Ho, Fatimeh! Ho, Khedijeh! Ho, Herifeh! Ho, Senineh!" Whereupon all those who were in the place of women and neighbours flocked to me and fell a-laughing at me and saying, "O blockhead, what ailed thee to meddle with gallantry?" Then one of them came and looked in my face and laughed, and another said, "By Allah, thou mightest have known that she lied, from the time she said she loved thee and was enamoured of thee? What is there in thee to love?" And a third said, "This is an old man without understanding." And they vied with each other in making mock of me, what while I suffered sore chagrin.

However, after awhile, one of the women took pity on me and brought me a rag of thin stuff and cast it on me. With this I covered my privities, and no more, and abode awhile thus. Then said I in myself, "The husbands of these women will presently gather together on me and I shall be disgraced." So I went out by another door of the house, and young and old crowded about me, running after me and saying, "A madman! A madman!" till I came to my house and knocked at the door; whereupon out came my wife and seeing me naked, tall, bareheaded, cried out and ran in again, saying,"This is a madman, a Satan!" But, when she and my family knew me, they rejoiced and said to me, "What aileth thee?" I told them that thieves had taken my clothes and stripped me and had been like to kill me; and when I told them that they would have killed me, they praised God the Most High and gave me joy of my safety. So consider the craft of this woman and this device that she practised upon me, for all my pretensions to sleight and quickwittedness.'

The company marvelled at this story and at the doings of women. Then came forward a fourth officer and said, 'Verily, that which hath betided me of strange adventures is yet more extraordinary than this; and it was on this wise.

THE FOURTH OFFICER'S STORY.

We were sleeping one night on the roof, when a woman made her way into the house and gathering into a bundle all that was therein, took it up, that she might go away with it. Now she was great with child and near upon her term and the hour of her deliverance; so, when she made up the bundle and offered to shoulder it and make off with it, she hastened the coming of the pangs of labour and gave birth to a child in the dark. Then she sought for the flint and steel and striking a light, kindled the lamp and went round about the house with the little one, and it was weeping. [The noise awoke us,] as we lay on the roof, and we marvelled. So we arose, to see what was to do, and looking down through the opening of the saloon,[377] saw a woman, who had kindled the lamp, and heard the little one weeping. She heard our voices and raising her eyes to us, said, "Are ye not ashamed to deal with us thus and discover our nakedness? Know ye not that the day belongeth to you and the night to us? Begone from us! By Allah, were it not that ye have been my neighbours these [many] years, I would bring down the house upon you!" We doubted not but that she was of the Jinn and drew back our heads; but, when we arose on the morrow, we found that she had taken all that was with us and made off with it; wherefore we knew that she was a thief and had practised [on us] a device, such as was never before practised; and we repented, whenas repentance advantaged us not.'

When the company heard this story, they marvelled thereat with the utmost wonderment. Then the fifth officer, who was the lieutenant of the bench,[378] came forward and said, '[This is] no wonder and there befell me that which is rarer and more extraordinary than this.

THE FIFTH OFFICER'S STORY.

As I sat one day at the door of the prefecture, a woman entered and said to me privily, "O my lord, I am the wife of such an one the physician, and with him is a company of the notables[379] of the city, drinking wine in such a place." When I heard this, I misliked to make a scandal; so I rebuffed her and sent her away. Then I arose and went alone to the place in question and sat without till the door opened, when I rushed in and entering, found the company engaged as the woman had set out, and she herself with them. I saluted them and they returned my greeting and rising, entreated me with honour and seated me and brought me to eat. Then I informed them how one had denounced them to me, but I had driven him[380] away and come to them by myself; wherefore they thanked me and praised me for my goodness. Then they brought out to me from among them two thousand dirhems[381] and I took them and went away.

Two months after this occurrence, there came to me one of the Cadi's officers, with a scroll, wherein was the magistrate's writ, summoning me to him. So I accompanied the officer and went in to the Cadi, whereupon the plaintiff, to wit, he who had taken out the summons, sued me for two thousand dirhems, avouching that I had borrowed them of him as the woman's agent.[382] I denied the debt, but he produced against me a bond for the amount, attested by four of those who were in company [on the occasion]; and they were present and bore witness to the loan. So I reminded them of my kindness and paid the amount, swearing that I would never again follow a woman's counsel. Is not this marvellous?'

The company marvelled at the goodliness of his story and it pleased El Melik ez Zahir; and the prefect said, 'By Allah, this story is extraordinary!' Then came forward the sixth officer and said to the company, 'Hear my story and that which befell me, to wit, that which befell such an one the assessor, for it is rarer than this and stranger.

THE SIXTH OFFICER'S STORY.

A certain assessor was one day taken with a woman and much people assembled before his house and the lieutenant of police and his men came to him and knocked at the door. The assessor looked out of window and seeing the folk, said, "What aileth you?" Quoth they, "[Come,] speak with the lieutenant of police such an one." So he came down and they said to him, "Bring forth the woman that is with thee." Quoth he, "Are ye not ashamed? How shall I bring forth my wife?" And they said, "Is she thy wife by contract[383] or without contract?" ["By contract,"] answered he, "according to the Book of God and the Institutes of His Apostle." "Where is the contract?" asked they; and he replied, "Her contract is in her mother's house." Quoth they, "Arise and come down and show us the contract." And he said to them, "Go from her way, so she may come forth." Now, as soon as he got wind of the matter, he had written the contract and fashioned it after her fashion, to suit with the case, and written therein the names of certain of his friends as witnesses and forged the signatures of the drawer and the wife's next friend and made it a contract of marriage with his wife and appointed it for an excuse.[384] So, when the woman was about to go out from him, he gave her the contract that be had forged, and the Amir sent with her a servant of his, to bring her to her father. So the servant went with her and when she came to her door, she said to him, "I will not return to the citation of the Amir; but let the witnesses[385] present themselves and take my contract."

Accordingly, the servant carried this message to the lieutenant of police, who was standing at the assessor's door, and he said, "This is reasonable." Then said [the assessor] to the servant, "Harkye, O eunuch! Go and fetch us such an one the notary;" for that he was his friend [and it was he whose name he had forged as the drawer-up of the contract]. So the lieutenant of police sent after him and fetched him to the assessor, who, when he saw him, said to him, "Get thee to such an one, her with whom thou marriedst me, and cry out upon her, and when she cometh to thee, demand of her the contract and take it from her and bring it to us." And he signed to him, as who should say, "Bear me out in the lie and screen me, for that she is a strange woman and I am in fear of the lieutenant of police who standeth at the door; and we beseech God the Most High to screen us and you from the trouble of this world. Amen."

So the notary went up to the lieutenant, who was among the witnesses, and said "It is well. Is she not such an one whose marriage contract we drew up in such a place?" Then he betook himself to the woman's house and cried out upon her; whereupon she brought him the [forged] contract and he took it and returned with it to the lieutenant of police. When the latter had taken cognizance [of the document and professed himself satisfied, the assessor] said [to the notary,] "Go to our lord and master, the Cadi of the Cadis, and acquaint him with that which befalleth his assessors." The notary rose to go, but the lieutenant of police feared [for himself] and was profuse in beseeching the assessor and kissing his hands, till he forgave him; whereupon the lieutenant went away in the utterest of concern and affright. On this wise the assessor ordered the case and carried out the forgery and feigned marriage with the woman; [and thus was calamity warded off from him] by the excellence of his contrivance."[386]

The folk marvelled at this story with the utmost wonderment and the seventh officer said, 'There befell me in Alexandria the [God-]guarded a marvellous thing, [and it was that one told me the following story].

THE SEVENTH OFFICER'S STORY.

There came one day an old woman [to the stuff-market], with a casket of precious workmanship, containing trinkets, and she was accompanied by a damsel great with child. The old woman sat down at the shop of a draper and giving him to know that the damsel was with child by the prefect of police of the city, took of him, on credit, stuffs to the value of a thousand dinars and deposited with him the casket as security. [She opened the casket and] showed him that which was therein; and he found it full of trinkets [apparently] of price; [so he trusted her with the goods] and she took leave of him and carrying the stuffs to the damsel, who was with her, [went her way]. Then the old woman was absent from him a great while, and when her absence was prolonged, the draper despaired of her; so he went up to the prefect's house and enquired of the woman of his household, [who had taken his stuffs on credit;] but could get no tidings of her nor lit on aught of her trace.

Then he brought out the casket of jewellery [and showed it to an expert,] who told him that the trinkets were gilt and that their worth was but an hundred dirhems. When he heard this, he was sore concerned thereat and presenting himself before the Sultan's deputy, made his complaint to him; whereupon the latter knew that a trick had been put off upon him and that the folk had cozened him and gotten the better of him and taken his stuffs. Now the magistrate in question was a man of good counsel and judgment, well versed in affairs; so he said to the draper, "Remove somewhat from thy shop, [and amongst the rest the casket,] and on the morrow break the lock and cry out and come to me and complain that they have plundered all thy shop. Moreover, do thou call [upon God for succour] and cry aloud and acquaint the folk, so that all the people may resort to thee and see the breach of the lock and that which is missing from thy shop; and do thou show it to every one who presenteth himself, so the news may be noised abroad, and tell them that thy chief concern is for a casket of great value, deposited with thee by a great man of the town and that thou standest in fear of him. But be thou not afraid and still say in thy converse, 'My casket belonged to such an one, and I fear him and dare not bespeak him; but you, O company and all ye who are present, I call you to witness of this for me.' And if there be with thee more than this talk, [say it;] and the old woman will come to thee."

The draper answered with "Hearkening and obedience" and going forth from the deputy's presence, betook himself to his shop and brought out thence [the casket and] somewhat considerable, which he removed to his house. At break of day he arose and going to his shop, broke the lock and cried out and shrieked and called [on God for help,] till the folk assembled about him and all who were in the city were present, whereupon he cried out to them, saying even as the prefect had bidden him; and this was bruited abroad. Then he made for the prefecture and presenting himself before the chief of the police, cried out and complained and made a show of distraction.

After three days, the old woman came to him and bringing him the [thousand dinars, the] price of the stuffs, demanded the casket.[387] When he saw her, he laid hold of her and carried her to the prefect of the city; and when she came before the Cadi, he said to her, "O Sataness, did not thy first deed suffice thee, but thou must come a second time?" Quoth she, "I am of those who seek their salvation[388] in the cities, and we foregather every month; and yesterday we foregathered." "Canst thou [bring me to] lay hold of them?" asked the prefect; and she answered, "Yes; but, if thou wait till to-morrow, they will have dispersed. So I will deliver them to thee to-night." Quoth he to her, "Go;" and she said, "Send with me one who shall go with me to them and obey me in that which I shall say to him, and all that I bid him he shall give ear unto and obey me therein." So he gave her a company of men and she took them and bringing them to a certain door, said to them, "Stand at this door, and whoso cometh out to you, lay hands on him; and I will come out to you last of all." "Hearkening and obedience," answered they and stood at the door, whilst the old woman went in. They waited a long while, even as the Sultan's deputy had bidden them, but none came out to them and their standing was prolonged. When they were weary of waiting, they went up to the door and smote upon it heavily and violently, so that they came nigh to break the lock. Then one of them entered and was absent a long while, but found nought; so he returned to his comrades and said to them,"This is the door of a passage, leading to such a street; and indeed she laughed at you and left you and went away."When they heard his words, they returned to the Amir and acquainted him with the case, whereby he knew that the old woman was a crafty trickstress and that she had laughed at them and cozened them and put a cheat on them, to save herself. Consider, then, the cunning of this woman and that which she contrived of wiles, for all her lack of foresight in presenting herself [a second time] to the draper and not apprehending that his conduct was but a trick; yet, when she found herself in danger, she straightway devised a shift for her deliverance.'

When the company heard the seventh officer's story, they were moved to exceeding mirth, and El Melik ez Zahir Bibers rejoiced in that which he heard and said, 'By Allah, there betide things in this world, from which kings are shut out, by reason of their exalted station!" Then came forward another man from amongst the company and said, 'There hath reached me from one of my friends another story bearing on the malice of women and their craft, and it is rarer and more extraordinary and more diverting than all that hath been told to you."

Quoth the company, 'Tell us thy story and expound it unto us, so we may see that which it hath of extraordinary.' And he said 'Know, then, that

THE EIGHTH OFFICER'S STORY.

A friend of mine once invited me to an entertainment; so I went with him, and when we came into his house and sat down on his couch, he said to me, "This is a blessed day and a day of gladness, and [blessed is] he who liveth to [see] the like of this day. I desire that thou practise with us and deny[389] us not, for that thou hast been used to hearken unto those who occupy themselves with this."[390] I fell in with this and their talk happened upon the like of this subject.[391] Presently, my friend, who had invited me, arose from among them and said to them, "Hearken to me and I will tell you of an adventure that happened to me. There was a certain man who used to visit me in my shop, and I knew him not nor he me, nor ever in his life had he seen me; but he was wont, whenever he had need of a dirhem or two, by way of loan, to come to me and ask me, without acquaintance or intermediary between me and him, [and I would give him what he sought]. I told none of him, and matters abode thus between us a long while, till he fell to borrowing ten at twenty dirhems [at a time], more or less.

One day, as I stood in my shop, there came up to me a woman and stopped before me; and she as she were the full moon rising from among the stars, and the place was illumined by her light. When I saw her, I fixed my eyes on her and stared in her face; and she bespoke me with soft speech. When I heard her words and the sweetness of her speech, I lusted after her; and when she saw that I lusted after her, she did her occasion and promising me [to come again], went away, leaving my mind occupied with her and fire kindled in my heart. Then I abode, perplexed and pondering my affair, whilst fire flamed in my heart, till the third day, when she came again and I scarce credited her coming. When I saw her, I talked with her and cajoled her and courted her and strove to win her favour with speech and invited her [to my house]; but she answered, saying, 'I will not go up into any one's house.' Quoth I, 'I will go with thee;' and she said, 'Arise and come with me.'

So I arose and putting in my sleeve a handkerchief, wherein was a good sum of money, followed the woman, who went on before me and gave not over walking till she brought me to a by-street and to a door, which she bade me open. I refused and she opened it and brought me into the vestibule. As soon as I had entered, she locked the door of entrance from within and said to me, 'Sit [here] till I go in to the slave-girls and cause them enter a place where they shall not see me.' 'It is well,' answered I and sat down; whereupon she entered and was absent from me a moment, after which she returned to me, without a veil, and said, 'Arise, [enter,] in the name of God.'[1392] So I arose and went in after her and we gave not over going till we entered a saloon. When I examined the place, I found it neither handsome nor agreeable, but unseemly and desolate, without symmetry or cleanliness; nay, it was loathly to look upon and there was a foul smell in it.

I seated myself amiddleward the saloon, misdoubting, and as I sat, there came down on me from the estrade seven naked men, without other clothing than leather girdles about their waists. One of them came up to me and took my turban, whilst another took my handkerchief, that was in my sleeve, with my money, and a third stripped me of my clothes; after which a fourth came and bound my hands behind me with his girdle. Then they all took me up, pinioned as I was, and casting me down, fell a-dragging me towards a sink-hole that was there and were about to cut my throat, when, behold, there came a violent knocking at the door. When they heard this, they were afraid and their minds were diverted from me by fear; so the woman went out and presently returning, said to them, 'Fear not; no harm shall betide you this day. It is only your comrade who hath brought you your noon-meal.' With this the new-comer entered, bringing with him a roasted lamb; and when he came in to them, he said to them, 'What is to do with you, that ye have tucked up [your sleeves and trousers]?' Quoth they, '[This is] a piece of game we have caught.'

When he heard this, he came up to me and looking in my face, cried out and said, 'By Allah, this is my brother, the son of my mother and father! Allah! Allah!' Then he loosed me from my bonds and kissed my head, and behold it was my friend who used to borrow money of me. When I kissed his head, he kissed mine and said, 'O my brother, be not affrighted.' Then he called for my clothes [and money and restored to me all that had been taken from me] nor was aught missing to me. Moreover, he brought me a bowl full of [sherbet of] sugar, with lemons therein, and gave me to drink thereof; and the company came and seated me at a table. So I ate with them and he said to me, 'O my lord and my brother, now have bread and salt passed between us and thou hast discovered our secret and [become acquainted with] our case; but secrets [are safe] with the noble.' Quoth I, 'As I am a lawfully-begotten child, I will not name aught [of this] neither denounce [you!*]' And they assured themselves of me by an oath. Then they brought me out and I went my way, scarce crediting but that I was of the dead.

I abode in my house, ill, a whole month; after which I went to the bath and coming out, opened my shop [and sat selling and buying as usual], but saw no more of the man or the woman, till, one day, there stopped before my shop a young man, [a Turcoman], as he were the full moon; and he was a sheep-merchant and had with him a bag, wherein was money, the price of sheep that he had sold. He was followed by the woman, and when he stopped at my shop, she stood by his side and cajoled him, and indeed he inclined to her with a great inclination. As for me, I was consumed with solicitude for him and fell to casting furtive glances at him and winked at him, till he chanced to look round and saw me winking at him; whereupon the woman looked at me and made a sign with her hand and went away. The Turcoman followed her and I counted him dead, without recourse; wherefore I feared with an exceeding fear and shut my shop. Then I journeyed for a year's space and returning, opened my shop; whereupon, behold, the woman came up to me and said, 'This is none other than a great absence.' Quoth I, 'I have been on a journey;' and she said, 'Why didst thou wink at the Turcoman?' 'God forbid!' answered I. 'I did not wink at him.' Quoth she, 'Beware lest thou cross me;' and went away.

 Awhile after this a friend of mine invited me to his house and when I came to him, we ate and drank and talked. Then said he to me, 'O my friend, hath there befallen thee in thy life aught of calamity?' 'Nay,' answered I; 'but tell me [first], hath there befallen thee aught?' ['Yes,'] answered he. 'Know that one day I espied a fair woman; so I followed her and invited her [to come home with me]. Quoth she, "I will not enter any one's house; but come thou to my house, if thou wilt, and be it on such a day." Accordingly, on the appointed day, her messenger came to me, purposing to carry me to her; so I arose and went with him, till we came to a handsome house and a great door. He opened the door and I entered, whereupon he locked the door [behind me] and would have gone in, but I feared with an exceeding fear and foregoing him to the second door, whereby he would have had me enter, locked it and cried out at him, saying, "By Allah, an thou open not to me, I will kill thee; for I am none of those whom thou canst cozen!" Quoth he, "What deemest thou of cozenage?" And I said, "Verily, I am affrighted at the loneliness of the house and the lack of any at the door thereof; for I see none appear." "O my lord," answered he, "this is a privy door." "Privy or public," answered I, "open to me."

So he opened to me and I went out and had not gone far from the house when I met a woman, who said to me, "Methinks a long life was fore-ordained to thee; else hadst thou not come forth of yonder house." "How so?" asked I, and she answered, "Ask thy friend [such an one," naming thee,] "and he will acquaint thee with strange things." So, God on thee, O my friend, tell me what befell thee of wonders and rarities, for I have told thee what befell me.' 'O my brother,' answered I, 'I am bound by a solemn oath.' And he said, 'O my friend, break thine oath and tell me.' Quoth I, 'Indeed, I fear the issue of this.' [But he importuned me] till I told him all, whereat he marvelled. Then I went away from him and abode a long while, [without farther news].

One day, another of my friends came to me and said 'A neighbour of mine hath invited me to hear [music]. [And he would have me go with him;] but I said, 'I will not foregather with any one.' However, he prevailed upon me [to accompany him]; so we repaired to the place and found there a man, who came to meet us and said, '[Enter,] in the name of God!' Then he pulled out a key and opened the door, whereupon we entered and he locked the door after us. Quoth I, 'We are the first of the folk; but where are their voices?'[393] '[They are] within the house,' answered he. 'This is but a privy door; so be not amazed at the absence of the folk.' And my friend said to me, 'Behold, we are two, and what can they avail to do with us?' [Then he brought us into the house,] and when we entered the saloon, we found it exceeding desolate and repulsive of aspect Quoth my friend, 'We are fallen [into a trap]; but there is no power and no virtue save in God the Most High, the Supreme!' And I said, 'May God not requite thee for me with good!'

Then we sat down on the edge of the estrade and presently I espied a closet beside me; so I looked into it and my friend said to me, 'What seest thou?' Quoth I, 'I see therein good galore and bodies of murdered folk. Look.' So he looked and said, 'By Allah, we are lost men!' And we fell a-weeping, I and he. As we were thus, behold, there came in upon us, by the door at which we had entered, four naked men, with girdles of leather about their middles, and made for my friend. He ran at them and dealing one of them a buffet, overthrew him, whereupon the other three fell all upon him. I seized the opportunity to escape, what while they were occupied with him, and espying a door by my side, slipped into it and found myself in an underground chamber, without window or other issue. So I gave myself up for lost and said, 'There is no power and no virtue save in God the Most High, the Supreme!' Then I looked to the top of the vault and saw in it a range of glazed lunettes; so I clambered up for dear life, till I reached the lunettes, and I distracted [for fear]. I made shift to break the glass and scrambling out through the frames, found a wall behind them. So I bestrode the wall and saw folk walking in the road; whereupon I cast myself down to the ground and God the Most High preserved me, so that I reached the earth, unhurt. The folk flocked round me and I acquainted them with my story.

As fate would have it, the chief of the police was passing through the market; so the people told him [what was to do] and he made for the door and burst it open. We entered with a rush and found the thieves, as they had overthrown my friend and cut his throat; for they occupied not themselves with me, but said, 'Whither shall yonder fellow go? Indeed, he is in our grasp.' So the prefect took them with the hand[394] and questioned them, and they confessed against the woman and against their associates in Cairo. Then he took them and went forth, after he had locked up the house and sealed it; and I accompanied him till he came without the [first] house. He found the door locked from within; so he bade break it open and we entered and found another door. This also he caused burst in, enjoining his men to silence till the doors should be opened, and we entered and found the band occupied with a new victim, whom the woman had just brought in and whose throat they were about to cut.

The prefect released the man and gave him back all that the thieves had taken from him; and he laid hands on the woman and the rest and took forth of the house treasures galore. Amongst the rest, they found the money-bag of the Turcoman sheep-merchant. The thieves they nailed up incontinent against the wall of the house, whilst, as for the woman, they wrapped her in one of her veils and nailing her [to a board, set her] upon a camel and went round about the town with her. Thus God razed their dwelling-places and did away from me that which I feared. All this befell, whilst I looked on, and I saw not my friend who had saved me from them the first time, whereat I marvelled to the utterest of marvel. However, some days afterward, he came up to me, and indeed he had renounced[395] [the world] and donned a fakir's habit; and he saluted me and went away.

Then he again began to pay me frequent visits and I entered into converse with him and questioned him of the band and how he came to escape, he alone of them all. Quoth he, 'I left them from the day on which God the Most High delivered thee from them, for that they would not obey my speech; wherefore I swore that I would no longer consort with them.' And I said, 'By Allah, I marvel at thee, for that thou wast the cause of my preservation!' Quoth he, 'The world is full of this sort [of folk]; and we beseech God the Most High for safety, for that these [wretches] practise upon men with every kind of device.' Then said I to him, 'Tell me the most extraordinary adventure of all that befell thee in this villainy thou wast wont to practise.' And he answered, saying, 'O my brother, I was not present when they did on this wise, for that my part with them was to concern myself with selling and buying and [providing them with] food; but I have heard that the most extraordinary thing that befell them was on this wise.

THE THIEF'S STORY.

The woman who used to act as decoy for them once caught them a woman from a bride-feast, under pretence that she had a wedding toward in her own house, and appointed her for a day, whereon she should come to her.

When the appointed day arrived, the woman presented herself and the other carried her into the house by a door, avouching that it was a privy door. When she entered [the saloon], she saw men and champions[396] [and knew that she had fallen into a trap]; so she looked at them and said, "Harkye, lads![397] I am a woman and there is no glory in my slaughter, nor have ye any feud of blood-revenge against me, wherefore ye should pursue me; and that which is upon me of [trinkets and apparel] ye are free to take." Quoth they, "We fear thy denunciation." But she answered, saying, "I will abide with you, neither coming in nor going out." And they said, "We grant thee thy life."

Then the captain looked on her [and she pleased him]; so he took her for himself and she abode with him a whole year, doing her endeavour in their service. till they became accustomed to her [and felt assured of her]. One night she plied them with drink and they drank [till they became intoxicated]; whereupon she arose and took her clothes and five hundred dinars from the captain; after which she fetched a razor and shaved all their chins. Then she took soot from the cooking-pots and blackening their faces withal, opened the doors and went out; and when the thieves awoke, they abode confounded and knew that the woman had practised upon them.""

The company marvelled at this story and the ninth officer came forward and said, 'I will tell you a right goodly story I heard at a wedding.

THE NINTH OFFICER'S STORY.

A certain singing-woman was fair of favour and high in repute, and it befell one day that she went out apleasuring. As she sat,[398] behold, a man lopped of the hand stopped to beg of her, and he entered in at the door. Then he touched her with his stump, saying, "Charity, for the love of God!" but she answered, "God open [on thee the gate of subsistence]!" and reviled him. Some days after this, there came to her a messenger and gave her the hire of her going forth.[399] So she took with her a handmaid and an accompanyist;[400] and when she came to the appointed place, the messenger brought her into a long passage, at the end whereof was a saloon. So (quoth she) we entered and found none therein, but saw the [place made ready for an] entertainment with candles and wine and dessert, and in another place we saw food and in a third beds.

We sat down and I looked at him who had opened the door to us, and behold he was lopped of the hand. I misliked this of him, and when I had sat a little longer, there entered a man, who filled the lamps in the saloon and lit the candles; and behold, he also was handlopped. Then came the folk and there entered none except he were lopped cf the hand, and indeed the house was full of these. When the assembly was complete, the host entered and the company rose to him and seated him in the place of honour. Now he was none other than the man who had fetched me, and he was clad in sumptuous apparel, but his hands were in his sleeves, so that I knew not how it was with them. They brought him food and he ate, he and the company; after which they washed their hands and the host fell to casting furtive glances at me.

Then they drank till they were drunken, and when they had taken leave [of their wits], the host turned to me and said, "Thou dealtest not friendly with him who sought an alms of thee and thou saidst to him, 'How loathly thou art!'" I considered him and behold, he was the lophand who had accosted me in my pleasaunce. So I said, "O my lord, what is this thou sayest?" And he answered, saying, "Wait; thou shall remember it." So saying, he shook his head and stroked his beard, whilst I sat down for fear. Then he put out his hand to my veil and shoes and laying them by his side, said to me, "Sing, O accursed one!" So I sang till I was weary, whilst they occupied themselves with their case and intoxicated themselves and their heat redoubled.[401] Presently, the doorkeeper came to me and said, "Fear not, O my lady; but, when thou hast a mind to go, let me know." Quoth I, "Thinkest thou to delude me?" And he said, "Nay, by Allah! But I have compassion on thee for that our captain and our chief purposeth thee no good and methinketh he will slay thee this night." Quoth I to him, "An thou be minded to do good, now is the time." And he answered, saying, "When our chief riseth to do his occasion and goeth to the draught-house, I will enter before him with the light and leave the door open; and do thou go whithersoever thou wilt."

Then I sang and the captain said, "It is good," Quoth I, "Nay, but thou art loathly." He looked at me and said, "By Allah, thou shalt never more scent the odour of the world!" But his comrades said to him, "Do it not," and appeased him, till he said, "If it must be so, she shall abide here a whole year, not going forth." And I said, "I am content to submit to whatsoever pleaseth thee. If I have erred, thou art of those to whom pertaineth clemency." He shook his head and drank, then arose and went out to do his occasion, what while his comrades were occupied with what they were about of merry-making and drunkenness and sport. So I winked to my fellows and we slipped out into the corridor. We found the door open and fled forth, unveiled and knowing not whither we went; nor did we halt till we had left the house far behind and happened on a cook cooking, to whom said I, "Hast thou a mind to quicken dead folk?" And he said, "Come up." So we went up into the shop, and he said, 'Lie down." Accordingly, we lay down and he covered us with the grass,[402] wherewith he was used to kindle [the fire] under the food.

Hardly had we settled ourselves in the place when we heard a noise of kicking [at the door] and people running right and left and questioning the cook and saying, "Hath any one passed by thee?" "Nay," answered he; "none hath passed by me." But they ceased not to go round about the shop till the day broke, when they turned back, disappointed. Then the cook removed the grass and said to us, "Arise, for ye are delivered from death." So we arose, and we were uncovered, without mantle or veil; but the cook carried us up into his house and we sent to our lodgings and fetched us veils; and we repented unto God the Most High and renounced singing,[403] for indeed this was a great deliverance after stress.'

The company marvelled at this story and the tenth officer came forward and said, 'As for me, there befell me that which was yet more extraordinary than all this.' Quoth El Melik ez Zahir, 'What was that?' And he said,

THE TENTH OFFICER'S STORY.

'A great theft had been committed in the city and I was cited,[404] I and my fellows. Now it was a matter of considerable value and they[405] pressed hard upon us; but we obtained of them some days' grace and dispersed in quest of the stolen goods. As for me, I sallied forth with five men and went round about the city that day; and on the morrow we fared forth [into the suburbs]. When we came a parasang or two parasangs' distance from the city, we were athirst; and presently we came to a garden. So I went in and going up to the water-wheel,[406] entered it and drank and made the ablution and prayed. Presently up came the keeper of the garden and said to me, "Out on thee! Who brought thee into this water-wheel?" And he cuffed me and squeezed my ribs till I was like to die. Then he bound me with one of his bulls and made me turn in the water-wheel, flogging me the while with a cattle whip he had with him, till my heart was on fire; after which he loosed me and I went out, knowing not the way.

When I came forth, I swooned away: so I sat down till my trouble subsided; then I made for my comrades and said to them, "I have found the booty and the thief, and I affrighted him not neither troubled him, lest he should flee; but now, come, let us go to him, so we may make shift to lay hold upon him." Then I took them and repaired to the keeper of the garden, who had tortured me with beating, meaning to make him taste the like of that which he had done with me and lie against him and cause him eat stick. So we rushed into the water-wheel and seizing the keeper, pinioned him.

Now there was with him a youth and he said, "By Allah, I was not with him and indeed it is six months since I entered the city, nor did I set eyes on the stuffs until they were brought hither." Quoth we, "Show us the stuffs." So he carried us to a place wherein was a pit, beside the water-wheel, and digging there, brought out the stolen goods, with not a stitch of them missing. So we took them and carried the keeper to the prefecture, where we stripped him and beat him with palm-rods till he confessed to thefts galore. Now I did this by way of mockery against my comrades, and it succeeded.'[407]

The company marvelled at this story with the utmost wonderment, and the eleventh officer rose and said, 'I know a story yet rarer than this: but it happened not to myself.

THE ELEVENTH OFFICER'S STORY.

There was once aforetime a chief officer [of police] and there passed by him one day a Jew, with a basket in his hand, wherein were five thousand dinars; whereupon quoth the officer to one of his slaves, "Canst thou make shift to take that money from yonder Jew's basket?" "Yes," answered he, nor did he tarry beyond the next day before he came to his master, with the basket in his hand. So (quoth the officer) I said to him, "Go, bury it in such a place." So he went and buried it and returned and told me. Hardly had he done this when there arose a clamour and up came the Jew, with one of the king's officers, avouching that the money belonged to the Sultan and that he looked to none but us for it. We demanded of him three days' delay, as of wont, and I said to him who had taken the money, "Go and lay somewhat in the Jew's house, that shall occupy him with himself." So he went and played a fine trick, to wit, he laid in a basket a dead woman's hand, painted [with henna] and having a gold seal- ring on one of the fingers, and buried the basket under a flagstone in the Jew's house. Then came we and searched and found the basket, whereupon we straightway clapped the Jew in irons for the murder of a woman.

When it was the appointed time, there came to us the man of the Sultan's guards, [who had accompanied the Jew, when he came to complain of the loss of the money,] and said, "The Sultan biddeth you nail up[408] the Jew and bring the money, for that there is no way by which five thousand dinars can be lost." Wherefore we knew that our device sufficed not. So I went forth and finding a young man, a Haurani,[409] passing the road, laid hands on him and stripped him and beat him with palm-rods. Then I clapped him in irons and carrying him to the prefecture, beat him again, saying to them, "This is the thief who stole the money." And we strove to make him confess; but he would not confess. So we beat him a third and a fourth time, till we were weary and exhausted and he became unable to return an answer. But, when we had made an end of beating and tormenting him, he said, "I will fetch the money forthright."

So we went with him till he came to the place where my slave had buried the money and dug there and brought it out; whereat I marvelled with the utmost wonder and we carried it to the prefect's house. When the latter saw the money, he rejoiced with an exceeding joy and bestowed on me a dress of honour. Then he restored the money straightway to the Sultan and we left the youth in prison; whilst I said to my slave who had taken the money, "Did yonder young man see thee, what time thou buriedst the money?" "No, by the Great God!" answered he. So I went in to the young man, the prisoner, and plied him with wine till he recovered, when I said to him, "Tell me how thou stolest the money." "By Allah," answered he, "I stole it not, nor did I ever set eyes on it till I brought it forth of the earth!" Quoth I, "How so?" And he said, "Know that the cause of my falling into your hands was my mother's imprecation against me; for that I evil entreated her yesternight and beat her and she said to me, 'By Allah, O my son, God shall assuredly deliver thee into the hand of the oppressor!' Now she is a pious woman. So I went out forthright and thou sawest me in the way and didst that which thou didst; and when beating was prolonged on me, my senses failed me and I heard one saying to me, 'Fetch it.' So I said to you what I said and he[410] guided me till I came to the place and there befell what befell of the bringing out of the money."

I marvelled at this with the utmost wonderment and knew that he was of the sons of the pious. So I bestirred myself for his release and tended him [till he recovered] and besought him of quittance and absolution of responsibility.'

All those who were present marvelled at this story with the utmost marvel, and the twelfth officer came forward and said, 'I will tell you a pleasant trait that I had from a certain man, concerning an adventure that befell him with one of the thieves. (Quoth he)

THE TWELFTH OFFICER'S STORY.

As I was passing one day in the market, I found that a thief had broken into the shop of a money-changer and taken thence a casket, with which he had made off to the burial-grounds. So I followed him thither [and came up to him, as] he opened the casket and fell a-looking into it; whereupon I accosted him, saying, "Peace be on thee!" And he was startled at me. Then I left him and went away from him.

Some months after this, I met him again under arrest, in the midst of the guards and officers of the police, and he said to them, "Seize yonder man." So they laid hands on me and carried me to the chief of the police, who said, "What hast thou to do with this fellow?" The thief turned to me and looking a long while in my face, said, "Who took this man?" Quoth the officers, "Thou badest us take him; so we took him." And he said, "I seek refuge with God! I know not this man, nor knoweth he me, and I said not that to you but of a man other than this." So they released me, and awhile afterward the thief met me in the street and saluted me, saying, "O my lord, fright for fright! Hadst thou taken aught from me, thou hadst had a part in the calamity."[411] And I said to him, "God [judge] between thee and me!" And this is what I have to tell'

Then came forward the thirteenth officer and said, 'I will tell you a story that a man of my friends told me. (Quoth he)

THE THIRTEENTH OFFICER'S STORY.

I went out one night to the house of one of my friends and when it was the middle of the night, I sallied forth alone [to go home]. When I came into the road, I espied a sort of thieves and they saw me, whereupon my spittle dried up; but I feigned myself drunken and staggered from side to side, crying out and saying, "I am drunken." And I went up to the walls right and left and made as if I saw not the thieves, who followed me till I reached my house and knocked at the door, when they went away.

Some days after this, as I stood at the door of my house, there came up to me a young man, with a chain about his neck and with him a trooper, and he said to me, "O my lord, charity for the love of God!" Quoth I, "God open!"[412] and he looked at me a long while and said, "That which thou shouldst give me would not come to the value of thy turban or thy waistcloth or what not else of thy raiment, to say nothing of the gold and the silver that was about thee." "How so?" asked I, and he said, "On such a night, when thou fellest into peril and the thieves would have stripped thee, I was with them and said to them, 'Yonder man is my lord and my master who reared me.' So was I the cause of thy deliverance and thus I saved thee from them." When I heard this, I said to him, "Stop;" and entering my house, brought him that which God the Most High made easy [to me].[413] So he went his way. And this is my story.'

Then came forward the fourteenth officer and said, 'Know that the story I have to tell is pleasanter and more extraordinary than this; and it is as follows.

THE FOURTEENTH OFFICER'S STORY.

Before I entered this corporation,[414] I had a draper's shop and there used to come to me a man whom I knew not, save by his face, and I would give him what he sought and have patience with him, till he could pay me. One day, I foregathered with certain of my friends and we sat down to drink. So we drank and made merry and played at Tab;[415] and we made one of us Vizier and another Sultan and a third headsman.

Presently, there came in upon us a spunger, without leave, and we went on playing, whilst he played with us. Then quoth the Sultan to the Vizier, "Bring the spunger who cometh in to the folk, without leave or bidding, that we may enquire into his case. Then will I cut off his head." So the headsman arose and dragged the spunger before the Sultan, who bade cut off his head. Now there was with them a sword, that would not cut curd;[416] so the headsman smote him therewith and his head flew from his body. When we saw this, the wine fled from our heads and we became in the sorriest of plights. Then my friends took up the body and went out with it, that they might hide it, whilst I took the head and made for the river.

Now I was drunken and my clothes were drenched with the blood; and as I passed along the road, I met a thief. When he saw me, he knew me and said to me, "Harkye, such an one!" "Well?" answered I, and he said, "What is that thou hast with thee?" So I acquainted him with the case and he took the head from me. Then we went on till we came to the river, where he washed the head and considering it straitly, said, "By Allah, this is my brother, my father's son. and he used to spunge upon the folk." Then he threw the head into the river. As for me, I was like a dead man [for fear]; but he said to me, "Fear not neither grieve, for thou art quit of my brother's blood."

Then he took my clothes and washed them and dried them, and put them on me; after which he said to me, "Get thee gone to thy house." So I returned to my house and he accompanied me, till I came thither, when he said to me, "May God not forsake thee! I am thy friend [such an one, who used to take of thee goods on credit,] and I am beholden to thee for kindness; but henceforward thou wilt never see me more."'

The company marvelled at the generosity of this man and his clemency[417] and courtesy, and the Sultan said, 'Tell us another of thy stories.'[418] 'It is well,' answered the officer, 'They avouch that

A MERRY JEST OF A THIEF.

A thief of the thieves of the Arabs went [one night] to a certain man's house, to steal from a heap of wheat there, and the people of the house surprised him. Now on the heap was a great copper measure, and the thief buried himself in the corn and covered his head with the measure, so that the folk found him not and went away; but, as they were going, behold, there came a great crack of wind forth of the corn. So they went up to the measure and [raising it], discovered the thief and laid hands on him. Quoth he, "I have eased you of the trouble of seeking me: for I purposed, [in letting wind], to direct you to my [hiding-]place; wherefore do ye ease me and have compassion on me, so may God have compassion on you!" So they let him go and harmed him not.

And for another story of the same kind,' continued the officer,

STORY OF THE OLD SHARPER.

'There was once an old man renowned for roguery, and he went, he and his mates, to one of the markets and stole thence a parcel of stuffs. Then they separated and returned each to his quarter. Awhile after this, the old man assembled a company of his fellows and one of them pulled out a costly piece of stuff and said, "Will any one of you sell this piece of stuff in its own market whence it was stolen, that we may confess his [pre-eminence in] sharping?" Quoth the old man, "I will;" and they said, "Go, and God the Most High prosper thee!"

So on the morrow, early, he took the stuff and carrying it to the market whence it had been stolen, sat down at the shop whence it had been stolen and gave it to the broker, who took it and cried it for sale. Its owner knew it and bidding for it, [bought it] and sent after the chief of the police, who seized the sharper and seeing him an old man of venerable appearance, handsomely clad, said to him, "Whence hadst thou this piece of stuff?" "I had it from this market," answered he, "and from yonder shop where I was sitting." Quoth the prefect, "Did its owner sell it to thee?" "Nay," replied the thief; "I stole it and other than it." Then said the magistrate, "How camest thou to bring it [for sale] to the place whence thou stolest it?" And he answered, "I will not tell my story save to the Sultan, for that I have an advertisement[419] wherewith I would fain bespeak him." Quoth the prefect, "Name it." And the thief said, "Art thou the Sultan?" "No," replied the other; and the old man said, "I will not tell it but to himself."

So the prefect carried him up to the Sultan and he said, "I have an advertisement for thee, O my lord." "What is thine advertisement?" asked the Sultan; and the thief said, "I repent and will deliver into thy hand all who are evildoers; and whomsoever I bring not, I will stand in his stead." Quoth the Sultan, "Give him a dress of honour and accept his profession of repentance." So he went down from the presence and returning to his comrades, related to them that which had passed and they confessed his subtlety and gave him that which they had promised him. Then he took the rest of the stolen goods and went up with them to the Sultan. When the latter saw him, he was magnified in his eyes and he commanded that nought should be taken from him. Then, when he went down, [the Sultan's] attention was diverted from him, little by little, till the case was forgotten, and so he saved the booty [for himself].' The folk marvelled at this and the fifteenth officer came forward and said, 'Know that among those who make a trade of knavery are those whom God the Most High taketh on their own evidence against themselves.' 'How so?' asked they; and he said.

THE FIFTEENTH OFFICER'S STORY.

'It is told of a certain doughty thief, that he used to rob and stop the way by himself upon caravans, and whenever the prefect of police and the magistrates sought him, he would flee from them and fortify himself in the mountains. Now it befell that a certain man journeyed along the road wherein was the robber in question, and this man was alone and knew not the perils that beset his way. So the highwayman came out upon him and said to him, "Bring out that which is with thee, for I mean to slay thee without fail." Quoth the traveller, "Slay me not, but take these saddle-bags and divide [that which is in] them and take the fourth part [thereof]." And the thief answered, "I will not take aught but the whole." "Take half," rejoined the traveller, "and let me go." But the robber replied, "I will take nought but the whole, and I will slay thee [to boot]." And the traveller said, "Take it."

So the highwayman took the saddle-bags and offered to kill the traveller, who said, "What is this? Thou hast no blood-feud against me, that should make my slaughter incumbent [on thee]. Quoth the other, "Needs must I slay thee;" whereupon the traveller dismounted from his horse and grovelled on the earth, beseeching the robber and speaking him fair. The latter hearkened not to his prayers, but cast him to the ground; whereupon the traveller [raised his eyes and seeing a francolin flying over him,] said, in his agony," O francolin, bear witness that this man slayeth me unjustly and wickedly; for indeed I have given him all that was with me and besought him to let me go, for my children's sake; yet would he not consent unto this. But be thou witness against him, for God is not unmindful of that which is done of the oppressors." The highwayman paid no heed to this speech, but smote him and cut off his head.

After this, the authorities compounded with the highwayman for his submission, and when he came before them, they enriched him and he became in such favour with the Sultan's deputy that he used to eat and drink with him and there befell familiar converse between them. On this wise they abode a great while, till, one day, the Sultan's deputy made a banquet, and therein, for a wonder, was a roasted francolin, which when the robber saw, he laughed aloud. The deputy was angered against him and said to him, "What is the meaning of thy laughter? Seest thou default [in the entertainment] or dost thou mock at us, of thy lack of breeding?" "Not so, by Allah, O my lord," answered the highwayman. "But I saw yonder francolin and bethought myself thereanent of an extraordinary thing; and it was on this wise. In the days of my youth, I used to stop the way, and one day I fell in with a man, who had with him a pair of saddle-bags and money therein. So I said to him, 'Leave these bags, for I mean to kill thee.' Quoth he, 'Take the fourth part of [that which is in] them and leave [me] the rest.' And I said, 'Needs must I take the whole and slay thee, to boot.' Then said he, 'Take the saddle-bags and let me go my way.' But I answered, 'Needs must I slay thee.' As we were in this contention, he and I, behold, he saw a francolin and turning to it, said, 'Bear witness against him, O francolin, that he slayeth me unjustly and letteth me not go to my children, for all he hath gotten my money.' However, I took no pity on him neither hearkened to that which he said, but slew him and concerned not myself with the francolin's testimony."

His story troubled the Sultan's deputy and he was sore enraged against him; so he drew his sword and smiting him, cut off his head; whereupon one recited the following verses:

An you'd of evil be quit, look that no evil yon do; Nay, but do good, for the like God will still render to you.
All things, indeed, that betide to you are fore-ordered of God; Yet still in your deeds is the source to which their fulfilment is due.

Now this[420] was the francolin that bore witness against him.'

The company marvelled at this story and said all, 'Woe to the oppressor!' Then came forward the sixteenth officer and said, 'And I also will tell you a marvellous story, and it is on this wise.

THE SIXTEENTH OFFICER'S STORY.

I went forth one day, purposing to make a journey, and fell in with a man whose wont it was to stop the way. When he came up with me, he offered to slay me and I said to him, "I have nothing with me whereby thou mayst profit." Quoth he, "My profit shall be the taking of thy life." "What is the cause of this?" asked I. "Hath there been feud between us aforetime?" And he answered, "No; but needs must I slay thee." Therewithal I fled from him to the river-side; but he overtook me and casting me to the ground, sat down on my breast. So I sought help of the Sheikh El Hejjaj[421] and said to him, "Protect me from this oppressor!" And indeed he had drawn a knife, wherewith to cut my throat, when, behold, there came a great crocodile forth of the river and snatching him up from off my breast, plunged with him into the water, with the knife still in his hand; whilst I abode extolling the perfection of God the Most High and rendering thanks for my preservation to Him who had delivered me from the hand of that oppressor.'

ABDALLAH BEN NAFI AND THE KING'S SON OF CASHGHAR[422]

THERE abode once, of old days and in bygone ages and times, in the city of Baghdad, the Abode of Peace, the Khalif Haroun er Reshid, and he had boon-companions and story-tellers, to entertain him by night Among his boon-companions was a man called Abdallah ben Nan, who was high in favour with him and dear unto him, so that he was not forgetful of him a single hour. Now it befell, by the ordinance of destiny, that it became manifest to Abdallah that he was grown of little account with the Khalif and that he paid no heed unto him; nor, if he absented himself, did he enquire concerning him, as had been his wont. This was grievous to Abdallah and he said in himself, "Verily, the heart of the Commander of the Faithful and his fashions are changed towards me and nevermore shall I get of him that cordiality wherewith he was wont to entreat me." And this was distressful to him and concern waxed upon him, so that he recited the following verses:

If, in his own land, midst his folk, abjection and despite Afflict a man, then exile sure were better for the wight.
So get thee gone, then, from a house wherein thou art abased And let not severance from friends lie heavy on thy spright.
Crude amber[423] in its native land unheeded goes, but, when It comes abroad, upon the necks to raise it men delight.
Kohl[424] in its native country, too, is but a kind of stone; Cast out and thrown upon the ways, it lies unvalued quite;
But, when from home it fares, forthright all glory it attains And 'twixt the eyelid and the eye incontinent 'tis dight.

Then he could brook this no longer; so he went forth from the dominions of the Commander of the Faithful, under pretence of visiting certain of his kinsmen, and took with him servant nor companion, neither acquainted any with his intent, but betook himself to the road and fared on into the desert and the sandwastes, knowing not whither he went. After awhile, he fell in with travellers intending for the land of Hind [and journeyed with them]. When he came thither, he lighted down [in a city of the cities of the land and took up his abode] in one of the lodging-places; and there he abode a while of days, tasting not food neither solacing himself with the delight of sleep; nor was this for lack of dirhems or dinars, but for that his mind was occupied with musing upon [the reverses of] destiny and bemoaning himself for that the revolving sphere had turned against him and the days had decreed unto him the disfavour of our lord the Imam.[425]

On this wise he abode a space of days, after which he made himself at home in the land and took to himself comrades and got him friends galore, with whom he addressed himself to diversion and good cheer. Moreover, he went a-pleasuring with his friends and their hearts were solaced [by his company] and he entertained them with stories and civilities[426] and diverted them with pleasant verses and told them abundance of histories and anecdotes. Presently, the report of him reached King Jemhour, lord of Cashghar of Hind, and great was his desire [for his company]. So he went in quest of him and Abdallah repaired to his court and going in to him, kissed the earth before him. Jemhour welcomed him and entreated him with kindness and bade commit him to the guest-house, where he abode three days, at the end of which time the king sent [to him] a chamberlain of his chamberlains and let bring him to his presence. When he came before him, he greeted him [with the usual compliment], and the interpreter accosted him, saying, "King Jemhour hath heard of thy report, that thou art a goodly boon-companion and an eloquent story-teller, and he would have thee company with him by night and entertain him with that which thou knowest of anecdotes and pleasant stories and verses." And he made answer with "Hearkening and obedience."

(Quoth Abdallah ben Nan) So I became his boon-companion and entertained him by night [with stories and the like]; and this pleased him to the utmost and he took me into especial favour and bestowed on me dresses of honour and assigned me a separate lodging; brief, he was everywise bountiful to me and could not brook to be parted from me a single hour. So I abode with him a while of time and every night I caroused with him [and entertained him], till the most part of the night was past; and when drowsiness overcame him, he would rise [and betake himself] to his sleeping-place, saying to me, "Forsake not my service for that of another than I and hold not aloof from my presence." And I made answer with "Hearkening and obedience."

Now the king had a son, a pleasant child, called the Amir Mohammed, who was comely of youth and sweet of speech; he had read in books and studied histories and above all things in the world he loved the telling and hearing of verses and stories and anecdotes. He was dear to his father King Jemhour, for that he had none other son than he on life, and indeed he had reared him in the lap of fondness and he was gifted with the utterest of beauty and grace and brightness and perfection. Moreover, he had learnt to play upon the lute and upon all manner instruments of music and he was used to [carouse and] company with friends and brethren. Now it was of his wont that, when the king rose to go to his sleeping-chamber, he would sit in his place and seek of me that I should entertain him with stories and verses and pleasant anecdotes; and on this wise I abode with them a great while in all cheer and delight, and the prince still loved me with an exceeding great love and entreated me with the utmost kindness.

It befell one day that the king's son came to me, after his father had withdrawn, and said to me, "Harkye, Ibn Nafil" "At thy service, O my lord," answered I; and he said, "I would have thee tell me an extraordinary story and a rare matter, that thou hast never related either to me or to my father Jemhour." "O my lord," rejoined I, "what story is this that thou desirest of me and of what kind shall it be of the kinds?" Quoth he, "It matters little what it is, so it be a goodly story, whether it befell of old days or in these times." "O my lord," said I, "I know many stories of various kinds; so whether of the kinds preferrest thou, and wilt thou have a story of mankind or of the Jinn?" "It is well," answered he; "if thou have seen aught with thine eyes and heard it with thine ears, [tell it me."Then he bethought himself] and said to me, "I conjure thee by my life, tell me a story of the stories of the Jinn and that which thou hast heard and seen of them!" "O my son," replied I, "indeed thou conjurest [me] by a mighty conjuration; so [hearken and thou shalt] hear the goodliest of stories, ay, and the most extraordinary of them and the pleasantest and rarest." Quoth the prince, "Say on, for I am attentive to thy speech." And I said, "Know, then, O my son, that

STORY OF THE DAMSEL TUHFET EL CULOUB AND THE KHALIF HAROUN ER RESHID.

The Vicar of the Lord of the Worlds[427] Haroun er Reshid had a boon-companion of the number of his boon-companions, by name Ishac ben Ibrahim en Nedim el Mausili,[428] who was the most accomplished of the folk of his time in the art of smiting upon the lute; and of the Commander of the Faithful's love for him, he assigned him a palace of the choicest of his palaces, wherein he was wont to instruct slave-girls in the arts of lute-playing and singing. If any slave-girl became, by his instruction, accomplished in the craft, he carried her before the Khalif, who bade her play upon the lute; and if she pleased him, he would order her to the harem; else would he restore her to Ishac's palace.

One day, the Commander of the Faithful's breast was straitened; so he sent after his Vizier Jaafer the Barmecide and Ishac the boon-companion and Mesrour the eunuch, the swordsman of his vengeance; and when they came, he changed his raiment and disguised himself, whilst Jaafer [and Ishac] and Mesrour and El Fezll[429] and Younus[430] (who were also present) did the like. Then he went out, he and they, by the privy gate, to the Tigris and taking boat, fared on till they came to near Et Taf,[431] when they landed and walked till they came to the gate of the thoroughfare street.[432] Here there met them an old man, comely of hoariness and of a venerable and dignified bearing, pleasing[433] of aspect and apparel. He kissed the earth before Ishac el Mausili (for that be knew but him of the company, the Khalif being disguised, and deemed the others certain of his friends) and said to him, 'O my lord, there is presently with me a slave-girl, a lutanist, never saw eyes the like of her nor the like of her grace, and indeed I was on my way to pay my respects to thee and give thee to know of her; but Allah, of His favour, hath spared me the trouble. So now I desire to show her to thee, and if she be to thy liking, well and good: else I will sell her.' Quoth Ishac, 'Go before me to thy barrack, till I come to thee and see her.'

The old man kissed his hand and went away; whereupon quoth Er Reshid to him, 'O Ishac, who is yonder man and what is his occasion?' 'O my lord,' answered the other, 'this is a man called Said the Slave-dealer, and he it is who buyeth us slave-girls and mamelukes.[434] He avoucheth that with him is a fair [slave-girl, a] lutanist, whom he hath withheld from sale, for that he could not fairly sell her till he had shown her to me.' 'Let us go to him,' said the Khalif,'so we may look on her, by way of diversion, and see what is in the slave-dealer's barrack of slave-girls.' And Ishac answered, 'Commandment belongeth to God and to the Commander of the Faithful.' Then he went on before them and they followed in his track till they came to the slave-dealer's barrack and found it high of building and spacious of continence, with sleeping-cells and chambers therein, after the number of the slave-girls, and folk sitting upon the benches.

Ishac entered, he and his company, and seating themselves in the place of honour, amused themselves by looking on the slave-girls and mamelukes and watching how they were sold, till the sale came to an end, when some of the folk went away and other some sat. Then said the slave-dealer, 'Let none sit with us except him who buyeth by the thousand [dinars] and upwards.' So those who were present withdrew and there remained none but Er Reshid and his company; whereupon the slave-dealer called the damsel, after he had caused set her a chair of fawwak,[435] furnished with Greek brocade, and it was as she were the sun shining in the clear sky. When she entered, she saluted and sitting down, took the lute and smote upon it, after she had touched its strings and tuned it, so that all present were amazed. Then she sang thereto the following verses:

Wind of the East, if thou pass by the land where my loved ones dwell, I pray, The fullest of greetings bear to them from me, their lover, and say
That I am the pledge of passion still and that my longing love And eke my yearning do overpass all longing that was aye.
O ye who have withered my heart and marred my hearing and my sight, Desire and transport for your sake wax on me night and day.
My heart with yearning is ever torn and tortured without cease, Nor can my lids lay hold on sleep, that Sees from them away.

'Well done, O damsel!' cried Ishac. 'By Allah, this is a fair hour!' Whereupon she rose and kissed his hand, saying, 'O my lord, the hands stand still in thy presence and the tongues at thy sight, and the eloquent before thee are dumb; but thou art the looser of the veil.'[436] Then she clung to him and said, 'Stand.' So he stood and said to her, 'Who art thou and what is thy need?' She raised a corner of the veil, and he beheld a damsel as she were the rising full moon or the glancing lightning, with two side locks of hair that fell down to her anklets. She kissed his hand and said to him, 'O my lord, know that I have been in this barrack these five months, during which time I have been withheld[437] from sale till thou shouldst be present [and see me]; and yonder slave-dealer still made thy coming a pretext to me[438] and forbade me, for all I sought of him night and day that he should cause thee come hither and vouchsafe me thy presence and bring me and thee together.' Quoth Ishac, 'Say what thou wouldst have.' And she answered, 'I beseech thee, by God the Most High, that thou buy me, so I may be with thee, by way of service.' 'Is that thy desire?' asked he, and she replied, ' Yes.'

So Ishac returned to the slave-dealer and said to him, 'Harkye, Gaffer Said!*' 'At thy service, O my lord,' answered the old man; and Ishac said, 'In the corridor is a cell and therein a damsel pale of colour. What is her price in money and how much dost thou ask for her?, Quoth the slave-dealer, 'She whom thou mentionest is called Tuhfet el Hemca.'[439] 'What is the meaning of El Hemca?' asked Ishac, and the old man replied, 'Her price hath been paid down an hundred times and she still saith, "Show me him who desireth to buy me;" and when I show her to him, she saith, "This fellow is not to my liking; he hath in him such and such a default." And in every one who would fain buy her she allegeth some default or other, so that none careth now to buy her and none seeketh her, for fear lest she discover some default in him.' Quoth Ishac, 'She seeketh presently to sell herself; so go thou to her and enquire of her and see her price and send her to the palace.' 'O my lord,' answered Said, 'her price s an hundred dinars, though, were she whole of this paleness that is upon her face, she would be worth a thousand; but folly and pallor have diminished her value; and behold, I will go to her and consult her of this.' So he betook himself to her, and said to her, 'Wilt thou be sold to Ishac ben Ibrahim el Mausili?' 'Yes,' answered she, and he said, 'Leave frowardness,[440] for to whom doth it happen to be in the house of Ishac the boon-companion?'[441]

Then Ishac went forth of the barrack and overtook Er Reshid [who had foregone him]; and they walked till they came to their [landing-]place, where they embarked in the boat and fared on to Theghr el Khanekah.[442] As for the slave-dealer, he sent the damsel to the house of Ishac en Nedim, whose slave-girls took her and carried her to the bath. Then each damsel gave her somewhat of her apparel and they decked her with earrings and bracelets, so that she redoubled in beauty and became as she were the moon on the night of its full. When Ishac returned home from the Khalifs palace, Tuhfeh rose to him and kissed his hand; and he saw that which the slave-girls had done with her and thanked them therefor and said to them, 'Let her be in the house of instruction and bring her instruments of music, and if she be apt unto singing, teach her; and may God the Most High vouchsafe her health and weal!' So there passed over her three months, what while she abode with him in the house of instruction, and they brought her the instruments of music. Moreover, as time went on, she was vouchsafed health and soundness and her beauty waxed many times greater than before and her pallor was changed to white and red, so that she became a ravishment to all who looked on her.

One day, Ishac let bring all who were with him of slave-girls from the house of instruction and carried them up to Er Reshid's palace, leaving none in his house save Tuhfeh and a cookmaid; for that he bethought him not of Tuhfeh, nor did she occur to his mind, and none of the damsels remembered him of her. When she saw that the house was empty of the slave-girls, she took the lute (now she was unique in her time in smiting upon the lute, nor had she her like in the world, no, not Ishac himself, nor any other) and sang thereto the following verses:

Whenas the soul desireth one other than its peer, It winneth not of fortune the wish it holdeth dear.
Him with my life I'd ransom whose rigours waste away My frame and cause me languish; yet, if he would but hear,
It rests with him to heal me; and I (a soul he hath Must suffer that which irks it), go saying, in my fear
Of spies, "How long, O scoffer, wilt mock at my despair, As 'twere God had created nought else whereat to jeer?"

Now Ishac had returned to his house upon an occasion that presented itself to him; and when he entered the vestibule, he heard a sound of singing, the like whereof he had never heard in the world, for that it was [soft] as the breeze and richer[443] than almond oil.[444] So the delight of it gat hold of him and joyance overcame him, and he fell down aswoon in the vestibule, Tuhfeh heard the noise of steps and laying the lute from her hand, went out to see what was to do. She found her lord Ishac lying aswoon in the vestibule; so she took him up and strained him to her bosom, saying, 'I conjure thee in God's name, O my lord, tell me, hath aught befallen thee?' When he heard her voice, he recovered from his swoon and said to her, 'Who art thou? ' Quoth she, 'I am thy slave-girl Tuhfeh.' And he said to her, 'Art thou indeed Tuhfeh?' 'Yes,' answered she; and he, 'By Allah, I had forgotten thee and remembered thee not till now!' Then he looked at her and said, 'Indeed, thy case is altered and thy pallor is grown changed to rosiness and thou hast redoubled in beauty and lovesomeness. But was it thou who was singing but now?' And she was troubled and affrighted and answered, 'Even I, O my lord.'

Then Ishac seized upon her hand and carrying her into the house, said to her, 'Take the lute and sing; for never saw I nor heard thy like in smiting upon the lute; no, not even myself!' 'O my lord,' answered she, 'thou makest mock of me. Who am I that thou shouldst say all this to me?

Indeed, this is but of thy kindness.' 'Nay, by Allah,' exclaimed he, 'I said but the truth to thee and I am none of those on whom pretence imposeth. These three months hath nature not moved thee to take the lute and sing thereto, and this is nought but an extraordinary thing. But all this cometh of strength in the craft and self-restraint.' Then he bade her sing; and she said, 'Hearkening and obedience.' So she took the lute and tightening its strings, smote thereon a number of airs, so that she confounded Ishac's wit and he was like to fly for delight. Then she returned to the first mode and sang thereto the following verses:

Still by your ruined camp a dweller I abide; Ne'er will I change nor e'er shall distance us divide.
Far though you dwell, I'll ne'er your neighbourhood forget, O friends, whose lovers still for you are stupefied.
Your image midst mine eye sits nor forsakes me aye; Ye are my moons in gloom of night and shadowtide.
Still, as my transports wax, grows restlessness on me And woes have ta'en the place of love-delight denied.

When she had made an end of her song and laid down the lute, Ishac looked fixedly on her, then took her hand and offered to kiss it; but she snatched it from him and said to him, 'Allah, O my lord, do not that!' Quoth he, 'Be silent. By Allah, I had said that there was not in the world the like of me; but now I have found my dinar[445] in the craft but a danic,[446] "for thou art, beyond comparison or approximation or reckoning, more excellent of skill than I! This very day will I carry thee up to the Commander of the Faithful Haroun er Reshid, and whenas his glance lighteth on thee, thou wilt become a princess of womankind. So, Allah, Allah upon thee, O my lady, whenas thou becomest of the household of the Commander of the Faithful, do not thou forget me!' And she replied, saying, 'Allah, O my lord, thou art the source of my fortunes and in thee is my heart fortified.' So he took her hand and made a covenant with her of this and she swore to him that she would not forget him.

Then said he to her, 'By Allah, thou art the desire of the Commander of the Faithful![447] So take the lute and sing a song that thou shalt sing to the Khalif, whenas thou goest in to him.' So she took the lute and tuning it, sang the following verses:

His love on him took pity and wept for his dismay: Of those that him did visit she was, as sick he lay.
She let him taste her honey and wine[448] before his death: This was his last of victual until the Judgment Day.

Ishac stared at her and seizing her hand, said to her, 'Know that I am bound by an oath that, when the singing of a damsel pleaseth me, she shall not make an end of her song but before the Commander of the Faithful. But now tell me, how came it that thou abodest with the slave-dealer five months and wast not sold to any, and thou of this skill, more by token that the price set on thee was no great matter?'

She laughed and answered, 'O my lord, my story is a strange one and my case extraordinary. Know that I belonged aforetime to a Mughrebi merchant, who bought me, when I was three years old, and there were in his house many slave-girls and eunuchs; but I was the dearest to him of them all. So he kept me with him and used not to call me but "daughterling," and indeed I am presently a clean maid. Now there was with him a damsel, a lutanist, and she reared me and taught me the craft, even as thou seest. Then was my master admitted to the mercy of God the Most High[449] and his sons divided his good. I fell to the lot of one of them; but it was only a little while ere he had squandered all his substance and there was left him no tittle of money. So I left the lute, fearing lest I should fall into the hand of a man who knew not my worth, for that I was assured that needs must my master sell me; and indeed it was but a few days ere he carried me forth to the barrack of the slave-merchant who buyeth slave-girls and showeth them to the Commander of the Faithful. Now I desired to learn the craft; so I refused to be sold to other than thou, till God (extolled be His perfection and exalted be He!) vouchsafed me my desire of thy presence; whereupon I came out to thee, whenas I heard of thy coming, and besought thee to buy me. Thou healedst my heart and boughtedst me; and since I entered thy house, O my lord, I have not taken up the lute till now; but to-day, whenas I was quit of the slave-girls, [I took it]; and my purpose in this was that I might see if my hand were changed[450] or no. As I was singing, I heard a step in the vestibule; so I laid the lute from my hand and going forth to see what was to do, found thee, O my lord, on this wise.'

Quoth Ishac, 'Indeed, this was of thy fair fortune. By Allah, I know not that which thou knowest in this craft!' Then he arose and going to a chest, brought out therefrom striped clothes of great price, netted with jewels and great pearls, and said to her, 'In the name of God, don these, O my lady Tuhfeh.' So she arose and donned those clothes and veiled herself and went up [with Ishac] to the palace of the Khalifate, where he made her stand without, whilst he himself went in to the Commander of the Faithful (with whom was Jaafer the Barmecide) and kissing the earth before him, said to him, 'O Commander of the Faithful, I have brought thee a damsel, never saw eyes her like for excellence in singing and touching the lute; and her name is Tuhfeh."[451] 'And where,' asked Er Reshed, 'is this Tuhfeh, who hath not her like in the world?' Quoth Ishac, 'Yonder she stands, O Commander of the Faithful;' and he acquainted the Khalif with her case from first to last. Then said Er Reshid, 'It is a marvel to hear thee praise a slave-girl after this fashion. Admit her, so we may see her, for that the morning may not be hidden.'

Accordingly, Ishac bade admit her; so she entered, and when her eyes fell upon the Commander of the Faithful, she kissed the earth before him and said, 'Peace be upon thee, O Commander of the Faithful and asylum of the people of the faith and reviver of justice among all creatures! May God make plain the treading of thy feet and vouchsafe thee enjoyment of that which He hath bestowed on thee and make Paradise thy harbourage and the fire that of thine enemies!' Quoth Er Reshid, 'And on thee be peace, O damsel! Sit.' So she sat down and he bade her sing; whereupon she took the lute and tightening its strings, played thereon in many modes, so that the Commander of the Faithful and Jaafer were confounded and like to fly for delight. Then she returned to the first mode and sang the following verses:

By Him whom I worship, indeed, I swear, O thou that mine eye dost fill, By Him in whose honour the pilgrims throng and fare to Arafat's hill,
Though over me be the tombstone laid, if ever thou call on me, Though rotten my bone should be, thy voice I'll answer, come what will.
I crave none other than thou for friend, beloved of my heart; So trust in my speech, for the generous are true and trusty still.

Er Reshid considered her beauty and the goodliness of her singing and her eloquence and what not else she comprised of qualities and rejoiced with an exceeding joyance; and for the stress of that which overcame him of delight, he descended from the couch and sitting down with her upon the ground, said to her, 'Thou hast done well, O Tuhfeh. By Allah, thou art indeed a gift'[452] Then he turned to Ishac and said to him, 'Thou dealtest not equitably, O Ishac, in the description of this damsel,[453] neither settest out all that she compriseth of goodliness and skill; for that, by Allah, she is incomparably more skilful than thou; and I know of this craft that which none knoweth other than I!' 'By Allah,' exclaimed Jaafer, 'thou sayst sooth, O my lord, O Commander of the Faithful. Indeed, this damsel hath done away my wit' Quoth Ishac, 'By Allah, O Commander of the Faithful, I had said that there was not on the face of the earth one who knew the craft of the lute like myself; but, when I heard her, my skill became nothing worth in mine eyes.'

Then said the Khalif to her, 'Repeat thy playing, O Tuhfeh.' So she repeated it and he said to her, 'Well done!' Moreover, he said to Ishac, 'Thou hast indeed brought me that which is extraordinary and worth in mine eyes the empire of the earth.' Then he turned to Mesrour the eunuch and said to him, 'Carry Tuhfeh to the lodging of honour.'[454] Accordingly, she went away with Mesrour and the Khalif looked at her clothes and seeing her clad in raiment of choice, said to Ishac, 'O Ishac, whence hath she these clothes?' 'O my lord, answered he, 'these are somewhat of thy bounties and thy largesse, and they are a gift to her from me. By Allah, O Commander of the Faithful, the world, all of it, were little in comparison with her!' Then the Khalif turned to the Vizier Jaafer and said to him, 'Give Ishac fifty thousand dirhems and a dress of honour of the apparel of choice.' 'Hearkening and obedience,' replied Jaafer and gave him that which the Khalif ordered him.

As for Er Reshid, he shut himself up with Tuhfeh that night and found her a clean maid and rejoiced in her; and she took high rank in his heart, so that he could not endure from her a single hour and committed to her the keys of the affairs of the realm, for that which he saw in her of good breeding and wit and modesty. Moreover, he gave her fifty slave-girls and two hundred thousand dinars and clothes and trinkets and jewels and precious stones, worth the kingdom of Egypt; and of the excess of his love for her, he would not entrust her to any of the slave-girls or eunuchs; but, whenas he went out from her, he locked the door upon her and took the key with him, against he should return to her, forbidding the damsels to go in to her, of his fear lest they should slay her or practise on her with knife or poison; and on this wise he abode awhile.

One day as she sang before the Commander of the Faithful, he was moved to exceeding delight, so that he took her and offered to kiss her hand; but she drew it away from him and smote upon her lute and broke it and wept

Er Reshid wiped away her tears and said, 'O desire of the heart, what is it maketh thee weep? May God not cause an eye of thine to weep!' 'O my lord,' answered she, 'what am I that thou shouldst kiss my hand? Wilt thou have God punish me for this and that my term should come to an end and my felicity pass away? For this is what none ever attained unto.' Quoth he, 'Well said, O Tuhfeh. Know that thy rank in my esteem is mighty and for that which wondered me of what I saw of thee, I offered to do this, but I will not return unto the like thereof; so be of good heart and cheerful eye, for I have no desire for other than thyself and will not die but in the love of thee, and thou to me art queen and mistress, to the exclusion of all humankind.' Therewith she fell to kissing his feet; and this her fashion pleased him, so that his love for her redoubled and he became unable to brook an hour's severance from her.

One day he went forth to the chase and left Tuhfeh in her pavilion. As she sat looking upon a book, with a candlestick of gold before her, wherein was a perfumed candle, behold, a musk-apple fell down before her from the top of the saloon.[455] So she looked up and beheld the Lady Zubeideh bint el Casim,[456] who saluted her and acquainted her with herself, whereupon Tuhfeh rose to her feet and said, 'O my lady, were I not of the number of the upstarts, I had daily sought thy service; so do not thou bereave me of thine august visits.'[457] The Lady Zubeideh called down blessings upon her and answered, 'By the life of the Commander of the Faithful, I knew this of thee, and but that it is not of my wont to go forth of my place, I had come out to do my service to thee.' Then said she to her, 'Know, O Tuhfeh, that the Commander of the Faithful hath forsaken all his concubines and favourites on thine account, even to myself. Yea, me also hath he deserted on this wise, and I am not content to be as one of the concubines; yet hath he made me of them and forsaken me, and I am come to thee, so thou mayst beseech him to come to me, though it be but once a month, that I may not be the like of the handmaids and concubines nor be evened with the slave-girls; and this is my occasion with thee.' 'Hearkening and obedience,' answered Tuhfeh. 'By Allah, O my lady, I would well that he might be with thee a whole month and with me but one night, so thy heart might be comforted, for that I am one of thy handmaids and thou art my lady in every event.' The Lady Zubeideh thanked her for this and taking leave of her, returned to her palace.

When the Khalif returned from the chase, he betook himself to Tuhfeh's pavilion and bringing out the key, opened the door and went in to her. She rose to receive him and kissed his hand, and he took her to his breast and seated her on his knee. Then food was brought to them and they ate and washed their hands; after which she took the lute and sang, till Er Reshid was moved to sleep. When she was ware of this, she left singing and told him her adventure with the Lady Zubeideh, saying, 'O Commander of the Faithful, I would have thee do me a favour and heal my heart and accept my intercession and reject not my word, but go forthright to the Lady Zubeideh's lodging.' Now this talk befell after he had stripped himself naked and she also had put off her clothes; and he said, 'Thou shouldst have named this before we stripped ourselves naked.' But she answered, saying, ' O Commander of the Faithful, I did this not but in accordance with the saying of the poet in the following verses:

All intercessions come and all alike do ill succeed, Save Tuhfeh's, daughter of Merjan, for that, in very deed,
The intercessor who to thee herself presenteth veiled Is not her like who naked comes with thee to intercede.'

When the Khalif heard this, her speech pleased him and he strained her to his bosom. Then he went forth from her and locked the door upon her, as before; whereupon she took the book and sat looking in it awhile. Presently, she laid it down and taking the lute, tightened its strings. Then she smote thereon, after a wondrous fashion, such as would have moved inanimate things [to delight], and fell to singing marvellous melodies and chanting the following verses:

Rail not at the vicissitudes of Fate, For Fortune still spites those who her berate.
Be patient under its calamities, For all things have an issue soon or late.
How many a mirth-exciting joy amid The raiment of ill chances lies in wait!
How often, too, hath gladness come to light Whence nought but dole thou didst anticipate!

Then she turned and saw within the chamber an old man, comely of hoariness, venerable of aspect, who was dancing on apt and goodly wise, a dance the like whereof none might avail unto. So she sought refuge with God the Most High from Satan the Stoned[458] and said, 'I will not give over what I am about, for that which God decreeth, He carrieth into execution.' Accordingly, she went on singing till the old man came up to her and kissed the earth before her, saying, 'Well done, O Queen of the East and the

West! May the world be not bereaved of thee! By Allah, indeed thou art perfect of qualities and ingredients, O Tuhfet es Sudour![459] Dost thou know me?' 'Nay, by Allah,' answered she; 'but methinks thou art of the Jinn.' Quoth he, 'Thou sayst sooth; I am the Sheikh Aboultawaif[460] Iblis, and I come to thee every night, and with me thy sister Kemeriyeh, for that she loveth thee and sweareth not but by thy life; and her life is not pleasant to her, except she come to thee and see thee, what while thou seest her not. As for me, I come to thee upon an affair, wherein thou shall find thine advantage and whereby thou shalt rise to high rank with the kings of the Jinn and rule them, even as thou rulest mankind; [and to that end I would have thee come with me and be present at the festival of my son's circumcision;[461]] for that the Jinn are agreed upon the manifestation of thine affair.' And she answered, 'In the name of God.'

So she gave him the lute and he forewent her, till he came to the house of easance, and behold, therein was a door and a stairway. When Tuhfeh saw this, her reason fled; but Iblis cheered her with discourse. Then he descended the stair and she followed him to the bottom thereof, where she found a passage and they fared on therein, till they came to a horse standing, ready saddled and bridled and accoutred. Quoth Iblis, '[Mount], in the name of God, O my lady Tuhfeh;' and he held the stirrup for her. So she mounted and the horse shook under her and putting forth wings, flew up with her, whilst the old man flew by her side; whereat she was affrighted and clung to the pummel of the saddle; nor was it but an hour ere they came to a fair green meadow, fresh-flowered as if the soil thereof were a goodly robe, embroidered with all manner colours.

Midmost that meadow was a palace soaring high into the air, with battlements of red gold, set with pearls and jewels, and a two-leaved gate; and in the gateway thereof were much people of the chiefs of the Jinn, clad in sumptuous apparel. When they saw the old man, they all cried out, saying, 'The Lady Tuhfeh is come!' And as soon as she reached the palace-gate, they came all and dismounting her from the horse's back, carried her into the palace and fell to kissing her hands. When she entered, she beheld a palace whereof never saw eyes the like; for therein were four estrades, one facing other, and its walls were of gold and its ceilings of silver. It was lofty of building, wide of continence, and those who beheld it would be puzzled to describe it. At the upper end of the hall stood a throne of red gold, set with pearls and jewels, unto which led up five steps of silver, and on the right thereof and on its left were many chairs of gold and silver; and over the dais was a curtain let down, gold and silver wrought and broidered with pearls and jewels.

The old man carried Tuhfeh up [to the dais and seated her] on a chair of gold beside the throne, whilst she was amazed at that which she saw in that place and magnified her Lord (extolled be His perfection and exalted be He!) and hallowed Him. Then the kings of the Jinn came up to the throne and seated themselves thereon; and they were in the semblance of mortals, excepting two of them, who were in the semblance of the Jinn, with eyes slit endlong and jutting horns and projecting tusks. After this there came up a young lady, fair of favour and pleasant of parts; the light of her face outshone that of the flambeaux, and about her were other three women, than whom there were no fairer on the face of the earth. They saluted Tuhfeh and she rose to them and kissed the earth before them; whereupon they embraced her and sat down on the chairs aforesaid.

Now the four women who thus accosted Tuhfeh were the princess Kemeriyeh, daughter of King Es Shisban, and her sisters; and Kemeriyeh loved Tuhfeh with an exceeding love. So, when she came up to her, she fell to kissing and embracing her, and Iblis said, 'Fair befall you! Take me between you.' At this Tuhfeh laughed and Kemeriyeh said, 'O my sister, I love thee and doubtless hearts have their evidences,[462] for, since I saw thee, I have loved thee.' 'By Allah,' replied Tuhfeh, 'hearts have deeps,[463] and thou, by Allah, art dear to me and I am thy handmaid.' Kemeriyeh thanked her for this and said to her, 'These are the wives of the kings of the Jinn: salute them. This is Queen Jemreh,[464] that is Queen Wekhimeh and this other is Queen Sherareh, and they come not but for thee.' So Tuhfeh rose to her feet and kissed their hands, and the three queens kissed her and welcomed her and entreated her with the utmost honour.

Then they brought trays and tables and amongst the rest a platter of red gold, inlaid with pearls and jewels; its margents were of gold and emerald, and thereon were graven the following verses:

For the uses of food I was fashioned and made; The hands of the noble me wrought and inlaid.
My maker reserved me for generous men And the niggard and sland'rer to use me forebade.
So eat what I offer in surety and be The Lord of all things with thanks-giving repaid!

So they ate and Tuhfeh looked at the two kings, who had not changed their favour and said to Kemeriyeh, 'O my lady, what is yonder wild beast and that other like unto him? By Allah, mine eye brooketh not the sight of them.' Kemeriyeh laughed and answered, 'O my sister, that is my father Es Shisban and the other is Meimoun the Sworder; and of the pride of their souls and their arrogance, they consented not to change their [natural] fashion. Indeed, all whom thou seest here are, by nature, like unto them in fashion; but, on thine account, they have changed their favour, for fear lest thou be disquieted and for the comforting of thy mind, so thou mightest make friends with them and be at thine ease.' 'O my lady,' quoth Tuhfeh, 'indeed I cannot look at them. How frightful is yonder Meimoun, with his [one] eye! Mine eye cannot brook the sight of him, and indeed I am fearful of him.' Kemeriyeh laughed at her speech, and Tuhfeh said, 'By Allah, O my lady, I cannot fill my eye with them!'[465] Then said her father Es Shisban to her, 'What is this laughing?' So she bespoke him in a tongue none understood but they [two] and acquainted him with that which Tuhfeh had said; whereat he laughed a prodigious laugh, as it were the pealing thunder.

Then they ate and the tables were removed and they washed their hands; after which Iblis the Accursed came up to Tuhfeh and said to her, 'O my lady Tuhfeh, thou gladdenest the place and with thy presence enlightenest and embellishest it; but now fain would these kings hear somewhat of thy singing, for the night hath spread its wings for departure and there abideth thereof but a little.' Quoth she, 'Hearkening and obedience.' So she took the lute and touching its strings on rare wise, played thereon after a wondrous fashion, so that it seemed to those who were present as if the palace stirred with them for the music. Then she fell a-singing and chanted the following verses:

Peace on you, people of my troth! With peace I do you greet. Said ye not truly, aforetime, that we should live and meet?
Ah, then will I begin on you with chiding than the breeze More soft, ay pleasanter than clear cold water and more sweet.
Indeed, mine eyelids still with tears are ulcered and to you My bowels yearn to be made whole of all their pain and heat.
Parting hath sundered us, belov'd; indeed, I stood in dread Of this, whilst yet our happiness in union was complete.
To God of all the woes I've borne I plain me, for I pine For longing and lament, and Him for solace I entreat

The kings of the Jinn were moved to delight by that fair singing and fluent speech and praised Tuhfeh; and Queen Kemeriyeh rose to her and embraced her and kissed her between the eyes, saying, 'By Allah, it is good, O my sister and solace of mine eyes and darling of my heart!' Then said she, 'I conjure thee by Allah, give us more of this lovely singing.' And Tuhfeh answered with 'Hearkening and obedience.' So she took the lute and playing thereon after a different fashion from the former one, sang the following verses:

Oft as my yearning waxeth, my heart consoleth me With hopes of thine enjoyment in all security.
Sure God shall yet, in pity, reknit our severed lives, Even as He did afflict me with loneness after thee.
Thou whose desire possesseth my soul, the love of whom Hold on my reins hath gotten and will not let me free,
Compared with thine enjoyment, the hardest things are light To win and all things distant draw near and easy be.
God to a tristful lover be light! A man of wit, Yet perishing for yearning and body-worn is he.
Were I cut off, beloved, from hope of thy return, Slumber, indeed, for ever my wakeful lids would flee.
For nought of worldly fortune I weep! my only joy In seeing thee consisteth and in thy seeing me.

At this the accursed Iblis was moved to delight and put his finger to his arse, whilst Meimoun danced and said, 'O Tuhfet es Sudour, soften the mode;[466] for, as delight, entereth into my heart, it bewildereth my vital spirits.' So she took the lute and changing the mode, played a third air; then she returned to the first and sang the following verses:

The billows of thy love o'erwhelm me passing sore; I sink and all in vain for succour I implore.
Ye've drowned me in the sea of love for you; my heart Denies to be consoled for those whom I adore.
Think not that I forget our trothplight after you. Nay; God to me decreed remembrance heretofore.[467]
Love to its victim clings without relent, and he Of torments and unease complaineth evermore.

The kings and all those who were present rejoiced in this with an exceeding delight and the accursed Iblis came up to Tuhfeh and kissing her hand, said to her, 'There abideth but little of the night; so do thou tarry with us till the morrow, when we will apply ourselves to the wedding[468] and the circumcision.' Then all the Jinn went away, whereupon Tuhfeh rose to her feet and Iblis said, 'Go ye up with Tuhfeh to the garden for the rest of the night.' So Kemeriyeh took her and carried her into the garden. Now this garden contained all manner birds, nightingale and mocking-bird and ringdove and curlew[469] and other than these of all the kinds, and therein were all kinds of fruits. Its channels[470] were of gold and silver and the water thereof, as it broke forth of its conduits, was like unto fleeing serpents' bellies, and indeed it was as it were the Garden of Eden.[471]

When Tuhfeh beheld this, she called to mind her lord and wept sore and said, 'I beseech God the Most High to vouchsafe me speedy deliverance, so I may return to my palace and that my high estate and queendom and glory and be reunited with my lord and master Er Reshid.' Then she walked in that garden and saw in its midst a dome of white marble, raised on columns of black teak and hung with curtains embroidered with pearls and jewels. Amiddleward this pavilion was a fountain, inlaid with all manner jacinths, and thereon a statue of gold, and [beside it] a little door. She opened the door and found herself in a long passage; so she followed it and behold, a bath lined with all kinds of precious marbles and floored with a mosaic of pearls and jewels. Therein were four cisterns of alabaster, one facing other, and the ceiling of the bath was of glass coloured with all manner colours, such as confounded the understanding of the folk of understanding and amazed the wit.

Tuhfeh entered the bath, after she had put off her clothes, and behold, the basin thereof was overlaid with gold set with pearls and red rubies and green emeralds and other jewels; so she extolled the perfection of God the Most High and hallowed Him for the magnificence of that which she saw of the attributes of that bath. Then she made her ablutions in that basin and pronouncing the Magnification of Prohibition,[472] prayed the morning prayer and what else had escaped her of prayers;[473] after which she went out and walked in that garden among jessamine and lavender and roses and camomile and gillyflowers and thyme and violets and sweet basil, till she came to the door of the pavilion aforesaid and sat down therein, pondering that which should betide Er Reshid after her, whenas he should come to her pavilion and find her not. She abode sunken in the sea of her solicitude, till presently sleep took her and she slept

Presently she felt a breath upon her face; whereupon she awoke and found Queen Kemeriyeh kissing her, and with her her three sisters, Queen Jemreh, Queen Wekhimeh and Queen Sherareh. So she arose and kissed their hands and rejoiced in them with the utmost joy and they abode, she and they, in talk and converse, what while she related to them her history, from the time of her purchase by the Mughrebi to that of her coming to the slave-dealers' barrack, where she besought Ishac en Nedim to buy her, and how she won to Er Reshid, till the moment when Iblis came to her and brought her to them. They gave not over talking till the sun declined and turned pale and the season of sundown drew near and the day departed, whereupon Tuhfeh was instant in supplication to God the Most High, on the occasion of the prayer of sundown, that He would reunite her with her lord Er Reshid.

After this, she abode with the four queens, till they arose and entered the palace, where she found the candles lit and ranged in candlesticks of gold and silver and censing-vessels of gold and silver, filled with aloes-wood and ambergris, and there were the kings of the Jinn sitting. So she saluted them, kissing the earth before them and doing them worship; and they rejoiced in her and in her sight. Then she ascended [the estrade] and sat down upon her chair, whilst King Es Shisban and King El Muzfir and Queen Louloueh and [other] the kings of the Jinn sat on chairs, and they brought tables of choice, spread with all manner meats befitting kings. They ate their fill; after which the tables were removed and they washed their hands and wiped them with napkins. Then they brought the wine-service and set on bowls and cups and flagons and hanaps of gold and silver and beakers of crystal and gold; and they poured out the wines and filled the flagons.

Then Iblis took the cup and signed to Tuhfeh to sing; and she said, 'Hearkening and obedience.' So she took the lute and tuning it, sang the following verses:

Drink ever, O lovers, I rede you, of wine And praise his desert who for yearning doth pine,
Where lavender, myrtle, narcissus entwine, With all sweet-scented herbs, round the juice of the vine.

So Iblis the Accursed drank and said, 'Well done, O desire of hearts! but thou owest me yet another song.' Then he filled the cup and signed to her to sing. Quoth she, 'Hearkening and obedience,' and sang the following verses:

Ye know I'm passion-maddened, racked with love and languishment, Yet ye torment me, for to you 'tis pleasing to torment.
Between mine eyes and wake ye have your dwelling-place, and thus My tears flow on unceasingly, my sighs know no relent.
How long shall I for justice sue to you, whilst, with desire For aid, ye war on me and still on slaying me are bent!
To me your rigour love-delight, your distance nearness is; Ay, your injustice equity, and eke your wrath consent.
Accuse me falsely, cruelly entreat me; still ye are My heart's beloved, at whose hands no rigour I resent.

All who were present were delighted and the sitting-chamber shook with mirth, and Iblis said, 'Well done, O Tuhfet es Sudour!' Then they gave not over wine-bibbing and rejoicing and making merry and tambourining and piping till the night waned and the dawn drew near; and indeed exceeding delight entered into them. The most of them in mirth was the Sheikh Iblis, and for the excess of that which betided him of delight, he put off all that was upon him of coloured clothes and cast them over Tuhfeh, and among the rest a robe broidered with jewels and jacinths, worth ten thousand dinars. Then he kissed the earth and danced and put his finger to his arse and taking his beard in his hand, said to her, 'Sing about this beard and endeavour after mirth and pleasance, and no blame shall betide thee for this.' So she improvised and sang the following verses:

Beard of the old he-goat, the one-eyed, what shall be My saying of a knave, his fashion and degree?
I rede thee vaunt thee not of praise from us, for lo! Even as a docktailed cur thou art esteemed of me.
By Allah, without fail, to-morrow thou shalt see Me with ox-leather dress and drub the nape of thee!

All those who were present laughed at her mockery of Iblis and marvelled at the goodliness of her observation[474] and her readiness in improvising verses; whilst the Sheikh himself rejoiced and said to her, 'O Tuhfet es Sudour, the night is gone; so arise and rest thyself ere the day; and to-morrow all shall be well.' Then all the kings of the Jinn departed, together with those who were present of guards, and Tuhfeh abode alone, pondering the affair of Er Reshid and bethinking her of how it was with him, after her, and of that which had betided him for her loss, till the dawn gleamed, when she arose and walked in the palace. Presently she saw a handsome door; so she opened it and found herself in a garden goodlier than the first, never saw eyes a fairer than it. When she beheld this garden, delight moved her and she called to mind her lord Er Reshid and wept sore, saying, 'I crave of the bounty of God the Most High that my return to him and to my palace and my home may be near at hand!'

Then she walked in the garden till she came to a pavilion, lofty of building and wide of continence, never saw mortal nor heard of a goodlier than it [So she entered] and found herself in a long corridor, which led to a bath goodlier than that whereof it hath been spoken, and the cisterns thereof were full of rose-water mingled with musk. Quoth Tuhfeh, 'Extolled be the perfection of God! Indeed, this[475] is none other than a mighty king.' Then she put off her clothes and washed her body and made her ablution, after the fullest fashion,[476] and prayed that which was due from her of prayer from the evening [of the previous day].[477] When the sun rose upon the gate of the garden and she saw the wonders thereof, with that which was therein of all manner flowers and streams, and heard the voices of its birds, she marvelled at what she saw of the surpassing goodliness of its ordinance and the beauty of its disposition and sat meditating the affair of Er Reshid and pondering what was come of him after her. Her tears ran down upon her cheek and the zephyr blew on her; so she slept and knew no more till she felt a breath on her cheek, whereupon she awoke in affright and found Queen Kemeriyeh kissing her face, and with her her sisters, who said to her, 'Arise, for the sun hath set.'

So she arose and making the ablution, prayed that which behoved her of prayers[478] and accompanied the four queens to the palace, where she saw the candles lighted and the kings sitting. She saluted them and seated herself upon her couch; and behold, King Es Shisban had changed his favour, for all the pride of his soul. Then came up Iblis (whom God curse!) and Tuhfeh rose to him and kissed his hands. He in turn kissed her hand and called down blessings on her and said, 'How deemest thou? Is [not] this place pleasant, for all its loneliness and desolation?' Quoth she, 'None may be desolate in this place;' and he said, 'Know that no mortal dare tread [the soil of] this place.' But she answered, 'I have dared and trodden it, and this is of the number of thy favours.' Then they brought tables and meats and viands and fruits and sweetmeats and what not else, to the description whereof mortal man availeth not, and they ate till they had enough; after which the tables were removed and the trays and platters[479] set on, and they ranged the bottles and flagons and vessels and phials, together with all manner fruits and sweet-scented flowers.

The first to take the cup was Iblis the Accursed, who said, 'O Tuhfet es Sudour, sing over my cup.' So she took the lute and touching it, sang the following verses:

Awaken, O ye sleepers all, and profit, whilst it's here By what's vouchsafed of fortune fair and life untroubled, clear.
Drink of the first-run wine, that shows as very flame it were, When from the pitcher 'tis outpoured, or ere the day appear.
O skinker of the vine-juice, let the cup 'twixt us go round, For in its drinking is my hope and all I hold most dear.
What is the pleasance of the world, except it be to see My lady's face, to drink of wine and ditties still to hear?

So Iblis drank off his cup, and when he had made an end of his draught, he waved his hand to Tuhfeh, and putting off that which was upon him of clothes, delivered them to her. Amongst them was a suit worth ten thousand dinars and a tray full of jewels worth a great sum of money. Then he filled again and gave the cup to his son Es Shisban, who took it from his hand and kissing it, stood up and sat down again. Now there was before him a tray of roses; so he said to her 'O Tuhfeh sing upon these roses.' Hearkening and obedience,' answered she and sang the following verses:

O'er all the fragrant flowers that be I have the prefrence aye, For that I come but once a year, and but a little stay.
And high is my repute, for that I wounded aforetime My lord,[480] whom God made best of all the treaders of the clay.

So Es Shisban drank off the cup in his turn and said, 'Well done, O desire of hearts!' And he bestowed on her that which was upon him, to wit, a dress of cloth-of-pearl, fringed with great pearls and rubies and broidered with precious stones, and a tray wherein were fifty thousand dinars. Then Meimoun the Sworder took the cup and fell to gazing intently upon Tuhfeh. Now there was in his hand a pomegranate-flower and he said to her, 'Sing upon this pomegranate-flower, O queen of men and Jinn; for indeed thou hast dominion over all hearts.' Quoth she, 'Hearkening and obedience;' and she improvised and sang the following verses:

The zephyr's sweetness on the coppice blew, And as with falling fire 'twas clad anew;
And to the birds' descant in the foredawns, From out the boughs it flowered forth and grew,
Till in a robe of sandal green 'twas clad And veil that blended rose and flame[481] in hue.

Meinsoun drank off his cup and said to her, 'Well done, O perfect of attributes!' Then he signed to her and was absent awhile, after which he returned and with him a tray of jewels worth an hundred thousand dinars, [which he gave to Tuhfeh]. So Kemeriyeh arose and bade her slave-girl open the closet behind her, wherein she laid all that wealth. Then she delivered the key to Tuhfeh, saying, 'All that cometh to thee of riches, lay thou in this closet that is by thy side, and after the festival, it shall be carried to thy palace on the heads of the Jinn.' Tuhfeh kissed her hand, and another king, by name Munir, took the cup and filling it, said to her, 'O fair one, sing to me over my cup upon the jasmine.' 'Hearkening and obedience,' answered she and improvised the following verses:

It is as the jasmine, when it I espy, As it glitters and gleams midst its boughs, were a sky
Of beryl, all glowing with beauty, wherein Thick stars of pure silver shine forth to the eye.

Munir drank off his cup and ordered her eight hundred thousand dinars, whereat Kemeriyeh rejoiced and rising to her feet, kissed Tuhfeh on her face and said to her, 'May the world not be bereaved of thee, O thou who lordest it over the hearts of Jinn and mortals!' Then she returned to her place and the Sheikh Iblis arose and danced, till all present were confounded; after which he said to Tuhfeh, 'Indeed, thou embellishest my festival, O thou who hast commandment over men and Jinn and rejoicest their hearts with thy loveliness and the excellence of thy faithfulness to thy lord. All that thy hands possess shall be borne to thee [in thy palace and placed] at thy service; but now the dawn is near at hand; so do thou rise and rest thee, as of thy wont' Tuhfeh turned and found with her none of the Jinn; so she laid her head on the ground and slept till she had gotten her rest; after which she arose and betaking herself to the pool, made the ablution and prayed. Then she sat beside the pool awhile and pondered the affair of her lord Er Reshid and that which had betided him after her and wept sore.

Presently, she heard a blowing behind her; so she turned and behold, a head without a body and with eyes slit endlong; it was of the bigness of an elephant's head and bigger and had a mouth as it were an oven and projecting tusks, as they were grapnels, and hair that trailed upon the earth. So Tuhfeh said, 'I take refuge with God from Satan the Stoned!' and recited the Two Amulets;[482] what while the head drew near her and said to her, 'Peace be upon thee, O princess of Jinn and men and unique pearl of her age and her time! May God still continue thee on life, for all the lapsing of the days, and reunite thee with thy lord the Imam!'[483] 'And upon thee be peace,' answered she, 'O thou whose like I have not seen among the Jinn!' Quoth the head, 'We are a people who avail not to charge their favours and we are called ghouls. The folk summon us to their presence, but we may not present ourselves before them [without leave]. As for me, I have gotten leave of the Sheikh Aboultawaif to present myself before thee and I desire of thy favour that thou sing me a song, so I may go to thy palace and question its haunters[484] concerning the plight of thy lord after thee and return to thee; and know, O Tuhfet es Sudour, that between thee and thy lord is a distance of fifty years' journey to the diligent traveller.' 'Indeed,' rejoined Tuhfeh, 'thou grievest me [for him] between whom and me is fifty years' journey. And the head said to her, 'Be of good heart and cheerful eye, for the kings of the Jinn will restore thee to him in less than the twinkling of an eye.' Quoth she,' I will sing thee an hundred songs, so thou wilt bring me news of my lord and that which hath befallen him after me.' And the head answered, saying, 'Do thou favour me and sing me a song, so I may go to thy lord and bring thee news of him, for that I desire, before I go, to hear thy voice, so haply my thirst[485] may be quenched.' So she took the lute and tuning it, sang the following verses:

They have departed; but the steads yet full of them remain: Yea, they have left me, but my heart of them doth not complain.
My heart bereavement of my friends forebode; may God of them The dwellings not bereave, but send them timely home again!
Though they their journey's goal, alas I have hidden, in their track Still will I follow on until the very planets wane.

Ye sleep; by Allah, sleep comes not to ease my weary lids; But from mine eyes, since ye have passed away, the blood doth rain.
The railers for your loss pretend that I should patient be: 'Away!' I answer them: ' 'tis I, not you, that feel the pain.'
What had it irked them, had they'd ta'en farewell of him they've left Lone, whilst estrangement's fires within his entrails rage amain?
Great in delight, beloved mine, your presence is with me; Yet greater still the miseries of parting and its bane.
Ye are the pleasaunce of my soul; or present though you be Or absent from me, still my heart and thought with you remain.

The head wept exceeding sore and said, 'O my lady, indeed thou hast solaced my heart, and I have nought but my life; so take it.' Quoth she, 'An I but knew that thou wouldst bring me news of my lord Er Reshid, it were liefer to me than the empery of the world.' And the head answered her, saying, 'It shall be done as thou desirest.' Then it disappeared and returning to her at the last of the night, said, 'Know, O my lady, that I have been to thy palace and have questioned one of the haunters thereof of the case of the Commander of the Faithful and that which befell him after thee; and he said, "When the Commander of the Faithful came to Tuhfeh's lodging and found her not and saw no sign of her, he buffeted his face and head and rent his clothes. Now there was in thy lodging the eunuch, the chief of thy household, and he cried out at him, saying, 'Bring me Jaafer the Barmecide and his father and brother forthright.' The eunuch went out, confounded in his wit for fear of the Commander of the Faithful, and whenas he came to Jaafer, he said to him, 'Come to the Commander of the Faithful, thou and thy father and brother.' So they arose in haste and betaking themselves to the Khalif's presence, said to him, 'O Commander of the Faithful, what is to do?' Quoth he, 'There is that to do which overpasseth description. Know that I locked the door and taking the key with me, betook myself to the daughter of mine uncle, with whom I lay the night; but, when I arose in the morning and came and opened the door, I found no sign of Tuhfeh.' 'O Commander of the Faithful,' rejoined Jaafer, 'have patience, for that the damsel hath been snatched away, and needs must she return, seeing she took the lute with her, and it is her [own] lute. The Jinn have assuredly carried her off and we trust in God the Most High that she will return.' Quoth the Khalif, ' This[486] is a thing that may nowise be' And he abode in her lodging, eating not neither drinking, what while the Barmecides besought him to go forth to the folk; and he weepeth and abideth on this wise till she shall return." This, then, is that which hath betided him after thee.'

When Tuhfeh heard this, it was grievous to her and she wept sore; whereupon quoth the head to her, 'The relief of God the Most High is near at hand; but now let me hear somewhat of thy speech.' So she took the lute and sang three songs, weeping the while. 'By Allah,' said the head, 'thou hast been bountiful to me, may God be with thee!' Then it disappeared and the season of sundown came. So she arose [and betook herself] to her place [in the hall]; whereupon the candles rose up from under the earth and kindled themselves. Then the kings of the Jinn appeared and saluted her and kissed her hands and she saluted them. Presently, up came Kemeriyeh and her three sisters and saluted Tuhfeh and sat down; whereupon the tables were brought and they ate. Then the tables were removed and there came the wine-tray and the drinking-service. So Tuhfeh took the lute and one of the three queens filled the cup and signed to Tuhfeh [to sing]. Now she had in her hand a violet; so Tuhfeh sang the following verses:

Behold, I am clad in a robe of leaves green And a garment of honour of ultramarine.
Though little, with beauty myself I've adorned; So the flowers are my subjects and I am their queen.
If the rose be entitled the pride of the morn, Before me nor after she wins it, I ween.

The queen drank off her cup and bestowed on Tuhfeh a dress of cloth-of-pearl, fringed with red rubies, worth twenty thousand dinars, and a tray wherein were ten thousand dinars.

All this while Meimoun's eye was upon her and presently he said to her, 'Harkye, Tuhfeh! Sing to me.' But Queen Zelzeleh cried out at him and said, 'Desist, O Meimoun. Thou sufferest not Tuhfeh to pay heed unto us.' Quoth he, 'I will have her sing to me.' And words waxed between them and Queen Zelzeleh cried out at him. Then she shook and became like unto the Jinn and taking in her hand a mace of stone, said to him, 'Out on thee! What art thou that thou shouldst bespeak us thus? By Allah, but for the king's worship and my fear of troubling the session and the festival and the mind of the Sheikh Iblis, I would assuredly beat the folly out of thy head!' When Meimoun heard these her words, he rose, with the fire issuing from his eyes, and said, 'O daughter of Imlac, what art thou that thou shouldst outrage me with the like of this talk?' 'Out on thee, O dog of the Jinn,' replied she, 'knowest thou not thy place?' So saying, she ran at him and offered to strike him with the mace, but the Sheikh Iblis arose and casting his turban on the ground, said, 'Out on thee, O Meimoun! Thou still dost with us on this wise. Wheresoever thou art present, thou troubleth our life! Canst thou not hold thy peace till thou goest forth of the festival and this bride-feast[487] be accomplished? When the circumcision is at an end and ye all return to your dwelling-places, then do as thou wilt. Out on thee, O Meimoun! Knowest thou not that Imlac is of the chiefs of the Jinn? But for my worship, thou shouldst have seen what would have betided thee of humiliation and punishment; but by reason of the festival none may speak. Indeed thou exceedest: knowest thou not that her sister Wekhimeh is doughtier than any of the Jinn? Learn to know thyself: hast thou no regard for thy life?'

Meimoun was silent and Iblis turned to Tuhfeh and said to her, 'Sing to the kings of the Jinn this day and to-night until the morrow, when the boy will be circumcised and each shall return to his own place.' So she took the lute and Kemeriyeh said to her, (now she had in her hand a cedrat), 'O my sister, sing to me on this cedrat.' 'Hearkening and obedience,' replied Tuhfeh, and improvising, sang the following verses:

My fruit is a jewel all wroughten of gold, Whose beauty amazeth all those that behold.
My juice among kings is still drunken for wine And a present am I betwixt friends, young and old.

At this Queen Kemeriyeh was moved to exceeding delight and drank off her cup, saying, 'Well done, O queen of hearts!' Moreover, she took off a surcoat of blue brocade, fringed with red rubies, and a necklace of white jewels, worth an hundred thousand dinars, and gave them to Tuhfeh. Then she passed the cup to her sister Zelzeleh, who had in her hand sweet basil, and she said to Tuhfeh, 'Sing to me on this sweet basil.' 'Hearkening and obedience,' answered she and improvised and sang the following verses:

The crown of the flow'rets am I, in the chamber of wine, And Allah makes mention of me 'mongst the pleasures divine; Yea, ease and sweet basil and peace, the righteous are told, In Eternity's Garden of sweets shall to bless them combine.[488] Where, then, is the worth that in aught with my worth can compare And where is the rank in men's eyes can be likened to mine?

Thereat Queen Zelzeleh was moved to exceeding delight and bidding her treasuress bring a basket, wherein were fifty pairs of bracelets and the like number of earrings, all of gold, set with jewels of price, the like whereof nor men nor Jinn possessed, and an hundred robes of coloured brocade and an hundred thousand dinars, gave the whole to Tuhfeh. Then she passed the cup to her sister Sherareh, who had in her hand a stalk of narcissus; so she took it from her and turning to Tuhfeh, said to her, 'O Tuhfeh, sing to me on this.' 'Hearkening and obedience,' answered she and improvised and sang the following verses:

Most like a wand of emerald my shape it is, trow I; Amongst the fragrant flow'rets there's none with me can vie.
The eyes of lovely women are likened unto me; Indeed, amongst the gardens I open many an eye.

When she had made an end of her song, Sherareh was moved to exceeding delight and drinking off her cup, said to her, 'Well done, O gift of hearts!' Then she ordered her an hundred dresses of brocade and an hundred thousand dinars and passed the cup to Queen Wekhimeh. Now she had in her hand somewhat of blood-red anemone; so she took the cup from her sister and turning to Tuhfeh, said to her, 'O Tuhfeh, sing to me on this.' Quoth she, 'I hear and obey,' and improvised the following verses:

The Merciful dyed me with that which I wear Of hues with whose goodliness none may compare.
The earth is my birth-place, indeed; but my place Of abidance is still in the cheeks of the fair.

Therewith Wekhimeh was moved to exceeding delight and drinking off the cup, ordered her twenty dresses of Greek brocade and a tray, wherein were thirty thousand dinars. Then she gave the cup to Queen Shuaaeh, Queen of the Fourth Sea, who took it and said, 'O my lady Tuhfeh, sing to me on the gillyflower.' Quoth she 'Hearkening and obedience,' and improvised the following verses:

The season of my presence is never at an end 'Mongst all their time in gladness and solacement who spend,

Whenas the folk assemble for birling at the wine, Whether in morning's splendour or when night's shades descend.
The pitcher then of goblets filled full and brimming o'er With limpid wine we plunder, that pass from friend to friend.

Queen Shuaaeh was moved to exceeding delight and emptying her cup, gave Tuhfeh an hundred thousand dinars. Then arose Iblis (may God curse him!) and said, 'Verily, the dawn gleameth.' Whereupon the folk arose and disappeared, all of them, and there abode not one of them save Tuhfeh, who went forth to the garden and entering the bath, made her ablutions and prayed that which had escaped her of prayers. Then she sat down and when the sun rose, behold, there came up to her near an hundred thousand green birds; the branches of the trees were filled with their multitudes and they warbled in various voices, whilst Tuhfeh marvelled at their fashion. Presently, up came eunuchs, bearing a throne of gold, set with pearls and jewels and jacinths white and red and having four steps of gold, together with many carpets of silk and brocade and Egyptian cloth of silk welted with gold. These latter they spread amiddleward the garden and setting up the throne thereon, perfumed the place with virgin musk and aloes and ambergris.

After that, there appeared a queen, never saw eyes a goodlier than she nor than her attributes; she was clad in rich raiment, embroidered with pearls and jewels, and on her head was a crown set with various kinds of pearls and jewels. About her were five hundred slave-girls, high-bosomed maids, as they were moons, screening her, right and left, and she among them as she were the moon on the night of its full, for that she was the most of them in majesty and dignity. She gave not over walking, till she came to Tuhfeh, whom she found gazing on her in amazement; and when the latter saw her turn to her, she rose to her, standing on her feet, and saluted her and kissed the earth before her.

The queen rejoiced in her and putting out her hand to her, drew her to herself and seated her by her side on the couch; whereupon Tuhfeh kissed her hands and the queen said to her, 'Know, O Tuhfeh, that all that thou treadest of these belong not to any of the Jinn,[489] for that I am the queen of them all and the Sheikh Aboultawaif Iblis sought my permission[490] and prayed me to be present at the circumcision of his son. So I sent to him, in my stead, a slave-girl of my slave-girls, to wit, Shuaaeh, Queen of the Fourth Sea, who is vice-queen of my kingdom. When she was present at the wedding and saw thee and heard thy singing, she sent to me, giving me to know of thee and setting forth to me thine elegance and pleasantness and the goodliness of thy breeding and thy singing. So I am come to thee, for that which I have heard of thy charms, and this shall bring thee great worship in the eyes of all the Jinn.'[491]

Tuhfeh arose and kissed the earth and the queen thanked her for this and bade her sit. So she sat down and the queen called for food; whereupon they brought a table of gold, inlaid with pearls and jacinths and jewels and spread with various kinds of birds and meats of divers hues, and the queen said, 'O Tuhfeh, in the name of God, let us eat bread and salt together, thou and I.' So Tuhfeh came forward and ate of those meats and tasted somewhat the like whereof she had never eaten, no, nor aught more delicious than it, what while the slave-girls stood compassing about the table and she sat conversing and laughing with the queen. Then said the latter, 'O my sister, a slave-girl told me of thee that thou saidst, "How loathly is yonder genie Meimoun! There is no eating [in his presence]."'[492] 'By Allah, O my lady,' answered Tuhfeh, 'I cannot brook the sight of him,[493] and indeed I am fearful of him.' When the queen heard this, she laughed, till she fell backward, and said, 'O my sister, by the virtue of the inscription upon the seal-ring of Solomon, prophet of God, I am queen over all the Jinn, and none dare so much as look on thee a glance of the eye.' And Tuhfeh kissed her hand. Then the tables were removed and they sat talking.

Presently up came the kings of the Jinn from every side and kissed the earth before the queen and stood in her service; and she thanked them for this, but stirred not for one of them. Then came the Sheikh Aboultawaif Iblis (God curse him!) and kissed the earth before her, saying, 'O my lady, may I not be bereft of these steps!'[494] O Sheikh Aboultawalf,' answered she, 'it behoveth thee to thank the bounty of the Lady Tuhfeh, who was the cause of my coming.' 'True,' answered he and kissed the earth. Then the queen fared on [towards the palace] and there [arose and] alighted upon the trees an hundred thousand birds of various colours. Quoth Tuhfeh, 'How many are these birds!' And Queen Wekhimeh said to her, 'Know, O my sister, that this queen is called Queen Es Shuhba and that she is queen over all the Jinn from East to West. These birds that thou seest are of her troops, and except they came in this shape, the earth would not contain them. Indeed, they came forth with her and are present with her presence at this circumcision. She will give thee after the measure of that which hath betided thee[495] from the first of the festival to the last thereof; and indeed she honoureth us all with her presence.'

Then the queen entered the palace and sat down on the throne of the circumcision[496] at the upper end of the hall, whereupon Tuhfeh took the lute and pressing it to her bosom, touched its strings on such wise that the wits of all present were bewildered and the Sheikh Iblis said to her, 'O my lady Tuhfeh, I conjure thee, by the life of this worshipful queen, sing for me and praise thyself, and gainsay me not.' Quoth she, 'Hearkening and obedience; yet, but for the adjuration by which thou conjurest me, I had not done this. Doth any praise himself? What manner of thing is this?' Then she improvised and sang the following verses:

In every rejoicing a boon[497] midst the singers and minstrels am I;
The folk witness bear of my worth and none can my virtues deny.
My virtues 'mongst men are extolled and my glory and station rank high.

Her verses pleased the kings of the Jinn and they said, 'By Allah, thou sayst sooth!' Then she rose to her feet, with the lute in her hand, and played and sang, whilst the Jinn and the Sheikh Aboultawaif danced. Then the latter came up to her and gave her a carbuncle he had taken from the hidden treasure of Japhet, son of Noah (on whom be peace), and which was worth the kingdom of the world; its light was as the light of the sun and he said to her, 'Take this and glorify thyself withal over[498] the people of the world.' She kissed his hand and rejoiced in the jewel and said, 'By Allah, this beseemeth none but the Commander of the Faithful.'

Now the dancing of Iblis pleased Queen Es Shuhba and she said to him, 'By Allah, this is a goodly dancing!' He thanked her for this and said to Tuhfeh, 'O Tuhfeh, there is not on the face of the earth a skilfuller than Ishac en Nedim; but thou art more skilful than he. Indeed, I have been present with him many a time and have shown him passages[499] on the lute, and there have betided me such and such things with him.[500] Indeed, the story of my dealings with him is a long one and this is no time to repeat it; but now I would fain show thee a passage on the lute, whereby thou shall be exalted over all the folk.' Quoth she to him, 'Do what seemeth good to thee.' So he took the lute and played thereon on wondrous wise, with rare divisions and extraordinary modulations, and showed her a passage she knew not; and this was liefer to her than all that she had gotten. Then she took the lute from him and playing thereon, [sang and] presently returned to the passage that he had shown her; and he said, 'By Allah, thou singest better than I!' As for Tuhfeh, it was made manifest to her that her former usance[501] was all of it wrong and that what she had learnt from the Sheikh Aboultawaif Iblis was the origin and foundation [of all perfection] in the art. So she rejoiced in that which she had gotten of [new skill in] touching the lute far more than in all that had fallen to her lot of wealth and raiment and kissed the Sheikh's hand.

Then said Queen Es Shuhba, 'By Allah, O Sheikh, my sister Tuhfeh is indeed unique among the folk of her time, and I hear that she singeth upon all sweet- scented flowers.' 'Yes, O my lady,' answered Iblis, 'and I am in the utterest of wonderment thereat. But there remaineth somewhat of sweet-scented flowers, that she hath not besung, such as the myrtle and the tuberose and the jessamine and the moss-rose and the like.' Then he signed to her to sing upon the rest of the flowers, that Queen Es Shuhba might hear, and she said, 'Hearkening and obedience.' So she took the lute and played thereon in many modes, then returned to the first mode and sang the following verses:

One of the host am I of lovers sad and sere For waiting long drawn out and expectation drear.
My patience underneath the loss of friends and folk With pallor's sorry garb hath clad me, comrades dear.
Abasement, misery and heart-break after those I suffer who endured before me many a year.
All through the day its light and when the night grows dark, My grief forsakes me not, no, nor my heavy cheer.
My tears flow still, nor aye of bitterness I'm quit, Bewildered as I am betwixten hope and fear.

Therewithal Queen Es Shuhba was moved to exceeding delight and said, 'Well done, O queen of delight! None can avail to describe thee. Sing to us on the apple,' Quoth Tuhfeh, 'Hearkening and obedience.' Then she improvised and sang the following verses:

Endowed with amorous grace past any else am I; Graceful of shape and lithe and pleasing to the eye.
The hands of noble folk do tend me publicly; With waters clear and sweet my thirsting tongue they ply.

My clothes of sendal are, my veil of the sun's light, The very handiwork of God the Lord Most High.

Whenas my sisters dear forsake me, grieved that they Must leave their native place and far away must hie,

The nobles' hands, for that my place I must forsake, Do solace me with beds, whereon at ease I lie.

Lo! in the garden-ways, the place of ease and cheer, Still, like the moon at full, my light thou mayst espy.

Queen Es Shubha rejoiced in this with an exceeding delight and said, 'Well done! By Allah, there is none surpasseth thee.' Tuhfeh kissed the earth, then returned to her place and improvised on the tuberose, saying:

My flower a marvel on your heads doth show, Yet homeless[502] am I in your land, I trow.

Make drink your usance in my company And flout the time that languishing doth go.

Camphor itself to me doth testify And in my presence owns me white as snow.

So make me in your morning a delight And set me in your houses, high and low;

So shall we quaff the cups in ease and cheer, In endless joyance, quit of care and woe.

At this Queen Es Shuhba was stirred to exceeding delight and said, 'Well done, O queen of delight! By Allah, I know not how I shall do to render thee thy due! May God the Most High grant us to enjoy thy long continuance [on life]!' Then she strained her to her breast and kissed her on the cheek; whereupon quoth Iblis (on whom be malison!), 'Indeed, this is an exceeding honour!' Quoth the queen, 'Know that this lady Tuhfeh is my sister and that her commandment is my commandment and her forbiddance my forbiddance. So hearken all to her word and obey her commandment.' Therewithal the kings rose all and kissed the earth before Tuhfeh, who rejoiced in this. Moreover, Queen Es Shuhba put off on her a suit adorned with pearls and jewels and jacinths, worth an hundred thousand dinars, and wrote her on a sheet of paper a patent in her own hand, appointing her her deputy. So Tuhfeh rose and kissed the earth before the queen, who said to her, 'Sing to us, of thy favour, concerning the rest of the sweet-scented flowers and herbs, so I may hear thy singing and divert myself with witnessing thy skill.' 'Hearkening and obedience, O lady mine,' answered Tuhfeh and taking the lute, improvised the following verses:

Midst colours, my colour excelleth in light And I would every eye of my charms might have sight.
My place is the place of the fillet and pearls And the fair are most featly with jasmine bedight,
How bright and how goodly my lustre appears! Yea, my wreaths are like girdles of silver so white.

Then she changed the measure and improvised the following:

I'm the crown of every sweet and fragrant weed; When the loved one calls, I keep the tryst agreed.
My favours I deny not all the year; Though cessation be desired, I nothing heed.
I'm the keeper of the promise and the troth, And my gathering is eath, without impede.

Then she changed the measure and the mode [and played] so that she amazed the wits of those who were present, and Queen Es Shuhba was moved to mirth and said, 'Well done, O queen of delight!' Then she returned to the first mode and improvised the following verses on the water-lily:

I fear to be seen in the air, Without my consent, unaware;
So I stretch out my root neath the flood And my branches turn back to it there.

Therewithal Queen Es Shuhba was moved to delight and said, 'Well done, O Tuhfeh! Let me have more of thy singing.' So she smote the lute and changing the mode, improvised the following verses on the moss-rose:

Look at the moss-rose, on its branches seen, Midmost its leafage, covered all with green.
Tis gazed at for its slender swaying shape And cherished for its symmetry and sheen.
Lovely with longing for its love's embrace, The fear of his estrangement makes it lean.

Then she changed the measure and the mode and sang the following verses:

O thou that questionest the lily of its scent, Give ear unto my words and verses thereanent.
Th' Amir (quoth it) am I whose charms are still desired; Absent or present, all in loving me consent.

When she had made an end of her song, Queen Es Shuhba arose and said, 'Never heard I from any the like of this.' And she drew Tuhfeh to her and fell to kissing her. Then she took leave of her and flew away; and all the birds took flight with her, so that they walled the world; whilst the rest of the kings tarried behind.

When it was the fourth night, there came the boy whom they were minded to circumcise, adorned with jewels such as never saw eye nor heard ear of, and amongst the rest a crown of gold, set with pearls and jewels, the worth whereof was an hundred thousand dinars. He sat down upon the throne and Tuhfeh sang to him, till the surgeon came and they circumcised him, in the presence of all the kings, who showered on him great store of jewels and jacinths and gold. Queen Kemeriyeh bade the servants gather up all this and lay it in Tuhfeh's closet, and it was [as much in value as] all that had fallen to her, from the first of the festival to the last thereof. Moreover, the Sheikh Iblis (whom God curse!) bestowed upon Tuhfeh the crown worn by the boy and gave the latter another, whereat her reason fled. Then the Jinn departed, in order of rank, whilst Iblis took leave of them, band by band.

Whilst the Sheikh was thus occupied with taking leave of the kings, Meimoun sought his opportunity, whenas he saw the place empty, and taking up Tuhfeh on his shoulders, soared up with her to the confines of the sky and flew away with her. Presently, Iblis came to look for Tuhfeh and see what she purposed, but found her not and saw the slave-girls buffeting their faces; so he said to them, 'Out on ye! What is to do?' 'O our lord,' answered they, 'Meimoun hath snatched up Tuhfeh and flown away with her.' When Iblis heard this, he gave a cry, to which the earth trembled, and said, 'What is to be done? Out on ye! Shall he carry off Tuhfeh from my very palace and outrage mine honour? Doubtless, this Meimoun hath lost his wits.' Then he cried out a second time, that the earth quaked therefor, and rose up into the air.

The news came to the rest of the kings; so they [flew after him and] overtaking him, found him full of trouble and fear, with fire issuing from his nostrils, and said to him, 'O Sheikh Aboultawaif, what is to do?' Quoth he, 'Know that Meimoun hath carried off Tuhfeh from my palace and outraged mine honour.' When they heard this, they said, 'There is no power and no virtue but in God the Most High, the Supreme! By Allah, he hath ventured upon a grave matter and indeed he destroyeth himself and his people!' Then the Sheikh Iblis gave not over flying till he fell in with the tribes of the Jinn, and there gathered themselves together unto him much people, none may tell the tale of them save God the Most High. So they came to the Fortress of Copper and the Citadel of Lead,[503] and the people of the strongholds saw the tribes of the Jinn issuing from every steep mountain-pass and said, 'What is to do?' Then Iblis went in to King Es Shisban and acquainted him with that which had befallen, whereupon quoth he, 'May God destroy Meimoun and his folk! He thinketh to possess Tuhfeh, and she is become queen of the Jinn! But have patience till we contrive that which befitteth in the matter of Tuhfeh.' Quoth Iblis, 'And what befitteth it to do?' And Es Shisban said, *We will fall upon him and slay him and his people with the sword.'

Then said the Sheikh Iblis, 'We were best acquaint Queen Kemeriyeh and Queen Zelzeleh and Queen Sherareh and Queen Wekhimeh; and when they are assembled, God shall ordain [that which He deemeth] good in the matter of her release.' 'It is well seen of thee,' answered Es Shisban and despatched to Queen Kemeriyeh an Afrit called Selheb, who came to her palace and found her asleep; so he aroused her and she said, 'What is to do, O Selheb?' 'O my lady,' answered he, 'come to the succour of thy sister Tuhfeh, for that Meimoun hath carried her off and outraged thine honour and that of the Sheikh Iblis.' Quoth she, 'What sayest thou?' And she sat up and cried out with a great cry. And indeed she feared for Tuhfeh and said, 'By Allah, indeed she used to say that he looked upon her and prolonged the looking on her; but ill is that to which his soul hath prompted him.' Then she arose in haste and mounting a she-devil of her devils, said to her, 'Fly.' So she flew off and alighted with her in the palace of her sister Sherareh, whereupon she sent for her sisters Zelzeleh and Wekhimeh and acquainted them with the news, saying, 'Know that Meimoun hath snatched up Tuhfeh and flown off with her swiftlier than the blinding lightning.'

[Then they all flew off in haste and] lighting down in the place where were their father Es Shisban and their grandfather the Sheikh Aboultawaif, found the folk on the sorriest of plights. When their grandfather Iblis saw them, he rose to them and wept, and they all wept for Tuhfeh. Then said Iblis to them, 'Yonder dog hath outraged mine honour and taken Tuhfeh, and I doubt not but that she is like to perish [of concern] for herself and her lord Er Reshid and saying "All that they said and did[504] was false."' Quoth Kemeriyeh, 'O grandfather mine, there is nothing left for it but [to use] stratagem and contrivance for her deliverance, for that she is dearer to me than everything; and know that yonder accursed one, whenas he is ware of your coming upon him, will know that he hath no power to cope with you, he who is the least and meanest [of the Jinn]; but we fear that, when he is assured of defeat, he will kill Tuhfeh; wherefore nothing will serve but that we contrive for her deliverance; else will she perish.' 'And what hast thou in mind of device?' asked he; and she answered, 'Let us take him with fair means, and if he obey, [all will be well]; else will we practise stratagem against him; and look thou not to other than myself for her deliverance.' Quoth Iblis, 'The affair is thine; contrive what thou wilt, for that Tuhfeh is thy sister and thy solicitude for her is more effectual than [that of] any.'

So Kemeriyeh cried out to an Afrit of the Afrits and a calamity of the calamities,[505] by name El Ased et Teyyar,[506] and said to him, 'Go with my message to the Crescent Mountain, the abiding-place of Meimoun the Sworder, and enter in to him and salute him in my name and say to him, "How canst thou be assured for thyself, O Meimoun?[507] Couldst thou find none on whom to vent thy drunken humour and whom to maltreat save Tuhfeh, more by token that she is a queen? But thou art excused, for that thou didst this not but of thine intoxication, and the Shekh Aboultawaif pardoneth thee, for that thou wast drunken. Indeed, thou hast outraged his honour; but now restore her to her palace, for that she hath done well and favoured us and done us service, and thou knowest that she is presently our queen. Belike she may bespeak Queen Es Shuhba, whereupon the matter will be aggravated and that wherein there is no good will betide. Indeed, thou wilt get no tittle of profit [from this thine enterprise]; verily, I give thee good counsel, and so peace be on thee!"'

'Hearkening and obedience,' answered El Ased and flew till he came to the Crescent Mountain, when he sought audience of Meimoun, who bade admit him. So he entered and kissing the earth before him, gave him Queen Kemeriyeh's message, which when he heard he said to the Afrit,

'Return whence thou comest and say to thy mistress, "Be silent and thou wilt do wisely." Else will I come and seize upon her and make her serve Tuhfeh; and if the kings of the Jinn assemble together against me and I be overcome of them, I will not leave her to scent the wind of this world and she shall be neither mine nor theirs, for that she is presently my soul[508] from between my ribs; and how shall any part with his soul?' When the Afrit heard Meimoun's words, he said to him, 'By Allah, O Meimoun, thou hast lost thy wits, that thou speakest these words of my mistress, and thou one of her servants!' Whereupon Meimoun cried out and said to him, 'Out on thee, O dog of the Jinn! Wilt thou bespeak the like of me with these words?' Then, he bade those who were about him smite El Ased, but he took flight and soaring into the air, betook himself to his mistress and told her that which had passed; and she said, 'Thou hast done well, O cavalier.'

Then she turned to her father and said to him, 'Give ear unto that which I shall say to thee.' Quoth he, 'Say on;' and she said, 'Take thy troops and go to him, for that, when he heareth this, he in his turn will levy h s troops and come forth to thee; wherepon do thou give him battle and prolong the fighting with him and make a show to him of weakness anc giving way. Meantime, I will practise a device for winning to Tuhfeh and delivering her, what while he is occupied with you in battle; and when my messenger cometh to thee and giveth thee to know that I have gotten possession of Tuhfeh and that she is with me, do thou return upon Meimoun forthright and destroy him, him and his hosts, and take him prisoner. But, if my device succeed not with him and we avail not to deliver Tuhfeh, he will assuredly go about to slay her, without recourse, and regret for her will abide in our hearts.' Quoth Iblis, 'This is the right counsel,' and let call among the troops to departure, whereupon an hundred thousand cavaliers, doughty men of war, joined themselves to him and set out for Meimoun's country.

As for Queen Kemeriyeh, she flew off to the palace of her sister Wekhimeh and told her what Meimoun had done and how [he avouched that], whenas he saw defeat [near at hand], he would slay Tuhfeh; and indeed,' added she, 'he is resolved upon this; else had he not dared to commit this outrage. So do thou contrive the affair as thou deemest well, for thou hast no superior in judgment.' Then they sent for Queen Zelzeleh and Queen Sherareh and sat down to take counsel, one with another, of that which they should do in the matter. Then said Wekhimeh, 'We were best fit out a ship in this island [wherein is my palace] and embark therein, in the guise of mortals, and fare on till we come to a little island, that lieth over against Meimoun's palace. There will we [take up our abode and] sit drinking and smiting the lute and singing. Now Tuhfeh will of a surety be sitting looking upon the sea, and needs must she see us and come down to us, whereupon we will take her by force and she will be under our hands, so that none shall avail more to molest her on any wise. Or, if Meimoun be gone forth to do battle with the Jinn, we will storm his stronghold and take Tuhfeh and raze his palace and put to death all who are therein. When he hears of this, his heart will be rent in sunder and we will send to let our father know, whereupon he will return upon him with his troops and he will be destroyed and we shall be quit of him.' And they answered her, saying, 'This is a good counsel.' Then they bade fit out a ship from behind the mountain,[509] and it was fitted out in less than the twinkling of an eye. So they launched it on the sea and embarking therein, together with four thousand Afrits, set out, intending for Meimoun's palace. Moreover, they bade other five thousand Afrits betake themselves to the island under the Crescent Mountain and lie in wait for them there.

Meanwhile, the Sheikh Aboultawaif Iblis and his son Es Shisban set out, as we have said, with their troops, who were of the doughtiest of the Jinn and the most accomplished of them in valour and horsemanship, [and fared on till they drew near the Crescent Mountain], When the news of their approach reached Meimoun, he cried out with a great cry to the troops, who were twenty thousand horse, [and bade them make ready for departure]. Then he went in to Tuhfeh and kissing her, said to her, 'Know that thou art presently my life of the world, and indeed the Jinn are gathered together to wage war on me on thine account. If I am vouchsafed the victory over them and am preserved alive, I will set all the kings of the Jinn under thy feet and thou shall become queen of the world.' But she shook her head and wept; and he said, 'Weep not, for, by the virtue of the mighty inscription engraven on the seal-ring of Solomon, thou shall never again see the land of men! Can any one part with his life? So give ear unto that which I say; else will I kill thee.' And she was silent.

Then he sent for his daughter, whose name was Jemreh, and when she came, he said to her, 'Harkye, Jemreh! Know that I am going to [meet] the clans of Es Shisban and Queen Kemeriyeh and the kings of the Jinn. If I am vouchsafed the victory over them, to Allah be the praise and thou shall have of me largesse; but, if thou see or hear that I am worsted and any come to thee with news of me [to this effect], hasten to slay Tuhfeh, so she may fall neither to me nor to them.' Then he took leave of her and mounted, saying, 'When this cometh about, pass over to the Crescent Mountain and take up thine abode there, and await what shall befall me and what I shall say to thee.' And Jemreh answered with 'Hearkening and obedience.'

When Tuhfeh heard this, she fell to weeping and wailing and said, 'By Allah, nought irketh me save separation from my lord Er Reshid; but, when I am dead, let the world be ruined after me.' And she doubted not in herself but that she was lost without recourse. Then Meimoun set forth with his army and departed in quest of the hosts [of the Jinn], leaving none in the palace save his daughter Jemreh and Tuhfeh and an Afrit who was dear unto him. They fared on till they met with the army of Es Shisban; and when the two hosts came face to face, they fell upon each other and fought a passing sore battle. After awhile, Es Shisban's troops began to give back, and when Meimoun saw them do thus, he despised them and made sure of victory over them.

Meanwhile, Queen Kemeriyeh and her company sailed on, without ceasing, till they came under the palace wherein was Tuhfeh, to wit, that of Meimoun the Sworder; and by the ordinance of destiny, Tuhfeh herself was then sitting on the belvedere of the palace, pondering the affair of Haroun er Reshid and her own and that which had befallen her and weeping for that she was doomed to slaughter. She saw the ship and what was therein of those whom we have named, and they in mortal guise, and said, 'Alas, my sorrow for yonder ship and the mortals that be therein!' As for Kemeriyeh and her company, when they drew near the palace, they strained their eyes and seeing Tuhfeh sitting, said, 'Yonder sits Tuhfeh. May God not bereave [us] of her!' Then they moored their ship and making for the island, that lay over against the palace, spread carpets and sat eating and drinking; whereupon quoth Tuhfeh, 'Welcome and fair welcome to yonder faces! These are my kinswomen and I conjure thee by Allah, O Jemreh, that thou let me down to them, so I may sit with them awhile and make friends with them and return.' Quoth Jemreh, 'I may on no wise do that.' And Tuhfeh wept. Then the folk brought out wine and drank, what while Kemeriyeh took the lute and sang the following verses:

By Allah, but that I trusted that I should meet you again. Your camel-leader to parting had summoned you in vain!

Parting afar hath borne you, but longing still is fain To bring you near; meseemeth mine eye doth you contain.

When Tuhfeh heard this, she gave a great cry, that the folk heard her and Kemeriyeh said, 'Relief is at hand.' Then she looked out to them and called to them, saying, 'O daughters of mine uncle, I am a lonely maid, an exile from folk and country. So, for the love of God the Most High, repeat that song!' So Kemeriyeh repeated it and Tuhfeh swooned away. When she came to herself, she said to Jemreh, 'By the virtue of the Apostle of God (whom may He bless and preserve!) except thou suffer me go down to them and look on them and sit with them awhile, [I swear] I will cast myself down from this palace, for that I am weary of my life and know that I am slain without recourse; wherefore I will slay myself, ere thou pass sentence upon me.' And she was instant with her in asking.

When Jemreh heard her words, she knew that, if she let her not down, she would assuredly destroy herself. So she said to her, 'O Tuhfeh, between thee and them are a thousand fathoms; but I will bring them up to thee.' 'Nay,' answered Tuhfeh, 'needs must I go down to them and take my pleasance in the island and look upon the sea anear; then will we return, thou and I; for that, if thou bring them up to us, they will be affrighted and there will betide them neither easance nor gladness. As for me, I do but wish to be with them, that they may cheer me with their company neither give over their merrymaking, so haply I may make merry with them, and indeed I swear that needs must I go down to them; else will I cast myself upon them.' And she cajoled Jemreh and kissed her hands, till she said, 'Arise and I will set thee down beside them.'

Then she took Tuhfeh under her armpit and flying up, swiftlier than the blinding lightning, set her down with Kemeriyeh and her company; whereupon she went up to them and accosted them, saying, 'Fear not, no harm shall betide you; for I am a mortal, like unto you, and I would fain look on you and talk with you and hear your singing.' So they welcomed her and abode in their place, whilst Jemreh sat down beside them and fell a-snuffing their odours and saying, 'I smell the scent of the Jinn! I wonder whence [it cometh!'] Then said Wekhimeh to her sister Kemeriyeh, 'Yonder filthy one [smelleth us] and presently she will take to flight; so what is this remissness concerning her?'[510] Thereupon Kemeriyeh put out a hand,[511] as it were a camel's neck,[512] and dealt Jemreh a buffet on the head, that made it fly from her body and cast it into the sea. Then said she, 'God is most great!' And they uncovered their faces, whereupon Tuhfeh knew them and said to them, 'Protection!'

Queen Kemeriyeh embraced her, as also did Queen Zelzeleh and Queen Wekhimeh and Queen Sherareh, and the former said to her, 'Rejoice in assured deliverance, for there abideth no harm for thee; but this is no time for talk.' Then they cried out, whereupon up came the Afrits ambushed in the island, with swords and maces in their hands, and taking up Tuhfeh, flew with her to the palace and made themselves masters thereof, whilst the Afrit aforesaid, who was dear to Meimoun and whose name was Dukhan, fled like an arrow and stayed not in his flight till he carne to Meimoun and found him engaged in sore battle with the Jinn. When his lord saw him, he cried out at him, saying, 'Out on thee! Whom hast thou left in the palace?' And Dukhan answered, saying, 'And who abideth in the palace? Thy beloved Tuhfeh they have taken and Jemreh is slain and they have gotten possession of the palace, all of it.' With this Meimoun buffeted his face and head and said, 'Out on it for a calamity!' And he cried aloud. Now Kemeriyeh had sent to her father and acquainted him with the news, whereat the raven of parting croaked for them. So, when Meimoun saw that which had betided him, (and indeed the Jinn smote upon him and the wings of death overspread his host,) he planted the butt of his spear in the earth and turning the point thereof to his heart, urged his charger upon it and pressed upon it with his breast, till the point came forth, gleaming, from his back.

Meanwhile the messenger had reached the opposite camp with the news of Tuhfeh's deliverance, whereat the Sheikh Aboultawaif rejoiced and bestowed on the bringer of good tidings a sumptuous dress of honour and made him commander over a company of the Jinn. Then they fell upon Meimoun's troops and destroyed them to the last man; and when they came to Meimoun, they found that he had slain himself and was even as we have said. Presently Kemeriyeh and her sister [Wekhimeh] came up to their grandfather and told him what they had done; whereupon he came to Tuhfeh and saluted her and gave her joy of her deliverance. Then he delivered Meimoun's palace to Selheb and took all the former's riches and gave them to Tuhfeh, whilst the troops encamped upon the Crescent Mountain. Moreover, the Sheikh Aboultawaif said to Tuhfeh, 'Blame me not,' and she kissed his hands. As they were thus engaged, there appeared to them the tribes of the Jinn, as they were clouds, and Queen Es Shuhba flying in their van, with a drawn sword in her hand.

When she came in sight of the folk, they kissed the earth before her and she said to them, 'Tell me what hath betided Queen Tuhfeh from yonder dog Meimoun and why did ye not send to me and tell me?' Quoth they, 'And who was this dog that we should send to thee, on his account? Indeed, he was the least and meanest [of the Jinn].' Then they told her what Kemeriyeh and her sisters had done and how they had practised upon Meimoun and delivered Tuhfeh from his hand, fearing lest he should slay her, whenas he found himself discomfited; and she said, 'By Allah, the accursed one was wont to prolong his looking upon her!' And Tuhfeh fell to kissing Queen Es Shuhba's hand, whilst the latter strained her to her bosom and kissed her, saying, 'Trouble is past; so rejoice in assurance of relief.'

Then they arose and went up to the palace, whereupon the trays of food were brought and they ate and drank; after which quoth Queen Es Shuhba, 'O Tuhfeh, sing to us, by way of thankoffering for thy deliverance, and favour us with that which shall solace our minds, for that indeed my mind hath been occupied with thee.' Quoth Tuhfeh 'Hearkening and obedience, O my lady.' So she improvised and sang the following verses:

Wind of the East, if thou pass by the land where my loved ones dwell, I pray, The fullest of greetings bear to them from me, their lover, and say
That I am the pledge of passion still and that my longing love And eke my yearning do overpass all longing that was aye.

Therewithal Queen Es Shuhba rejoiced and all who were present rejoiced also and admired her speech and fell to kissing her; and when she had made an end of her song, Queen Kemeriyeh said to her, 'O my sister, ere thou go to thy palace, I would fain bring thee to look upon El Anca, daughter of Behram Gour, whom El Anca, daughter of the wind, carried off, and her beauty; for that there is not her match on the face of the earth.' And Queen Es Shuhba said, 'O Kemeriyeh, I [also] have a mind to see her.' Quoth Kemeriyeh, 'I saw her three years agone; but my sister Wekhimeh seeth her at all times, for that she is near unto her, and she saith that there is not in the world a fairer than she. Indeed, this Queen El Anca is become a byword for loveliness and proverbs are made upon her beauty and grace' And Wekhimeh said, 'By the mighty inscription [on the seal-ring of Solomon], there is not her like in the world!' Then said Queen Es Shuhba, 'If it needs must be and the affair is as ye say, I will take Tuhfeh and go with her [to El Anca], so she may see her.'

So they all arose and repaired to El Anca, who abode in the Mountain Caf.[513] When she saw them, she rose to them and saluted them, saying, 'O my ladies, may I not be bereaved of you!' Quoth Wekhimeh to her, 'Who is like unto thee, O Anca? Behold, Queen Es Shuhba is come to thee.' So El Anca kissed the queen's feet and lodged them in her palace; whereupon Tuhfeh came up to her and fell to kissing her and saying, 'Never saw I a goodlier than this favour.' Then she set before them somewhat of food and they ate and washed their hands; after which Tuhfeh took the lute and played excellent well; and El Anca also played, and they fell to improvising verses in turns, whilst Tuhfeh embraced El Anca every moment. Quoth Es Shuhba, 'O my sister, each kiss is worth a thousand dinars; and Tuhfeh answered, 'Indeed, a thousand dinars were little for it.' Whereat El Anca laughed and on the morrow they took leave of her and went away to Meimoun's palace.[514]

Here Queen Es Shuhba bade them farewell and taking her troops, returned to her palace, whilst the kings also went away to their abodes and the Sheikh Aboultawaif addressed himself to divert Tuhfeh till nightfall, when he mounted her on the back of one of the Afrits and bade other thirty gather together all that she had gotten of treasure and raiment and jewels and dresses of honour. [Then they flew off,] whilst Iblis went with her, and in less than the twinkling of an eye he set her down in her sleeping-chamber. Then he and those who were with him took leave of her and went away. When Tuhfeh found herself in her own chamber and on her couch, her reason fled for joy and it seemed to her as if she had never stirred thence. Then she took the lute and tuned it and touched it on wondrous wise and improvised verses and sang.

The eunuch heard the smiting of the lute within the chamber and said, 'By Allah, that is my lady Tuhfeh's touch!' So he arose and went, as he were a madman, falling down and rising up, till he came to the eunuch on guard at the door at the Commander of the Faithful and found him sitting. When the latter saw him, and he like a madman, falling down and rising up, he said to him, 'What aileth thee and what bringeth thee hither at this hour?' Quoth the other, 'Wilt thou not make haste and awaken the Commander of the Faithful?' And he fell to crying out at him; whereupon the Khalif awoke and heard them bandying words together and Tuhfeh's servant saying to the other, 'Out on thee! Awaken the Commander of the Faithful in haste.' So he said, 'O Sewab, what aileth thee?' And the chief eunuch answered, saying, 'O our lord, the eunuch of Tuhfeh's lodging hath taken leave of his wits and saith, "Awaken the Commander of the Faithful in haste!"' Then said Er Reshid to one of the slave-girls, 'See what is to do.'

So she hastened to admit the eunuch, who entered; and when he saw the Commander of the Faithful, he saluted not neither kissed the earth, but said, 'Quick, quick! Arise in haste! My lady Tuhfeh sitteth in her chamber, singing a goodly ditty. Come to her in haste and see all that I say to thee! Hasten! She sitteth [in her chamber].' The Khalif was amazed at his speech and said to him, 'What sayst thou?' 'Didst thou not hear the first of the speech?' replied the eunuch. 'Tuhfeh sitteth in the sleeping-chamber, singing and playing the lute. Come thy quickliest! Hasten!' So Er Reshid arose and donned his clothes; but he credited not the eunuch's words and said to him, 'Out on thee! What is this thou sayst? Hast thou not seen this in a dream?' 'By Allah,' answered the eunuch, 'I know not what thou sayest, and I was not asleep.' Quoth Er Reshid, 'If thy speech be true, it shall be for thy good luck, for I will enfranchise thee and give thee a thousand dinars; but, if it be untrue and thou have seen this in sleep, I will crucify thee.' And the eunuch said in himself, 'O Protector,[515] let me not have seen this in Sleep!' Then he left the Khalif and going to the chamber-door, heard the sound of singing and lute-playing; whereupon he returned to Er Reshid and said to him, 'Go and hearken and see who is asleep.'

When Er Reshid drew near the door of the chamber, he heard the sound of the lute and Tuhfeh's voice singing; whereat he could not restrain his reason and was like to swoon away for excess of joy. Then he pulled out the key, but could not bring his hand to open the door. However, after awhile, he took heart and applying himself, opened the door and entered, saying, 'Methinks this is none other than a dream or an illusion of sleep.' When Tuhfeh saw him, she rose and coming to meet him, strained him to her bosom; and he cried out with a cry, wherein his soul was like to depart, and fell down in a swoon. She strained him to her bosom and sprinkled on him rose-water, mingled with musk, and washed his face, till he came to himself, as he were a drunken man, for the excess of his joy in Tuhfeh's return to him, after he had despaired of her.

Then she took the lute and smote thereon, after the fashion she had learnt from the Sheikh Iblis, so that Er Reshid's wit was dazed for excess of delight and his understanding was confounded for joy; after which she improvised and sang the following verses:

My heart will never credit that I am far from thee; In it thou art, nor ever the soul can absent be.
Or if to me "I'm absent" thou sayest, "'Tis a lie," My heart replies, bewildered 'twixt doubt and certainty.

When she had made an end of her verses, Er Reshid said to her, 'O Tuhfeh, thine absence was extraordinary, but thy presence[516] is yet more extraordinary.' 'By Allah, O my lord,' answered she, 'thou sayst sooth.' And she took his hand and said to him, 'See what I have brought with me.' So he looked and saw riches such as neither words could describe nor registers avail to set out, pearls and jewels and jacinths and precious stones and great pearls and magnificent dresses of honour, adorned with pearls and jewels and embroidered with red gold. Moreover, she showed him that which Queen Es Shuhba had bestowed on her of those carpets, which she had brought with her, and that her throne, the like whereof neither Chosroes nor Cassar possessed, and those tables inlaid with pearls and jewels and those vessels, that amazed all who looked on them, and the crown, that was on the head of the circumcised boy, and those dresses of honour, which Queen Es Shuhba and the Sheikh Aboultawaif had put off upon her, and the trays wherein were those riches; brief, she showed him treasures the like whereof he had never in his life set eyes on and which the tongue availeth not to describe and whereat all who looked thereon were amazed.

Er Reshid was like to lose his wits for amazement at this sight and was confounded at this that he beheld and witnessed. Then said he to Tuhfeh, 'Come, tell me thy story from first to last, [and let me know all that hath betided thee,] as if I had been present' She answered with 'Hearkening and obedience,' and fell to telling him [all that had betided her] first and last, from the time when she first saw the Sheikh Aboultawaif, how he took her and descended with her through the side of the draught-house; and she told him of the horse she had ridden, till she came to the meadow aforesaid and described it to him, together with the palace and that which was therein of furniture, and related to him how the Jinn rejoiced in her and that which she had seen of the kings of them, men and women, and of Queen Kemeriyeh and her sisters and Queen Shuaaeh, Queen of the Fourth Sea, and Queen Es Shuhba, Queen of Queens, and King Es Shisban, and that which each one of them had bestowed upon her. Moreover, she told him the story of Meimoun the Sworder and described to him his loathly favour, which he had not consented to change, and related to him that which befell her from the kings of the Jinn, men and women, and the coming of the Queen of Queens, Es Shuhba, and how she had loved her and appointed her her vice-queen and how she was thus become ruler over all the kings of the Jinn; and she showed him the patent of investiture that Queen Es Shuhba had written her and told him that which had betided her with the Ghoul-head, whenas it appeared to her in the garden, and how she had despatched it to her palace, beseeching it to bring her news of the Commander of the Faithful and that which had betided him after her. Then she described to him the gardens, wherein she had taken her pleasure, and the baths inlaid with pearls and jewels and told him that which had befallen Meimoun the Sworder, whenas he carried her off, and how he had slain himself; brief, she told him all that she had seen of wonders and rarities and that which she had beheld of all kinds and colours among the Jinn.

Then she told him the story of Anca, daughter of Behram Gour, with Anca, daughter of the wind, and described to him her dwelling-place and her island, whereupon quoth Er Reshid, 'O Tuhfet es Sedr,[517] tell me of El Anca, daughter of Behram Gour; is she of the Jinn or of mankind or of the birds? For this long time have I desired to find one who should tell me of her.' 'It is well, O Commander of the Faithful,' answered Tuhfeh. 'I asked the queen of this and she acquainted me with her case and told me who built her the palace.' Quoth Er Reshid, 'I conjure thee by Allah, tell it me.' And Tuhfeh answered, 'It is well,' and proceeded to tell him. And indeed he was amazed at that which he heard from her and what she told him and at that which she had brought back of jewels and jacinths of various colours and preciots stones of many kinds, such as amazed the beholder and confounded thought and mind. As for this, it was the means of the enrichment of the Barmecides and the Abbasicles, and they abode in their delight.

Then the Khalif went forth and bade decorate the city: [so they decorated it] and the drums of glad tidings were beaten. Moreover they made banquets to the people and the tables were spread seven days. And Tuhfeh and the Commander of the Faithful ceased not to be in the most delightsome of life and the most prosperous thereof till there came to them the Destroyer of Delights and the Sunderer of Companies; and thu is all that hath come down to as of their story."

Calcutta (1814-18) Text.

The following story occupies the last five Nights (cxcv-cc) of the unfinished Calcutta Edition of 1814-18. The only other text of it known to me is that published by Monsieur Langles (Paris, 1814), as an appendix to his Edition of the Voyages of Sindbad, and of this I have freely availed myself in making the present translation, comparing and collating with it the Calcutta (1814-18) Text and filling up and correcting omissions and errors that occur in the latter. In the Calcutta (1814-18) Text this story (Vol. II. pp. 367-378) is immediately succeeded by the Seven Voyages of Sindbad (Vol. II. pp. 378-458), which conclude the work.

WOMEN'S CRAFT

It is told that there was once, in the city of Baghdad, a comely and well-bred youth, fair of face, tall of stature and slender of shape. His name was Alaeddin and he was of the chiefs of the sons of the merchants and had a shop wherein he sold and bought One day, as he sat in his shop, there passed by him a girl of the women of pleasure,[518] who raised her eyes and casting a glance at the young merchant, saw written in a flowing hand on the forepart[519] of the door of his shop, these words, "VERILY, THERE IS NO CRAFT BUT MEN'S CRAFT, FORASMUCH AS IT OVERCOMETH WOMEN'S CRAFT." When she beheld this, she was wroth and took counsel with herself, saying, "As my head liveth, I will assuredly show him a trick of the tricks of women and prove the untruth of[520] this his inscription!"

So, on the morrow, she made her ready and donning the costliest of apparel, adorned herself with the most magnificent of ornaments and the highest of price and stained her hands with henna. Then she let down her tresses upon her shoulders and went forth, walking along with coquettish swimming gait and amorous grace, followed by her slave-girls, till she came to the young merchant's shop and sitting down thereat, under colour of seeking stuffs, saluted him and demanded of him somewhat of merchandise. So he brought out to her various kinds of stuffs and she took them and turned them over, talking with him the while. Then said she to him, "Look at the goodliness of my shape and my symmetry. Seest thou in me any default?" And he answered, "No, O my lady." "Is it lawful," continued she, "in any one that he should slander me and say that I am hump-backed?"

Then she discovered to him a part of her bosom, and when he saw her breasts, his reason took flight from his head and he said to her, "Cover it up, so may God have thee in His safeguard!" Quoth she, "Is it fair of any one to missay of my charms?" And he answered, "How shall any missay of thy charms, and thou the sun of loveliness?" Then said she, "Hath any the right to say of me that I am lophanded? "And tucking up her sleeves, showed him forearms, as they were crystal; after which she unveiled to him a face, as it were a full moon breaking forth on its fourteenth night, and said to him, "Is it lawful for any to missay of me [and avouch] that my face is pitted with smallpox or that I am one-eyed or crop-eared?" And he answered her, saying, "O my lady, what is it moveth thee to discover unto me that lovely face and those fair members, [of wont so jealously] veiled and guarded? Tell me the truth of the matter, may I be thy ransom!" And he recited the following verses:

A white one, from her sheath of tresses now laid bare And now again concealed in black, luxuriant hair;[521]
As if the maid the day resplendent and her locks The night that o'er it spreads its shrouding darkness were.

"Know, O my lord," answered she, "that I am a maiden oppressed of my father, for that he misspeaketh of me and saith to me, 'Thou art foul of favour and it befitteth not that thou wear rich clothes; for thou and the slave-girls, ye are equal in rank, there is no distinguishing thee from them.' Now he is a rich man, having wealth galore, [and saith not on this wise but] because he is a niggard and grudgeth the spending of a farthing; [wherefore he is loath to marry me,] lest he be put to somewhat of charge in my marriage, albeit God the Most High hath been bountiful to him and he is a man puissant in his time and lacking nothing of the goods of the world." "Who is thy father," asked the young merchant, "and what is his condition?" And she replied, "He is the Chief Cadi of the Supreme Court, under whose hand are all the Cadis who administer justice in this city."

The merchant believed her and she took leave of him and went away, leaving in his heart a thousand regrets, for that the love of her had gotten possession of him and he knew not how he should win to her; wherefore he abode enamoured, love-distraught, unknowing if he were alive or dead. As soon as she was gone, he shut his shop and going up to the Court, went in to the Chief Cadi and saluted him. The magistrate returned his salutation and entreated him with honour and seated him by his side. Then said Alaeddin to him, "I come to thee, a suitor, seeking thine alliance and desiring the hand of thy noble daughter." "O my lord merchant," answered the Cadi, "indeed my daughter beseemeth not the like of thee, neither sorteth she with the goodliness of thy youth and the pleasantness of thy composition and the sweetness of thy discourse;" but Alaeddin rejoined, saying, "This talk behoveth thee not, neither is it seemly in thee; if I be content with her, how should this irk thee?" So they came to an accord and concluded the treaty of marriage at a dower precedent of five purses[522] paid down then and there and a dower contingent of fifteen purses,[523] so it might be uneath unto him to put her away, forasmuch as her father had given him fair warning, but he would not be warned.

Then they drew up the contract of marriage and the merchant said, "I desire to go in to her this night." So they carried her to him in procession that very night, and he prayed the prayer of eventide and entered the privy chamber prepared for him; but, when he lifted the veil from the face of the bride and looked, he saw a foul face and a blameworthy aspect; yea, he beheld somewhat the like whereof may God not show thee! loathly, dispensing from description, inasmuch as there were reckoned in her all legal defects.[524] So he repented, whenas repentance availed him not, and knew that the girl had cheated him. However, he lay with the bride, against his will, and abode that night sore troubled in mind, as he were in the prison of Ed Dilem.[525] Hardly had the day dawned when he arose from her and betaking himself to one of the baths, dozed there awhile, after which he made the ablution of defilement[526] and washed his clothes. Then he went out to the coffee-house and drank a cup of coffee; after which he returned to his shop and opening the door, sat down, with discomfiture and chagrin written on his face.

Presently, his friends and acquaintances among the merchants and people of the market began to come up to him, by ones and twos, to give him joy, and said to him, laughing, "God's blessing on thee! Where an the sweet-meats? Where is the coffee?[527] It would seem thou hast forgotten us; surely, the charms of the bride have disordered thy reason and taken thy wit, God help thee! Well, well; we give thee joy, we give thee joy." And they made mock of him, whilst he gave them no answer and was like to tear his clothes and weep for vexation. Then they went away from him, and when it was the hour of noon, up came his mistress, trailing her skirts and swaying in her gait, as she were a cassia-branch in a garden. She was yet more richly dressed and adorned and more bewitching[528] in her symmetry and grace than on the previous day, so that she made the passers stop and stand in ranks to look on her.

When she came to Alaeddin's shop, she sat down thereat and said to him, "May the day be blessed to thee, O my lord Alaeddin! God prosper thee and be good to thee and accomplish thy gladness and make it a wedding of weal and content!" He knitted his brows and frowned in answer to her; then said he to her, "Tell me, how have I failed of thy due, or what have I done to injure thee, that thou shouldst play me this trick?" Quoth she, "Thou hast no wise offended against me; but this inscription that is written on the door of thy shop irketh me and vexeth my heart. If thou wilt change it and write up the contrary thereof, I will deliver thee from thy predicament." And he answered, "This that thou seekest is easy. On my head and eyes be it." So saying, he brought out a ducat[529] and calling one of his mamelukes, said to him, "Get thee to such an one the scribe and bid him write us an inscription, adorned with gold and ultramarine, in these words, to wit, 'THERE IS NO CRAFT BUT WOMEN'S CRAFT, FOR THAT INDEED THEIR CRAFT IS A MIGHTY CRAFT AND OVERCOMETH AND HUMBLETH THE FABLES[530] OF MEN.'" And she said to the servant, "Go forthright."

So he repaired to the scribe, who wrote him the scroll, and he brought it to his master, who set it on the door and said to the damsel, "Art thou satisfied?" "Yes," answered she. "Arise forthright and get thee to the place before the citadel, where do thou foregather with all the mountebanks and ape-dancers and bear-leaders and drummers and pipers and bid them come to thee to-morrow early, with their drums and pipes, what time thou drinkest coffee with thy father-in-law the Cadi, and congratulate thee and wish thee joy, saying, 'A blessed day, O son of our uncle! Indeed, thou art the vein[531] of our eye! We rejoice for thee, and if thou be ashamed of us, verily, we pride ourselves upon thee; so, though thou banish us from thee, know that we will not forsake thee, albeit thou forsakest us.' And do thou fall to strewing dinars and dirhems amongst them; whereupon the Cadi will question thee, and do thou answer him, saying, 'My father was an ape-dancer and this is our original condition; but out Lord opened on us [the gate of fortune] and we have gotten us a name among the merchants and with their provost.'

Then will he say to thee, 'Then thou art an ape-leader of the tribe of the mountebanks?' And do thou reply, 'I may in nowise deny my origin, for the sake of thy daughter and in her honour.' The Cadi will say, 'It may not be that thou shalt be given the daughter of a sheikh who sitteth upon the carpet of the Law and whose descent is traceable by genealogy to the loins of the Apostle of God,[532] nor is it seemly that his daughter be in the power of a man who is an ape-dancer, a minstrel.' And do thou rejoin, 'Nay, O Effendi, she is my lawful wife and every hair of her is worth a thousand lives, and I will not let her go, though I be given the kingship of the world.' Then be thou persuaded to speak the word of divorce and so shall the marriage be dissolved and ye be delivered from each other."

Quoth Alaeddin, "Thou counsellest well," and locking up his shop, betook himself to the place before the citadel, where he foregathered with the drummers and pipers and instructed them how they should do, [even as his mistress had counselled him,] promising them a handsome reward. So they answered him with "Hearkening and obedience" and on the morrow, after the morning-prayer, he betook himself to the presence of the Cadi, who received him with obsequious courtesy and seated him beside himself. Then he turned to him and fell to conversing with him and questioning him of matters of selling and buying and of the price current of the various commodities that were exported to Baghdad from all parts, whilst Alaeddin replied to him of all whereof he asked him.

As they were thus engaged, behold, up came the dancers and mountebanks, with their pipes and drums, whilst one of their number forewent them, with a great banner in his hand, and played all manner antics with his voice and limbs. When they came to the Courthouse, the Cadi exclaimed, "I seek refuge with God from yonder Satans!" And the merchant laughed, but said nothing. Then they entered and saluting his highness the Cadi, kissed Alaeddin's hands and said, "God's blessing on thee, O son of our uncle! Indeed, thou solacest our eyes in that which thou dost, and we beseech God to cause the glory of our lord the Cadi to endure, who hath honoured us by admitting thee to his alliance and allotted us a part in his high rank and dignity." When the Cadi heard this talk, it bewildered his wit and he was confounded and his face flushed with anger and he said to his son-in-law, "What words are these?" Quoth the merchant, "Knowest thou not, O my lord, that I am of this tribe? Indeed this man is the son of my mother's brother and that other the son of my father's brother, and I am only reckoned of the merchants [by courtesy]!"

When the Cadi heard this, his colour changed and he was troubled and waxed exceeding wroth and was rike to burst for excess of rage. Then said he to the merchant, "God forbid that this should be! How shall it be permitted that the daughter of the Cadi of the Muslims abide with a man of the dancers and vile of origin? By Allah, except thou divorce her forthright,

I will bid beat thee and cast thee into prison till thou die! Had I foreknown that thou wast of them, I had not suffered thee to approach me, but had spat in thy face, for that thou art filthier[533] than a dog or a hog." Then he gave him a push and casting him down from his stead, commanded him to divorce; but he said, "Be clement to me, O Effendi, for that God is clement, and hasten not. I will not divorce my wife, though thou give me the kingdom of Irak."

The Cadi was perplexed and knew that constraint was not permitted of the law;[534] so he spoke the young merchant fair and said to him, "Protect me,[535] so may God protect thee. If thou divorce her not, this disgrace will cleave to me till the end of time." Then his rage got the better of him and he said to him, "An thou divorce her not with a good grace, I will bid strike off thy head forthright and slay myself; rather flame[536] than shame." The merchant bethought himself awhile, then divorced her with a manifest divorcement[537] and on this wise he delivered himself from that vexation. Then he returned to his shop and sought in marriage of her father her who had played him the trick aforesaid and who was the daughter of the chief of the guild of the blacksmiths. So he took her to wife and they abode with each other and lived the most solaceful of lives, in all prosperity and contentment and joyance, till the day of death; and God [alone] is All-Knowing.

VOLUME THE THIRD

NOUREDDIN ALI OF DAMASCUS AND THE DAMSEL SITT EL MILAH[538]

THERE was once, of old days and in bygone ages and times, a merchant of the merchants of Damascus, by name Aboulhusn, who had money and riches and slaves and slave-girls and lands and houses and baths; but he was not blessed with a child and indeed his years waxed great; wherefore he addressed himself to supplicate God the Most High in private and in public and in his inclining and his prostration and at the season of the call to prayer, beseeching Him to vouchsafe him, before his admittance [to His mercy], a son who should inherit his wealth and possessions; and God answered his prayer. So his wife conceived and the days of her pregnancy were accomplished and her months and her nights and the pangs of her travail came upon her and she gave birth to a male child, as he were a piece of the moon. He had not his match for beauty and he put to shame the sun and the resplendent moon; for he had a shining face and black eyes of Babylonian witchery[539] and aquiline nose and ruby lips; brief, he was perfect of attributes, the loveliest of the folk of his time, without doubt or gainsaying.

His father rejoiced in him with the utmost joy and his heart was solaced and he was glad; and he made banquets to the folk and clad the poor and the widows. He named the boy Sidi[540] Noureddin Ali and reared him in fondness and delight among the slaves and servants. When he came to seven years of age, his father put him to school, where he learned the sublime Koran and the arts of writing and reckoning: and when he reached his tenth year, he learned horsemanship and archery and to occupy himself with arts and sciences of all kinds, part and parts.[541] He grew up pleasant and subtle and goodly and lovesome, ravishing all who beheld him, and inclined to companying with brethren and comrades and mixing with merchants and travellers. From these latter he heard tell of that which they had seen of the marvels of the cities in their travels and heard them say, "He who leaveth not his native land diverteth not himself [with the sight of the marvels of the world,] and especially of the city of Baghdad."

So he was concerned with an exceeding concern for his lack of travel and discovered this to his father, who said to him, "O my son, why do I see thee chagrined?" And he answered, "I would fain travel." Quoth Aboulhusn, "O my son, none travelleth save those whose occasion is urgent and those who are compelled thereunto [by need]. As for thee, O my son, thou enjoyest ample fortune; so do thou content thyself with that which God hath given thee and be bounteous [unto others], even as He hath been bounteous unto thee; and afflict not thyself with the toil and hardship of travel, for indeed it is said that travel is a piece of torment."[542] But the youth said, "Needs must I travel to Baghdad, the abode of peace."

When his father saw the strength of his determination to travel, he fell in with his wishes and equipped him with five thousand dinars in cash and the like in merchandise and sent with him two serving-men. So the youth set out, trusting in the blessing of God the Most High, and his father went out with him, to take leave of him, and returned [to Damascus]. As for Noureddin Ali, he gave not over travelling days and nights till he entered the city of Baghdad and laying up his loads in the caravanserai, made for the bath, where he did away that which was upon him of the dirt of the road and putting off his travelling clothes, donned a costly suit of Yemen stuff, worth an hundred dinars. Then he put in his sleeve[543] a thousand mithcals[544] of gold and sallied forth a-walking and swaying gracefully as he went. His gait confounded all those who beheld him, as he shamed the branches with his shape and belittled the rose with the redness of his cheeks and his black eyes of Babylonian witchcraft; indeed, thou wouldst deem that whoso looked on him would surely be preserved from calamity; [for he was] even as saith of him one of his describers in the following verses:

Thy haters say and those who malice to thee bear A true word, profiting its hearers everywhere;
"The glory's not in those whom raiment rich makes fair, But those who still adorn the raiment that they wear."

So he went walking in the thoroughfares of the city and viewing its ordinance and its markets and thoroughfares and gazing on its folk. Presently, Abou Nuwas met him. (Now he was of those of whom it is said, "They love the fair,"[545] and indeed there is said what is said concerning him.[546] When he saw Noureddin Ali, he stared at him in amazement and exclaimed, "Say, I take refuge with the Lord of the Daybreak!"[547] Then he accosted the young Damascene and saluting him, said to him, "Why do I see my lord alone and forlorn? Meseemeth thou art a stranger and knowest not this country; so, with my lord's permission, I will put myself at his service and acquaint him with the streets, for that I know this city." Quoth Noureddin, "This will be of thy favour, O uncle." Whereat Abou Nuwas rejoiced and fared on with him, showing him the markets and thoroughfares, till they came to the house of a slave-dealer, where he stopped and said to the youth, "From what city art thou?" "From Damascus," answered Noureddin; and Abou Nuwas said, "By Allah, thou art from a blessed city, even as saith of it the poet in the following verses:

Damascus is all gardens decked for the pleasance of the eyes; For the seeker there are black-eyed girls and boys of Paradise."

Noureddin thanked him and they entered the slave-merchant's house. When the people of the house saw Abou Nuwas, they rose to do him worship, for that which they knew of his station with the Commander of the Faithful. Moreover, the slave-dealer himself came up to them with two chairs, and they seated themselves thereon. Then the slave-merchant went into the house and returning with the slave-girl, as she were a willow-wand or a bamboo-cane, clad in a vest of damask silk and tired with a black and white turban, the ends whereof fell down over her face, seated her on a chair of ebony; after which quoth he to those who were present, "I will discover to you a face as it were a full moon breaking forth from under a cloud." And they said, "Do so." So he unveiled the damsel's face and behold, she was like the shining sun, with comely shape and day-bright face and slender [waist and heavy] hips; brief, she was endowed with elegance, the description whereof existeth not, [and was] even as saith of her the poet:

A fair one, to idolaters if she herself should show, They'd leave their idols and her face for only Lord would know;
And if into the briny sea one day she chanced to spit, Assuredly the salt sea's floods straight fresh and sweet would grow.

The dealer stood at her head and one of the merchants said, "I bid a thousand dinars for her." Quoth another, "I bid eleven hundred dinars;" [and a third, "I bid twelve hundred"]. Then said a fourth merchant, "Be she mine for fourteen hundred dinars." And the biddings stood still at that sum. Quoth her owner, "I will not sell her save with her consent. If she desire to be sold, I will sell her to whom she willeth." And the slave-dealer said to him, "What is her name?" "Her name is Sitt el Milah,"[548] answered the other; whereupon the dealer said to her, "By thy leave, I will sell thee to yonder merchant for this price of fourteen hundred dinars." Quoth she, "Come hither to me." So he came up to her and when he drew near, she gave him a kick with her foot and cast him to the ground, saying, "I will not have that old man." The slave-dealer arose, shaking the dust from his clothes and head, and said, "Who biddeth more? Who is desirous [of buying?]" Quoth one of the merchants, "I," and the dealer said to her, "O Sitt el Milah, shall I sell thee to this merchant?" "Come hither to me," answered she; but he said "Nay; speak and I will hearken to thee from my place, for I will not trust myself to thee," And she said, "I will not have him."

Then he looked at her and seeing her eyes fixed on the young Damascene, for that in very deed he had ravished her with his beauty and grace, went up to the latter and said to him, "O my lord, art thou a looker-on or a buyer? Tell me." Quoth Noureddin, "I am both looker-on and buyer. Wilt thou sell me yonder slave-girl for sixteen hundred dinars?" And he pulled out the purse of gold. So the dealer returned, dancing and clapping his hands and saying, "So be it, so be it, or not [at all]!" Then he came to the damsel and said to her, "O Sitt el Milah, shall I sell thee to yonder young Damascene for sixteen hundred dinars?" But she answered, "No," of shamefastness before her master and the bystanders; whereupon the people of the bazaar and the slave-merchant departed, and Abou Nuwas and Ali Noureddin arose and went each his own way, whilst the damsel returned to her master's house, full of love for the young Damascene.

When the night darkened on her, she called him to mind and her heart clave to him and sleep visited her not; and on this wise she abode days and nights, till she sickened and abstained from food. So her lord went in to her and said to her, "O Sitt el Milah, how findest thou thyself?" "O my lord," answered she, "I am dead without recourse and I beseech thee to bring me my shroud, so I may look on it before my death." Therewithal he went out from her, sore concerned for her, and betook himself to a friend of his, a draper, who had been present on the day when the damsel was cried [for sale]. Quoth his friend to him, "Why do I see thee troubled?" And he answered, "Sitt el Milah is at the point of death and these three days she hath neither eaten nor drunken. I questioned her to-day of her case and she said, 'O my lord, buy me a shroud, so I may look on it before my death.'" Quoth the draper, "Methinks nought ails her but that she is enamoured of the young Damascene and I counsel thee to mention his name to her and avouch to her that he hath foregathered with thee on her account and is desirous of coming to thy house, so he may hear somewhat of her singing. If she say, 'I reck not of him, for there is that to do with me which distracteth me from the Damascene and from other than he,' know that she saith sooth concerning her sickness; but, if she say to thee other than this, acquaint me therewith.'"

So the man returned to his lodging and going in to his slave-girl, said to her, "O Sitt el Milah, I went out on thine occasion and there met me the young man of Damascus, and he saluted me and saluteth thee. Indeed, he seeketh to win thy favour and would fain be a guest in our dwelling, so thou mayst let him hear somewhat of thy singing." When she heard speak of the young Damascene, she gave a sob, that her soul was like to depart her body, and answered, saying, "He knoweth my plight and is ware that these three days past I have eaten not nor drunken, and I beseech thee, O my lord, by the Great God, to accomplish the stranger his due and bring him to my lodging and make excuse to him for me."

When her master heard this, his reason fled for joy and he went to his friend the draper and said to him, "Thou wast right in the matter of the damsel, for that she is enamoured of the young Damascene; so how shall I do?" Quoth the other, "Go to the bazaar and when thou seest him, salute him and say to him, 'Indeed, thy departure the other day, without accomplishing thine occasion, was grievous to me; so, if thou be still minded to buy the girl, I will abate thee an hundred dinars of that which thou badest for her, by way of hospitable entreatment of thee and making myself agreeable to thee; for that thou art a stranger in our land.' If he say to thee, 'I have no desire for her' and hold off from thee, know that he will not buy; in which case, let me know, so I may contrive thee another device; and if he say to thee other than this, conceal not from me aught.

So the girl's owner betook himself to the bazaar, where he found the youth seated at the upper end of the merchants' place of session, selling and buying and taking and giving, as he were the moon on the night of its full, and saluted him. The young man returned his salutation and he said to him, "O my lord, be not thou vexed at the girl's speech the other day, for her price shall be less than that [which thou badest], to the intent that I may propitiate thy favour. If thou desire her for nought, I will send her to thee, or if thou wouldst have me abate thee of her price, I will well, for I desire nought but what shall content thee; for that thou art a stranger in our land and it behoveth us to entreat thee hospitably and have consideration for thee." "By Allah," answered the youth, "I will not take her from thee but at an advance on that which I bade thee for her aforetime; so wilt thou now sell her to me for seventeen hundred dinars?" And the other answered," O my lord, I sell her to thee, may God bless thee in her."

So the young man went to his lodging and fetching a purse, returned to the girl's owner and counted out to him the price aforesaid, whilst the draper was between them. Then said he, "Bring her forth;" but the other answered, "She cannot come forth at this present; but be thou my guest the rest of this day and night, and on the morrow thou shall take thy slave-girl and go in the protection of God." The youth fell in with him of this and he carried him to his house, where, after a little, he let bring meat and wine, and they [ate and] drank. Then said Noureddin to the girl's owner, "I beseech thee bring me the damsel, for that I bought her not but for the like of this time." So he arose and [going in to the girl], said to her, "O Sitt el Milan, the young man hath paid down thy price and we have bidden him hither; so he hath come to our dwelling and we have entertained him, and he would fain have thee be present with him."

Therewithal the damsel rose briskly and putting off her clothes, washed and donned sumptuous apparel and perfumed herself and went out to him, as she were a willow-wand or a bamboo-cane, followed by a black slave girl, bearing the lute. When she came to the young man, she saluted him and sat down by his side. Then she took the lute from the slave-girl and tuning it, smote thereon in four-and-twenty modes, after which she returned to the first mode and sang the following verses:

Unto me the world's whole gladness is thy nearness and thy sight; All incumbent thy possession and thy love a law of right.
In my tears I have a witness; when I call thee to my mind, Down my cheeks they run like torrents, and I cannot stay their flight.
None, by Allah, 'mongst all creatures, none I love save thee alone! Yea, for I am grown thy bondman, by the troth betwixt us plight.
Peace upon thee! Ah, how bitter were the severance from thee! Be not this thy troth-plight's ending nor the last of our delight!

Therewithal the young man was moved to delight and exclaimed, "By Allah, thou sayest well, O Sitt el Milan! Let me hear more." Then he handselled her with fifty dinars and they drank and the cups went round among them; and her seller said to her, "O Sitt el Milah, this is the season of leave-taking; so let us hear somewhat on the subject." Accordingly she struck the lute and avouching that which was in her heart, sang the following verses:

I am filled full of longing pain and memory and dole, That from the wasted body's wounds distract the anguished soul.
Think not, my lords, that I forget: the case is still the same. When such a fever fills the heart, what leach can make it whole?
And if a creature in his tears could swim, as in a sea, I to do this of all that breathe were surely first and sole.
O skinker of the wine of woe, turn from a love-sick maid, Who drinks her tears still, night and morn, thy bitter-flavoured bowl.
I had not left you, had I known that severance would prove My death; but what is past is past, Fate stoops to no control.

As they were thus in the enjoyment of all that in most delicious of easance and delight, and indeed the wine was sweet to them and the talk pleasant, behold, there came a knocking at the door. So the master of the house went out, that he might see what was to do, and found ten men of the Khalif's eunuchs at the door. When he saw this, he was amazed and said to them, "What is to do?" Quoth they, "The Commander of the Faithful saluteth thee and requireth of thee the slave-girl whom thou hast for sale and whose name is Sitt el Milah." By Allah," answered the other, "I have sold her." And they said, "Swear by the head of the Commander of the Faithful that she is not in thy dwelling." He made oath that he had sold her and that she was no longer at his disposal; but they paid no *need to his word and forcing their way into the house, found the damsel and the young Damascene in the sitting-chamber. So they laid hands upon her, and the youth said, "This is my slave-girl, whom I have bought with my money." But they hearkened not to his speech and taking her, carried her off to the Commander of the Faithful.

Therewithal Noureddin's life was troubled; so he arose and donned his clothes, and his host said, "Whither away this night, O my lord?" Quoth Noureddin, "I mean to go to my lodging, and to-morrow I will betake myself to the palace of the Commander of the Faithful and demand my slave-girl." "Sleep till the morning," said the other, "and go not forth at the like of this hour." But he answered, "Needs must I go;" and the host said to him, "[Go] in the safeguard of God." So Noureddin went forth, and drunkenness had got the mastery of him, wherefore he threw himself down on [a bench before one of] the shops. Now the watch were at that hour making their round and they smelt the sweet scent [of essences] and wine that exhaled from him; so they made for it and found the youth lying on the bench, without sense or motion. They poured water upon him, and he awoke, whereupon they carried him to the house of the Chief of the Police and he questioned him of his affair. "O my lord," answered Noureddin, "I am a stranger in this town and have been with one of my friends. So I came forth from his house and drunkenness overcame me."

The prefect bade carry him to his lodging; but one of those in attendance upon him, by name El Muradi, said to him, "What wilt thou do? This man is clad in rich clothes and on his finger is a ring of gold, the beazel whereof is a ruby of great price; so we will carry him away and slay him and take that which is upon him of raiment [and what not else] and bring t to thee; for that thou wilt not [often] see profit the like thereof, more by token that this fellow is a stranger and there is none to enquire concerning him." Quoth the prefect, "This fellow is a thief and that which he sa'th is leasing." And Noureddin said, "God forbid that I should be a thief!" But the prefect answered, "Thou liest." So they stripped him of his clothes and taking the ring from his finger, beat him grievously, what while he cried out for succour, but none succoured him, and besought protection, but none protected him. Then said he to them, "O folk, ye are quit of[549] that which ye have taken from me; but now restore me to my lodging." But they answered, saying, "Leave this knavery, O cheat! Thine intent is to sue us for thy clothes on the morrow." "By Allah, the One, the Eternal," exclaimed he, "I will not sue any for them!" But they said, "We can nowise do this." And the prefect bade them carry him to the Tigris and there slay him and cast him into the river.

So they dragged him away, what while he wept and spoke the words which whoso saith shall nowise be confounded, to wit, "There is no power and no virtue save in God the Most High, the Sublime!" When they came to the Tigris, one of them drew the sword upon him and El Muradi said to the swordbearer, "Smite off his head." But one of them, Ahmed by name, said, "O folk, deal gently with this poor wretch and slay him not unjustly and wickedly, for I stand in fear of God the Most High, lest He burn me with his fire." Quoth El Muradi, "A truce to this talk!" And Ahmed said, "If ye do with him aught, I will acquaint the Commander of the Faithful." "How, then, shall we do with him?" asked they; and he answered, 'Let us deposit him in prison and I will be answerable to you for his provision; so shall we be quit of his blood, for indeed he is wrongfully used." So they took him up and casting him into the Prison of Blood,[550] went away.

Meanwhile, they carried the damsel into the Commander of the Faithful and she pleased him; so he assigned her a lodging of the apartments of choice. She abode in the palace, eating not neither drinking and ceasing not from weeping night nor day, till, one night, the Khalif sent for her to his sitting-chamber and said to her, "O Sitt el Milah, be of good heart and cheerful eye, for I will make thy rank higher than [any of] the concubines and thou shall see that which shall rejoice thee." She kissed the earth and wept; whereupon the Khalif called for her lute and bade her sing. So she improvised and sang the following verses, in accordance with that which was in her heart:

Say, by the lightnings of thy teeth and thy soul's pure desire, Moan'st thou as moan the doves and is thy heart for doubt on fire?
How many a victim of the pangs of love-liking hath died! Tired is my patience, but of blame my censors never tire.

When she had made an end of her song, she cast the lute from her hand and wept till she swooned away, whereupon the Khalif bade carry her to her chamber. Now he was ravished with her and loved her with an exceeding love; so, after awhile, he again commanded to bring her to his presence, and when she came, he bade her sing. Accordingly, she took the lute and spoke forth that which was in her heart and sang the following verses:

What strength have I solicitude and long desire to bear? Why art thou purposed to depart and leave me to despair?
Why to estrangement and despite inclin'st thou with the spy? Yet that a bough[551] from side to side incline[552] small wonder 'twere.
Thou layst on me a load too great to bear, and thus thou dost But that my burdens I may bind and so towards thee fare.

Then she cast the lute from her hand and swooned away; so she was carried to her chamber and indeed passion waxed upon her. After a long while, the Commander of the Faithful sent for her a third time and bade her sing. So she took the lute and sang the following verses:

O hills of the sands and the rugged piebald plain, Shall the bondman of love win ever free from pain!

I wonder, shall I and the friend who's far from me Once more be granted of Fate to meet, we twain!

Bravo for a fawn with a houri's eye of black, Like the sun or the shining moon midst the starry train!

To lovers, "What see ye?" he saith, and to hearts of stone, "What love ye," quoth he, "[if to love me ye disdain?"]

I supplicate Him, who parted us and doomed Our separation, that we may meet again.

When she had made an end of her song, the Commander of the Faithful said to her, "O damsel, thou art in love." "Yes," answered she. And he said, "With whom?" Quoth she, "With my lord and my master, my love for whom is as the love of the earth for rain, or as the love of the female for the male; and indeed the love of him is mingled with my flesh and my blood and hath entered into the channels of my bones. O Commander of the Faithful, whenas I call him to mind, mine entrails are consumed, for that I have not accomplished my desire of him, and but that I fear to die, without seeing him, I would assuredly kill myself." And he said, "Art thou in my presence and bespeakest me with the like of these words? I will assuredly make thee forget thy lord."

Then he bade take her away; so she was carried to her chamber and he sent her a black slave-girl, with a casket, wherein were three thousand dinars and a carcanet of gold, set with pearls, great and small, and jewels, worth other three thousand, saying to her, "The slave-girl and that which is with her are a gift from me to thee." When she heard this, she said, "God forbid that I should be consoled for the love of my lord and my master, though with the earth full of gold!" And she improvised and recited the following verses:

I swear by his life, yea, I swear by the life of my love without peer, To please him or save him from hurt, I'd enter the fire without fear!

"Console thou thyself for his love," quoth they, "with another than he;" But, "Nay, by his life," answered I, "I'll never forget him my dear!"

A moon is my love, in a robe of loveliness proudly arrayed, And the splendours of new-broken day from his cheeks and his forehead shine clear.

Then the Khalif summoned her to his presence a fourth time and said to her, "O Sitt el Milah, sing." So she improvised and sang the following verses:

To his beloved one the lover's heart's inclined; His soul's a captive slave, in sickness' hands confined.
"What is the taste of love?" quoth one, and I replied, "Sweet water 'tis at first; but torment lurks behind."
Love's slave, I keep my troth with them; but, when they vowed, Fate made itself Urcoub,[553] whom never oath could bind.
What is there in the tents? Their burdens are become A lover's, whose belov'd is in the litters' shrined.
In every halting-place like Joseph[554] she appears And he in every stead with Jacob's grief[555] is pined.

When she had made an end of her song, she threw the lute from her hand and wept till she swooned away. So they sprinkled on her rose-water, mingled with musk, and willow-flower water; and when she came to herself, Er Reshid said to her, "O Sitt el Milah, this is not fair dealing in thee. We love thee and thou lovest another." "O Commander of the Faithful," answered she, "there is no help for it." Therewithal he was wroth with her and said, "By the virtue of Hemzeh[556] and Akil[557] and Mohammed, Prince of the Apostles, if thou name one other than I in my presence, I will bid strike off thy head!" Then he bade return her to her chamber, whilst she wept and recited the following verses:

If I must die, then welcome death to heal My woes; 'twere lighter than the pangs I feel.
What if the sabre cut me limb from limb! No torment 'twere for lovers true and leal.

Then the Khalif went in to the Lady Zubeideh, pale with anger, and she noted this in him and said to him, "How cometh it that I see the Commander of the Faithful changed of colour?" "O daughter of my uncle," answered he, "I have a beautiful slave-girl, who reciteth verses and telleth stories, and she hath taken my whole heart; but she loveth other than I and avoucheth that she loveth her [former] master; wherefore I have sworn a great oath that, if she come again to my sitting-chamber and sing for other than I, I will assuredly take a span from her highest part."[558] Quoth Zubeideh, "Let the Commander of the Faithful favour me with her presence, so I may look on her and hear her singing." So he bade fetch her and she came, whereupon the Lady Zubeideh withdrew behind the curtain, whereas she saw her not, and Er Reshid said to her, "Sing to us." So she took the lute and tuning it, sang the following verses:

Lo, since the day I left you, O my masters, Life is not sweet, no aye my heart is light.
Yea, in the night the thought of you still slays me; Hidden are my traces from the wise men's sight,
All for a wild deer's love, whose looks have snared me And on whose brows the morning glitters bright
I am become, for severance from my loved one, Like a left hand, forsaken of the right.
Beauty on his cheek hath written, "Blest be Allah, He who created this enchanting wight!"
Him I beseech our loves who hath dissevered, Us of his grace once more to reunite.

When Er Reshid heard this, he waxed exceeding wroth and said, "May God not reunite you twain in gladness!" Then he summoned the headsman, and when he presented himself, he said to him, "Strike off the head of this accursed slave-girl." So Mesrour took her by the hand and [led her away; but], when she came to the door, she turned and said to the Khalif, "O Commander of the Faithful, I conjure thee, by thy fathers and forefathers, give ear unto that I shall say!" Then she improvised and recited the following verses:

O Amir of justice, be kind to thy subjects; For justice, indeed, of thy nature's a trait.
O thou my inclining to love him that blamest, Shall lovers be blamed for the errors of Fate?
Then spare me, by Him who vouchsafed thee the kingship; For a gift in this world is the regal estate.

Then Mesrour carried her to the other end of the sitting-chamber and bound her eyes and making her sit, stood awaiting a second commandment; whereupon quoth the Lady Zubeideh, "O Commander of the Faithful, with thy permission, wilt thou not vouchsafe this damsel a share of thy clemency? Indeed, if thou slay her, it were injustice." Quoth he, "What is to be done with her?" And she said, "Forbear to slay her and send for her lord.

If he be as she describeth him in grace and goodliness, she is excused, and if he be not on this wise, then slay her, and this shall be thy justification against her."[559]

"Be it as thou deemest," answered Er Reshid and caused return the damsel to her chamber, saying to her, "The Lady Zubeideh saith thus and thus." Quoth she, "God requite her for me with good! Indeed, thou dealest equitably, O Commander of the Faithful, in this judgment." And he answered, "Go now to thy place, and to-morrow we will let bring thy lord." So she kissed the earth and recited the following verses:

I am content, for him I love, to all abide; So, who will, let him blame, and who will, let him chide.
At their appointed terms souls die; but for despair My soul is like to die, or ere its term betide.
O thou with love of whom I'm smitten, yet content, I prithee come to me and hasten to my side.

Then she arose and returned to her chamber.

On the morrow, the Commander of the Faithful sat [in his hall of audience] and his Vizier Jaafer ben Yehya the Barmecide came in to him; whereupon he called to him, saying, "I would have thee bring me a youth who is lately come to Baghdad, hight [Sidi Noureddin Ali] the Damascene." Quoth Jaafer, "Hearkening and obedience," and going forth in quest of the youth, sent to the markets and khans and caravanserais three days' space, but found no trace of him, neither lit upon tidings of him. So on the fourth day he presented himself before the Khalif and said to him, "O our lord, I have sought him these three days, but have not found him." Quoth Er Reshid, "Make ready letters to Damascus. Belike he hath returned to his own land." So Jaafer wrote a letter and despatched it by a dromedary-courier to the city of Damascus; and they sought him there and found him not.

Meanwhile, news was brought that Khorassan had been conquered;[560] whereupon Er Reshid rejoiced and bade decorate Baghdad and release all who were in the prisons, giving each of them a dinar and a dress. So Jaafer addressed himself to the decoration of the city and bade his brother El Fezl ride to the prison and clothe and release the prisoners. El Fezl did his brother's bidding and released all but the young Damascene, who abode still in the Prison of Blood, saying, "There is no power and no virtue save in

God the Most High, the Sublime! Verily, we are God's and to Him we return." Then said El Fezl to the gaoler, "Is there any prisoner left in the prison?" "No," answered he, and El Fezl was about to depart, when Noureddin called out to him from within the prison, saying, "O my lord, tarry, for there remaineth none in the prison other than I and indeed I am oppressed. This is a day of clemency and there is no disputing concerning it." El Fezl bade release him; so they set him free and he gave him a dress and a dinar. So the young man went out, bewildered and knowing not whither he should go, for that he had abidden in the prison nigh a year and indeed his condition was changed and his favour faded, and he abode walking and turning round, lest El Muradi should come upon him and cast him into another calamity.

When El Muradi heard of his release, he betook himself to the chief of the police and said to him, "O our lord, we are not assured from yonder youth, [the Damascene], for that he hath been released from prison and we fear lest he complain of us." Quoth the prefect, "How shall we do?" And El Muradi answered, saying, "I will cast him into a calamity for thee." Then he ceased not to follow the young Damascene from place to place till he came up with him in a strait place and a by-street without an issue; whereupon he accosted him and putting a rope about his neck, cried out, saying, "A thief!" The folk flocked to him from all sides and fell to beating and reviling Noureddin, whilst he cried out for succour, but none succoured him, and El Muradi still said to him, "But yesterday the Commander of the Faithful released thee and to-day thou stealest!" So the hearts of the folk were hardened against him and El Muradi carried him to the master of police, who bade cut off his hand.

Accordingly, the hangman took him and bringing out the knife, offered to cut off his hand, what while El Muradi said to him, "Cut and sever the bone and sear[561] it not for him, so he may lose his blood and we be rid of him." But Ahmed, he who had aforetime been the means of his deliverance, sprang up to him and said, "O folk, fear God in [your dealings with] this youth, for that I know his affair from first to last and he is void of offence and guiltless. Moreover, he is of the folk of condition,[552] and except ye desist from him, I will go up to the Commander of the Faithful and acquaint him with the case from first to last and that the youth is guiltless of crime or offence." Quoth El Muradi, "Indeed, we are not assured from his mischief." And Ahmed answered, "Release him and commit him to me and I will warrant you against his affair, for ye shall never see him again after this." So they delivered Noureddin to him and he took him from their hands and said to him, "O youth, have compassion on thyself, for indeed thou hast fallen into the hands of these folk twice and if they lay hold of thee a third time, they will make an end of thee; and [in dealing thus with thee], I aim at reward and recompense for thee[563] and answered prayer."[564]

Noureddin fell to kissing his hand and calling down blessings on him and said to him, "Know that I am a stranger in this your city and the completion of kindness is better than the beginning thereof; wherefore I beseech thee of thy favour that thou complete to me thy good offices and kindness and bring me to the gate of the city. So will thy beneficence be accomplished unto me and may God the Most High requite thee for me with good!" ["Fear not,"] answered Ahmed; "no harm shall betide thee. Go; I will bear thee company till thou come to thy place of assurance." And he left him not till he brought him to the gate of the city and said to him, "O youth, go in the safeguard of God and return not to the city; for, if they fall in with thee [again], they will make an end of thee." Noureddin kissed his hand and going forth the city, gave not over walking till he came to a mosque that stood in one of the suburbs of Baghdad and entered therein with the night.

Now he had with him nought wherewithal he might cover himself; so he wrapped himself up in one of the rugs of the mosque [and abode thus till daybreak], when the Muezzins came and finding him sitting in that case, said to him, "O youth, what is this plight?" Quoth he, "I cast myself on your hospitality, imploring your protection from a company of folk who seek to kill me unjustly and oppressively, without cause." And [one of] the Muezzin[s] said, "Be of good heart and cheerful eye." Then he brought him old clothes and covered him withal; moreover, he set before him somewhat of meat and seeing upon him signs of gentle breeding, said to him, "O my son, I grow old and desire thee of help, [in return for which] I will do away thy necessity." "Hearkening and obedience," answered Noureddin and abode with the old man, who rested and took his ease, what while the youth [did his service in the mosque], celebrating the praises of God and calling the faithful to prayer and lighting the lamps and filling the ewers[565] and sweeping and cleaning out the place.

Meanwhile, the Lady Zubeideh, the wife of the Commander of the Faithful, made a banquet in her palace and assembled her slave-girls. As for Sitt el Milah, she came, weeping-eyed and mournful-hearted, and those who were present blamed her for this, whereupon she recited the following verses:

Ye chide at one who weepeth for troubles ever new; Needs must th' afflicted warble the woes that make him rue.
Except I be appointed a day [to end my pain], I'll weep until mine eyelids with blood their tears ensue.

When she had made an end of her verses, the Lady Zubeideh bade each damsel sing a song, till the turn came round to Sitt el Milah, whereupon she took the lute and tuning it, sang thereto four-and-twenty songs in four-and-twenty modes; then she returned to the first mode and sang the following verses:

Fortune its arrows all, through him I love, let fly At me and parted me from him for whom I sigh.
Lo, in my heart the heat of every heart burns high And in mine eyes unite the tears of every eye.

When she had made an end of her song, she wept till she made the bystanders weep and the Lady Zubeideh condoled with her and said to her, "God on thee, O Sitt el Milah, sing us somewhat, so we may hearken to thee." "Hearkening and obedience," answered the damsel and sang the following verses:

Assemble, ye people of passion, I pray; For the hour of our torment hath sounded to-day.
The raven of parting croaks loud at our door; Alas, for our raven cleaves fast to us aye!
For those whom we cherish are parted and gone; They have left us in torment to pine for dismay.
So arise, by your lives I conjure you, arise And come let us fare to our loved ones away.

Then she cast the lute from her hand and wept till she made the Lady Zubeideh weep, and she said to her, "O Sitt el Milah, methinks he whom thou lovest is not in this world, for that the Commander of the Faithful hath sought him in every place, but hath not found him." Whereupon the damsel arose and kissing the Lady Zubeideh's hands, said to her, "O my lady, if thou wouldst have him found, I have a request to make to thee, wherein thou mayst accomplish my occasion with the Commander of the Faithful." Quoth the princess, "And what is it?" "It is," answered Sitt el Milah, "that thou get me leave to go forth by myself and go round about in quest of him three days, for the adage saith, 'She who mourneth for herself is not the like of her who is hired to mourn.'[566] If I find him, I will bring him before the Commander of the Faithful, so he may do with us what he will; and if I find him not, I shall be cut off from hope of him and that which is with me will be assuaged." Quoth the Lady Zubeideh, "I will not get thee leave from him but for a whole month; so be of good heart and cheerful eye." Whereupon Sitt el Milah was glad and rising, kissed the earth before her once more and went away to her own place, rejoicing.

As for Zubeideh, she went in to the Khalif and talked with him awhile; then she fell to kissing him between the eyes and on his hand and asked him that which she had promised Sitt el Milah, saying, "O Commander of the Faithful, I doubt me her lord is not found in this world; but, if she go about in quest of him and find him not, her hopes will be cut off and her mind will be set at rest and she will sport and laugh; for that, what while she abideth in hope, she will never cease from her frowardness." And she gave not over cajoling him till he gave Sitt el Milah leave to go forth and make search for her lord a month's space and ordered her an eunuch to attend her and bade the paymaster [of the household] give her all she needed, were it a thousand dirhems a day or more. So the Lady Zubeideh arose and returning to her palace, sent for Sitt el Milah and acquainted her with that which had passed [between herself and the Khalif]; whereupon she kissed her hand and thanked her and called down blessings on her.

Then she took leave of the princess and veiling her face, disguised herself; [567]after which she mounted the mule and sallying forth, went round about seeking her lord in the thoroughfares of Baghdad three days' space, but lit on no tidings of him; and on the fourth day, she rode forth without the city. Now it was the noontide hour and great was the heat, and she was aweary and thirst waxed upon her. Presently, she came to the mosque, wherein the young Damascene had taken shelter, and lighting down at the door, said to the old man, [the Muezzin], "O elder, hast thou a draught of cold water? Indeed, I am overcome with heat and thirst." Quoth he, "[Come up] with me into my house." So he carried her up into his lodging and spreading her [a carpet and cushions], seated her [thereon]; after which he brought her cold water and she drank and said to the eunuch, "Go thy ways with the mule and on the morrow come back to me here." [So he went away] and she slept and rested herself.

When she awoke, she said to the old man, "O elder, hast thou aught of food?" And he answered, "O my lady, I have bread and olives." Quoth she, "That is food fit but for the like of thee. As for me, I will have nought but roast lamb and broths and fat rissoled fowls and stuffed ducks and all manner meats dressed with [pounded nuts and almond-]kernels and sugar." "O my lady," replied the Muezzin, "I never heard of this chapter in the Koran, nor was it revealed unto our lord Mohammed, whom God bless and keep!"[568] She laughed and said, "O elder, the matter is even as thou sayest; but bring me inkhorn and paper." So he brought her what she sought and she wrote a letter and gave it to him, together with a seal-ring from her finger, saying, "Go into the city and enquire for such an one the money-changer and give him this my letter."

The old man betook himself to the city, as she bade him, and enquired for the money-changer, to whom they directed him. So he gave him the ring and the letter, which when he saw, he kissed the letter and breaking it open, read it and apprehended its purport. Then he repaired to the market and buying all that she bade him, laid it in a porter's basket and bade him go with the old man. So the latter took him and went with him to the mosque, where he relieved him of his burden and carried the meats in to Sitt el Milah. She seated him by her side and they ate, he and she, of those rich meats, till they were satisfied, when the old man rose and removed the food from before her.

She passed the night in his lodging and when she arose in the morning, she said to him, "O elder, may I not lack thy kind offices for the morning-meal! Go to the money-changer and fetch me from him the like of yesterday's food." So he arose and betaking himself to the money-changer, acquainted him with that which she had bidden him. The money-changer brought him all that she required and set it on the heads of porters; and the old man took them and returned with them to Sitt el Milah. So she sat down with him and they ate their sufficiency, after which he removed the rest of the food. Then she took the fruits and the flowers and setting them over against herself, wrought them into rings and knots and letters, whilst the old man looked on at a thing whose like he had never in his life seen and rejoiced therein.

Then said she to him, "O elder, I would fain drink." So he arose and brought her a gugglet of water; but she said to him, "Who bade thee fetch that?" Quoth he, "Saidst thou not to me, 'I would fain drink'?" And she answered, "I want not this; nay, I want wine, the delight of the soul, so haply, O elder, I may solace myself therewith." "God forbid," exclaimed the old man, "that wine should be drunk in my house, and I a stranger in the land and a Muezzin and an imam,[569] who prayeth with the true-believers, and a servant of the house of the Lord of the Worlds! "Quoth she, "Why wilt thou forbid me to drink thereof in thy house?" "Because," answered he, "it is unlawful." "O elder," rejoined she, "God hath forbidden [the eating of] blood and carrion and hog's flesh. Tell me, are grapes and honey lawful or unlawful?" Quoth he, "They are lawful;" and she said, "This is the juice of grapes and the water of honey." But he answered, "Leave this thy talk, for thou shall never drink wine in my house." "O Sheikh," rejoined she, "folk eat and drink and enjoy themselves and we are of the number of the folk and God is very forgiving, clement."[570] Quoth he, "This is a thing that may not be." And she said, "Hast thou not heard what the poet saith ... ?" And she recited the following verses:

O son of Simeon, give no ear to other than my say. How bitter from the convent 'twas to part and fare away!
Ay, and the monks, for on the Day of Palms a fawn there was Among the servants of the church, a loveling blithe and gay.
By God, how pleasant was the night we passed, with him for third! Muslim and Jew and Nazarene, we sported till the day.
The wine was sweet to us to drink in pleasance and repose, And in a garden of the garths of Paradise we lay,
Whose streams beneath the myrtle's shade and cassia's welled amain And birds made carol jubilant from every blossomed spray.
Quoth he, what while from out his hair the morning glimmered white, "This, this is life indeed, except, alas! it doth not stay."

"O elder," added she, "if Muslims and Jews and Nazarenes drink wine, who are we [that we should abstain from it]?" "By Allah, O my lady," answered he, "spare thine endeavour, for this is a thing to which I will not hearken." When she knew that he would not consent to her desire, she said to him, "O elder, I am of the slave-girls of the Commander of the Faithful and the food waxeth on me[571] and if I drink not, I shall perish,[572] nor wilt thou be assured against the issue of my affair. As for me, I am quit of blame towards thee, for that I have made myself known to thee and have bidden thee beware of the wrath of the Commander of the Faithful."

When the old man heard her words and that wherewith she menaced him, he arose and went out, perplexed and knowing not what he should do, and there met him a Jew, who was his neighbour, and said to him, "O Sheikh, how cometh it that I see thee strait of breast? Moreover, I hear in thy house a noise of talk, such as I use not to hear with thee." Quoth the Muezzin, "Yonder is a damsel who avoucheth that she is of the slave-girls of the Commander of the Faithful Haroun er Reshid; and she hath eaten food and now would fain drink wine in my house, but I forbade her. However she avoucheth that except she drink thereof, she will perish, and indeed I am bewildered concerning my affair." "Know, O my neighbour," answered the Jew, "that the slave-girls of the Commander of the Faithful are used to drink wine, and whenas they eat and drink not, they perish; and I fear lest some mishap betide her, in which case thou wouldst not be safe from the Khalifs wrath." "What is to be done?" asked the Sheikh; and the Jew replied, "I have old wine that will suit her." Quoth the old man, "[I conjure thee] by the right of neighbourship, deliver me from this calamity and let me have that which is with thee!" "In the name of God," answered the Jew and going to his house, brought out a flagon of wine, with which the Sheikh returned to Sitt el Milah. This pleased her and she said to him, "Whence hadst thou this?" "I got it from my neighbour the Jew," answered he. "I set out to him my case with thee and he gave me this."

Sitt el Milah filled a cup and emptied it; after which she drank a second and a third. Then she filled the cup a fourth time and handed it to the old man, but he would not accept it from her. However, she conjured him, by her own head and that of the Commander of the Faithful, that he should take it from her, till he took the cup from her hand and kissed it and would have set it down; but she conjured him by her life to smell it. So he smelt it and she said to him, "How deemest thou?" "Its smell is sweet," replied he; and she conjured him, by the life of the Commander of the Faithful, to taste it. So he put it to his mouth and she rose to him and made him drink; whereupon, "O princess of the fair," said he, "this is none other than good." Quoth she, "So deem I. Hath not our Lord promised us wine in Paradise?" And he answered, "Yes. Quoth the Most High, 'And rivers of wine, a delight to the drinkers.'[573] And we will drink it in this world and the world to come." She laughed and emptying the cup, gave him to drink, and he said, "O princess of the fair, indeed thou art excusable in thy love for this." Then he took from her another and another, till he became drunken and his talk waxed great and his prate.

The folk of the quarter heard him and assembled under the window; and when he was ware of them, he opened the window and said to them, "Are ye not ashamed, O pimps? Every one in his own house doth what he will and none hindereth him; but we drink one poor day and ye assemble and come, cuckoldy varlets that ye are! To-day, wine, and to-morrow [another] matter; and from hour to hour [cometh] relief." So they laughed and dispersed. Then the girl drank till she was intoxicated, when she called to mind her lord and wept, and the old man said to her, "What maketh thee weep, O my lady?" "O elder," replied she, "I am a lover and separated [from him I love]." Quoth he, "O my lady, what is this love?" "And thou," asked she, "hast thou never been in love?" "By Allah, O my lady," answered he, "never in all my life heard I of this thing, nor have I ever known it! Is it of the sons of Adam or of the Jinn?" She laughed and said, "Verily, thou art even as those of whom the poet speaketh, when as he saith ..." And she repeated the following verses:

How long will ye admonished be, without avail or heed? The shepherd still his flocks forbids, and they obey his rede.
I see yon like unto mankind in favour and in form; But oxen,[574] verily, ye are in fashion and in deed.

 The old man laughed at her speech and her verses pleased him. Then said she to him, "I desire of thee a lute."[575] So he arose and brought her a piece of firewood. Quoth she, "What is that?" And he said, "Didst thou not bid me bring thee wood?" "I do not want this," answered she, and he rejoined, "What then is it that is called wood, other than this?" She laughed and said, "The lute is an instrument of music, whereunto I sing." Quoth he, "Where is this thing found and of whom shall I get it for thee?" And she said, "Of him who gave thee the wine." So he arose and betaking himself to his neighbour the Jew, said to him, "Thou favouredst us aforetime with the wine; so now complete thy favours and look me out a thing called a lute, to wit, an instrument for singing; for that she seeketh this of me and I know it not" "Hearkening and obedience," replied the Jew and going into his house, brought him a lute. [The old man took it and carried it to Sitt el Milah,] whilst the Jew took his drink and sat by a window adjoining the other's house, so he might hear the singing.

The damsel rejoiced, when the old man returned to her with the lute, and taking it from him, tuned its strings and sang the following verses:

After your loss, nor trace of me nor vestige would remain, Did not the hope of union some whit my strength sustain.
Ye're gone and desolated by your absence is the world: Requital, ay, or substitute to seek for you 'twere vain.
Ye, of your strength, have burdened me, upon my weakliness, With burdens not to be endured of mountain nor of plain.
When from your land the breeze I scent that cometh, as I were A reveller bemused with wine, to lose my wits I'm fain.
Love no light matter is, O folk, nor are the woe and care And blame a little thing to brook that unto it pertain.
I wander seeking East and West for you, and every time Unto a camp I come, I'm told, "They've fared away again."
My friends have not accustomed me to rigour; for, of old, When I forsook them, they to seek accord did not disdain.

When she had made an end of her song, she wept sore, till presently sleep overcame her and she slept.

On the morrow, she said to the old man, "Get thee to the money-changer and fetch me the ordinary." So he repaired to the money-changer and delivered him the message, whereupon he made ready meat and drink, as of his wont, [with which the old man returned to the damsel and they ate till they had enough. When she had eaten,] she sought of him wine and he went to the Jew and fetched it. Then they sat down and drank; and when she grew drunken, she took the lute and smiting it, fell a-singing and chanted the following verses:

How long shall I thus question my heart that's drowned in woe? I'm mute for my complaining; but tears speak, as they flow.
They have forbid their image to visit me in sleep; So even my nightly phantom forsaketh me, heigho!

And when she had made an end of her song, she wept sore.

All this time, the young Damascene was hearkening, and whiles he likened her voice to that of his slave-girl and whiles he put away from him this thought, and the damsel had no whit of knowledge of him. Then she broke out again into song and chanted the following verses:

"Forget him," quoth my censurers, "forget him; what is he?" "If I forget him, ne'er may God," quoth I, "remember me!"
Now God forbid a slave forget his liege lord's love! And how Of all things in the world should I forget the love of thee?
Pardon of God for everything I crave, except thy love, For on the day of meeting Him, that will my good deed be.

Then she drank three cups and filling the old man other three, sang the following verses:

His love he'd have hid, but his tears denounced him to the spy, For the heat of a red-hot coal that 'twixt his ribs did lie.
Suppose for distraction he seek in the Spring and its blooms one day, The face of his loved one holds the only Spring for his eye.
O blamer of me for the love of him who denieth his grace, Which be the delightsome of things, but those which the people deny?
A sun [is my love;] but his heat in mine entrails still rageth, concealed; A moon, in the hearts of the folk he riseth, and not in the sky.

When she had made an end of her song, she threw the lute from her hand and wept, whilst the old man wept for her weeping. Then she fell down in a swoon and presently coming to herself, filled the cup and drinking it off, gave the old man to drink, after which she took the lute and breaking out into song, chanted the following verses:

Thy loss is the fairest of all my heart's woes; My case it hath altered and banished repose.
The world is upon me all desolate grown. Alack, my long grief and forlornness! Who knows
But the Merciful yet may incline thee to me And unite us again, in despite of our foes!

Then she wept till her voice rose high and her lamentation was discovered [to those without]; after which she again began to drink and plying the old man with wine, sang the following verses:

They have shut out thy person from my sight; They cannot shut thy memory from my spright.
Favour or flout me, still my soul shall be Thy ransom, in contentment or despite.
My outward of my inward testifies And this bears witness that that tells aright.[576]

When she had made an end of her song, she threw the lute from her hand and wept and lamented. Then she slept awhile and presently awaking, said, "O elder, hast thou what we may eat?" "O my lady," answered the old man, "there is the rest of the food;" but she said, "I will not eat of a thing I have left. Go down to the market and fetch us what we may eat." Quoth he, "Excuse me, O my lady; I cannot stand up, for that I am overcome with wine; but with me is the servant of the mosque, who is a sharp youth and an intelligent. I will call him, so he may buy thee that which thou desirest." "Whence hast thou this servant?" asked she; and he replied, "He is of the people of Damascus." When she heard him speak of the people of Damascus, she gave a sob, that she swooned away; and when she came to herself, she said, "Woe's me for the people of Damascus and for those who are therein! Call him, O elder, that he may do our occasions."

So the old man put his head forth of the window and called the youth, who came to him from the mosque and sought leave [to enter]. The Muezzin bade him enter, and when he came in to the damsel, he knew her and she knew him; whereupon he turned back in bewilderment and would have fled; but she sprang up to him and seized him, and they embraced and wept together, till they fell down on the ground in a swoon. When the old man saw them in this plight, he feared for himself and fled forth, seeing not the way for drunkenness. His neighbour the Jew met him and said to him, "How comes it that I see thee confounded?" "How should I not be confounded," answered the old man, "seeing that the damsel who is with me is fallen in love with the servant of the mosque and they have embraced and fallen down in a swoon? Indeed, I fear lest the Khalif come to know of this and be wroth with me; so tell me thou what is to be done in this wherewith I am afflicted of the affair of this damsel." Quoth the Jew, "For the nonce, take this casting-bottle of rose-water and go forth-right and sprinkle them therewith. If they be aswoon for this their foregathering and embracement, they will come to themselves, and if otherwise, do thou flee."

The old man took the casting-bottle from the Jew and going up to Noureddin and the damsel, sprinkled their faces, whereupon they came to themselves and fell to relating to each other that which they had suffered, since their separation, for the anguish of severance. Moreover, Noureddin acquainted Sitt el Milah with that which he had endured from the folk who would have slain him and made away with him; and she said to him, "O my lord, let us presently give over this talk and praise God for reunion of loves, and all this shall cease from us." Then she gave him the cup and he said, "By Allah, I will nowise drink it, whilst I am in this plight!" So she drank it off before him and taking the lute, swept the strings and sang the following verses:

Thou that wast absent from my stead, yet still with me didst bide, Thou wast removed from mine eye, yet still wast by my side.
Thou left'st unto me, after thee, languor and carefulness; I lived a life wherein no jot of sweetness I espied.
For thy sweet sake, as 'twere, indeed, an exile I had been, Lone and deserted I became, lamenting, weeping-eyed.
Alack, my grief! Thou wast, indeed, grown absent from my yiew, Yet art the apple of mine eye nor couldst from me divide.

When she had made an end of her song, she wept and Noureddin wept also. Then she took the lute and improvised and sang the following verses:

God knows I ne'er recalled thy memory to my thought, But still with brimming tears straightway mine eyes were fraught;
Yea, passion raged in me and love-longing was like To slay me; yet my heart to solace still it wrought.
Light of mine eyes, my hope, my wish, my thirsting eyes With looking on thy face can never sate their drought.

When Noureddin heard these his slave-girl's verses, he fell a-weeping, what while she strained him to her bosom and wiped away his tears with her sleeve and questioned him and comforted his mind. Then she took the lute and sweeping its strings, played thereon, after such a wise as would move the phlegmatic to delight, and sang the following verses:

Whenas mine eyes behold thee not, that day As of my life I do not reckon aye;

And when I long to look upon thy face, My life is perished with desire straightway.

On this wise they abode till the morning, tasting not the savour of sleep; and when the day lightened, behold, the eunuch came with the mule and said to Sitt el Milah, "The Commander of the Faithful calleth for thee." So she arose and taking her lord by the hand, committed him to the old man, saying, "I commend him to thy care, under God,[577] till this eunuch cometh to thee; and indeed, O elder, I owe thee favour and largesse such as filleth the interspace betwixt heaven and earth."

Then she mounted the mule and repairing to the palace of the Commander of the Faithful, went in to him and kissed the earth before him. Quoth he to her, as who should make mock of her, "I doubt not but thou hast found thy lord." "By thy felicity and the length of thy continuance [on life,]" answered she, "I have indeed found him!" Now Er Reshid was leaning back; but, when he heard this, he sat up and said to her, "By my life, [is this thou sayest] true?" "Ay, by thy life!" answered she; and he said, "Bring him into my presence, so I may see him." But she replied, "O my lord, there have betided him many stresses and his charms are changed and his favour faded; and indeed the Commander of the Faithful vouchsafed me a month; wherefore I will tend him the rest of the month and then bring him to do his service to the Commander of the Faithful." Quoth Er Reshid, "True; the condition was for a month; but tell me what hath betided him." "O my lord," answered she, "may God prolong thy continuance and make Paradise thy place of returning and thy harbourage and the fire the abiding-place of thine enemies, when he presenteth himself to pay his respects to thee, he will expound to thee his case and will name unto thee those who have wronged him; and indeed this is an arrear that is due to the Commander of the Faithful, in[578] whom may God fortify the Faith and vouchsafe him the mastery over the rebel and the froward!"

Therewithal he ordered her a handsome house and bade furnish it with carpets and other furniture and vessels of choice and commanded that all she needed should be given her. This was done during the rest of the day, and when the night came, she despatched the eunuch with the mule and a suit of clothes, to fetch Noureddin from the Muezzin's lodging. So the young man donned the clothes and mounting; rode to the house, where he abode in luxury and delight a full-told month, what while she solaced him with four things, to wit, the eating of fowls and the drinking of wine and the lying upon brocade and the entering the bath after copulation. Moreover, she brought him six suits of clothes and fell to changing his apparel day by day; nor was the appointed time accomplished ere his beauty returned to him and his goodliness; nay, his charms waxed tenfold and he became a ravishment to all who looked on him.

One day the Commander of the Faithful bade bring him to the presence; so his slave-girl changed his raiment and clothing him in sumptuous apparel, mounted him on the mule. Then he rode to the palace and presenting himself before the Khalif, saluted him with the goodliest of salutations and bespoke him with eloquent and deep-thoughted speech. When Er Reshid saw him, he marvelled at the goodliness of his favour and his eloquence and the readiness of his speech and enquiring of him, was told that he was Sitt el Milah's lord; whereupon quoth he, "Indeed, she is excusable in her love for him, and if we had put her to death unrighteously, as we were minded to do, her blood would have been upon our heads." Then he turned to the young man and entering into discourse with him, found him well bred, intelligent, quick of wit and apprehension, generous, pleasant, elegant, erudite. So he loved him with an exceeding love and questioned him of his native city and of his father and of the manner of his journey to Baghdad. Noureddin acquainted him with that which he would know in the goodliest of words and with the concisest of expressions; and the Khalif said to him, "And where hast thou been absent all this while? Indeed, we sent after thee to Damascus and Mosul and other the towns, but lit on no tidings of thee." "O my lord," answered the young man, "there betided thy slave in thy city that which never yet betided any." And he acquainted him with his case from first to last and told him that which had befallen him of evil [from El Muradi and his crew].

When Er Reshid heard this, he was sore chagrined and waxed exceeding wroth and said, "Shall this happen in a city wherein I am?" And the Hashimi vein[579] started out between his eyes. Then he bade fetch Jaafer, and when he came before him, he acquainted him with the matter and said to him, "Shall this come to pass in my city and I have no news of it?" Then he bade Jaafer fetch all whom the young Damascene had named [as having maltreated him], and when they came, he let smite off their heads. Moreover, he summoned him whom they called Ahmed and who had been the means of the young man's deliverance a first time and a second, and thanked him and showed him favour and bestowed on him a sumptuous dress of honour and invested him with the governance over his city.[580]

Then he sent for the old man, the Muezzin, and when the messenger came to him and told him that the Commander of the Faithful sought him, he feared the denunciation of the damsel and accompanied him to the palace, walking and letting wind[581] as he went, whilst all who passed him by laughed at him. When he came into the presence of the Commander of the Faithful, he fell a-trembling and his tongue was embarrassed, [so that he could not speak]. The Khalif laughed at him and said to him, "O elder, thou hast done no offence; so [why] fearest thou?" "O my lord,' answered the old man (and indeed he was in the sorest of that which may be of fear,) "by the virtue of thy pure forefathers, indeed I have done nought, and do thou enquire of my conduct." The Khalif laughed at him and ordering him a thousand dinars, bestowed on him a sumptuous dress of honour and made him chief of the Muezzins in his mosque.

Then he called Sitt el Milah and said to her, "The house [wherein thou lodgest] and that which is therein Is a guerdon [from me] to thy lord. So do thou take him and depart with him in the safeguard of God the Most High; but absent not yourselves from our presence." [So she went forth with Noureddin and] when she came to the house, she found that the Commander of the Faithful had sent them gifts galore and abundance of good things. As for Noureddin, he sent for his father and mother and appointed him agents and factors in the city of Damascus, to take the rent of the houses and gardens and khans and baths; and they occupied themselves with collecting that which accrued to him and sending it to him every year. Meanwhile, his father and mother came to him, with that which they had of monies and treasures and merchandise, and foregathering with their son, saw that he was become of the chief officers of the Commander of the Faithful and of the number of his session-mates and entertainers, wherefore they rejoiced in reunion with him and he also rejoiced in them.

The Khalif assigned them pensions and allowances and as for Noureddin, his father brought him those riches and his wealth waxed and his case was goodly, till he became the richest of the folk of his time in Baghdad and left not the presence of the Commander of the Faithful night or day. Moreover, he was vouchsafed children by Sitt el Milah, and he ceased not to live the most delightsome of lives, he and she and his father and mother, a while of time, till Aboulhusn sickened of a sore sickness and was admitted to the mercy of God the Most High. After awhile, his mother died also and he carried them forth and shrouded them and buried and made them expiations and nativities.[582] Then his children grew up and became like unto moons, and he reared them in splendour and fondness, what while his wealth waxed and his case flourished. He ceased not to pay frequent visits to the Commander of the Faithful, he and his children and his slave-girl Sitt el Milah, and they abode, he and they, in all solace of life and prosperity till there came to them the Destroyer of Delights and the Sunderer of Companies; and extolled be the perfection of the Abiding One, the Eternal! This is all that hath come down to us of their story.

EL ABBAS AND THE KING'S DAUGHTER OF BAGHDAD[583]

THERE was once, of old days and in bygone ages and times, in the city of Baghdad, the Abode of Peace, a king mighty of estate, lord of understanding and beneficence and liberality and generosity, and he was strong of sultanate and endowed with might and majesty and magnificence. His name was Ins ben Cais ben Rebiya es Sheibani,[584] and when he took horse, there rode unto him [warriors] from the farthest parts of the two Iraks.[585] God the Most High decreed that he should take to wife a woman hight Afifeh, daughter of Ased es Sundusi, who was endowed with beauty and grace and brightness and perfection and justness of shape and symmetry; her face was like unto the new moon and she had eyes as they were gazelle's eyes and an aquiline nose like the crescent moon. She had learned horsemanship and the use of arms and had thoroughly studied the sciences of the Arabs; moreover, she had gotten by heart all the dragomanish[586] tongues and indeed she was a ravishment to mankind.

She abode with Ins ben Cais twelve years, during which time he was blessed with no children by her; wherefore his breast was straitened, by reason of the failure of lineage, and he besought his Lord to vouchsafe him a child. Accordingly the queen conceived, by permission of God the Most High; and when the days of her pregnancy were accomplished, she gave birth to a maid-child, than whom never saw eyes a goodlier, for that her face was as it were a pure pearl or a shining lamp or a golden[587] candle or a full moon breaking forth of a cloud, extolled be the perfection of Him who created her from vile water[588] and made her a delight to the beholders! When her father saw her on this wise of loveliness, his reason fled for joy, and when she grew up, he taught her the art of writing and polite letters[589] and philosophy and all manner of tongues. So she excelled the folk of her time and overpassed her peers;[590] and the sons of the kings heard of her and all of them desired to look upon her.

The first who sought her in marriage was King Nebhan of Mosul, who came to her with a great company, bringing with him an hundred she-camels laden with musk and aloes-wood and ambergris and as many laden with camphor and jewels and other hundred laden with silver money and yet other hundred laden with raiment of silken and other stuffs and brocade, besides an hundred slave-girls and an hundred magnificent horses of swift and generous breeds, completely housed and accoutred, as they were brides; and all this he laid before her father, demanding her of him in marriage. Now King Ins ben Cais had bound himself by an oath that he would not marry his daughter but to him whom she should choose; so, when King Nebhan sought her in marriage, her father went in to her and consulted her concerning his affair. She consented not and he repeated to Nebhan that which she said, whereupon he departed from him. After this came King Behram, lord of the White Island, with riches more than the first; but she accepted not of him and he returned, disappointed; nor did the kings give over coming to her father, on her account, one after other, from the farthest of the lands and the climes, each glorying in more[591] than those who forewent him; but she paid no heed unto any of one them.

Presently, El Abbas, son of King El Aziz, lord of the land of Yemen and Zebidoun[592] and Mecca (which God increase in honour and brightness and beauty!), heard of her; and he was of the great ones of Mecca and the Hejaz[593] and was a youth without hair on his cheeks. So he presented himself one day in his father's sitting-chamber,[594] whereupon the folk made way for him and the king seated him on a chair of red gold, set with pearls and jewels. The prince sat, with his head bowed to the ground, and spoke not to any; whereby his father knew that his breast was straitened and bade the boon-companions and men of wit relate marvellous histories, such as beseem the assemblies of kings; nor was there one of them but spoke forth the goodliest of that which was with him; but El Abbas still abode with his head bowed down. Then the king bade his session-mates withdraw, and when the chamber was void, he looked at his son and said to him, "By Allah, thou rejoicest me with thy coming in to me and chagrinest me for that thou payest no heed to any of the session-mates nor of the boon-companions. What is the cause of this?"

"O father mine," answered the prince, "I have heard tell that in the land of Irak is a woman of the daughters of the kings, and her father is called King Ins ben Cais, lord of Baghdad; she is renowned for beauty and grace and brightness and perfection, and indeed many folk have sought her in marriage of the kings; but her soul consented not unto any one of them. Wherefore I am minded to travel to her, for that my heart cleaveth unto her, and I beseech thee suffer me to go to her." "O my son," answered his father, "thou knowest that I have none other than thyself of children and thou art the solace of mine eyes and the fruit of mine entrails; nay, I cannot brook to be parted from thee an instant and I purpose to set thee on the throne of the kingship and marry thee to one of the daughters of the kings, who shall be fairer than she." El Abbas gave ear to his father's word and dared not gainsay him; so he abode with him awhile, whilst the fire raged in his entrails.

Then the king took counsel with himself to build his son a bath and adorn it with various paintings, so he might show it to him and divert him with the sight thereof, to the intent that his body might be solaced thereby and that the obsession of travel might cease from him and he be turned from [his purpose of] removal from his parents. So he addressed himself to the building of the bath and assembling architects and builders and artisans from all the towns and citadels and islands [of his dominions], assigned them a site and marked out its boundaries. Then the workmen occupied themselves with the making of the bath and the setting out and adornment of its cabinets and roofs. They used paints and precious stones of all kinds, according to the variousness of their hues, red and green and blue and yellow and what not else of all manner colours; and each artisan wrought at his handicraft and each painter at his art, whilst the rest of the folk busied themselves with transporting thither varicoloured stones.

One day, as the [chief] painter wrought at his work, there came in to him a poor man, who looked long upon him and observed his handicraft; whereupon quoth the painter to him, "Knowest thou aught of painting?" "Yes," answered the stranger; so he gave him tools and paints and said to him, "Make us a rare piece of work." So the stranger entered one of the chambers of the bath and drew [on the walls thereof] a double border, which he adorned on both sides, after a fashion than which never saw eyes a fairer. Moreover, [amiddleward the chamber] he drew a picture to which there lacked but the breath, and it was the portraiture of Mariyeh, the king's daughter of Baghdad. Then, when he had made an end of the portrait, he went his way [and told none of what he had done], nor knew any the chambers and doors of the bath and the adornment and ordinance thereof.

Presently, the chief workman came to the palace and sought an audience of the king, who bade admit him. So he entered and kissing the earth, saluted him with a salutation beseeming kings and said, "O king of the time and lord of the age and the day, may felicity endure unto thee and acceptance and be thy rank exalted over all the kings both morning and evening![595] The work of the bath is accomplished, by the king's fair fortune and the eminence of his magnanimity,[596] and indeed we have done all that behoved us and there remaineth but that which behoveth the king." El Aziz ordered him a sumptuous dress of honour and expended monies galore, giving unto each who had wroughten, after the measure of his work. Then he assembled in the bath all the grandees of his state, amirs and viziers and chamberlains and lieutenants, and the chief officers of his realm and household, and sending for his son El Abbas, said to him,"O my son, I have builded thee a bath, wherein thou mayst take thy pleasance; so enter thou therein, that thou mayst see it and divert thyself by gazing upon it and viewing the goodliness of its ordinance and decoration." "With all my heart," replied the prince and entered the bath, he and the king and the folk about them, so they might divert themselves with viewing that which the workmen's hands had wroughten.

El Abbas went in and passed from place to place and chamber to chamber, till he came to the chamber aforesaid and espied the portrait of Mariyeh, whereupon he fell down in a swoon and the workmen went to his father and said to him, "Thy son El Abbas hath swooned away." So the king came and finding the prince cast down, seated himself at his head and bathed his face with rose-water. After awhile he revived and the king said to him, "God keep thee,[597] O my son! What hath befallen thee?" "O my father," answered the prince, "I did but look on yonder picture and it bequeathed me a thousand regrets and there befell me that which thou seest." Therewithal the king bade fetch the [chief] painter, and when he stood before him, he said to him, "Tell me of yonder portrait and what girl is this of the daughters of the kings; else will I take thy head." "By Allah, O king," answered the painter, "I limned it not, neither know I who she is; but there came to me a poor man and looked at me. So I said to him, 'Knowest thou the art of painting?' And he replied, 'Yes.' Whereupon I gave him the gear and said to him, 'Make us a rare piece of work.' So he wrought yonder portrait and went away and I know him not neither have I ever set eyes on him save that day."

Therewithal the king bade all his officers go round about in the thorough-fares and colleges [of the town] and bring before him all strangers whom they found there. So they went forth and brought him much people, amongst whom was the man who had painted the portrait. When they came into the presence, the Sultan bade the crier make proclamation that whoso wrought the portrait should discover himself and have whatsoever he desired. So the poor man came forward and kissing the earth before the king, said to him, "O king of the age, I am he who painted yonder portrait." Quoth El Aziz, "And knowest thou who she is?" "Yes," answered the other; "this is the portrait of Mariyeh, daughter of the king of Baghdad." The king ordered him a dress of honour and a slave-girl [and he went his way]. Then said El Abbas, "O father mine, give me leave to go to her, so I may look upon her; else shall I depart the world, without fail." The king his father wept and answered, saying, "O my son, I builded thee a bath, that it might divert thee from leaving me, and behold it hath been the cause of thy going forth; but the commandment of God is a foreordained[598] decree."[599]

Then he wept again and El Abbas said to him, "Fear not for me, for thou knowest my prowess and my puissance in returning answers in the assemblies of the land and my good breeding[600] and skill in rhetoric; and indeed he whose father thou art and whom thou hast reared and bred and in whom thou hast united praiseworthy qualities, the repute whereof hath traversed the East and the West, thou needest not fear for him, more by token that I purpose but to seek diversion[601] and return to thee, if it be the will of God the Most High." Quoth the king, "Whom wilt thou take with thee of attendants and [what] of good?" "O father mine," replied El Abbas, "I have no need of horses or camels or arms, for I purpose not battle, and I will have none go forth with me save my servant Aamir and no more."

As he and his father were thus engaged in talk, in came his mother and caught hold of him; and he said to her, "God on thee, let me go my gait and strive not to turn me from my purpose, for that needs must I go." "O my son," answered she, "if it must be so and there is no help for it, swear to me that thou wilt not be absent from me more than a year." And he swore to her. Then he entered his father's treasuries and took therefrom what he would of jewels and jacinths and everything heavy of worth and light of carriage. Moreover, he bade his servant Aamir saddle him two horses and the like for himself, and whenas the night darkened behind him,[602] he rose from his couch and mounting his horse, set out for Baghdad, he and Aamir, whilst the latter knew not whither he intended.

He gave not over going and the journey was pleasant to him, till they came to a goodly land, abounding in birds and wild beasts, whereupon El Abbas started a gazelle and shot it with an arrow. Then he dismounted and cutting its throat, said to his servant, "Alight thou and skin it and carry it to the water." Aamir answered him [with "Hearkening and obedience"] and going down to the water, kindled a fire and roasted the gazelle's flesh. Then they ate their fill and drank of the water, after which they mounted again and fared on diligently, and Aamir still unknowing whither El Abbas was minded to go. So he said to him, "O my lord, I conjure thee by God the Great, wilt thou not tell me whither thou intendest?" El Abbas looked at him and made answer with the following verses:

In my soul the fire of yearning and affliction rageth aye; Lo, I burn with love and longing; nought in answer can I say.
To Baghdad upon a matter of all moment do I fare, For the love of one whose beauties have my reason led astray.
Under me's a slender camel, a devourer of the waste; Those who pass a cloudlet deem it, as it flitteth o'er the way.
So, O Aamir, haste thy going, e'en as I do, so may I Heal my sickness and the draining of the cup of love essay;
For the longing that abideth in my heart is hard to bear. Fare with me, then, to my loved one. Answer nothing, but obey.

When Aamir heard his lord's verses, he knew that he was a slave of love [and that she of whom he was enamoured abode] in Baghdad. Then they fared on night and day, traversing plains and stony wastes, till they came in sight of Baghdad and lighted down in its suburbs[603] and lay the night there. When they arose in the morning, they removed to the bank of the Tigris and there they encamped and sojourned three days.

As they abode thus on the fourth day, behold, a company of folk giving their beasts the rein and crying aloud and saying, "Quick! Quick! Haste to our rescue, O King!" Therewithal the king's chamberlains and officers accosted them and said to them, "What is behind you and what hath befallen you?" Quoth they, "Bring us before the king." [So they carried them to Ins ben Cais;] and when they saw him, they said to him, "O king, except thou succour us, we are dead men; for that we are a folk of the Benou Sheiban,[604] who have taken up our abode in the parts of Bassora, and Hudheifeh the Arab[605] hath come down on us with his horses and his men and hath slain our horsemen and carried off our women and children; nor was one saved of the tribe but he who fled; wherefore we crave help [first] by God the Most High, then by thy life."

When the king heard their speech, he bade the crier make proclamation in the thoroughfares of the city that the troops should prepare [for the march] and that the horsemen should mount and the footmen come forth; nor was it but the twinkling of the eye ere the drums beat and the trumpets sounded; and scarce was the forenoon of the day passed when the city was blocked with horse and foot. So the king passed them in review and behold, they were four-and-twenty thousand in number, horsemen and footmen. He bade them go forth to the enemy and gave the commandment over them to Said ibn el Wakidi, a doughty cavalier and a valiant man of war. So the horsemen set out and fared on along the bank of the Tigris.

El Abbas looked at them and saw the ensigns displayed and the standards loosed and heard the drums beating; so he bade his servant saddle him a charger and look to the girths and bring him his harness of war. Quoth Aamir, "And indeed I saw El Abbas his eyes flash and the hair of his hands stood on end, for that indeed horsemanship[606] abode [rooted in his heart]."So he mounted his charger, whilst Aamir also bestrode a war-horse, and they went forth with the troops and fared on two days. On the third day, after the hour of the mid-afternoon prayer, they came in sight of the enemy and the two armies met and the ranks joined battle. The strife raged amain and sore was the smiting, whilst the dust rose in clouds and hung vaulted [over them], so that all eyes were blinded; and they ceased not from the battle till the night overtook them, when the two hosts drew off from the mellay and passed the night, perplexed concerning themselves [and the issue of their affair].

When God caused the morning morrow, the two armies drew out in battle array and the troops stood looking at one another. Then came forth El Harith ibn Saad between the two lines and played with his lance and cried out and recited the following verses:

Algates ye are our prey become; this many a day and night Right instantly of God we've craved to be vouchsafed your sight.
So hath the Merciful towards Hudheifeh driven you, A champion ruling over all, a lion of great might.
Is there a man of you will come, that I may heal his pairt With blows right profitful for him who's sick for lust of fight?

By Allah, come ye forth to me, for lo, I'm come to you | May he who's wronged the victory get and God defend the right![607]

Thereupon there sallied forth to him Zuheir ben Hebib, and they wheeled about and feinted awhile, then came to dose quarters and exchanged strokes. El Harith forewent his adversary in smiting and stretched him weltering in his gore; whereupon Hudheifeh cried out to him, saying, "Gifted of God art thou, O Harith! Call another of them." So he cried out, saying, "Is there a comer-forth [to battle?]" But they of Baghdad held back froni him; and when it appeared to El Harith that confusion was amongst them, he fell upon them and overthrew the first of them upon their last and slew of them twelve men. Then the evening overtook him and the Baghdadis addressed themselves to flight.

When the morning morrowed, they found themselves reduced to a fourth part of their number and there was not one of them had dismounted from his horse. So they made sure of destruction and Hudheifeh came out between the ranks (now he was reckoned for a thousand cavaliers) and cried out, saying, "Harkye, my masters of Baghdad! Let none come forth to me but your Amir, so I may talk with him and he with me; and he shall meet me in single combat and I will meet him, and may he who is void of offence come off safe!" Then he repeated his speech and said, "Why do I not hear your Amir return me an answer?" But Saad, the amir of the army of Baghdad, [replied not to him], and indeed his teeth chattered in his head, whenas he heard him summon him to single combat.

When El Abbas heard Hudheifeh's challenge and saw Saad in this case, he came up to the latter and said to him, "Wilt thou give me leave to reply to him and I will stand thee in stead in the answering of him and the going forth to battle with him and will make myself thy sacrifice?" Saad looked at him and seeing valour shining from between his eyes, said to him, "O youth, by the virtue of the Chosen [Prophet,] (whom God bless and keep,) tell me [who thou art and] whence thou comest to our succour." "This is no place for questioning," answered the prince; and Saad said to him, "O champion, up and at Hudheifeh! Yet, if his devil prove too strong for thee, afflict not thyself in thy youth."[608] Quoth El Abbas, "It is of Allah that help is to be sought,"[609] and taking his arms, fortified his resolution and went down [into the field], as he were a castle of the castles or a piece of a mountain.

[When] Hudheifeh [saw him], he cried out to him, saying, "Haste thee not, O youth! Who art thou of the folk?" And he answered, "I am Saad [ibn] el Wakidi, commander of the host of King Ins, and but that thou vauntedst thyself in challenging me, I had not come forth to thee; for that thou art not of my peers neither art counted equal to me in prowess and canst not avail against my onslaught. Wherefore prepare thee for departure,[610] seeing that there abideth but a little of thy life." When Hudheifeh heard this his speech, he threw himself backward,[611] as if in mockery of him, whereat El Abbas was wroth and called out to him, saying, "O Hudheifeh, guard thyself against me." Then he rushed upon him, as he were a swooper of the Jinn,[612] and Hudheifeh met him and they wheeled about a long while.

Presently, El Abbas cried out at Hudheifeh a cry that astonied him and dealt him a blow, saying, "Take this from the hand of a champion who feareth not the like of thee." Hudheifeh met the stroke with his shield, thinking to ward it off from him; but the sword shore the target in sunder and descending upon his shoulder, came forth gleaming from the tendons of his throat and severed his arm at the armpit; whereupon he fell down, wallowing in his blood, and El Abbas turned upon his host; nor had the sun departed the pavilion of the heavens ere Hudheifeh's army was in full flight before El Abbas and the saddles were empty of men. Quoth Saad, "By the virtue of the Chosen [Prophet], whom God bless and keep, I saw El Abbas with the blood upon his saddle pads, [in gouts] like camels' livers, smiting with the sword right and left, till he scattered them abroad in every mountain-pass and desert; and when he turned [back to the camp], the men of Baghdad were fearful of him."

When the Baghdadis saw this succour that had betided them against their enemies [and the victory that El Abbas had gotten them], they turned back and gathering together the spoils [of the defeated host], arms and treasures and horses, returned to Baghdad, victorious, and all by the valour of El Abbas. As for Saad, he foregathered with the prince, and they fared on in company till they came to the place where El Abbas had taken horse, whereupon the latter dismounted from his charger and Saad said to him, "O youth, wherefore alightest thou in other than thy place? Indeed, thy due is incumbent upon us and upon our Sultan; so go thou with us to the dwellings, that we may ransom thee with our souls." "O Amir Saad," replied El Abbas, "from this place I took horse with thee and herein is my lodging.

So, God on thee, name me not to the king, but make as if thou hadst never seen me, for that I am a stranger in the land."

So saying, he turned away from him and Saad fared on to the palace, where he found all the suite in attendance on the king and recounting to him that which had betided them with El Abbas. Quoth the king, "Where is he?" And they answered, "He is with the Amir Saad." [So, when the latter entered], the king [looked, but] found none with him; and Saad, seeing that he hankered after the youth, cried out to him, saying, "God prolong the king's days! Indeed, he refuseth to present himself before thee, without leave or commandment." "O Saad," asked the king, "whence cometh this man?" And the Amir answered, "O my lord, I know not; but he is a youth fair of favour, lovesome of aspect, accomplished in discourse, goodly of repartee, and valour shineth from between his eyes."

Quoth the king, "O Saad, fetch him to me, for indeed thou describest to me a masterful man."[613] And he answered, saying, "By Allah, O my lord, hadst thou but seen our case with Hudheifeh, what while he challenged me to the field of war and the stead of thrusting and smiting and I held back from doing battle with him! Then, whenas I thought to go forth to him, behold, a cavalier gave loose to his bridle-rein and called out to me, saying, 'O Saad, wilt thou suffer me to fill thy room in waging war with him and I will ransom thee with myself?' And I said, 'By Allah, O youth, whence cometh thou?' Quoth he, 'This is no time for thy questions.'" Then he recounted to the king all that had passed between himself and El Abbas from first to last; whereupon quoth Ins ben Cais, "Bring him to me in haste, so we may learn his tidings and question him of his case." "It is well," answered Saad, and going forth of the king's presence, repaired to his own house, where he put off his harness of war and took rest for himself.

To return to El Abbas, when he alighted from his charger, he put off his harness of war and rested awhile; after which he brought out a shirt of Venetian silk and a gown of green damask and donning them, covered himself with a turban of Damietta stuff and girt his middle with a handkerchief. Then he went out a-walking in the thoroughfares of Baghdad and fared on till he came to the bazaar of the merchants. There he found a merchant, with chess before him; so he stood watching him and presently the other looked up at him and said to him, "O youth, what wilt thou stake upon the game?" And he answered, "Be it thine to decide." "Then be it a hundred dinars," said the merchant, and El Abbas consented to him, whereupon quoth he, "O youth, produce the money, so the game may be fairly stablished." So El Abbas brought out a satin purse, wherein were a thousand dinars, and laid down an hundred dinars therefrom on the edge of the carpet, whilst the merchant did the like, and indeed h.s reason fled for joy, whenas he saw the gold in El Abbas his possession.

The folk flocked about them, to divert themselves with watching the play, and they called the bystanders to witness of the wager and fell a-playing. El Abbas forbore the merchant, so he might lead him on, and procrastinated with him awhile; and the merchant won and took of him the hundred dinars. Then said the prince, "Wilt thou play another game?" And the other answered, "O youth, I will not play again, except it be for a thousand dinars." Quoth the prince, "Whatsoever thou stakest, I will match thy stake with the like thereof." So the merchant brought out a thousand dinars and the prince covered them with other thousand. Then they fell a-playing, but El Abbas was not long with him ere he beat him in the square of the elephant,[614] nor did he leave to do thus till he had beaten him four times and won of him four thousand dinars.

This was all the merchant's good; so he said, "O youth, I will play thee another game for the shop." Now the value of the shop was four thousand dinars; so they played and El Abbas beat him and won his shop, with that which was therein; whereupon the other arose, shaking his clothes, and said to him, "Up, O youth, and take thy shop." So El Abbas arose and repairing to the shop, took possession thereof, after which he returned to [the place where he had left] his servant [Aamir] and found there the Amir Saad, who was come to bid him to the presence of the king. El Abbas consented to this and accompanied him till they came before King Ins ben Cais, whereupon he kissed the earth and saluted him and exceeded[615] in the salutation. Quoth the king to him, "Whence comest thou, O youth?" and he answered, "I come from Yemen."

Then said the king, "Hast thou a need we may accomplish unto thee? For indeed we are exceeding beholden to thee for that which thou didst in the matter of Hudheifeh and his folk." And he let cast over him a mantle of Egyptian satin, worth an hundred dinars. Moreover, he bade his treasurer give him a thousand dinars and said to him, "O youth, take this in part of that which thou deservest of us; and if thou prolong thy sojourn with us, we will give thee slaves and servants." El Abbas kissed the earth and said, "O king, may grant thee abiding prosperity, I deserve not all this." Then he put his hand to his poke and pulling out two caskets of gold, in each of which were rubies, whose value none could tell, gave them to the king, saying, "O king, God cause thy prosperity to endure, I conjure thee by that which God hath vouchsafed thee, heal my heart by accepting these two caskets, even as I have accepted thy present." So the king accepted the two caskets and El Abbas took his leave and went away to the bazaar.

When the merchants saw him, they accosted him and said, "O youth, wilt thou not open thy shop?" As they were bespeaking him, up came a woman, having with her a boy, bareheaded, and [stood] looking at El Abbas, till he turned to her, when she said to him, "O youth, I conjure thee by Allah, look at this boy and have pity on him, for that his father hath forgotten his cap in the shop [he lost to thee]; so if thou will well to give it to him, thy reward be with God! For indeed the child maketh our hearts ache with his much weeping, and God be witness for us that, were there left us aught wherewithal to buy him a cap in its stead, we had not sought it of thee." "O adornment of womankind," replied El Abbas, "indeed, thou bespeakest me with thy fair speech and supplicatest me with thy goodly words ...But bring me thy husband." So she went and fetched the merchant, whilst the folk assembled to see what El Abbas would do. When the man came, he returned him the gold he had won of him, all and part, and delivered him the keys of the shop, saying, "Requite us with thy pious pray-ers."Therewithal the woman came up to him and kissed his feet, and on like wise did the merchant her husband; and all who were present blessed him, and there was no talk but of El Abbas.

As for the merchant, he bought him a sheep and slaughtering it, roasted it and dressed birds and [other] meats of various kinds and colours and bought dessert and sweetmeats and fresh fruits. Then he repaired to El Abbas and conjured him to accept of his hospitality and enter his house and eat of his victual. The prince consented to his wishes and went with him till they came to his house, when the merchant bade him enter. So El Abbas entered and saw a goodly house, wherein was a handsome saloon, with a vaulted estrade. When he entered the saloon, he found that the merchant had made ready food and dessert and perfumes, such as overpass description; and indeed he had adorned the table with sweet-scented flowers and sprinkled musk and rose-water upon the food. Moreover, he had smeared the walls of the saloon with ambergris and set [the smoke of burning] aloes-wood abroach therein.

Presently, El Abbas looked out of the window of the saloon and saw thereby a house of goodly ordinance, lofty of building and abounding in chambers, with two upper stories; but therein was no sign of inhabitants. So he said to the merchant, "Indeed, thou exceedest in doing us honour; but, by Allah, I will not eat of thy victual till thou tell me what is the reason of the emptiness of yonder house." "O my lord," answered the other, "that was El Ghitrif's house and he was admitted to the mercy of God[616] and left none other heir than myself; so it became mine, and by Allah, if thou hast a mind to sojourn in Baghdad, do thou take up thine abode in this house, so thou mayst be in my neighbourhood; for that indeed my heart inclineth unto thee with love and I would have thee never absent from my sight, so I may still have my fill of thee and hearken to thy speech." El Abbas thanked him and said to him, "Indeed, thou art friendly in thy speech and exceedest [in courtesy] in thy discourse, and needs must I sojourn in Baghdad. As for the house, if it like thee, I will abide therein; so take of me its price."

So saying, he put his hand to his poke and bringing out therefrom three hundred dinars, gave them to the merchant, who said in himself, "Except I take the money, he will not abide in the house." So he pouched the money and sold him the house, taking the folk to witness against himself of the sale. Then he arose and set food before El Abbas and they ate of the good things which he had provided; after which he brought him dessert and sweetmeats. They ate thereof till they had enough, when the tables were removed and they washed their hands with rose-water and willow-flower-water. Then the merchant brought El Abbas a napkin perfumed with the fragrant smoke of aloes-wood, on which he wiped his hand,[617] and said to him, "O my lord, the house is become thy house; so bid thy servant transport thither the horses and arms and stuffs." El Abbas did this and the merchant rejoiced in his neighbourhood and left him not night nor day, so that the prince said to him, "By Allah, I distract thee from thy livelihood." "God on thee, O my lord," replied the merchant, "name not to me aught of this, or thou wilt break my heart, for the best of traffic is thy company and thou art the best of livelihood." So there befell strait friendship between them and ceremony was laid aside from between them.

Meanwhile the king said to his vizier, "How shall we do in the matter of yonder youth, the Yemani, on whom we thought to confer largesse, but he hath largessed us with tenfold [our gift] and more, and we know not if he be a sojourner with us or no?" Then he went into the harem and gave the rubies to his wife Afifeh, who said to him, "What is the worth of these with thee and with [other] the kings?" And he answered, "They are not to be found save with the greatest of kings and none may avail to price them with money." Quoth she, "Whence gottest thou them?" So he recounted to her the story of El Abbas from first to last, and she said, "By Allah, the claims of honour are imperative on us and the king hath fallen short of his due; for that we have not seen him bid him to his assembly, nor hath he seated him on his left hand."

[When the king heard his wife's words], it was as if he had been asleep and awoke; so he went forth of the harem and bade slaughter fowls and dress meats of all kinds and colours. Moreover, he assembled all his retainers and let bring sweetmeats and dessert and all that beseemeth unto kings' tables. Then he adorned his palace and despatched after El Abbas a man of the chief officers of his household, who found him coming forth of the bath, clad in a doublet of fine goats' hair and over it a Baghdadi scarf; his waist was girt with a Rustec[618] kerchief and on his head he wore a light turban of Damietta make.

The messenger wished him joy of the bath and exceeded in doing him worship. Then he said to him, "The king biddeth thee in weal."[619] "Hearkening and obedience," answered El Abbas and accompanied the messenger to the king's palace.

Now Afifeh and her daughter Mariyeh were behind the curtain, looking at him; and when he came before the king, he saluted him and greeted him with the greeting of kings, whilst all who were present stared at him and at his beauty and grace and perfection. The king seated him at the head of the table; and when Afifeh saw him and straitly considered him, she said, "By the virtue of Mohammed, prince of the Apostles, this youth is of the sons of the kings and cometh not to these parts but for some high purpose!" Then she looked at Mariyeh and saw that her face was changed, and indeed her eyes were dead in her face and she turned not her gaze from El Abbas a glance of the eyes, for that the love of him had gotten hold upon her heart. When the queen saw what had befallen her daughter, she feared for her from reproach concerning El Abbas; so she shut the wicket of the lattice and suffered her not to look upon him more. Now there was a pavilion set apart for Mariyeh, and therein were privy chambers and balconies and lattices, and she had with her a nurse, who served her, after the fashion of kings' daughters.

When the banquet was ended and the folk had dispersed, the king said to El Abbas, "I would fain have thee [abide] with me and I will buy thee a house, so haply we may requite thee the high services for which we are beholden to thee; for indeed thy due is imperative [upon us] and thy worth is magnified in our eyes; and indeed we have fallen short of thy due in the matter of distance."[620] When the prince heard the king's speech, he rose and sat down[621] and kissing the earth, returned thanks for his bounty and said, "I am the king's servant, wheresoever I may be, and under his eye." Then he recounted to him the story of the merchant and the manner of the buying of the house, and the king said, "Indeed, I would fain have had thee with me and in my neighbourhood."

Then El Abbas took leave of the king and went away to his own house. Now it befell that he passed under the palace of Mariyeh the king's daughter, and she was sitting at a window. He chanced to look round and his eyes met those of the princess, whereupon his wit departed and he was like to swoon away, whilst his colour changed and he said, "Verily, we are God's and to Him we return!" But he feared for himself lest estrangement betide him; so he concealed his secret and discovered not his case to any of the creatures of God the Most High. When he reached his house, his servant Aamir said to him, "O my lord, I seek refuge for thee with God from change of colour! Hath there betided thee a pain from God the Most High or hath aught of vexation befallen thee? Verily, sickness hath an end and patience doth away vexation." But the prince returned him no answer. Then he brought out inkhorn [and pen] and paper and wrote the following verses:

Quoth I (and mine a body is of passion all forslain, Ay, and a heart that's all athirst for love and longing pain
And eye that knoweth not the sweet of sleep; yet she, who caused My dole, may Fortune's perfidies for aye from her abstain!
Yea, for the perfidies of Fate and sev'rance I'm become Even as was Bishr[622] of old time with Hind,[623] a fearful swain;
A talking-stock among the folk for ever I abide; Life and the days pass by, yet ne'er my wishes I attain),
"Knoweth my loved one when I see her at the lattice high Shine as the sun that flameth forth in heaven's blue demesne?"
Her eye is sharper than a sword; the soul with ecstasy It takes and longing leaves behind, that nothing may assain.
As at the casement high she sat, her charms I might espy, For from her cheeks the envious veil that hid them she had ta'en.

She shot at me a shaft that reached my heart and I became The bond-man of despair, worn out with effort all in vain.
Fawn of the palace, knowst thou not that I, to look on thee, The world have traversed, far and wide, o'er many a hill and plain?
Read then my writ and pity thou the blackness of my fate, Sick, love-distraught, without a friend to whom I may complain.

Now the merchant's wife aforesaid, who was the nurse of the king's daughter, was watching him from a window, unknown of him, and [when she heard his verses], she knew that there hung some rare story by him; so she went in to him and said, "Peace be on thee, O afflicted one, who acquaintest not physician with thy case! Verily, thou exposest thyself unto grievous peril! I conjure thee by the virtue of Him who hath afflicted thee and stricken thee with the constraint of love-liking, that thou acquaint me with thine affair and discover to me the truth of thy secret; for that indeed I have heard from thee verses that trouble the wit and dissolve the body." So he acquainted her with his case and enjoined her to secrecy, whereof she consented unto him, saying, "What shall be the recompense of whoso goeth with thy letter and bringeth thee an answer thereto?" He bowed his head for shamefastness before her [and was silent]; and she said to him, "Raise thy head and give me thy letter." So he gave her the letter and she took it and carrying it to the princess, said to her, "Read this letter and give me the answer thereto."

Now the liefest of all things to Mariyeh was the recitation of poems and verses and linked rhymes and the twanging [of the strings of the lute], and she was versed in all tongues; so she took the letter and opening it, read that which was therein and apprehended its purport. Then she cast it on the ground and said, "O nurse, I have no answer to make to this letter." Quoth the nurse, "Indeed, this is weakness in thee and a reproach unto thee, for that the people of the world have heard of thee and still praise thee for keenness of wit and apprehension; so do thou return him an answer, such as shall delude his heart and weary his soul." "O nurse," rejoined the princess, "who is this that presumeth upon me with this letter? Belike he is the stranger youth who gave my father the rubies." "It is himself," answered the woman, and Mariyeh said, "I will answer his letter on such a wise that thou shalt not bring me other than it [from him]." Quoth the nurse, "So be it." So the princess called for inkhorn and paper and wrote the following verses:

O'erbold art thou in that to me, a stranger, thou hast sent These verses; 'twill but add to thee unease and miscontent.

Now God forbid thou shouldst attain thy wishes! What care I If thou have looked on me a look that caused thee languishment?

Who art thou, wretch, that thou shouldst hope to win me? With thy rhymes What wouldst of me? Thy reason, sure, with passion is forspent.

If to my favours thou aspire and covet me, good lack! What leach such madness can assain or what medicament?

Leave rhyming, madman that thou art, lest, bound upon the cross, Thou thy presumption in the stead of abjectness repent.

Deem not, O youth, that I to thee incline; indeed, no part Have I in those who walk the ways, the children of the tent.[624]

In the wide world no house thou hast, a homeless wanderer thou: To thine own place thou shall be borne, an object for lament.[625]

Forbear thy verse-making, O thou that harbourest in the camp, Lest to the gleemen thou become a name of wonderment.

How many a lover, who aspires to union with his love, For all his hopes seem near, is baulked of that whereon he's bent!

Then get thee gone nor covet that which thou shall ne'er obtain; So shall it be, although the time seem near and the event.

Thus unto thee have I set forth my case; consider well My words, so thou mayst guided be aright by their intent.

When she had made an end of her verses, she folded the letter and delivered it to the nurse, who took it and went with it to El Abbas. When she gave it to him, he took it and breaking it open, read it and apprehended its purport; and when he came to the end of it, he swooned away. After awhile, he came to himself and said, "Praised be God who hath caused her return an answer to my letter! Canst thou carry her another letter, and with God the Most High be thy requital?" Quoth she, "And what shall letters profit thee, seeing she answereth on this wise?" But he said, "Belike, she may yet be softened." Then he took inkhorn and paper and wrote the following verses:

Thy letter reached me; when the words thou wrot'st therein I read, My longing waxed and pain and woe redoubled on my head.

Yea, wonder-words I read therein, my trouble that increased And caused emaciation wear my body to a shred.

Would God thou knewst what I endure for love of thee and how My vitals for thy cruelty are all forspent and dead!

Fain, fain would I forget thy love. Alack, my heart denies To be consoled, and 'gainst thy wrath nought standeth me in stead.

An thou'dst vouchsafe to favour me,'twould lighten my despair, Though but in dreams thine image 'twere that visited my bed.

Persist not on my weakliness with thy disdain nor be Treason and breach of love its troth to thee attributed;

For know that hither have I fared and come to this thy land, By hopes of union with thee and near fruition led.

How oft I've waked, whilst over me my comrades kept the watch! How many a stony waste I've crossed, how many a desert dread!

From mine own land, to visit thee, I came at love's command, For all the distance did forbid,'twixt me and thee that spread.

Wherefore, by Him who letteth waste my frame, have ruth on me And quench my yearning and the fires by passion in me fed.

In glory's raiment clad, by thee the stars of heaven are shamed And in amaze the full moon stares to see thy goodlihead.

All charms, indeed, thou dost comprise; so who shall vie with thee And who shall blame me if for love of such a fair I'm sped?

When he had made an end of his verses, he folded the letter and delivering it to the nurse, charged her keep the secret. So she took it and carrying it to Mariyeh, gave it to her. The princess broke it open and read it and apprehended its purport. Then said she, "By Allah, O nurse, my heart is burdened with an exceeding chagrin, never knew I a dourer, because of this correspondence and of these verses." And the muse made answer to her, saying, "O my lady, thou art in thy dwelling and thy place and thy heart is void of care; so return him an answer and reck thou not" Accordingly, the princess called for inkhorn and paper and wrote the following verses:

Thou that the dupe of yearning art, how many a melting wight In waiting for the unkept tryst doth watch the weary night!

If in night's blackness thou hast plunged into the desert's heart And hast denied thine eyes the taste of sleep and its delight,

If near and far thy toiling feet have trod the ways and thou Devils and Marids hast ensued nor wouldst be led aright,

And dar'dst, O dweller in the tents, to lift thine eyes to me, Hoping by stress to win of me the amorous delight,

Get thee to patience fair, if thou remember thee of that Whose issues (quoth the Merciful) are ever benedight.[626]

How many a king for my sweet sake with other kings hath v'ed, Still craving union with me and suing for my sight!

Whenas En Nebhan strove to win my grace, himself to me With camel-loads he did commend of musk and camphor white,

And aloes-wood, to boot, he brought and caskets full of pearls And priceless rubies and the like of costly gems and bright;

Yea, and black slaves he proffered me and slave-girls big with child And steeds of price, with splendid arms and trappings rich bedight.

Raiment of silk and sendal, too, he brought to us for gift, And me in marriage sought therewith; yet, all his pains despite,

Of me he got not what he sought and brideless did return, For that estrangement and disdain were pleasing in my sight.

Wherefore, O stranger, dare thou not approach me with desire, Lest ruin quick and pitiless thy hardihood requite.

When she had made an end of her verses, she folded the letter and delivered it to the nurse, who took it and carried it to El Abbas. He broke it open and read it and apprehended its purport; then took inkhorn and paper and wrote the following verses:

Indeed, thou'st told the tale of kings and men of might, Each one a lion fierce, impetuous in the fight,

Whose wits (like mine, alack!) thou stalest and whose hearts With shafts from out thine eyes bewitching thou didst smite.

Yea, and how slaves and steeds and good and virgin girls Were proffered thee to gift, thou hast not failed to cite,

How presents in great store thou didst refuse and eke The givers, great and small, with flouting didst requite.

Then came I after them, desiring thee, with me No second save my sword, my falchion keen and bright.

No slaves with me have I nor camels swift of foot, Nor slave-girls have I brought in curtained litters dight.

Yet, an thou wilt vouchsafe thy favours unto me, My sabre thou shalt see the foemen put to flight;

Ay, and around Baghdad the horsemen shalt behold, Like clouds that wall the world, full many a doughty knight,

All hearkening to my word, obeying my command, In whatsoever thing is pleasing to my sight.

If slaves thou fain wouldst have by thousands every day Or, kneeling at thy feet, see kings of mickle might,

And horses eke wouldst have led to thee day by day And girls, high-breasted maids, and damsels black and white,

Lo under my command the land of Yemen is And trenchant is my sword against the foe in fight.

Whenas the couriers came with news of thee, how fair Thou wast and sweet and how thy visage shone with light,

All, all, for thy sweet sake, I left; ay, I forsook Aziz, my sire, and those akin to me that hight

And unto Irak fared, my way to thee to make, And crossed the stony wastes i' the darkness of the night.

Then sent I speech to thee in verses such as burn The heart; reproach therein was none nor yet unright;

Yet with perfidiousness (sure Fortune's self as thou Ne'er so perfidious was) my love thou didst requite

And deemedst me a waif, a homeless good-for-nought, A slave-begotten brat, a wanton, witless wight.

Then he folded the letter and committed it to the nurse and gave her five hundred dinars, saying, "Accept this from me, for that indeed thou hast wearied thyself between us." "By Allah, O my lord," answered she, "my desire is to bring about union between you, though I lose that which my right hand possesseth." And he said, "May God the Most High requite thee with good!" Then she carried the letter to Mariyeh and said to her, "Take this letter; belike it may be the end of the correspondence." So she took it and breaking it open, read it, and when she had made an end of it, she turned to the nurse and said to her, "This fellow putteth off lies upon me and avoucheth unto me that he hath cities and horsemen and footmen at his command and submitting to his allegiance; and he seeketh of me that which he shall not obtain; for thou knowest, O nurse, that kings' sons have sought me in marriage, with presents and rarities; but I have paid no heed unto aught of this; so how shall I accept of this fellow, who is the fool[627] of his time and possesseth nought but two caskets of rubies, which he gave to my father, and indeed he hath taken up his abode in the house of El Ghitrif and abideth without silver or gold? Wherefore, I conjure thee by Allah, O nurse, return to him and cut off his hope of me."

Accordingly the nurse returned to El Abbas, without letter or answer; and when she came in to him, he saw that she was troubled and noted the marks of chagrin on her face; so he said to her, "What is this plight?" Quoth she, "I cannot set out to thee that which Mariyeh said; for indeed she charged me return to thee without letter or answer." "O nurse of kings," rejoined El Abbas, "I would have thee carry her this letter and return not to her without it." Then he took inkhorn and paper and wrote the following verses:

My secret is disclosed, the which I strove to hide; Of thee and of thy love enough have I abyed.

My kinsmen and my friends for thee I did forsake And left them weeping tears that poured as 'twere a tide.

Yea, to Baghdad I came, where rigour gave me chase And I was overthrown of cruelty and pride.

Repression's draught, by cups, from the beloved's hand I've quaffed; with colocynth for wine she hath me plied.

Oft as I strove to make her keep the troth of love, Unto concealment's ways still would she turn aside.

My body is dissolved with sufferance in vain; Relenting, ay, and grace I hoped should yet betide;

But rigour still hath waxed on me and changed my case And love hath left me bound, afflicted, weeping-eyed.

How long shall I anights distracted be for love Of thee? How long th' assaults of grief and woes abide?

Thou, thou enjoy'st repose and comfortable sleep, Nor of the mis'ries reckst by which my heart is wried.

I watch the stars for wake and pray that the belov'd May yet to me relent and bid my tears be dried.

The pains of long desire have wasted me away; Estrangement and disdain my body sore have tried.

"Be thou not hard of heart," quoth I. Had ye but deigned To visit me in dreams, I had been satisfied.

But when ye saw my writ, the standard ye o'erthrew Of faith, your favours grudged and aught of grace denied.

Nay, though ye read therein discourse that sure should speak To heart and soul, no word thereunto ye replied,

But deemed yourself secure from every changing chance Nor recked the ebb and flow of Fortune's treacherous tide.

Were my affliction thine, love's anguish hadst thou dreed And in the flaming hell of long estrangement sighed.

Yet shall thou suffer that which I from thee have borne And with love's woes thy heart shall yet be mortified.

The bitterness of false accusing shall thou taste And eke the thing reveal that thou art fain to hide;
Yea, he thou lov'st shall be hard-hearted, recking not Of fortune's turns or fate's caprices, in his pride.
Wherewith farewell, quoth I, and peace be on thee aye, What while the branches bend, what while the stars abide.

When he had made an end of his verses, he folded the letter and gave it to the nurse, who took it and carried it to Mariyeh. When she came into the princess's presence, she saluted her; but Mariyeh returned not her salutation and she said, "O my lady, how hard is thy heart that thou grudgest to return the salutation! Take this letter, for that it is the last of that which shall come to thee from him." Quoth Mariyeh, "Take my warning and never again enter my palace, or it will be the cause of thy destruction; for I am certified that thou purposest my dishonour. So get thee gone from me." And she commanded to beat the nurse; whereupon the latter went forth fleeing from her presence, changed of colour and absent of wits, and gave not over going till she came to the house of El Abbas.

When the prince saw her in this plight, he was as a sleeper awakened and said to her, "What hath befallen thee? Set out to me thy case." "God on thee," answered she, "nevermore send me to Mariyeh, and do thou protect me, so may God protect thee from the fires of hell!" Then she related to him that which had bedded her with Mariyeh; which when he heard, there took him the shamefastness of the generous and this was grievous unto him. The love of Mariyeh fled forth of his heart and he said to the nurse, "How much hadst thou of Mariyeh every month?" "Ten dinars," answered she, and he said, "Be not concerned." Then he put his hand to his poke and bringing out two hundred dinars, gave them to her and said, "Take this for a whole year's wage and turn not again to serve any one. When the year is out, I will give thee two years' wage, for that thou hast wearied thyself with us and on account of the cutting off of thy dependence upon Mariyeh."

Moreover, he gave her a complete suit of clothes and raising his head to her, said, "When thou toldest me that which Mariyeh had done with thee, God rooted out the love of her from my heart, and never again will she occur to my mind; so extolled be the perfection of Him who turneth hearts and eyes! It was she who was the cause of my coming out from Yemen, and now the time is past for which I engaged with my people and I fear lest my father levy his troops and come forth in quest of me, for that he hath no child other than myself and cannot brook to be parted from me; and on like wise is it with my mother." When the nurse heard his words, she said to him, "O my lord, and which of the kings is thy father?" "My father is El Aziz, lord of Yemen and Nubia and the Islands[628] of the Benou Kehtan and the Two Noble Sanctuaries[629] (God the Most High have them in His keeping!)," answered El Abbas; "and whenas he taketh horse, there mount with him an hundred and twenty and four thousand horsemen, all smiters with the sword, let alone attendants and servants and followers, all of whom give ear unto my word and obey my commandment." "Why, then, O my lord," asked the nurse, "didst thou conceal the secret of thy rank and lineage and passedst thyself off for a wayfarer? Alas for our disgrace before thee by reason of our shortcoming in rendering thee thy due! What shall be our excuse with thee, and thou of the sons of the kings?" But he rejoined, "By Allah, thou hast not fallen short! Nay, it is incumbent on me to requite thee, what while I live, though I be far distant from thee."

Then he called his servant Aamir and said to him, "Saddle the horses." When the nurse heard his words and indeed [she saw that] Aamir brought him the horses and they were resolved upon departure, the tears ran down upon her cheeks and she said to him, "By Allah, thy separation is grievous to me, O solace of the eye!" Then said she, "Where is the goal of thine intent, so we may know thy news and solace ourselves with thy report?" Quoth he, "I go hence to visit Akil, the son of my father's brother, for that he hath his sojourn in the camp of Kundeh ben Hisham, and these twenty years have I not seen him nor he me; wherefore I purpose to repair to him and discover his news and return hither. Then will I go hence to Yemen, if it be the will of God the Most High."

So saying, he took leave of the woman and her husband and set out, intending for Akil, his father's brother's son. Now there was between Baghdad and Akil's abiding-place forty days' journey; so El Abbas settled himself on the back of his courser and his servant Aamir mounted also and they fared forth on their way. Presently, El Abbas turned right and left and recited the following verses:

I am the champion-slayer, the warrior without peer; My foes I slay, destroying the hosts, when I appear.
Tow'rds El Akil my journey I take; to visit him, The wastes in praise and safety I traverse, without fear,

And all the desert spaces devour, whilst to my rede, Or if in sport or earnest,[630] still Aamir giveth ear.

Who letteth us or hind'reth our way, I spring on him, As springeth lynx or panther upon the frighted deer;

With ruin I o'erwhelm him and abjectness and woe And cause him quaff the goblet of death and distance drear.

Well-ground my polished sword is and thin and keen of edge And trenchant, eke, for smiting and long my steel-barbed spear.

So fell and fierce my stroke is, if on a mountain high It lit, though all of granite, right through its midst 'twould shear.

Nor troops have I nor henchmen nor one to lend me aid Save God, to whom, my Maker, my voice in praise I rear.

'Tis He who pardoneth errors alike to slave and free; On Him is my reliance in good and evil cheer.

Then they fell to journeying night and day, and as they went, behold, they sighted a camp of the camps of the Arabs. So El Abbas enquired thereof and was told that it was the camp of the Benou Zuhreh. Now there were around them sheep and cattle, such as filled the earth, and they were enemies to El Akil, the cousin of El Abbas, upon whom they still made raids and took his cattle; wherefore he used to pay them tribute every year, for that he availed not to cope with them. When El Abbas came near the camp, he dismounted from his courser and his servant Aamir also dismounted; and they set down the victual and ate their sufficiency and rested awhile of the day. Then said the prince to Aamir, "Fetch water and give the horses to drink and draw water for us in thy water-bag, by way of provision for the road."

So Aamir took the water-skin and made for the water; but, when he came to the well, behold, two young men with gazelles, and when they saw him, they said to him, "Whither wilt thou, O youth, and of which of the Arabs art thou?" "Harkye, lads," answered he, "fill me my water-skin, for that I am a stranger man and a wayfarer and I have a comrade who awaiteth me." Quoth they, "Thou art no wayfarer, but a spy from El Akil's camp." Then they took him and carried him to [their king] Zuheir ben Shebib; and when he came before him, he said to him, "Of which of the Arabs art thou?" Quoth Aamir, "I am a wayfarer." And Zuheir said, "Whence comest thou and whither wilt thou?" "I am on my way to Akil," answered Aamir. When he named Akil, those who were present were agitated; but Zuheir signed to them with his eyes and said to him, "What is thine errand with Akil?" Quoth he, "We would fain see him, my friend and I."

When Zuheir heard his words, he bade smite off his head; but his Vizier said to him, "Slay him not, till his friend be present." So he commanded the two slaves to fetch his friend; whereupon they repaired to El Abbas and called to him, saying, "O youth, answer the summons of King Zuheir." "What would the king with me?" asked he, and they answered, "We know not." Quoth he, "Who gave the king news of me?" "We went to draw water," answered they, "and found a man by the water. So we questioned him of his case, but he would not acquaint us therewith; wherefore we carried him perforce to King Zuheir, who questioned him of his case and he told him that he was going to Akil. Now Akil is the king's enemy and he purposeth to betake himself to his camp and make prize of his offspring and cut off his traces." "And what," asked El Abbas, "hath Akil done with King Zuheir?" And they replied, "He engaged for himself that he would bring the king every year a thousand dinars and a thousand she-camels, besides a thousand head of thoroughbred horses and two hundred black slaves and fifty slave-girls; but it hath reached the king that Akil purposeth to give nought of this; wherefore he is minded to go to him. So hasten thou with us, ere the king be wroth with thee and with us."

Then said El Abbas to them, "O youths, sit by my arms and my horse till I return." But they answered, saying, "By Allah, thou prolongest discourse with that which beseemeth not of words! Make haste, or we will go with thy head, for indeed the king purposeth to slay thee and to slay thy comrade and take that which is with you." When the prince heard this, his skin quaked and he cried out at them with a cry that made them tremble. Then he sprang upon his horse and settling himself in the saddle, galloped till he came to the king's assembly, when he cried out at the top of his voice, saying ["To horse,] cavaliers!" And levelled his spear at the pavilion wherein was Zuheir. Now there were about him a thousand smiters with the sword; but El Abbas fell in upon them and dispersed them from around him, and there abode none in the tent save Zuheir and his vizier.

Then came up El Abbas to the door of the tent, and therein were four-and-twenty golden doves; so he took them, after he had beaten them down with the end of his lance. Then he called out, saying, "Harkye, Zuheir! Doth it not suffice thee that thou hast quelled El Akil's repute, but thou art minded to quell that of those who sojourn round about him? Knowest thou not that he is of the lieutenants of Kundeh ben [Hisham of the Benou] Sheiban, a man renowned for prowess? Indeed, covetise of him hath entered into thee and jealousy of him hath gotten possession of thee. Doth it not suffice thee that thou hast orphaned his children[631] and slain his men? By the virtue of the Chosen Prophet, I will make thee drink the cup of death!" So saying, he drew his sword and smiting Zuheir on his shoulder, caused the steel issue, gleaming, from the tendons of his throat. Then he smote the vizier and clove his head in sunder.

As he was thus, behold, Aamir called out to him and said, "O my lord, come to my help, or I am a dead man!" So El Abbas went up to him and found him cast down on his back and chained with four chains to four pickets of iron. He loosed his bonds and said to him, "Go before me, O Aamir." So he fared on before him a little, and presently they looked, and behold, horsemen making to Zuheir's succour, to wit, twelve thousand cavaliers, with Sehl ben Kaab in their van, mounted upon a jet-black steed. He charged upon Aamir, who fled from him, then upon El Abbas, who said, "O Aamir, cleave fast to my horse and guard my back." Aamir did as he bade him, whereupon El Abbas cried out at the folk and falling upon them, overthrew their braves and slew of them nigh two thousand cavaliers, whilst not one of them knew what was to do nor with whom he fought. Then said one of them to other, "Verily, the king is slain; so with whom do we wage war? Indeed ye flee from him; so do ye enter under his banners, or not one of you will be saved."

Thereupon they all dismounted and putting off that which was upon them of harness of war, came before El Abbas and tendered him allegiance and sued for his protection. So he held his hand from them and bade them gather together the spoils. Then he took the riches and the slaves and the camels, and they all became his liege-men and his retainers, to the number (according to that which is said) of fifty thousand horse. Moreover, the folk heard of him and flocked to him from all sides; whereupon he divided [the spoil amongst them] and gave gifts and abode thus three days, and there came presents to him. Then he bade set out for Akil's abiding-place; so they fared on six days and on the seventh day they came in sight of the camp. El Abbas bade his man Aamir forego him and give Akil the glad news of his cousin's coming. So he rode on to the camp and going in to Akil, gave him the glad news of Zuheir's slaughter and the conquest of his tribe.

Akil rejoiced in the coming of El Abbas and the slaughter of his enemy and all in his camp rejoiced also and cast dresses of honour upon Aamir. Moreover, Akil bade go forth to meet El Abbas, and commanded that none, great or small, freeman or slave, should tarry behind. So they did his bidding and going forth all, met El Abbas at three parasangs' distance from the camp. When they met him, they all dismounted from their horses and Akil and he embraced and clapped hands.[632] Then they returned, rejoicing in the coming of El Abbas and the slaughter of their enemy, to the camp, where tents were pitched for the new-comers and carpets spread and game killed and beasts slaughtered and royal guest-meals spread; and on this wise they abode twenty days, in the enjoyment of all delìght and solace of life.

To return to King El Aziz. When his son El Abbas left him, he was desolated for him with an exceeding desolation, he and his mother; and when tidings of him tarried long and the appointed time passed [and the prince returned not], the king caused public proclamation to be made, commanding all his troops to make ready to mount and go forth in quest of his son El Abbas at the end of three days, after which time no cause of hindrance nor excuse should be admitted unto any. So on the fourth day, the king bade number the troops, and behold, they were four-and-twenty thousand horse, besides servants and followers. Accordingly, they reared the standards and the drums beat to departure and the king set out [with his army], intending for Baghdad; nor did he cease to fare on with all diligence, till he came within half a day's journey of the city and bade his troops encamp in [a place there called] the Green Meadow. So they pitched the tents there, till the country was straitened with them, and set up for the king a pavilion of green brocade, broidered with pearls and jewels.

When El Aziz had sat awhile, he summoned the mamelukes of his son El Abbas, and they were five-and-twenty in number, besides half a score slave-girls, as they were moons, five of whom the king had brought with him and other five he had left with the prince's mother. When the mamelukes came before him, he cast over each of them a mantle of green brocade and bade them mount like horses of one and the same fashion and enter Baghdad and enquire concerning their lord El Abbas. So they entered the city and passed through the [streets and] markets, and there abode in Baghdad nor old man nor boy but came forth to gaze on them and divert himself with the sight of their beauty and grace and the goodliness of their aspect and of their clothes and horses, for that they were even as moons.

They gave not over going till they came to the royal palace, where they halted, and the king looked at them and seeing their beauty and the goodliness of their apparel and the brightness of their faces, said, "Would I knew of which of the tribes these are!" And he bade the eunuch bring him news of them.

So he went out to them and questioned them of their case, whereupon, "Return to thy lord," answered they, "and question him of Prince El Abbas, if he have come unto him, for that he left his father King El Aziz a full-told year agone, and indeed longing for him troubleth the king and he hath levied a part of his army and his guards and is come forth in quest of his son, so haply he may light upon tidings of him." Quoth the eunuch, "Is there amongst you a brother of his or a son?" "Nay, by Allah!" answered they. "But we are all his mamelukes and the boughten of his money, and his father El Aziz hath despatched us to make enquiry of him. So go thou to thy lord and question him of the prince and return to us with that which he shall answer you." "And where is King El Aziz?" asked the eunuch; and they replied, "He is encamped in the Green Meadow."[633]

The eunuch returned and told the king, who said, "Indeed, we have been neglectful with regard to El Abbas. What shall be our excuse with the king? By Allah, my soul misdoubted me that the youth was of the sons of the kings!" The Lady Afifeh, his wife, saw him lamenting for [his usage of] El Abbas and said to him, "O king, what is it thou regrettest with this exceeding regret?" Quoth he, "Thou knowest the stranger youth, who gave us the rubies?" "Assuredly," answered she; and he said, "Yonder youths, who have halted in the palace court, are his mamelukes, and his father King El Aziz, lord of Yemen, hath pitched his camp in the Green Meadow; for he is come with his army to seek him, and the number of his troops is [four-and-] twenty thousand men." [Then he went out from her], and when she heard his words, she wept sore for him and had compassion on his case and sent after him, counselling him to send for the mamelukes and lodge them [in the palace] and entertain them.

The king gave ear to her counsel and despatching the eunuch for the mamelukes, assigned them a lodging and said to them, "Have patience, till the king give you tidings of your lord El Abbas." When they heard his words, their eyes ran over with plenteous tears, of their much longing for the sight of their lord. Then the king bade the queen enter the privy chamber[634] and let down the curtain[635] [before the door thereof]. So she did this and he summoned them to his presence. When they stood before him, they kissed the earth, to do him worship, and showed forth their breeding[636] and magnified his dignity. He bade them sit, but they refused, till he conjured them by their lord El Abbas. So they sat down and he caused set before them food of various kinds and fruits and sweetmeats. Now within the Lady Afifeh's palace was an underground way communicating with the palace of the princess Mariyeh. So the queen sent after her and she came to her, whereupon she made her stand behind the curtain and gave her to know that El Abbas was the king's son of Yemen and that these were his mamelukes. Moreover, she told her that the prince's father had levied his troops and was come with his army in quest of him and that he had pitched his camp in the Green Meadow and despatched these mamelukes to make enquiry of their lord. So Mariyeh abode looking upon them and upon their beauty and grace and the goodliness of their apparel, till they had eaten their fill of food and the tables were removed; whereupon the king recounted to them the story of El Abbas and they took leave of him and went away.

As for the princess Mariyeh, when she returned to her palace, she bethought herself concerning the affair of El Abbas, repenting her of that which she had done, and the love of him took root in her heart. So, when the night darkened upon her, she dismissed all her women and bringing out the letters, to wit, those which El Abbas had written, fell to reading them and weeping. She gave not over weeping her night long, and when she arose in the morning, she called a damsel of her slave-girls, Shefikeh by name, and said to her, "O damsel, I purpose to discover to thee mine affair, and I charge thee keep my secret; to wit, I would have thee betake thyself to the house of the nurse, who used to serve me, and fetch her to me, for that I have grave occasion for her."

Accordingly, Shefikeh went out and repairing to the nurse's house, found her clad in apparel other[637] than that which she had been wont to wear aforetime. So she saluted her and said to her, "Whence hadst thou this dress, than which there is no goodlier?" "O Shefikeh," answered the nurse, "thou deemest that I have gotten[638] no good save of thy mistress; but, by Allah, had I endeavoured for her destruction, I had done [that which was my right], for that she did with me what thou knowest[639] and bade the eunuch beat me, without offence of me committed; wherefore do thou tell her that he, on whose behalf I bestirred myself with her, hath made me quit of her and her humours, for that he hath clad me in this habit and given me two hundred and fifty dinars and promised me the like thereof every year and charged me serve none of the folk."

Quoth Shefikeh, "My mistress hath occasion for thee; so come thou with me and I will engage to restore thee to thy dwelling in weal and safety." But the nurse answered, saying, "Indeed, her palace is become forbidden[640] to me and never again will I enter therein, for that God (extolled be His perfection and exalted be He!) of His favour and bounty hath rendered me independent of her." So Shefikeh returned to her mistress and acquainted her with the nurse's words and that wherein she was of affluence; whereupon Mariyeh confessed the unseemliness of her dealing with her and repented, whenas repentance profited her not; and she abode in that her case days and nights, whilst the fire of longing flamed in her heart.

Meanwhile, El Abbas abode with his cousin Akil twenty days, after which he made ready for the journey to Baghdad and letting bring the booty he had gotten of King Zuheir, divided it between himself and his cousin. Then he set out for Baghdad, and when he came within two days' journey of the city, he called his servant Aamir and bade him mount his charger and forego him with the baggage-train and the cattle. So Aamir [took horse and] fared on till he came to Baghdad, and the season of his entering was the first of the day; nor was there little child or hoary old man in the city but came forth to divert himself with gazing on those flocks and herds and upon the goodliness of those slave-girls, and their wits were amazed at what they saw. Presently the news reached the king that the young man El Abbas, who had gone forth from him, was come back with herds and rarities and slaves and a mighty host and had taken up his sojourn without the city, whilst his servant Aamir was presently come to Baghdad, so he might make ready dwelling- places for his lord, wherein he should take up his abode.

When the king heard these tidings of Aamir, he sent for him and let bring him before him; and when he entered his presence, he kissed the earth and saluted and showed forth his breeding and greeted him with the goodliest of compliments. The king bade him raise his head and questioned him of his lord El Abbas; whereupon he acquainted him with his tidings and told him that which had betided him with King Zuheir and of the army that was become at his commandment and of the spoil that he had gotten. Moreover, he gave him to know that El Abbas was coming on the morrow, and with him more than fifty thousand cavaliers, obedient to his commandment. When the king heard his speech, he bade decorate Baghdad and commanded [the inhabitants] to equip themselves with the richest of their apparel, in honour of the coming of El Abbas. Moreover, he sent to give King El Aziz the glad tidings of his son's return and acquainted him with that which he had heard from the prince's servant.

When the news reached El Aziz, he rejoiced with an exceeding joy in the coming of his son and straightway took horse, he and all his army, what while the trumpets sounded and the musicians played that the earth quaked and Baghdad also trembled, and it was a notable day. When Mariyeh beheld all this, she repented with the uttermost of repentance of that which she had wroughten against El Abbas his due and the fires still raged in her vitals. Meanwhile, the troops[641] sallied forth of Baghdad and went out to meet those of El Abbas, who had halted in a meadow called the Green Island. When he espied the approaching host, he knew not what they were; so he strained his sight and seeing horsemen coming and troops and footmen, said to those about him, "Among yonder troops are ensigns and banners of various kinds; but, as for the great green standard that ye see, it is the standard of my father, the which is reserved [unto him and never displayed save] over his head, and [by this] I know that he himself is come out in quest of me." And he was certified of this, he and his troops.

[So he fared on towards them] and when he drew near unto them, he knew them and they knew him; whereupon they lighted down from their horses and saluting him, gave him joy of his safety and the folk flocked to him. When he came to his father, they embraced and greeted each other a long time, whilst neither of them availed unto speech, for the greatness of that which betided them of joy in reunion. Then El Abbas bade the folk mount; so they mounted and his mamelukes surrounded him and they entered Baghdad on the most magnificent wise and in the highest worship and glory.

The wife of the shopkeeper, to wit, the nurse, came out, with the rest of those who came out, to divert herself with gazing upon the show, and when she saw El Abbas and beheld his beauty and the goodliness of his army and that which he had brought back with him of herds and slaves and slave-girls and mamelukes, she improvised and recited the following verses:

El Abbas from Akil his stead is come again; Prize hath he made of steeds and many a baggage-train;
Yea, horses hath he brought, full fair of shape and hue, Whose collars, anklet-like, ring to the bridle-rein.
Taper of hoofs and straight of stature, in the dust They prance, as like a flood they pour across the plain;
And on their saddles perched are warriors richly clad, That with their hands do smite on kettle-drums amain.
Couched are their limber spears, right long and lithe of point, Keen- ground and polished sheer, amazing wit and brain.
Who dares with them to cope draws death upon himself; Yea, of the deadly lance incontinent he's slain.
Come, then, companions mine, rejoice with me and say, "All hail to thee, O friend, and welcome fair and fain!"
For whoso doth rejoice in meeting him shall have Largesse and gifts galore at his dismounting gain.

When the troops entered Baghdad, each of them alighted in his pavilion, whilst El Abbas encamped apart in a place near the Tigris and commanded to slaughter for the troops, each day, that which should suffice them of oxen and sheep and bake them bread and spread the tables. So the folk ceased not to come to him and eat of his banquet. Moreover, all the people of the country came to him with presents and rarities and he requited them many times the like of their gifts, so that the lands were filled with his tidings and the report of him was bruited abroad among the folk of the deserts and the cities.

Then, when he rode to his house that he had bought, the shopkeeper and his wife came to him and gave him joy of his safety; whereupon he ordered them three swift thoroughbred horses and ten dromedaries and an hundred head of sheep and clad them both in sumptuous dresses of honour. Then he chose out ten slave-girls and ten black slaves and fifty horses and the like number of she- camels and three hundred head of sheep, together with twenty ounces of musk and as many of camphor, and sent all this to the King of Baghdad. When this came to Ins ben Cais, his wit fled for joy and he was perplexed wherewithal to requite him. Moreover, El Abbas gave gifts and largesse and bestowed dresses of honour upon great and small, each after the measure of his station, save only Mariyeh; for unto her he sent nothing.

This was grievous to the princess and it irked her sore that he should not remember her; so she called her slave- girl Shefikeh and said to her, "Go to El Abbas and salute him and say to him, 'What hindereth thee from sending my lady Mariyeh her part of thy booty?'" So Shefikeh betook herself to him and when she came to his door, the chamberlains refused her admission, until they should have gotten her leave and permission. When she entered, El Abbas knew her and knew that she had somewhat of speech [with him]; so he dismissed his mamelukes and said to her, "What is thine errand, O handmaid of good?" "O my lord," answered she, "I am a slave-girl of the Princess Mariyeh, who kisseth thy hands and commendeth her salutation to thee. Indeed, she rejoiceth in thy safety and reproacheth thee for that thou breakest her heart, alone of all the folk, for that thy largesse embraceth great and small, yet hast thou not remembered her with aught of thy booty. Indeed, it is as if thou hadst hardened thy heart against her." Quoth he, "Extolled be the perfection of him who turneth hearts! By Allah, my vitals were consumed with the love of her [aforetime] and of my longing after her, I came forth to her from my native land and left my people and my home and my wealth, and it was with her that began the hardheartedness and the cruelty. Nevertheless, for all this, I bear her no malice and needs must I send her somewhat whereby she may remember me; for that I abide in her land but a few days, after which I set out for the land of Yemen."

Then he called for a chest and bringing out thence a necklace of Greek handiwork, worth a thousand dinars, wrapped it in a mantle of green silk, set with pearls and jewels and inwrought with red gold, and joined thereto two caskets of musk and ambergris. Moreover, he put off upon the girl a mantle of Greek silk, striped with gold, wherein were divers figures and semblants depictured, never saw eyes its like. Therewithal the girl's wit fled for joy and she went forth from his presence and returned to her mistress. When she came in to her, she acquainted her with that which she had seen of El Abbas and that which was with him of servants and attendants and [set out to her] the loftiness of his station and gave her that which was with her.

Mariyeh opened the mantle, and when she saw that necklace, and indeed the place was illumined with the lustre thereof, she looked at her slave-girl and said to her, "By Allah, O Shefikeh, one look at him were liefer to me than all that my hand possesseth! Would I knew what I shall do, whenas

Baghdad is empty of him and I hear no tidings of him!" Then she wept and calling for inkhorn* and paper and pen of brass, wrote the following verses:

Still do I yearn, whilst passion's fire flames in my liver aye; For parting's shafts have smitten me and done my strength away.
Oft for thy love as I would be consoled, my yearning turns To-thee- ward still and my desires my reason still gainsay.
My transports I conceal for fear of those thereon that spy; Yet down my cheeks the tears course still and still my case bewray.
No rest is there for me, no life wherein I may delight, Nor pleasant meat nor drink avails to please me, night or day.
To whom save thee shall I complain, of whom relief implore, Whose image came to visit me, what while in dreams I lay?
Reproach me not for what I did, but be thou kind to one Who's sick of body and whose heart is wasted all away.
The fire of love-longing I hide; severance consumeth me, A thrall of care, for long desire to wakefulness a prey.
Midmost the watches of the night I see thee, in a dream; A lying dream, for he I love my love doth not repay.
Would God thou knewest that for love of thee which I endure! It hath indeed brought down on me estrangement and dismay.
Read thou my writ and apprehend its purport, for my case This is and fate hath stricken me with sorrows past allay.
Know, then, the woes that have befall'n a lover, neither grudge Her secret to conceal, but keep her counsel still, I pray.

Then she folded the letter and giving it to her slave-girl, bade her carry it to El Abbas and bring back his answer thereto. Accordingly, Shefikeh took the letter and carried it to the prince, after the doorkeeper had sought leave of him to admit her. When she came in to him, she found with him five damsels, as they were moons, clad in [rich] apparel and ornaments; and when he saw her, he said to her, "What is thine occasion, O handmaid of good?" So she put out her hand to him with the letter, after she had kissed it, and he bade one of his slave-girls receive it from her. Then he took it from the girl and breaking it open, read it and apprehended its purport; whereupon "We are God's and to Him we return!" exclaimed he and calling for ink- horn and paper, wrote the following verses:

I marvel for that to my love I see thee now incline, What time my heart, indeed, is fain to turn away from thine.

Whilere, the verses that I made it was thy wont to flout, Saying, "No passer by the way[642] hath part in me or mine.

How many a king to me hath come, of troops and guards ensued, And Bactrian camels brought with him, in many a laden line,

And dromedaries, too, of price and goodly steeds and swift Of many a noble breed, yet found no favour in my eyne!"

Then, after them came I to thee and union did entreat And unto thee set forth at length my case and my design;

Yea, all my passion and desire and love-longing in verse, As pearls in goodly order strung it were, I did enshrine.

Yet thou repaidst me with constraint, rigour and perfidy, To which no lover might himself on any wise resign.

How many a bidder unto love, a secret-craving wight, How many a swain, complaining, saith of destiny malign,

"How many a cup with bitterness o'erflowing have I quaffed! I make my moan of woes, whereat it boots not to repine."

Quoth thou, "The goodliest of things is patience and its use: Its practice still mankind doth guide to all that's fair and fine."

Wherefore fair patience look thou use, for sure 'tis praiseworthy; Yea, and its issues evermore are blessed and benign;

And hope thou not for aught from me, who reck not with a folk To mix, who may with abjectness infect my royal line.

This is my saying; apprehend its purport, then, and know I may in no wise yield consent to that thou dost opine.

Then he folded the letter and sealing it, delivered it to the damsel, who took it and carried it to her mistress. When the princess read the letter and apprehended its contents, she said, "Meseemeth he recalleth to me that which I did aforetime." Then she called for inkhorn and paper and wrote the following verses:

Me, till I stricken was therewith, to love thou didst excite, And with estrangement now, alas! heap'st sorrows on my spright.

The sweet of slumber after thee I have forsworn; indeed The loss of thee hath smitten me with trouble and affright.

How long shall I, in weariness, for this estrangement pine, What while the spies of severance[643] do watch me all the night?

My royal couch have I forsworn, sequestering myself From all, and have mine eyes forbid the taste of sleep's delight.

Thou taught'st me what I cannot bear; afflicted sore am I; Yea, thou hast wasted me away with rigour and despite.
Yet, I conjure thee, blame me not for passion and desire, Me whom estrangement long hath brought to sick and sorry plight.
Sore, sore doth rigour me beset, its onslaughts bring me near Unto the straitness of the grave, ere in the shroud I'm dight.
So be thou kind to me, for love my body wasteth sore, The thrall of passion I'm become its fires consume me quite.

Mariyeh folded the letter and gave it to Shefikeh, bidding her carry it to El Abbas. So she took it and going with it to his door, would have entered; but the chamberlains and serving-men forbade her, till they had gotten her leave from the prince. When she went in to him, she found him sitting in the midst of the five damsels aforesaid, whom his father had brought him. So she gave him the letter and he took it and read it. Then he bade one of the damsels, whose name was Khefifeh and who came from the land of China, tune her lute and sing upon the subject of separation. So she came forward and tuning the lute, played thereon in four-and-twenty modes; after which she returned to the first mode and sang the following verses:

Upon the parting day our loves from us did fare And left us to endure estrangement and despair.
Whenas the burdens all were bounden on and shrill The camel-leader's call rang out across the air,
Fast flowed my tears; despair gat hold upon my soul And needs mine eyelids must the sweet of sleep forbear.
I wept, but those who spied to part us had no ruth On me nor on the fires that in my vitals flare.
Woe's me for one who burns for love and longing pain! Alas for the regrets my heart that rend and tear!
To whom shall I complain of what is in my soul, Now thou art gone and I my pillow must forswear?
The flames of long desire wax on me day by day And far away are pitched the tent-poles of my fair.
O breeze of heaven, from me a charge I prithee take And do not thou betray the troth of my despair;
Whenas thou passest by the dwellings of my love, Greet him for me with peace, a greeting debonair,
And scatter musk on him and ambergris, so long As time endures; for this is all my wish and care.

When the damsel had made an end of her song, El Abbas swooned away and they sprinkled on him rose-water, mingled with musk, till he came to himself, when he called another damsel (now there was on her of linen and clothes and ornaments that which beggareth description, and she was endowed with brightness and loveliness and symmetry ard perfection, such as shamed the crescent moon, and she was a Turkish girl from the land of the Greeks and her name was Hafizeh) and said to her, "O Hafizeh, close thine eyes and tune thy lute and sing to us upon the days of separation." She answered him with "Hearkening and obedience" and taking the lute, tuned its strings and cried out from her head,[644] in a plaintive voice, and sang the following verses:

O friends, the tears flow ever, in mockery of my pain; My heart is sick for sev'rance and love-longing in vain.
All wasted is my body and bowels tortured sore; Love's fire on me still waxeth, mine eyes with tears still rain.
Whenas the fire of passion flamed in my breast, with tears, Upon the day of wailing, to quench it I was fain.
Desire hath left me wasted, afflicted, sore afraid, For the spy knows the secret whereof I do complain.
When I recall the season of love-delight with them, The sweet of sleep forsakes me, my body wastes amain.
Those who our parting plotted our sev'rance still delights; The spies, for fearful prudence, their wish of us attain.
I fear me for my body from sickness and unrest, Lest of the fear of sev'rance it be betrayed and slain.

When Hafizeh had made an end of her song, El Abbas said to her, "Well done! Indeed, thou quickenest hearts from sorrows." Then he called another damsel of the daughters of the Medes, by name Merjaneh, and said to her, "O Merjaneh, sing to me upon the days of separation." "Hearkening and obedience," answered she and improvsing, sang the following verses:

"Fair patience practise, for thereon still followeth content." So runs the rede 'mongst all that dwell in city or in tent.
How oft of dole have I made moan for love and longing pain, What while my body for desire in mortal peril went!
How oft I've waked, how many a cup of sorrow have I drained, Watching the stars of night go by, for sleepless languishment!

It had sufficed me, had thy grace with verses come to me; My expectation still on thee in the foredawns was bent.

Then was my heart by that which caused my agitation seared, And from mine eyelids still the tears poured down without relent.

Yea, nevermore I ceased from that wherewith I stricken was; My night with wakefulness was filled, my heart with dreariment.

But now hath Allah from my heart blotted the love of thee, After for constancy I'd grown a name of wonderment.

Hence on the morrow forth I fare and leave your land behind; So take your leave of us nor fear mishap or ill event.

Whenas in body ye from us are far removed, would God I knew who shall to us himself with news of you present!

And who can tell if ever house shall us together bring In union of life serene and undisturbed content?

When Merjaneh had made an end of her song, the prince said to her, "Well done, O damsel! Indeed, thou sayest a thing that had occurred to my mind and my tongue was like to speak it." Then he signed to the fourth damsel, who was a Cairene, by name Sitt el Husn, and bade her tune her lute and sing to him upon the [same] subject. So she tuned her lute and sang the following verses:

Fair patience use, for ease still followeth after stress And all things have their time and ordinance no less.

Though Fortune whiles to thee belike may be unjust, Her seasons change and man's excused if he transgress.

In her revolving scheme, to bitter sweetness still Succeeds and things become straight, after crookedness.

Thine honour, therefore, guard and eke thy secret keep, Nor save to one free-born and true thy case confess.

The Lord's alternatives are these, wherewith He's wont The needy wretch to ply and those in sore duresse.

When El Abbas heard her verses, they pleased him and he said to her, "Well done, O Sitt el Husn! Indeed, thou hast done away trouble from my heart and [banished] the things that had occurred to my mind." Then he heaved a sigh and signing to the fifth damsel, who was from the land of the Persians and whose name was Merziyeh (now she was the fairest of them all and the sweetest of speech and she was like unto a splendid star, endowed with beauty and loveliness and brightness and perfection and justness of shape and symmetry and had a face like the new moon and eyes as they were gazelle's eyes) and said to her, "O Merziyeh, come forward and tune thy lute and sing to us on the [same] subject, for indeed we are resolved upon departure to the land of Yemen." Now this damsel had met many kings and had consorted with the great; so she tuned her lute and sang the following verses:

May the place of my session ne'er lack thee I Oh, why, My heart's love, hast thou saddened my mind and mine eye?[645]
By thy ransom,[646] who dwellest alone in my heart, In despair for the loss of the loved one am I.
So, by Allah, O richest of all men in charms, Vouchsafe to a lover, who's bankrupt well-nigh
Of patience, thy whilom endearments again, That I never to any divulged, nor deny
The approof of my lord, so my stress and unease I may ban and mine enemies' malice defy,
Thine approof which shall clothe me in noblest attire And my rank in the eyes of the people raise high.

When she had made an end of her song, all who were in the assembly wept for the daintiness of her speech and the sweetness of her voice and El Abbas said to her, "Well done, O Merziyeh I Indeed, thou confoundest the wits with the goodliness of thy verses and the elegance o⁼ thy speech." All this while Shefikeh abode gazing upon her, and when she beheld El Abbas his slave-girls and considered the goodliness of their apparel and the nimbleness of their wits and the elegance of their speech, her reason was confounded. Then she sought leave of El Abbas and returning to her mistress Mariyeh, without letter or answer, acquainted her with his case and that wherein he was of puissance and delight and majesty and venerance and loftiness of rank. Moreover, she told her what she had seen of the slave-girls and their circumstance and that which they had said and how they had made El Abbas desireful of returning to his own country by the recitation of verses to the sound of the strings.

When the princess heard this her slave-girl's report, she wept and lamented and was like to depart the world. Then she clave to her pillow and said, "O Shefikeh, I will instruct thee of somewhat that is not hidden from God the Most High, and it is that thou watch over me till God the Most High decree the accomplishment of His commandment, and when my days are ended, take thou the necklace and the mantle that El Abbas gave me and return them to him. Indeed, I deem not he will live after me, and if God the Most High decree against him and his days come to an end, do thou give one charge to shroud us and bury us both in one grave."

Then her case changed and her colour paled; and when Shefikeh saw her mistress in this plight, she repaired to her mother and told her that the lady Mariyeh refused meat and drink. "Since when hath this befallen her?" asked the queen, and Shefikeh answered, "Since yesterday;" whereat the queen was confounded and betaking herself to her daughter, that she might enquire into her case, found her as one dead. So she sat down at her head and Mariyeh opened her eyes and seeing her mother sitting by her, sat up for shamefastness before her. The queen questioned her of her case and she said, "I entered the bath and it stupefied me and weakened me and left an exceeding pain in my head; but I trust in God the Most High that it will cease."

When her mother went out from her, Mariyeh fell to chiding the damsel for that which she had done and said to her, "Verily, death were leifer to me than this; so look thou discover not my affair to any and I charge thee return not to the like of this fashion." Then she swooned away and lay awhile without life, and when she came to herself, she saw Shefikeh weeping over her; whereupon she took the necklace from her neck and the mantle from her body and said to the damsel, "Lay them in a napkin of damask and carry them to El Abbas and acquaint him with that wherein I am for the persistence of estrangement and the effects of forbiddance." So Shefikeh took them and carried them to El Abbas, whom she found in act to depart, for that he was about to take horse for Yemen. She went in to him and gave him the napkin and that which was therein, and when he opened it and saw what it contained, to wit, the mantle and the necklace, his vexation was excessive and his eyes were distorted, [so that the whites thereof appeared] and his rage was manifest in them.

When Shefikeh saw that which betided him, she came forward and said to him, "O bountiful lord, indeed my mistress returneth not the mantle and the necklace despitefully; but she is about to depart the world and thou hast the best right to them." "And what is the cause of this?" asked he. Quoth Shefikeh, "Thou knowest. By Allah, never among the Arabs nor the barbarians nor among the sons of the kings saw I a harder of heart than thou! Is it a light matter to thee that thou troublest Mariyeh's life and causest her mourn for herself and depart the world on acccunt of[647] thy youth? Indeed, thou wast the cause of her acquaintance with thee and now she departeth the world on thine account, she whose like God the Most High hath not created among the daughters of the kings."

When El Abbas heard these words from the damsel, his heart irked him for Mariyeh and her case was grievous to him; so he said to Shefikeh, "Canst thou avail to bring me in company with her, so haply I may discover her affair and allay that which aileth her?" "Yes," answered the damsel, "I can do that, and thine will be the bounty and the favour." So he arose and followed her, and she forewent him, till they came to the palace. Then she [opened and] locked behind them four-and-twenty doors and made them fast with bolts; and when he came to Mariyeh, he found her as she were the setting sun, cast down upon a rug of Taifi leather,[648] among cushions stuffed with ostrich down, and not a limb of her quivered. When her maid saw her in this plight, she offered to cry out; but El Abbas said to her, "Do it not, but have patience till we discover her affair; and if God the Most High have decreed the ending of her days, wait till thou have opened the doors to me and I have gone forth. Then do what seemeth good to thee."

So saying, he went up to the princess and laying his hand upon her heart, found it fluttering like a doveling and the life yet clinging to[649] her bosom. So he laid his hand upon her cheek, whereupon she opened her eyes and beckoning to her maid, signed to her, as who should say, "Who is this that treadeth my carpet and transgresseth against me?"[650] "O my lady," answered Shefikeh, "this is Prince El Abbas, for whose sake thou departest the world." When Mariyeh heard speak of El Abbas, she raised her hand from under the coverlet and laying it upon his neck, inhaled his odour awhile. Then she sat up and her colour returned to her and they sat talking till a third part of the night was past.

Presently, the princess turned to her maid and bade her fetch them somewhat of food and sweetmeats and dessert and fruits. So Shefikeh brought what she desired and they ate and drank [and abode on this wise] without lewdness, till the night departed and the day came. Then said El Abbas, "Indeed, the day is come. Shall I go to my father and bid him go to thy father and seek thee of him in marriage for me, in accordance with the Book of God the Most High and the Institutes of His Apostle (whom may He bless and keep!) so we may not enter into transgression?" And Mariyeh answered, saying, "By Allah, it is well counselled of thee!" So he went away to his lodging and nought befell between them; and when the day lightened, she improvised and recited the following verses:

O friends, the East wind waxes, the morning draweth near; A plaintive voice[651] bespeaks me and I rejoice to hear.
Up, to our comrade's convent, that we may visit him And drink of wine more subtle than dust;[652] our trusty fere
Hath spent thereon his substance, withouten stint; indeed, In his own cloak he wrapped it, he tendered it so dear.[653]
Whenas its jar was opened, the singers prostrate fell In worship of its brightness, it shone so wonder-clear.
The priests from all the convent came flocking onto it: With cries of joy and welcome their voices they did rear.
We spent the night in passing the cup, my mates and I, Till in the Eastward heaven the day-star did appear.
No sin is there in drinking of wine, for it affords All that's foretold[654] of union and love and happy cheer.
O morn, our loves that sunder'st, a sweet and easeful life Thou dost for me prohibit, with thy regard austere.
Be gracious, so our gladness may be fulfilled with wine And we of our beloved have easance, without fear.
The best of all religions your love is, for in you Are love and life made easeful, untroubled and sincere.

Meanwhile, El Abbas betook himself to his father's camp, which was pitched in the Green Meadow, by the side of the Tigris, and none might make his way between the tents, for the much interlacement of the tent-ropes. When the prince reached the first of the tents, the guards and servants came out to meet him from all sides and escorted him till he drew near the sitting-place of his father, who knew of his coming. So he issued forth of his pavilion and coming to meet his son, kissed him and made much of him. Then they returned together to the royal pavilion and when they had seated themselves and the guards had taken up their station in attendance on them, the king said to El Abbas, "O my son, make ready thine affair, so we may go to our own land, for that the folk in our absence are become as they were sheep without a shepherd." El Abbas looked at his father and wept till he swooned away, and when he recovered from his swoon, he improvised and recited the following verses:

I clipped her[655] in mine arms and straight grew drunken with the scent Of a fresh branch that had been reared in affluence and content.

'Twas not of wine that I had drunk; her mouth's sweet honeyed dews It was intoxicated me with bliss and ravishment.

Upon the table of her cheek beauty hath writ, "Alack, Her charms! 'Twere well thou refuge sought'st with God incontinent."[656]

Since thou hast looked on her, mine eye, be easy, for by God Nor mote nor ailment needst thou fear nor evil accident.

Beauty her appanage is grown in its entirety, And for this cause all hearts must bow to her arbitrament.

If with her cheek and lustre thou thyself adorn,[657] thou'lt find But chrysolites and gold, with nought of baser metal blent.

When love-longing for her sweet sake I took upon myself, The railers flocked to me anon, on blame and chiding bent;

But on no wise was I affrayed nor turned from love of her; So let the railer rave of her henceforth his heart's content.

By God, forgetfulness of her shall never cross my mind, What while I wear the bonds of life nor when of death they're rent

An if I live, in love of her I'll live, and if I die Of love and longing for her sight, O rare! O excellent!

When El Abbas had made an end of his verses, his father said to him, "I seek refuge for thee with God, O my son! Hast thou any want unto which thou availest not, so I may endeavour for thee therein and lavish my treasures in quest thereof?" "O father mine," answered El Abbas, "I have, indeed, an urgent want, on account whereof I came forth of my native land and left my people and my home and exposed myself to perils and stresses and became an exile from my country, and I trust in God that it may be accomplished by thine august endeavour." "And what is thy want?" asked the king. Quoth El Abbas, "I would have thee go and demand me in marriage Mariyeh, daughter of the King of Baghdad, for that my heart is distraught with love of her." And he recounted to his father his story from first to last.

When the king heard this from his son, he rose to his feet and calling for his charger of state, took horse with four-and-twenty amirs of the chief officers of his empire. Then he betook himself to the palace of the King of Baghdad, who, when he saw him coming, bade his chamberlains open the doors to him and going down himself to meet him, received him with all worship and hospitality and entreated him with the utmost honour.

Moreover, he carried him [and his suite] into the palace and causing make ready for them carpets and cushions, sat down upon a chair of gold, with traverses of juniper- wood, set with pearls and jewels. Then he bade bring sweetmeats and confections and odoriferous flowers and commanded to slaughter four-and-twenty head of sheep and the like of oxen and make ready geese and fowls, stuffed and roasted, and pigeons and spread the tables; nor was it long before the meats were set on in dishes of gold and silver. So they ate till they had enough and when they had eaten their fill, the tables were removed and the wine-service set on and the cups and flagons ranged in order, whilst the mamelukes and the fair slave- girls sat down, with girdles of gold about their middles, inlaid with all manner pearls and diamonds and emeralds and rubies and other jewels. Moreover, the king bade fetch the musicians; so there presented themselves before him a score of damsels, with lutes and psalteries and rebecks, and smote upon instruments of music, on such wise that they moved the assembly to delight.

Then said El Aziz to the King of Baghdad, "I would fain speak a word to thee; but do thou not exclude from us those who are present. If thou consent unto my wish, that which is ours shall be thine and that which is incumbent on thee shall be incumbent on us,[658] and we will be to thee a mighty aid against all enemies and opposites." Quoth Ins ben Cais, "Say what thou wilt, O King, for indeed thou excellest in speech and attainest [the mark] in that which them sayest" So El Aziz said to him," I desire that thou give thy daughter Mariyeh in marriage to my son El Abbas, for thou knowest that wherewithal he is gifted of beauty and loveliness and brightness and perfection and how he beareth himself in the frequentation of the valiant and his constancy in the stead of smiting and thrusting." "By Allah, O king," answered Ins ben Cais, "of my love for Mariyeh, I have appointed her disposal to be in her own hand; wherefore, whomsoever she chooseth of the folk, I will marry her to him."

Then he arose and going in to his daughter, found her mother with her; so he set out to them the case and Mariyeh said, "O father mine, my wish is subject unto[659] thy commandment and my will ensueth thy will; so whatsoever thou choosest, I am still obedient unto thee and under thy dominion." Therewithal the King knew that Mariyeh inclined unto El Abbas; so he returned forthright to King El Aziz and said to him, "May God amend the King! Verily, the occasion is accomplished and there is no opposition unto that which thou commandest" Quoth El Aziz, "By God's leave are occasions accomplished. How deemest thou, O King, of fetching El Abbas and drawing up the contract of marriage between Mariyeh and him?" And Ins ben Cais answered, saying, "Thine be it to decide."

So El Aziz sent after his son and acquainted him with that which had passed; whereupon El Abbas called for four-and-twenty males and half a score horses [and as many camels] and loaded the mules with pieces of silk and rags of leather and boxes of camphor and musk and the camels [and horses] with chests of gold and silver. Moreover, he took the richest of the stuffs and wrapping them in pieces of gold-striped silk, laid them on the heads of porters, and they fared on with the treasures till they reached the King of Baghdad's palace, whereupon all who were present dismounted in honour of El Abbas and escorting him to the presence of King Ins ben Cais, displayed unto the latter all that they had with them of things of price. The king bade carry all this into the harem and sent for the Cadis and the witnesses, who drew up the contract and married Mariyeh to Prince El Abbas, whereupon the latter commanded to [slaughter] a thousand head of sheep and five hundred buffaloes. So they made the bride-feast and bade thereto all the tribes of the Arabs, Bedouins and townsfolk, and the tables abode spread for the space of ten days.

Then El Abbas went in to Mariyeh in a happy and praiseworthy hour[660] and found her an unpierced pearl and a goodly filly that had never been mounted; wherefore he rejoiced and was glad and made merry, and care and sorrow ceased from him and his life was pleasant and trouble departed and he abode with her in the gladsomest of case and in the most easeful of life, till seven days were past, when King El Aziz determined to set out and return to his kingdom and bade his son seek leave of his father-in-law to depart with his wife to his own country. [So El Abbas bespoke King Ins of this] and he granted him the leave he sought; whereupon he chose out a red camel, taller[661] than the [other] camels, and mounting Mariyeh in a litter thereon, loaded it with apparel and ornaments.

Then they spread the ensigns and the standards, whilst the drums beat and the trumpets sounded, and set out upon the homeward journey. The King of Baghdad rode forth with them and brought them three days' journey on their way, after which he took leave of them and returned with his troops to Baghdad. As for King El Aziz and his son, they fared on night and day and gave not over going till there abode but three days' journey between them and Yemen, when they despatched three men of the couriers to the prince's mother [to acquaint her with their return], safe and laden with spoil, bringing with them Mariyeh, the king's daughter of Baghdad. When the queen-mother heard this, her wit fled for joy and she adorned El Abbas his slave-girls after the goodliest fashion. Now he had ten slave-girls, as they were moons, whereof his father had carried five with him to Baghdad, as hath aforetime been set out, and other five abode with his mother. When the dromedary-posts[662] came, they were certified of the approach of El Abbas, and when the sun rose and their standards appeared, the prince's mother came out to meet her son; nor was there great or small, old man or infant, but went forth that day to meet the king.

The drums of glad tidings beat and they entered in the utmost of worship and magnificence. Moreover, the tribes heard of them and the people of the towns and brought them the richest of presents and the costliest of rarities and the prince's mother rejoiced with an exceeding joy. Then they slaughtered beasts and made mighty bride-feasts to the people and kindled fires, that it might be visible afar to townsman [and Bedouin] that this was the house of the guest-meal and the wedding, festival, to the intent that, if any passed them by, [without partaking of their hospitality], it should be of his own fault[663] So the folk came to them from all parts and quarters and on this wise they abode days and months.

Then the prince's mother bade fetch the five slave-girls to that assembly; whereupon they came and the ten damsels foregathered. The queen seated five of them on her son's right hand and other five on his left and the folk assembled about them. Then she bade the five who had remained with her speak forth somewhat of verse, so they might entertain therewith the assembly and that El Abbas might rejoice therein. Now she had clad them in the richest of raiment and adorned them with trinkets and ornaments and wroughten work of gold and silver and collars of gold, set with pearls and jewels. So they came forward, with harps and lutes and psalteries and recorders and other instruments of music before them, and one of them, a damsel who came from the land of China and whose name was Baoutheh, advanced and tightened the strings of her lute. Then she cried out from the top of her head[664] and improvising, sang the following verses:

Unto its pristine lustre your land returned and more, Whenas ye came, dispelling the gloom that whiles it wore.

Our stead, that late was desert, grew green and eke our trees, That barren were, grew loaded with ripened fruits galore.

Yea, to the earth that languished for lack of rain, the clouds Were bounteous; so it flourished and plenteous harvests bore;

And troubles, too, forsook us, who tears like dragons' blood, O lordings, for your absence had wept at every pore.

Indeed, your long estrangement hath caused my bowels yearn. Would God I were a servant in waiting at your door!

When she had made an end of her song, all who were present were moved to delight and El Abbas rejoiced in this. Then he bade the second damsel sing somewhat on the like subject. So she came forward and tuning the strings of her harp, which was of balass ruby,[665] warbled a plaintive air and improvising, sang the following verses;

The absent ones' harbinger came us unto With tidings of those who[666] had caused us to rue.

"My soul be thy ransom,"quoth I,"for thy grace! Indeed, to the oath that thou swor'st thou wast true."

On the dear nights of union, in you was our joy, But afflicted were we since ye bade us adieu.

You swore you'd be faithful to us and our love, And true to your oath and your troth-plight were you;

And I to you swore that a lover I was; God forbid that with treason mine oath I ensue!

Yea, "Welcome! Fair welcome to those who draw near!' I called out aloud, as to meet you I flew.

The dwellings, indeed, one and all, I adorned, Bewildered and dazed with delight at your view;

For death in your absence to us was decreed; But, when ye came back, we were quickened anew.

When she had made an end of her verses, El Abbas bade the third damsel, who came from Samarcand of the Persians and whose name was Rummaneh, sing, and she answered with "Hearkening and obedience." Then she took the psaltery and crying out from the midst of her bead[667] improvised and sang the following verses:

My watering lips, that cull the rose of thy soft cheek. declare My basil,[668] lily mine, to be the myrtles of thy hair.

Sandhill[669] and down[670] betwixt there blooms a yellow willow-flower,[671] Pomegranate-blossoms[672] and for fruits pomegranates[673] that doth bear.

His eyelids' sorcery from mine eyes hath banished sleep; since he From me departed, nought see I except a drowsy fair.[674]

He shot me with the shafts of looks launched from an eyebrow's[675] bow; A chamberlain[676] betwixt his eyes hath driven me to despair.

My heart belike shall his infect with softness, even as me His body with disease infects, of its seductive air.

Yet, if with him forgotten be the troth-plight of our loves, I have a king who of his grace will not forget me e'er.

His sides the tamarisk's slenderness deride, so lithe they are, Whence for conceit in his own charms still drunken doth he fare.

Whenas he runs, his feet still show like wings,[677] and for the wind When was a rider found, except King Solomon it were?[678]

Therewithal El Abbas smiled and her verses pleased him. Then he bade the fourth damsel come forward and sing. Now she was from the land of Morocco and her name was Belekhsha. So she came forward and taking the lute and the psaltery, tightened the strings thereof and smote thereon in many modes; then returned to the first mode and improvising, sang the following verses:

When in the sitting-chamber we for merry-making sate, With thine eyes' radiance the place thou didst illuminate

And pliedst us with cups of wine, whilst from the necklace pearls[679] A strange intoxicating bliss withal did circulate,

Whose subtleness might well infect the understanding folk; And secrets didst thou, in thy cheer, to us communicate.

Whenas we saw the cup, forthright we signed to past it round And sun and moon unto our eyes shone sparkling from it straight.

The curtain of delight, perforce, we've lifted through the friend,[680] For tidings of great joy, indeed, there came to us of late.

The camel-leader singing came with the belov'd; our wish Accomplished was and we were quit of all the railers' prate.

When clear'd my sky was by the sweet of our foregathering And not a helper there remained to disuniting Fate,

I shut myself up with my love; no spy betwixt us was; We feared no enemies' despite, no envious neighbour's hate.

Life with our loves was grown serene, estrangement was at end: Our dear ones all delight of love vouchsafed to us elate,

Saying, "Thy fill of union take; no spy is there on us, Whom we should fear, nor yet reproach our gladness may abate."
Our loves are joined and cruelty at last is done away; Ay, and the cup of love-delight 'twixt us doth circulate.
Upon yon be the peace of God! May all prosperity, For what's decreed of years and lives, upon you ever wait!

When Belekhsha had made an end of her verses, all present were moved to delight and El Abbas said to her, "Well done, O damsel!" Then he bade the fifth damsel come forward and sing. Now she was from the land of Syria and her name was Rihaneh; she was surpassing of voice and when she appeared in an assembly, all eyes were fixed upon her. So she came forward and taking the rebeck (for that she was used to play upon [all manner] instruments) improvised and sang the following verses:

Your coming to-me-ward, indeed, with "Welcome! fair welcome!" I hail. Your sight to me gladness doth bring and banisheth sorrow and bale;
For love with your presence grows sweet, untroubled and life is serene And the star of our fortune burns bright, that clouds in your absence did veil.
Yea, by Allah, my longing for you ne'er waneth nor passetb away; For your like among creatures is rare and sought for in mountain and vale.
Ask mine eyes whether slumber hath lit on their lids since the hour of your loss Or if aye on a lover they've looked. Nay, an ye believe not their tale,
My heart, since the leave-taking day afflicted, will tell of my case, And my body, for love and desire grown wasted and feeble and frail.
Could they who reproach me but see my sufferings, their hearts would relent; They'd marvel, indeed, at my case and the loss of my loved ones bewail.
Yea, they'd join me in pouring forth tears and help me my woes to lament, And like unto me they'd become all wasted and tortured and pale.
How long did the heart for thy love that languished with longing endure A burden of passion, 'neath which e'en mountains might totter and fail!
By Allah, what sorrows and woes to my soul for thy sake were decreed! My heart is grown hoar, ere eld's snows have left on my tresses their trail.
The fires in my vitals that rage if I did but discover to view, Their ardour the world to consume, from the East to the West, might avail.
But now unto me of my loves accomplished are joyance and cheer And those whom I cherish my soul with the wine of contentment regale.
Our Lord, after sev'rance, with them hath conjoined us, for he who doth good Shall ne'er disappointed abide and kindnesses kindness entail.

When King El Aziz heard the damsel's song, her speech and her verses pleased him and he said to El Abbas, "O my son, verily, these damsels are weary with long versifying, and indeed they make us yearn after the dwellings and the homesteads with the goodliness of their songs. Indeed, these five have adorned our assembly with the excellence of their melodies and have done well in that which they have said before those who are present; wherefore we counsel thee to enfranchise them for the love of God the Most High." Quoth El Abbas, "There is no commandment but thy commandment;" and he enfranchised the ten damsels in the assembly; whereupon they kissed the hands of the king and his son and prostrated themselves in thanksgiving to God the Most High. Then they put off that which was upon them of ornaments and laying aside the lutes [and other] instruments of music, clave to their houses, veiled, and went not forth.[681]

As for King El Aziz, he lived after this seven years and was admitted to the mercy of God the Most High; whereupon his son El Abbas carried him forth to burial on such wise as beseemeth unto kings and let make recitations and readings of the Koran, in whole or in part, over his tomb. He kept up the mourning for his father a full-told month, at the end of which time he sat down on the throne of the kingship and judged and did justice and distributed silver and gold. Moreover, he loosed all who were in the prisons and abolished grievances and customs dues and did the oppressed justice of the oppressor; wherefore the people prayed for him and loved him and invoked on him endurance of glory and kingship and length of continuance [on life] and eternity of prosperity and happiness. Moreover, the troops submitted to him and the hosts from all parts of the kingdom, and there came to him presents from all the lands. The kings obeyed him and many were his troops and his grandees, and his subjects lived with him the most easeful and prosperous of lives.

Meanwhile, he ceased not, he and his beloved, Queen Mariyeh, in the most delightsome of life and the pleasantest thereof, and he was vouchsafed by her children; and indeed there befell friendship and love between them and the longer their companionship was prolonged, the more their love waxed, so that they became unable to endure from each other a single hour, save the time of his going forth to the Divan, when he would return to her in the utterest that might be of longing. Aud on this wise they abode in all solace and delight of life, till there came to them the Destroyer of Delights and the Sunderer of Companies. So extolled be the perfection of Him whose kingdom endureth for ever, who is never heedless neither dieth nor sleepeth! This is all that hath come down to us of their story, and so peace [be on you!]

SHEHRZAD AND SHEHRIYAR[682]

King Shehriyar marvelled [at this story[683]] and said "By Allah, verily, injustice slayeth its folk!"[684] And he was edified by that wherewith Shehrzad bespoke him and sought help of God the Most High. Then said he to her, "Tell me another of thy stories, O Shehrzad; let it be a pleasant one and this shall be the completion of the story-telling." "With all my heart," answered Shehrzad. "It hath reached me, O august King, that a man once said to his fellows, 'I will set forth to you a means[685] of security[686] against vexation.[687] A friend of mine once related to me and said, "We attained [whiles] to security[688] against vexation,[689] and the origin of it was other than this; to wit, it was as follows.[690]

THE TWO KINGS AND THE VIZIER'S DAUGHTERS

[Aforetime] I journeyed in [many] lands and climes and towns and visited the great cities and traversed the ways and [exposed myself to] dangers and hardships. Towards the last of my life, I entered a city [of the cities of China],[691] wherein was a king of the Chosroes and the Tubbas[692] and the Caesars.[693] Now that city had been peopled with its inhabitants by means of justice and equitable dealing; but its [then] king was a tyrant, who despoiled souls and [did away] lives; there was no wanning oneself at his fire,[694] for that indeed he oppressed the true believers and wasted the lands. Now he had a younger brother, who was [king] in Samarcand of the Persians, and the two kings abode a while of time, each in his own city and place, till they yearned unto each other and the elder king despatched his vizier in quest of his younger brother.

When the vizier came to the King of Samarcand [and acquainted him with his errand], he submitted himself to the commandment [of his brother and made answer] with 'Hearkening and obedience.' Then he equipped himself and made ready for the journey and brought forth his tents and pavilions. A while after midnight, he went in to his wife, that he might take leave of her, and found with her a strange man, sleeping with her in one bed. So he slew them both and dragging them out by the feet, cast them away and set forth incontinent on his journey. When he came to his brother's court, the latter rejoiced in him with an exceeding joy and lodged him in the pavilion of entertainment, [to wit, the guest-house,] beside his own palace. Now this pavilion overlooked a garden belonging to the elder king and there the younger brother abode with him some days. Then he called to mind that which his wife had done with him and remembered him of her slaughter and bethought him how he was a king, yet was not exempt from the vicissitudes of fortune; and this wrought upon him with an exceeding despite, so that it caused him abstain from meat and drink, or, if he ate anything, it profited him not.

When his brother saw him on this wise, he doubted not but that this had betided him by reason of severance from his people and family and said to him, 'Come, let us go forth a-hunting.' But he refused to go with him; so the elder brother went forth to the chase, whilst the younger abode in the pavilion aforesaid. As he was diverting himself by looking out upon the garden from the window of the palace, behold, he saw his brother's wife and with her ten black slaves and as many slave-girls. Each slave laid hold of a damsel [and swived her] and another slave [came forth and] did the like with the queen; and when they had done their occasions, they all returned whence they came. Therewithal there betided the King of Samarcand exceeding wonder and solacement and he was made whole of his malady, little by little.

After a few days, his brother returned and finding him healed of his sickness, said to him, 'Tell me, O my brother, what was the cause of thy sickness and thy pallor, and what is the cause of the return of health to thee and of rosiness to thy face after this?' So he acquainted him with the whole case and this was grievous to him; but they concealed their affair and agreed to leave the kingship and fare forth pilgrim-wise, wandering at a venture, for they deemed that there had befallen none the like of this which had befallen them. [So they went forth and wandered on at hazard] and as they journeyed, they saw by the way a woman imprisoned in seven chests, whereon were five locks, and sunken in the midst of the salt sea, under the guardianship of an Afrit; yet for all this that woman issued forth of the sea and opened those locks and coming forth of those chests, did what she would with the two brothers, after she had circumvented the Afrit.

When the two kings saw that woman's fashion and how she circumvented the Afrit, who had lodged her at the bottom of the sea, they turned back to their kingdoms and the younger betook himself to Samarcand, whilst the elder returned to China and established unto himself a custom in the slaughter of women, to wit, his vizier used to bring him a girl every night, with whom he lay that night, and when he arose in the morning, he gave her to the vizier and bade him put her to death. On this wise he abode a great while, whilst the people murmured and the creatures [of God] were destroyed and the commons cried out by reason of that grievous affair whereinto they were fallen and feared the wrath of God the Most High, dreading lest He should destroy them by means of this. Still the king persisted in that fashion and in that his blameworthy intent of the killing of women and the despoilment of the curtained ones,[695] wherefore the girls sought succour of God the Most High and complained to Him of the tyranny of the king and of his oppressive dealing with them.

Now the king's vizier had two daughters, own sisters, the elder of whom had read books and made herself mistress of [all] sciences and studied the writings of the sages and the histories of the boon-companions,[696] and she was possessed of abundant wit and knowledge galore and surpassing apprehension. She heard that which the folk suffered from the king and his despiteous usage of their children; whereupon compassion gat hold upon her for them and jealousy and she besought God the Most High that He would bring the king to renounce that his heresy,[697] and God answered her prayer. Then she took counsel with her younger sister and said to her, 'I mean to contrive somewhat for the liberation of the people's children; and it is that I will go up to the king [and offer myself to him], and when I come to his presence, I will seek thee. When thou comest in to me and the king hath done his occasion [of me], do thou say to me, 'O my sister, let me hear and let the king hear a story of thy goodly stories, wherewithal we may beguile the waking hours of our night, till we take leave of each other.' 'It is well,' answered the other. 'Surely this contrivance will deter the king from his heresy and thou shalt be requited with exceeding favour and abounding recompense in the world to come, for that indeed thou adventurest thyself and wilt either perish or attain to thy desire.'

So she did this and fair fortune aided her and the Divine favour was vouchsafed unto her and she discovered her intent to her father, who forbade her therefrom, fearing her slaughter. However, she repeated her speech to him a second and a third time, but he consented not. Then he cited unto her a parable, that should deter her, and she cited him a parable in answer to his, and the talk was prolonged between them and the adducing of instances, till her father saw that he availed not to turn her from her purpose and she said to him, 'Needs must I marry the king, so haply I may be a sacrifice for the children of the Muslims; either I shall turn him from this his heresy or I shall die.' When the vizier despaired of dissuading her, he went up to the king and acquainted him with the case, saying, 'I have a daughter and she desireth to give herself to the king.' Quoth the king, 'How can thy soul consent unto this, seeing that thou knowest I lie but one night with a girl and when I arise on the morrow, I put her to death, and it is thou who slayest her, and thou hast done this again and again?' 'Know, O king,' answered the vizier, 'that I have set forth all this to her, yet consented she not unto aught, but needs must she have thy company and still chooseth to come to thee and present herself before thee, notwithstanding that I have cited to her the sayings of the sages; but she hath answered me to the contrary thereof with more than that which I said to her.' And the king said, 'Bring her to me this night and to-morrow morning come thou and take her and put her to death; and by Allah, an thou slay her not, I will slay thee and her also!'

The vizier obeyed the king's commandment and going out from before him, [returned to his own house. When it was night, he took his elder daughter and carried her up to the king; and when she came into his presence,] she wept; whereupon quoth he to her, 'What causeth thee weep? Indeed, it was thou who willedst this.' And she answered, saying, 'I weep not but for longing after my little sister; for that, since we grew up, I and she, I have never been parted from her till this day; so, if it please the king to send for her, that I may look on her and take my fill of her till the morning, this were bounty and kindness of the king.'

Accordingly, the king bade fetch the girl [and she came]. Then there befell that which befell of his foregathering with the elder sister, and when he went up to his couch, that he might sleep, the younger sister said to the elder, 'I conjure thee by Allah, O my sister, an thou be not asleep, tell us a story of thy goodly stories, wherewithal we may beguile the watches of our night, against morning come and parting.' 'With all my heart,' answered she and fell to relating to her, whilst the king listened. Her story was goodly and delightful, and whilst she was in the midst of telling it, the dawn broke. Now the king's heart clave to the hearing of the rest of the story; so he respited her till the morrow, and when it was the next night, she told him a story concerning the marvels of the lands and the extraordinary chances of the folk, that was yet stranger and rarer than the first. In the midst of the story, the day appeared and she was silent from the permitted speech. So he let her live till the ensuing night, so he might hear the completion of the story and after put her to death.

Meanwhile, the people of the city rejoiced and were glad and blessed the vizier's daughter, marvelling for that three days had passed and that the king had not put her to death and exulting in that, [as they deemed,] he had turned [from his purpose] and would never again burden himself with blood-guiltiness against any of the maidens of the city. Then, on the fourth night, she related to him a still more extraordinary story, and on the fifth night she told him anecdotes of kings and viziers and notables. On this wise she ceased not [to do] with him [many] days and nights, what while the king still said in himself, 'When I have heard the end of the story, I will put her to death,' and the people waxed ever in wonder and admiration.

Moreover, the folk of the provinces and cities heard of this thing, to wit, that the king had turned from his custom and from that which he had imposed upon himself and had renounced his heresy, wherefore they rejoiced and the folk returned to the capital and took up their abode therein, after they had departed thence; yea, they were constant in prayer to God the Most High that He would stablish the king in that his present case; and this," said Shehrzad, "is the end of that which my friend related to me."

"O Shehrzad," quoth Shehriyar, "finish unto us the story that thy friend told thee, for that it resembleth the story of a king whom I knew; but fain would I hear that which betided the people of this city and what they said of the affair of the king, so I may return from that wherein I was." "With all my heart," answered Shehrzad. "Know, O august king and lord of just judgment and praiseworthy excellence and exceeding prowess, that, when the folk heard that the king had put away from him his custom and returned from that which had been his wont, they rejoiced in this with an exceeding joy and offered up prayers for him. Then they talked with one another of the cause of the slaughter of the girls, and the wise said, 'They[698] are not all alike, nor are the fingers of the hand alike.'"

<h2 style="text-align:center">SHEHRZAD AND SHEHRIYAR[699]
(Conclusion)</h2>

When King Shehriyar heard this story, he came to himself and awaking from his drunkenness,[700] said, "By Allah, this story is my story and this case is my case, for that indeed I was in wrath[701] and [danger of] punishment till thou turnedst me back from this into the right way, extolled be the perfection of the Causer of causes and the Liberator of necks! Indeed, O Shehrzad," continued he, "thou hast awakened me unto many things and hast aroused me from mine ignorance."

Then said she to him, "O chief of the kings, the wise say, 'The kingship is a building, whereof the troops are the foundation,' and whenas the foundation is strong, the building endureth; wherefore it behoveth the king to strengthen the foundation, for that they say, 'Whenas the foundation is weak, the building falleth.' On like wise it behoveth the king to care for his troops and do justice among his subjects, even as the owner of the garden careth for his trees and cutteth away the weeds that have no profit in them; and so it behoveth the king to look into the affairs of his subjects and fend off oppression from them. As for thee, O king," continued Shehrzad, "it behoveth thee that thy vizier be virtuous and versed in the knowledge of the affairs of the folk and the common people; and indeed God the Most High hath named his name[702] in the history of Moses (on whom be peace!) whenas He saith, [Quoth Moses] 'And make me a vizier of my people, Aaron [my brother].[703] Could a vizier have been dispensed withal, Moses ben Imran had been worthier [than any of this dispensation].[704]

As for the vizier, the sultan discovereth unto him his affairs, private and public; and know, O king, that the similitude of thee with the people is that of the physician with the sick man; and the condition[705] of the vizier is that he be truthful in his sayings, trustworthy in all his relations, abounding in compassion for the folk and in tender solicitude over them. Indeed, it is said, O king, that good troops[706] are like the druggist; if his perfumes reach thee not, thou still smallest the sweet scent of them; and ill troops are like the black-smith; if his sparks burn thee not, thou smellest his nauseous smell. So it behoveth thee take unto thyself a virtuous vizier, a man of good counsel, even as thou takest unto thee a wife displayed before thy face, for that thou hast need of the man's righteousness for thine own amendment,[707] seeing that, if thou do righteously, the commons will do likewise, and if thou do evil, they also will do evil."

When the king heard this, drowsiness overcame him and he slept and presently awaking, called for the candles. So they were lighted and he sat down on his couch and seating Shehrzad by him, smiled in her face. She kissed the earth before him and said, "O king of the age and lord of the time and the day, extolled be the perfection of [God] the Forgiving One, the Bountiful Giver, who hath sent me unto thee, of His favour and beneficence, so I have informed thee with longing after Paradise; for that this which thou wast used to do was never done of any of the kings before thee. As for women, God the Most High [in His Holy Book] maketh mention of them, [whenas He saith, 'Verily, men who submit [themselves unto God] and women who submit] and true-believing men and true-believing women and obedient men and obedient women and soothfast men and soothfast women [and long-suffering men and long-suffering women and men who order themselves humbly and women who order themselves humbly and charitable men and charitable women and men who fast and women who fast] and men who guard their privities and women who guard their privities [and men who are constantly mindful of God and women who are constantly mindful, God hath prepared unto them forgiveness and a mighty recompense].[708]

As for that which hath befallen thee, verily, it hath befallen [many] kings before thee and their women have played them false, for all they were greater of puissance than thou, yea, and mightier of kingship and more abounding in troops. If I would, I could relate unto thee, O king, concerning the wiles of women, that whereof I could not make an end all my life long; and indeed, aforetime, in all these my nights that I have passed before thee, I have told thee [many stories and anecdotes] of the artifices of women and of their craft and perfidy; but indeed the things abound on me;[709] wherefore, if it like thee, O king, I will relate unto thee [somewhat] of that which befell kings of old time of the perfidy of their women and of the calamities which overtook them by reason of these latter." "How so?" asked the king. "Tell on." "Hearkening and obedience," answered Shehrzad. "It hath been told me, O king, that a man once related to a company and spoke as follows:

THE FAVOURITE AND HER LOVER[710]

ONE day, a day of excessive heat, as I stood at the door of my house, I saw a fair woman approaching, and with her a slave-girl carrying a parcel. They gave not over going till they came up to me, when the woman stopped and said to me, 'Hast thou a draught of water?' 'Yes,' answered I. 'Enter the vestibule, O my lady, so thou mayst drink.' Accor-dingly, she entered and I went up into the house and fetched two mugs of earthenware, perfumed with musk[711] and full of cold water. She took one of them and discovered her face, [that she might drink]; whereupon I saw that she was as the shining sun or the rising moon and said to her, 'O my lady, wilt thou not come up into the house, so thou mayst rest thyself till the air grow cool and after go away to thine own place?' Quoth she, 'Is there none with thee?' 'Indeed,' answered I, 'I am a [stranger] and a bachelor and have none belonging to me, nor is there a living soul in the house.' And she said, 'An thou be a stranger, thou art he in quest of whom I was going about.'

Then she went up into the house and put off her [walking] clothes and I found her as she were the full moon. I brought her what I had by me of meat and drink and said to her, 'O my lady, excuse me: this is that which is ready.' Quoth she, 'This is abundant kindness and indeed it is what I sought' And she ate and gave the slave-girl that which was left; after which I brought her a casting-bottle of rose-water, mingled with musk, and she washed her hands and abode with me till the season of afternoon-prayer, when she brought out of the parcel that she had with her a shirt and trousers and an upper garment[712] and a kerchief wroughten with gold and gave them to me; saying, 'Know that I am one of the favourites of the Khalif, and we are forty favourites, each one of whom hath a lover who cometh to her as often as she would have him; and none is without a lover save myself, wherefore I came forth to-day to find me a gallant and behold, I have found thee. Thou must know that the Khalif lieth each night with one of us, whilst the other nine-and-thirty favourites take their ease with the nine-and-thirty men, and I would have thee be with me on such a day, when do thou come up to the palace of the Khalif and wait for me in such a place, till a little eunuch come out to thee and say to thee a [certain] word, to wit, "Art thou Sendel?" And do thou answer, "Yes," and go with him.'

Then she took leave of me and I of her, after I had strained her to my bosom and embraced her and we had kissed awhile. So she went away and I abode expecting the appointed day, till it came, when I arose and went forth, intending for the trysting-place; but a friend of mine met me by the way [and would have me go home with him. So I accompanied him to his house] and when I came up [into his sitting-chamber] he locked the door on me and went forth to fetch what we might eat and drink. He was absent till mid-day, then till the hour of afternoon-prayer, whereat I was sore disquieted. Then he was absent till sundown, and I was like to die of chagrin and impatience; [and indeed he returned not] and I passed my night on wake, nigh upon death, for that the door was locked on me, and my soul was like to depart my body on account of the tryst.

At daybreak, my friend returned and opening the door, came in, bringing with him meat-pottage[713] and fritters and bees' honey,[714] and said to me, 'By Allah, thou must needs excuse me, for that I was with a company and they locked the door on me and have but now let me go.' But I returned him no answer. Then he set before me that which was with him and I ate a single mouthful and went out, running, so haply I might overtake that which had escaped me.[715] When I came to the palace, I saw over against it eight-and-thirty gibbets set up, whereon were eight-and-thirty men crucified, and under them eight-and-thirty concubines as they were moons. So I enquired of the reason of the crucifixion of the men and concerning the women in question, and it was said unto me, 'The men [whom thou seest] crucified the Khalif found with yonder damsels, who are his favourites.' When I heard this, I prostrated myself in thanksgiving to God and said, 'God requite thee with good, O my friend!' For that, had he not invited me [and kept me perforce in his house] that night, I had been crucified with these men, wherefore praise be to God!

Thus," continued Shehrzad, "none is safe from the calamities of fortune and the vicissitudes of time, and [in proof of this], I will relate unto thee yet another story still rarer and more extraordinary than this. Know, O King, that one said to me, 'A friend of mine, a merchant, told me the following story. Quoth he,

THE MERCHANT OF CAIRO AND THE FAVOURITE OF THE KHALIF EL MAMOUN EL HAKIM BI AMRILLAH[716]

AS I sat one day in my shop, there came up to me a fair woman, as she were the moon at its rising, and with her a slave-girl. Now I was a handsome man in my time; so the lady sat down on [the bench before] my shop and buying stuffs of me, paid down the price and went away. I questioned the girl of her and she said, "I know not her name." Quoth I, "Where is her abode?" "In heaven," answered the slave-girl; and I said, "She is presently on the earth; so when doth she ascend to heaven and where is the ladder by which she goeth up?" Quoth the girl, "She hath her lodging in a palace between two rivers,[717] to wit, the palace of El Mamoun el Hakim bi Amrillah."[718] Then said I, "I am a dead man, without recourse; "but she replied, "Have patience, for needs must she return unto thee and buy stuffs of thee yet again." "And how cometh it," asked I, "that the Commander of the Faithful trusteth her to go out?" "He loveth her with an exceeding love," answered she, "and is wrapped up in her and gain-sayeth her not."

Then the girl went away, running, after her mistress, whereupon I left the shop and set out after them, so I might see her abiding-place. I followed after them all the way, till she disappeared from mine eyes, when I returned to my place, with a heart on fire. Some days after, she came to me again and bought stuffs of me. I refused to take the price and she said, "We have no need of thy goods." Quoth I, "O my lady, accept them from me as a gift;" but she said, "[Wait] till I try thee and make proof of thee." Then she brought out of her pocket a purse and gave me therefrom a thousand dinars, saying, "Trade with this till I return to thee." So I took the purse and she went away [and returned not to me] till six months had passed by. Meanwhile, I traded with the money and sold and bought and made other thousand dinars profit [on it].

Presently, she came to me again and I said to her, "Here is thy money and I have gained [with it] other thousand dinars." Quoth she, "Keep it by thee and take these other thousand dinars. As soon as I have departed from thee, go thou to Er Rauzeh[719] and build there a goodly pavilion, and when the building thereof is accomplished, give me to know thereof." So saying, she left me and went away. As soon as she was gone, I betook myself to Er Rauzeh and addressed myself to the building of the pavilion, and when it was finished, I furnished it with the goodliest of furniture and sent to the lady to tell her that I had made an end of its building; whereupon she sent back to me, saying, "Let him meet me to-morrow at daybreak at the Zuweyleh gate and bring with him a good ass." So I got me an ass and betaking myself to the Zuweyleh gate, at the appointed time, found there a young man on horse- back, awaiting her, even as I awaited her.

As we stood, behold, up came the lady, and with her a slave-girl. When she saw the young man, she said to him, "Art thou here?" And he answered, "Yes, O my lady." Quoth she, "To-day I am bidden by this man. Wilt thou go with us?" And he replied, "Yes." Then said she, "Thou hast brought me [hither] against my will and perforce. Wilt thou go with us in any event?"[720] "Yes, yes," answered he and we fared on, [all three,] till we came to Er Rauzeh and entered the pavilion. The lady diverted herself awhile with viewing its ordinance and furniture, after which she put off her [walking-]clothes and sat down [with the young man] in the goodliest and chiefest place. Then I went forth and brought them what they should eat at the first of the day; moreover, I went out also and fetched them what they should eat at the last of the day and brought them wine and dessert and fruits and flowers. On this wise I abode in their service, standing on my feet, and she said not unto me, "Sit," nor "Take, eat" nor "Take, drink," what while she and the young man sat toying and laughing, and he fell to kissing her and pinching her and hopping about upon the ground and laughing.

They abode thus awhile and presently she said, "Up to now we have not become drunken; let me pour out." So she took the cup and gave him to drink and plied him with liquor, till he became drunken, when she took him and carried him into a closet. Then she came out, with his head in her hand, what while I stood silent, fixing not mine eyes on hers neither questioning her of this; and she said to me, "What is this?" "I know not," answered I; and she said, "Take it and cast it into the river." I obeyed her commandment and she arose and stripping herself of her clothes, took a knife and cut the dead man's body in pieces, which she laid in three baskets, and said to me, "Throw them into the river."

I did as she bade me and when I returned, she said to me, "Sit, so I may relate to thee yonder fellow's case, lest thou be affrighted at that which hath befallen him. Thou must know that I am the Khalif's favourite, nor is there any more in honour with him than I; and I am allowed six nights in each month, wherein I go down [into the city and take up my abode] with my [former] mistress, who reared me; and when I go down thus, I dispose of myself as I will. Now this young man was the son of neighbours of my mistress, when I was a virgin girl. One day, my mistress was [engaged] with the chief [officers] of the palace and I was alone in the house. When the night came on, I went up to the roof, so I might sleep there, and before I was aware, this youth came up from the street and falling upon me, knelt on my breast. He was armed with a poniard and I could not win free of him till he had done away my maidenhead by force; and this sufficed him not, but he must needs disgrace me with all the folk, for, as often as I came down from the palace, he would lie in wait for me by the way and swive me against my will and follow me whithersoever I went. This, then, is my story, and as for thee, thou pleasest me and thy patience pleaseth me and thy good faith and loyal service, and there abideth with me none dearer than thou." Then I lay with her that night and there befell what befell between us till the morning, when she gave me wealth galore and fell to coming to the pavilion six days in every month.

On this wise we abode a whole year, at the end of which time she was absent[721] from me a month's space, wherefore fire raged in my heart on her account. When it was the next month, behold, a little eunuch presented himself to me and said, "I am a messenger to thee from such an one," [naming my mistress], "who giveth thee to know that the Commander of the Faithful hath sentenced her to be drowned, her and those who are with her, six-and-twenty slave-girls, on such a day at Deir et Tin,[722] for that they have confessed against one another of lewdness, and she biddeth thee look how thou mayst do with her and how thou mayst contrive to deliver her, even if thou gather together all her money and spend it upon her, for that this is the time of manhood."[723] Quoth I, "I know not this woman; belike it is other than I [to whom this message is addressed]; so beware, O eunuch, lest thou cast me into stress." Quoth he, "Behold, I have told thee [that which I had to say,"] and went away, leaving me in concern [on her account].

[When the appointed day arrived], I arose and changing my clothes and favour, donned sailor's apparel; then I took with me a purse full of gold and buying good [victual for the] morning-meal, accosted a boatman [at Deir et Tin] and sat down and ate with him; after which said I to him, "Wilt thou hire me thy boat?" Quoth he, "The Commander of the Faithful hath commanded me to be here;" and he told me the story of the concubines and how the Khalif purposed to drown them that day. When I heard this from him, I brought out to him half a score dinars and discovered to him my case, whereupon quoth he to me, "O my brother, get thee empty calabashes, and when thy mistress cometh, give me to know of her and I will contrive the trick."

I kissed his hand and thanked him, and as I was walking about, [waiting,] up came the guards and eunuchs with the women, who were weeping and crying out and taking leave of one another. The eunuchs cried out to us, whereupon we came with the boat, and they said to the boatman, "Who is this?" "This is my mate," answered he, "[whom I have brought,] to help me, so one of us may keep the boat, whilst another doth your service." Then they brought out to us the women, one by one, saying, "Throw them [in] by the Island;" and we answered, "It is well." Now each of them was shackled and they had made a jar of sand fast about her neck. We did as the eunuchs bade us and ceased not to take the women, one after another, and cast them in, till they gave us my mistress and I winked to my comrade. So we took her and carried her out into mid-stream, where I gave her the empty calabashes[724] and said to her, "Wait for me at the mouth of the canal." Then we cast her in, after we had loosed the jar of sand from her neck and done off her fetters, and returned.

Now there remained one after her; so we took her and drowned her and the eunuchs went away, whilst we dropped down the river with the boat till we came to the mouth of the canal, where I saw my mistress awaiting me. So we took her up into the boat and returned to our pavilion on Er Rauzeh. Then I rewarded the boatman and he took his boat and went away; whereupon quoth she to me, "Thou art indeed a friend in need."[725] And I abode with her some days; but the shock wrought upon her so that she sickened and fell to wasting away and redoubled in languishment and weakness till she died. I mourned for her with an exceeding mourning and buried her; after which I removed all that was in the pavilion to my own house [and abandoned the former].

Now she had brought to the pavilion aforetime a little brass coffer and laid it in a place whereof I knew not; so, when the inspector of inheritances[726] came, he searched the pavilion and found the coffer, with the key in the lock. So he opened it and finding it full of jewels and jacinths and earrings and seal-rings and precious stones, such as are not found save with kings and sultans, took it, and me with it, and ceased not to put me to the question with beating and torment till I confessed to them the whole affair from beginning to end, whereupon they carried me to the Khalif and I told him all that had passed between me and her; and he said to me, "O man, depart from this city, for I acquit thee for thy valiance sake and because of thy [constancy in] keeping thy secret and thy daring in exposing thyself to death." So I arose forthright and departed his city; and this is what befell me.'"

SHEHRZAD AND SHEHRIYAR.

King Shehriyar marvelled at these things and Shehrzad said to him, "Thou marvelledst at that which befell thee on the part of women; yet hath there befallen the kings of the Chosroes before thee what was more grievous than that which befell thee, and indeed I have set forth unto thee that which betided khalifs and kings and others than they with their women, but the exposition is long and hearkening groweth tedious, and in this [that I have already told thee] is sufficiency for the man of understanding and admonishment for the wise."

Then she was silent, and when the king heard her speech and profited by that which she said, he summoned up his reasoning faculties and cleansed his heart and caused his understanding revert [to the right way] and turned [with repentance] to God the Most High and said in himself, "Since there befell the kings of the Chosroes more than that which hath befallen me, never, whilst I abide [on life], shall I cease to blame myself [for that which I did in the slaughter of the daughters of the folk]. As for this Shehrzad, her like is not found in the lands; so extolled be the perfection of Him who appointed her a means for the deliverance of His creatures from slaughter and oppression!" Then he arose from his session and kissed her head, whereat she rejoiced with an exceeding joy, she and her sister Dinarzad.

When the morning morrowed, the king went forth and sitting down on the throne of the kingship, summoned the grandees of his empire; whereupon the chamberlains and deputies and captains of the host went in to him and kissed the earth before him. He distinguished the vizier with his especial favour and bestowed on him a dress of honour and entreated him with the utmost kindness, after which he set forth briefly to his chief officers that which had betided him with Shehrzad and how he had turned from that his former usance and repented him of what he had done aforetime and purposed to take the vizier's daughter Shehrzad to wife and let draw up the contract of marriage with her.

When those who were present heard this, they kissed the earth before him and offered up prayers for him and for the damsel Shehrzad, and the vizier thanked her. Then Shehriyar made an end of the session in all weal, whereupon the folk dispersed to their dwelling-places and the news was bruited abroad that the king purposed to marry the vizier's daughter Shehrzad. Then he proceeded to make ready the wedding gear, and [when he had made an end of his preparations], he sent after his brother King Shahzeman, who came, and King Shehriyar went forth to meet him with the troops. Moreover, they decorated the city after the goodliest fashion and diffused perfumes [from the censing-vessels] and [burnt] aloes-wood and other perfumes in all the markets and thoroughfares and rubbed themselves with saffron, what while the drums beat and the flutes and hautboys sounded and it was a notable day.

When they came to the palace, King Shehriyar commanded to spread the tables with beasts roasted [whole] and sweetmeats and all manner viands and bade the crier make proclamation to the folk that they should come up to the Divan and eat and drink and that this should be a means of reconciliation between him and them. So great and small came up unto him and they abode on that wise, eating and drinking, seven days with their nights. Then the king shut himself up with his brother and acquainted him with that which had betided him with the vizier's daughter [Shehrzad] in those three years [which were past] and told him what he had heard from her of saws and parables and chronicles and pleasant traits and jests and stories and anecdotes and dialogues and histories and odes and verses; whereat King Shahzeman marvelled with the utterest of marvel and said, "Fain would I take her younger sister to wife, so we may be two own brothers to two own sisters, and they on likewise be sisters unto us; for that the calamity which befell me was the means of the discovering of that which befell thee and all this time of three years past I have taken no delight in woman, save that I lie each night with a damsel of my kingdom, and when I arise in the morning, I put her to death; but now I desire to marry thy wife's sister Dinarzad."

When King Shehriyar heard his brother's words he rejoiced with an exceeding joy and arising forthright, went in to his wife Shehrzad and gave her to know of that which his brother purposed, to wit, that he sought her sister Dinarzad in marriage; whereupon, "O king of the age, ' answered she, "we seek of him one condition, to wit, that he take up his abode with us, for that I cannot brook to be parted from my sister an hour, because we were brought up together and may not brook severance from each other. If he accept this condition, she is his handmaid." King Shehriyar returned to his brother and acquainted him with that which Shehrzad had said; and he answered, saying, "Indeed, this is what was in my mind, for that I desire nevermore to be parted from thee. As for the kingdom, God the Most High shall send unto it whom He chooseth, for that there abideth to me no desire for the kingship."

When King Shehriyar heard his brother's words, he rejoiced with an exceeding joy and said, "Verily, this is what I had wished, O my brother. So praised be God who hath brought about union between us!" Then he sent after the Cadis and learned men and captains and notables, and they married the two brothers to the two sisters. The contracts were drawn up and the two kings bestowed dresses of honour of silk and satin on those who were present, whilst the city was decorated and the festivities were renewed. The king commanded each amir and vizier and chamberlain and deputy to decorate his palace and the folk of the city rejoiced in the presage of happiness and content. Moreover, King Shehriyar bade slaughter sheep and get up kitchens and made bride-feasts and fed all comers, high and low.

Then the eunuchs went forth, that they might perfume the bath [for the use of the brides]; so they essenced it with rose-water and willow-flower-water and bladders of musk and fumigated it with Cakili[727] aloes-wood and ambergris. Then Shehrzad entered, she and her sister Dinarzad, and they cleansed their heads and clipped their hair. When they came forth of the bath, they donned raiment and ornaments, [such as were] prepared for the kings of the Chosroes; and among Shehrzad's apparel was a dress charactered with red gold and wroughten with semblants of birds and beasts. Moreover, they both encircled their necks with necklaces of jewels of price, in the like whereof Iskender[728] rejoiced not, for therein were great jewels such as amazed the wit and the eye, and the thought was bewildered at their charms, for indeed, each of them was brighter than the sun and the moon. Before them they kindled lighted flambeaux in torch-holders of gold, but their faces outshone the flambeaux, for that they had eyes sharper than drawn swords and the lashes of their eyelids ensorcelled all hearts.

Their cheeks were rosy and their necks and shapes swayed gracefully and their eyes wantoned. And the slave-girls came to meet them with instruments of music.

Then the two kings entered the bath, and when they came forth, they sat down on a couch, inlaid with pearls and jewels, whereupon the two sisters came up to them and stood before them, as they were moons, swaying gracefully from side to side in their beauty and grace. Presently they brought forward Shehrzad and displayed her, for the first dress, in a red suit; whereupon King Shehriyar rose to look upon her and the wits of all present, men and women, were confounded, for that she was even as saith of her one of her describers:

Like a sun at the end of a cane in a hill of sand, She shines in a dress of the hue of pomegranate flower.
She gives me to drink of her cheeks and her honeyed lips And quenches the worst of the fires that my heart devour.

Then they attired Dinarzad in a dress of blue brocade and she became as she were the full moon, whenas it shineth forth. So they displayed her in this, for the first dress, before King Shahzeman, who rejoiced in her and well-nigh took leave of his wits for longing and amorous desire; yea, he was distraught with love for her, whenas he saw her, for, indeed, she was as saith of her one of her describers in the following verses:

She comes in a robe the colour of ultramarine, Blue as the stainless sky, unflecked with white;
I view her with yearning eyes and she seems to me A moon of the summer, set in a winter's night.

Then they returned to Shehrzad and displayed her in the second dress. They clad her in a dress of surpassing goodliness, and veiled her face to the eyes with her hair. Moreover, they let down her side locks and she was even as saith of her one of her describers in the following verses:

Bravo for her whose loosened locks her cheeks do overcloud! She slays me with her cruelty, so fair she is and proud.
Quoth I, "Thou overcurtainest the morning with the night;" And she, "Not so; it is the moon that with the dark I shroud."

Then they displayed Dinarzad in a second and a third and a fourth dress and she came forward, as she were the rising sun, and swayed coquettishly to and fro; and indeed she was even as saith the poet of her in the following verses:

A sun of beauty she appears to all who look on her, Glorious in arch and amorous grace, with coyness beautified;
And when the sun of morning sees her visage and her smile, O'ercome. he hasteneth his face behind the clouds to hide.

Then they displayed Shehrzad in the third dress and the fourth and the fifth, and she became as she were a willow-wand or a thirsting gazelle, goodly of grace and perfect of attributes, even as saith o͞f her one in the following verses:

Like the full moon she shows upon a night of fortune fair, Slender of shape and charming all with her seductive air.
She hath an eye, whose glances pierce the hearts of all mankind, Nor can cornelian with her cheeks for ruddiness compare.
The sable torrent of her locks falls down unto her hips; Beware the serpents of her curls, I counsel thee, beware!
Indeed her glance, her sides are soft; but none the less, alas! Her heart is harder than the rock; there is no mercy there.
The starry arrows of her looks she darts above her veil; They hit and never miss the mark, though from afar they fare.

Then they returned to Dinarzad and displayed her in the fifth dress and in the sixth, which was green. Indeed, she overpassed with her loveliness the fair of the four quarters of the world and outshone, with the brightness of her countenance, the full moon at its rising; for she was even as saith of her the poet in the following verses:

A damsel made for love and decked with subtle grace; Thou'dst deem the very sun had borrowed from her face.
She came in robes of green, the likeness of the leaf That the pomegranate's flower doth in the bud encase.
"How call'st thou this thy dress?" quoth we, and she replied A word wherein the wise a lesson well might trace;
"Breaker of hearts," quoth she, "I call it, for therewith I've broken many a heart among the amorous race."

Then they displayed Shehrzad in the sixth and seventh dresses and clad her in youths' apparel, whereupon she came forward, swaying coquettishly from side to side; and indeed she ravished wits and hearts and ensorcelled with her glances [all who looked on her]. She shook her sides and wagged her hips, then put her hair on the hilt of her sword and went up to King Shehriyar, who embraced her, as the hospitable man embraces the guest, and threatened her in her ear with the taking of the sword; and indeed she was even as saith of her the poet in these verses:

Were not the darkness[729] still in gender masculine, As ofttimes is the case with she-things passing fine,
Tirewomen to the bride, who whiskers, ay, and beard Upon her face produce, they never would assign.[730]

On this wise they did with her sister Dinarzad, and when they had made an end of displaying the two brides, the king bestowed dresses of honour on all who were present and dismissed them to their own places. Then Shehrzad went in to King Shehriyar and Dinarzad to King Shahzeman and each of them solaced himself with the company of his beloved and the hearts of the folk were comforted. When the morning morrowed, the vizier came in to the two kings and kissed the ground before them; wherefore they thanked him and were bountiful to him. Then they went forth and sat down upon couches of estate, whilst all the viziers and amirs and grandees and the chief officers of the realm and the household presented themselves before them and kissed the earth. King Shehriyar ordered them dresses of honour and largesse and they offered up prayers for the abiding continuance [on life] of the king and his brother.

Then the two kings appointed their father-in-law the vizier to be viceroy in Samarcand and assigned him five of the chief amirs to accompany him, charging them attend him and do him service. The vizier kissed the earth and prayed that they might be vouchsafed length of life. Then he went in to his daughters, whilst the eunuchs and ushers walked before him, and saluted them and bade them farewell. They kissed his hands and gave him joy of the kingship and bestowed on him treasures galore. Then he took leave of them and setting out, journeyed days and nights till he came within three days' journey of Samarcand, where the townspeople met him and rejoiced in him with an exceeding joy. So he entered Samarcand and they decorated the city, and it was a notable day. He sat down on the throne of his kingship and the viziers did him homage and the grandees and amirs of Samarcand and prayed that he might be vouchsafed justice and victory and length of continuance [on life]. So he bestowed on them dresses of honour and entreated them with worship and they made him Sultan over them.

As soon as his father-in-law had departed for Samarcand, King Shehriyar summoned the grandees of his realm and made them a magnificent banquet of all manner rich meats and exquisite sweetmeats. Moreover, he bestowed on them dresses of honour and guerdoned them and divided the kingdoms between himself and his brother in their presence, whereat the folk rejoiced. Then the two kings abode, ruling each a day in turn and they accorded with each other, what while their wives continued in the love of God the Most High and in thanksgiving to Him; and the subjects and the provinces were at peace and the preachers prayed for them from the pulpits, and their report was bruited abroad and the travellers bore tidings of them [to all countries].

Moreover, King Shehriyar summoned chroniclers and copyists and bade them write all that had betided him with his wife, first and last; so they wrote this and named it "The Stories of the Thousand Nights and One Night." The book came to[731] thirty volumes and these the king laid up in his treasury. Then the two kings abode with their wives in all delight and solace of life, for that indeed God the Most High had changed their mourning into joyance; and on this wise they continued till there took them the Destroyer of Delights and Sunderer of Companies, he who maketh void the dwelling-places and peopleth the tombs, and they were translated to the mercy of God the Most High; their houses were laid waste and their palaces ruined and the kings inherited their riches.

Then there reigned after them an understanding king, who was just, keen-witted and accomplished and loved stories, especially those which chronicle the doings of kings and sultans, and he found [in the treasuries of the kings who had foregone him] these marvellous and rare and delightful stories, [written] in the thirty volumes aforesaid. So he read in them a first book and a second and a third and [so on] to the last of them, and each book pleased him more than that which forewent it, till he came to the end of them. Then he marvelled at that which he had read [therein] of stories and discourse and witty traits and anecdotes and moral instances and reminiscences and bade the folk copy them and publish them in all lands and climes; wherefore their report was bruited abroad and the people named them "The marvels and rarities of the Thousand Nights and One Night." This is all that hath come down to us of [the history of] this book, and God is All-Knowing.[732]

SINDBAD THE SAILOR AND HINDBAD THE PORTER

ON the morrow they[733] returned to their place, as of their wont, and betook themselves to eating and drinking and merry-making and sporting till the last of the day, when Sindbad bade them hearken to his relation concerning his sixth voyage, the which (quoth he) is of the most extraordinary of pleasant stories and the most startling [for that which it compriseth] of tribulations and disasters. Then said he,

THE SIXTH VOYAGE OF SINDBAD THE SAILOR

"When I returned from my fifth voyage, I gave myself up to eating and drinking and passed my time in solace and delight and forgot that which I had suffered of stresses and afflictions, nor was it long before the thought of travel again presented itself to my mind and my soul hankered after the sea. So I brought out the goods and binding up the bales, departed from Baghdad, [intending] for certain of the lands, and came to the sea-coast, where I embarked in a stout ship, in company with a number of other merchants of like mind with myself, and we [set out and] sailed till we came among certain distant islands and found ourselves in difficult and dangerous case.

[One day], as the ship was sailing along, and we unknowing where we were, behold, the captain came down [from the mast] and casting his turban from his head, fell to buffeting his face and plucking at his beard and weeping and supplicating [God for deliverance]. We asked him what ailed him, and he answered, saying, 'Know, O my masters, that the ship is fallen among shallows and drifteth upon a sand-bank of the sea. Another moment [and we shall be upon it]. If we clear the bank, [well and good]; else, we are all dead men and not one of us will be saved; wherefore pray ye to God the Most High, so haply He may deliver us from these deadly perils, or we shall lose our lives.' So saying, he mounted [the mast] and set the sail, but at that moment a contrary wind smote the ship, and it rose upon the crest of the waves and sank down again into the trough of the sea.

Now there was before us a high mountain,[734] rising [abruptly] from the sea, and the ship fell off into an eddy,[735] which bore it on till presently it struck upon the skirt[736] of the mountain and broke in sunder; whereupon the captain came down [from the mast], weeping, and said, 'God's will be done! Take leave of one another and look yourselves out graves from to-day, for we have fallen into a predicament[737] from which there is no escape, and never yet hath any been cast away here and come off alive.' So all the folk fell a-weeping and gave themselves up for lost, despairing of deliverance; friend took leave of friend and sore was the mourning and lamentation; for that hope was cut off and they were left without guide or pilot.[738] Then all who were in the ship landed on the skirt of the mountain and found themselves on a long island, whose shores were strewn with [wrecks], beyond count or reckoning, [of] ships that had been cast away [there] and whose crews had perished; and there also were dry bones and dead bodies, heaped upon one another, and goods without number and riches past count So we abode confounded, drunken, amazed, humbling ourselves [in supplication to God] and repenting us [of having exposed ourselves to the perils of travel]; but repentance availed not in that place.

In this island is a river of very sweet water, issuing from the shore of the sea and entering in at a wide cavern in the skirt of an inaccessible mountain, and the stones of the island are all limpid sparkling crystal and jacinths of price. Therein also is a spring of liquid, welling up like [molten] pitch, and when it cometh to the shore of the island, the fish swallow it, then return and cast it up, and it becometh changed from its condition and that which it was aforetime; and it is crude ambergris. Moreover, the trees of the island are all of the most precious aloes-wood, both Chinese and Comorin; but there is no way of issue from the place, for it is as an abyss midmost the sea; the steepness of its shore forbiddeth the drawing up of ships, and if any approach the mountain, they fall into the eddy aforesaid; nor is there any resource[739] in that island.

So we abode there, daily expecting death, and whoso of us had with him a day's victual ate it in five days, and after this he died; and whoso had with him a month's victual ate it in five months and died also. As for me, I had with me great plenty of victual; so I buried it in a certain place and brought it out, [little by little,] and fed on it; and we ceased not to be thus, burying one the other, till all died but myself and I abode alone, having buried the last of my companions, and but little victual remained to me. So I said in myself, 'Who will bury me in this place?' And I dug me a grave and abode in expectation of death, for that I was in a state of exhaustion. Then, of the excess of my repentance, I blamed and reproached myself for my much [love of] travel and said, 'How long wilt thou thus imperil thyself?' And I abode as I were a madman, unable to rest; but, as I was thus melancholy and distracted, God the Most High inspired me with an idea, and it was that I looked at the river aforesaid, as it entered in at the mouth of the cavern in the skirt of the mountain, and said in myself, 'Needs must this water have issue in some place.'

So I arose and gathering wood and planks from the wrecks, wrought of them the semblance of a boat [to wit, a raft,] and bound it fast with ropes, saying, 'I will embark thereon and fare with this water into the inward of the mountain. If it bring me to the mainland or to a place where I may find relief and safety, [well and good]; else I shall [but] perish, even as my companions have perished.' Then I collected of the riches and gold and precious stuffs, cast up there, whose owners had perished. a great matter, and of jacinths and crude ambergris and emeralds somewhat past count, and laid all this on the raft [together with what was left me of victual]. Then I launched it on the river and seating myself upon it, put my trust in God the Most High and committed myself to the stream.

The raft fared on with me, running along the surface of the river, and entered into the inward of the mountain, where the light of day forsook me and I abode dazed and stupefied, unknowing whither I went. Whenas I hungered, I ate a little of the victual I had with me, till it was all spent and I abode expecting the mercy of the Lord of all creatures.[740] Presently I found myself in a strait [channel] in the darkness and my head rubbed against the roof of the cave; and in this case I abode awhile, knowing not night from day, whilst anon the channel grew straiter and anon widened out; and whenas my breast was straitened and I was confounded at my case, sleep took me and I knew neither little nor much.

When I awoke and opened my eyes, I found myself [in the open air] and the raft moored to the bank of the stream, whilst about me were folk of the blacks of Hind. When they saw that I was awake, they came up to me, to question me; so I rose to them and saluted them. They bespoke me in a tongue I knew not, whilst I deemed myself in a dream, and for the excess of my joy, I was like to fly and my reason refused to obey me. Then there came to my mind the verses of the poet and I recited, saying:

Let destiny with loosened rein its course appointed fare And lie thou down to sleep by night, with heart devoid of care;
For 'twixt the closing of an eye and th'opening thereof, God hath it in His power to change a case from foul to fair.

When they heard me speak in Arabic, one of them came up to me and saluting me [in that language], questioned me of my case. Quoth I, 'What [manner of men] are ye and what country is this?' 'O my brother,' answered he, 'we are husbandmen and come to this river, to draw water, wherewithal to water our fields; and whilst we were thus engaged to-day, as of wont, this boat appeared to us on the surface of the water, issuing from the inward of yonder mountain. So we came to it and finding thee asleep therein, moored it to the shore, against thou shouldst awake. Acquaint us, therefore, with thy history and tell us how thou camest hither and whence thou enteredst this river and what land is behind yonder mountain, for that we have never till now known any make his way thence to us.' But I said to them, 'Give me somewhat to eat and after question me.' So they brought me food and I ate and my spirits revived and I was refreshed. Then I related to them all that had befallen me, whereat they were amazed and confounded and said, 'By Allah, this is none other than a marvellous story, and needs must we carry thee to our king, that thou mayst acquaint him therewith.' So they carried me before their king, and I kissed his hand and saluted him.

Now he was the king of the land of Serendib,[741] and he welcomed me and entreated me with kindness, bidding me be seated and admitting me to his table and converse. So I talked with him and called down blessings upon him and he took pleasure in my discourse and showed me satisfaction and said to me, 'What is thy name?' 'O my lord,' answered I, 'my name is Sindbad the Sailor;' and he said, 'And what countryman art thou?' Quoth I, 'I am of Baghdad.' 'And how earnest thou hither?' asked he. So I told him my story and he marvelled mightily thereat and said, 'By Allah, O Sindbad, this thy story is marvellous and it behoveth that it be written in characters of gold.'

Then they brought the raft before him and I said to him, 'O my lord, I am in thy hands, I and all my good.' He looked at the raft and seeing therein jacinths and emeralds and crude ambergris, the like whereof was not in his treasuries, marvelled and was amazed at this. Then said he, 'O Sindbad, God forbid that we should covet that which God the Most High hath vouchsafed unto thee! Nay, it behoveth us rather to further thee on thy return to thine own country.' So I called down blessings on him and thanked him. Then he signed to one of his attendants, who took me and established me in a goodly lodging, and the king assigned me a daily allowance and pages to wait on me. And every day I used to go in to him and he entertained me and entreated me friendly and delighted in my converse; and as often as our assembly broke up, I went out and walked about the town and the island, diverting myself by viewing them.

Now this island is under the Equinoctial line; its night is still twelve hours and its day the like. Its length is fourscore parasangs and its breadth thirty, and it is a great island, stretching between a lofty mountain and a deep valley. This mountain is visible at a distance of three days' journey and therein are various kinds of jacinths and other precious stones and metals of all kinds and all manner spice-trees, and its soil is of emery, wherewith jewels are wrought. In its streams are diamonds, and pearls are in its rivers.[742] I ascended to its summit and diverted myself by viewing all the marvels therein, which are such as beggar description; after which I returned to the king and sought of him permission to return to my own country. He gave me leave, after great pressure, and bestowed on me abundant largesse from his treasuries. Moreover, he gave me a present and a sealed letter and said to me, 'Carry this to the Khalif Haroun er Reshid and salute him for us with abundant salutation.' And I said, 'I hear and obey.'

Now this letter was written with ultramarine upon the skin of the hog-deer, the which is goodlier than parchment or paper and inclineth unto yellow, and was to the following effect: 'From the King of Hind, before whom are a thousand elephants and on the battlements of his palace a thousand jewels, [to the Khalif Haroun er Reshid, greeting]. To proceed:[743] we send thee some small matter of presents, which do thou accept and be to us as a brother and a friend, for that the love of thee aboundeth in our heart and we would have thee to know that we look to thee for an answer. Indeed, we are sharers with thee in love and fear, ceasing[744] never to do thee honour; and for a beginning, we send thee the Book of the Quintessence of Balms and a present after the measure of that which is fallen to our lot. Indeed, this is unworthy of thy rank, but we beseech thee, O brother, to favour us by accepting it, and peace be on thee!'

Now this present was a cup of ruby, a span high and a finger's length broad, full of fine pearls, each a mithcal[745] in weight and a bed covered with the skin of the serpent that swalloweth the elephant, marked with spots, each the bigness of a dinar, whereon whoso sitteth shall never sicken; also an hundred thousand mithcals of Indian aloes-wood and thirty grains of camphor, each the bigness of a pistachio-nut, and a slave-girl with her paraphernalia, a charming creature, as she were the resplendent moon. Then the king took leave of me, commending me to the merchants and the captain of the ship, and I set out, with that which was entrusted to my charge and my own good, and we ceased not to pass from island to island and from country to country, till we came to Baghdad, when I entered my house and foregathered with my family and brethren.

Then I took the present and a token of service from myself to the Khalif and [presenting myself before him], kissed his hands and laid the whole before him, together with the King of Hind's letter. He read the letter and taking the present, rejoiced therein with an exceeding joy and entreated me with the utmost honour. Then said he to me, 'O Sindbad, is this king, indeed, such as he avoucheth in this letter?' I kissed the earth and answered, saying, 'O my lord, I myself have seen the greatness of his kingship to be manifold that which he avoucheth in his letter. On the day of his audience,[746] there is set up for him a throne on the back of a huge elephant, eleven cubits high, whereon he sitteth and with him are his officers and pages and session-mates, standing in two ranks on his right hand and on his left. At his head standeth a man, having in his hand a golden javelin, and behind him another, bearing a mace of the same metal, tipped with an emerald, a span long and an inch thick. When he mounteth, a thousand riders take horse with him, arrayed in gold and silk; and whenas he rideth forth, he who is before him proclaimeth and saith, "This is the king, mighty of estate and high of dominion!" And he proceedeth to praise him on this wise and endeth by saying, "This is the king, lord of the crown the like whereof nor Solomon[747] nor Mihraj[748] possessed!" Then is he silent, whilst he who is behind the king proclaimeth and saith, "He shall die! He shall die! And again I say, he shall die!" And the other rejoineth, saying, "Extolled be the perfection of the Living One who dieth not!" And by reason of his justice and judgment[749] and understanding, there is no Cadi in his [capital] city; but all the people of his realm distinguish truth from falsehood and know [and practise] truth and right for themselves.'

The Khalif marvelled at my speech and said, 'How great is this king! Indeed, his letter testifieth of him; and as for the magnificence of his dominion, thou hast acquainted us with that which thou hast seen; so, by Allah, he hath been given both wisdom and dominion.' Then he bestowed on me largesse and dismissed me, so I returned to my house and paid the poor-rate[750] and gave alms and abode in my former easy and pleasant case, forgetting the grievous stresses I had suffered. Yea, I cast out from my heart the cares of travel and traffic and put away travail from my thought and gave myself up to eating and drinking and pleasure and delight."

SINDBAD THE SAILOR AND HINDBAD THE PORTER.

When Sindbad the Sailor had made an end of his story, all who were present marvelled at that which had befallen him. Then he bade his treasurer give the porter an hundred mithcals of gold and dismissed him, charging him return on the morrow, with the rest of the folk, to hear the history of his seventh voyage. So the porter went away to his house, rejoicing; and on the morrow he presented himself with the rest of the guests, who sat down, as of their wont, and occupied themselves with eating and drinking and merry-making till the end of the day, when their host bade them hearken to the story of his seventh voyage. Quoth Sindbad the Sailor,

THE SEVENTH VOYAGE OF SINDBAD THE SAILOR

"when I [returned from my sixth voyage, I] forswore travel and renounced commerce, saying in myself, 'What hath befallen me sufficeth me.' So I abode at home and passed my time in pleasance and delight, till, one day, as I sat at mine ease, plying the wine-cup [with my friends], there came a knocking at the door. The doorkeeper opened and found without one of the Khalif's pages, who came in to me and said, 'The Commander of the Faithful biddeth thee to him.' So I accompanied him to the presence of the Khalif and kissing the earth before him, saluted him. He bade me welcome and entreated me with honour and said to me, 'O Sindbad, I have an occasion with thee, which I would have thee accomplish for me.' So I kissed his hand and said, 'O my lord, what is the lord's occasion with the slave?' Quoth he, 'I would have thee go to the King of Serendib anc carry him our letter and our present, even as he sent us a present and a letter.'

At this I trembled and replied, 'By the Most Great God, O my lord, I have taken a loathing to travel, and whenas any maketh mention to me of travel by sea or otherwise, I am like to swoon for affright, by reason of that which hath befallen me and what I have suffered of hardships and perils. Indeed, I have no jot of inclination left for this, and I have sworn never again to leave Baghdad.' And I related to him all that had befallen me, first and last; whereat he marvelled exceedingly and said, 'By the Most Great God, O Sindbad, never was heard from time immemorial of one whom there betided that which hath betided thee and well may it behove thee never again to mention travel! But for my sake go thou this once and carry my letter to the King of Serendib and return in haste, if it be the will of God the Most High, so we may not remain indebted to the king for favour and courtesy.' And I answered him with 'Hearkening and obedience,' for that I dared not gainsay his commandment

Then he gave me the present and letter and money for my expenses. So I kissed his hand and going out from before him, repaired to the sea-coast, where I took ship with many other merchants and we sailed days and nights, till, after a prosperous voyage, God vouchsafed us a safe arrival at the island of Serendib. We landed and went up to the city, where I carried the letter and present to the king and kissing the earth fell [prostrate before him], invoking blessings on him. When he saw me, 'Welcome to thee, O Sindbad!' quoth he. 'By the Most Great God, we have longed for thy sight and the day is blessed on which we behold thee once more.' Then he took my hand and seating me by his side, welcomed me and entreated me friendly and rejoiced in me with an exceeding joy; after which he fell to conversing with me and caressing me and said, 'What brings thee to us, O Sindbad?' I kissed his hand and thanking him, said, 'O my lord, I bring thee a present and a letter from my lord the Khalif Haroun er Reshid.' Then I brought out to him the present and the letter and he read the latter and accepted the former, rejoicing therein with an exceeding joy.

Now this present was a horse worth ten thousand dinars and all its housings and trappings of gold set with jewels, and a book and five different kinds of suits of apparel and an hundred pieces of fine white linen cloths of Egypt and silks of Suez and Cufa and Alexandria and a crimson carpet and another of Tebaristan[751] make and an hundred pieces of cloth of silk and flax mingled and a goblet of glass of the time of the Pharaohs, a finger-breadth thick and a span wide, amiddleward which was the figure of a lion and before him an archer kneeling, with his arrow drawn to the head, and the table of Solomon son of David,[752] on whom be peace; and the contents of the letter were as follows: 'From the Khalif Haroun er Reshid, unto whom and to his forefathers (on whom be peace) God hath vouchsafed the rank of the noble and exceeding glory, to the august, God-aided Sultan, greeting. Thy letter hath reached us and we rejoiced therein and have sent thee the book [called] "The Divan of Hearts and the Garden of Wits," of the translation whereof when thou hast taken cognizance, its excellence will be established in thine eyes; and the superscription of this book we have made unto thee. Moreover, we send thee divers other kingly presents;[753] so do thou favour us by accepting them, and peace be on thee!'

When the king had read this letter, he rejoiced with an exceeding joy and bestowed on me great store of presents and entreated me with the utmost honour. Some days after this, I sought of him leave to depart, but he granted it not to me save after much pressing. So I took leave of him and shipped with divers merchants and others, intending for my own country and having no desire for travel or traffic. We sailed on, without ceasing, till we had passed many islands; but, one day, as we fared on over a certain tract of the sea, there came forth upon us a multitude of boats full of men like devils, clad in chain-mail and armed with swords and daggers and bows and arrows, and surrounded us on every side. They entreated us after the cruellest fashion, smiting and wounding and slaying those who made head against them, and taking the ship, with the crew and all that were therein, carried us to an island, where they sold us all for a low price. A rich man bought me and taking me into his house, gave me to eat and drink and clothed me and entreated me kindly, till my heart was comforted and I was somewhat restored.

One day my master said to me, 'Knowest thou not some art or handicraft?' And I answered, saying, 'O my lord, I am a merchant and know nought but traffic.' Quoth he, 'Knowest thou how to shoot with a bow and arrows?' And I replied, 'Yes, I know that.' So he brought me a bow and arrows and mounting me behind him on an elephant, set out with me, at the last of the night, and fared on till we came to a forest of great trees; whereupon he made me climb a high and stout tree and giving me the bow and arrows, said to me, 'Sit here, and when the elephants come hither by day, shoot at them, so haply thou shalt hit one of them; and if any of them fall, come at nightfall and tell me.' Then he went away and left me trembling and fearful. I abode hidden in the tree till the sun rose, when the elephants came out and fared hither and thither among the trees, and I gave not over shooting at them with arrows, till I brought down one of them. So, at eventide, I went and told my master, who rejoiced in me and rewarded me; then he came and carried away the dead elephant.

On this wise I abode a while of time, every day shooting an elephant, whereupon my master came and carried it away, till, one day, as I sat hidden in the tree, there came up elephants without number, roaring and trumpeting, so that meseemed the earth trembled for the din. They all made for the tree whereon I was and the girth whereof was fifty cubits, and compassed it about. Then a huge elephant came up to the tree and winding his trunk about it, tugged at it, till he plucked it up by the roots and cast it to the ground. I fell among the elephants, and the great elephant, coming up to me, as I lay aswoon for affright, wound his trunk about me and tossing me on to his back, made off with me, accompanied by the others; nor did he leave faring on with me, and I absent from the world, till he brought me to a certain place and casting me down from off his back, went away, followed by the rest. I lay there awhile, till my trouble subsided and my senses returned to me, when I sat up, deeming myself in a dream, and found myself on a great hill, stretching far and wide and all of elephants' bones. So I knew that this was their burial-place and that they had brought me thither on account of the bones.

Then I arose and fared on a day and a night, till I came to the house of my master, who saw me pale and disfeatured for fear and hunger. He rejoiced in my return and said to me, 'By Allah, thou hast made my heart ache on thine account; for I went and finding the tree torn up by the roots, doubted not but the elephants had destroyed thee. Tell me then how it was with thee.' So I told him what had befallen me and he marvelled exceedingly and rejoiced, saying, 'Knowst thou where this hill is?' 'Yes, O my lord,' answered I. So he took me up with him on an elephant and we rode till we came to the elephants' burial-place.

When he saw those many bones, he rejoiced therein with an exceeding joy and carried away what he had a mind to thereof. Then we returned to his house and he entreated me with increased favour and said to me, 'Verily, O my son, thou hast directed us to a passing great gain, may God requite thee with all good! Thou art free for the sake of God the Most High. Every year these elephants used to kill of us much people on account of these bones; but God delivered thee from them and thou hast done us good service in the matter of these bones, of which thou hast given us to know; wherefore thou meritest a great recompense, and thou art free.' 'O my lord,' answered I, 'may God free thy neck from the fire! I desire of thee that thou give me leave to return to my own country.' 'So be it,' replied he; 'but we have a fair, on occasion whereof the merchants come hither to us and take of us these elephants' bones. The time of the fair is now at hand, and when they come to us, I will send thee with them and give thee somewhat to bring thee to thine own country.'

I blessed him and thanked him and abode with him in all honour and consideration, till, after a little, the merchants came, even as he had said, and bought and sold and bartered; and when they were about to depart, my master came to me and said, 'The merchants are about to depart; arise, that thou mayst go with them to thy country.' So I betook myself to the folk, and behold, they had bought great store of elephants' bones and bound up their loads and embarked in the ship; and my master took passage for me with them and paid my hire and all that was chargeable upon me.[754] Moreover, he gave me great store of goods and we set sail and passed from island to island, till we traversed the sea and arrived at the port of our destination; whereupon the merchants brought out their goods and sold; and I also brought out that which was with me and sold it at a good profit.

Then I bought of the best and finest of the produce and rarities of the country and all I had a mind to and a good hackney[755] and we set out again and traversed the deserts from country to country till we came to Baghdad. Then I went in to the Khalif and saluted him and kissed his hand; after which I acquainted him with all that had passed and that which had befallen me. He rejoiced in my deliverance and thanked God the Most High; then he caused write my story in letters of gold and I betook myself to my house and foregathered with my brethren and family. This, then," added Sindbad, "is the last of that which befell me in my travels, and praise be to God, the One, the Creator, the Maker!"

When Sindbad the Sailor had made an end of his story, he bade his servant give the porter an hundred mithcals of gold and said to him, "How now, my brother! Hast ever in the world heard of one whom such calamities have betided as have betided me and hath any suffered that which I have suffered of afflictions or undergone that which I have undergone of hardships? Wherefore it behoveth that I have these pleasures in requital of that which I have undergone of travail and humiliations." So the porter came forward and kissing the merchant's hands, said to him, "O my lord, thou hast indeed suffered grievous perils and hast well deserved these bounteous favours [that God hath vouchsafed thee]. Abide, then, O my lord, in thy delights and put away from thee [the remembrance of] thy troubles; and may God the Most High crown thine enjoyments with perfection and accomplish thy days in pleasance until the hour of thine admission [to His mercy]!"

Therewithal Sindbad the Sailor bestowed largesse upon him and made him his boon-companion, and he abode, leaving him not night or day, to the last of their lives. Praise be to God the Glorious, the Omnipotent, the Strong, the Exalted of estate, Creator of heaven and earth and land and sea, to whom belongeth glorification! Amen. Amen. Praise be to God, the Lord of the Worlds! Amen.

NOTE

AS stated In the Prefatory Note to my "Book of the Thousand Nights and One Night," four printed Editions (of which three are more or less complete) exist of the Arabic text of the original work, namely those of Calcutta (1839-42), Boulac (Cairo), Breslau (Tunis) and Calcutta (1814-18). The first two are, for purposes of tabulation, practically identical, one whole story only,[756] of those that occur in the Calcutta (1839-42) Edition, (which is the most complete of all,) being omitted from that of Boulac; and I have, therefore, given but one Table of Contents for these two Editions. The Breslau Edition, though differing widely from those of Calcutta (1839-42) and Boulac in contents, resembles them in conta ning the full number (a thousand and one) of Nights, whilst that of Calcutta (1814-18) is but a fragment, comprising only the first two hundred Nights and the Voyages of Sindbad, as a separate Tale.

The subscribers to my "Book of the Thousand Nights and One Night" and the present "Tales from the Arabic" have now before them a complete English rendering (the first ever made) of all the tales contained in the four printed (Arabic) Texts of the original work and I have, therefore, thought it well to add to this, the last Volume of my Translation, full Tables of Contents of these latter, a comparison of which will show the exact composition of the different Editions and the particulars in which they differ from one another, together with the manner n which the various stories that make up the respective collections are distributed over the Nights. In each Table, the titles of the stories occurring only in the Edition of which it gives the contents are printed in Italics and each Tale is referred to the number of the Night on which it is begun.

The Breslau Edition, which was printed from a Manuscript of the Book of the Thousand Nights and One Night alleged to have been furnished to the Editor by a learned Arab of Tunis, whom he styles "Herr M. Annaggar" (Quære En Nejjar, the Carpenter), the lacunes found in which were supplemented from various other MS. sources indicated by Silvestre de Sacy and other eminent Orientalists, is edited with a perfection of badness to which only German scholars (at once the best and worst editors in the world) can attain. The original Editor, Dr. Maximilian Habicht, was during the period (1825- 1839) of publication of the first eight Volumes, engaged in continual and somewhat acrimonious[757] controversy concerning the details of his editorship with Prof. H. L. Fleischer, who, after his death, undertook the completion of his task and approved himself a worthy successor of his whilom adversary, his laches and shortcomings in the matter of revision and collation of the text being at least equal in extent and gravity to those of his predecessor, whilst he omitted the one valuable feature of the latter's work, namely, the glossary of Arabic words, not occurring in the dictionaries, appended to the earlier volumes.

As an instance of the extreme looseness with which the book was edited, I may observe that the first four Vols. were published without tables of contents, which were afterwards appended en bloc to the fifth Volume. The state of corruption and incoherence in which the printed Text was placed before the public by the two learned Editors, who were responsible for its production, is such as might well drive a translator to despair: the uncorrected errors of the press would alone fill a volume and the verse especially is so corrupt that one of the most laborious of English Arabic scholars pronounced its translation a hopeless task. I have not, however, in any single instance, allowed myself to be discouraged by the difficulties presented by the condition of the text, but have, to the best of my ability, rendered into English, without abridgment or retrenchment, the whole of the tales, prose and verse, contained in the Breslau Edition, which are not found in those of Calcutta (1839-42) and Boulac. In this somewhat ungrateful task, I have again had the cordial assistance of Captain Burton, who has (as in the case of my "Book of the Thousand Nights and One Night") been kind enough to look over the proofs of my translation and to whom I beg once more to tender my warmest thanks.

Some misconception seems to exist as to the story of Seif dhoul Yezen, a fragment of which was translated by Dr. Habicht and included, with a number of tales from the Breslau Text, in the fourteenth Vol. of the extraordinary gallimaufry published by him in 1824-5 as a complete translation of the 1001 Nights[758] and it has, under the mistaken impression that this long but interesting Romance forms part of the Book of the Thousand Nights and One Night, been suggested that a complete transla- tion of it should be included in the present publication. The Romance in question does not, however, in any way, belong to my original and forms no part of the Breslau Text, as will be at once apparent from an examination of the Table of Contents of the latter (see post, p. 261), by which all the Nights are accounted for. Dr. Habicht himself tells us, in his preface to the first Vol. of the Arabic Text, that he found the fragment (undivided into Nights) at the end of the fifth Volume of his MS., into which other detached tales, having no connection with the Nights, appear to have also found their way. This being the case, it is evident that the Romance of Seif dhoul Yezen in no way comes within the scope of the present work and would (apart from the fact that its length would far overpass my limits) be a manifestly improper addition to it. It is, however, possible that, should I come across a suitable text of the work, I may make it the subject of a separate publication; but this is, of course, a matter for future considera-tion.

ENDNOTES

---

[1] Breslau Text, vol. iv. pp. 134-189, Nights cclxxii.-ccxci. This is the story familiar to readers of the old "Arabian Nights" as "Abon Hassan, or the Sleeper Awakened" and is the only one of the eleven tales added by Galland to his version of the (incomplete) MS. of the Book of the Thousand Nights and One Night procured by him from Syria, the Arabic original of which has yet been discovered. (See my "Book of the Thousand Nights and One Night," Vol. IX. pp. 264 et seq.) The above title is of course intended to mark the contrast between the everyday (or waking) hours of Aboulhusn and his fantastic life in the Khalif's palace, supposed by him to have passed in a dream, and may also be rendered "The Sleeper and the Waker." (p. 2)

[2] i.e. The Wag. (p. 2)

[3] Always noted for debauchery. (p. 2)

[4] i.e. the part he had taken for spending money. (p. 2)

[5] i.e. "those," a characteristic Arab idiom. (p. 2)

[6] Lit. draw thee near (to them). (p. 2)

[7] i.e. that over the Tigris. (p. 2)

[8] "Platter bread," i.e. bread baked in a platter, instead of, as usual with the Arabs, in an oven or earthen jar previously heated, to the sides of which the thin cakes of dough are applied, "is lighter than oven bread, especially if it be made thin and leavened."--Shecouri, a medical writer quoted by Dozy. (p. 3)

[9] Or cooking-pots. (p. 4)

[10] Or fats for frying. (p. 4)

[11] Or clarified. (p. 4)

[12] Taam, lit. food, the name given by the inhabitants of Northern Africa to the preparation of millet-flour (something like semolina) called kouskoussou, which forms the staple food of the people. (p. 4)

13 Or "In peace." (p. 4)

14 Eastern peoples attach great importance, for good or evil omen, to the first person met or the first thing that happens in the day. (p. 4)

15 Or "attributed as sin." (p. 4)

16 A common Eastern substitute for soap. (p. 6)

17 This common formula of assent is an abbreviation of "Hearkening and obedience are due to God and to the Commander of the Faithful" or other the person addressed. (p. 7)

18 Dar es Selam, one of the seven "Gardens" into which the Mohammedan Paradise is divided. (p. 8)

19 i.e. a mattrass eighteen inches thick. (p. 8)

20 Complimentary form of address to eunuchs, generally used by inferiors only. (p. 9)

21 The morning-prayer consists of four inclinations (rekäat) only. A certain fixed succession of prayers and acts of adoration is called a rekah (sing, of rekäat) from the inclination of the body that occurs in it. (p. 9)

22 i.e. the terminal formula of prayer, "Peace be on us and on all the righteous servants of God!" (p. 9)

23 i.e. said "I purpose to make an end of prayer." (p. 9)

24 Or "linen." (p. 9)

25 A well-known poet of the time. (p. 9)

26 i.e. Ibrahim of Mosul, the greatest musician of his day. (p. 9)

27 i.e., doughty men of war, guards. (p. 9)

28 The Abbaside Khalifs traced their descent from Abbas, the uncle of Mohammed, and considered themselves, therefore, as belonging to the family of the Prophet. (p. 10)

29 i.e. May thy dwelling-place never fall into ruin. (p. 10)

[30] i.e. the raised recess situate at the upper end of an Oriental saloon, wherein is the place of honour. (p. 10)

[31] ie, the necromancers. (p. 13)

[32] Lit. I have not found that thou hast a heel blessed (or propitious) to me. (p. 14)

[33] i.e. O thou who art a calamity to those who have to do with thee! (p. 16)

[34] Abou Nuwas ibn Hani, the greatest poet of the time. (p. 16)

[35] As a charm against evil spirits. (p. 17)

[36] i.e. the vein said to have been peculiar to the descendants of Hashim, grandfather of Abbas and great-grandson of Mohammed, and to have started out between their eyes in moments of anger. (p. 19)

[37] Lit. that I may do upon her sinister deeds. (p. 21)

[38] "The pitcher comes not always back unbroken from the well."--English proverb. (p. 22)

[39] i.e. of sorrow for his loss. (p. 22)

[40] i.e. of grief for her loss. (p. 22)

[41] Breslau Text, vol. vl. pp. 182-188, Nights ccccxxxii-ccccxxxiv. (p. 24)

[42] The eighth Khalif (A.D. 717-720) of the house of Umeyyeh and the best and most single-hearted of all the Khalifs, with the exception of the second, Omar ben Khettab, from whom he was descended. (p. 24)

[43] A celebrated statesman of the time, afterwards governor of Cuia* and Bassora under Omar ben Abdulaziz. (p. 24)

[44] The most renowned poet of the first century of the Hegira. He is said to have been equally skilled in all styles of composition grave and gay. (p. 24)

[45] Or eternal. (p. 24)

[46] Or "in him." (p. 24)

47 Chief of the tribe of the Benou Suleim. Et Teberi tells this story in a different way. According to him, Abbas ben Mirdas (who was a well-known poet), being dissatisfied with the portion of booty allotted to him by the Prophet, refused it and composed a lampoon against Mohammed, who said to Ali, "Cut off this tongue which attacketh me," i.e. "Silence him by giving what will satisfy him," whereupon Ali doubled the covetous chief's share. (p. 24)

48 Bilal ibn Rebeh was the Prophet's freedman and crier. The word bilal signifies "moisture" or (metonymically) "beneficence" and it may well be in this sense (and not as a man's name) that it is used in the text. (p. 24)

49 Said to have been the best poet ever produced by the tribe of Cureish. His introduction here is an anachronism, as he died A.D. 712, five years before Omar's accession. (p. 25)

50 i.e. odorem pudendorum amicæ? (p. 25)

51 A famous poet of the tribe of the Benou Udhreh, renowned for their passionate sincerity in love-matters. He is celebrated as the lover of Butheineh, as Petrarch of Laura, and died A.D. 701, sixteen years before Omar's accession. (p. 25)

52 A friend of Jemil and a poet of equal renown. He is celebrated as the lover of Azzeh, whose name is commonly added to his, and kept a grocer's shop at Medina. (p. 25)

53 i.e. in the attitude of prayer. (p. 25)

54 A famous satirical poet of the time, afterwards banished by Omar for the virulence of his lampoons. His name is wrongly given by the text; it should be El Ahwes. He was a descendant of the Ansar or (Medinan) helpers of Mohammed. (p. 25)

55 A famous poet of the tribe of the Benou Temim and a rival of Jerir, to whom he was by some preferred. He was a notorious debauchee and Jerir, in one of the satires that were perpetually exchanged between himself and El Ferezdec, accuses his rival of having "never been a guest in any house, but he departed with ignominy and left behind him disgrace." (p. 26)

56 A Christian and a celebrated poet of the time. (p. 26)

57 The poet apparently meant to insinuate that those who professed to keep the fast of Ramazan ate flesh in secret. The word rendered "in public," i.e. openly, avowedly, may also perhaps be translated "in the forenoon," and in this El Akhtel

may have meant to contrast his free-thinking disregard of the ordinances of the fast with the strictness of the orthodox Muslim, whose only meals in Ramazan-time are made between sunset and dawn-peep. As soon as a white thread can be distinguished from a black, the fast is begun and a true believer must not even smoke or swallow his saliva till sunset. (p. 26)

[58] Prominent words of the Muezzin's fore-dawn call to prayer. (p. 26)

[59] i.e. fall down drunk. (p. 26)

[60] i.e. she who ensnares [all] eyes. (p. 26)

[61] Imam, the spiritual title of the Khalif, as head of the Faith and leader (lit. "foreman") of the people at prayer. (p. 26)

[62] Or "worldly." (p. 26)

[63] Or "worldly." (p. 26)

[64] A town and province of Arabia, of which (inter alia) Omar ben Abdulaziz was governor, before he came to the Khalifate. (p. 27)

[65] Syn. munificence. (p. 27)

[66] About 2 pounds sterling 10 s. (p. 27)

[67] i.e. what is thy news? (p. 27)

[68] Or "I approve of him." (p. 27)

[69] Breslau Text, vol. vi. pp. 188-9, Night ccccxxxiv. (p. 28)

[70] El Hejjaj ben Yousuf eth Thekefi, a famous statesman and soldier of the seventh and eighth centuries. He was governor of Chaldaea (Irak Arabi), under the fifth and sixth Khalifs of the Ommiade dynasty, and was renowned for his cruelty, but appears to have been a prudent and capable administrator, who used no more rigour than was necessary to restrain the proverbially turbulent populations of Bassora and Cufa, Most of the anecdotes of his brutality and tyranny, which abound in Arab authors, are, in all probability, apocryphal. (p. 28)

[71] Used, by synecdoche, for "heads." (p. 28)

[72] i.e. the governed, to wit, he who is led by a halter attached (metaphorically of course) to a ring passed through his nose, as with a camel. (p. 28)

[73] i.e. the governor or he who is high of rank. (p. 28)

[74] i.e. their hair, which may be considered the wealth of the head. This whole passage is a description a double-entente of a barber-surgeon. (p. 28)

[75] Syn. cooking-pot. (p. 28)

[76] Syn. be lowered. This passage is a similar description of an itinerant hot bean-seller. (p. 28)

[77] The rows of threads on a weaver's loom. (p. 28)

[78] Syn. levelleth. (p. 28)

[79] i.e. that of wood used by the Oriental weaver to govern the warp and weft. (p. 28)

[80] Syn. behave aright. (p. 28)

[81] The loop of thread so called in which the weaver's foot rests. (p. 28)

[82] Syn. eloquence. (p. 28)

[83] Adeb, one of the terribly comprehensive words which abound in Arabic literature for the confusion of translators. It signifies generally all kinds of education and means of mental and moral discipline and seems here to mean more particularly readiness of wit and speech or presence of mind. (p. 28)

[84] Breslau Text, vol. vi. pp. 189-191, Night ccccxxxiv. (p. 29)

[85] Syn. (Koranic) "Thou hast swerved from justice" or "been unjust" (adeita). (p. 29)

[86] Syn. (Koranic) "Thou hast transgressed" (caset-ta). (p. 29)

[87] Or falling-away. (p. 29)

[88] Koran vi. 44. (p. 29)

[89] Or do injustice, tadilou (syn. do justice). (p. 29)

[90] Koran iv. 134. (p. 29)

[91] El casitouna (syn. those who act righteously or equitably). (p. 29)

[92] Koran lxxii. 15. (p. 29)

[93] Name of the Persian ancestor of the Barmecide (properly Bermeki) family. (p. 29)

[94] Breslau Text, vol. vi. pp. 191-343, Nights ccccxxv-cccclxxxvii. This is the Arab version of the well-known story called, in Persian, the Bekhtyar Nameh, i.e. the Book of Bekhtyar, by which name the prince, whose attempted ruin by the envious viziers is the central incident of the tale, is distinguished in that language. The Arab redaction of the story is, to my mind, far superior to the Persian, both in general simplicity and directness of style and in the absence of the irritating conceits and moral digressions with which Persian (as well as Indian) fiction is so often overloaded. The Persian origin of the story is apparent, not only in the turn of the incidents and style and the names of the personages, but in the fact that not a single line of verse occurs in it. (p. 30)

[95] Rawi; this is probably a copyist's mistake for raai, a beholder, one who seeth. (p. 30)

[96] Lit. what was his affair? It may be here observed that the word keif (how?) is constantly used in the Breslau Text in the sense of ma (what?). (p. 32)

[97] A district of Persia, here probably Persia itself. (p. 33)

[98] Probably a corruption of Kisra (Chosroës). (p. 33)

[99] i.e. waylaying travellers, robbing on the high road. (p. 33)

[100] Or skill. (p. 34)

[101] Lit. the descended fate. (p. 34)

[102] The Arabs attribute to a man's parentage absolute power in the determination of his good and evil qualities; eg. the son of a slave, according to them, can possess none of the virtues of the free-born, whilst good qualities are in like manner considered congenitally inherent in the latter. (p. 35)

[103] Or "business." (p. 37)

[104] i.e. whither he should travel. (p. 37)

[105] About half-a-crown. (p. 38)

[106] It is a common practice with Eastern nations to keep a child (especially a son and one of unusual beauty) concealed until a certain age, for fear of the evil eye. See my "Book of the Thousand Nights and One Night," Vol. III. p. 234; Vol. IX. p. 67, etc., etc. (p. 42)

[107] i.e. killing a man. (p. 44)

[108] i.e., it will always be in our power to slay him, when we will. (p. 44)

[109] i.e. the grave. (p. 50)

[110] i.e. the wedding-day. (p. 53)

[111] i.e. thy women (p. 53)

[112] i.e. hath been unduly prolonged. (p. 54)

[113] i.e. Let thy secret thoughts and purposes be righteous, even as thine outward profession. (p. 55)

[114] See my "Book of the Thousand Nights and One Night," Vol. V. p. 264. (p. 55)

[115] Afterwards called his "chamberlain," i.e. the keeper of the door of the harem or chief eunuch. See post, p. III. (p. 56)

[116] i.e. the eunuch who had dissuaded Dadbin from putting her to death. (p. 57)

[117] Apparently referring to Aboulkhair (see ante p. 107), whom Dabdin would seem to have put to death upon the vizier's false accusation, although no previous mention of this occurs. (p. 58)

[118] The Arabs believe that each man's destiny is charactered, could we decipher it, in the sutures of his skull. (p. 58)

[119] ie. the lex talionis, which is the essence of Muslim jurisprudence. (p. 58)

[120] i.e. a soldier of fortune, going about from court to court, in quest of service. (p. 60)

[121] This phrase refers to the Arab idiom, "His hand (or arm) is long or short," i.e. he is a man of great or little puissance. (p. 68)

[122] The Arabs consider it a want of respect to allow the hands or feet to remain exposed in the presence of a superior. (p. 68)

[123] Adeb. See ante, p. 54, note 9. (p. 69)

[124] i.e. that he become my son-in-law. (p. 69)

[125] It is a common Eastern practice to have the feet kneaded and pressed (shampooed) for the purpose of inducing sleep, and thus the king would habitually fall asleep with his feet on the knees of his pages. (p. 69)

[126] Syn. whoso respecteth not his lord's women. (p. 70)

[127] i.e. a domed tomb. (p. 71)

[128] Of a man's life. The Muslims believe each man's last hour to be written in a book called "The Preserved Tablet." (p. 78)

[129] i.e, the Autumnal Equinox, one of the two great festival days (the other being the New Year) of the Persians. See my "Book of the Thousand Nights and One Night," Vol. IV. p. 144. (p. 78)

[130] i.e. heritage. (p. 81)

[131] i.e. The Emperor of the Romans of the Lower Empire, so called by the Arabs. "Caesar" is their generic term for the Emperors of Constantinople, as is Kisra (Chosroës) for the ancient Kings of Persia. (p. 81)

[132] i.e. Shah Khatoun. (p. 82)

[133] i.e. our power increased by his alliance, a. familiar Arab idiom. (p. 82)

[134] In token of deputation of authority, a ceremony usual on the appointment of a governor of a province. (p. 84)

[135] Or enigma. (p. 85)

[136] i.e. if my death be ordained of destiny to befall on an early day none may avail to postpone it to a later day. (p. 88)

[137] Of life. See supra, note, p. 147. (p. 91)

[138] The hoopoe is fabled by the Muslim chroniclers to have been to Solomon what Odin's ravens were to the Norse god. It is said to have known all the secrets of the earth and to have revealed them to him; hence the magical virtues attributed by the Mohammedans to its heart. (p. 92)

[139] This phrase may be read either literally or in its idiomatic sense, i.e., "Folk convicted or suspected of murder or complicity in murder." (p. 94)

[140] Or purse-belt. (p. 94)

[141] See supra, p. 66. (p. 95)

[142] Khilaah, lit. that which one takes off from one's own person, to bestow upon a messenger of good tidings or any other whom it is desired especially to honour. The literal meaning of the phrase, here rendered "he bestowed on him a dress of honour," is "he put off on him [that which was upon himself." A Khilaah commonly includes a horse, a sword, a girdle or waist-cloth and other articles, according to the rank of the recipient, and might more precisely be termed "a complete equipment of honour." (p. 96)

[143] An economical mode of rewarding merit, much in favour with Eastern monarchs. (p. 96)

[144] Breslau Text, vol. vii. pp. 251-4, Night dlxv. (p. 97)

[145] Syn. doorkeper (hajib). (p. 97)

[146] Ibn Khelbkan, who tells this story in a somewhat different style, on the authority of Er Reshid's brother Ibrahim ben El Mehdi, calls the person whom Jaafer expected "Abdulmelik ben Behran, the intendant of his demesnes." (p. 97)

[147] The wearing of silk and bright colours is forbidden to the strict Muslim and it is generally considered proper, in a man of position, to wear them only on festive occasions or in private, as in the text. (p. 97)

[148] The Abbasides or descendants of El Abbas, the Prophet's uncle, were noted for their excessive pride and pretensions to strict orthodoxy in all outward observances. Abdulmelik ben Salih, who was a well-known general and statesman of the time, was especially renowned for pietism and austerity of manners. (p. 97)

[149] i.e. Do not let my presence trouble you. (p. 97)

---

[150] As a member of the reigning family, he of course wore black clothes, that being the especial colour of the house of Abbas, adopted by them in opposition to the rival (and fallen) dynasty of the Benou Umeyyeh, whose family colour was white, that of the house of Ali being green. (p. 97)

[151] About £25,000. Ibn Khellikan makes the debt four millions of dirhems or about £100,000 (p. 98)

[152] Breslau text, vol vii, pp.258-60, Night dlxvii. (p. 99)

[153] Fourth Khalif of the house of Abbas, A.D. 785-786. (p. 99)

[154] Third Khalif of the house of Abbas, A.D. 775-785. (p. 99)

[155] The following is Et Teberi's version of this anecdote. El Mehdi had presented his son Haroun with a ruby ring, worth a hundred thousand dinars, and the latter being one day with his brother [the then reigning Khalif], El Hadi saw the ring on his finger and desired it. So, when Haroun went out from him, he sent after him, to seek the ring of him. The Khalif's messenger overtook Er Reshid on the bridge over the Tigris and acquainted him with his errand; whereupon the prince enraged at the demand, pulled off the ring and threw it into the river. When El Hadi died and Er Reshid succeeded to the throne, he went with his suite to the bridge in question and bade his Vizier Yehya ben Khalid send for divers and cause them make search for the ring. It had then been five months in the water and no one believed it would be found. However, the divers plunged into the river and found the ring in the very place where he had thrown it in, whereat Haroun rejoiced with an exceeding joy, regarding it as a presage of fair fortune. (p. 99)

[156] This is an error. Jaafer's father Yehya was appointed by Haroun his vizier and practically continued to exercise that office till the fall of the Barmecides (A.D. 803), his sons Fezl and Jaafer acting only as his assistants or lieutenants. See my Essay on the History and Character of the Book of the Thousand Nights and One Night. (p. 99)

[157] Another mistake. It was Fezl, the Khalif's foster-brother, to whom he used to give this title. (p. 99)

[158] A third mistake. The whole period during which the empire was governed by Yehya and his sons was only seventeen years, i.e. A.D 786-803, but see my Essay. (p. 99)

[159] The apparent meaning of this somewhat obscure saying is, "Since fortune is uncertain, conciliate the favour of those with whom thou hast to do by kind offices, so thou mayst find refuge with them in time of need." (p. 99)

[160] For a detailed account of the Barmecides and of their fall, see my Essay. (p. 100)

[161] Breslau Text, vol. vii. pp. 260-1, Night dlxviii. (p. 101)

[162] Aboulabbas Mohammed Ibn Sabih, surnamed Ibn es Semmak (son of the fishmonger), a well-known Cufan jurisconsult and ascetic of the time. He passed the latter part of his life at Baghdad and enjoyed high favour with Er Reshid, as the only theological authority whom the latter could induce to promise him admission to Paradise. (p. 101)

[163] Breslau Text, vol. vii. pp. 261-2, Night dlxviii. (p. 102)

[164] Seventh Khalif of the house of Abbas, A.D. 813-33. (p. 102)

[165] Sixth Khalif of the house of Abbas, A.D. 809-13, a sanguinary and incapable prince, whose contemplated treachery against his brother El Mamoun, (whom, by the advice of his vizier, the worthless intriguer Fezl ben Rebya, the same who was one of the prime movers in the ruin of the illustrious Barmecide family and who succeeded Yehya and his sons in the vizierate (see my Essay), he contemplated depriving of his right of succession and murdering,) was deservedly requited with the loss of his own kingdom and life. He was, by the way, put to death by El Mamoun's general, in contravention of the express orders of that generous and humane prince, who wished his brother to be sent prisoner to him, on the capture of Baghdad. (p. 102)

[166] i.e. forfeits. It is a favourite custom among the Arabs to impose on the loser of a game, in lieu of stakes, the obligation of doing whatsoever the winner may command him. For an illustration of this practice, see my "Book of the Thousand Nights and One Night," Vol. V. pp. 336-41, Story of the Sandalwood Merchant and the Sharpers. (p. 102)

[167] El Mamoun was of a very swarthy complexion and is said to have been the son of a black slave-girl. Zubeideh was Er Reshid's cousin, and El Amin was, therefore, a member of the house of Abbas, both on the father's and mother's side. Of this purity of descent from the Prophet's family (in which he is said to have stood alone among the Khalifs of the Abbaside dynasty) both himself and his mother were exceedingly proud, and it was doubtless this circumstance which led Er Reshid to prefer El Amin and to assign him the precedence in the succession over the more capable and worthier El Mamoun. (p. 102)

[168] Breslau Text, vol. viii. pp. 226-9, Nights dclx-i. (p. 103)

[169] A pre-Mohammedan King of the Arab kingdom of Hireh (a town near Cufa on the Euphrates), under the suzerainty of the Chosroes of Persia, and a cruel and fantastic tyrant. (p. 103)

[170] The tribe to which belonged the renowned pre-Mohammedan chieftain and poet, Hatim Tal, so celebrated in the East for his extravagant generosity and hospitality. (p. 103)

[171] i.e. I will make a solemn covenant with him before God. (p. 103)

[172] i.e. he of the tribe of Tai. (p. 103)

[173] In generosity. (p. 104)

[174] A similar anecdote is told of Omar ben el Khettab, second successor of Mohammed, and will be found in my "Book of the Thousand Nights and One Night," Vol. IV. p. 239. (p. 104)

[175] Breslau Text, vol. viii. pp. 273-8, Nights dclxxv--vi. (p. 105)

[176] A similar story will be found in my "Book of the Thousand Nights and One Night", Vol. V. p. 263. (p. 107)

[177] Breslau Text, vol xi. pp. 84-318, Nights dccclxxv-dccccxxx. (p. 108)

[178] i.e. A pilgrimage. Pilgrimage is one of a Muslim's urgent duties. (p. 109)

[179] By a rhetorical figure, Mecca is sometimes called El Hejj (the Pilgrimage) and this appears to be the case here. It is one of the dearest towns in the East and the chief occupation of its inhabitants a the housing and fleecing of pilgrims. An Arab proverb says, "There is no place in which money goes [so fast] as it goes in Mecca." (p. 110)

[180] lit. loved with it. (p. 110)

[181] It is not clear what is here meant by El Hejj; perhaps Medina, though this is a "visitation" and not an obligatory part of the pilgrimage. The passage is probably corrupt. (p. 110)

[182] It is not clear what is here meant by El Hejj; perhaps Medina, though this is a "visitation" and not an obligatory part of the pilgrimage. The passage is probably corrupt. (p. 111)

[183] Syn. whole or perfect (sehik). (p. 111)

[184] i.e. in white woollen garments. (p. 111)

[185] i.e. I desire a privy place, where I may make the preliminary ablution and pray. (p. 111)

[186] It is customary in the East to give old men and women the complimentary title of "pilgrim," assuming, as a matter of course, that they have performed the obligatory rite of pilgrimage. (p. 112)

[187] Or saint. (p. 112)

[188] Keniseh, a Christian or other non-Muslim place of worship. (p. 112)

[189] Apparently the harem. (p. 113)

[190] i.e. otherwise than according to God's ordinance. (p. 115)

[191] A city of Persian Irak. (p. 115)

[192] Lit. its apparatus, i.e. spare strings, etc.? (p. 115)

[193] i.e. the woman whose face he saw. (p. 116)

[194] Lit. the place of battle, i.e. that where they had lain. (p. 116)

[195] A common Eastern fashion of securing a shop, when left for a short time. The word shebekeh (net) may also be tendered a grating or network of iron or other metal. (p. 117)

[196] i.e. gave her good measure. (p. 117)

[197] i.e. she found him a good workman. Equivoque erotique, apparently founded on the to-and-fro movement of the shuttle in weaving. (p. 117)

[198] Equivoque érotique. (p. 117)

---

[199] i.e. removed the goods exposed for sale and laid them up in the inner shop or storehouse. (p. 118)

[200] The Eastern oven is generally a great earthenware jar sunken in the earth. (p. 118)

[201] i.e. a boughten white slave (memlouk). (p. 119)

[202] Apparently changing places. The text is here fearfully corrupt and (as in many other parts of the Breslau Edition) so incoherent as to be almost unintelligible. (p. 119)

[203] i.e. in the (inner) courtyard. (p. 119)

[204] i.e. the essential nature, lit. jewel. (p. 120)

[205] i.e. in proffering thee the kingship. (p. 121)

[206] Without the city. (p. 122)

[207] According to the conclusion of the story, this recompense consisted in an augmentation of the old man's allowances of food. See post, p. 245. (p. 122)

[208] i.e. I have given my opinion. (p. 123)

[209] This passage is evidently corrupt. I have amended it, on conjecture, to the best of my power. (p. 123)

[210] The words ruteb wa menazil, here rendered "degrees and dignities," may also be rendered, "stations and mansions (of the moon and planets)." (p. 124)

[211] Syn. "ailing" or "sickly." (p. 124)

[212] i.e. the caravan with which he came. (p. 125)

[213] i.e. I seek to marry thy daughter, not for her own sake, but because I desire thine alliance. (p. 126)

[214] i.e. the face of his bride. (p. 126)

[215] i.e. his wife. (p. 126)

[216] i.e. his wife. (p. 127)

[217] Naming the poor man. (p. 127)

[218] Naming his daughter. (p. 127)

[219] i.e. united. (p. 128)

[220] Or "humble." (p. 128)

[221] i.e. one another. (p. 128)

[222] Or "conquer." (p. 128)

[223] Or "commandment." (p. 128)

[224] Lit. "will be higher than." (p. 128)

[225] Syn. device or resource (hileh). (p. 129)

[226] Syn. chasten or instruct. (p. 129)

[227] Students of our old popular poetry will recognize, in the principal incident of this story, the subject of the well-known ballad, "The Heir of Linne." (p. 129)

[228] i.e. Turcomans; afterwards called Sejestan. (p. 131)

[229] With a pile of stones or some such landmark. (p. 132)

[230] i.e. the extraordinary resemblance of the supposed sister to his wife. (p. 134)

[231] The foregoing passage is evidently very corrupt and the meaning is by no means plain, but, in the absence of a parallel version, it is impossible to clear up the obscurity of the text. (p. 136)

[232] This appears to be the sense of the text; but the whole passage is to obscure and corrupt that it is impossible to make sure of its exact meaning. (p. 137)

[233] Meaning apparently, "thou puttest my devices to nought" or (perhaps) "thou art so skilful that I fear lest thou undermine my favour with the king and oust me from my post of vizier." (p. 138)

[234] Lit. "land;" but the meaning is evidently as in the text. (p. 139)

[235] The reader will recognize the well-known story used by Chaucer, Boccaccio and La Fontaine. (p. 139)

[236] Syn. flourishing. (p. 140)

[237] Syn. depopulated. (p. 140)

[238] Lit. an oppressor. (p. 140)

[239] i.e. a man of commanding presence. (p. 140)

[240] Syn. cause flourish. (p. 140)

[241] Syn. depopulateth. (p. 140)

[242] Lit. the year. (p. 140)

[243] The whole of the tither's account of himself is terribly obscure and so corrupt that it is hardly possible to make sense of it. The same remark applies to much of the rest of the story. (p. 140)

[244] Or "cause flourish." (p. 141)

[245] Lit. a better theologian. The Muslim law being entirely based on the Koran and the Traditions of the Prophet, the terms "lawyer" and "theologian" are necessarily synonymous among Mohammedan peoples. (p. 141)

[246] A danic is the sixth of a dirhem, i.e. about one penny. (p. 142)

[247] i.e. say, "May I be [triply] divorced from my wife, if etc.!" By the Muslim law, a divorce three times pronounced is irrevocable, and in case of its appearing that the user of such an oath as the above had sworn falsely, his wife would become divorced by operation of law, without further ceremony. Hence the frequency and binding nature of the oath in question. (p. 143)

[248] i.e. thousandfold cuckold. (p. 143)

[249] i.e. the blows which the thief had given him. (p. 143)

[250] i.e. at least, at the most moderate reckoning. (p. 144)

[251] Or "Breath of God," a title given to Jesus by the Mohammedans. (p. 145)

[252] i.e. attaineth his desire. (p. 145)

[253] Syn. guards. (p. 146)

[254] i.e. the husbandman. (p. 148)

[255] i.e. those bound to render suit and service to the king, as hclders of fiefs. (p. 148)

[256] Syn. the revenue or rent-charge of thy fief. (p. 148)

[257] Heads of families? (p. 148)

[258] Or "caused flourish." (p. 149)

[259] Or froward. (p. 150)

[260] i.e. sold and spent the price of. (p. 151)

[261] i.e. his lack of means to entertain her. (p. 151)

[262] i.e. all that can conduce to. (p. 151)

[263] i.e. it is for you (after God) to excuse me. (p. 152)

[264] i.e. the [supposed] rest of his hoard. (p. 154)

[265] Apparently the idiot's name. (p. 154)

[266] i.e. had he been on his own guard against that, etc. (p. 156)

[267] A town of Khoiassan. (p. 158)

[268] i.e., he dared not attempt to force her? (p. 158)

[269] i.e. her "yes" meant "yes" and her "no" "no." (p. 158)

[270] Lit. ignorance. (p. 158)

[271] Lit. spoke against her due. (p. 160)

[272] i.e. a domed monument. (p. 161)

---

[273] Lit "ignorance," often used in the sense of "forwardness." (p. 162)

[274] i.e. my present plight. (p. 163)

[275] i.e. ten thousand dinars. (p. 164)

[276] A similar story to this, though differing considerably in detail, will be found in my "Book of the Thousand Nights and One Night," Vol. V. p. 9, The Jewish Cadi and his pions wife. (p. 164)

[277] Or divineress (kahinek). (p. 165)

[278] i.e. whoredom. (p. 165)

[279] Or "scar" (ather). (p. 165)

[280] ie. hearken to. (p. 166)

[281] i.e. Persia. (p. 167)

[282] i.e. the case with which he earned his living. (p. 167)

[283] i.e. the ten thousand dirhems of the bond. (p. 167)

[284] i.e. exhorted her to patience. (p. 167)

[285] Or performing surgical operations (ilaj). (p. 168)

[286] i.e. the open space before his house. (p. 168)

[287] Or "drew near unto." (p. 168).

[288] i.e. a descendant of Mohammed. (p. 169)

[289] Or the art of judging from external appearances (firaseh). (p. 169)

[290] Sic in the text; but the passage is apparently corrupt. It is not plain why a rosy complexion, blue eyes and tallness should be peculiar to women in love. Arab women being commonly short, swarthy and black eyed, the attributes mentioned appear rather to denote the foreign origin of the woman; and it is probable, therefore, that this passage has by a copyist's error, been mixed up with that which related to the signs by which the mock physician recognized her strangehood, the clause specifying the symptoms of her love lorn condition having been crowded

out in the process, an accident of no infrequent occurrence in the transcription of Oriental works. (p. 169)

[291] Yellow was the colour prescribed for the wearing of Jews by the Muslim lawm in accordance with the decree issued by Khalif Omar ben el Khettab after the taking of Jerusalem in A.D. 636. (p. 170)

[292] i.e. Sunday. (p. 170)

[293] Herais, a species of "risotto," made of pounded wheat or rice and meat in shreds. (p. 170)

[294] Lit. "That have passed the night," i.e. are stale and therefore indigestable. (p. 170)

[295] i.e. Saturday. (p. 170)

[296] i.e. native of Merv. (p. 170)

[297] Or "ruined," lit. "destroyed." (p. 170)

[298] i.e. native of Rei, a city of Khorassia. (p. 170)

[299] The text has khenadic, ditches or valleys; but this is, in all probability, a clerical or typographical error for fenadic, inns or caravanserais. (p. 170)

[300] It is a paramount duty of the Muslim to provide his dead brother in the faith with decent interment; it is, therefore, a common practice for the family of a poor Arab to solicit contributions toward the expenses of his burial, nor is the well-to-do true believer safe from imposition of the kind described in the text. (p. 171)

[301] i.e. the recompense in the world to come promised to the performer of a charitable action. (p. 172)

[302] i.e. camphor and lote-tree leaves dried and powdered (sometimes mixed with rose-water) which are strewn over the dead body, before it is wrapped in the shroud. In the case of a man of wealth, more costly perfumes (such as musk, aloes and ambergris) are used. (p. 172)

[303] All the ablutions prescribed by the Mohammedan ritual are avoided by the occurrence, during the process, of any cause of ceremonial impurty (such as the mentioned in the text) and must be recommenced. (p. 172)

[304] Having handled a corpse, he had become in a state of legal impurity and it beloved him therefore to make the prescribed ablution. (p. 172)

[305] Which he had taken off for the purpose of making abulution. This was reversing the ordinary course of affairs, the dead man's clothes being the washer's prequisite. (p. 172)

[306] i.e. till it was diminished by evaporation to two-thirds of its original volume. (p. 173)

[307] The Mohammedan grave is a cell, hollowed out in the sides of a trench and so constructed as to keep out the earth, that the deceased may be able to sit up and answer the examining angels when they visit him in the tomb. There was, therefore, nothing improbable in Er Razi's boast that he could abide two days in the tomb. (p. 174)

[308] Nawous, a sort of overground well or turricle of masonry, surmounted by an iron grating, on which the Gueber's body is placed for devoration by the birds. (p. 174)

[309] Munkir [Munker] and Nakir [Nekir] are the two angels that preside at 'the examination of the tomb.' They visit a man in his grave directly after he has been buried and examine him concerning his faith; if he acknowledge that there is but one God and that Mohammed is His prophet [apostle], they suffer him to rest in peace; otherwise they beat him with [red-hot] iron maces, till he roars so loud[ly] that he is heard by all from east to west, except by man and Ginns [Jinn]."-- Palmer's Koran, Introduction. (p. 174)

[310] Lit. the oven (tennour); but this is obviously a mistake for "tombs" (cubour). (p. 174)

[311] i.e. as a propitiatory offering on behalf of. (p. 175)

[312] i.e. though he remain at thy charge or (as we should say) on thy hands. (p. 178)

[313] About twenty-five shillings. (p. 178)

[314] About £137 10s. (p. 178)

[315] Meaning the sharper. (p. 180)

[316] i.e. he asketh nought but that which is reasonable. (p. 180)

[317] The strict Muslim is averse from taking an oath, even in support at the truth, and will sometimes submit to a heavy loss rather than do so. For an instance of this, see my "Book of the Thousand Nights and One Night," Vol. V. p. 44, The King of the Island. (p. 180)

[318] To wit, the merchant and his officious friend. (p. 181)

[319] There appears to be some mistake here, but I have no means of rectifying it. The passage is probably hopelessly corrupt and a portion of the conclusion of the story seems to have dropped out. (p. 182)

[320] i.e. well-guarded, confined in the harem. (p. 184)

[321] i.e. an old woman to crafty that she was a calamity to those against whom she plotted. (p. 184)

[322] i.e. the amount of the contingent dowry and of the allowance which he was bound to make her for her support during the four months and some days which must elapse before she could lawfully marry again. (p. 185)

[323] i.e. thou wilt have satisfied us all. (p. 185)

[324] With the smoke of burning aloes-wood or other perfume, a common practice among the Arabs. The aloes-wood is placed upon burning charcoal in a censer perforated with holes, which is swung towards the person to be fumigated, whose clothes and hair are thus impregnated with the grateful fragrance of the burning wood. An accident such as that mentioned in the text might easily happen during the process of fumigation. (p. 186)

[325] i.e. by God. The old woman is keeping up her assumption of the character of a devotee by canting about Divine direction. (p. 186)

[326] This is the same story as "The House with the Belvedere." See my "Book of the Thousand Nights and one Night," Vol. V. p. 323. (p. 186)

[327] See note, Vol. I. p. 212. Also my "Book of the Thousand Nights and One Night," Vol. V. p. 263, The King and his Vizier's wife. (p. 186)

[328] Or experienced. (p. 188)

[329] i.e. the inhabitants of the island and the sailors? (p. 190)

[330] i.e. postponed the fulfilment of his promise. (p. 193)

[331] Sic; but apparently a state-prison or place of confinement for notable offenders is meant. (p. 195)

[332] Or "getting hold of." (p. 195)

[333] Lit. "betrothed." (p. 196)

[334] Or "in." (p. 199)

[335] i.e. if his appearance be such as to belie the possibility of his being a thief. (p. 199)

[336] i.e. people of power and worship. (p. 199)

[337] i.e. of wine. (p. 201)

[338] i.e. all his former afflictions or (perhaps) all His commandments. (p. 202)

[339] i.e. a more venial sin. (p. 202)

[340] i.e. I have a proposal to make thee. (p. 202)

[341] i.e. he was brought up in my house. (p. 210)

[342] i.e. prayed for him by name, as the reigning sovereign, in the Khutbeh, a sort of homily made up of acts of prayer and praise and of exhortations to the congregation, which forms part of the Friday prayers. The mention of a newly-appointed sovereign's name in the Khutbeh is equivalent with the Muslims to a solemn proclamation of his accession. (p. 211)

[343] i.e. deprive him of his rank. (p. 212)

[344] Or perverted belief, i.e. an infidel. (p. 212)

[345] i.e. not God. (p. 213)

[346] Or corrupt belief, i.e. that the destinies of mankind were governed by the planets and not by God alone. (p. 213)

[347] i.e. "him who is to me even as mine own soul," to wit, the king. (p. 214)

[348] The whole of this story (which is apparently intended as an example of the flowery style (el bediya) of Arab prose) is terribly corrupt and obscure, and in the absence of a parallel version, with which to collate it, it is impossible to be sure that the exact sense has been rendered. (p. 214)

[349] i.e. the first or Beherite dynasty of the Mameluke Sultans, the founder of which was originally a Turkish (i.e. Turcoman) slave. (p. 216)

[350] Fourth Sultan of the above dynasty. (p. 216)

[351] i.e. Palestine (Es Sahil) so styled by the Arabs. (p. 216)

[352] Lit. his nightly entertainers, i.e. those whose place it was to entertain him by night with the relation of stories and anecdotes and the recitation of verses, etc. (p. 216)

[353] i.e. the perfect of police. (p. 217)

[354] About fifty shillings. (p. 217)

[355] i.e. those of the visible and invisible worlds. (p. 217)

[356] i.e. of the Sultan's officers of the household. The Sultan's palace and the lodgings of his chief officers were situate, according to Eastern custom, in the citadel or central fortress of the city. (p. 218)

[357] Lit. [self-]possession (temkin). (p. 218)

[358] God forbid! (p. 219)

[359] Or strong place. (p. 219)

[360] i.e. lest ill-hap betide her and you be held responsible for her. (p. 219)

[361] Which was in his custody in his ex-officio capacity of guardian, orphans in Muslim countries being, by operation of law, wards of the Cadi of their district. (p. 219)

[362] Altogether six thousand dinars or about £3000. (p. 219)

[363] i.e. except thou give me immediate satisfaction, I will complain of thee to the Sultan. (p. 219)

---

[364] i.e. forgetting all that is enjoined upon the true-believer by the Institutes of the Prophet (Sunneh) and the Canons (Fers) of the Divine Law, as deduced from the Koran. (p. 219)

[365] Lit. red i.e. violent or bloody) death. (p. 220)

[366] Lit. the conquered one. (p. 221)

[367] i.e. my view of the matter differs from that of the Cadi, but I cannot expect a hearing against a personage of his rank. (p. 221)

[368] And therefore freshly shed. (p. 221)

[369] For redness. (p. 221)

[370] Or parties. (p. 222)

[371] Lit. quench that fire from him. (p. 222)

[372] Of Cairo or (quære) the two Egyptian provinces known as Es Sherkiyeh (The Eastward) and El Gherbiyeh (The Westward). (p. 223)

[373] i.e, he was a man of ready wit and presence of mind. (p. 223)

[374] Or (in modern slang) "There are good pickings to be had out of this job." (p. 223)

[375] Lit "the douceur of the key," i.e. the gratuity which it is customary to give to the porter or portress on hiring a house or lodging. Cf. the French denier à Dieu, Old English "God's penny." (p. 225)

[376] i.e. made the complete ablution prescribed by the Muslim law after copulation. (p. 225)

[377] i.e. the round opening made in the ceiling for ventilation. (p. 227)

[378] i.e. he who sits on the bench outside the police-office, to attend to emergencies. (p. 227)

[379] Lit. witnesses, i.e. those who are qualified by their general respectability and the blamelessness of their lives, to give evidence in the Mohamedan courts of law. (p. 228)

[380] Sic. (p. 228)

[381] About 50 pounds. (p. 228)

[382] Or guardian. (p. 228)

[383] Syn. book (kitab). (p. 229)

[384] Or made it a legal deed. (p. 229)

[385] Lit. assessors. (p. 229)

[386] This sentence is almost unintelligible, owing to the corruptness and obscurity of the text; but the sense appears to be as above. (p. 230)

[387] Apparently supposing the draper to have lost it and purposing to require a heavy indemnity for its loss. (p. 231)

[388] Apparently, a cant phrase for "thieve." (p. 231)

[389] or disapprove of. (p. 232)

[390] This passage is unintelligible; the text is here again, to all appearance, corrupt. (p. 232)

[391] i.e. women's tricks? (p. 232)

[392] Muslim formula of invitation. (p. 233)

[393] i.e. the singers? (p. 236)

[394] i.e. easily. (p. 236)

[395] Or made a show of renouncing. (p. 237)

[396] i.e. strong men (or athletes) armed. (p. 238)

[397] Fityan, Arab cant name for thieves. (p. 238)

[398] Apparently in a pavillion in some garden or orchard, the usual pleasure of the Arabs. (p. 238)

---

[399] i.e. engaged her to attend an entertainment and paid her her hire in advance. (p. 238)

[400] Lit. a [she-]partner, i.e. one who should relieve her, when she was weary of singing, and accompany her voice on the lute. (p. 238)

[401] i.e. they grew ever more heated with drink. (p. 239)

[402] Helfeh or helfaa (vulg. Alfa), a kind of coarse, rushy grass (Pos. multiflora), used in the East as fuel. (p. 240)

[403] Lit. "we repented to God, etc, of singing." The practice of music, vocal and instrumental, is deprecated by the strict Muslim, in accordance with a tradition by which the Prophet is said to have expressed his disapproval of these arts. (p. 240)

[404] i.e. required to find the thief or make good the loss. (p. 240)

[405] i.e. the parties aggrieved. (p. 240)

[406] Or irrigation-work, usually a bucket-wheel, worked by oxen. (p. 240)

[407] Or "came true." (p. 241)

[408] i.e. crucify. (p. 242)

[409] i.e. a native of the Hauran, a district East of Damascus. (p. 242)

[410] i.e. the mysterious speaker. (p. 242)

[411] i.e. in the punishment that overtook me. (p. 243)

[412] The well-known Arab formula of refusal to a beggar, equivalent to the Spanish "Perdoneme por amor de Dios, hermano!" (p. 244)

[413] i.e. what I could afford. (p. 244)

[414] i.e. that of the officers of police. (p. 244)

[415] A common Oriental game, something like a rude out-door form of back-gammon, in which the players who throw certain numbers are dubbed Sultan and Vizier. (p. 244)

[416] Lit. milk (leben), possibly a copyist's error for jubn (cheese). (p. 244)

[417] i.e. his forbearance in relinquishing his blood-revenge for his brother. (p. 245)

[418] In the text, by an evident error, Shehriyar is here made to ask Shehrzad for another story and she to tell it him. (p. 245)

[419] Nesiheh. (p. 246)

[420] i.e. the mysterious speaker? (p. 248)

[421] Apparently some famous saint. The El Hajjaj whose name is familiar to readers of the Thomsand and One Night (see supra, Vol. I. p. 53, note 2) was anything but a saint, if we may believe the popular report of him. (p. 249)

[422] Breslan Text, vol. xi. pp. 400-473 and vol. xii. pp. 4-50, Nights dccccvli-dcccclvii. (p. 250)

[423] The usual meaning of the Arab word anber (pronounced amber) a ambergris, i.e. the morbid secretion of the sperm-whale; but the context appears to point to amber, i.e. the fossil resin used for necklaces, etc.; unless, indeed, the allusion of the second hemistich is to ambergris, as worn, for the sake of the perfume, in amulets or pomanders (Fr. pomme d'ambre) slung about the neck. (p. 250)

[424] i.e. galena or sulphuret of lead, of which, reduced to powder, alone or in combination with other ingredients, the well-known cosmetic or eye-powder called kohl consists. (p. 250)

[425] See supra, Vol. 1. p. 50, note 2. (p. 251)

[426] Or "accomplishments" (adab). (p. 251)

[427] Title of the Khalif. (p. 252)

[428] i.e. Isaac of Mosul, the greatest of Arab musicians. (p. 252)

[429] Elder brother of Jaafer; see my "Book of the Thousand Nights and One Night," Vol. IX. p. 342 et seq. (p. 253)

[430] Yonnus ibn Hebib, a renowned grammarian and philologer of the day, who taught at Bassora and whose company was much sought after by distinguished men of letters and others. He was a friend of Isaac of Mosul. (p. 253)

[431] Apparently a suburb of Baghdad. (p. 253)

[432] i.e. the principal street of Et Taf. (p. 253)

[433] Or "elegant." (p. 253)

[434] See supra, Vol. I. p. 236, note 1. (p. 253)

[435] ? (p. 254)

[436] A passage has apparently dropped out here. The Khalif seems to have gone away without buying, leaving Ishac behind, whereupon the latter was accosted by another slave-girl, who came out of a cell in the corridor. (p. 254)

[437] Or "have withheld myself." (p. 254)

[438] For not selling me? (p. 254)

[439] i.e. Tuhfeh the fool. Hemca is the feminine form of ahmec, fool. If by a change in the (unwritten) vowels, we read Humeca, which is the plural form of ahmec, the title will signify, "Gift (Tuhfeh) of fools" and would thus represent a jesting alteration of the girl's real name (Tuhfet el Culoub, Gift of hearts), in allusion to her (from the slave-merchant's point of view) foolish and vexatious behaviour in refusing to be sold to the first comer, as set out below. (p. 255)

[440] Or "folly" (hemakeh). (p. 255)

[441] i.e. not every one is lucky enough to be in Ishac's house. (p. 255)

[442] Apparently some part of Baghdad adjoining the Tigris. Khanekah means "a convent of dervishes." (p. 255)

[443] Lit. stronger (acwa). (p. 256)

[444] The gist of this curious comparison is not very apparent. Perhaps "blander" is meant. (p. 256)

[445] About 10s. (p. 257)

[446] About a penny; i.e. I have found all my skill in the craft but a trifle in comparison with thine. (p. 257)

[447] i.e. thou art what he wants. (p. 257)

[448] i.e. the dews of her mouth, commonly compared by Oriental writers to wine and honey. (p. 258)

[449] i.e. he died. (p. 258)

[450] i.e. if my hand were out for want of practice. (p. 258)

[451] i.e. a gift or rarity. (p. 259)

[452] Or "rarity" (tuhfeh) (p. 259)

[453] i.e. thou didst her not justice. (p. 260)

[454] i.e. that set apart for the chief of the concubines. (p. 260)

[455] i.e. from the opening made in the ceiling for ventilation. Or the saloon in which she sat may have been open to the sky, as is not uncommon in the East. (p. 261)

[456] Zubeideh was the daughter of Jaafer, son of El Mensour, second Khalif of the house of Abbas, and was therefore Er Reshid's first cousin. It does not appear why she is called daughter (bint) of El Casim. (p. 261)

[457] Lit. "of those noble steps." (p. 261)

[458] So styled by the Muslums, because Abraham is fabled by them to have driven him away with stones, when he strove to prevent him from sacrificing Ishmael, whom they substitute for Isaac as the intended victim. (p. 262)

[459] i.e. Gift of Breasts. The word "breasts" here is, of course, used (metonymically) for "hearts." (p. 263)

[460] i.e. "He (lit. father) of the hosts of tribes." (p. 263)

[461] See post, passim. (p. 263)

[462] Lit. witnesses (shawahid). (p. 264)

[463] Lit. seas (behar). (p. 264)

[464] Afterwards called Zelzeleh; see post, p. 245 et seq. (p. 264)

[465] i.e. I cannot look long on them. (p. 265)

[466] i.e. change the sir to one less poignant? Or (perhaps) "lower thy voice." (p. 266)

[467] i.e. from time immemorial, before the creation of the world. The most minute details of every man's life in the world are believed by the Mohammedans to have been fore-ordained by God from all eternity. This belief is summed up in the Koranic saying, "Verily, the commandment of God is a prevenient decree." (p. 266)

[468] No mention is afterward made of any wedding, and the word is, therefore, probably used here in its implied sense of "festival," "merry-making." I am not, however acquainted with any instance of this use of the word urs. (p. 267)

[469] Or "peewit." (p. 267)

[470] i.e. those that led the water to the roots of the trees, after the manner of Eastern gardeners. (p. 267)

[471] One of the seven "Gardens" or stages for the Mohammedan heaven. (p. 267)

[472] "God is Most Great!" So called because its pronunciation, after that of the niyeh or intent (i.e. "I purpose to pray such and such prayers"), prohibits the speaking of any words previous to prayer. (p. 267)

[473] i.e. those of the five daily prayers (due at daybreak, noon, mid-afternoon, sundown, and nightfall respectively) which she had been prevented from praying on the previous evening, through having passed it in carousing with the Jinn. It is incumbent on the strict Muslim to make up his arrears of prayer in this manner. (p. 267)

[474] Lit. skill in physiognomy (firaseh). (p. 269)

[475] i.e. the owner of this palace. (p. 270)

[476] The Mohammedan rite of ablution, previous to prayer, is a very elaborate and complicated process, somewhat "scamped" by the ordinary "true-believer." See my "Book of the Thousand Nights and One Night," Vol. IV. pp. 332-4. (p. 270)

[477] i.e. the prayers of nightfall, in addition to those of daybreak. (p. 270)

[478] i.e. those of noon, mid-afternoon and sundown. (p. 270)

[479] Containing the dessert. (p. 271)

[480] i.e. Mohammed, who was passionately fond of flowers and especially of the rose, which is fabled to have blossomed from his sweat. (p. 271)

[481] The Arab name (julnar) of the promegranate is made up of the Persian word for rose (gul) and the Arabic fire (nar). (p. 272)

[482] i.e. Chapters cxiii. and cxiv. of the Koran, respectively known as the Chapter of the [Lord of the] Daybreak and the Chapter of [The Lord of] Men. These chapters, which it is the habit of the Muslim to recite as a talisman or preventive against evil, are the last and shortest in the book and run as follows. Chapter cxiii.--"In the name of the Compassionate, the Merciful! Say [quoth Gabriel] 'I take refuge with the Lord of the Daybreak from the evil of that which He hath created and from the evil of the beginning of the night, whenas it invadeth [the world], and from the mischief of the women who blow on knots (i.e. witches) and from the mischief of the envier, whenas he envieth.'" Chapter cxiv.--"In the name of God the Compassionate, the Merciful! Say [quoth Gabriel] 'I take refuge with the Lord of Men, the King of Men, the God of Men, from the mischief of the stealthy Tempter (i.e. the devil) who whispereth (i.e. insinuateth evil) into the breasts (hearts) of mankind, from Jinn and men!'" These two chapters are often written on parchment etc. and worn as an amulet about the person--hence their name. (p. 273)

[483] Hieratic title of the Khalif, as foreman (imam) of the people at prayer. (p. 273)

[484] i.e. the Jinn that dwell therein. Each house, according to Muslim belief, has its haunter or domestic spirit. (p. 273)

[485] i.e. yearning. (p. 273)

[486] i.e. her return. (p. 274)

[487] See ante, p. 229, note 2. (p. 276)

[488] "As for him who is of those brought near unto God, [for him shall be] easance and sweet basil (syn. victual, rihan), and a garden of pleasance."--Koran lvi. 87-8. It will be observed that this verse is somewhat garbled in the quotation. (p. 277)

[489] Meaning apparently, "None of the Jinn may tread these carpets, etc., that thou treadest." (p. 278)

[490] i.e. to hold festival. (p. 278)

[491] This passage may also be rendered, "And in this I do thee a great favour [and honour thee] over all the Jinn." (p. 279)

---

[492] Lit. "How loathly is that which yonder genie Meimoun eateth!" But this is evidently a mistake. See ante, p. 226. (p. 279)

[493] Lit. "I have not an eye that availeth to look upon him." (p. 279)

[494] i.e. "May I not lack of thy visits!" (p. 279)

[495] i.e. "As much again as all thou hast given." (p. 280)

[496] The attainment by a boy of the proper age for circumcision, or (so to speak) his religious majority, in a subject for great rejoicing with the Mohammedans, and the occasion is celebrated by the giving of as splendid an entertainment as the means of his family will afford, during which he is displayed to view upon a throne or raised seat, arrayed in the richest and ornaments that can be found, hired or borrowed for the purpose. (p. 280)

[497] Tuhfeh. (p. 280)

[498] Lit. "be equitable therewith unto;" but the meaning appears to be as above. (p. 280)

[499] Lit. "places" (mawazi). Quaere "shifts" or "positions." (p. 280)

[500] See my "Book of the Thousand Nights and One Night," Vol. VI. p. 226, Isaac of Mosul and his Mistress and the Devil. (p. 280)

[501] i.e. method of playing the lute. (p. 281)

[502] i.e. not indigenous? (p. 282)

[503] Apparently the residence of King Es Shisban. (p. 285)

[504] i.e. all the Jinn's professions of affection to me and promises of protection, etc. (p. 286)

[505] i.e. one so crafty that he was a calamity to his enemies, a common Arab phrase used in a complimentary sense. (p. 286)

[506] i.e. the Flying Lion. (p. 286)

[507] i.e. How canst thou feel assured of safety, after that which thou hast done? (p. 286)

[508] Or "life" (ruh). (p. 287)

[509] Quaere the mountain Cat. (p. 288)

[510] i.e. why tarriest thou to make an end of her? (p. 290)

[511] i.e. arm. (p. 290)

[512] i.e. for length. (p. 290)

[513] A fabulous mountain-range, believed by the Arabs to encompass the world and by which they are supposed to mean the Caucasus. (p. 293)

[514] The Anca, phoenix or griffin, is a fabulous bird that figures largely in Persian romance. It is fabled to have dwelt in the Mountain Caf and to have once carried off a king's daughter on her wedding-day. It is to this legend that the story-teller appears to refer in the text; but I am not aware that the princess in question is represented to have been the daughter of Behram Gour, the well-known King of Persia, who reigned in the first half of the fifth century and was a contemporary of the Emperors Theodosius the Younger and Honorius. (p. 293)

[515] One of the names of God. (p. 294)

[516] i.e. thy return. (p. 295)

[517] Gift of the Breast (heart). (p. 296)

[518] Binat el hawa, lit. daughters of love. This is the ordinary meaning of the phrase; but the girl in question appears to have been of good repute and the expression, as applied to her, is probably, therefore, only intended to signify a sprightly, frolicsome damsel. (p. 297)

[519] Lit. the forehead, quare the lintel. (p. 297)

[520] Or "put to nought" (p. 297)

[521] Comparing her body, now hidden in her flowing stresses and now showing through them, to a sword, as it flashes in and out of its sheath. (p. 298)

[522] About £25. (p. 299)

[523] About £75. (p. 299)

[524] i.e. all defects for which a man is by law entitled to return a slave-girl to her seller. (p. 299)

[525] Ed Dilem is the ancient Media. The allusion to its prison or prisons I do not understand. (p. 299)

[526] i.e. the complete ablution prescribed by the Mohammedan law after sexual intercourse. (p. 299)

[527] It is customary for a newly-married man to entertain his male acquaintances with a collation on the morning after the wedding. (p. 299)

[528] Lit. more striking and cutting. (p. 299)

[529] Sherifi, a small gold coin, worth about 6s. 8d. (p. 300)

[530] Or "false pretences." (p. 300)

[531] Or, as we should say, "the apple." (p. 300)

[532] Apparently the Cadi was our claimed to be a seyyid i.e. descendant of Mohammed, through his daughter Fatmeh. (p. 301)

[533] Lit. more ill-omened. (p. 302)

[534] i.e. that the law would not allow him to compel the young merchant to divorce his wife. (p. 302)

[535] i.e. veil in honour. (p. 302)

[536] Lit the fire, i.e. hell. (p. 302)

[537] i.e. by an irrevocable divorcement (telacan bainan), to wit, such a divorcement as estops the husband from taking back his divorced wife, except with her consent and after the execution of a fresh contract of marriage. (p. 302)

[538] Breslau Text, vol. xii. pp. 50-116, Nights dcccclviii-dcccclxv. (p. 304)

[539] Babylon, according to the Muslims, is the head-quarters of sorcery and it is there that the two fallen angels, Harout and Marout, who are appointed to tempt mankind by teaching them the art of magic, are supposed to be confined. (p. 304)

540 i.e. "my lord," a title generally prefixed to the names of saints. It is probable, therefore, that the boy was named after some saint or other, whose title, as well as name, was somewhat ignorantly appropriated to him. (p. 304)

541 i.e. one and all? (p. 304)

542 i.e. a foretaste of hell. (p. 305)

543 Lit. he loaded his sleeve with. (p. 305)

544 A mithcal is the same as a dinar, i.e. about ten shillings. (p. 305)

545 Masculine. (p. 305)

546 He was a noted debauchee, as well as the greatest poet of his day See my "Book of the Thousand Nights and One Night," Vol. IV. p. 205, and Vol. IX. p. 332. (p. 305)

547 See ante, Vol. II. p. 240. note. (p. 305)

548 Princess of the Fair. (p. 307)

549 i.e. Ye are welcome to. (p. 311)

550 i.e. the place in which those accused or convicted of crimes of violence were confined. (p. 312)

551 i.e. a youth slender and flexile as a bough. (p. 312)

552 i.e. sway gracefully. A swimming gait is the ideal of elegance to the Arab. (p. 312)

553 An Arab of Medina, proverbial for faithlessness. (p. 314)

554 Joseph is the Mohammedan prototype of beauty. (p. 314)

555 For the loss of Joseph. Jacob, in like manner, is the Muslim type of inconsolable grief. (p. 314)

556 Uncle of the Prophet. (p. 314)

557 First cousin of the Prophet. (p. 314)

558 i.e. cut off her head. (p. 314)

---

[559] When asked, on the Day of Judgment, why he had slain her. (p. 316)

[560] i.e. that some one of the many risings in Khorassan (which was in a chronic state of rebellion during Er Reshid's reign) had been put down. (p. 316)

[561] Lit. fry. The custom is to sear the stump by plunging it into boiling oil. (p. 317)

[562] Lit. of those having houses. (p. 317)

[563] i.e. from God in the world to come. (p. 318)

[564] I look to get God's favour in consequence of thy fervent prayers for me. (p. 318)

[565] Provided for ablution. (p. 318)

[566] i.e. if you want a thing done, do it yourself. (p. 320)

[567] i.e. put on the ordinary walking dress of the Eastern lady, which completely hides the person. (p. 320)

[568] This is apparently said in jest; but the Muslim Puritan (such as the strict Wehhabi) is often exceedingly punctilious in refusing to eat or use anything that is not sanctified by mention in the Koran or the Traditions of the Prophet, in the same spirit as the old Calvinist Scotchwoman of popular tradition, who refused to eat muffins, because they "warna mentioned in the Bible." (p. 321)

[569] i.e. a leader (lit. foreman, antistes) of the people at prayer. (p. 322)

[570] Koran ii. 168. (p. 322)

[571] i.e. I have eaten largely and the food lies heavy on my stomach. (p. 322)

[572] Wine is considered by the Arabs a sovereign digestive. See my "Book of the Thousand Nights and One Night," Vol. IV. p. 357. (p. 322)

[573] "The similitude of Paradise, the which is promised unto those who fear [God]. Therein are rivers of water incorruptible and rivers of milk, the taste whereof changeth not, and rivers of wine, a delight to the drinkers, and rivers of clarified honey."--Koran xlvii. 16, 17. (p. 323)

[574] The ox is the Arab type of stupidity, as with us the ass. (p. 324)

[575] Syn. wood (oud). (p. 324)

[576] i.e. my pallor and emaciation testify to the affliction of my heart and the latter bears witness that the external symptoms correctly indicate the internal malady. (p. 327)

[577] Lit. he is [first] the deposit of God, then thy deposit. (p. 329)

[578] Or "by." (p. 329)

[579] See supra, Vol. I. p. 35, note. (p. 330)

[580] i.e. made him Chief of the Police of Baghdad, in place of the former Prefect, whom he had put to death with the rest of Noureddin's oppressors. (p. 330)

[581] For affright. (p. 331)

[582] i.e. religious ceremonies so called. See my "Book of the Thousand Nights and One Night," Vol. IX. p. 113, note. (p. 332)

[583] Breslau Text, vol. xii. pp. 116-237, Nights dcccclxvi-dcccclxxix. (p. 333)

[584] i.e. A member of the tribe of Sheiban. No such King of Baghdad (which was not founded till the eighth century) as Ins ben Cais is, I believe, known to history. (p. 333)

[585] The cities and provinces of Bassora and Cufa are generally known as "The Two Iraks"; but the name is here in all probability used in its wider meaning of Irak Arabi (Chaldaea) and Irak Farsi (Persian Irak). (p. 333)

[586] i.e. all those languages the knowledge whereof is necessary to an interpreter or dragoman (properly terjeman). Or quaere is the word terjemaniyeh (dragomanish) here a mistranscription for turkumaniyeh (Turcoman). (p. 333)

[587] i.e. gilded? (p. 333)

[588] i.e. sperma hominis. (p. 333)

[589] Syn. good breeding. (p. 333)

[590] i.e. those women of equal age and rank with herself. (p. 333)

[591] i.e. vaunting himself of offering richer presents. (p. 334)

---

[592] Apparently Zebid, the ancient capital of the province of Tehameh in Yemen, a town on the Red Sea, about sixty miles north of Mocha. The copyist of the Tunis MS. appears to have written the name with the addition of the characteristic desinence (oun) of the nominative case, which is dropped except in the Koran and in poetry. (p. 334)

[593] Name of the province in which Mecca is situated. (p. 334)

[594] Syn. assembly. (p. 334)

[595] i.e. day and night, to wit, for ever. (p. 336)

[596] Syn. the loftiness of his purpose. (p. 336)

[597] Lit "I charm thee by invoking the aid of God for thee against evil" or "I seek refuge with God for thee." (p. 336)

[598] Or "determinate." (p. 337)

[599] Koran xxxiii. 38. (p. 337)

[600] Or "accomplishments." (p. 337)

[601] i.e. to make a pleasure-excursion. (p. 337)

[602] Lit. beset his back. (p. 337)

[603] Lit. in its earth. (p. 338)

[604] The king's own tribe. (p. 338)

[605] i.e. the Arab of the desert or Bedouin (el Aarabi), the nomad. (p. 338)

[606] i.e. the martial instinct. (p. 339)

[607] Lit. "And he who is oppressed shall become oppressor." (p. 340)

[608] i.e. be not ashamed to flee rather than perish in thy youth, if his prowess (attributed to diabolical aid or possession) prove too much for thee. (p. 340)

[609] A periphrastic way of saying, "I look to God for help." (p. 340)

[610] i.e. from the world. (p. 341)

[611] In laughter. (p. 341)

[612] i.e. as he were a flying genie, swooping down upon a mortal from the air, hawk-fashion. (p. 341)

[613] Syn. "Thou settest out to me a mighty matter." (p. 342)

[614] i.e. the castle. (p. 343)

[615] i.e. was eloquent and courtly to the utmost. (p. 343)

[616] i.e. died. (p. 345)

[617] The Arabs use the right hand only in eating. (p. 345)

[618] Name of a quarter of Baghdad. (p. 346)

[619] i.e. he summoneth thee to his presence by way of kindness and not because he is wroth with thee. (p. 346)

[620] i.e. in allowing thee hitherto to remain at a distance from as and not inviting thee to attach thyself to our person. (p. 347)

[621] An Arab idiom, meaning "he showed agitation." (p. 347)

[622] Apparently two well-known lovers. (p. 347)

[623] Apparently two well-known lovers. (p. 347)

[624] i.e. the wandering Arabs. (p. 349)

[625] i.e. slain. (p. 349)

[626] "O ye who believe, seek aid of patience and prayer; verily God is with the patient."--Koran ii. 148. (p. 350)

[627] Lit. "ignorant one" (jahil). (p. 352)

[628] i.e. Peninsula. Jezireh (sing, of jezair, islands) is constantly used by the Arabs in this sense; hence much apparent confusion in topographical passages. (p. 355)

---

[629] i.e. Mecca and Medina. (p. 355)

[630] i.e. whether on a matter of sport, such as the chase, or a grave matter, such as war, etc. (p. 356)

[631] i.e. the children of his fighting-men whom thou slewest. (p. 358)

[632] Arab fashion of shaking hands. See my "Book of the Thousand Nights and One Night," Vol. IX p. 171, note. (p. 359)

[633] Lit. a cleft meadow (merj selia). This is probably a mistranscription for merj sselia, a treeless champaign. (p. 360)

[634] i.e. one of the small rooms opening upon the hall of audience at saloon of estate. (p. 360)

[635] So she might hear and see what passed, herself unseen. (p. 360)

[636] Or knowledge of court etiquette. (p. 361)

[637] i.e. richer. (p. 361)

[638] Lit. seen. (p. 361)

[639] Lit. what she did. (p. 361)

[640] i.e. tabooed or unlawful in a religious sense (heram). (p. 362)

[641] i.e. those of El Aziz, who had apparently entered the city or passed through it on their way to the camp of El Abbas. (p. 363)

[642] Lit. none of the sons of the road. (p. 367)

[643] i.e. the stars. (p. 367)

[644] i.e. in falsetto? (p. 369)

[645] by thine absence. (p. 371)

[646] Common abbreviation for "May I be thy ransom!" (p. 371)

[647] i.e. for love of and longing for. (p. 373)

[648] i.e. leather from Et Taif, a town of the Hejaz, renowned for the manufacture of scented goats' leather. (p. 373)

[649] Or "suspended in." (p. 373)

[650] i.e. violateth my privacy. (p. 373)

[651] i.e. the plaintive song of a nightingale or turtle-dove. (p. 374)

[652] This curious comparison appears to be founded upon the extreme tenuity of the particles of fine dust, so minutely divided as to seem almost fluid. (p. 374)

[653] i.e. he carried it into the convent, hidden under his cloak. (p. 374)

[654] i.e. all the delights of Paradise, as promised to the believer by the Koran. (p. 374)

[655] "Him" in the text and so on throughout the piece; but Mariyeh is evidently the person alluded to, according to the common practice of Muslim poets of a certain class, who consider it indecent openly to mention a woman as an object of love. (p. 375)

[656] i.e. from the witchery of her beauty. See Vol. II. p. 240, note. (p 375)

[657] Lit "if thou kohl thyself" i.e. use them as a cosmetic for the eye. (p. 375)

[658] i.e. we will assume thy debts and responsibilities. (p. 376)

[659] Lit "behind." (p. 376)

[660] i.e. a specially auspicious hour, as ascertained by astrological calculations. Eastern peoples have always laid great stress upon the necessity of commencing all important undertakings at an (astrologically) favourable time. (p. 377)

[661] Or "more valuable." Red camels are considered better than those of other colours by some of the Arabs. (p. 377)

[662] i.e. couriers mounted on dromedaries, which animals are commonly used for this purpose, being (for long distances) swifter and more enduring than horses. (p. 378)

[663] Lit. he sinned against himself. (p. 378)

---

[664] i.e. in falsetto? (p. 378)

[665] i.e. of gold or rare wood, set with balass rubies. (p. 379)

[666] i.e. whose absence. (p. 379)

[667] i.e. in a throat voice? (p. 379)

[668] Koranic synonym, victual (rihan). See Vol. II. p. 247, note. (p. 380)

[669] Apparently, the apple of the throat. (p. 380)

[670] Apparently, the belly. (p. 380)

[671] Apparently, the bosom. (p. 380)

[672] Cf. Fletcher's well-known song in The Bloody Brother;

"Hide, O hide those hills of snow, That thy frozen bosom bears, On Whose Tops the Pinks That Grow Are of those that April wears." (p. 380)

[673] i.e. the breasts themselves. (p. 380)

[674] i.e. your languishing beauties are alone present to my mind's eye. A drowsy voluptuous air of languishment is considered by the Arabs an especial charm. (p. 380)

[675] Syn. chamberlain (hajib). (p. 380)

[676] Syn. eyebrow (hajib). The usual trifling play of words is of course intended. (p. 380)

[677] Lit. feathers. (p. 380)

[678] Solomon is fabled by the Muslims to have compelled the wind to bear his throne when placed upon his famous magic carpet. See my "Book of the Thousand Nights and One Night," Vol. V. pp. 235-6. (p. 380)

[679] Quære the teeth. (p. 380)

[680] i.e. the return of our beloved hath enabled us to remove the barriers that stood between us and delight. (p. 380)

[681] Singing (as I have before pointed out) is not, in the eyes of the strict Muslim, a reputable occupation and it is, therefore, generally the first idea of the "repentant" professional songstress or (as in this case) enfranchised slave-girl, who has been wont to entertain her master with the display of her musical talents, to free herself from all signs of her former profession and identify herself as closely as possible with the ordinary "respectable" bourgeoise of the harem, from whom she has been distinguished hitherto by unveiled face and freedom of ingress and egress; and with this aim in view she would naturally be inclined to exaggerate the rigour of Muslim custom, as applied to herself. (p. 382)

[682] Breslau Text, vol. xii. pp. 383-4 (Night mi). (p. 383)

[683] i.e. that of the king, his seven viziers, his son and his favourite, which in the Breslau Edition immediately follows the Story of El Abbas and Mariyeh and occupies pp. 237-383 of vol. xii. (Nights dcccclxxix-m). It will be found translated in my "Book of the Thousand Nights and One Night," Vol. V. pp. 260-346, under the name of "The Malice of Women." (p. 383)

[684] i.e. those who practise it. (p. 383)

[685] Or "cause" (sebeb). (p. 383)

[686] Or "preservation" (selameh). (p. 383)

[687] Or "turpitude, anything that is hateful or vexatious" (keraheh). (p. 383)

[688] Or "preservation" (selameh). (p. 383)

[689] Or "turpitude, anything that is hateful or vexatious" (keraheh). (p. 383)

[690] These preliminary words of Shehrzad have no apparent connection with the story that immediately follows and which is only her own told in the third person, and it is difficult to understand why they should be here introduced. The author may have intended to connect them with the story by means of a further development of the latter and with the characteristic carelessness of the Eastern story-teller, forgotten or neglected to carry out his intention; or, again, it is possible that the words in question may have been intended as an introduction to the Story of the Favourite and her Lover (see post, p. 165), to which they seem more suitable, and have been misplaced by an error of transcription. In any case, the text is probably (as usual) corrupt. (p. 383)

[691] The kingdom of the elder brother is afterwards referred to as situate in China. See post, p. 150. (p. 384)

[692] Tubba was the dynastic title of the ancient Himyerite Kings of Yemen, even as Chosroës and Cæsar of the Kings of Persia and the Emperors of Constantinople respectively. (p. 384)

[693] i.e. a king similar in magnificence and dominion to the monarchs of the three dynasties aforesaid, whose names are in Arab literature synonyms for regal greatness. (p. 384)

[694] i.e. his rage was ungovernable, so that none dared approach him in his heat of passion. (p. 384)

[695] i.e. maidens cloistered or concealed behind curtains and veiled in the harem. (p. 385)

[696] i.e. those whose business it is to compose or compile stories, verses, etc., for the entertainment of kings and grandees. (p. 386)

[697] i.e. that his new and damnable custom. The literal meaning of bidah is "an innovation or invention, anything new;" but the word is commonly used in the sense of "heresy" or "heterodox innovation," anything new being naturally heretical in the eyes of the orthodox religionist. (p. 386)

[698] i.e. women. (p. 388)

[699] Breslau Text, vol. xii. pp. 394-398. (p. 388)

[700] i.e. his apathy or indifference to the principles of right and wrong and the consequences of his wicked behaviour. (p. 388)

[701] i.e. in a state of reprobation, having incurred the wrath of God. (p. 388)

[702] hath mentioned the office of vizier. (p. 389)

[703] Koran xx. 30. (p. 389)

[704] i.e. none had been better qualified to dispense with a vizier than he. (p. 389)

[705] i.e. the essential qualification. (p. 389)

[706] The word jeish (troops) is here apparently used in the sense at officials, ministers of government. (p. 389)

[707] Or "rectification." (p. 389)

[708] Koran xxxiii. 35. (p. 390)

[709] i.e. I know not which to choose of the superabundant material at my command in the way of instances of women's craft. (p. 390)

[710] Breslau Text, vol xii. pp. 398-402. (p. 391)

[711] i.e. incensed with the smoke of burning musk. It is a common practice in the East to fumigate drinking-vessels with the fragrant smoke of aloes-wood and other perfumes, for the purpose of giving a pleasant flavour to the water, etc., drunk from them. (p. 391)

[712] Huneini foucaniyeh. Foucaniyeh means "upper" (fem.); but the meaning of huneini is unknown to me. (p. 391)

[713] Heriseh. See supra, Vol. II. p. 26, note 4. (p. 392)

[714] The Arabs distinguish three kinds of honey, i.e. bees' honey, cane honey (treacle or syrup of sugar) and drip-honey (date-syrup). (p. 392)

[715] i.e. yet arrive in time for the rendezvous. (p. 392)

[716] Breslau Text, pp. 402-412. (p. 393)

[717] i.e. on an island between two branches of the Nile. (p. 393)

[718] It is not plain what Khalif is here meant, though it is evident, from the context, that an Egyptian prince is referred to, unless the story is told of the Abbaside Khalif El Mamoun, son of Er Reshid (A.D. 813-33), during his temporary residence in Egypt, which he is said to have visited. This is, however, unlikely, as his character was the reverse of sanguinary; besides, El Mamoun was not his name, but his title (Aboulabbas Abdallah El Mamoun Billah). Two Khalifs of Egypt assumed the title of El Hakim bi Amrillah (He who rules or decrees by or in accordance with the commandment of God), i.e. the Fatimite Abou Ali El Mensour (A.D. 995-1021), and the faineant Abbaside Aboulabbas Ahmed (A.D. 1261-1301); but neither of these was named El Mamoun. It is probable, however, that the first named is the prince referred to in the story, the latter having neither the power nor the inclination for such wholesale massacres as that described in the text, which are perfectly in character with the brutal and fantastic nature of the founder of the Druse religion. (p. 393)

[719] i.e. the well-known island of that name (The Garden). (p. 393)

[720] i.e. "whatever may betide" or "will I, nill I"? (p. 394)

[721] Lit. she was cut off or cut herself off. (p. 395)

[722] Lit. "The convent of Clay." (p. 395)

[723] i.e. this is the time to approve thyself a man. (p. 395)

[724] To keep her afloat. (p. 396)

[725] Lit "Thou art the friend who is found (or present) (or the vicissitudes of Time (or Fortune)." (p. 396)

[726] i.e. the officer whose duty it is to search out the estates of intestates and lay hands upon such property as escheats to the Crown for want of heirs. (p. 396)

[727] i.e. Sumatran. (p. 399)

[728] i.e. Alexander. (p. 399)

[729] i.e. the blackness of the hair. (p. 402)

[730] The ingenuity of the bride's attendants, on the occasion of a wedding, is strained to the utmost to vary her attire and the manner in which the hair is dressed on the occasion of her being displayed to her husband, and one favourite trick consists in fastening her tresses about her chin and cheeks, so as to produce a sort of imitation of beard and whiskers. (p. 402)

[731] Literal. (p. 403)

[732] i.e. God only knows if it be true or not. (p. 404)

[733] i.e. the porter and the other guests. (p. 405)

[734] i.e. a mountainous island. (p. 406)

[735] Kherabeh, lit. a hole. Syn. ruin or destruction. (p. 406)

[736] i.e. an outlying spur or reef. (p. 406)

[737] Syn. perilous place. (p. 406)

---

[738] Lit. their guide was disappointed. (p. 406)

[739] i.e. means (hileh) of sustaining life. (p. 406)

[740] i.e. death. (p. 407)

[741] i.e. Ceylon. (p. 408)

[742] Audiyeh (plural of wadi, a valley). The use of the word in this sense points to an African origin of this version of the story. The Moors of Africa and Spain commonly called a river "a valley," by a natural figure of metonymy substituting the container for the contained; e.g. Guadalquiver (Wadi el Kebir, the Great River), Guadiana, etc. (p. 409)

[743] i.e. after the usual compliments, the letter proceeded thus. (p. 409)

[744] i.e. we are thine allies in peace and war, for offence and defence. Those whom thou lovest we love, and those whom thou hatest we hate. (p. 409)

[745] About seventy-two grains. (p. 410)

[746] Or public appearance. (p. 410)

[747] Solomon was the dynastic name of the kings of the prae-Adamite Jinn and is here used in a generic sense, as Chosroes for the ancient Kings of Persia, Caesar for the Emperors of Constantinople, Tubba for the Himyerite Kings of Yemen, etc., etc. (p. 410)

[748] i.e. Maharajah. (p. 410)

[749] Or "government." (p. 410)

[750] Every Muslim is bound by law to give alms to the extent of two and half per cent. of his property. (p. 411)

[751] In North-east Persia. (p. 412)

[752] Alleged to have been found by the Arab conquerors of Spain on the occasion of the sack of Toledo and presented by them to the Ommiade Khalif El Welid ben Abdulmelik (A.D. 705-716). See my "Book of the Thousand Nights and One Night," Vol. III. p. 331. (p. 413)

---

[753] i.e. such as are fit to be sent from king to king. (p. 413)

[754] i.e, the price of his victual and other necessaries for the voyage. (p. 415)

[755] Lit. riding-beast (French monture, no exact English equivalent), whether camel, mule or horse does not appear. (p. 415)

[756] The Envier and the Envied. (p. 417)

[757] After the manner of Orientalists, a far more irritable folk than any poets. (p. 418)

[758] By the by, apropos of this soi-disant complete translation of the great Arabian collection of romantic fiction, it is difficult to understand how an Orientalist of repute, such as Dr. Habicht, can have put forth publication of this kind, which so swarms with blunders of every description as to throw the mistakes of all other translators completely into the shade and to render it utterly useless to the Arabic scholar as a book of reference. We can only conjecture that he must have left the main portion of the work to be executed, without efficient supervision, by incapable collaborators or that he undertook and executed the translation in such haste as to preclude the possibility of any preliminary examination and revision, worthy of the name, of the original MS.; and this latter supposition appears to be borne out by the fact that the translation was entirely published before the appearance of any portion of the Arabic Text, as printed from the Tunis Manuscript. Whilst on the subject of German translations, it may be well to correct an idea, which appears to prevail among non-Arabic scholars, to the effect that complete translations of the Book of the Thousand Nights and One Night exist in the language of Hoffmann and Heine, and which is (as far, at least, as my own knowledge extends) a completely erroneous one. I have, I believe, examined all the German translations in existence and have found not one of them worthy of serious consideration; the best, that of Hammer-Purgstall, to which I had looked for help in the elucidation of doubtful and corrupt passages, being so loose and unfaithful, so disfigured by ruthless retrenchments and abridgments, no less than by gross errors of all kinds, that I found myself compelled to lay it aside as useless. It is but fair, however, to the memory of the celebrated Austrian Orientalist, to state that the only form in which Von Hammer's translation is procurable is that of the German rendering of Prof. Zinserling (1823-4), executed from the original (French) manuscript, which latter was unfortunately lost before publication. (p. 418)